RUNNER IN THE SUN

A Story of Indian Maize

By D'ARCY McNICKLE

Illustrated by ALLAN C. HOUSER

THE vast peaceful expanse of America before the coming of the white man is D'Arcy McNickle's background for this finely wrought story of Indian life. The author re-creates the atmosphere and problems of the ancient cliff-dwelling settlements of the Southwest through full-bodied characterization and a plot alive with mystery and suspense.

Readers will follow in the footsteps of Salt, a teen-age boy being groomed to lead his people, who, as he grows to manhood, is accepted into the tribe and makes a life-and-death trek to the opulent cities of the ancient Aztecs in search of a hardier kind of Indian maize. Rich with Indian lore that is deftly woven into a taut, fast-paced plot, RUNNER IN THE SUN is an adventure, not only in good reading but into the history of a fascinating people nearly lost in the mists of history.

★ ★ ★ ★ ★

D'ARCY McNICKLE is a full-blooded American Indian who is now director of American Indian Development. He was educated at the University of Montana, Oxford University in England and at the University of Grenoble, France. He has been the U. S. representative at inter-American conferences on Indian life in Mexico and Peru and is widely respected as a spokesman for the Indian minority. One of the few Indians to do professional writing, the author has two other books to his credit, *The Surrounded* and *They Came Here First*.

ALLAN C. HOUSER, whose illustrations so perfectly catch the flavor of RUNNER IN THE SUN, is a full-blooded Apache. A versatile artist, whose illustrations have appeared in other books for young readers, he is also winning a reputation as a sculptor. Already a war memorial in stone by him stands at Haskell Institute, the Indian school at Lawrence, Kansas.

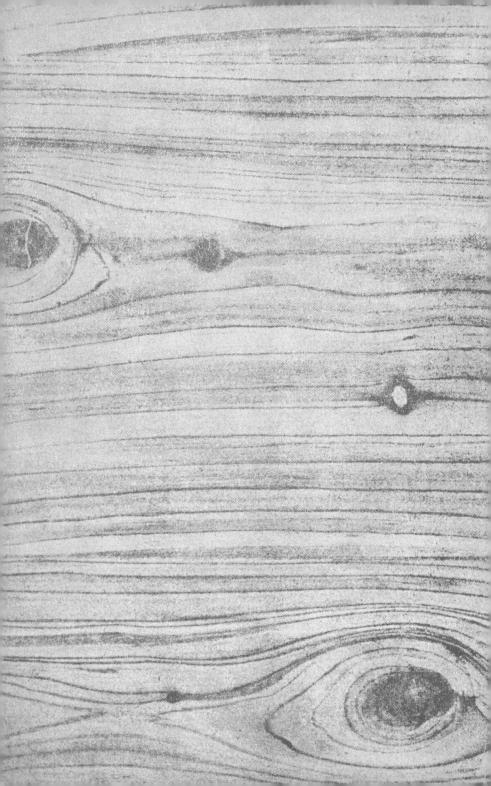

RUNNER
IN THE
SUN

A Story of Indian Maize

RUNNER IN THE SUN

By D'ARCY McNICKLE

Illustrated by Allan C. Houser

THE JOHN C. WINSTON COMPANY
Philadelphia · Toronto

FIRST EDITION

R0191081545

Ref

JM 234 mw

To Roma, Toni, and Kay

LAND OF THE FREE SERIES

Edited by ERICK BERRY

Other titles forthcoming

Foreword

Most of us grow up believing that the history of America begins with the men who came across from Europe and settled in New World wilderness. The real story of our country is much older, much richer, than this usual history book account.

Thousands of years before Europeans, by accident, stumbled upon the American continents, men were living here, scattered between the two polar oceans. They lived under a variety of conditions, and they developed tools, clothing, shelter, food habits, customs, and beliefs to fit their conditions. In some areas, they felled trees in the forest and built houses out of planks split from the trees. Elsewhere, they erected great mounds of earth and stone and placed their houses and temples on the summits. In still other places, they quarried rock and built houses of stone.

They were skilled craftsmen and artists: weaving baskets; fashioning fine pottery; carving in wood, stone, and ivory; molding copper, silver, and gold ornaments; and rearing monumental public buildings. Some were fishermen and sea-mammal hunters, following their game in wooden boats far out in the open ocean. Others were renowned hunters of land animals. But by far the greater part of this population depended upon agriculture, and some groups even constructed irrigation works to reclaim otherwise worthless desert lands.

Salt's people lived without written records, but the shape and content of their lives have been pieced together by scientists examining the houses, tools, weapons, clothing, ceremonial objects, and other evidences of their existence. We know approximately when they lived, and what happened to them.

They were real people, as were all the people Salt encountered on his journey south into the country we call Mexico. They lived, looking into the very skies we look into, hundred of years before Columbus and his three little ships set sail from Isabella's Spain.

They and their racial kinsmen, scattered over the two continents, domesticated many of the food, fiber, and medicinal plants we use today; not alone the corn which plays a part in our story, but tobacco, white and sweet potatoes, long staple cotton, beans, pumpkins, squash, cocoa, quinine, tomatoes, maguey fiber (henequen), and cassava (tapioca), to mention the best known. The tribes inhabiting the highlands of Peru used no fewer than seventy different plants for food and other purposes.

The world was enriched by such a material contribution as maize, or Indian corn, which quickly spread to all continents after New World discovery. The world might have been even richer today if the first Europeans had adopted and carried away with them the respect for peaceful living which characterized the first Americans.

Columbus remarked their gentle quality: "No request of anything from them is ever refused, but they rather invite acceptance of what they possess, and manifest such a generosity that they would give away their own hearts."

Later Europeans, coming as permanent settlers, would learn to dread the war cry of the wilderness, and they would depict the Indian as a dull, revengeful savage. Unfortunately for the Indian people, this latter judgment has prevailed.

The gentle, friendly people Columbus encountered did not physically disappear, but something happened to that openhanded generosity with which they met him. Tribes dislodged from their homes along the Atlantic coast had either to fight or perish. They turned upon other tribes, seeking territory, and soon Indian fought against Indian throughout the land. With mounting ferocity, they attacked white settlements as well, and border warfare did not finally subside until an awful morning in December 1890, when a camp of Sioux Indians was slaughtered in the snow on Wounded Knee Creek, South Dakota, by United States soldiers.

Scientists digging into old village sites tell us of tribes living side by side for hundreds of years without warfare. The myths and legends of the many tribes are not battle stories, but convey instead a feeling for the dignity of man and reverence for all of nature. Best of all evidence of the innate peace-seeking habits of the first Americans are the living Indian societies of today. Here one finds true concern for the well-being of each least member, respect for the elders, and devotion to the needs of the spirit.

Corn was, indeed, a great gift to the world; but a greater gift was one that the world let lie and never gathered up for its own. That was the gift of peace on earth.

Yes, these were real people. They broke the trails which our railways and highways follow today. Their names are upon our land, upon the rivers, lakes, and mountains we love.

They belong in the great tradition we call American.

CONTENTS

xiii

xiii

RUNNER IN THE SUN

Chapter 1

Call to the Kiva

THIS is the story of a town that refused to die. It is the story of the angry men who tried to destroy, and of the Indian boy called Salt, in the language of his people, who stood against them.

It was not an ordinary town. It did not rise from the crown of a hill and flash views of its towers and steeples to an approaching stranger. Neither did it fit snugly in a valley against the bend of a sparkling river. One might travel close by and never know the town existed, unless one had been told about it.

1

The country which held this town was so broad and flat that the horizon seemed to lie at the end of the world. The soil underfoot was light gray in color, but so thickly was the land covered with pinon and juniper and dwarf oak that the distances looked black. It was high country, a land of little rain, where rocks turned black under the sun's intensity. At day's end, after heat had poured for long hours upon the parched earth, waves of blue haze rose against the horizon until earth and sky blurred and the tops of distant turreted rocks seemed to float on empty space. The people living there sometimes called it the Enchanted Land.

If one traveled across the countryside looking for the town, one would come without warning to the edge of space. The broad plain with its grass and sage and pinion trees ceased to be. Looking down into the void one would see shadows, and at first it might seem that there was no bottom. The sun striking from an angle made a shimmering screen that blocked vision. After one's eyes became adjusted to the tricky light, a rock wall would float into view, ghostlike, across a wide chasm. By shielding one's eyes, details would come into focus. A jutting pinnacle of rock rose from the bottom. Pine and spruce trees appeared far below. A shaft of light might strike the bronze of an eagle's wings as it pivoted on a current of rising air.

At last the town would emerge out of shadow. It was not at the bottom of the chasm, but in the wall of gray rock standing opposite. Streaks of brown weathering extended downward from the top of the canyon, then disappeared where the rock bulged inward to form the roof of a cave. The houses inside the cave were perfectly sheltered. They were built of stone and stood in some places four stories high.

No smoke would rise from cooking fires; no life would be visible. Sun and shadow alone would be there. But listening carefully, it might seem, after a while, that sounds were rising from the canyon depths. Voices would be chanting faintly. The dead air would stir between the rock walls. The lazily vaulting eagle would clap its wings in startled energy and sail away.

This was the town where the boy called Salt lived many centuries ago. The path to the town—White Rock Place or Village, they called it—started from the bottom of a canyon. There was also a way to reach it from on top, where the people had their planted fields. In addition, a certain few old men knew of a secret trail, but this knowledge they guarded carefully, lest enemies learn of it and steal in upon the people while they slept.

The canyon floor was a clutter of great boulders fallen from the cliff during the centuries, when frost and wind and rain were gouging out the cave. Rocks had also decayed into earth and the earth produced a thick growth of succulent grasses and shrubs. The bottom of the canyon was cool and moist. A stream of clear water, starting from a gushing spring at the head of the canyon, twisted over and around the crowding boulders. The water flowed not so strongly as it once had; it made a feeble music among the

boulders, but still it left the air smelling of sweet dampness. Willows, wild cherry, cottonwood, cedar, and tall
yellow pines followed the stream bed, while hardier sage
and juniper scrambled up the slope of the canyon until
solid rock was encountered. Juniper is not easily discouraged, and single bushes clung to the rock wall, wherever
a crack had allowed a seed to lodge. The canyon bottom
was a pleasant place, where meadow larks sang even in the
heat of midday and mourning doves talked to each other
in pine tree shade.

The trail climbed an easy slope of fractured rock lying
at the base of the cliff. Where the slope ended at the cliff
wall, the trail followed a shelf of rock, then disappeared
into a narrow cleft or chimney. It ascended by a succession
of natural and carved steps until it reached another hori-
zontal shelf. The last steep pitch was bridged by three
thick logs, placed one above the other against rock but-
tresses. In time, children learned to run up and down these
notched logs as if they were following a path on level
ground. In case of attack the logs could be tossed down
and the cave was then inaccessible from below.

The boy called Salt climbed the last log and stood finally
within the cave, where he paused for breath. A burning
early summer sun struck back from the gray walls across
the canyon and even the deep interior of the cave was
unusually bright. The boy liked the brightness and the
burning feeling on his skin. He wanted not to move from
the hot boulder against which he leaned.

This was the high end of the cave, and standing with his
back to the wall he could see down into the village. People

he talked to every day were moving about. A woman who often visited his mother was climbing the ladder that led into her house. No doors or windows occurred at the ground level and entrances were from the roof. An old blind man sat in the full sun spinning cotton into thread by rolling the loose fiber across his bare thigh. A second old man sat nearby and talked, no doubt about what everybody was talking about these days—the diminishing flow of the spring at the bottom of the canyon. Children and their dogs made faint shouting noises at the far end of the village. Salt watched them, then watched a man appear on the roof of the Chief's House. The man's voice came clearly, though faintly, up to Salt.

"Now hear your father speak!" Salt heard. The shell ornament at the man's throat flashed a miniature sun.

This was the Crier, and Salt knew without hearing the words what he would announce, and he knew without going further what the village fathers might talk about when in response to the announcement they assembled in the kiva of the Turquoise people.

A boy of sixteen already knew many things. Climbing about, and poking about, as a boy must if he is to learn things, Salt had seen men meeting when they thought they went unobserved. He had heard words exchanged in the darkness of night. He had come upon these things unexpectedly, then had crept closer, practicing his stealth. Then he realized that he was not playing a boy's game, and he became afraid.

Salt was slender, with a man's height. He was a straight line from shoulder to hip, and his long muscled legs sug-

gested a tireless runner. His clothing was simple: a band
of cloth wrapped around his shoulder-length black hair,
and a kind of kilt held at his waist by a belt. The kilt was
woven of white cotton with black zigzags running up and
down. His feet were covered with sandals made of twisted
yucca fiber which curved up and over his toes and were
fastened by thongs crossing over the instep. Around his
neck he wore white shells strung on a buckskin thong with
a central ornament of turquoise inlaid in bone. But this was
more than ornament—it signified his initiation into manhood. His frequent touching of it disclosed how new a
thing it was for him to wear.

His face, as he watched in repose, had a gentle look.
The eyes were large and set wide; the nose high and
straight; the lips thin—a countenance promising intelli-
gence and quick feeling. He tried to close his ears to the
words rising from below, to pretend he did not hear and
did not have to respond.

"Now hear, O children! The world once before died in
fire and our fathers ran into the unwatered desert and
slaked their thirst on burning sand. Do not bring the fires
again to ravage us from our homes and drive livid snakes
upon us! Heed this! Turquoise men, you are called by
your fathers. Come at once to the underground house.
Turquoise men, come to the clan house!"

Salt frowned. The words, born of a long-ago fear, were
intended to bend the mind and compel instant obedience.

He recognized that the summons was for him. He was
of the Turquoise people, and he must go. But he would go

warily. If those men, those secret meeting men, charged him with spying, he would not be frightened. But really he would rather not go to the meeting!

The boy walked along the path which ran just inside a low masonry wall at the cliff's edge. He could peer easily over the wall into the depths of the canyon where, far below, pine and cedar made a deeper gloom. It was a view he gazed upon so many times a day that now he did not even see it.

Within the cave no space went unused. The buildings followed the contours of the cave floor and, where it sloped sharply, a house might be two stories in front and a single story in back. At the highest arch of the cave, buildings of three and four stories reached to the roof. One principal street, besides the path at the cliff's edge, ran the length of the village. It was a crooked street, narrow and wide by turns, as it crossed the village. A single opening led inward from the cliff path, but a stranger might never find the opening because it seemed to end against a blank wall. A sharp turn to the left, a narrow passage, then a flight of steps, led at last to an open space where public gatherings were held and where outdoor cooking fireplaces filled the air with the odor of sweet-smelling cedar.

Salt turned from the cliff path and at the stone steps found his way blocked by several small, naked children, watched over by two older girls wearing skirts, with woven bands to hold back their hair. The girls looked up, saw that the passage was blocked, but giggled and made no attempt to get their young charges out of the way. Salt

felt affronted by their failure to recognize the urgency of
his mission.

"I am called to the House of the Turquoise people. The
men are gathering," he explained. The girls eyed him, but
only giggled the harder.

A boy of four, round and brown, looked and grinned.
Next moment, he came charging at Salt's legs and almost
bowled him over. Salt saved himself by reaching down and
lifting the urchin, legs flying, high over his head.

"So, birdling! You charge like a buck deer! Do not the
silly girls teach manners?"

"Down! Down!" the peewee squealed, not frightened,
not happy.

At that, one of the girls, the elder of the two, soberly
offered to take the boy. She was taller than the other, her
face pleasant and already beginning to look womanly. As
she held out her hands for the four-year-old, her eyes
sparkled.

"He is my brother. Let me have him and I will clear
the others away. We should have noticed that you were
a personage." She pointed to the turquoise ornament.
"See," she told her mate. "He is a man." Then her eyes
flashed mischief: "It is hard to tell nowadays who are our
elders."

Salt handed over the struggling boy and was promptly
butted from behind by another seeking his attention. This
made it difficult for him to remove himself with dignity,
but he managed it as a man should.

"Your beauty shines forth. May it remain with you,"
he blurted out, with the formality of an elderly uncle

speaking to a female relative. Behind him he heard suppressed laughter, and hurried his steps to escape from the sound.

Now the sharp glare of the sun was screened by the outer row of buildings and only a soft twilight penetrated the street. The cave, in fact, seemed quite dark to anyone entering from the cliff path. The air became chill and stagnant. In winter, when clouds hung low and for days no wind moved the stale air, the stench of people living together within the cave penetrated everywhere.

He thought he heard his name called and wondered if his mother would be here in the large plaza or at the smaller one farther along. Then he heard the same voice call his name again and his arm was grasped.

"We are the late ones again. What will our clan fathers say this time?"

Salt turned to the speaker, and showed his annoyance by frowning. The boy, of his own age, was called Star Climber, and Salt considered this an inappropriate name. The two had grown up together, played the same games, and now they had been initiated into the men's society together. Salt thought Star Climber was dull and slow. He would never make a hunter because of his clumsiness on the trail. He would never make a fighter because he hung back when the play got rough. He would never make a leader of the people because he believed everything he was told and never knew what he believed himself. He was a tiresome companion, but they had come all this way together and nothing could be done about it. Salt walked on without pausing.

"I suppose you were sleeping again," he said.

Star Climber smiled foolishly. "No one waked me when it was time. And what about you—I suppose you were doing something important."

For a moment Salt thought he would ignore the question, but presently he found himself explaining: "I was up before the sun and ran for two hours in the desert. Then I had other things to do—down there. I was just returning when I heard the call."

As they passed an open space between the buildings on their right, a narrow alley leading away into the deeper shadows of the inner cave, they heard the familiar sound of many turkeys gobbling. The boys paused and looked toward the sound.

"Should we go see what makes them talk?" Star Climber asked.

It was a foolish question which Salt did not answer. Star Climber often said things that left Salt wondering whether he realized that they were nonsense, or whether he said them only to tease. If they had been babes they might have followed the suggestion of going to look at the turkeys. Once, as children, they had gone to play with the carefully guarded birds, and had been soundly scolded. No one took it seriously then, since they knew no better, but such an escapade now would bring more than a scolding. Turkeys were called "divining birds," and were held in high regard. The flesh was never eaten and the birds were treated as if they were spokesmen and leaders of the people. When it was necessary to foretell some future event, certain priests consulted the turkeys, following a prescribed ceremony, and announced the findings in language which could be understood only with the greatest difficulty.

When a passer-by heard the turkeys talking among themselves, it was not seemly to stop and listen. Salt glared at his companion, who should have known better.

The street now led into a small plaza, where the sun again shone in full brightness. The buildings on the cliff-side had ended in a low parapet wall; women sat here in the sun, with their backs to a wall, their legs extending straight before them. Their dresses, of cotton, were fastened over the right shoulder, leaving the left shoulder free. Their hair was cut shoulder length and hung loose, for they were all wives and mothers. They were working from mounds of pottery clay, fashioning the moist earth into coils for the walls of various shapes of vessels. As they worked they chattered.

The women looked up as the boys approached, and Salt saw that his mother was one of the pottery workers. For a fleet second he watched her small strong hands add a slender coil of moist clay to the top of what would be a water jar and smooth the coil inside and out until a perfect joint had been made. Her fingers darted like swallows as they moved to the nearby basin of water, then to the clay, then back to the water. Surely there was no better potter in the White Rock Village!

His mother caught his look and smiled. "I believe you are awaited over there," she motioned with her lips.

Salt was aware that the guard at the ladder leading

down into the kiva was annoyed from too much waiting.
Nevertheless, it was necessary to pause to look at his
mother's flying fingers.

Another woman in the group spoke up. "Now that they
have made a man of you, they'll not lose a chance to make
you feel like a child. That's the way men are." The voice
was half scolding, but it was not unpleasant. His mother's
younger sister had spoken.

"As soon as you have finished, come to our house and
eat." That was his mother again, her fingers never pausing.

"I leave you in happiness," he said, moving on.

"Go then in happiness," his mother answered, smiling
fleetingly.

Star Climber had already descended the ladder into the
kiva. The impatient guard was the very man who had
called from the housetop, a little man with a large face.
His chin, instead of coming to a point, looked like a round
swelling in his neck, and his mouth usually hung half
open as if from the weight of his baggy chin.

"When the Turquoise men are called, you will learn to
come," the crier-guard said. The words seemed to come
out of his nose, because his sagging lower lip hardly moved.
He was called Stone Man. Salt placed his hand on the
protruding ends of the ladder and step by step descended
into the darkness.

He remembered again the man he had trailed at night-
fall. He heard the man's low whistle, like the night hawk's,
and the answering whistle. He had watched as a second
figure emerged out of shadow, and he had crept closer to
learn who the second person might be and to hear, if he

could, what words passed. Then the scene seemed to dissolve, he lost track of the stealthy men—until he was grabbed from behind and sent spinning down the trail. He tried afterward to remember and to identify the voice of the speaker who had hissed at him: "Come this way again and your ears will be sliced off!"

Would someone, here in the kiva, reveal himself as one of those who met by darkness and by stealth? Would he be accused? And by whom? And of what?

Chapter 2

Voice of the Enemy

THE KIVA, a circular room without windows, could be entered only by the square opening in the roof, at once a smoke hole and a doorway. This was the meeting place for the men of the clan, but it was more than that. In it, Salt and boys of his own age, and boys before his time, were taught the art and skills of manhood. History and legend were told here, and the manner in which a man should stand before the world was proclaimed in many long speeches.

14

The interior was not entirely dark, since a fan of light came from above and a bed of red coals in the fire pit near the center of the room produced a faint glow, but it was so dim that Salt stood with one hand on the ladder until his eyes would save him from colliding with people. A knot of older men sat in a tight ring near the fire pit. They were passing a short-stemmed pottery pipe from one to another, each man puffing four times, then twice more, then handing it on.

As his eyes adjusted themselves and Salt could make his way to the seat assigned to him, his mind reached out to the men, his fathers, whose hands had worked so cleverly to lay together the stones for these walls. Men talked of kinship, but the laying up of a wall for one's children to use was a real thing. It bridged and held together those who had gone on and those who remained, in everlasting kinship. Salt always felt this when he looked upon the walls of his kiva.

Against the outer wall, at even intervals, six pillars reached to the top like six strong men and supported the pine beams on which the roof rested. In between these pillars ran a waist-high bench of stone. Those who sat on the bench were elevated above others, hence the seats were reserved for certain officers called "Speakers."

In the south wall of the kiva a square hole just above the floor brought fresh air. A slab of stone standing upright between the fresh-air opening and the fire pit deflected the current of air and caused it to circulate around the room and to create a draft for the fire. The walls were whitewashed frequently, as Salt and the other young men

knew, since they performed the work. Once a year, when
the clan leaders prepared for the Earth Renewing ceremony, the leader of the Masked God society repainted the
sacred symbols on the facing side of the stone pillars.

The men who had been smoking near the center of the
room presently rose and moved to their seats on the
benches. The talk would begin. Speaking in the kiva followed a regular procedure. Each of the principal officers
had a spokesman to talk for him. Sometimes a spokesman
came to a situation when he did not know what his man
wanted said, and in that case the meeting might break up,
or others might change the subject.

As the meeting began, Salt's attention wandered. From
thinking of ancient kinship with his fathers, his mind had
skipped to his morning run and he was again chasing a
rabbit through the sagebrush in the half-light. A man had
duties to perform, and meeting in the kiva was one of the
ways in which a man fulfilled himself. But the boy could
still remind the man that nothing in the world was as
pleasant as running free and alone in a great space, when
the stars are dimming and soft winds rise in the west! To
such an extent had Salt's thoughts strayed that he did not
hear at once the words directed at him, and did not see the
pointing hand.

"That boy will destroy us! You have heard me say this
before and I say it again!"

The speaker was rather short, with strong legs and
chest and long, powerful arms. His head seemed large
for the size of his body. He moved in bursts of speed, as
if something were ever on the point of getting away, and

he must ever be pouncing upon it. He spoke angrily, in a hoarse voice. This was Flute Man, who had no ceremonial office in the kiva but whose position was nonetheless important. As War Chief, or, as they sometimes said, Outside Chief, he was expected to see that men observed the fasts and purification rites required before they took part in important ceremonies. If such rules were disregarded, a ceremony might fail, and failure might mean that the corn would not grow, that men might become bewitched, or that enemies might steal their women and children. Men of the kiva were careful not to arouse Flute Man's suspicion or displeasure.

When Salt realized at last that all eyes were turned upon him, he stiffened. Flute Man belonged in his mother's family, yet he never seemed to be part of it. A man belonged to the house of his mother and his sisters, never to a house of his own. But Flute Man seemed to come and go according to some plan of his own. Salt could never remember a time when there had been any closeness between them. Older men were always quick to throw protecting arms around the younger boys of a family. They were the teachers, the sponsors, the go-betweens. Flute Man had been none of these, and Salt had never understood him. To be attacked by him was a double burden, since it was difficult to answer a relative.

"This is a serious thing, this talk against my son. We wait to hear the rest."

It was Shield, tall and stooping, who spoke. He used the term "son" in speaking of Salt, by which he meant that he regarded the boy as his young clansman. Shield,

an elder, was held in great respect and in his time had
filled many offices in clan and village.

Flute Man, the accuser, was not abashed at having his
words challenged by such a man as Shield.

"I speak of serious things, indeed. We expect our young
people to work in the cornfields, to learn what they need
to know, and to respect holy things. If you ask whether
this boy cares for such things, my duty requires me to tell
you he cares very little. When I go to the fields, he is
nowhere to be seen. But walk out on the desert down
there, beyond where our sacred stream vanished into the
earth—there you will find him, sitting on a rock idling
away his time. Or he will tell you he is hunting rabbits,
but I can say he rarely brings game home to his house. I
have watched, since that is part of my duty."

He paused to give his words effect, and a memory stirred
in Salt. He waited in a daze.

"As for learning what he will need to know when he
must go to war or help his people in time of trouble—I
can only say a boy sitting on a rock or running like a wolf
in the desert learns nothing to benefit himself, or his people. As for respecting holy things—you saw today how
he was last to come to our kiva meeting when, being a
young man, he should be among the earliest to arrive. Nor
is this the first time."

Shield listened to the end, then waited, allowing Flute
Man to continue further if he desired. When nothing more
came, the thin old man lifted his long face, framed by
straggling ends of graying hair, and gazed long at the
accused boy.

"Son," the tone was gentle, "we will give you permission to talk, if you wish it. What can you say in answer to our brother? As he says, these are serious matters."

Salt had never before been invited to speak in the kiva; seldom was a young man so asked. His feelings came up in a lump as he glanced at the set faces before him. Only Flute Man stared back. The others regarded the earth at their feet and indicated neither favor nor disfavor. To speak out forcefully and win the minds of men—that was the thing any boy might dream about from his first kiva meeting. How different, when the time came! He looked again at the lowered heads and wondered if it would not be wiser to hold his tongue and not risk offending his elders. Perhaps he would have chosen the latter course if Climbing Star, seated next to him, had not nudged him and hissed: "Better not speak! Flute Man is watching you!"

The cautioning words stung Salt. He must speak.

"Flute Man, my uncle, knows that our corn grows badly." Courtesy was prized by his people as one of the first virtues, and Salt was careful to show courtesy by word and tone. "Each year it gets worse. I spoke of this. I said our people should move their fields from the land above, where there are many rocks and no water, and plant them down there in the canyon. The spring water disappears into the earth just where the canyon opens and grows wide. The sagebrush is thick at that place and willows grow there also, drinking up the water. When I spoke of this, he answered that such things are not for me to think about. So I made a place in the sagebrush—I chopped it away and dug it out. Then I planted corn there. It is now

three times as high as the corn in the upper fields. I think
my uncle does not like this."

Several of the listening men sat back and looked at the
boy. He could hear the quick sucking in of breath. Flute
Man called out. "You see! Just hear how he talks!" His
face was shining with a victor's glee. "His own words
condemn him."

Shield persisted in his gentle voice: "You know, boy,
that our fields above were laid out by our fathers, and that
is where we plant. The ground below has never been con-
secrated. Who goes there, goes in peril."

"Uncle, I knew of that. Yet, I knew how in our family
field every year we have less corn, hardly enough to eat;
none to store for the bad year when all corn will fail. I
think that bad year will come soon."

Confirming voices sounded around the room. "The boy
says well. This is a true thing."

Flute Man was quick to interrupt the agreeing tones.

"Is a boy to set aside our accepted way of living? I
warned you he does not respect holy things. Now you
hear for yourselves. The corn he planted will have to be
pulled up. Otherwise, who knows what may befall our
people. The very spring by which we live may fail us.
Destroy the corn, I say, then consider what to do with him.
For something must be done."

Shield once more pressed into the discussion. "I think
we will first look at the boy's corn before we pull it up.
Others say the bad year might be coming soon. I agree.
Each year our sacred spring gives a smaller stream of
water, as we all know. When this boy was an infant, you

could hear the water roar as it came down from the mountain wall. Now you have to listen carefully on the quietest night to hear it from up here. What will happen to these people when the water is gone?"

Salt, listening, suddenly heard the voice again, and excitement burned in his eyes. The voice was speaking, not about the planting of corn. It was nighttime, and out of the shadow it hissed, "Come this way again——" Salt looked away, fearful that his burning eyes would give him away. Better that he say no more.

Flute Man, showing unhappiness, rose to his feet. Speakers did not rise except on formal occasions, but Flute Man was too excited to think about that. "This cannot be! The boy will destroy us!" He looked challengingly from face to face until he had surveyed every man in the kiva.

At that point an aged blind man, who sat in the back row with Salt and the newly initiated men, spoke up in the quaver of the ancient.

"I can't see Flute Man but I know he is looking at me. His eyes poke at me like willow sticks. I will only ask him if he is a priest to decide where we may plant."

Flute Man, of course, was not a priest, and the remark fetched a sprinkling of laughter.

At that point, one of the speakers slid from his place on the high bench. He was a stout man, of a serious expression, as was proper in one of his position. His graying hair was tied down with a band of red woven stuff that circled his head. They called him Day Singer.

"I think the boy should go now. We will take this into our thoughts. Surely a strange thing has happened and must be answered in some fashion." In that there was agreement.

Salt hurried up the ladder when told that he could go, and once he reached the open air his pent-up breath burst from him. Something surely was happening, something beyond anything he had ever imagined. Who were these men who had met in stealth? Who, besides this one whose name he now knew?

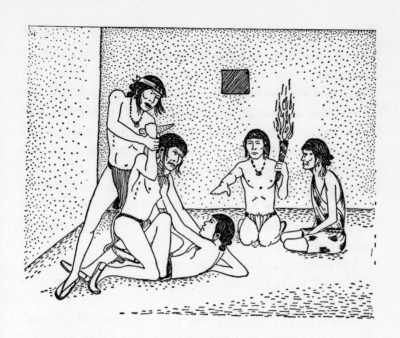

Chapter 3

Face to Face

D ARKNESS crept up the canyon wall like flood waters rising against the banks of a stream. By the time the sun crossed the arc of sky above the towering rock walls, the flood of shadow was at the brim. At that moment, a chilling wind blew into the cave of White Rock Village.

When Salt stepped from the ladder to the roof of the kiva and found that he had missed the sun, it was as if a friend had gone ahead without waiting. He stood at the edge of the little plaza and gazed upward. Stars were

23

already visible in the blue depths above. A nighthawk hurtled through the air, startling the silence. The cave was a lonely place at the moment between daylight and darkness.

His mother had gone with the warmth of the day. He paused near where she and the other women had worked in the sun. Evening chill shook him; then he was hungry.

From the darkening canyon, he turned to the still darker cave. Cooking fires glowed on roof terraces and threw feeble shadows on house and cave walls. Cedarwood gave off no smoke when it burned, but it left a sweet stinging odor in the air.

He climbed a short ladder to one terrace, crossed to a shadowed wall, climbed a steeper ladder, then stood in firelight. A voice called.

"Here is our youngest father returning from the council. He has discovered that hunger grows faster than wisdom."

It was his mother's youngest sister, Shell Woman, laughing as always. He did not mind being chided by her. It brought a feeling of well-being.

"We kept the pot near the fire all afternoon. Is the talking finished?"

His mother had stepped to his side and he could see the firelight glow in her searching eyes. His head was already above hers.

"Ah, no," she continued before he spoke. "You left before the others. And you are troubled."

The people called her Becoming Day, and she had the trick of knowing when he was tired or sick or downcast. After she satisfied herself with a look, she lost no time preparing a remedy.

"Food first," she ordered. "Sit, and I will bring it to you."

The warm food, tasting fragrantly of the sage his mother cooked with the meat, brought a certain peace. Whatever the voices in the kiva might be saying, here for a moment was forgetfulness. The glowing embers of the cooking fire gave light and comfort. Let Flute Man talk in shadow and anger; it was of no concern here. He gathered his feet close under and sat firm on a mound of mountain-goat skin.

A lesser figure moved away from the fire glow, then merged in shadow. His name was called softly, but not the name his elders called him by. It was a secret name, used only by his younger sister.

"Muddy-O" was the whispered sound. And hearing it, he smiled in the secret shadow.

It was as if a bright light burst upon him, as when the sun suddenly shoots from behind a thundercloud and fashions a new landscape. It was a name of laughter and games, a name that went with leaping from stone to stone, of plunging into the cool waters that flowed at the bottom of the canyon. On one such day, he being a boy of ten and his sister a child of six years, they had played until exhaustion caught up with them and they lay down at the mossy edge of the canyon stream. First they lay and told stories about the beasts of earth and sky—idle caricatures of the stories their elders told in high seriousness. The stories grew drowsier, and presently they both slept. When Salt awoke (at the time he was called simply the Youngest Boy), it was to a sound of laughter. He lay a moment to get his wits together, fearing that he had slept too long. Then quickly he put his hands to his itching face and found that he had been plastered with mud! His sister, by then, was already out of range and as she danced away, leaping up the trail to the cave village, she chanted, "Brother has a mud face! Brother has a mud face!"

He smiled in the shadows, remembering how the words echoed back at him from the canyon walls. By the time he reached the village, running to catch his taunting sister when he should have stopped to wash, the name "Mud Face" was tossed back at him from every household.

Only his sister still remembered, but she had softened her conquest with the years.

"Muddy-O" was the sound he heard.

Young people grew up early in the Village of the White Rocks. His sister, Morning Shell, at eleven, was already a cook, a potter and a weaver of sorts. A woman of the household.

She came quite close before she spoke further.

"Our mother did not speak of this. She wanted you to eat first. But there is to be trouble. Word has come from the kiva that you did some bad thing, and that you will be punished. I did not believe it, my brother. How can they punish you in that case?"

"They will not ask what you believe, little mustard seed, though I am happy to hear you speak in my favor."

"What will they do, and why do they say you have done a bad thing?"

"You might agree with them if I told you. Then I would have no one to talk for me."

"You speak in fun. Our mother will speak out for you. But you must tell me."

"This much I tell you truly. I know what is said against me, but my accuser says one thing and means something else. Only time will answer the riddle."

The answer did not satisfy the girl, who moaned softly in the darkness. Salt had to stare hard at the shadowy form at his side to be sure it was his child sister, she sounded so like a woman full grown.

"They will send the masked gods to whip you with rawhide knots. Blood will run from your skin. I see it, Brother! You must go away!"

He reached across and touched her arm. "You frighten yourself—"

Forms had appeared above the parapet. Now they were moving forms, approaching the fire. He twisted his sister's shoulder to turn her toward the fire.

"See, these are not masked gods. They are—"

His sister trembled under his hand.

First came Eldest Woman, his mother's mother, who lived alone in the Chief's Tower, with only a granddaughter to cook for her. Age and shortness of breath had slowed her, but she still climbed ladders and busied herself in the village. They could hear her mighty gasps as she threw her short legs over the parapet. Next to come was Shield, tall and stooped, who had questioned Flute Man in the kiva. Then came the man wearing the red woven band around his head, the one called Day Singer. Last of all to scramble out of the shadow into the firelight, Flute Man himself.

* * * * *

All sat in the room, their forms imperfectly revealed in the light of a pinon torch whose resins smoked and sputtered. Only the Eldest Woman showed clearly, since the flame was held near her to help her in her half-blindness. Once she had been fat, then she had wasted, and folds of skin now hung loosely under her chin. The brown scalp showed in patches through the thin mat of gray hair. She spoke first.

"I want to know what is being said about my grandson. If it is idle talk, it must stop. Well, who waits? Speak up!"

Flute Man thrust his large head forward into the light.

"It is not what people are saying, Grandmother, but what the boy himself says. Call upon him to speak."

"In due time," the ancient one answered. "It is reported that you accuse the boy of placing a curse on his people. If you have a reason, I came to hear it."

Flute Man was not tall, but when he arose his head almost touched the low ceiling. A robe of rabbit's wool was thrown over his left shoulder, leaving his right arm free to gesture. The flaring torch was a bright spark in his wild eyes.

Salt, looking up at the speaker, saw the angry eyes. But he also saw the tuft of eagle feathers hanging from the center beam. This would keep evil from the room, he thought, and no harm would come to him. That, at least, was what the old people believed; but one could not always count on it. An accident could befall an unlucky person.

"These men were present." Flute Man motioned into the shadows. "They know what was said."

Salt felt his breath rise and fall. Now he was tempted

to speak and put an end to this wasting of words; now he would hold his tongue. In his indecision, he waited and heard Flute Man repeat again the blind and ugly words he had uttered in the kiva.

"If our sacred spring dries up entirely, this witless boy will be the cause, since he goes against the ways of our people."

The speaker stared at each shadowy figure in turn. Then when his eyes came to Eldest Woman, he drew back and presently was seated again.

"Well!" Impatience exploded in the clan mother's single word. "Who else will speak?"

The boy's face grew hot, but still he held back. Eldest Woman had always been ancient in Salt's memory. She had a longer name, but no one spoke it. Other women might visit his mother and smile upon her family. Not this mother of mothers, as older women were sometimes called. On the rare occasions when children encountered her in the plaza or on the trail, her eyes were far away and took no notice of what laughter, fear or sorrow might be in the young faces she encountered. To speak in her presence, to risk her rebuke, was a fearful thing. As the silence endured, Salt grew tense; then, gratefully, he saw Shield rising out of the shadows. The pressure in his chest at once escaped in a great sigh that the clan mother heard. She raised one ragged eyebrow in his direction, but Salt was too preoccupied to notice.

Shield talked in wispy, dry tones. "We are children of the Turquoise Clan gathered here. We dwell all in the same house. We know that beyond our walls other clans-

men watch us jealously. Our legends tell us that Turquoise
men were the first to occupy the Village of the White
Rocks. As the first, we were the most powerful. It was for
us to decide who might live in the village and who might
not."

Shield did not speak hurriedly. He let each sentence
linger before starting another. His stooped figure fitted
just under the ceiling, so that his voice seemed to cling to
the yellow pine beams.

"Our power is not what it was. Our numbers grow less.
Then, as you know, the Holy One, our true leader, moved
out of our village and lives alone. I speak no more of
that, but it is a certainty that since that day of misfortune
our strength has been drying up like a field without water.
Beyond our walls, people watch. They are hungry. They
may be our younger children, but they sharpen their flint
knives for our throats. Take care that our own actions do
not split us apart and leave us ready for those knives."

The speaker halted on a tone of uncertainty, then
seemed to decide against saying more. Cautiously he moved
backward until he found his place in the shadows.

Eldest Woman frowned. "Shield talks strangely. Who
is splitting us apart?"

Shield rose to his feet again, but did not move forward
into the flickering light. He was a voice without form.

"The spring in the canyon is life-giver to us all. Without
the water, the Village of the White Rocks would be filled
with our bleached bones. When a speaker in the kiva blames
a Turquoise man for the failing spring, by morning every
child in the village will point at that man. Our kiva talks

are supposed to be kept within the kiva, but everyone
knows that stones have ears. Such a story will grow, until
it is claimed that our clan itself is at fault—and thus our
enemies, the envious ones of our village, will be made
bolder."

Flute Man came forward into the light, impatient to
answer Shield, but Eldest Woman held him back with a
gesture.

"Do you still insist that this grandson, who wears the
badge of a Turquoise man, is destroying our spring?"

Salt moved his hand in the dark, feeling for the turquoise ornament. The elders had told him at the time of
his initiation that the touch of that stone would drive fear
out of a true Turquoise man. In time of danger, it would
protect him from harm; it would insure a full and happy
life. For was not the turquoise the gift of the blue sky,
where the Sun Father traveled? Sun Old Man, he was also
called. The people prayed to him at his rising, they prayed
to him when he stood still at midday, and again when he
entered his evening house. Turquoise reminded a man of
the peace that dwelt in the sky. It said to the mind, Behold,
here is the way to live, at peace with your brothers!

Fingering the blue stone, Salt felt the turmoil subside
in his breast. Let Flute Man say what he would!

His thoughts strayed and he did not follow closely on
Flute Man's opening words. What he finally heard drove
thoughts of peace from his mind and left him shivering.
It was difficult, he was learning, to hold a thing fast in his
thinking.

"—and that is why I say he is a meddling child and

must be corrected. What matter, O Grandmother, whether the Turquoise Clan be split asunder by what happens among us, if our entire Seven Clans are to be destroyed? Do you wish us to bind up our mouths while this impure child remains among us, bringing us to shame and destruction?"

"I've heard enough! Let the boy speak. You, Grandson! Come where I can see your face. Now, tell me if you understand what has been said against you, and how you answer."

The slender boy stood straight before his elders. His breathing rose and fell, and he hardly knew at first whether any words would come.

"I understand it well, my Grandmother. My mother's youngest brother wants our people to plant corn where there is no water. He says the corn land is the high land. Yet he knows, even as I know, that up there the corn plants are weaker each year and bear fewer ears. I think in the days of our elders more rain fell on the high land. The stream beds are there still, but now they are dry. It looks as though those streams have been dry a long time—"

Eldest Woman muttered to herself, but loud enough to be heard: "The boy obviously uses his eyes. We had mighty rains in my childhood. Continue!" she called out, aware of her interruption.

"With my digging stick I made a deep hole, and the earth was dry to the depth of my stick. I mean no disrespect, but I say it is better to plant our corn down in the canyon where the water from the spring sinks into the ground.

"But that is not all I understand—" The boy turned suddenly in the direction of Flute Man.

"Now you have heard him!" the angry accuser interrupted. "This is no simple child."

"Be quiet, you! I wish to hear him."

Salt breathed deeply for strength. "My uncle speaks of the corn I planted below. He shames me before others. He wishes you not to listen to me, not to believe me. Because I know something about him. This he knows—"

"I warn you, you mud-faced child! Watch your tongue!"

"He talks in dark corners with men whose faces I could not see—but I can name one."

Eldest Woman gasped. "Child—" she began.

Salt rushed on. The words were crowding for utterance and he must say them before his breath failed.

"My uncle knows what I saw—and he would silence me. He talks to the one we call Dark Dealer—"

Flute Man hurled himself against the boy, crying, "A knife! A knife! I'll cut out his black tongue!"

As they crashed to the floor, Salt felt sharp fingers at his throat. He lashed out with hands and feet, but still the clawing fingers squeezed. He struck blindly.

Then his throat was suddenly free. The weight lifted from his body.

It was the stocky, gray-haired Day Singer who had plunged in and grasped Flute Man by the hair.

Then there was silence, save for the harsh gasping breath that seemed to fill the place. Salt sat cross-legged in the middle of the room, his heart pounding at his ribs.

Eldest Woman, having reflected on what she had heard and seen, spoke at last. She looked at Flute Man.

"Now you must leave." Her voice, flat and cold, was not accusing. "We will talk again of this. Shield and Day Singer I ask to stay."

Flute Man was enraged. "You will listen to this boy's lies. I insist on hearing him out!"

"You will go," Eldest Woman replied and did not even glance up.

As Flute Man turned, he kicked out at Salt, but the blow fell short. Day Singer had nudged him with his shoulder enough to throw him off balance. They heard him on the roof terrace a moment later. He had bumped against a shadowed form.

"O you snooping women! Get to your beds!"

A silence fell upon the room again. Once the commotion had ceased, the pinon torch burned quietly.

The boy remained cross-legged in the center of the room, waiting. He did not regret what he had said; his eyes had not deceived him. But he was not so long removed from childhood as to forget how grown people often treated the words of a young person. They would ask him how he knew. Was he sure? Did he realize what he was saying? He waited.

At last Eldest Woman sighed, as one who comes from a deep sleep.

"The Dark Dealer has killed men. Everyone speaks of it."

Salt knew this and said nothing.

"It is known that he talks to the Cloud People—the Dead. He has the power of witchcraft."

This also Salt knew, and he said nothing.

"He is the only man in all the village who dares to look into a spring when the sun stands at the high point of the day. And we know why he can do that and not be stricken with a blank mind. Only one man stands against the Dark Dealer. Him we call the Holy One. Shield and Day Singer know why the Holy One lives in a cave by himself, and there's no need to tell that story now."

Eldest Woman had been talking, as if to herself, gazing straight ahead. Now she looked down at Salt squatting on the floor.

The tuft of eagle feathers hanging overhead turned halfway in a draft of air, then turned back, like something alive. Would those feathers still protect him, or would he be one of the unlucky ones?

"If Flute Man has been talking to Dark Dealer, it was wrong of you, child, to speak of it when Flute Man was here among us. Now you have put him on his guard and we may not find out what scheme they are plotting until it is too late."

She fell silent but all knew she would speak again. Her thoughts were traveling afar, but would return.

"What it is to be, we will know in time. I am not thinking about that now. I am thinking of how we will protect you. Trouble may fall on you first, before anything else is tried. To protect you, we must take your manhood badge away from you. That is my thought."

Salt, startled by the words, clutched the turquoise pendant.

"The kiva must be asked to reverse the ceremony which made you a man. As a child, no one will touch you, for Sun Old Man is the special protector of children. Even Dark Dealer knows that. The village people will force him to respect that much of our law."

Salt rose to his knees, and stayed there. His eyes urged the right to speak.

"What you are saying—surely this cannot be. I am not afraid. The stone will protect me, as it protects all Turquoise men. Without it, as you say, I would be a child again; and what can a child do for his people! Let me remain a man, my Grandmother, and I will show you how I can protect us all!"

The voice of Eldest Woman grew sharp and crisp.

"Now you are showing us that you are indeed a child. You will protect us! Do you think it not possible for your elders to take care of themselves, and of you as well? We will talk no more of this. Remove the stone from his neck. I am going to bed. Tomorrow make the announcement."

And that night the boy Salt did indeed become a child again. In the lowermost room where he went to sleep, in utter darkness, his tears poured over his hands as he held them to his mouth to stifle his own outcries. He shuddered, but made no sound. The hours went by, shrouded in darkness, and in time his limbs began to slacken and stretch their length.

At the very end of that night, almost as sleep caught him, a last moment of alertness held him fast. In that moment came a sound which, as a very young child, he had often heard. Or was it a sound? Like stones dropping, one by one, into a hole of deep water. Like the beat of a very distant drum. Or was it only tears dropping from his eyes upon the packed earth floor? His eyes by then were quite dry, but still he heard the throb of something, perhaps the very heart of the earth itself.

Chapter 4

The Owl's Claw

WHEN Flute Man left the house of Salt's mother, he scrambled over parapet, ladder, and roof until he reached the dark inner street of the cliff village. There, safely in shadow, he waited. No one moved. No sounds came. Still he waited.

When he moved finally, no one could have said he moved. He simply became one with the shadow and was no longer there.

Staying within the deep shadows, he hurried, slipping through the village until he reached the high place, where the log ladder led downward. Quickly he descended, his feet finding the notches unerringly. Halfway down the cliff, he paused again. Waited and listened. Then he followed a ledge of rock which went, not downward as the villagers went when they descended into the canyon, but off to his left, seemingly into the void. The ledge was only the width of a moccasined foot. Then presently there was no ledge at all, only toe- and handholds in the solid rock. Flute Man moved more slowly, feeling each grappling place, pulling himself upward over the waiting emptiness of the canyon. He breathed without effort, seeming to feel neither fear nor uncertainty. At last he pulled himself over the edge and into a narrow crack in the cliff. With a last flip of his feet, he disappeared into the rock.

In the blackness, after he had crawled a body's length, he could feel himself descending. He rose to his knees, then stood at full height. It was a lesser cave, lying just below the great cave of the village.

He moved no further, for just as he got to his feet the point of a flint knife lodged against his ribs. A voice growled in his ear.

"Are you alone?"

"Of course, fool!"

"Then who saw you come?"

"Worse-than-fool! No one saw me."

Flute Man was pushed roughly forward into the darkness and the voice behind him rasped, "Save your brave words for the one in there."

For a moment, unbalanced in the utter darkness, Flute

Man struck against sharp rocks and in the black record
of his mind vowed that he would repay the guard. The
power would be his someday, and not far off, to repay all
who had abused him.

A low fire burning in the pit threw a vague and waver-
ing light over the faces of three seated men. The man,
Dark Dealer, with two others sat in the kiva of the Spider
Clan.

Dark Dealer was not an old man, yet he occupied a
place of leadership which normally fell to only the oldest
men in a clan. Power and position usually came to men
late in life, after they had survived the accidents of existence and had arrived at wisdom and tolerance. Dark Dealer
was the youngest son of a family which, before him, had
not been noted for wisdom or bravery. If he had gone the
normal course, his voice would never have been heard in
the kiva meeting, and if he had risen to speak none would
have listened.

But his life had not taken the usual course. It was ru-
mored that at his birth, when he was carried outdoors to
be presented to the sun, a dark cloud suddenly appeared
and remained over the sun until the godparents and infant
returned to the house. He was taken out a second day, and
again a cloud covered the sun. On a third occasion, it was
the same. And when it happened even on a fourth attempt,
the godparents refused to have anything more to do with
the child. Thus, he was never presented to the sun and,
in a manner of speaking, was never properly brought into

life. That was the rumor, but doubtless like all rumors it had grown with the telling.

People also remembered that when Dark Dealer came up for initiation and one of the masked figures stepped forward to whip him across the back with a willow sapling, in token of his acceptance into the clan, the sapling broke in the masked figure's hand and the boy was never touched. Later, people pointed to this as a sign that the boy possessed special powers. Not even the masked impersonator of one of the supernatural people could touch him.

Then came the time when the office of War Chief in the Spider Clan was to be filled. The prior War Chief, as he lay dying, named as his successor a nephew whom he had been training for years. But this nephew, even before the ceremony could be performed which would accomplish his chieftainship, fell over a cliff and broke his neck. In such a situation, the next male relative in the mother's line was usually chosen. But when a candidate had been selected in this instance and announcement of the coming ceremony was made, the candidate was struck by lightning as he went out to gather pinon nuts. The clansmen hesitated to name a third candidate, but while they hesitated Dark Dealer offered himself and was able to prove that his mother's family was distantly related to the late War Chief.

So began his climb to power. The very name, Dark Dealer, was first used then, but as only a whisper passing to and fro. Until hearing of it, he proclaimed it as his own. He even laughed about it.

"The people will remember that name. We'll make it stand for something," he told his clansmen in the kiva. They laughed with him, but none knew for sure whether it was a thing to laugh about, or not.

The War Chief, it was believed, had control over the enemy. His was the power to protect his people against the spirits of enemies slain in battle. His also was the power, it was said, to control the actions of the dead, and to thrust witches away from the people. These were dangerous tasks, but they must be performed by someone. The War Chief had never been an important office in the clan—until Dark Dealer came along and made it so. The clan was led nominally by an old man, Dawn Child, who bore the title of Sun Watcher. This was a position of unusual holiness, since the person in it had the duty of keeping the calendar and of naming the days of important ceremonies. To miscalculate in reckoning these propitious dates might destroy the crops, the very people themselves.

Of him, Dark Dealer said: "Let this old man watch the rocks where the sun passes in his journeys, and let him make the proper prayer sticks for offerings. But look to me; I will make our Spider Clan powerful. It is for Spider Clan men to decide who may live in the Village of the White Rocks. The Turquoise Clan has held this power too long. We live here only by their good will, and who knows when our children may be driven over the cliff? We have a duty to our children to make ourselves powerful. Does any man disagree?"

And none disagreed.

So, through many twistings and turnings, schemes, and

secret meetings, Flute Man, who was not a man of power, but who had his own ambitions within the Turquoise Clan, came to the kiva of the Spider Clan.

Like all other kivas, this one had a daylight entrance through a hole in the roof. A ladder led down into it and anyone could see who came and went by the ladder. But there was also a secret entrance, up the face of the cliff, through a crack in the rock which in daylight was hardly visible from below, then through a narrow cave and the ventilator shaft which led from the cave into the kiva.

Flute Man crawled into the ventilator shaft, and waited. He was still angry with the guard who had pushed him, but not so angry as to forget caution. He crawled silently forward, until by the dim light in the fire pit he could observe who was present. When he satisfied himself that Dark Dealer was alone with his two assistants, he made the chipping sound of a chipmunk. Then waited again.

Inside the kiva, the men moved like machines set in motion by a spring. Dark Dealer arose at once and held up his hand, demanding caution. One of the assistants went to the ladder and climbed out on the roof. The second assistant stopped at the foot of the ladder and took a position where he could watch the man above. Dark Dealer then dropped his hand to his side.

"You risk us all, coming thus without forewarning. I have a flint knife for anyone who ruins our plans." Dark Dealer's voice was low, scarcely audible, yet there was energy in what he said.

Flute Man felt the sting. "When knives are used, mine will not be idle."

The two men were about of the same height, but Dark Dealer was the more powerful. His shoulders and arms were better muscled and his hands were larger. In grappling with a man, he could surely break an arm or a windpipe. Knowing his strength, Dark Dealer said no more, but smiled.

"My sister's youngest boy, that meddler Salt, has been talking with Eldest Woman."

"Well, continue! What did he say?"

Flute Man had come to Dark Dealer's kiva with a purpose, and not merely to report a conversation. That was why, meeting Dark Dealer's gaze squarely, he lied, saying: "The boy accused you of planning to destroy Turquoise Clan."

"How does he say this? What does he know?" The questioner's eyes blazed sharply.

"He makes wild guesses, hoping to win attention. He knows nothing. But he talks, and he must be stopped."

"He'll be stopped—but I want to know why he talks. A child does not speak unless he sees something. Has he seen you climb the cliff up here?"

"He said he saw—but he was lying."

Dark Dealer moved quickly and with one powerful hand grasped the other by the throat.

"It's as I thought. That night you met me at the edge of the village—and said you had to go back. The boy trailed you! So! A child, for all your talk, is smarter than you are. You want to know our plans? You want to take part in them? Then I tell you what you must do. Destroy this boy! Get him out of my way. If you do that without getting caught in a trap, come back, and I will tell you how you can help, and what part you will play."

A shove of the powerful hand sent Flute Man stumbling across the room, until he collapsed against the wall. Dark Dealer sprang forward and stood over him, threatening to seize him once more.

"Only remember. If you are caught, the blame is yours. I will say I know nothing of what you do. I have ears everywhere; if you talk, you will never talk again."

In shame, Flute Man arose. In shame, he moved away from the hurler of threats and toward the ventilator shaft. This was a square opening, no wider than a man's shoulders, placed at the level of the floor. It brought in fresh air for the fire and kept the kiva sweet-smelling.

"You will need help," Dark Dealer spoke up in softer tones. "We want no failure in what you do. I give you this owl's claw to hide on your person. It will protect you against witching powers and give you the cunning to do what must be done."

Flute Man glanced with horror at the sharp claw nestled in a ball of feathers. He backed away.

"This I cannot do. You know our people stone to death any man who is found bearing any part of an owl. Such help is not needed to carry out this little task. I will find pleasure in it, I assure you."

"Take it, I say!"

"It isn't needed. Wait and see."

"You refuse? Too bad, then, because I have decided you can't leave here without it. Too much is at stake. Fire Striker!"

At the sound of his name, the man at the foot of the ladder moved toward the two.

"Is all clear up above?" Dark Dealer asked.

"The short-legged one has given no signal."

"Go up and tell him to be watchful. I will need your help for a minute."

"What will you do?" Alarm entered Flute Man's voice. "We are friends together in this. You will need my help before you finish."

"I decide what help I need. Just now I have decided that I can manage without you. In the morning they will find you at the bottom of the cliff."

Flute Man dived headfirst toward the ventilator shaft. But not quickly enough. He was seized around the knees and brought to the earth-packed floor. After a brief tussle he lay still.

The one called Fire Striker was back from the ladder and ready to take a hand. "How will we do it?" the man asked.

"Wait until this one gets his breath again. Then I'll ask him once more which way he chooses."

But Flute Man did not have to wait. He had heard the words and was ready to speak.

"Give me the owl's claw. I can see your plan is best. When the task is finished, I will return it."

"When the task is finished, yes. Then we will talk again. Do not come here until you have completed it. The guard out there will be watching."

Flute Man squirmed his way through the air shaft. A

moment later he could be heard quarreling with the guard in the cave.

Dark Dealer smiled. "In this way," he told his companion at the fire pit, "we get rid of one, maybe two. With good planning it may be two. Spread the word that Flute Man carries the owl's claw. That will set people to watching him—and when he strikes, they will also be ready to strike."

Chapter 5

Nothing Is Built on Fear

THE MAN called the Holy One lived alone in his rock shelter high above the great cave of the village. Sometimes, looking up, people could see him hopping around like a child at play. "See Grandfather Grasshopper," mothers told their children.

And the same mothers would say to each other, out of hearing of their children: "The fool will fall and break his neck. Not that it would make any difference, since he has deserted us."

Men with serious village problems frequently went up to ask his advice, but they never knew how they would be received. At times they found him crawling around on all fours, and for every question they asked, his only answer was to bark, doglike. At other times he curled up like a bear in hibernation, and no amount of coaxing would cause him to heed their talk. On still other occasions he stood on the rock ledge in front of his cave house and threw stones at anyone trying to climb the steep trail to his abode. When he did respond to questions, and this was a rare occasion, his talk was so difficult that the men spent days in the kiva afterward trying to unravel his words. He resorted to backward talk—a trick of saying the opposite of what he meant. In order to understand his true meaning, the men had to remember the exact wording of the questions they asked and the answers he gave.

No one could have told his age in years, since the people of those times were not so much concerned with the passage of years as they were with the happenings of nature which were encompassed in a man's lifetime. Some could remember back to an early autumn when many families from the Village of the White Rocks were trapped and frozen to death in an unseasonable blizzard which struck while they were gathering pinon nuts. Even farther back in memory was the winter when a heavy wet snow fell, then froze sharply, and a great ledge of rock broke from the opposite cliff and crashed to the canyon bottom with a roar that seemed to shatter the world. Two little girls were crushed at the spring and the spring itself was almost destroyed.

The Holy One had lived through those and many other

dire events. His long, unkempt hair was almost white.
Even his skin seemed bleached, when he sat opposite a
younger tribesman. The deer-hide garments he wore,
black and shiny with grime, appeared to be as ancient as he.
He had never been a large man, but the years had wasted
him until the bones of his face and his limbs looked too big
for the skin that stretched over them. His eyes alone
looked keen and ageless—but that was when he was by
himself, gazing off across the world of broken rock and
black pine headlands. When people came from below to
complain of things in the village, most likely his eyes
would roll until only the whites showed, or he would
simply close them and pucker up his face like the pumpkin
slices the people dried on their roof tops.

They called him the Holy One because it was thought
that he had been touched by the spirits of the other world
—hence, no longer entirely a part of the world of men.
He was entitled, therefore, to a special kind of respect
by men.

That morning as the old man watched the boy Salt
scramble upward over the path of loose rocks, he indulged
in no strange antics and no stone-throwing. But he moved
away from the rock on which he had been sitting in plain
view of the village, and retreated into his cave. There Salt
found him, his eyes looking up brightly.

It was a morning when the air over the mountains hung
clear and tender. Smoke rising from a cooking fire
ascended in a straight line until it finally dissolved high
up against the arching sky. Meadow larks called clearly
and the drumming sound of doves came up from the can-

yon. A pine squirrel ran his long trill with the chirping
sounds at the end. Each stir of air brought a smell of
sage and juniper, commingled as one scent.

"May you have happiness today, Grandfather," the boy
greeted.

"Peace to you, boy." The old man pointed to a flat
rock slightly below his own.

"Here you can sit and look out upon the world, and
watch who comes up the trail. Also, it is easier to talk when
another is not watching your face."

Salt's eyes widened in surprise. The old man seemed to
know that he had come to talk of difficult things.

"You never come unless you have serious problems to
solve," the Holy One said, as if the boy had expressed his
surprise aloud. "Anyhow, your turquoise badge is missing
and that troubles you. So speak, boy. No one will stop you
or accuse you."

"You know what was said, then? You know what happened?"

"I only know what comes drifting to me on the wind."

It was often said that nothing happened in the cliff
village that was not reported in full to the Eagle's Nest,
as the Holy One's cave was called.

For a long time after Salt had finished his story, beginning with the scene in the kiva, and while the sun climbed
midway up the morning sky, the old man made no com-
ment. Once Salt looked back over his shoulder to assure
himself that his listener had not fallen asleep. When he
found the ancient eyes burning fiercely, he looked away
quickly.

"My people think my mind is gone," the old one said finally.

The boy was silent, ashamed to admit that the village talked of this.

"It surprises me that I have my senses still. I know how it is down there. They tell lies. They meet in secret. I am old, but I am still Chief, and some don't like that."

"Eldest Woman said I talked too big. But maybe I could help a little, if I had my turquoise badge."

Salt was surprised to hear the old man laugh—a dry cackling sound.

"We are captives, you and I. To protect you, they take away your badge. For my own protection, I leap around like a goat. We won't be touched while we are as we are, but it has its disadvantages. It is a game to play while we wait, and you must understand that."

"That is what I don't understand, Grandfather. What do we wait for?"

"For the enemy to show who he is, and how he intends to move."

"The enemy has already shown himself."

"Flute Man? Yes, I have known that for some time. Dark Dealer is his master, as I also know. But who else? There are others moving around down there. Stories come up to me."

"I am ashamed to be a child again."

"Ah, no doubt. You are young and want to grow fast. Do you know what—I am ashamed, even in my age when I should outgrow such things, I am ashamed to act like an old fool! It's a game. But do you know why I do it?"

"To wait, you said."

"Yes. But if I lived down there, with those lies and those secret meetings, I would forget my duty. You know how our people say that the Chief should be pure of heart, never become angry. He works for peace. Yes. But if I were down there, I might take my knife or my club and destroy these troublemakers."

"Somebody will have to do it, I think."

"The people will do it, once they know."

"They will poison the minds of the people."

"You think things out. And so I am sure you will be a great leader of the people someday. Also that is why I talk to you freely, and someday may depend on you. But these men are not strong enough to win the people over. They will use fear if they can. They will try to make the people afraid of me, or of you, or of anyone who is trusted by the people. A few weak ones will accept fear as a way of action—and out of fear they may use knives and spill blood. But nothing is built on fear, and they will pass away."

"I believe this, Grandfather. But as a child, I have no part in anything. How long will it be?"

The sun stood in his midday house, where he pauses to catch his breath after the long climb up the morning sky. It was the time when a prayer is said and no one stays out of doors or in the full glare of the sun if he can avoid it. Salt waited until the old man raised his head again.

"We have talked a long time, yet there is still much that must be said another time. Only I will say this, Grandson. Eldest Woman acted in her right and her power in returning you to childhood. She is your godmother. She presented you to the sun at your birth hour. So she is responsible for you and she did this to protect you. But there is a way to win back your manhood badge."

"That is what I want! Only tell me!"

"I will set you a task. Maybe there will be a second task after that."

"Good. I will perform anything you say."

"These will not be easy tasks. I cannot tell you all I have in mind, but this much I will say. Three different times I have had a certain dream. Each time a sacred person talks about our village and tells me that our troubles will not be solved by ourselves alone, that we must go outside of ourselves to find help. I don't know yet what this means. But meantime we must prepare. Someone may have to make a journey, and at my age that is out of the question. If a journey must be attempted, it will have to fall on a young man; one who thinks of his people, not of himself; one who will give his life, if necessary, in order to save his people."

"This I would do if you asked me. When will you name the first task?"

For some time Salt had sat facing the Holy One. Now he saw the tight skin pucker around the eyes and he heard the old man's cackling laugh.

"You are so anxious to be away, you hardly hear what I am telling you. I tell you again, you are starting something which may end with your giving your life."

"Better that than fall down the cliff and break my neck.

If I give my life helping the people, I cannot give it stupidly. I am listening, Grandfather."

"Good. Now, let me tell you. I want to know how good your wits really are. If you were in a strange country and had to find your way where no way was known to you, or lose your life, how would you succeed? That is your first task."

The words puzzled Salt. "I don't understand."

"Patience, clansman. I haven't explained yet. Look, the Village of the White Rocks was built a long time ago. It already existed when my grandfather was born. Before it was built, according to the story he told, our people lived to the south and west of here. Their houses were small, families were scattered, and they lived in a broad valley where abundant waters flowed, and their corn and bean patches stretched all across that valley. I can believe how happy those people were, with their storage houses always full and never a poor growing season. Then a terrible thing happened. Without warning, Sun Father, whether it was in wrath that people who enjoyed abundance should somehow fail in their duties to him, no one knew, but he threw a great flaming mountain at our people. When it struck, a powerful explosion occurred and burning rock flowed into the fields, and even dried up some of the streams. The people threw down whatever they held in their hands and fled. Mothers even threw down their babies, but afterward went back to find them—and sometimes the babies were not there—nothing was there but smoke and devastation."

"That is why our Sun Crier speaks of the world that died in fire!" The words burst from Salt, heedlessly interrupting the ancient speaker.

"You are correct, but you interrupt."

"I ask to be forgiven."

"It is forgotten. Our people left that broad, pleasant valley and journeyed a long time, seeking safety and new places to plant their crops. They came to the mountains and moved up into many sheltering canyons. Not only the people of our village, but many others had lived in the open valley where the mountain of fire struck the earth. They say that for a long time those people kept moving into the mountains, and into the canyons where they could feel safe from Sun Father. They went into caves, like our own great cave of the White Rocks. There they felt secure, since He Who Rides the Sky could observe their houses for only a few hours of each day."

The Holy One paused when he came to that point. Another thought came upon him and diverted his story.

"Maybe they were foolish—but remember, they were frightened."

"I say nothing against our grandfathers," Salt announced solemnly. He missed the sudden sparkle in the old eyes watching him. "It is not proper for me to speak against the ancient ones. But in our time, much foolishness is talked, and our people live in dark holes like animals. Grandfather, I love the Sun, our Father Sun, and I believe we should no longer dwell in caves."

Salt glanced up, and his face felt suddenly hot when he saw how the Holy One smiled at him.

"Perhaps you will be the one to lead them away from here. Perhaps you will return our people to the broad valley and the gleaming waters."

"I don't know about that, but I would like to lead them down below, where their cornfields would receive the water from our spring."

The smile passed from the old man's face and his voice deepened. "Our corn crop suffers from something more than the want of water. I cannot talk of that now. Another time. Only I must tell you that by planting where you did, you offended the feelings of many. But worse, you gave somebody who moves against us in the dark a chance to blame you for the disaster which may be planned. Thus would you be destroyed, and with you our leadership as Turquoise men."

The words were spoken softly, almost in kindness, but each struck Salt with the force of a blow from a man's hand and set his ears to ringing. Never had he been so sternly rebuked.

Weakly he encountered: "I was a child, I see. You have said our people live in darkness, and I thought I would find the light for them to follow."

The old man tossed the matted gray hair back from his eyes, and was smiling once more.

"True, I have told you that our people live in darkness. An old man may talk thus if, in addition to his years, he has listened to many, has reflected on what was said, and maybe learned something of the purpose of life. It is not a rebuke, but I remind you to expect faults in others and to bend your words to travel around their faults.

"But now we have got ourselves on a strange trail and have to go back. Your task—that is what I must talk about."

"Yes, Grandfather."

"When our people moved into the cave of the White Rocks and built the village, they made a secret trail from the village to the flat land above. It was thought that, if ever disaster should come, the people should have a secret way of escape. Only three living men know about the trail, where it starts and where it ends. When one of the three is about to die, he passes his knowledge on to his successor. If more people knew of it, an enemy might come to know, and we could be destroyed.

"My clansman, you are to find this secret road—and when you find it you are to tell no one. I will have to warn you also that if two of the three discover what you are trying to do, they may destroy you. I, the third one, will be your only protection if you are discovered, but they may act without asking who sent you, and I cannot tell them beforehand that I intend you to be my successor."

Now he looked at the boy. "That is your task. Are you afraid?"

Salt sat speechless, feeling his heart pump loudly—for a moment he actually heard it in his ears.

"This is a heavy task, Grandfather." In his mind, he thought that he must not be rash; he must consider carefully before he spoke.

"One more warning, clansman." The man's voice turned suddenly harsh and cold. "If you decide you cannot or will not try it, I will have to put my flint knife to your throat with my own hand. No one can know there is a secret trail from our village unless he is one of the three. If you know that such a thing exists, you must become one of us. You cannot know about it and remain apart from us. So what is your choice?"

It seemed to Salt that a wind out of the dead of winter swept up his back and brushed the hair at his neck.

"I will find this road, Grandfather. And I will live to come back and tell you of it."

Chapter 6

Friend and Foe Together

WHEN Salt reached the middle street running through the cliff village he walked swiftly, silently. He was relieved to find the street empty. It seemed quite possible that he could reach his mother's house and climb the ladder without being observed. He need only tread lightly, hold his breath, and presently he would be out of sight. He looked ahead, measuring the short distance still to cover.

He had just passed a jutting wall, when he heard suppressed laughter, the sound he had dreaded. Good sense told him that he should not turn to look, but he turned, nevertheless, and saw the same young girls who had blocked his path the day before. In one voice they sang out: "Did you lose your pretty badge? Did you lose your pretty badge?"

And the voice of the older girl rose up above the others: "Hush, children! Our uncle is trying to find out where the men are meeting. They forgot to tell him!"

The laughter rang out clear and shrill. Salt desired above all else to run the last few steps, but he held to his stride. A moment later he was at the foot of the ladder that would rescue him from shame.

In reality, his progress through the street had been observed from within the shadows of many house openings and from roof tops as well. The seemingly deserted village was alive that morning with gossip and rumor. People might stand out of the boy's way, as they would turn their gaze away from any person who would be embarrassed by their watching, but they were not any less curious about the things that were being told. It was a courtesy not to pry openly into another's affairs.

One who watched from a shadowed doorway was Flute Man, his mind still aflame from the indignities heaped upon him since the previous day. He would be on the watch henceforth, until his hand performed the deed which his wits had not shifted to another.

Another watcher was Star Climber, Salt's age mate, who had been thunderstruck when he was told the purpose of the kiva meeting. His hands trembled and he felt a tightening in his chest, as if he expected a similar blow to fall upon him.

When the words of the Sun Crier had died away, Star Climber heard himself muttering: "They will turn him into a child again. Surely he has done some terrible thing. Never have I heard of this before. What may happen to me, for have I not been his friend since we were children together? But if they ask me, I shall say I know nothing, and whatever it is, I don't approve. I cannot be blamed."

Star Climber was so slow of understanding and so timid at the same time, it was just as well he stayed out of sight and made no effort to catch up with his hurrying friend. Salt was not in a mood to explain what was to happen.

An air of foreboding and a reluctance to proceed lay heavily upon that meeting. Each man as he descended the ladder felt that some decision would be required of him, and each felt that someone else should be responsible. This reluctance even reached to the four principal officers, who sat near the weak fire in the center of the room and passed the short-stemmed pipe from hand to hand. When one pipe had been smoked cold, a second pipe was prepared and sent around. Then, instead of opening the meeting, the one having the title of Fire Tender or Fire Chief was directed to bring cedar bark for the fire, and as the pungent smoke arose it was aspersed to the four directions by the Sun Watcher. Still no one spoke.

The only one in the room who wished the meeting to proceed was Flute Man. He sat restlessly while the kiva officers prolonged their smoking. A number of times he straightened his shoulders, as if preparing himself to speak. Then he would look at his near neighbors on either side, perhaps to encourage them to call for action. But it was a reluctant meeting.

The boy, Star Climber, had found a spot in the deepest shadow. He was wishing that no one would even notice his presence in the room. He kept his eyes to the ground immediately in front of his folded legs.

Finally, the four officers arose from their places around the fire pit and moved to their appointed seats. Trailing Cloud, who had the title of Sun Watcher and was the senior officer of the kiva, indicated that he would speak. He coughed, then he sighed. "If anyone is to speak, let him start now." He sighed once more and relaxed.

The rule of procedure required a formal statement of the business to come before the meeting, a statement usually given by the leader of the society concerned. In a question involving hunting, the War Chief spoke first. In this case, Cloud Head, the chief of the Masked God society which conducted the initiation ceremonies, was responsible. But Cloud Head, like the others, did not want to start.

Flute Man fidgeted. Staring at Cloud Head, he all but called upon him to begin.

Finally, Cloud Head rose; a short, stout man, with a surprisingly powerful voice. His black hair was cropped in jagged edges and bound by a band of twisted material.

"I did not call this meeting," he announced in a voice that battered the walls. "But you know what was announced at sunrise. Eldest Woman sent word to deal with this boy. Someone else may know the reason for this. I do not. If you want it done, I will carry out your wishes. That is all I have to say at this time."

When Cloud Head returned to his seat, breathing loudly, the room was silent again. A man coughed, another scratched loudly.

Trailing Cloud looked up in surprise. He had expected the meeting to start, but instead it was back in his hands. He was fretful in his old age, and the fact that he had to be helped to his feet irritated him. Surely so much trouble was unnecessary.

"Someone will have to speak," he said sharply. He was too shortsighted to recognize faces at arm's length away, but he squinted around him as if he could see plainly. "You know it is not my place to begin. We have been called together, now it is for you to explain why we are here. Start the meeting!" He did not sit down at once but continued to squint into vacancy.

Flute Man arose. It was still not his turn, but he wanted something to happen. The others might hesitate to act because they did not want to shame that boy, or because they were in the dark. But he knew what he wanted. Let them get started!

When the squinting Sun Watcher failed to see him in the dim room, Flute Man spoke out: "I am ready, Grandfather. This boy of whom we speak is my sister's child. I know about this matter."

Trailing Cloud not only ignored him but turned his face in the other direction.

"I know the speaker, Flute Man, and I don't want to hear him. Let someone else speak at this time."

Flute Man was shocked by the harshness of the old man's rebuff. It was the first hint that the meeting might go against him. These men would not bend to him, as he intended they should, unless he could stand straight before them and speak with the weight of his office. They must remember that the War Chief could retaliate.

The exchange of words started a murmuring, a general stirring and shifting of bodies, as if the men had become aware of tension. Cloud Head stood up, frowning, seeming to suggest that he had been ready all the time.

"This is not my wish," he boomed. "Our young clansman, the boy we call Salt, is accused of acting in some manner, I don't know what, to bring shame upon himself and upon us, his elder brothers. We are asked to put him out of the kiva and turn him back to the children. This has never been done in my lifetime, though I know it was done in other times. We have a way of doing it. Our Masked God society must be called together for the initiation ceremony, only we will perform it backward. This will take practice, since none of us have done it before. If you want this done, tell us, so we will know. We must take the whip from the boy's back if he is to be put out of the kiva."

"Why do this to one of our brothers?" The question came out of the shadows.

"I tell you all I know," Cloud Head thundered back. "Eldest Woman sent word that it should be done. Indeed, she has already taken away the turquoise badge, so the boy is now without protection."

The Sun Watcher spoke from where he sat. "It is only our protection which is taken away. He is now, like all

children, protected by Sun, our Father. He is safe enough.
If Eldest Woman wishes the wrongway ceremony performed, I think we must do it. She has her reasons for what
she asks. It is something for all of us to decide."

Star Climber, in his shadowed spot, had raised his head.
He began to feel that these men, with their reluctance,
were not bent upon destroying him or his friend, although
he could not fully understand the turns and twists in their
talk. He watched the firelight play upon the faces, his ears
alert to each voice, to anger or treachery. Flute Man had
attacked Salt at other kiva meetings. Did he now speak as
enemy, or as friend?

Flute Man had risen again, and the boy in the shadows
hugged his knees tightly. He thought: Now it will come.
Something terrible will happen, and I am here watching it.

The voice of Flute Man was subdued, as if he had decided to guard his words and his manner. "I ask permission
to speak."

Trailing Cloud, in the place of authority, waved his
assent. "The matter has been stated. You may speak."

"I am grateful. I speak for this boy, whose mother is
my sister. You have heard me speak harshly to him, even
here in this kiva. That was when he deserved rebuke. Now
I speak in his favor, for I am one who knows how to be
fair. It is a shameful thing we talk of doing to this boy.
We are told that Eldest Woman wants this done. Are we
to act blindly and shame our younger brother? We are
men, here, and the decision is with us, as our Sun Watcher
reminds us. I say the boy should have his badge restored
and he should come back to the kiva."

Flute Man glanced here and there, as if to see who would support him. His long thin face seemed to float by itself in the pale light that spread downward from the square opening in the kiva roof.

Silence, then. Until a voice hissed out of the shadows, "A child that walks in the protection of the sun, will not be killed in darkness."

Flute Man jumped forward, trembling. "Who speaks?" he shouted. He would have leaped over the seated forms in front of him, if a hand had not grasped his arm.

"Easy, brother. Here we are having a kiva meeting."

"Someone speaks lies!" Flute Man struggled, but could not loosen the grip.

Star Climber, who had put his hands over his face, glanced through open fingers and saw Flute Man straining. Perhaps there will be a fight, here in the kiva! he thought. The very possibility made him tremble. The kiva was a place for calmness and order; it was the place where one made prayer sticks and honored the supernatural people.

Across the room the voice of Trailing Cloud snapped like a whip. He did not rise, but it was as if he suddenly towered over all.

"Turn that man loose! And you, Flute Man, stand back! There, now. When you ask for permission to speak, and it is granted, you are expected to act properly. You know it without my telling you."

"I am at fault," acknowledged Flute Man, still panting. He saw clearly that he would not have his way. It might even go harder against him.

"Very well. Now, you say a lie has been spoken. What is the lie?"

Flute Man opened his mouth to speak boldly. Then closed it as quickly.

"I couldn't tell who spoke. Someone over there," he jutted chin and lips to indicate the opposite side of the room.

"I did not ask who. I asked what lie was spoken."

"Perhaps I spoke too fast. I did not intend to say that word."

"All right. Then no lie was spoken. Who was it that talked?"

Day Singer rose across the room. In the dull light the red cloth which bound his graying hair looked black. His broad, unsmiling face was a pale moon.

"I was the one who spoke. I wish to ask this man why he wants our young brother brought back to the kiva. I say it is not because he loves him. And I remind every man here that whoever harms a child harms us all, and we will pay it back."

Flute Man looked here and there at the faces around him, wondering what was known, what guessed at, and what hands would be raised against him.

He gestured, as if to brush the matter aside. "I spoke for the sake of the boy. He is my sister's child. I wish him respected."

"Then," Day Singer continued, relentlessly, "you will be content to see his childhood protected. Respect and protect are twins."

"Who says he needs protection?" Flute Man fired back.

"We are all brothers here. If I am accused of something, let me know what it is." People of the village often said they could not understand Flute Man. His voice was hard when there seemed to be no need of it. He always talked louder than was necessary. When a kiva leader placed him in charge of some small office, even if it was no more than gathering and storing the corn from the clan lands, he issued orders, as if the entire village were under his command.

Day Singer stood staring. He started to reply, then checked himself. He turned to the officers in the center of the room. "I have decided that Shield should answer this man. I have a rude tongue and I may say something to harm us all. Shield, my uncle in the clan, knows what is in my mind. He will answer as he sees fit."

"Shield can answer, if he desires," Trailing Cloud said in a tone that indicated clearly that he did not care. "For myself, I think the man needs no answer. He questions our wisdom for wanting to protect the boy. Let it rest there."

"I will answer for our wisdom," Shield replied, rising tall among them. The bones in his face made shadows in the half-light, as did the wells of his eyes. Seen with these shadows upon it, it was a face of thoughtfulness and hidden purposes.

"We accuse no man here," the quiet voice said. Shield stood not far from Flute Man, regarding him. "It is of the boy, Salt, we are thinking. He will be a leader among us someday; only now he is impatient and wants to be a leader at once, before he has grown into it. We think it best that he have a little time to think about the duties of

a leader. Our clansman here, Flute Man, knows that we
are not looking for harm to come to the boy. The sun will
truly watch his movements, and if the sun fails, which is
unthinkable, there will be eyes to watch. Our clansman
knows this."

When Shield withdrew to his stone bench against the
wall, there was murmured approval. Tension seemed to
go out of the room. Flute Man had been warned, but so
skilfully that it was as the shadow of a bird passing out of
sight. He must know how the kiva felt about this, yet
nothing had been said to offend him. He could withdraw
decently. Shield was a clever man in such matters. The
murmuring went all around the room.

Star Climber, in his corner, breathed freely at last. His
hands no longer covered his face and he felt happy to be
present at a meeting where everything was turning out so
well.

Trailing Cloud put his approval on Shield's words by
declaring the meeting at an end. But first, he gave instruc-
tions: "We will proceed with the wrongway ceremony.
Cloud Head will instruct his people in the Masked God
society. In four days, we will return, and the boy, Salt,
will be brought in. The whip will be taken from his back."

The men responded with their calls of "Good! Good!"

Flute Man was at the ladder. Then he was gone. Only
he knew how frightened he had been toward the end.
Frightened at the thought that someone in the kiva knew
of the owl's claw tucked away under his belt. Day Singer
might be the one, or even Shield, in all his mildness.

Fear still went with him into the open air, like a thong looped around his middle and biting the flesh. If his Turquoise clansmen were truly against him and waited only for the time when they might destroy him, then he must know and join openly with Dark Dealer and the Spider Clan. But he would not do that until the last moment, when he knew certainly that he could not retreat. For there was no safety in Dark Dealer.

Chapter 7

Beware of Owls

IT WAS hard to believe in a secret trail. Salt had been born in a house lying under the cliff and lived all his days scrambling over the rubble of rock, exploring eagles' nests on high crags, hunting rabbits in the flat land above the cliff. He knew the trail that led from the village to the bottom of the canyon and also the trail that twisted and climbed to the upper country. No secret about these, since the people of the village used them every day. It wasn't that he doubted the word of the Holy One, but it was like being told that summer comes twice in a year or that he could enter his own house without going through the opening in the roof.

After leaving the cave house of the Holy One that morning, he spent the entire day alone, stopping at home only long enough to put two handfuls of parched corn in the buckskin bag he carried at his waist. He would find the secret trail, as he had promised, though he would start with a heavy heart. He fled to the flat country above the canyon to begin the search, but most of all to be by himself.

For he was troubled. In the course of one day's journey of the sun, he had himself traveled from a boy's concern with the hunting of rabbits to a knowledge of the dangers with which his elders lived. It was a long journey to make in so short a time. His mind had to take it in. His flesh had to find warmth again. He had to learn how to act in a threatening world.

The elders were fond of saying that, if a man expected to find truth, he should seek it alone. Salt was not sure it meant the same thing, but he had discovered that he could think better, and indeed he often felt better, when he went off by himself. On some of his lonely excursions, he thought only of going as far and as fast as he could, and he would run and walk by turns, until at day's end he had passed beyond his known world. Then, if he had killed a rabbit with his throwing stick or snared a bird in his net of woven hair, he would kindle a fire and eat. Or if his running and walking left him too exhausted to hunt, he fed meagerly on parched corn and crawled among warm rocks to sleep. His mother never fretted over these absences; she knew that they were a part of his growing time.

On other excursions, he delighted himself just in looking at things. He might sit on a rock while the sun moved
all the way across the sky and watch the comings and goings
of a colony of ants. He would shred the tip of a sliver of
yucca to make a fine brush, and with a quick paint of
saliva and white clay, he would daub the backs of some
ants to tell them apart. Then he would smile to himself
as he began to understand which ones went out to forage
for food, which others labored at hauling grains of sand
out of the underground house, and which appeared to act
as guards or warriors of the house. It was a fine thing, he
thought, just to watch an ant making a world for itself.
That was almost as good as running to cover distance and
get away from human talk.

That day when Salt went to the flat country above the
cliffs, it was to look again at a land that he knew well. The
people called it the flat country, but really it was not flat.
The earth rose in round hills, with shallow valleys between,
or it lay in long ridges out of which an edge of broken
brown rocks showed like the teeth of a monster. The low-
growing pinon and cedar trees which, close at hand, appeared so green, turned blue-black in the distance. Knife-
leafed yucca plants and cholla cactus grew between the
trees. The women prized the yucca, because from its roots
they made a fine froth in which they washed their hair.
In other clear spaces the grass grew thick and made moving
patterns in the wind, and the grass was prized by the deer
and antelope, whose flashing tails might be seen through
the pine trees on almost any day one came up from the
canyon.

One breathed freer in this open country. One's fears and doubts, if they were the fears and doubts of a boy growing up, fell away, and one's heart grew light again.

Up here in the flat country were the planted fields from which the Village of the White Rocks drew life and the songs that fill a life. These fields stretched from almost the rim of the canyon to the very point at which the sky came down to the land. Along this entire reach, the earth was quite level, except that it sloped from each side toward the center, as if it had been the bowl of an old lake. The field that belonged to Salt's family was about midway along and toward the low center. Each family placed a boundary of sticks and stones around its plot. Each of the Seven Clans making up the village had its own land, and these lands, too, were marked off and a boundary post gave the sign for the clan.

The fields were never deserted. Even when the cleaning out of weeds had been completed and the plants had only to grow and fulfil themselves, men from the village remained close by. They might be out of sight in a clump of cedar trees, but they were there, watching. Deer liked the tender top growth of corn; ground squirrels were fond of succulent roots; crows waited for the ears to fill. Many walking and crawling animals besides the people of the village waited to feast on the corn, beans, and squash that grew in those fields. An even greater danger, one that folk preferred not to mention, were the hungry peoples who came down from the north, sometimes from the east, and carried off entire crops. They too waited until the ripening time, and when they came, the flat country was filled with

fierce shouting and moans and the sound of clubs and
stones striking dully on flesh.

Today, Salt was mindful of the men watching from
the trees. He must be careful not to appear to be looking
for anything, or they would come and offer to join in the
search. He knew how tiresome it became sitting through
the day with nothing to do but watch clouds and learn new
songs from an elder uncle, and he decided it would be
better to act the part of a child at play, wandering aimlessly in the sun. It would be reported in the kiva, of
course, that he was not performing his duties as he should,
and not helping his family. That could not be helped.

In considering the secret trail, he had decided that it
was impossible to look for it in the village. It might start
from one of the seven kivas, or even from under the floor
of a house. Prying into such places was unlikely to accomplish results. But since the trail was planned as an escape
to the country above the cliffs, it could be assumed that
somewhere up here he would find the other end. That is,
if the trail really existed.

He worked out a game of playing eagle; at least anyone
watching him from the trees would guess it was that. To
play the game, he would find a mound of rocks or a low
hill. There he would stand poised, appearing to survey
the land stretched out below his perch. He would move
his head from side to side. Then, with outstretched arms,
he would swoop down from his high place and run, not too
fast, in long sweeping curves that took him through pine
thickets and open spaces, and he would tilt his arms as he

turned and peered at the ground. When he pounced for the kill, he would leap high and come down on all fours. That allowed him time to search the mound of earth around a badger hole or to scratch away the brown needles at the base of a pine tree. He hardly knew what he was looking for, but somewhere, if his eyes were sharp, he would find a sign, a stray footprint, a worn place in the grass, a marking on a rock, something that would lead him to his goal.

As he played his game into the afternoon, with one part of his mind always aware of the men and boys who might be watching from the planted fields, Salt forgot about two others who might also be watching.

The Holy One had said that the secret of the hidden trail was known to three, of which he was himself one. That was all he said, except to warn Salt that he would go in peril when he tried to find the trail.

And thus it happened, on that first day of Salt's searching, that two watched from a hiding place which gave them a view over the entire sweep of land. They watched, and were puzzled.

One of these, Day Singer, was especially concerned. He was stocky and powerful, though his hair was beginning to gray and deep erosions crossed his brow. His headband of red woven stuff marked him as one of the speakers in the kiva. His manners were blunt, yet he was known in his family for his gentleness with children. The women complained that he spoiled the children, would not make

them mind; but possibly that was because the children
flocked to him when he entered a house and became deaf
to their mothers.

His companion was Turtle, of the Water-Reed Clan—
sometimes called the Younger Sister Clan, since the legend
told that these people followed closely behind the Turquoise clansmen in their trip from the south. Turtle was
older, thin and tall; talkative and complaining. He found
fault with his relatives, his health, the conduct of kiva
officials, the lack of rain, and the failure of the young
people to listen when their elders spoke. He carried always
a long staff, which he claimed his aging legs required, but
the young men jeered that he used the staff for probing
and prying. He too bound his hair with a band of woven
cotton, its color a turquoise blue.

Looking out from the hiding place where they sat side
by side, Day Singer expressed his concern: "What is that
boy doing up here? I have already protected him in the
kiva—what must I do now?"

He continued to watch and to frown.

Turtle added his own grumbling: "He is too big a boy
for playing that kind of nonsense. What is he up to? He
runs back and forth like a dog searching for something."

The boy was not too far away, and it almost seemed as
if he were following some design which brought him closer
and closer. Day Singer moved restlessly.

"If he should find this trail—" Turtle asked, but felt
too uncomfortable to finish his question.

"Our duty is to destroy him," Day Singer replied,
unhappy.

"But he is your kinsman. If he comes, I will take care of him."

"No. We are both responsible. My hand will be against him too."

They pursued the matter no further, for at that moment their attention was drawn to a second figure moving in the country below them.

Salt had been playing his game for several hours when an owl called out, faintly, as if from a great distance.

No one liked to hear owl talk. It was bad enough at night, though that was the normal time for the creatures to converse among themselves. But an owl in the daytime could only mean danger, bad luck, or someone passing into death.

Owls were the spirits of the dead. Since they were not human, not limited by human weaknesses, they could perform alarming feats of strength and magic. Every household had owl stories—a certain man was lured to his death over a cliff; another man rolled dice for his own head, and lost; a woman followed an owl, crying like a child, and was lost in a blizzard. Children, listening, never forgot such stories.

One story was told of a handsome young man who was crushed to death by a stone rolling from a mountain ledge just as he was on his way to the house of the beautiful girl he was to marry. Immediately after that unhappy event, a snow-white owl appeared in a tall hemlock tree that rose from the canyon bottom. For several nights the villagers saw and heard the great white bird. It talked in low mourning tones. On the fourth day, just as dusk gathered in the cliff village, the large white creature sailed on spread wings into the village itself, plucked the girl from a gathering of people who were too frightened even to utter a sound, beat its wings rapidly until it was clear of the cliff walls, and sailed to a pinnacle of rock that stood by itself far down the canyon. The walls of this pinnacle were so sheer and high that no man could climb it. For days afterward, the people in the village could hear the girl crying to be rescued, but none could reach her, though many tried. Finally, they heard her no more, nor did they ever see the white owl again.

The cry of an owl in midafternoon was certainly a bad thing. As soon as Salt heard it, he stopped his game. It was as if a black cloud had come swiftly up the sky to blot out the sun. The suddenness of it left him in breathless confusion.

He stood rigid for several moments, as his thoughts darted about. An instinct told him to run, but he seemed to know that if he ran, his fear would increase, until he would be running away from the thought of being afraid. While he stood swaying between the impulse to run and the impulse to stand his ground, he looked into the near trees, but saw nothing. Then with great effort of mind, he turned around, moved a few feet and looked in the direction of the ridge of broken rocks.

He expected to see nothing. No bird. No movement among the treetops or in the knee-high grass. No sound. Small desert birds which had been chirping, stopped, as if they were watching something. A hunter following game knew the sensation. Salt remembered just in time. Or maybe it was the single snapping sound behind him.

He leaped sharply to his right. An arrow whistled past his head and drove itself into the ground a few feet beyond where he had been standing. He heard the muffled crack of the flint head as it struck a buried stone.

In one forward motion, he grabbed the arrow, snapping the shaft at the point where it entered the hard ground, and ran.

As he ran, he realized that he was not frightened. He was angry, but not frightened or confused. He was running from a living man, an armed enemy, who might be notching another arrow. That was something one knew and understood. Not an owl talking of death, but a prowling hunter.

Salt ran on, as swift and sure-footed as the deer that flashed through the woods. And as he ran he examined the feathered shaft in his hand and recognized the workmanship. No man could disguise his own handiwork.

Chapter 8

Conversation at Dawn

THE WOMAN called The Eldest had a longer, more formal name, which the people of the village rarely used; many perhaps had forgotten that she was The-Woman-Who-Rises-to-the-Top-of-Dawn-Mountain. The name Eldest Woman was actually a title, borne in each generation by the oldest woman in the direct line of descent from the legendary founder of the clan; she need not be the oldest woman in age within the clan; in fact, The-Woman-Who-Rises had been called Eldest Woman ever since she was a young married woman, and everyone knew her in that way.

82

Although advanced in years and short of breath, she still arose in the early dawn and started her day of toil. Upon arising, she ran a brush of shredded yucca fibers through her thinning gray hair. Then she picked up the little bag of corn pollen from its place in a wall niche and anointed first her forehead, then her lips, and finally a few grains of the powdery substance were allowed to fall upon the pallet upon which she had lain. Thus, with her head blessed for clear thoughts, her lips reminded to speak truthfully, and her bed commended for having given rest, she hunched herself together and squeezed through the narrow opening which led to the roof terrace outside her topmost room. Her house, which was the tallest in the village, reached almost to the overlying rock, and at dawn it was still black night under the roof of the cave.

Age had not destroyed her sense of balance. When she came to the ladder projecting up from the terrace below, she threw her short leg over the parapet and walked down without touching her hands to the ladder.

A figure shrouded in darkness moved on this lower terrace. Coals glowed red for a moment, subsided, then glowed again. A breath was bringing them to life. A tiny flame spurted.

"May you have happiness in this new day, young one," Eldest Woman greeted the fire maker.

A young woman's face was dimly lighted by the pale fire. "You move like a star, Grandmother. I heard nothing. May all days bring peace to you," came the reply.

"I go below, but will return soon."

"The heated pot and I will be waiting."

When she had descended two more ladders, walking
erect and facing forward, Eldest Woman emerged in a
kind of courtyard. Walls surrounded the small square,
where people waited. The darkness was so intense that the
waiting ones were sensed rather than seen; anyway, they
were expected. As soon as Eldest Woman touched her feet
to the stone pavement, voices uttered greetings of the
morning. Bodies moved about. The odor of smoke, cling-
ing to hair and clothing, identified the shadows as women.
Their cooking fires were with them, even when they were
not laboring at their pots.

"Are we all here? Are more to come?" Eldest Woman
tried to make out the number of forms around her.

"I think we have one more than usual—I can't rightly
tell," a voice explained.

"So? Is there a new one present? Speak up. All are
welcome."

"I came, not for food, Mother, but to speak with you."

Eldest Woman moved forward, raising a hand to avoid
colliding with anyone who might stand in the way.

"Who is it, then, my Daughter?"

Then her hands cupped themselves around the form of
a face. She knew finally who it was.

"Ah, yes. Indeed. We will talk. Just wait."

She moved across the enclosure and squeezed herself
through an entrance as narrow as the one from her sleeping
room. House doors were built with a high sill that helped
to check cold air from creeping in at the floor level, and
their narrowness also made it easier to keep out an unwel-

come intruder. In really cold weather a hanging of thick cotton cloth or a fur robe was placed over the opening.

"Now, my daughters, bring your jars, or whatever you have. Here is corn, dried squash, beans, and dried meat for your babes and your ailing ones. Bring a jar here, where my hand is reaching. Our storeroom may not be bottomless, but for our mothers who are without men and our children who are without elders, we always have enough. Bring your jars or your baskets. You belong to the House of Turquoise, and there is abundance among us."

Eldest Woman continued to chatter as she filled jars and baskets. Each woman, upon receiving a brimming measure in her receptacle, murmured a blessing and hurried away. In the darkness of the early dawn, none might see who came to the clan storehouse to receive a gift of food. No one ever spoke of such things. The names of the women, or the children, who appeared at the storehouse were never uttered in the hearing of others.

They had gone at last, except one who waited by the ladder descending into the courtyard. Eldest Woman squeezed her way through the storehouse doorway and moved toward the waiting figure.

"Now, mother of the boy Salt, you wish to talk and I am ready to listen. It is as well that we stay where we are, since we will not be interrupted."

Salt's mother, Becoming Day, was small and slender. She made only a slight shadow at the foot of the ladder. The hands that moved so swift and true in pottery making held firm to a mantle of woven cotton that covered her head and was gathered under her chin. Her upturned eyes caught a glint from an early morning fire and seemed like dark wells of questioning.

"How will it end, my Mother? I have a heaviness in my heart that I speak to no one about, only to you. How will it end? At tomorrow's sunrise the men in the kiva will begin the ceremony which returns my son to childhood. Perhaps a mother should rejoice to have a child restored— but I cannot rejoice. They tell me this is a protection for him—that no one will harm him. Yet, two days ago, as he walked on the land above, someone shot an arrow that would have pierced him through the back, if he had not leaped aside. And yesterday, as he followed the trail which leads from our village to the land above, a stone gave way under his foot. If he had not made a strong leap, he would have been dashed to the bottom. How is he being protected, I ask myself, when these things occur?"

The soft, hurried voice caught for a moment, as if the dark eyes were staring into a chasm and watching a boulder, which might have been her son, strike on stone, and fly far out into space.

Eldest Woman stood silently, waiting. She knew the other woman must talk, so she waited with bowed head.

"He had not strayed from the path, he tells me. It was a stone right there before him, one on which he had trod many times. I knew the place well when he described it. It is a stone we have all trod on. Somehow it had been loosened, and was waiting for him.

"What will happen before another sun sets? What will happen after they hold this wrongway ceremony? He will be a child and will go unarmed. How will he defend himself against this enemy who shoots from ambush and lays traps for him? How will it end? That is what lies in my heart."

Eldest Woman reached across to touch the cheek of the other woman. That was the only mark of tenderness she displayed and it was more than usual.

"I cannot answer these questions. They must lie with you, must twist your heart, until they are answered."

Daylight was now seeping in under the cliff, bringing the forms of houses out of darkness. The two women standing so close together could each see the troubled face of the other. Each knew that talk would solve nothing, yet talk was still a comfort.

"Men are moving, here and there, out of our sight," Eldest Woman continued. "They move against all of us, not against your boy alone. You say the boy is not protected, because he goes unarmed, as a child should. But why did he leap away from the arrow shot from ambush? Why was he not swept into the canyon with the rock that turned under his foot? I say he is protected by Father Sun. Remember it."

The clan mother moved away, looking carefully for eyes that might be watching from the walls and terraces above; then returned. Her voice dropped to a thin whisper.

"This day, and the night to come, will be decisive. Before another sun rises from his morning bed, some men will stand and some will fall. How it will be, I cannot yet tell. It is not clear. The boy, Salt, will have his part in it.

"Now, we must go. A pair of eyes watches from somewhere. I cannot find them, but they are there. We will mount the ladder and go to our morning work."

When they had reached the first terrace, Eldest Woman paused to look again. Then she whispered, her voice so low that Salt's mother almost imagined rather than heard the words:

"Your boy will want to go again to the flat country. Do not stop him, but tell him to watch carefully. Today, the coyotes will be around. Go now."

She watched Salt's mother cross the terrace and climb to a set of buildings standing in the opposite direction from her own tower house. Then she turned to go her way. Her eyes missed nothing. She saw the quick withdrawal of a head within a doorway halfway across the village. Today would be the day, surely.

In the few minutes it took for her to reach her own cooking fire, The-Woman-Who-Rises-to-the-Top-of-Dawn-Mountain remembered many things out of her life. Some of them she remembered with sorrow. They came into mind without bidding because, in some way unknown to herself, she had a feeling, or an insight, of what was to come. This would be a day when the good that was in men would prove itself or be destroyed. And in such a day were the seeds of future sorrows.

It brought a moment of pain still, after almost fifty years, to recall the loss of her son child. She had been gathering pinon nuts up in the flat country and had left her first-born on a blanket of woven rabbit fur. She was a short distance away, reaching with a long pole to dislodge the fat cones. At first she had the impression of a cloud passing over the sun—after all these years, when the sun disappeared under a fast-moving cloud, she felt a sudden fright. On that day, the shadow swept over her, then she heard rather than saw the beating of heavy wings. They made a rumbling in the air. She rushed from behind the spreading limbs of the pinon tree, just in time to see a golden eagle of massive wingspread rise into flight. Its talons were securely locked in the flesh of the infant. She heard no outcry.

In her effort to erase the pain, her mind rushed on, into a scene of later anguish.

In the Village of the White Rocks, brother and sister relations were always close, but Eldest Woman and her brother were especially so, since both parents had perished in a snowstorm and left them in the care of aged grandparents whose household was made up of a great crowd of quarrelsome children and grandchildren. Through the shoutings and rivalries of many years, the orphaned pair protected and supported each other. When Eldest Woman married, she returned to her mother's house, as was proper; and her brother, on his marriage, went to the house of his wife's kin. That, too, was proper. He gathered the load of wood for his wife's mother which made him as one with the new household. As the years passed, brother and sister saw little of each other, though actually no day went by without one hearing news of the other.

After many years the brother, because he was trusted, as his family had been trusted before him, and because he was a man of peace, rose to be Village Chief. His name was then Blue Evening Sky, a good name, since

blue was the color of the west and the color, as well, of
peace and serenity. In a word, it was the color of turquoise.

He served the people and observed the duties of his
office with great care. It was not an easy load to carry. The
Village Chief was, in a way, a prisoner of his people. He
might never leave the village, because if he did the crops
might fail, springs might run dry, and people might perish
of hunger and thirst. So faithfully did Blue Evening Sky
observe this rule, that he rarely went even to the limits of
the village, but on any day could be found either in his
house, in the kiva, or in the plaza, which was in fact the
roof of the kiva. When he sat in the plaza, it was a signal
for people to come to him for help or advice.

Above everything, the Village Chief must persuade the
people to accept peaceful ways of settling differences. He
was not free to go to war, or even to hunt. A hunter always
ran the risk of offending the animal world, members of
which could retaliate by causing sickness among men, or
failure of crops. The chief of the village could not take
such a risk. Meat for his table was procured by others, and
others also brought wood for his household and planted his
crops. Thus, he was free to devote his entire time to the
needs of the people. He could keep his thoughts moving
toward the ways of peace.

After Blue Evening Sky became chief the years passed
quietly; neither hunger nor war interrupted the flow of
days. Babes born in the first year of his leadership grew
up, married, and started families of their own, and in all
that time nothing occurred to trouble the village.

Eldest Woman remembered these years in the minutes

of climbing from the courtyard where she gave out corn and beans to the waiting women. In all that span of years, her brother had kept the people together, kept them free of disastrous quarrels, and they prospered.

She paused at the top of the ladder and tried, as she had many times before, to understand what happened next. Her gaze swept over the tops of buildings into the void that lay beyond, but her eyes were not searching out any object. It was the mind that groped. What had happened? Perhaps—she had thought many times—men are not made for peace. They are animals that must fight among themselves when they have no enemies to contend against. Give them a full meal, and still they hunger for another's food.

Standing at the top of the ladder, she shuddered, trying to shake off troubled thoughts as a dog will shake off water.

It was difficult, indeed, to understand why the men of the Spider Clan, led by Dark Dealer, their new War Chief, came in a body to Blue Evening Sky and demanded that he retire as Chief of the Village of the White Rocks.

Dark Dealer was the spokesman, and a brazen one. He accosted Blue Evening Sky in the little plaza, and stood spread-legged, his men arrayed behind him. They at least observed the courtesy of lowering their eyes.

"We have come to say that we of the Spider Clan can no longer accept your leadership."

That was what Dark Dealer shouted, and what Eldest Woman, years later, still labored to understand. How could a man move so far beyond good manners and still be as one of them?

"You men of the Turquoise Clan have made the people

believe that you were the first to come, and therefore
have the right to decide all matters concerning the village. My clansmen are tired of believing that. Our legends
state that we are an older people, the oldest in the world.
It was Spider who carried the first earth up from the sea
and made the world. So why should we step aside? We
have as much right as the Turquoise people to rule the
village. We think you should share the leadership with
us—let us be the head for a while."

Up to that point, Dark Dealer had talked with loud
arrogance. It was clear that he wanted as many people as
possible to overhear him and to be struck by his fearless-
ness. Never before had anyone addressed the Village Chief
in such a manner. Blue Evening Sky was seated all that
time. He wore a sleeveless tunic of pale-blue cloth, a rope
of many strands of tiny pink shells around his neck,
earrings of sparkling shell, and a dark-blue twisted band
around his bristling gray hair. His manner was calm, and
a smile even played on his lips.

Dark Dealer shifted his feet, he bent his head down
toward the seated leader. He whispered, but the whisper
could be heard beyond the tiny plaza, so quiet was the
waiting crowd.

"Last night one of our strongest men died of an agony
in his belly. Only yesterday he was among us, a powerful
man. Why did he die? My people believe he was bewitched. I am prepared to tell them that a man of the
Turquoise Clan is the witch."

Dark Dealer pulled back, and for the first time smiled.
"Now, what do you say? Will you agree to let a Spider

Clan man succeed you as Village Chief, or shall we come among you and look for our witch?"

It was long afterward that Blue Evening Sky told all this to his sister. He told how at first he could not believe his ears. How he sat and stared at the arrogant speaker, expecting him to remember his manners and go away. He had heard about Dark Dealer, had even seen him around the village, but could not recall ever talking to him.

"When he continued that way," Blue Evening Sky explained, "I could feel something die within me. My lifetime, all I had done to teach peaceful living to our people, died, piece by piece, while that man talked."

When no answer came, Dark Dealer looked annoyed. He shouted: "Well? What have you to say?"

Blue Evening Sky was not a tall man, but neither was Dark Dealer, and when the Village Chief rose to his feet, his face was on a level with his adversary.

The Chief uttered not a word. He stood staring into the eyes that were on a level with his own. Then he spat straight into the arrogant face.

Still without speaking, he resumed his seat.

By that time the plaza had filled with Turquoise men, attracted by the loud voice. Quickly they saw what was happening and moved to cut off Dark Dealer from his bodyguard. Dark Dealer had not noticed that he was now alone, and when he advanced upon the Chief, shouting, "Now, you have done it! Now, you will pay! This is the end of your accursed clan!" he was quickly surrounded. Not a hand touched him, yet he was all but lifted off his feet and rushed from the plaza.

That was how it started. The web of quiet days was
torn apart and nothing could put it back. Before long, a
Turquoise man was found at dawn with an arrow through
his heart. He lay in the center of the plaza, where Dark
Dealer had shouted at Blue Evening Sky. Owl feathers
were tied to the protruding shaft of the arrow, which
meant that the dead man was accused by his killer of witchcraft.

The Village Chief aged swiftly. He tried to keep his
own men from committing crimes in retaliation, but he
found his strength not equal to it. A Spider clansman was
caught alone and hurled over the cliff.

To his sister, Blue Evening Sky lamented: "I am at
fault. Through all these years I talked against anger and
bad thoughts. I told others to be peaceful. Yet now, when
I had a chance to show my people how a man can put aside
anger and bad thoughts, just see what I do! An untaught
babe could not have done worse!"

He would not be consoled. Indeed, after a while he
would not even discuss the matter. When men came to
report later acts of bad faith or evildoing, he would babble
back at them until they were bewildered.

Before another year had passed, he moved out of the
village, to the rock shelter high up in the face of the cliff.
He meant it as an act of abdication, but his clansmen, and
in fact the villagers as a whole, would not accept the act
and still looked to him as leader.

They said: "He is now touched by the powers of the
Other World. He is the Holy One, and let no man put a
hand on him."

In the Turquoise Clan it was known that the trouble had not ended. Dark Dealer would not let it end. He continued to move against them, and would strike when he was ready.

This was the anguish that Eldest Woman felt in her heart that morning, as she climbed the last ladder and stood finally before her cooking fire.

The face of the young girl was upturned in daylight at last, and she was smiling. "You bring happiness, Grandmother," she murmured.

The searching, searing eyes of the older woman faltered at the words. She looked about, as if on returning from a distant journey she felt surprise at a familiar face and voice.

"You give happiness, child," she said, barely audible.

Chapter 9

Disaster in the Canyon

THAT was the day of the summer solstice—the day on which the sun reached its farthest advance into the northern sky. On that day, and at the winter solstice as well, the village people felt uneasy. Partly, this uneasiness resulted from what they could see with their own eyes: each day in summer the sun rose and set at a place farther to the north. The Sun Watcher, whose task it was to observe this movement, peered through a slit in the Sun Tower at each rising and setting of the sun. On the wall opposite the slit, he made a check against markings which had been scratched into the stone by Sun Watchers long before his time. So the people knew of this movement of the sun northward in summer, and they feared that if it did not check itself, it might desert the earth entirely. In the winter, it moved in the contrary direction and threatened to leave the world buried in snow and ice.

The principal cause of uneasiness, however, was the stories that were told of occasions when the sun disappeared out of the sky entirely. As the people watched in terror it seemed to die by degrees. True, it had always reappeared again, according to these stories, but such occurrences left men's minds with the unhappy feeling that the sun was a living substance, and like all living substances was mortal and was subject to whimsical behavior. Since their own lives, they knew, depended on the sun to warm their bodies and bring growth to their crops, they felt somewhat as children feel toward an elderly parent—they must be respectful and considerate.

Before dawn, runners had gone forth from each of the Seven Clan houses, or kivas. They would visit all the outlying shrines, some of which were at great distances, to place prayer feathers and offerings of sacred meal. They started early, because it was necessary to be back in the village before the sun reached its highest midday point.

Meantime, while the runners were out, officers of each of the Seven Clans took turns marching into the largest plaza, where they danced in two rows. They dressed bravely in many-colored knee-length aprons and sashes, and on their breasts and arms were ornaments of turquoise, shell, feathers, and animal teeth. The costumes were intended

to be gay and bright, to persuade the sun that his earth
children loved him and desired his presence. The songs
they sang were quick and sparkling:

> Behold us here,
> Behold us here,
> Brothers all, ai-ay-ai.
>
> Here we sing,
> Here we sing,
> Brothers all, ai-ay-ai.
>
> Here is food,
> Here is food,
> Brothers all, ai-ay-ai,
> Ai-ay-ai-ai-ai-ai.
>
> Behold us here,
> Behold us here,
> Brothers all, ai-ay-ai.
>
> Here is rest,
> Here is rest,
> Brothers all, ai-ay-ai.
>
> Comes the sun,
> Sparkling sun,
> Brothers all, ai-ay-ai,
> Ai-ay-ai-ai-ai-ai.

The song would go on like that, without stopping, for
several hours, as first one set of singers, then another,
chanted the words. Even the smallest children were en-

couraged to join in these dances and songs, since the sun was fond of children.

As midday approached, the dancers began to leave the central plaza to return to their kivas. People who had been watching, retreated toward their houses. All who could, tried to be out of the direct glare of the midday sun. If a man found himself in the field, he sought a spreading tree or an overhanging rock, there to sit out the sun's climb to its zenith. On this day of the solstice, people waited through the high-noon period for word that the sun had arrived in his northern house and was content not to travel beyond.

The noise of the singing had died away, people everywhere in the village were moving out of sight—then it happened!

First one voice, then several voices, carried the news. The voices came from the far end of the village, toward the south, where the trail came up from the bottom of the canyon. People who had been on the point of entering their houses stopped in their tracks and looked down that way. Others, who were already inside, came out again. No one moved at first, but all stood watching. On a day when people were naturally uneasy, any unexpected happening filled the air with excitement.

Three women had reached the top of the trail and were running toward the village. Their hands were empty of water jars. They were screaming.

"Our spring! Oh, fathers! Our spring!"

As the three women reached the first house, wide-eyed

and panting, other women moved forward in a group and swallowed them.

"What of the spring? What are you saying?" the women were asked.

A babble of sound followed. Meantime, other women were running forward. Men could now be seen standing in doorways or in the shadow of a building. They watched, but did not advance.

"What of the spring, Crane Woman?"

The woman thus called by name, eldest of the three, caught her breath and looked around.

"The spring, my people, is dead," she announced flatly.

The statement shocked everyone into silence. Minds groped with the words, turned them over and over. How could a spring die? What kind of nonsense was the woman talking?

After a moment, everyone talked at once, showering questions upon the three women. What had they seen? What happened?

Crane Woman was the first to collect her senses. She listened for a moment, started to answer a question, then threw up her hands and demanded silence.

"Peace! Peace! We have no time to stand babbling. The clan fathers must be told of this at once. Someone go to each kiva. Tell whomever you find that our spring has stopped flowing. It exists no more."

"At first, when we arrived to fill our jars, muddy water was flowing," the second woman explained. She too had sobered after the battering of questions. "We waited for it to clear. Then it stopped altogether."

The third woman of the group, hardly more than a girl but already a mother, was the last to speak out. Her voice was still strained. "We waited, and it seemed just to sink into the sand. We were frightened."

By that time, the first men had joined the group, and when they heard these reports they refused to believe them.

"Just wait, now," an old man said. He had a withered right leg and walked with the aid of a thick crutch which his bad leg wrapped itself around. He went by the name of Mountain Walker.

"Our clan fathers should not be disturbed here in the middle of the day. You women should take yourselves inside, away from the sun, instead of spreading this fantastic story about our spring drying up. What would we do without our spring?"

Crane Woman threw back her head. "Father, this is no time to worry about the sun, and if we don't tell this to the kiva leaders at once, we will all be sorry. I tell you, our spring is no more; it is dead, it runs no water. I saw it with my own eyes. These women, too. Ask them! Don't tell us we are spreading a fantasy! Just trot down there yourself, if you like."

"Peace, peace, woman!" the old man pleaded. "Obviously, I cannot trot anywhere. You say it ran dirty water first, then stopped. Perhaps a boulder fell from the cliff and blocked it for a while. It will flow again, just you see. In all our lifetimes, and the lifetimes of our fathers, our spring has never failed us. It cannot fail us now. Here, you young fellows, run down and look. Just see if the

water hasn't worked its way around the boulder and started
to flow again."

"There was no boulder—" Crane Woman started to
protest, then stopped, as if she could not be sure. She
looked at her two companions, but they only returned her
stare. They could not remember whether they had seen a
boulder lying in the stream or not.

"Maybe Mountain Walker is right. Maybe it will flow
again," a voice came from the group of women.

"We are wasting time, and the kiva leaders will be
angry," Crane Woman insisted, but she did not move away.

Two young men had already detached themselves from
the group and were disappearing over the edge of the
cliff. They would scramble down the log ladder and race
for the bottom of the canyon.

The waiting group did not stand in its uncertainty for
long, before men began to emerge from the seven kivas.
The men of the Turquoise Clan came first. Some even had
parts of their ceremonial dress still attached—anklets of
eagle feathers, a kilt of black and red design. One man was
absent-mindedly carrying an eagle-wing fan. The startling
news had caught them as they were undressing.

Following close upon them, came men from the Water-
Reed Clan, the Hawk Clan, the Stone Flute Clan, the
Gray Badger Clan, the Yellow Rod Clan, and lastly the
Spider Clan. Many of these had been taken by surprise
too, since they came daubed with the white clay markings
and bits of the ceremonial dress in which they had been
performing. They streamed up the kiva ladders and out
into the street.

The men of the Spider Clan were slower than the others in reaching the street, and only three came forth. Dark Dealer was not among these, though as War Chief and protector of the clan, he should have been among the first. People of the village did not recall this until later.

Now the houses too were emptying. On every terrace and roof top, women and children and old people gathered in silent clusters. "What is it?" was asked everywhere. No one yet knew, or they would not talk about it. "Something. Just wait," mothers told their young ones.

Star Climber had been in his own Turquoise kiva when the Sun Crier, the man who kept vigilance for the clan and made public announcements, scrambled down the ladder and held a whispered conversation. Whatever he said reached only to the ears of the leaders in the center of the room, but from their startled expressions and sharp exclamations, Star Climber knew that a terrible thing had happened. He had come to the kiva, as a dutiful young man should, to help the elders remove their cumbersome dance costumes and do whatever else was required. It filled him with dismay, therefore, when these sober, meticulous men cast aside costumes without regard and sprang for the kiva ladder. All without saying a word to him.

He climbed to the plaza, not sure in his mind whether to leave the kiva unprotected, but pulled strongly by the desire to know what was happening. He could see men hurrying toward the place where the trail came up from the canyon.

He went forward, staying close to the walls of the buildings along the central street. In a moment he arrived op-

posite the opening which led from the street into the dark
interior of the cave. The sacred turkeys were kept there,
always guarded and a damp, sour odor seemed to blow out
from that dark alleyway. On certain days, in winter especially, when the air in the cave seemed not to stir for weeks
at a time, the smell was so bad that people coughed and
their eyes watered when they got near. They always
hurried to pass it.

Children were warned never to go in that passage, and
Star Climber still remembered the time when he forgot
the warning, or decided to go in without regard to the
warning. He had not explored far within the passage when
a masked figure rushed out of the darkness, bellowing,
and lashing at him with a whip of many thongs. He was
a long time getting over the fright; it left him sick and
trembling in every part of his body. Even after many years
he would not even look in the dark entrance, if he were
alone, for fear of finding himself staring into the dead
eyes of a mask. He hurried away.

At last he reached the fringe of the crowd. The women
had made way for the men pouring up from the kivas, and
all waited at the corner of the last building of the village.
The runners who had been sent into the canyon to verify
the stories told by the three women were just then coming
into view.

The head of the trail was above the village and anyone
coming up from the canyon was immediately visible in the
village. The young men waved their arms and shouted
something which Star Climber at least could not hear

clearly. Then they ran forward and were encompassed by the crowd.

"It is true, O fathers," one gasped. "Our spring has stopped flowing."

His breath gave out, and the second runner continued: "We looked for a boulder or rock slide, but there was nothing. The water—just stopped."

"A few pools still hold water," the first speaker resumed. "I think the women should go with their jars. Before it disappears in the ground."

A profound silence fell upon the crowd. If the sun had fallen out of the clear sky on that equinoctial day, the people could not have been more deeply shocked. The spring was life, as was the sun. To be deprived of either, they knew in their hearts at once, meant the end of life. Without water, where would they go? What would they do? Each man and woman pondered these questions as if they had been passed from mouth to mouth, though no word was uttered.

It was Trailing Cloud, the Sun Watcher of the Turquoise Clan, who broke into the shocked silence. His eyesight was dim and his legs unsteady, but his voice was a firm check on their mounting fear. He spoke as if the future were already clear and he knew what each must do.

"Let a woman from each of the clans go with storage jars and collect the water in the pools. Then see that each family gets a fair share. When the pools have been drained, let men from the clans dig pits in the sand. These may fill by morning. But someone will need to watch, to see that the water does not seep away and that no one takes more than his share."

The elder paused for thought, then resumed. "We must get word at once to the man up there." All looked toward the rock shelter in the cliff, knowing that he meant the Holy One. "Shield will go to him. We will ask his help."

He squinted at the crowd that pressed around him. "I cannot tell who is here. I do not see Eldest Woman. Is she here?"

The men looked over the crowd, then at each other. No one had seen her.

"Then send for her," the old man ordered. A younger woman hurried from the crowd. Eldest Woman had been known to refuse to come at the bidding of a man.

Trailing Cloud's mouth quivered, but he held firm. "Tell the Rain Makers to prepare their prayer sticks and their holy meal. We will go down to the spring and speak for the lives of our people."

All at once his strength failed. "I want to sit down," he rasped irritably. His assistants led him to some stone steps where the street climbed up between houses.

The crowd fell apart then. The Rain Makers of each clan went to their kivas to prepare for the ceremony at the spring. Others could not decide whether to go below and see with their own eyes, or whether to wait. Most of the crowd simply stayed together, saying little, scarcely moving. They stood in the full glare of the midday sun and thought nothing of it.

Women, meanwhile, were arriving with jars of all sizes, including some very large storage jars which when filled would be too heavy for a single person to carry up the trail. These would be left below and water would be dipped from them into smaller vessels. Men with digging tools of sharp sticks and stone hand shovels came out of the houses and started down the trail.

"This may be the end of our ancient village," Trailing Cloud spoke as though from a dream. His kiva leaders, the Fire Chief, Tobacco Chief, and Sand Chief stayed with him. At a little distance, the boy, Star Climber, squatted on his heels. He was fearful of approaching too close to the leaders, because of the dread things he might hear, and equally fearful of not being on hand if they should ask for him.

"The people will survive," the old man went on, held in the grip of his dreaming vision. "But they will have to scatter. Who knows what will become of us? By tonight we will start runners out. They will have to range far and wide, to places we have never been, in search of living water. We know all the waters nearby; they are small streams, not enough for all our people, or they flow for only a short time each year."

Then he shook his head and came back to one thought, from which he never strayed far. Many that day kept returning to the same thought.

"This is strange, indeed. Our spring has never failed us before. In my lifetime, and in my father's lifetime, and I do not know for how long before that, the spring never failed. It almost seems as if someone among us has offended the Cloud People and our Guardian Spirits in some grievous way. But who among us will want to say

who is responsible for such a thing! Who among us understands such things!"

The Rain Makers were now returning, but they were
troubled. For each clan there was a Rain Maker Chief and
two assistants. Now they came with their cedar branches,
their prayer sticks topped with kingfisher feathers, their
pouches filled with water-washed stones, and their reed
flutes. All were together and ready, except for the men
from the Spider Clan. They had waited at the Spider Clan
kiva and finally sent someone to ask for the Rain Chief.
No one could say where he was. The sun was now halfway
across the afternoon sky. What were they to do?

Trailing Cloud rose shakily to his feet. In his heart he
knew that something was very wrong; a chill crept through
his body. But a decision had to be made, and he would
make it. He reached out to find a shoulder for support.

"We will go below," he said in a voice turned weak.
"We will go without Spider Clan, though never before
have we acted without all the clans together. Send word
throughout the village that all are to come below, to pray
for our spring and for our people."

Then he asked again for Eldest Woman, and when it
was reported that she had been sent for and could not be
found, a tremor went through his body. Clearly, it was an
evil day.

Criers called through the village and their voices echoed
back as they spread the word.

The clan leaders went first, and as they filed out of the
village, they began to chant of the Far Reaching One and
the Dawn Sky Woman, for these were the first Beings and

all things came from them. First the clan leaders took up the chant and were heard until, group by group, they started down the log ladder and their voices were lost in the chasm. Then, as people of the village followed after the leaders, they continued the chant, until their voices were also lost. It took some time for the village to empty itself. No one hurried. The people walked in what seemed a reluctant procession, as if their minds already assured them that they would fail in this attempt. Finally, all had departed and their singing came more faintly, echoed back from the far side of the canyon.

The people of the Spider Clan had not joined in the procession, but at the time no one seemed to notice that.

Chapter 10

Water Seeks Its Level

B Y THE TIME Salt reached the flat country above, day
had fully arrived. The sun was at the very edge of
the eastern world, resting on the land for a moment
before starting his sky walk, and pushing before him giant
tree shadows across the land.

Salt remembered his mother's words at morning blessing
time—that coyotes would be around that day. It had been
owls' talk the first day; then desert doves had called. Now
it would be coyotes.

He did not need the warning. Somewhere the enemy waited, behind any pinon tree or crouching boulder. Moving as noiselessly as a shadow, he sped out of the village and up the steep trail to the land above. He paused often to listen and to watch for movement. At those moments of waiting, his hand would move to his chest and the missing turquoise stone—and each time as his hand came away he felt the shock of being alone.

Salt looked carefully around, then crawled to the top of a grassy mound. There he could watch all sides and plan his next move. The land sloped downward toward the planted fields. The fields themselves were hidden behind the ridge that extended eastward from the canyon's edge. In places the ridge consisted of shattered rocks, protruding from the earth like the broken teeth of a monster; elsewhere, the rocks, collapsing entirely, had spilled down the slope in sun-blackened fragments. His eyes came to rest finally at a point along the ridge, where two slabs leaned against each other. These slabs seemed to stand at the top of a heap of loose stone. He had intended to climb those rocks, but the labor of scrambling over the loose gravel had discouraged his curiosity.

He studied the rocks, then turned to other features in the land that stretched out before him. All of it was familiar. All of it had been visited. Today he had to try something, or think of something that he had not tried or thought about before. Tomorrow morning the men would meet in the kiva to perform the wrongway ceremony. If they went through with it, he would have to wait a year before he would be eligible for initiation.

He turned his gaze to the upended slabs of rock and began to plan how he would move across the terrain. He selected the clumps of pinon and the sheltering rocks he would move to, in succession, when he left his sheltered post. If he went carefully, keeping under cover, crawling like brother-snake when he had to cross open space, and if luck were with him, he might make it without being observed; there would be no coyote cries. It was possible, of course, that an arrow would find his back and no sound be heard. Not by his ears.

Once more he looked carefully, then slid down the grassy hill and reached the first grove of pinon trees. There he waited, while he tried to decide whether the birds had been disturbed. He listened for a song broken off too suddenly, or an unusually long interval between bursts of song, a warning that he was not alone in the land. But if another was present, he too remembered the habits of birds.

Walking, crawling, he reached the next pinon shelter, then ran between the sheltering banks of a dry stream bed. The sun was well into the sky when finally he came to the last protective cover. The ridge then lay just in front of him and the ground between lay barren of any growth. A body moving up that exposed surface would be seen.

Day advanced and he could wait no longer. No arrow yet, no coyote cry. Finding hopefulness in this, he rose among the low-growing junipers where he had been crouching, and ran like the nimble-footed deer. Even when the ground rose sharply and he found himself among a waste of loose rocks, he still ran. His breath came in gasps, his heart seemed about to burst through his chest, but he bounded from footing to footing until he reached the top of the ridge. He looked back. Amazing, the distance he had covered and the height he had reached!

The planted fields lay directly before him now, on the other side of the ridge; and to the west, which was to his left as he reached the summit, he could see the edge of the canyon. The village was below, out of sight.

He did not know that at this moment, as he looked at the sky space above the village, disaster awaited his people. If he had known what was happening that morning, he might have understood why no one had attempted to ambush him. His fears would have seemed foolish, swallowed up in an anxiety greater than anything he had imagined.

The upended rock slabs rose massive, now that he stood at their base. Wind and frost had battered them and sent chips and splinters showering down the sloping sides. What remained was still a mighty thrust of brown and golden rock standing taller than any pine tree.

Salt began a careful study of the rock giants. He crawled over large detached boulders, already scorching hot. By midday, with the sun straight overhead, the heat of those rocks would be unbearable. He had to find what he wanted, and get out. But what did he seek?

The old people had a saying: "Looking for what you want but can't find, is like looking for the hole in the wind."

The entrance to the secret trail *had* to be in the land

above the canyon. But that was all he knew. The sun burned his flesh and sweat trickled from under his hair and down his face and neck, where it dried in trails of salt.

These rocks must hold the answer; he had sought everywhere else. In all the country lying below the ridge, hardly a tree or rock or clump of yucca had been missed. He had crisscrossed the earth, running in long, jolting strides and listening for the rumbling sound of a hollow place beneath the surface; he had thumped the boles of pinon trees and crashed rocks against larger boulders. Without avail.

The more he thought about these spires of rock, these teeth of the monster, the more certain he felt that this time he would find more than the hole in the wind. Working his way around the base of the first rock, he searched each crack and fault, and studied with special care the point at which the naked stone emerged from the surrounding rubble.

Finally, he arrived at the western face of the spire, where it was split at the base. From a distance this split gave the spire the appearance of two rock slabs leaning against each other. The appearance was false. It was all one mass, pyramid-shaped, but material had broken away from the inner side, leaving a hollow shell.

Then something checked his growing excitement. He was looking down into a depression at the base of the rock spire. The overhanging rock blocked out the sun, leaving the bottom of the depression in deep shadow. Almost at the bottom, he saw the stretched-out form of a man. He did not need to go nearer to know the man was dead.

The second shock came immediately. He crept down

the sloping stone. Then stopped. It was Flute Man. A club or a heavy stone had crushed his head; and this had happened some hours before.

Long ago Salt had learned to use his eyes. Two things explained what had happened. Flute Man had not been killed on the spot, for he had not bled here. And beside the body lay a long torch made from a lightning-killed pinon tree. Such wood was pitch-laden and burned brightly. The torch had been used, either by Flute Man or by those who had carried him to this place. This suggested an underground cave or passage, where a light was needed.

One more thing he saw, but the meaning was not clear. On Flute Man's breast lay an owl's claw, imbedded in feathers. Whether Flute Man had been killed by someone claiming the powers of witchcraft, or whether Flute Man was himself accused of witchcraft, Salt could not tell. He did not touch the evil object.

Almost immediately he found the trail. Even so, he might have missed it, if he had not expected it to be near. No one liked to touch the dead, and therefore Flute Man had not been carried far. But at first, as he sought, Salt seemed to face nothing but rock; the solid rock of the walls that rose above him, and shattered fragments lying in heaps. Still he continued his search. He turned over boulders that might be used to plug a hole, he tapped stone walls for hollow sounds.

Suddenly he knew that he had been staring for a long time at the answer. The rock, which had fallen away from the inner side of the spire, had left a narrow ledge running across the face of the break. This ledge was high, at least

the height of two men. But on close examination he saw
that in the wall were obvious hand- and footholds. When
he tried them, they were perfectly spaced for climbing.
He returned to the body of Flute Man and picked up the
pinon torch.

The sun, now at the mid-point of the sky, poured relent-
less heat upon the exposed rocks. Salt reached up to the
first handhold, climbed.

The narrow ledge, barely offering space for a man's
body, sloped downward to the left. The footing was pre-
carious. Salt leaned sharply inward, his hands raised above
his head, his palms flat against the hot stone. Thus he
moved sideways along the rock face. At the lower end of
the ledge, where it beveled down to the outer edge of the
spire, he observed a narrow space between the main body
of rock and a lesser slab. This slab, fracturing away, had
fallen back against the larger mass. A man could just
squeeze through the narrow opening.

He had found what he had come for . . . and with
swelling heart he thought of how he could report to the
Holy One. He looked back where the sunlight burned so
fiercely over the ground he had covered. Flat faces of rock
shot the blinding sun back into his eyes. He smiled at
how he had worried out there in the sun; how he had run
here and there.

He turned from the view, and as he stooped to explore
the opening, he remembered something else. The Holy One
had told him: "You are starting something which may end
with giving your life." The words, sounding in memory,

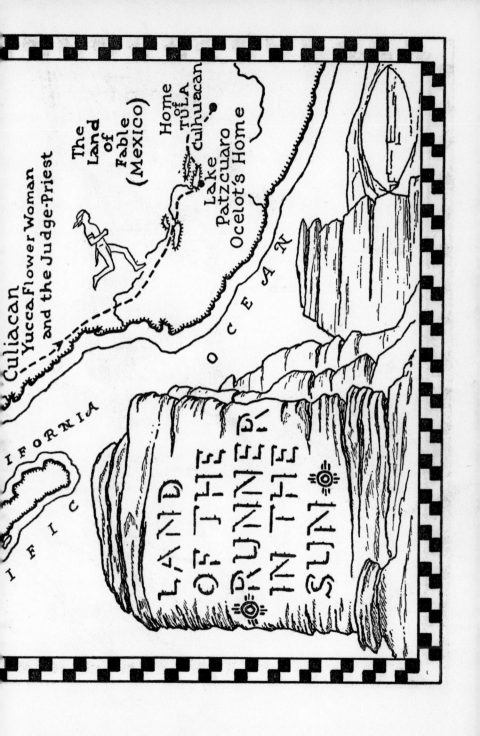

choked off the elation which rose like bird song in his throat.

"But what could happen now?" he heard himself whisper. "The arrow was shot out there in the open. The rock fell as I climbed the cliff. Here I am safe from watching eyes."

No voice was there to answer, else he might have learned that the secret trail was already discovered and invaded. What generations of his people had guarded carefully, was secret no more. And the same voice might have persuaded him that wisdom and safety lay in retreat, rather than in advancing. Because he knew nothing of the occurrence at the spring, and in his ignorance pushed forward into the unknown, he almost failed his people.

For Dark Dealer, the days of angry waiting were ending.

He had said to his clansmen: "Look to me, I will make our Spider Clan powerful! *We* will decide who lives in this village and who goes."

Before he became War Chief of Spider Clan, Dark Dealer had accomplished little that was either good or bad. His family had not been large. It might be said he belonged to no one. He ate wherever he found himself at mealtime. No household would turn a child away from food, but with him it was more than courtesy. His mother, a small, waspish person, was always quarreling with her neighbors and scolding her three children. Out of pity for the boy and his two sisters, other households took them in and showed them kindness.

As War Chief, new energies seemed to be released in this man who was nobody's child. Impatient in kiva meetings, he succeeded after a while in compelling his clansmen to abandon many of the courteous customs which governed such meetings. He would state what was to be discussed and who was to speak, and if he was displeased with a meeting, he broke it up. He had won over a group of younger men by favors and promises, and when he decided that a meeting had gone far enough and he wanted it ended, he gave the nod and the young men talked in loud tones, laughed, called out insulting words when anyone tried to speak, until peaceful men gave up in disgust.

But Dark Dealer's greatest weapon lay in witchcraft. The village lived in great fear of sickness, since sickness often struck without warning. It brought pain and even death. It might go away, too, but not one could tell whether sickness when it came would destroy a man or let him go. It was easy to believe that sickness was caused by unseen powers striking back at an individual who broke some rule of conduct. But if a man searched his mind and could find no wrongdoing, then he worried. He would think over who might be his enemies, who might wish him evil, and if he concluded that someone had used evil power against him, fear would enter his mind and he might become sick indeed.

Many were the ways of using evil power. When a man cut his hair, he was careful to bury the cuttings secretly; otherwise they might fall into the hands of a witch. Bones that remained from a meal must be thrown into the fire. Danger could come from an article of clothing or an ornament lost or misplaced outside of a man's home. Any personal possession, falling into unfriendly hands, could be used to destroy the owner.

Dark Dealer knew these things, and more.

When, after two candidates had already met untimely deaths, he proposed himself as War Chief, he hardly expected to be accepted. He was still young, he had accomplished nothing. He made his proposal to the Chief of the Summer House, it being the period of the year when authority over all political affairs of the clan was held by that chief. The expected rejection followed. The Summer Chief, a man called Echo, was polite but definite in his reaction.

"It pleases me that you offer yourself. I thought these matters did not interest you."

Dark Dealer considered. The two stood alone just outside the Spider Clan kiva. Afternoon brightness had faded and long slanting shadows reached across the canyon. In the distance children played a singing game.

"Why do you say I am not the right one, when my mother is of the same family as that of the last War Chief?"

The tone of the other was still firm. "That is a point in your favor. But to be War Chief, you need to be older. The people need to know what you can do. It requires much learning besides."

"I can learn as well as anyone else."

"No doubt. Still . . . up to now, you *haven't* learned."

The more firmly the Summer Chief spoke against him, the more decided became Dark Dealer's ambitions. Moreover, he had prepared himself for the interview. So he posed a question:

"The other two who were considered, and who died as soon as they were named . . . might it not be that they were not the right ones, after all?"

"What do you say? I do not understand."

"To be War Chief, a man must be able to destroy. If he is destroyed instead, clearly he does not have the power needed by the people."

"Perhaps so. Do you have this power?"

"The one who fell over the cliff . . . I can show you a strand of his hair. The other, killed by lightning . . . I can show you his sandal. And you, Uncle, you lost the shells which you use to pluck the hair from your face. I will return these shells, if you like."

The Summer Chief was thunderstruck. His hand reached for the skin pouch at his belt, then halted. He had known for several days that these shells were missing; he had been troubled by the loss. He saw Dark Dealer in quite a new light and continued to stare at him for some moments. It had grown dusk by then, but the elder man, Echo, saw enough.

So it happened that Dark Dealer was named War Chief.

That success led to bolder ventures, until in time he convinced himself and his followers that he could take over the leadership of the entire village. He discovered, as he went along, that the men who held positions of authority in his clan were not able to fight him. They had been taught by their seniors to do things in a certain way. Any other way seemed wrong, but they had no reasons in support of the old way, except that it had been taught them. Dark Dealer found that when he ignored the old men, or acted in a manner contrary to old practices, they were help-less. They grumbled, but they did nothing.

Then he made a discovery which opened the way for domination of the entire Village of the White Rocks.

The discovery grew out of an idle question. One of the younger men had asked in a kiva meeting: "I wonder what is back of the wall where the sacred turkeys are kept?"

Dark Dealer answered.

"What wall? And why shouldn't there be a wall? To make a room you build a wall."

"But this wall," the young man answered, "is not part of a room. The turkeys are kept in an open space between buildings. Guards stand in front to keep the creatures from getting into the street and keep anyone else from getting into them. The rear of the space should be the cliff itself. But instead, a wall of fitted stones is built across, blocking the passage to the cliff."

"How do you know this? The guards will not let any-one through there."

The young man, who was called Open Face, saw that Dark Dealer was interested, which was what he wanted.

"It is nothing," he said and gestured to signify nothing. "One of the guards likes to sleep; if you watch him, you can manage it."

"The place has such a bad smell, who would want to go in there? It is probably nothing. Some guard built the wall while he had nothing to do."

Open Face had no intention of stopping at that. "I

thought it was nothing, until I went in there. The guard stirred in his sleep, so I crouched down to keep in shadow. My head was against the wall. I heard footsteps, and thought they were in the street, or perhaps in one of the houses nearby. They were faint at first, then they seemed to come near. Finally they stopped. After a while I heard other steps. I heard voices. Even a name was spoken."

Dark Dealer leaned forward. "A name? What name?"

"I think it was Day Singer. That was how it sounded."

"Day Singer!"

The name was enough. It meant that the Turquoise Clan had a secret behind the rock wall; Dark Dealer would not let the matter rest until he knew that secret.

It was easy to dispose of the guard, who belonged to the Turquoise Clan. Dark Dealer appeared one day, when no one was within earshot, and threatened to expose the guard as a witch. The man protested angrily that he would break any man's head who claimed he was a witch. He had been seated on a stone bench just inside the entrance to the turkey pens. The shocking accusation brought him to his feet.

"I am glad to hear you say that," Dark Dealer answered, as if he had been made quite happy. "It shows that you realize what a serious matter it is to go around with witches, or to be one yourself. I have been told that you carry an owl's claw in your belt pouch. If the one who told me this is wrong, I will denounce him myself. So open your pouch and prove that you are innocent."

The guard did not hesitate. He plucked the pouch from his belt, opened it; and there was the owl's claw!

His eyes bulged and the pouch fell to the ground. "How can it be? I never saw it before!"

Dark Dealer dropped his pretense of pleasantness. "So! Just what I was told! You never saw it before! Miserable liar! A lucky thing for our village that you are discovered. Now I can tell the criers to warn the people."

The guard, a big man, was stupefied. He looked steadily at the object on the ground and seemed to pay no attention to Dark Dealer's words. Yet he must have heard, for presently he protested: "It is a lie."

"When I tell about you, the people won't listen to your excuses. It will be the end for you."

The guard looked up. His eyes searched the man facing him. He had begun to guess at the truth of what had happened, but he said nothing.

Dark Dealer continued. "But I want to be your friend, and I will make a bargain. I will save your life, if you will help me."

The guard was convinced then that he had been tricked. Still he said nothing.

"There is a stone wall back here. I want you to help me make an opening in that wall so I can get through and see what is on the other side."

At that, the guard's anger exploded. He hurled himself forward and, with a mighty blow, sent Dark Dealer reeling across the entranceway. It was a blow struck in vain. Three young men who had been concealed just outside, rushed in and subdued the angry man. One was ready to club him, after the other two had pinned his arms behind his back, but Dark Dealer interfered.

"My friend made a mistake," he said. He gasped noisily through a bloody mouth, but tried to make his voice sound natural. "He is going to help us. He knows what happens to witches. Don't you, friend?"

Gaining access to the secret trail made easy everything that followed, though at first Dark Dealer did not realize the value of his discovery. He could understand the trail as a means of escape, but that was of no use unless the village was under attack. His first conclusion was that the Turquoise men had kept the trail secret to save their own members in case of enemy attack.

Only after he had explored the full length of the trail, was he able to appreciate what power had come into his hands.

The trail ran underground, from the innermost part of the cave to the outlet among the rock spires. Originally it was an underground water channel. The rocky ridge, at some far distant time, had thrust upward as a molten mass through the surrounding sandstone. When the rock cooled, it was quite hard, much harder than the sandstone, and it lay like a great dike across the land. Waters flowing along the surface of the earth were stopped by the dike, and at one time a great lake had formed behind the rock barrier. Thousands of years later, Salt's people planted their fields in this old lake bed, rich in silt.

Water is always hungry; it is always eating away at earth and rock, and if it finds a crack it will soon make a chasm. The water in the ancient lake, finding a soft spot where the sandstone had been split by the erupting volcanic rock, seeped downward, eating its way by dissolving the surrounding material, always seeking a lower-flowing level. At one time the underground channel emptied into the cave of the White Rocks, then spilled over into the canyon in a great splashing waterfall.

Long before Salt's ancestors moved to the cave, the waterfall had ceased to exist. The first people saw no sign that water had ever flowed through the cave; boulders and rock trash had fallen from the ceiling and buried the channel. The water, always hungry, had found another soft spot along its underground course and worked its way to a lower-flowing level. In time it emerged at the bottom of the canyon as the bubbling spring which the people called sacred, and praised in song and legend. It meant life; it meant the end of wandering.

Water no longer flowed on the surface, in the flat country among the planted fields. But it seeped down from the far mountains, it crawled through the gravels that lay beneath the surface, and when it came to the volcanic dike, it was diverted as of old into the channel under the old lake bed, and emerged in the spring at the bottom of the canyon. The volume of water had been decreasing in late years and that was cause for worry; but so long as the spring flowed at all the people felt secure.

Dark Dealer and his young men had an imperfect understanding of what had happened in the underground region, but it was easy enough to see, by the aid of their smoking pinon torches, that an underground stream flowed at their feet and disappeared, with a roar, into a black abyss. Damp rocks gleamed in the torchlight like a thousand watchful eyes, and dampness filled the air. It was a frightening place, and when they came upon it, they were terrified. Dark Dealer was the first to approach for a closer view. He even handed his torch to one of his companions while he threw boulders into the yawning pit. His thought was to discover how deep was the hole. But he heard only the thunder of the rushing water.

That night, when he was back in the village and heard the women in his own household complain that the spring water had turned muddy during the afternoon, he began to understand what had happened.

The next day he returned, walking past a guard whose eyes burned fear and hatred, and threw more boulders into the roaring pit. One of his men was stationed at the spring, and by comparing notes afterward they were able to tell almost exactly how long it took the water to flow from the secret trail to the spring.

In a matter of days, Dark Dealer had worked out the plan which was to place himself and his Spider Clan in possession of the Village of the White Rocks.

Chapter 11

The Ambush

SALT, crawling from the hot midday sun into the dark opening in the rocks, realized that he had acted foolishly. In his excitement he had pushed through the outer cleft in the rock, and found that the opening widened and was high enough for him to stand erect. When he spread his arms, he could barely touch the rock walls. This pleased him. But then the passage narrowed; as he stooped to wedge his head and shoulders into the opening, he discovered that the passage took a sharp downward pitch.

He stayed for some time on his knees, trying to see into the slanting shaft. Since his body blocked out the light he stared into darkness. He knew that he must crawl into the black hole, and he hesitated. Darkness was an enemy that could attack at any time, from any side. Only a prodding sense of what was expected forced him at last to crawl into the passage. He stopped after a moment and lay still, hoping that his eyes would adjust themselves and he might see what lay ahead. But this was hopeless; he must depend entirely on his hands to guide him down into this darkness.

After a few feet, the space became so cramped he could not free the pinon torch on which he was lying. The weight of his body wedged the torch securely and he could not move it. When he tried to reverse himself and crawl backward, the steep angle stopped him.

It had been foolish, he thought, lying there, not to have lighted the torch before he started. Not only was the thick pine wood now useless to him, but it dug into his ribs, wedging him into a space already too narrow.

And now, a further concern—how could he be sure that he had found the right opening? He had crawled into the first hole he saw; perhaps there was another. This one seemed to get narrower with every inch he moved forward. Would he wedge himself hopelessly between jagged rocks and never again see daylight?

"What you are starting may end with giving your life." Was that what the Holy One meant? That he would die right here in this black tunnel?

Thought of the Holy One brought other thoughts. Would all this trouble in the kiva have started, he won-

dered, if he had not planted corn in the canyon? Asking
this of himself, he remembered vividly the pleasant days
down there, when between planting and tending his secret
corn, he would race in the sun and hurl his curved stick at
a bounding rabbit. No thought to kill on those occasions,
only the enjoyment of feeling the tug on his throwing
muscles.

Memory darkened then, as he heard the Holy One rebuke him for planting that very corn. What was meant in
his saying, "Our corn suffers from something more than
want of water"? What would be revealed?

In his vexation, he drove hard to free himself and move
forward, deeper into the black uncertainty. His body broke
into sweat, yet he was chilled.

The passage dipped downward still more sharply. Presently he faced a new problem. The tunnel had grown
larger again; his body no longer touched its sides. But now,
because it was so steep, he began to slide. When he struck
out for a handhold, a jagged point slashed the flesh, and he
jerked back. He dared not rise to his knees; he might not
hold his balance, and would fall face downward. His belt
caught on an unevenness in the floor, holding him for an
instant. He moved cautiously, trying to turn sidewise, to
find some way to brace himself.

But the angle was too steep. He slipped, and this time
went plunging on, down the steep incline. It was a moment
when courage meant nothing; duty meant nothing. This
being taken by surprise, with no chance to help himself,
filled him with despair.

His plunge ended in a clatter of loose stones; clouds of

bitter dust struck his eyes and filled his mouth. He rolled over several times and heard himself groan. For several moments he lay without moving, as he waited for courage to return.

Then he sat up. He was bruised and scratched; his hands seemed to be bleeding. But that didn't matter. A sound so unexpected caught his attention that every other sensation was lost.

It was the sound of water flowing, whispering as it coursed over rocks and into little pools. He heard it clearly. In the blackness, he even imagined that he saw clear water running over bright pebbles. It was like human speech; a familiar thing in a world of blackness and confusion.

He crawled a few feet to the edge of the stream and bathed his hands in the ice-cold water, nor did he mind the sting of the water on the lacerated flesh. He put his mouth to the water and drank deeply. Cautiously he rose, first to his knees, then to his full height. The discovery that he could stand erect still further renewed his courage. His shivering ceased. All he now needed was light!

It took some moments of prowling on hands and knees to locate the pine torch. He found it at last, not in the loose gravel at the bottom of the steep incline, but partway up; it had lodged itself crosswise in the passageway.

Then something happened which brought back all the fear he had felt in the black of the tunnel. With the fire rocks and tinder from his belt pouch he was preparing to start a blaze to ignite his pine torch. It was not easy to arrange these materials in the dark, and he spent some moments finding a level spot and laying out the tinder where sparks from the flint rocks would be sure to fall upon it. He also carried short splinters of pitch to pick up the flame from the tinder, and these had to be placed where his fingers could find them quickly. As he worked carefully with these materials, he glanced up.

At first Salt could not believe what he saw. He sat back on his haunches and stared, thinking that, whatever it was, it would go away. It did not go away, so he picked up the materials he had laid out and put them back in the pouch. He did this without thinking, in a daze.

What he saw was a glow of light, like feeble torchlight, rising and falling; but so commonplace an explanation seemed impossible. Salt's world was a world of witches; they were a part of everyday conversation; they came and went according to mysterious ways, with the power to corrupt and to destroy. A cry that was an echo out of his childhood escaped him. Surely, he had fallen into the underground home of the witch people!

For a moment, when it seemed as if the light was coming toward him, he thought wildly of scrambling back up the tunnel. But standing, he forced himself to face the light. It was still there, its feeble glow still rose and fell gently. He decided, after a moment, it was not coming any nearer. Whatever the source, it was far away, like faint lightning flashing below the horizon.

A weak and wavering confidence returned to him, though he was baffled. He knew himself to be in the secret trail, which only the Holy One and two others in the village knew about. How could there be a light, unless a hand was there to make it? And whose would be the hand? Those sworn to keep the secret of the trail—or some other?

The urge to turn and run shook him powerfully. He wanted to be back in the sunlight! Only he dared not report to the Holy One that he had seen a strange light and had been frightened. He dared not ask to be returned to his place among the men, when he had not carried out the task given him.

Once more he faced the flickering light. He began moving down the trail; half crouching, feeling through his moccasins for loose stones and obstructions. The sound of the whispering water journeyed with him; the voice of a friend, there in the darkness.

The light was farther away than he had judged, and he walked for some time before he seemed to come any nearer. The sound of voices halted him at last. Men were speaking, but so far away he could only guess he heard speech; he could not make out any words. He squatted on his heels and waited, listening for a footfall. Soon he heard the sound again, and was more certain that it was human speech. Again he waited, until he was satisfied that the speakers were not coming toward him.

He rose and moved ahead, crouching, and feeling still more carefully for stones that might rattle underfoot. The light was stronger now. Patterns of light and shadow reflected back from the roof of the tunnel, which now stood higher than his outstretched arms could reach. The stream, dropping down over shelves of rock into little pools, looked black in the reflected light.

He rounded a bend in the trail, and dropped flat. He had almost walked into the middle of a group of men, some of whom held pine torches high above their heads, while others moved with burdens on their backs.

Salt observed, as soon as he dared lift his head, that the tunnel had opened into a wide, low-ceilinged cavern, irregular in shape. The torches flared and fell, sending up great clouds of smoke. In this uncertain light it was hard to tell how wide the room was or how far ahead it extended. Brown-skinned men moved in and out of shadow. Salt trembled as he watched them, still inclined to think of them as creatures belonging to another world. When he recognized the speech of his own people and saw familiar faces, he almost ran forward to join them. Luckily, he stayed low. Some instinct told him that he had moved from unknown fears into certain danger, that he was facing desperate men.

The little stream had now turned into a lake. Lights glinted on a surface of water. As he continued to watch, lying in shadow, he noticed that the men with burdens were actually loaded down with carrying-baskets, filled with rock and dirt. They were transporting this material downstream, from the place where he had almost stumbled upon them, and depositing it in the stream bed—building a dam. They were hurrying, constantly trotting, from the bank where they scooped up the material, to the dike downstream which rose several feet above the surface of the water. He could hear their gasping breaths, echoed back from the low ceiling.

He could not understand the purpose of the labor.

Building a dam here in the underground would flood the secret trail—but why? He realized, unhappily, that he must creep closer. He must get a better view of what these men were doing; perhaps their talk would explain their action. Only when he had done this could he make a useful report to the Holy One.

While seeking some way to advance, he almost changed his mind. The torches flickered uncertainly and sent up clouds of smoke, but the light was still strong enough to reach into the deepest nooks and corners. Shadow and light chased each other back and forth across the low chamber. It seemed impossible for anyone to creep any closer and not be discovered.

Then watching for some time, he discovered that the four torchbearers never looked behind. They held their torches aloft to guide the burden bearers as they came with their empty baskets; and the men carrying the baskets, because of the light that shone in their eyes, could scarcely see behind the torchbearers. Each was intent on his own task, with thought only for that.

Salt waited for the right moment, when the burden bearers had filled their baskets and were trotting downstream, then he slipped over the ground, keeping close to the sandstone wall. The torchbearers turned downstream with extended arms, their bodies producing a vague and faltering shadow. He inched forward, then lay still. Head down, he watched only the pebbles and stones in front of him. At any moment might come a cry of discovery.

About half the distance between his starting place and the dike the trail curved to the left, away from the water.

The underground chamber broadened out into a kind of bay, not visible from where he first watched. Should he follow the wall of the chamber, retreating from the scene of action, or stay close to the torchbearers and risk discovery? He had already passed two men, but the other two were ahead.

Then he made a further discovery.

As he raised his head to study his next move, he saw what he took to be the bodies of two dead men. They were trussed securely with thongs of hide. Why, if they were dead, were they bound? The bodies lay in shadow, away from the dike. He moved in that direction.

He was still some distance away, crawling painfully over jagged rocks, when he realized that one of the bound men was Day Singer. The second man, Turtle, was someone Salt knew only casually, and he did not recognize him now. He might not have recognized Day Singer, so badly was he beaten about the face, but his was a familiar form and manner of dress.

Now, more than ever, Salt sensed the nearness of danger. Some terrible thing had happened, and he was caught in it. The realization hit him hard, and for a moment he could not move at all.

It was thought of Day Singer that stirred him again. When he had crawled closer and found the men breathing, he felt better. But now he had the problem of what to do. The men were too badly hurt to help themselves even if he succeeded in cutting their bonds. He would need help to set them free. But how could he risk leaving Day Singer and Turtle while he went for help?

As he lay puzzling about this, he failed to notice a shadow detaching itself from the background of shadow behind him. And when the club came down on his head, he saw only a burst of light, but felt no pain.

Neither did he hear a heavy voice speak out a moment later:

"Carry him and the other two below to the kiva. They will decide down there what to do with so many nosey people. Here, our work is finished."

Chapter 12

Dark Dealer Takes Command

THE SUN had already passed beyond the far rim, and deepening shadow was moving up from the bottom of the canyon when chanting voices were again heard. Prayers had been said at the spring and the people were returning up the trail. Each in his heart was thinking that this day of the solstice had been a day of disaster. They thought of their homes, where fires should already be burning but had not even been lighted, and wondered how long they would be able to remain in the

141

security they had known. Without water, it could not be for long. But where would they go? That was a question never out of their minds.

They came up the trail in the same order in which they went from the village—first the clan leaders, followed by the older men, then the older women; then young families, man and wife; then the children. And as they came up the trail, they were again chanting of the Far Reaching One and the Dawn Sky Woman.

Suddenly the procession stopped. Turquoise Clan men, led by Trailing Cloud, the Sun Watcher, and his four assistants, had reached the walls of the first buildings, where the long central street began.

They stopped before a barricade of rocks, built from wall to wall, blocking the street completely.

Trailing Cloud, walking slowly and with bent head, came to the barricade; he almost fell against it, before he realized that it was there. His white hair made a faint glow in the gathering darkness.

He stopped, then put out his hand, thinking that his failing eyesight had played him a trick. But the stones were there, just as his eyes had observed them. He looked around for the men at his side.

"What is it? What has happened?" he asked, as if arousing from a dream.

The others had been looking, too. They saw the wall, saw that it rose to the height of two men and looked most solid, but what it was or how it came to be there they could not explain.

"We cannot say, brother," Between Feathers answered.

He was Fire Tender in the kiva. "It was not here before. Now it is here."

"It was built to keep us out of the village," the Sand Chief growled. "But who could do it? We all went to pray at the spring."

Farther back in the crowd, which by then had massed close against the barricade, a woman's voice spoke out: "Where were your eyes, old men, if you thought everybody went to the spring? I looked, and saw not a single man, woman, child or dog from the Spider Clan. They stayed up here while we went to pray—they are the ones who are taking our homes."

The speaker was Crane Woman, one of the three women who had discovered the failing spring.

At these words, spoken with rising anger, laughter came from above. All heads turned and all eyes gazed upward. Then all knew what had happened.

Dark Dealer stood on the roof top, looking down. His laughter was not of the kind that rises out of pleasure or gives pleasure.

"One at least among you is clever enough to understand a simple thing. No surprise to me that a woman should see it first. You Turquoise men are too blind to be of any use to yourselves—or any use to our village. Now that is ended."

The same laughter slashed through the words.

"The woman is right. This is now the village of the Spider Clan. The houses are our houses. We will divide the kivas among our societies. We always needed space." The voice trailed off. In the following silence, men heard their own breathing.

"Well! Aren't you going to object? You, Trailing Cloud! I see no other leader among you. You are deserted. What have you to say?"

The old Sun Watcher took a step forward. He stood quite alone. He wore a loose shirt of white cotton that covered him to his knees, with a red sash around his waist. His failing eyes could not take in the man who taunted him, but sight was not needed—the fading light caught itself in his white hair and glowed for a moment.

"We are not without our leaders," the words came thin and sharp from the old man. "You will reckon with them before this time is passed."

"You think so, old man? And what will they feast on, these leaders? What food and water have they stored up for the fools who will follow them?"

Trailing Cloud's head was tilted upward as if his eyes really saw—his infirm muscles had found the strength to hold him without faltering.

"We have stored up peace in our hearts, something you have forgotten. Men may die for want of food and water, and death is miserable. But would it not be more miserable for us if, through fear of death, we yielded to you? You must know, since you were born among us, that when our Mother Corn came to our elders, we were told to keep peace in our minds and in all our actions. Those who remember this and live accordingly will never be destroyed. If you forgot to take this into account when you captured our houses and our food, I remind you of it now. We will survive, will we not?" The old man turned with the words to face the men and women crowding close behind him. "Will we not?"

The crash of many voices echoed against the inner wall of the cavern and rolled out across the canyon: "We will take care of ourselves. We spit upon this traitor!"

The words were like a whiplash across the face of Dark Dealer. He had enjoyed the taunts he threw down at the massed bodies. Now, he would sting them. Now, he would show who was master.

He turned to others who until then had not been visible.

"They speak of their leaders. Good! Bring one of them here. Let them see for themselves."

The crowd below could not observe what was happening, but men moved across the roof, dragging something with them. They approached Dark Dealer with their burden. He reached down, and when he straightened up again, an anguished gasp rose from the crowd below.

Dark Dealer had placed his foot on the low parapet that ran along the roof. With one hand he pulled Eldest Woman into view, holding her by the hair for them to see. Her eyes were closed in death.

"Here is one who stood against me. Here is one of your leaders. Will you be next, old man, down there? Look, I give her back to you!" With that, he rolled the body over the parapet. It fell clumsily over the heaped rocks and came to rest at the feet of Trailing Cloud.

Cries of amazement changed into shouts of anger. "We can't stand for this! See what he has done! The man must be destroyed! Destroy him!"

The shouting died suddenly. The leader on the roof had summoned his young men to his side, and they appeared armed with bows, lances, and war clubs.

A fresh outburst of laughter from Dark Dealer.

"You see? You forgot your weapons when you left your houses. My men collected them from every hiding place. If you want to attack us, we will be happy to shoot you down with your own arrows."

Trailing Cloud turned to his people. "He speaks a terrible truth. While we prayed for our village, even for these thieves, they were destroying us. There is nothing for us to do but take our beloved Eldest Woman away from here and make a grave for her. Then we shall see. The day has not ended."

Above the grumbling of many voices rose that of Crane Woman: "But what are we to do? Our food is in there, in our houses. Our children are hungry."

"Peace, woman," Trailing Cloud answered in a voice dazed with anger and weariness. "We must get away from here and talk among ourselves. We must make plans. The Holy One will be with us, I promise you."

"But where? Where is he?" Crane Woman insisted. "You asked Shield to go for him. Where are they?"

The people were beginning to move, all unwillingly, when the voice called to them from the roof top once more.

"Why do you hurry? Wouldn't you like to know what plans I have for our village?"

"What plans can he have but to murder us all?" asked Crane Woman.

No one would have lingered, so hateful had become

that voice. Yet the people could not move away. As they
talked among themselves they cast angry glances at the
man on the roof, who seemed to wait at his ease, knowing
they would listen to him. It did not ease their humiliation
to realize that they could do nothing. To try to climb the
wall of rock with armed men shooting down into them
meant certain death, and defeat. Even so, the younger men
would try it and came crowding forward amid cries of
"No! No! Stop them!"

So the people milled about in that narrow upward trail.
Children, big-eyed with fear, pressed against their mothers.
Some whimpered, but were silenced when a mother put
her hand over a trembling mouth.

The watchers on the roof had built up a fire, which
threw a feeble, wavering light over the watching faces
below. It was full dark when Trailing Cloud called back to
Dark Dealer.

"The choice is not ours, so we will listen. What have you
to say to us?"

"A simple thing." The voice seemed so free of trickery,
the listeners marveled at the shamelessness. "A simple
thing," he repeated. "You saw the spring die today—the
spring which gives life to your children and to all of us.
Is that not enough to persuade you that the men who have
been leaders in our village have lost their power? Who can
say what wrongful thing they have done? Certainly a
wrong was committed, or we would not be punished in
this way. I accuse no one, but I ask each of you to think
about it. Who is our Village Chief? Where does he live?
Can he be found in the village, where he is needed? Can

our mothers and our children and our clan leaders go to
him in time of trouble?"

He waited, but not for answers to his questions. He
would convince them, if he could, that he was an elder
brother, concerned with their comfort and safety.

"Where your Village Chief has failed you, I can protect
you. I can bring back the water to the spring. Do you hear?
Do you believe me? I can make the spring flow again."

He paused, but there was no silence. Instead, many
voices broke into sounds of surprise, disbelief, mockery.

"What trick is this?" asked a voice from the darkness.

"We waste our time listening to him," the Sand Chief
growled. "He cares nothing for us or for our village."

"Wait!" Trailing Cloud spoke. "Whether we trust his
words or not, we must hear him. Stay and listen." He
turned to face Dark Dealer, on whom the firelight flickered. "You speak of bringing the water back to the spring.
How can you do this? How are we to know that you can
do it?"

"I can do it because I have the power. I tell you nothing
beyond that. But this I tell you." The voice on the roof top
turned wrathful, as though the patience of a just man had
come to an end. "This I will tell you—you no longer deal
with a fool. You no longer deal with foolish old men who
have outlived their usefulness. When I tell you that my
power can bring the water back to the spring, I know
whereof I speak.

"Now! I will cause the spring to flow again. On one condi-
tion. Bring the Holy One here before me. I shall be named
Village Chief. In the presence of all of you, he shall name

me to that office. The altar which is in his keeping shall be turned over to me. The shrines which he protects, and all the duties which he performs, shall be turned over to me. You will witness these things, and you will approve. Spider Clan shall be the first clan in the village, going before all others in our village ceremonies. These things you will approve. And when this has been done, the water will flow again in the spring. All this can come to pass before Sun, our Father, rises from his morning bed, if you are so minded. This is what I have to say, these are my conditions. Now, what have you to say?"

The people were left without voice. Never had they imagined an utterance so shameless and so bold. They were as captives in the hands of an enemy.

Finally, Trailing Cloud found the words that must be said. "This is not for us to decide. We are but children who dwell here in the house of our fathers. Neither is it for you to decide, though you may beat us with clubs and drive arrows through us. But we will find the Holy One, and pass on your words to him."

He turned his back on the man on the roof and in his customary soft voice he said to the people: "I think we have already stayed too long. Take up the burden of our dead one. We must shelter her."

As the people moved away, they could not hear Dark Dealer's wrathful tones as he turned to his followers: "Where is that old goat-leaping fool? I counted on him to be leading those people. I counted on bargaining with him. We can't hold that water back forever—and once it breaks free, our advantage will be gone and we will have to fight to hold what we now have." He paced rapidly back and forth across the narrow roof space and as he crossed in front of the fire, his body, which was not that of a giant, threw the shadow of a giant across the roof of the cavern.

"Some of you will have to slip out there, among those people, and try to find that old goat. He can't be far away. I advise you," he stopped, and his lips pulled back from his teeth, "to be careful. You are Spider Clan men, and if you are discovered out there your bodies will wind up at the bottom of the canyon."

Chapter 13

Let Him Live—Despised

SALT realized that his name had been whispered over and over again. At first it formed part of a frightening dream. He was being pursued in the flat country above the canyon, and as he ran seeking shelter, trees and rocks eluded him, disappearing into the air just as he reached them, leaving him no choice but to run on, while his lungs burst and his legs turned lifeless, and all the while the pursuing voice called, "Salt! Salt! Wait for my arrow! I am aiming between your shoulders! Just wait! Salt! Salt!"

He escaped the dream at last. When he opened his eyes it was to find himself in darkness, his head throbbing with pain. He remained motionless, searching the darkness with his eyes.

Again the voice called his name. So there had been a reality in the dream after all! When it came again, he knew it as the voice of Day Singer; it seemed to be right at his ear.

He inclined his head slightly, to indicate his wakefulness. Then he heard: "We are in the kiva of the Spider Clan. There are four guards. Don't move. Be quiet." A long silence followed, until Salt began to wonder once more whether he was awake or dreaming. He wanted to move his head and examine his surroundings, but checked the action. Then the voice again.

"I must speak only a few words at a time. Wait. Don't move."

Thus, through long aching minutes, Salt learned what had happened. Day Singer had regained consciousness while he was being carried out of the underground passage, but he had concealed the fact. Turtle must have come to at about the same time, and they had managed to let each other know that they were alive and awake.

He and Turtle had been unwise. They had discovered the dam being built in the underground passage, had realized the purpose of it, and then had let themselves be struck down from behind. They had also recognized that the men in the underground passage were all of the Spider Clan, though they had not seen Dark Dealer.

All this he told in sounds that almost eluded Salt, hardly more than a word or two at a time, and Salt strained at listening until he thought his nerves would crack.

Then Day Singer said: "My bonds are untied. My hands are free . . . I also untied Turtle's hands . . . We waited until you were awake . . . Now I am going to untie your hands . . . Be careful, two guards back of us—I can't see them . . . Listen carefully . . . Turtle and I will rush guards standing by kiva ladder . . . We will grab their clubs if we can . . . Do our best to overpower them . . . That will bring the other guards to help . . . When you see four guards piling on us . . . Jump up and crawl through the ventilator hole . . . Holy One has plan for you . . . It is important that you get away . . . You will find him above . . . Entrance to secret trail . . . He is waiting . . . Now I will slide down toward your hands . . . If the guard is not watching . . ."

Nothing further happened. Salt heard nothing, no movement, no further words. When this silence had continued for some time, he began to wonder if Day Singer had fainted. He had been badly hurt and must have lost a quantity of blood. Yet Salt dared not look, dared not move. The agony of waiting was now greater than ever, since his hopes had been raised by Day Singer's plan of action. He knew how to lie waiting for game and to endure blistering sun or biting wind; he had practiced that through many hours. But this was a new experience. He was now the hunted, and the hunter stood somewhere out of sight. He had no signs to go by; no bird song breaking off at mid-point; no bright-eyed squirrel watching from a tree limb. Here was nothing but an agony of nerve and muscle.

His hands were tied behind and the thong which bound them passed down to his feet, which were doubled backward and tied together. A second thong passed from his hands upward and was fastened in a slip knot around his neck. Thus he could move neither hands nor feet without tightening the thong around his neck.

When it seemed that he could wait no longer and must shift his head or his body, he felt a movement at his back; it was so slight, so almost imperceptible, that he thought he must be mistaken. It seemed impossible that knots in a leather thong could be untied without tugging and pulling. Day Singer must be exploring the knots and deciding how to attack them. What was his amazement, then, when he felt his hands fall apart and the thong fall slack around his throat!

Day Singer's whisper came again: "Don't move! . . . Your feet are still tied . . . Turtle is ready . . . I will count ten . . . It will be up to you . . . to reach Holy One . . ."

Then—feet pounded on the roof overhead. Before Day Singer could even start his count, men were pouring down the kiva ladder. Salt lost track of their number. They sounded like men released from duty. They spoke loudly, laughing, "It is over! Now we have done it!"

This meant nothing to Salt; probably it meant nothing to Day Singer or Turtle either. But what would happen here in the kiva?

The guards who had been somewhere in the shadow

back of Salt moved toward the group gathered at the bottom of the ladder. "What has happened? We had to stay on guard duty. Tell us!"

Many explanations followed; many voices spoke at once. Salt felt shame and anger. He realized that disaster had fallen upon the village. He even understood that Eldest Woman had been murdered. Dark Dealer and the Spider Clan had captured the village. And he could do nothing! Surely it was impossible to carry out Day Singer's plan. They must die here, with nothing accomplished.

Perhaps Day Singer's thoughts moved in the same direction. He must have seen the hopeless situation. But his conclusion was different. At that moment he rose and his piercing yell rattled around the circular room. He hurled himself at a guard.

Next moment he had a war club. Still yelling, he swung right and left. Men reeled away from him.

Turtle, tall and thin, was alive and amazingly swift. An instant later, he hit the second guard. He too now held a war club.

Salt leaped as Day Singer lunged forward, and fell flat. He had forgotten to untie his legs! His numbed fingers fumbled at the knot. He tried to break the thong. The seconds passed. Day Singer and Turtle could not stand up against so many men for long. They still shouted, taunting the men they fought. The kiva ladder went down. No reinforcements could get into the kiva, but neither could Day Singer or Turtle escape.

Salt finally hobbled across the room toward the ventilator shaft, praying that no one saw him. He squirmed into the opening. Pulling with his hands, he went quickly. He was about to crawl into the larger opening beyond the kiva wall, when the leather thong jerked tight around his neck! He had been discovered! Someone had grabbed it from the other end! He reached for the thong, jerked it mightily. It came loose in his hands. It had caught against the edge of a rock! He was free!

At that moment a body fell upon him in the darkness. A hot stinking breath closed upon him. He heard words: "Not so fast, whoever you are. No one leaves by this door."

As Salt felt hands at his throat, his unseen, foul-smelling adversary made a sound that was half-groan and half-belch. The hands relaxed and Salt heard a familiar voice.

"The Holy One thinks you will be a leader, so you had better live a while longer." It was Shield.

"How did you know—" Salt began.

"We will talk later," Shield answered. "Day Singer and Turtle can't last long. This will stop pursuit for a while—" He moved in the darkness and Salt knew he was dragging the dead guard and crowding him into the narrow ventilator shaft.

Salt had freed his feet and slipped the thong from his neck. Moments later, Shield leading, they crawled through the crack in the outer rock and moved sideways across the cliff.

The stars shone clear and the smell of the pine trees and damp coolness came up from the canyon. The silence of the night came like a roar of mighty voices.

* * * * *

Shield did not take the upward trail as Salt expected. Instead, he scrambled across the face of the cliff until he reached the village trail, then started down. Salt almost called out that he was expecting to meet the Holy One in the country above, but perhaps it was better to travel in silence. He followed Shield and said nothing.

Within a very few minutes they had reached the bottom, were hurrying toward the spring; then Salt understood. There, where the canyon ended in a great half-circle, scattered among the boulders and the tall spruce and pine trees, the people of the Village of the White Rocks had gathered. A fire had been built, and the flames, leaping upward, cast a dancing, wavering light high against the canyon walls. It also lighted the faces of the people. At the center of them all, Salt saw, wonderingly, their leader, Blue Evening Sky, he whom they called Holy One.

As Salt approached, a small, quick-moving woman drew away from the crowd and came to him first. She stopped when she was still a few feet away and a clear shining smile lighted her face. His mother, Becoming Day, took one step closer and touched his arm.

"You are well. I rejoice. Happiness be yours."

It was a pleasant voice, as Salt would always remember. He answered: "May you have happiness, my Mother. I walk in your beauty."

They looked once more at each other and saw that all was well. Then Salt stood before the Holy One.

The old man smiled, and an expression of mischief seemed to play about his eyes.

"Peace, boy. We hoped you would finish sooner with entertaining that man up there."

"May your days and nights be in peace, Grandfather. The entertainment was not to my liking. What of Day Singer and Turtle?"

"You ask a hard question, my son." The old man turned back to the broken boulder on which he had been seated.

Men piled fresh logs on the fire and a burst of fiery sparks flew upward into the night. Salt saw that the people had been eating . . . the pots of cooked food were standing away from the fire. Even as he noticed this, his mother came bearing a bowl in which dried meat and corn had been cooked together.

"Our grandfather is cunning. He had food stored in his rock house." As she murmured the words, she looked shyly at the Holy One.

"Sit, boy, and eat," the Village Chief ordered. "You ask a difficult question. Some of us went up there and will try to get to Day Singer and Turtle before they are beaten to death. Other men wait at the barricade, threatening to attack from that side. I want no attack, if it can be avoided. Women and children are in there . . . our people if not our clansmen. You see," he smiled mockingly, "I am now a warrior, planning battles; not a man of peace."

"I cannot understand all that happened." Salt found eating difficult. "When I saw Flute Man murdered, I knew something was wrong. Maybe I should have reported this to you and the rest would not have happened."

The old one waved his hand. "You would not have

found me. I was up there ahead of you. I saw Flute Man
and waited. When he came to the entrance, there he stayed,
and there you found him. You were frightened . . . but
you went on, and proved to all of us that you have a man's
courage.

"If a mistake was made, I made it." The village leader
showed that he was troubled. "A great anger rose in me
when I realized that Flute Man had discovered the trail.
I slew him, the first man I ever slew with my hands. In
the quiet after anger, I went away. So, you would not have
found me."

Clearly he was troubled. The firelight revealed a look
of sorrow on his face. He turned to the elder men nearby:
Shield, Trailing Cloud, Cloud Head, Between Feathers
. . . all the leaders of the six clans represented there.

Shield answered, "The failing was not in you, but in
that man up there. He turned loose the anger that is in
us all. Many feel that he must be destroyed before we can
have peaceful minds again."

The Holy One pulled himself straight. "When I
walked alone up there, I decided that it is better for Dark
Dealer to destroy himself. This he will do. This he is already doing. He told the people that he has the power to
stop the spring, or to let it flow. This, of course, is a lie. He
built a dam of rocks, hoping that it would hold the water
long enough for him to win the village. But water is strong
even stronger than Dark Dealer or any of us. It will break
the dam, and we will have our spring again. And thus,
Dark Dealer destroys himself, step by step. I say there is
no need to have his blood on our hands."

Salt saw that Trailing Cloud, the Sun Watcher, was rising to his feet, trembling in his infirmity, but borne up by resolution. Erect at last, the old man held up his hand: "Holy One's decision is wise, and we will abide with it. But our hearts are heavy with grief for Eldest Woman. And Day Singer and Turtle . . . what of them? Will they also come to us lifeless? And are we to live with this too?"

Salt put aside his bowl, the food gone cold. Here were terrible questions.

The Holy One, turning to Trailing Cloud, spoke in a strong voice that carried to all the people. "We have a law among us which can demand that a man give his life for taking the life of another. We have many laws, demanding penalties. It is not enough to have a law. We still must decide whether to use the full force of the law, or to use it only in part. A law by itself cannot cure a man; that is for us to accomplish, if it can be accomplished. This I ask you: If we take the life of Dark Dealer in return for the lives he has taken, that will finish it. He will be no more, but will pass beyond our reach. But what if we hold him here, alive, where the minds and the tongues of men can play upon him? Is it not a greater justice that he should stay, despised, in the company of men? He will resist, he will plot against us, he will harm us if he can. But a man is not a rock, he is not beyond touch, and his flesh and his spirit can be hurt. I say, let this man live among us, despised. Let children spit in his footprints. Let women turn their faces from him. Let men refuse to hear him in the kiva councils. This is what he will come to. The young men who follow him today, even they will despise him.

"If he is at bottom a coward, and I think he may be, his own flint knife will save us the dishonor of taking his blood. But if he has the substance of a man, he will in time come to us and ask to start again. I say, let him live among us, despised."

Salt felt his blood warm at the fire of this old man's wisdom. Shame and outrage could come to a people, but they could still save themselves so long as their leaders remained firm.

No one voiced objection to the words of the Holy One.

The people began to consider other problems. Crane Woman expressed the concern which faced them all. Out of the shadows she faced the Village Chief. "Perhaps we will agree to let Dark Dealer live with us. But where will we live? He has taken our village, our houses, our food. Unless we are willing to battle him and throw him out of there, I see no place to invite him to share with us." Crane Woman often spoke boldly, in a strong voice, then became shy immediately afterward, as if she had said more than she intended. Having spoken out in this forthright manner, she ducked her head and retreated back into the shadows.

The Village Chief was not embarrassed by such bold questioning. He thanked Crane Woman for speaking. Then he explained his plan. "We have not forgotten how to build houses, so let us build for our needs, here where we stand tonight. Stone and timber are here in abundance. Our spring will be restored and we will have water. We will keep a guard in the trail to prevent Dark Dealer from interfering with our water again. I think we will not have to remain here long. When Dark Dealer took our village, he forgot that he has only one clan on his side. We are six clans. We have ten men for every man of his, and the fields are in our possession. Our guard in the trail will prevent his people from going out to their farms. When he has eaten the food in our storehouses up there, he will realize his mistake. I think he will realize it long before the food is gone. As for ourselves, we will live well. Our crops will soon be ripe, and while we wait for them to ripen, our men will prove that they are still good hunters. Is this not enough? Will we not survive, my children?"

Probably no one would have dissented. Their leader, who this night had put aside the masquerade of wild talk and goatish capers, had thought out their problems for them. His plan was good, they would survive. Probably no questions would have been asked, but as it turned out, there was no opportunity that night for any further discussion.

The people heard first a rumble, as of thunder muttering in the distant mountains. Then it grew louder at once. It came closer. Then it was upon them with a shattering roar. People who had turned to listen, suddenly leaped to their feet and were terrified. They looked here and there but could not locate the source of the fearful cascading sound.

Then a shout went up! "The water! Our father, the spring!"

It was true. Water in great rolling muddy waves shot out of the rock at the bottom of the canyon, splashing high against obstructing boulders, sweeping along with a thunder of stones. The dam built by Dark Dealer had burst! The water would run in a mad flood until it had drained the underground lake.

Now people ran madly, crying their joy, to meet the rushing water. In the roar of the water their fears were drowned and washed away.

Only the Holy One failed to move, and Salt, of course, since he had been stopped by a gesture of the old man.

"They will not worry now. They will be content to build a new village, if necessary, and go on living as they always have. I think Dark Dealer will not hold out too long, and the people can move back into their homes.

"But what has happened will not be mended tonight, or tomorrow, or ever. You, my son, have lived to see the end of the life which our fathers lived before us. I have watched it coming a long time. Dark Dealer was not created from nothing, like a poisonous mushroom that seems to come from nowhere. Such a man is born only when the time and place are ready for him. The shell in which we lived is broken and may never be put together again. I told you, when last we talked, that you might be the one to save us. I want you to go on a journey, a long and dangerous journey, from which you may never return."

Now. It had come. Salt felt his scalp move and the muscles across his belly tighten. He remembered the moment underground, when he thought to perish in darkness. And he sensed that in this new venture, such moments of uncertainty and fear would occur again and again.

"My Grandfather," he said slowly, pondering his words,

"am I the one to do this? Have I the courage? Can I endure?"

In the darkness he did not observe that the older man smiled. "You have learned something in three days. When we talked before, you had not yet been frightened. Yes, you are the one to go. We have no other to send. Those of us who have the experience for such a journey have not the strength. Others, who might be stronger, have not your desire to help your people. I am only sorry that you must go at once; better if you could train for this journey, but we have no choice. We will survive what Dark Dealer has done, but our life here is broken and will never be put together again in the way it was before. We must find a new way, and I have no knowledge of what that will be."

"But how am I to do this?" The venture, alone, with no hand upon his shoulder, became suddenly real. Salt saw himself failing, and his people with him. His heart seemed to die. Weakly he asked: "How will I know what to bring back to our people?"

Silence followed, a long silence. The fire had died, the men who had been feeding logs to it had all rushed off to watch the spouting water. As the fire died, night flowed back into the canyon. Out of that night, Holy One spoke at last.

"I cannot tell you what to look for, or what to bring back. That is the terrible thing about this journey of yours. I can only tell you that somewhere in the south lies a land our fathers called the Land of Fable. We know nothing about it, but we are told that our songs, our dances, and our Mother Corn came from there.

"One day we talked about the corn you planted down here in the canyon. What I didn't tell you then is something I heard my father talk about, and something I have watched myself. A field of corn is like a village of people —so my father would say. If people stay too long among themselves, they weaken themselves, some families die out entirely. He encouraged young men from other villages to come among us, marry our girls, and become part of us. He also encouraged our men to go elsewhere to find wives. On your journey south, you will find some of our people.

"A race of corn will become weak in the same way. No man among us can say how long we have had our corn. It has been too long. Water will make the stalks grow tall, as you discovered by planting down here. But we looked at your corn—and while the ears are not fully formed, they will be no thicker and no longer than the ears of the plants in the dry land above. I have watched this since my father's time, and I now understand what he talked about.

"Is it a new race of corn that is needed, then? I cannot say. Maybe what is needed is that our people should change. We are no longer the children we were when our songs, our dances, and our Mother Corn first came among us. We cannot live in fullness with these things as once we did. We try to reach beyond them.

"So, whether it is corn, or people, at fault, I cannot say. I have helped as much as I can. The rest is up to you.

"I cannot even say whether I will be here when you return. But if you are successful, our people will honor you. You will be their leader, and you will make their lives whole again. I think that what you must look for will be something that comes from our Father the Sun. It will live in him. It will lift up our hearts.

"And now, my son, I give you this turquoise stone from my own neck. It is as a part of my body; it will keep you secure against all enemies; it will hold up your heart when you are troubled."

The giving of the turquoise, there in the darkness, was the most shattering experience of all that long day. Salt felt as if the image in which he had been born had been broken, and he had been born a new person.

"We will talk again tomorrow," the Holy One was saying. "There will be much to discuss, many things that you must carry in your mind as you journey from us."

Chapter 14

Southward

T HE EAGLE spread its wings and plunged free of the brown crag. It drifted downward, following the high slope of the barren mountain, then caught the hot-air currents rising from the valley and let itself be swept higher and higher until it seemed to pass beyond the empty sky.

The man-creature moved alone, like a mole blindly groping. Twice the hard-eyed eagle circled the broad valley, watching.

The sands of a dried-up stream bed gleamed white as bone. A chain of low rounded hills showed red scars where wind and water had cut through the surface of grass and soil. The eagle tilted downward, descended rapidly out of the blue, leveled and circled. It flew up to the end of the long valley, skirted the apron of the high mountains in the north, wheeled and, descending still lower, hovered in space.

When the man-creature still moved, the great bird pumped its wings and sailed away.

Salt had come down out of the mountains, out of the timbered coolness and the tumbling streams, and journeyed now in low hot country. It was only midmorning, but the sun burned with an intensity he had never before experienced. He would not walk much farther into the heat of the day, only as far as the low-lying hills before him, where a pocket of dark green promised water. He saw the circling eagle, watched it soar westward up the long running valley and return. But the boy was not dismayed. The heat was great, but not unbearable; he felt strong, tireless. He was embarked on a journey which no other man in his village had been asked to make. The eagle did not worry him.

It was important to go swiftly, yet it was also important to reach his goal. He must not try too much in one day, for what he gained in overexertion he would lose afterward in resting. He trotted, then walked, then rested. Trotted, walked, rested. He had no way of telling time, but he tried to keep to the same time intervals in trotting and walking, and to rest lying flat on his back only long enough to get his breath and give his leg muscles time to relax.

Walking alone, he thought of the things he had been told by the Village Chief, by his mother, and by others at leave-taking: the world in which he moved was less strange and less empty when he kept his mind on such things.

The Village Chief—they would always call him the Holy One, even though he had left the rock shelter, talked straight, and was leader of his people again—had not said much. "You will be gone a long time . . . you will cover great distances . . . you will not remember too many things. Besides, I do not know the road you are taking and I cannot tell you all that you will meet."

The Chief was concerned that the boy conduct himself properly. "Be friendly," he told him. "If you show no fear of strangers, they will respect you. They may help you."

Salt thought of these words, as he trotted, walked and rested. He thought about them against the background of his knowledge of people. If he met a stranger who was un-afraid, would he be friendly? Helpful? He could answer for himself, but he did not know about others. Some men would be rude to strangers, as they were rude to anyone else. Perhaps if you took no notice of rudeness and continued being friendly, it would work. He would remember the advice.

The Chief also said: "Be watchful. You will be in strange country and none of us can tell you which turn to take, what river to follow, how to cross a mountain which may lie before you. Only remember that you will be traveling south all the time. You must have the sun on your left when you start in the morning. You must have it on your right when you stop at night. If you must go around a mountain, take the side that will lead you soonest south. When you cross a stream, look for the place where the current breaks into many ripples, for there it will be shallow and you will have rock underfoot. Watch everything as you go."

When Salt reached the low-lying hills and sought out the pocket of green, he found no live stream, but the water oozed to the surface in shallow pools. He also found sharp hoofprints and knew that an occasional deer stopped to drink. With a pointed rock, he dug out one of these pools and made a trench leading away from it. This would drain off the stagnant water and let fresh water enter. Then he lay down to rest in the shade of tall mesquite trees.

He had been told that when he came down out of the mountains he would find a river flowing from the east, and following downstream, he would find a second river coming up from the south. It was important to find this second stream, because living near it were friendly people who could tell him about the road southward.

He thought about this as he lay resting. The season had matured into full summer; ripened corn and beans were being gathered in all the fields he passed. He had not realized, setting out, how many people, how many villages, lay beyond the Village of the White Rocks. He even met people who spoke his own language, and this too surprised him. When these strangers found they could talk to him, they asked where he came from, what house or clan he belonged to, and they wondered where he was going. In offering food, they suggested that he might not find food where he was going, or he might not find friendly people. To all these invitations to discuss his journey, Salt only thanked them for their kindness and remarked that he had a long way to go and must not delay. All were friendly, even those who did not speak his language. None tried to detain him.

Of the people who lived on the stream flowing from the south, some were men and women from his own village. The Holy One spoke of them. They had married down there and no longer belonged to the north. But they would speak his language and would help him.

He rested until the greatest heat had gone out of the day, then climbed to the top of the low hill and looked across the wide valley for a landmark. Heat ran fluidly across the horizon and a distant purple mountain seemed to hang, without foundation, from the sky.

When he left the low-lying hill and started down through the desert's thorny brush and cactus, a gray wolf jumped from a ledge of rock on a neighboring hill and followed cautiously after him.

He camped that night without water, but at least he had the flesh of a rabbit to roast. His camp was in a dry arroyo where a fire could be built without arousing curiosity.

Salt's traveling equipment was simple. To get food, he carried a curved rabbit stick, a sling, a flint knife, and a long net made of fine brown cotton thread. On his feet he wore moccasins, the soles of heavy rawhide; an extra pair hung from his belt. A pouch of dried corn and a second pouch of dried meat constituted his reserve food supply, and a small pitch-covered basket carried water. His breech-clout was a long piece of white cotton material doubled over his belt at front and back with the ends hanging to his knees. A sleeveless jacket hung from a thong that crossed over one shoulder and under the opposite arm.

On the fourth day after coming down from the mountains, Salt found the river and the people dwelling there, a country of willows and great crowned cottonwood trees. Their houses, stretching for miles along the river, filled him with wonder. They were simple houses, flat-roofed, made of poles and intertwined willow saplings covered with adobe mud. Inside, even in the great heat of midday, these dwellings were dim and cool. Before each house rose a shaded shelter of poles covered with brush. Here in coolness the people cooked their meals, told their stories, and slept at night.

What astonished Salt were the irrigated fields. The people built dams of brush and stone at many places along the river and trenched canals that carried water far out into the flat valley. Looking at these canals for the first time, he was both joyful and sad . . . joyful to behold so much water, but sad that his own people did not share it.

Salt found the people from his village and was made welcome, as if he had been a younger brother. He must stay to be feasted. Indeed, he was feasted by each of the headmen in turn. The time was not lost, they assured him, when they heard of his plans for journeying south; and when they told him of the great summer rains which turned shallow desert rivers into whirling torrents that flooded entire valleys, he was content to stay. So he waited in that pleasant land, feasted, and heard stories of the people he would meet and the things he would see.

Even as he enjoyed himself, however, Salt examined the corn that he ate, and was disappointed to find that it was identical with the corn his people grew at home. Then he would recall those who waited for him . . . he would wonder if the new houses were built, if his people had food. Then becoming restless, he begged to be allowed to resume his journey.

In the end, the leader of the clan insisted on sending his own son, River Fighter, to accompany Salt as far as certain kinsmen living many days' journey to the south.

When Salt left that land of water, planted fields and crowned cottonwood trees, the fierce heat of summer had passed. The people, having become fond of him, uttered last words of advice, of what he should do, how to conduct himself, even words of regret. They gave him thick-soled sandals woven of tough yucca fibers and would have loaded him down with food and gifts if he had not protested that he was too frail for their bounty.

As he took to the trail, his heart sang as on a morning in spring. River Fighter was almost his own age and, like his tribesmen, was burned quite dark by the southern sun. He was handsome, good-natured, full of laughter, a happy traveling companion.

They set forth at dawn and followed the shallow valley of the northward-flowing river. They passed between the shadows of low, boulder-strewn mountains into a seemingly endless valley that opened before them. After many days they reached a height of land from which, henceforth, all streams would flow southward; all streams would carry Salt farther and farther into the Land of Fable, the Red Land of the South.

Soon they picked up the headwaters of one of these southward-flowing streams and on a morning when the desert doves talked and the rising sun stood in golden haze, Salt and his companion said farewell and Salt went on alone.

Distances were great, but it was not a lonely land. Hardly a day passed when he did not see a cluster of mud-roofed houses. Sometimes the clusters were large enough to be called a village, stretching along the banks of a swift stream pouring from a mountainside; sometimes only a few lonely dwellings scattered at the edge of a cornfield.

The land, except in rocky stretches and in flats where the earth glistened white with alkali, was everywhere clothed in fierce tangles of scrubby brush and branched cactus trees that stood above the scrub like silent men watching children at play. When he came to these thickets, he watched carefully to distinguish between game trails and the paths of men. The game trails might lead only to a water hole or a feeding ground, but man-trails would lead him on his way. Often he had to backtrack for hours before he found the road he wanted.

It was not a lonely land. The farther south he traveled, the more thickly populated he found it. Even when he encountered no man or woman, he knew that people were nearby. Everywhere along the trail, he found wayside shrines. These might appear to be no more than a heap of rocks piled at the trailside, with bright-colored feathers attached to protruding sticks. But he never failed to take up a rock from the roadside, breathe upon it, and, as taught him in childhood, lay it atop the pile. This in courtesy to the Cloud People.

This practice, unwittingly on his part, had several times saved his life. Men of strange tribes had followed him, distrusting him as they distrusted any stranger. Trailing him silently, as a wolf or a puma might have trailed him, they saw him perform his act of grace; thereafter he went on unmolested.

It was not a lonely land.

Day followed day. Days of hunger. Days of thirst. Days when insects swarmed about him, stinging and biting. Days of longing for his people, for the look of searching tenderness of his mother, for the kindly speech of the Holy One. Days of fever and quick, shuddering chills, when the food he ate was vomited up again and his legs seemed ready to break under the effort of walking.

At last the houses as well as the people were new and strange. The dwellings were circular with dome-shaped roofs. Long slender poles were bent into arches, tied at the top, and roofed with mats woven from palm leaves. Clusters of these houses, with their shaded outdoor living places, were found in clearings, a stream running by. It was surprising to see men from these villages trotting ahead of him down a trail, with quarters of a deer or other burden suspended from each end of a pole carried across the shoulders. It was a thing to remember and to tell about when he returned home . . . if he ever returned.

The excitement of new things passed, but weariness remained. If Salt could have seen himself, he would hardly have recognized his own image. His ribs, the bones at his elbows, shoulders, hips and knees showed through the thin flesh. Arms and legs were gashed by many thorns, some of them poisonous, causing his flesh to swell and mortify. Such wounds were slow in healing. His body was often mud-spattered, his long hair matted and unkempt.

He crossed some five or six large rivers and numerous branch streams—he tried to keep count of the rivers, for he knew that after a certain number he would come to one which he must follow inland, away from the sea—but in time the many crossings blurred together and he lost count.

Finally he stood upon a low foothill that extended like an arm out of the mountains to the east, and he looked down into a broad flood-plain at his feet. He had come upon a world still different from any he had ever known.

The land had continued to change, growing warmer, damper, more densely forested. Now, impenetrable jungles ranged before him. Vines and creepers twined themselves around all growth, lashing it together. But the trail was now a broad avenue leading southward . . . at times a kind of tunnel through a green underworld. The pounding feet of many generations of men had kept it clear of growth, its direction certain. Here, trade and communication flourished.

It was more than the countryside that had altered. Looking down in astonishment upon the flood-plain, he saw a community of houses exceeding in number anything he had ever imagined. In the broad valley it seemed as if dwellings extended all the way to the horizon; not scattered aimlessly across the valley, but divided into planned sections, with roads between. The houses were of mud, fashioned in square blocks like the stones of which his own village was built, the roofs a thick covering of long bleached grass. Here and there among the houses, on low man-built earth hills, large buildings had been erected. Salt recognized these as holy places.

His wonder increased when, descending, he followed a road wide enough for ten men to walk abreast, and came at last among the houses. People gazed upon him curiously, but unlike the villagers whom he had met back in the mountains, they made no effort to stop him or talk to him. They were taller than any people he knew, and they dressed in bright colors. The women wore an upper garment, loose at the neck, with wide, flowing sleeves, and a skirt reaching below the knees. Intertwined in their dark braided hair were bright ribbons and feathers of many colors. They wore necklaces and ear and arm ornaments of sparkling shells, pearls, turquoise, and little copper bells. Some men wore robes reaching from the shoulder almost to the ground, and some, whom he took to be warriors, wore headdresses with brilliant plumage flashing as they walked. These carried round shields covered with leather, on which curious designs were painted.

He came to an open place within the town where people crowded elbow to elbow. Around the four sides of this open place stood small booths in which were displayed a great wealth of foods, cooked and uncooked; goods woven of cotton, feathers, and strange fibers; ornaments of gold

and shell; baskets; pottery of many curious designs; caged
birds and small animals; carved objects of wood and stone
—countless things he had never seen or imagined. Here
was pottery that surpassed belief; of black and red with
brown and cream lines and whirls; some with a fluting up
and down the sides; and so highly polished as to reflect
his image. But what held his attention longest were small
jars, dark brown, highly polished, and engraved with a
sharp point in designs that suggested the delicacy of
feathers. He stared a long time at this, and somehow felt
here all the alien quality, the foreboding, the hidden
dangers of this new world into which he had come.

As he lingered in the open place gazing about him, he
was a strange figure. His sandals were frayed to shreds;
his legs covered with scratches and angry sores; his body
streaked with dust and mud; his hair matted. He seemed
not to be aware of this, and the people who brushed past
him seemed scarcely to look his way. But he was noticed.

He was accosted by two men bearing tall painted
wooden staffs and wearing headdresses from which dangled
eagle claws. They spoke to him in an unknown tongue;
but when they touched his elbows, one on each side, and
motioned to a large flat-roofed building facing the open
square, he knew that he was to go with them.

But for what purpose? Instinctively, his hand sought
the protecting turquoise at his neck.

Chapter 15

Still Southward

SALT was led through an open doorway into a courtyard, in the center of which lay a pool, green with
lily pads. Doorways opened upon this courtyard
from the rooms surrounding it on all sides.

The men walking on either side led him past the pool,
which he would have stopped to admire if he had been
alone. A fingerling fish flashed silver at him from the
shadows beneath the lilies. When his escorts reached the
open doorway opposite the street entrance, one went
ahead into the room, while the second, after motioning to
Salt to proceed, followed in the rear.

179

They entered a long narrow room, and, though the walls were whitewashed, Salt coming from bright sunlight found it dark. Several moments passed before he discerned three men seated at a table at the far end of the room. Silently they observed this stranger, then the middle one spoke sharply. He was answered by one of the escorts. Salt then realized that the man behind the table was speaking to him. The man spoke again, repeating his words, each time in a louder voice.

"I am Salt," said the boy proudly. "My people live there, in the north," he gestured northward.

The men all stared at him, then at each other. His speech was as strange to them as theirs to him.

The trio at the table spoke among themselves, pointing several times at Salt. It seemed they were more interested in the turquoise at his neck than in him. One of his guards approached closely and examined the stone. Presently the center man at the table clapped his hands. He seemed to give orders to one of the guards, who went out.

Again the men at the table talked among themselves, while Salt, trying to assure himself that their voices were friendly, began to feel uneasy. He tried again to explain himself, pointing to the north and to the south, but they only regarded him coldly.

In a little while the messenger returned and was followed by five other people, one an elderly woman. More talk, more pointing at Salt. One by one, the newcomers stepped forward and addressed Salt, each in a different language. So the men were seeking an interpreter.

The last to try was the woman. She wore the shoulder

mantle and the knee-length skirt customary with those people, and her hair in two braids tied together at the back. In her small round face her quiet eyes studied him before she spoke. This time the attempt was successful; it was reassuring to hear words in his own tongue even though pronounced haltingly, and with a strange accent. The three men, she told him, one a judge-priest and the other two his assistants, suspected him of being a spy, from a tribe north across the river. This city, she told him, was called Culiacan; its inhabitants were as numberless as the pines on the mountain, and they were suspicious of strangers among them. Then she asked why he wore a turquoise stone.

He understood that he was in danger. He must choose his words with care, must make the woman understand. He told her of the Village of the White Rocks; that his people were poor, but were men of peace who never made war or sent out spies. He had come this long journey seeking help. With many gestures he explained that the turquoise stood for the sky, where the sun lived; that it also stood for peace and long life, and it was the badge of his Turquoise Clan. He added, "Whoever wears the turquoise, travels in the protection of the gods." When he had finished, he looked for understanding in the woman's face.

While he watched in growing anxiety she explained at length to the three men who listened, eying him thoughtfully. Again they consulted among themselves. Then the one in the center, the judge-priest, rose from the wooden bench. As his cape of a pale-blue material fell back Salt saw, on his bare chest, a large disk in which turquoise, obsidian, white shell and some kind of pink stone were inlaid in an intricate mosaic.

He spoke first to the woman, quietly; then turning to Salt's guards his tone grew more peremptory. They left the room.

The woman, touching Salt's arm, said: "You come."

Salt, puzzled, looked to the men behind the table. Their gesture seemed to dismiss him.

In the street, the woman repeated, "You come."

She took him to her house, a few doors away, where were her two young daughters and an older boy. She gave orders, and the children brought cook pots, blew life into the fire in the outdoors cooking place, and fetched articles of clothing. That was like his mother. In a daze he stood watching the activity until the woman pushed him into an enclosed yard. He recognized the pot of yucca suds which the two daughters had just prepared. Presently he was kneeling while the woman washed his hair. This too was like being home again. Surely he was now safe with these people.

Meanwhile, the son of the household prepared the sweat bath which stood in the corner of the walled yard. When this was ready, the woman and her daughters retired. Salt went in to steam, and to wash himself afterward with water dipped in a gourd ladle from a large pottery jar. The son helped in this, smiling, and afterward showed Salt how to array himself in the new and curious garb of these people. The breechclout, a long strip of soft woven material, was passed between the legs, wrapped twice around the body, and the loose ends, tucked under and over at front and back, hung to the knees. New sandals made with a stiff leather sole; a robe of white cloth, on which a border of geometrical figures was embroidered in many colors, completed the costume.

When Salt returned to the house the woman was waiting, smiling a vague welcome. Then he saw waiting the two men who had led him before the judge-priest. His feeling of well-being died within him. So it had not been dismissal; some further ordeal awaited him.

But the woman must have guessed his emotion; her smile quickened reassuringly.

"You go to feast at priest's house," she said. "These people have Turquoise Clan, like you people. The priest belong that clan. Good fortune for you." And clapped her hands together, like a child who takes delight in a trick.

Salt could only ask, "What is your name? What may I call you?"

"They call me Yucca Flower Woman."

That night Salt ate strange foods from the sea, meats like no other he knew, and fruits beyond any dream. Many sat at the table, their faces gleaming in torchlight, Salt among them. From a ragged stranger looked upon with distrust, he had been transformed into an honored guest. The Holy One had spoken with truth when he said of the turquoise, "It will keep you secure."

So Salt went on from Culiacan. In the weeks that followed, he traveled through a country of marshes and lagoons, where sea birds wheeled and screamed. Villages built on broad earthen mounds above the surrounding land.

Then the trail turned away from salt water and the marsh-
lands and followed a river that clove the mountains lying
to the east. Now he had reached the last stage of his
journey. The Land of Fable lay somewhere beyond the
mountains which, as he traveled eastward in suffocating
jungle heat, arose in great blue ridges that seemed to climb
into the sky itself.

He was troubled now by a new concern. Culiacan had
taught him that without knowledge of the language of the
people he was to meet, he could never explain his mission,
nor understand whatever they tried to tell him. Indeed,
for lack of their speech, he might be slain as an enemy spy.

Also, coming to the end of his journey, what was he to
bring back with him? Would it be an object that he could
carry in his hands? Would it be something he could observe, and carry back as a picture in his mind? Or something to hear, such as a ritual, a nine days' recitation of
songs? If it was the corn spoken of by the Holy One, how
could he know when he had found the right kind? He had
come a long and difficult journey, and the thought that he
might return home empty-handed filled him with anguish
for his people.

On many nights, as he lay down to sleep in desert arroyo
or leafy jungle, he saw the faces of the people in the Village of the White Rocks and wondered what had happened
to them. Was Dark Healer still holding out in the village?
Had the new houses been built in the canyon? Who had
been ambushed? Murdered? Winter was now upon them,
and he wondered if the fields had yielded enough to feed
the people through the bleak months. And what of his

mother and his young sister? These were heavy thoughts to carry up a mountain trail. Unlike a burden strapped to one's back, they could not be put down for a resting period.

Finally, he was out of the suffocating heat of the coast jungle and journeying in the highlands where pine trees flashed their red trunks and fir and spruce brought a smell of home. He crossed the main range of the west and began to pass from one broad mountain valley to another. The villages increased in size again, the valley lands were richly tilled. He saw houses of stone, temples reared against the sky.

The trail had become a busy highway. Each day he encountered travelers. Sometimes he would pass a long file of villagers, each of whom would glance up, touch hand to forehead, then pass on, making no attempt to stop or to talk. At other times, hearing voices in speech or in song behind him, he would step off the trail and watch a file of men and women come trotting along, the men burdened with great piles of pottery ware, baskets, fibers for weaving, animal hides, while the women carried the burden of a child slung in a shawl at their backs. They too would touch hand to forehead as they passed Salt at the roadside, and resume a song broken off.

One afternoon he approached a large lake that spread its blue waters between mountain headlands. As he neared, a flight of ducks passed overhead, circled, and came to light close to the lake shore. He was hungry; duck flesh, after a steady diet of rabbit, squirrel and dried deer meat would be delicious. He hurried to the lake's edge, grabbing up small stones for his sling, and seeking a hiding place among the reeds. At the water's edge he crouched, waiting. The ducks should soon swim within range.

After a moment he noticed a number of large gourds floating on the water close to shore. The ducks were swimming around these gourds, diving into the shallow bottom, and discussing the things that ducks talk about among themselves. A light warm breeze blew off the lake, pushing ahead small shallow waves to splash upon the shore. The floating gourds bobbed up and down in the restless water, but moved no closer inland.

And even stranger, one of the gourds was floating away from its fellows, toward the place where the ducks were thickest. In amazement, he saw a duck disappear from the surface of the water, not in a dive, but seeming to plunge down all at once. A streak of red appeared on the surface of the water and spread in a circle.

Immediately a second duck disappeared beneath the surface; again that streak of red. Surely some strange animal had got among the ducks and was destroying them.

Salt rose then, fitted a stone to his sling, swung it around his head. It flew like a speeding arrow. The stone cracked squarely in the center of the floating gourd.

The gourd seemed to explode. A pair of eyes, human eyes, gazed at him through the fragments of the gourd shell.

The ducks rose in wild clamor, their wings whistling as they took to the air in panic. The person in the water moved a few feet toward shore, then slowly emerged.

Salt stared in amazement at the man standing half submerged. He shook off the fragments of gourd shell and two ducks dangled from his belt. Their heads had been twisted off under water.

It was an awkward moment. Salt knew he must act quickly. He raised his hand, palm forward, moving it back and forth. Among the people in the north, this was a sign for negation. It could mean "no," "nothing," "no more." Then he made the gesture for eating, moving his index finger forward toward his mouth, and pointing in the direction taken by the flight of ducks.

After that, he could only wait. The man in the water continued to stare, then waded ashore. This stranger, while not much older than himself, was taller, and probably more powerful in combat. He wore a knife in his belt.

The stranger spoke at last, in speech unknown to Salt.

Salt smiled, answering in his own tongue: "In the north, a stranger is a friend until he shows himself to be otherwise. I hope your people have the same custom." He smiled again, to show his friendly intentions.

The stranger spoke again, jerked his chin toward a spot farther down the lake shore, and moved in that direction. Salt followed him, happily interpreting this as an invitation.

Around a low head of land a canoe was drawn up on the beach. The boy dropped his two ducks in the bottom of the canoe and motioned Salt to take a place in the bow. The canoe, hollowed out of a cedar log, was long and narrow, and the paddle a round piece of cedarwood fastened with thongs to a slender pole. They shoved off from shore.

On impulse, Salt patted the side of the craft and asked

how it was named. He repeated the gesture several times, saying, "What do you call this? How is it said?"

The canoeman, facing Salt from the stern, puzzled over Salt's words. Then his face cleared. He freed his right hand from the paddle, patted the side of the canoe and gave the word "icharuta."

Salt repeated the word "icharuta, icharuta." Then he pointed to some fish in the bottom of the boat and repeated his question, "How is it said?"

The answer came at once, "Akumara."

The strangeness between them seemed to disappear, and Salt decided that whoever this young man was, whatever his family might be, he would remain long enough to learn the language.

Spring came gently in that land. The oak forests on the hillside turned from brown to green in a matter of days. The heavy winter rains slacked off and after a few days of steaming, the earth appeared fresh-washed and bright with new color. Almost immediately, the warmth of summer descended.

Salt, in these months, became a member of a family— the family of the duck hunter, whose name Salt soon learned meant the ocelot, the wildcat of this region. Bringing Salt home that first day, he told of the meeting at the lake as a joke on himself. It produced laughter in the family and Salt was accepted almost at once. They made him display his slingshot and later he demonstrated his marksmanship with it.

Ocelot's family lived in a whitewashed adobe house, one

of many houses facing on a long street that curved with the shore of the blue lake, Patzcuaro. The house roofs were of thatch and sloped in four directions from a high ridge.

The father belonged to the family of the calzonci, the ruling chief of the area. As a member of that family, he was an official of the state and had charge of the fields which each year produced revenue for the state's upkeep. In the household were the grandfather and grandmother, who kept themselves busy; Ocelot's married sister, with her husband and two small children; and two younger brothers, who ate the morning and evening meal with the family, but in between times, as they said, practiced at being hunters and warriors. They accepted Salt as their instructor in the use of the slingshot and the rabbit stick.

Salt was awed by Ocelot's mother, since he had never before known a woman who did not grind her own corn, cook her own meals, and plaster her own house. Women and girls from nearby houses came each day to grind corn on the stone metate, an older woman prepared the family meals, and still another woman went each morning to the market in the center of the city and obtained the day's food. The mother, whose name meant Flowering Shaft of the Yucca, walked in the garden which swept down a long hill, bordered by an adobe wall, where birds of many plumages lived in reed cages, and a tame deer came to feed from her hand.

This city beside the lake seemed a place of wonder. In Salt's country, each man tilled his own field, hunted for his own meat, obtained his own firewood, held office in

clan or village, and had his own place in the ceremonies
of the people; but here a man did but one thing and had
to depend upon others for those needs which he could not
supply himself. Some men were carpenters, others were
stonemasons, and some even devoted their whole time to
building and repairing temples. Among the most highly
regarded of all craftsmen were the men who worked in
gold, silver, and precious stones.

Religious ceremonies were occasions involving large
masses of people and solemn spectacles. The temples, built
high on a squared-off pyramid, stood out in bold relief
against the sky. Great fires were built before these temples and the people moved in slow processionals, clothed
in bright costumes, chanting through the days and nights.

By spring Salt could speak the new language well enough
to explain what had happened to his people and why he
had come on this journey. When he turned to Ocelot's
father, however, and asked for help and advice, he was
not encouraged. The old man either frowned and walked
away, or refused to continue the discussion.

But one day he said suddenly, "It is the Valley of
Mexico of which you speak. A sorry land it is. Once the
gods smiled upon it, and in gratitude the people built
temples, cities of stone. If you go, you will see all these,
but you will see them in ruins. Jaguars come out of the
hills and walk the ruined streets. Thieves and murderers
too roam the streets. What was once great is so no more.
I would not urge you to go there. A slashed throat may
be all you will find."

But Salt refused to be discouraged. The Mother Corn

of his people had come from this far land, what Ocelot's father called the Valley of Mexico. Now that the Land of Fable bore a name, it became a place in reality, no longer a legend. In such a place he would find people, and the people would help him. This he believed, as the young will always believe.

Salt poured out his hopes to Ocelot. They talked together into the night; and Ocelot, obedient son though he was, was finally captured by the excitement of Salt's quest.

His decision to accompany Salt was, after some hesitancy, reported to his father. His father stifled his anger; fathers, in that land, trained their sons to be independent of spirit, as well as obedient, so now Ocelot's parent acknowledged within himself that the son had the right to come to his own decision, however foolish it might appear to be.

"If you must go, I won't prevent it," the elder said, not wholly hiding his displeasure. More calmly, he continued: "I will give you the name of a friend in that land; if he has not been murdered, he will be an old man now. He is master over a large household; his clansmen will still acknowledge his leadership. See him; he will help if he can."

It was a strange farewell, offering little comfort, and no blessing.

Within a few days Salt and Ocelot left the city on the lake and traveled eastward.

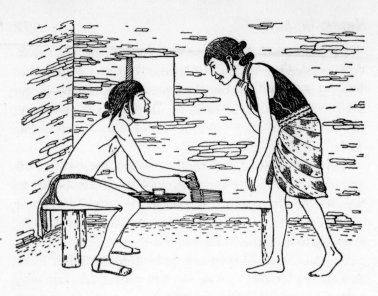

Chapter 16

Houses in the Sky

SALT knew that at last he had come to the end of his journey. During the last days of travel with Ocelot, they passed greater and greater numbers of people on the broad road. Here were buildings of stone, larger buildings, before which stood great carved pillars. The towns grew larger, and in the center of each was a high pyramid standing above the surrounding buildings, surmounted by a temple and often a curl of smoke rising from a sacrificial fire.

As they walked along, Salt expressed his amazement at these sights, and at each outburst his companion would voice a different view. If Salt remarked on the crowds of people they were passing, Ocelot pointed out that quite as many people came to the market in his town. If Salt bent his head backward to gaze at a temple standing against the hot blue sky, Ocelot commented: "We have just such temples. You saw them in the middle of Tzintzuntzan, our town."

They were too good friends to argue, but Salt would smile. Maybe the crowds only seemed larger, the buildings and temples more beautiful, because he expected them to be. This was what he had been sent to find, in this land of great expectation!

He and Ocelot had come to be as close as brothers since that day on the lake, when Salt had proved his skill with a sling. In spite of his slight advantage in age, Ocelot was content to follow behind the purposeful boy from the north.

When at last they mounted the last ridge lying to the west and started down in the valley where lay the lakes and their girdle of cities, no doubt or question remained. Even Ocelot stood and looked wonderingly. Mist hung low above lake water and spread out over the neighboring land, where it was pierced by rows of cypress spires. Pine-covered islands and headlands floated upon this mist. Nearer at hand, where the sun plunged into the mist and gave it liveliness, a pyramid and its surmounting temple, sparkling in morning light, seemed to be of the sky, not of the earth.

The young travelers looked long at the view below them, then at each other, and neither uttered a word. This truly was the Land of Fable.

Tenayuca was that first city. In the next days, following the marshy lake shore alive with birds, they passed through Azcapotzalco, Coyotlatelco, Tlacopan, Chapultepec and Coyoacan. From the latter town, a roadway extended across the entrance to Lake Xochimilco. The lake was shallow, and the roadway was built by driving logs into the mud in two rows and filling the space between with stones and dirt. An opening midway between the two shores, covered over by a bridge, allowed the water to circulate as the lake level rose and fell.

At last they came to Culhuacan, the end of the journey, where lived the friend of Ocelot's family.

Days later, when Salt had accustomed himself somewhat to the great strange house and the people in it, he thought back over the long journey and, for the first time, felt astonished at what he had accomplished. If he had known of the thirst and the hunger, the poisonous thorns, and the long empty spaces through which he had traveled, would he have dared to start? Would he have the courage to return when the time came? It seemed to him, now that he knew the perils, impossible.

Here in the pleasant security of Tula's house, the Village of the White Rocks was like a dream that begins to fade from memory. The moments of fear, anger, and high resolve once real, were becoming like parts of a tale he might have heard at some long-ago time. Difficult to feel that he himself had been involved. So he felt less need to act recklessly or with speed.

The house of Tula was built on northward sloping land. At the foot of the slope, stretching beyond the horizon to the north, the great Lake Texcoco lay speckled by the sun. Back of the house rose the cone-shaped Hill of the Star, surmounted by a temple whose white stone flashed sunrays as if it were itself a star.

This house of Tula was a house of peace and quiet. Its great courtyard was large enough to have included the entire Village of the White Rocks, Salt thought. Cypress and pine ran in rows across the lower end where, catching the prevailing wind, they made a pleasant murmur. A covered walk ran along the four sides of the courtyard, shading the rooms which opened on it.

An arched gate led to a garden on the east, enclosed within a fence of living cactus. This gateway also led into a smaller courtyard beyond the main building, where the women had their quarters along with the cooking fires and baking ovens. At the head of the courtyard was the council room where Tula's clansmen met.

After his first meeting with the master of the house, which occurred late one afternoon, Salt had no occasion to meet and talk with Tula again for many days, though he was sometimes present, silent and preoccupied, at the evening meal.

The first person in the household with whom Salt became acquainted was the slave girl who came each morning bearing a lacquered tray, on which were a cup of hot chocolate and a rolled tortilla pierced with a cactus thorn. She never looked up, but after placing the tray on a low bench backed away, her eyes downcast.

At first Salt assumed that she was a younger daughter of the family, until Ocelot explained that women of the family stayed within their own quarters. Only a slave girl was allowed to serve strangers.

Even when he talked to her, Salt could not get the girl to look up. She came each morning, placed the chocolate on the bench, backed away, paused, then turned to go. Her costume, always the same, was a skirt of dark material wrapped several times around her waist and held up by a narrow belt of red cloth, and a sleeveless blouse covering the right shoulder. Even though she held her head down, he could see that her nose stood high and her mouth was thin and well shaped.

She was called Quail, though a full translation of her name, Ocelot explained, meant Young-Quail-Who-Dis-appears-in-Prairie-Grass-and-Whose-Crest-Stands-Above-the-Grass. This obviously had to be shortened.

She came originally from the hill country of the west, and her dialect differed from that spoken by the people of Culhuacan. Salt would ask her the names of things when she came in the morning, but even as she struggled to understand him, she refused to raise her eyes.

Having failed to get her to look up, he finally resorted to a trick. He spent an entire afternoon catching butterflies of many sizes and colors, and placed them in a little cage of green willow shoots. When she came the next morning, he waited until she had set down the tray. Then he pushed the little cage toward her and popped open its lid. But in the cool morning air the butterflies were sluggish and refused to fly up.

The girl looked into the little cage, with its collection

of dormant butterflies. Then she looked squarely at him and began to laugh. They both laughed, and there was never any strangeness between them after that.

Quail had no parents. Her father had been taken as a prisoner of war and, his heart torn from his body, sacrificed on one of the high altars. Her mother died soon afterward, of grief or witchcraft. Two younger brothers were taken by grandparents to rear, but as it was a poor mountain village lying in the path of war parties, the corn and beans raised by the people were frequently seized by one army or another and the people left to await another harvest. Since a girl was a burden to a poor family, Quail was sold and eventually found herself in Tula's household. Here she was well treated and here she hoped to stay for the rest of her life. She told these things in snatches of words, which Salt put together as best he could. Sometimes he had to call upon Ocelot to explain what she told him, but he enjoyed her halting speech and preferred to struggle with it alone. She seemed more willing to talk without a third person present.

The most noticeable thing about her—the tattooed slave mark in the center of her forehead—drew his gaze constantly, but he never asked her about it. It was a small circle, with parallel lines shooting away in the four directions. Though he could not ask about that, he did ask indirect questions about her life.

Salt said to her one day, "Here you will never have your own life. You will have no family, no people of your own."

The girl surprised him with her reply. "Here it is better not to have people of your own. Who can say what bitterness may come to any of us?"

Then she asked in her turn, gaining ease as they talked, "You—and what do you expect to find among these people?"

"Corn! I came to find corn." He had not expected to describe his quest with that single word, but now that he had uttered it, he felt relief. Maybe it was the thing for which he had traveled across mountain and desert. At least it was something the girl would understand.

But she laughed, thinking he had given her a foolish answer.

"Corn," she said after a moment, "you can find anywhere. It must grow everywhere in the world. It even grows in the mountains where I was born."

"It grows in my country also, but hear what troubles we have—" He told her about the dried-up fields, the failing spring, and the corn that seemed to be dying of its own weakness.

And he added, "I have come to find the Mother Corn from which ours came."

Her face brightened. "When I was a child in our mountain village, we sang a song. Maybe it is for you. Listen.

> O sweet light,
> In my eyes see truth.
> O sweet sound,
> In my ears hear truth.
> O sweet mother corn,
> In my heart live truth.

"Maybe this is the Mother Corn you seek."

Salt was pleased.

He had been a guest in Tula's house for many weeks before he ever spoke more than the greetings of the day to the master. Tula was a tall man, of great physical power in spite of advanced years, and a man who obviously exerted authority over the lives of the people around him. His wife had been dead many years and, being an old-fashioned man, as he called himself, he had never remarried. Of his five sons, two had been killed in battle, two were gone to manage farms in distant captured territory, and one lived in the House of the Soldiers in Culhuacan. Three married daughters lived in houses adjoining Tula's city house, but they were usually under Tula's roof with their children, since their husbands were warriors fighting in foreign fields. An ancient woman, Tula's grandmother, or perhaps only an old woman of the clan (Salt could not be sure that he understood the terms of relationship), occupied an apartment to herself and only occasionally came to sun herself in the courtyard.

In addition, a constant stream of guests poured into Tula's house, stayed for a meal or a night's lodging, or remained for weeks. One could never be sure how many people would sit down to the evening table. Tula fed them all. He ate sparingly, but for his guests the serving-women loaded the table with many kinds of meat, baked or cooked in stews; fish served with sweet potatoes; corn flavored with certain herbs and steamed in a husk of leaves; jars of honey and sweet syrup extracted from the maguey plant.

In such a constant crowd, it was not surprising that Salt's

presence should hardly be noticed. But he had come for
a purpose, and he was not content to watch white clouds
sail over the temple on the Hill of the Star or to lose himself in the crowded streets and the public market.

When Tula finally set aside a time for an audience and
notified Salt, he apologized for his neglect. "As you see,
I lead a busy life. It has not been of my own choosing,
but the people of my clan keep me as their spokesman.
We have twenty clans in our tribe, and I represent my clan
in the council of the whole tribe. In addition, I sit as one
of the judges to hear appeals, and sometimes I must argue
these appeals before our High Chief. All of this takes time
and causes me to neglect a man's first duty, which is always
to his guest."

Listening to Tula talk of his duties and responsibilities,
Salt could not understand what Ocelot's father meant when
he spoke of him as a man deprived of power. He wore the
headdress of bright feathers and the purple cape belonging
to a man of high rank. His manner betrayed no uneasiness.
He listened closely, never breaking in while another talked,
never hurrying to finish a conversation.

He showed interest in the things Salt told him. In time,
Tula sensed the perplexity that lay in the mind of the boy
from the north. He invited him to sit at his side at clan
meetings. He took him to visit in the countryside. He
introduced him to priests and military leaders. Salt was
able to visit the schools where boys were trained to be
leaders and warriors.

It must be, Salt thought, that Ocelot's father had forgotten what Tula was like. For here, surely, was a man of

strength, a man of wisdom, a man to whom one would look for help.

No Land of Fable any longer, but a land of men; a land of cities, of buildings, of bridges across lakes, of armies on the march, of temples which thousands of men labored a lifetime in building; a land of cornfields stretching to the skyline; where courts measured out justice; where men were carried in gold-bossed chairs. Not a land of fable, Tula's country.

As Salt looked about, seeking understanding, he remembered the words of the slave girl: "Who knows what bitterness may come to any of us?" What did she mean? Why should anyone speak of bitterness in a land stamped with its own greatness?

Of Tula he asked: "What has made your people powerful? I have only my two hands. What can I carry in them that will help my people to grow strong, as yours have?"

No prompt reply came. The question troubled Tula. He sat in a great square chair, the arms carved into the likeness of gaping snakes, which climbed over the back and entwined their glistening bodies at the top. When Tula was not speaking, he leaned back, and the fingers of his right hand played over the smooth texture of the fangs and nostrils of the snake head.

Salt offered further explanation. "You find it hard to see in your mind what a poor country we have, how weak my people are. The rains no longer come, the crops grow less each year. We have so little, you might expect us to live in peace among ourselves, to share what we have and to support each other. Instead, as I have told you before, we cut each other down. Our Village Chief can no longer hold us together, good man that he is. How may we have peace again? Or must we utterly destroy ourselves?"

Still Tula did not answer. Instead, he rose from his chair, uttered, "Come!" and strode from the room.

Salt, puzzled, followed. Tula's long strides took him through the courtyard into the garden with its living fence of cactus. The land sloped upward to a row of cypress trees growing across the upper end. Maguey plants in rows followed the curve of sloping land and Tula walked on until he came to the topmost part of the garden. There he waited for Salt.

From that point, the view was across the lake toward the northeast and the east. Tula moved his arm in an arc connecting these two points.

"You can't see what I point out, so you must take my word for what I tell you. Before you leave this country, you may even go to see these things for yourself. In any case, there—" His long, strong finger seemed to poke a hole in the sky toward the east. "There, in a great dead city, my people lived, honored their fathers, and kept peace among themselves. How long ago this was, I cannot tell you. Our oldest temple priests have no memory of it. Our tradition tells us that in the city, when our people were young, our god Quetzalcoatl came to us."

Salt stared into a milk-blue sky without blinking, as if by the very strength of looking he might bring into view the dead city of which his host talked. When he took his eyes away at last, he realized that Tula was staring as if he could indeed see beyond the horizon.

"I cannot tell you everything that came to us through Quetzalcoatl. I only say this, that the breath which is life, which is seen as a feather on the face of still water, and again in the movement of the Evening Star through the night sky—that is Quetzalcoatl. The least thing, and at once the greatest also. Through his help, our people learned to write upon paper and upon stone. They were told about corn, our Mother—but as I told you, the things we received from him are many and I'll not recount them all."

When he turned away from gazing at the sky, it was as if a shadow fell over his face.

"One thing more, a truth which travels at the side of everything else, as night travels with day, and as death travels at the side of life: man lives in the face of many enemies. His life is a gift, given without his asking, and payment must be made to the giver. A man may try to avoid the payment, but he is a fool if he thinks he can escape and keep the whole gift to himself."

Tula looked up from his speaking as if to satisfy himself that he was understood. His face relented.

"I'm sure that I have talked too hard. You don't have our language fully, so we will return and let your companion help you. Only, before we go—" Tula turned once more to the horizon and pointed southward.

"Off there lies Cholula, the greatest temple in all this land. I hope you will see it."

Tula did not finish everything he wanted to say that first day, but came back to the subject again and again. With Ocelot to help, Salt began to understand that his

host was an unhappy man, that he spoke often out of deep
bitterness, out of a sense of irredeemable loss. Salt began
to understand too what Ocelot's father had meant when
he had said that Tula was a man whose power was passing.

In one of these long conversations, Tula said: "Quetzalcoatl, who ruled the lives of our fathers, here in this valley,
is not fashionable now. His name is not spoken. Soon even
his temples and monuments will be lost. We now have
coming from all corners of the world, it seems, a race of
men who have neither reason nor shame. Being without
reason, they understand nothing; nothing can be explained
to them. Being without shame, they are not humble, and
cannot be humbled. They think only in terms of size and
numbers. The great temples built by our fathers these men
covered over, not with masonry and carved stone such as
our fathers used, but with the coarsest rocks, even dirt
from the fields, so they might have the satisfaction of
having built a greater temple!

"That is a vanity they may have—I care nothing about
it. But in another matter the change is more serious. These
later comers, these men without reason and without shame,
are devouring our people. You tell me that your small
village is faced with destruction. What if I should tell you
that my country, great as it is in people and in land, is
destroying itself! Yet, it is so."

In the anxiety of his speech, Tula left his chair often
to pace the length of his council hall, along a colonnade
of wooden figures bearing the faces of many gods. Blue
cloth painted with designs hung against the white walls,

and on a central table large bowls, some of dark-brown pottery and some with images of birds and animals worked in gold, were reflected in dark polished wood.

"In former days it was our custom to draw blood from our bodies as a token in payment for the gift of life. This was done with a thorn at many ceremonies. Life must be paid for, and this was a token of our payment. Now come these men, without reason and without shame, these believers in numbers and in size, and they turn the simple ceremonies of our fathers into spectacles of horror. Our temples are washed in blood. Each year great throngs of our own people, as well as armies of captive tribes, are slaughtered.

"And here am I, Tula. My name is the name of my race. I am the head of my clan and spokesman for my clan in the Supreme Council of all the people. Yet I am helpless to hold back this tide which sweeps over us. I have many brother tribesmen who believe as I do in the older religion, but all of us together are powerless to save our people from destruction.

"So when you ask me how to save your village, I can only turn and ask, how may I save my own people?"

Tula's words, as Salt absorbed their cumulative effect, were sufficiently shattering. But they would have ended as words; nothing would have come of them, if it had not been for what Tula finally said, almost casually, as if it had slipped his mind:

"We are soon to celebrate the Feast of the Eighth Month. Perhaps you do not know this feast . . . in which the maturing of the new corn is honored by cutting off the head of a young girl . . . in the sight of the multitude . . .

"Well, we shall have the feast. And my household has been commanded to deliver an honored victim. I am powerless. Up to now, I have evaded these demands. If I continue to evade, I may lose my entire family, my sons and daughters, and my own life, useless as it is."

Salt was frightened. All that Tula had been saying became clear at last. This pleasant house, the pleasant sunshine in the courtyard, turned deathly cold. He shivered and would have turned away, to hear no more. But too late. Tula had been gazing at him; now he looked away. His words fell like petals from a dead flower.

"I have consented. The girl who came to us from the mountains—whom we call Quail—she will go to the temple and be sacrificed."

A parrot screamed in the courtyard. Even the distant barking of a dog pierced Salt's consciousness. But these sensations were detached from him. His mind and spirit had fled his mute body. So he stood, wounded deeply, wordless.

When thought unfroze at last and he could look upon Tula and upon the things standing in the room, he knew that his quest in behalf of his people had ended, here. He had not found the power that would help them; he would not find it; not here, not in death.

Tula, having finally unburdened himself, walked from the room, his stiff back suggesting the aloofness of the defeated.

Salt watched Tula go and hoped that he would never again have to speak with him.

Chapter 17

Flight from the Valley of Bitterness

O CELOT was terrified when Salt came to him with his plan. In the depth of the night, Salt had awakened Ocelot by placing his hand over his friend's mouth. In whispers the mad plan was broached: "The mountain girl is to be killed unless we save her."

That was how it started. Ocelot protested; he would have no part of it. He explained the dangers, the almost certain death. He explained the distances that must be traveled before they would be beyond the reach of Culhuacan soldiers. Even Tula would be bound to use his clansmen against them. As a slave, with the slave's mark tattooed on her forehead, no household would dare take them in, no one could protect them.

They talked most of that night, in whispers no louder than the sound of the wind in the leaves of the pepper trees. Salt would not be moved from his decision. Ocelot's pleading turned to anger, and finally into a threat of exposing the plan.

To everything, Salt made the steadfast reply: "Tula himself would do this if he could. He is unhappy about the girl. We do this for Tula."

Salt did not believe this, but he tried to will it to be true.

To which Ocelot replied over and over, "Then let Tula do it."

In the morning they went up through the town, saying nothing, but marking the streets and roads they would follow, the traps they must avoid.

In midafternoon, as they sat on a grass slope high above the city, the lake spread out before them, Ocelot remarked, without previous indication that he had even been thinking about the matter: "We must have a canoe ready. We could never make it by land. We would be caught at the bridge, if not before. We will have to go by water."

No more was said. They went down the hill, knowing that they would work together. At Tula's house they separated, Ocelot saying that he would go to find a canoe, while Salt went to the market to trade cacao beans for food and the articles they would need for the journey.

Tula was not present at the evening meal, and the boys

were saved the embarrassment of conversing with him. Salt dreaded a meeting. His anger at Tula, added to the fear he felt, made him unsure of himself.

They must start that night. Salt knew this. If they calculated their chances, tried to plan more carefully, they might lose their courage. When he realized that Ocelot was of the same mind, his spirits rose. They waited together for the summer twilight to pass and the night to arrive. Neither spoke, but each feared the moment when they must act. So at last they came to the point of action.

The greatest danger lay at the very outset. No man, other than an immediate member of the family, might enter the women's quarters. To be found there was to risk instant death.

Every large house had its own watchman, to guard against prowlers, watch for fires, easily started in a community of thatched roofs. He also watched for falling stars and other portents in the night sky that might bear upon the fortunes of the household.

The watchman in Tula's house was an ancient soldier with one eye, but a sharp eye. He often remained motionless for hours on end, leaning against a wall or tree. He seemed to have no regular sleeping time, but when he tired he might lie down on a rush mat near the street entrance. At all cost, they must avoid an encounter with him.

The last-quarter moon would not rise until after the middle of the night, a point in their favor when they started. Waiting just outside his door, Salt heard his heart pound. His hand touched Ocelot close by. Then they moved forward. The guard, they hoped, was stretched out asleep on his mat.

Salt knew where the girl slept, sharing her room with a single companion, an older woman. They crept out of the courtyard into the women's quarters.

Ocelot waited at Quail's door when Salt slipped inside. In the windowless room, utter darkness faced him. He was not sure where the sleeping pallets were. Most likely, toward the back. He dropped to his knees, crept forward.

Sweeping his hands before him, he touched a pallet. But whose? He leaned as far forward as he dared, sniffing at the air. A sour, forbidding odor.

Across the room, then. Again he sniffed. Now he smiled. The girl's breath was like the sage at dawn. He put his hand to her mouth; even that did not waken her at once. But when he squeezed her nostrils together, she gave a start.

Lying in the darkness, explaining why he had come and what he wanted her to do, it seemed to Salt he could never make her understand or persuade her to move. She offered no response at all, not even to indicate that she heard.

At the door, meantime, Ocelot rubbed his thumb over his fingertips, making a dry whisper. Was he urging speed, or warning of danger?

Just as Salt decided to crawl to the doorway and learn the reason for the signal, Quail shook her head affirmatively and began to rise. Her hand fumbled in the darkness, drawing a pouch from under her pallet. But Salt, in his eagerness to be away, did not observe this movement. He went quickly and found Ocelot crouching just inside the doorway.

He caught the whispered warning: "Stay low. I think One-Eye comes this way."

Hardly had he given the warning when they heard the footstep just beyond the open door. Had Ocelot's whisper carried out there? Salt, crouching opposite, dared not move, even to warn Quail. He feared she would come forward and, by whispered word or otherwise, reveal their presence. The watchman must be standing just outside. Time dragged so slowly.

When Quail did come, she was as stealthy as night itself. She touched him; otherwise he might not have felt her presence.

The girl seemed to sense the reason for their waiting. After a moment, she pressed her hand on Salt's shoulder, signaling him to stay. She rose to her feet and stepped through the doorway.

Too late, Salt realized what she was doing. If he had sensed it sooner, he would have pulled her back. She was gone, leaving him terrified.

But she had reasoned soundly. The watchman could not have suspected her action. It was her room, and she was free to get up during the night.

When she found no one outside, the boys could not be sure whether they had imagined a presence or whether the guard had moved to another vantage point and might still be waiting.

Now it was time to move. Ocelot, bending low, went first; then Quail; then Salt. They reached the entrance to the garden. Nothing happened.

Then, running feet! A shout!

No word was needed. As one, the three raced down the long rows of maguey plants. The direction of their flight had not yet been noticed. The torches blooming into sudden light were still within the courtyard. They had reached the far end of the garden and were slashing a hole through the cactus fence when the first torch entered the garden behind them.

Their wild flight led them away from the lake and the spot where Ocelot had hidden the canoe. They had to backtrack, keeping to a wide circle, and risk an encounter with townsmen or soldiers attracted by the lights and the shouts at Tula's house. They ran on, staying in the shadow of the walls and trees. Several times they lost themselves in roads and alleyways that ended dead against a house or high wall.

But it was a relief to be running, to be away. The long journey ahead concerned Salt not at all.

Waiting in shadow while Ocelot scouted ahead, Salt explained what he had been told by Tula. So far he had been able to tell Quail only that her life was threatened, and she must escape. When she understood that she had been destined to perform in the Eighth Month ceremony, celebrating the ripening of the corn, she whispered:

"But that is a great honor! In that ceremony a slave girl rises above all the people in the nation. She gives her life to bring a good harvest."

Astonishing words! They left Salt feeling foolish. Was it possible that she preferred to stay and enjoy the honor? He realized how little he understood this girl, or the people in this strange land. How foolish to expect strangers to be like his own people!

As he puzzled, he heard soft laughter. He turned to the girl; she had put her hand over her mouth to suppress her mirth.

"It *is* an honor. But I am happy to pass it on to somebody else. Did you think I wished to go back?"

Salt floundered. "You spoke of bitterness one day. I thought that meant that you would escape if you could. But just now—I was lost. It is better to live, I think."

"Yes, it is better to live. But I just now thought of that. If you had not asked me to come, the other would have seemed all right, I guess. One changes."

While they talked, Ocelot had been motioning them from a shadowing hedge. He had to come halfway across the open space and hiss sharply before they were aware of him.

Then they were running again, down a long incline leading to the water's edge. Ocelot, still beckoning, crept along a marshy shore to the hiding place of the canoe. Breathless, they came up with him and found him staring at a place where the reeds had been flattened. Only muddy water showed.

The canoe was gone! Frightened, they looked at each other. In growing panic, each ran in a different direction, plunging in among the tall reeds and sinking in the muddy ooze.

A moment later, Ocelot called. They found him laughing. He had been looking for the canoe in the wrong place. Now he had found it just where he left it.

By the time they pushed away from the shore, the summer dawn was almost upon them. A mist would be upon the lake at daylight, and they could hope to go unobserved. When they were well out from shore, Salt untied the bundle at his waist and brought out a skirt and blouse. These he had bought at the market, paying in cacao beans taken from Tula's house. The girl threw her old garments into the water. He could think of no way for her to cover the tattoo mark on her forehead, but when daylight came he discovered that she had plaited her hair in two braids and wrapped them around her head so that nothing showed.

Paddling southward, they kept well away from either shore. The mist was not as heavy as usual, but there was enough to curtain them from the land. However, it would lift when the sun warmed the air, and they must leave the water before that happened. They drove the canoe into a narrow inlet, where a stream poured down from a mountain headland.

Now they were with danger again. They must travel for many days through a countryside, well peopled, and risk encounter with soldiers or agents of Culhuacan or of Tula himself. A slave, at any time, was not given up easily. A slave who had been chosen by the temple for its uses would be searched for with diligence. Tula would certainly be accused of plotting Quail's escape; he would make a special effort to find her and bring her back.

With the canoe well hidden, the three fugitives crawled into the underbrush along the stream bed. There they stayed all through the heat of that first day. They watched the herons stand motionless, then stab the muck for a frog morsel. Ducks streaked low over the water, seeking a feeding ground. Gulls rose from a distant headland, complaining, headed toward the outer lake, then tilted upward, swerved, still complaining, returned shoreward, and finally came to rest riding high in the water.

Salt turned to the girl: "Where will you go? Will you be safe among your people in the mountains?"

Quail had given it thought, and her answer came at once. "I have no people."

Ocelot passed out food, a tortilla and a portion of beancake to each. "My family will be happy to have you. You will be one of us, not a slave."

Salt looked at the girl but could not tell how she would respond. She would do well to accept; she would be safe. A place would be made for her. But he hoped she would not accept, or would put off a decision. He could not say why he wanted this, since he had nothing to suggest in its place.

To Ocelot he remarked: "Your father is Tula's friend. He may not want to offend Tula by taking this girl."

A hard quality came into Ocelot's voice. "Perhaps you want to take her with you, through the desert and mountains?"

The question startled Salt. He had given it no thought, but he answered, "Perhaps. It will be up to her."

Ocelot's voice had softened again when he said, "My father will not let her return, even to Tula, when he understands what they would do to her."

The girl had not looked up while they talked. Now she spread her hands as if to end the talk. "We have not escaped yet. Who knows whether we will? We can talk about this again."

That evening they left their shelter and climbed a sloping hill. Presently they came upon a trail leading inland and followed it. The trail joined a road northward. Following along it, they soon came to the edge of the town of Cuecuilco.

There, for a moment, their adventure seemed to come to an end.

Since darkness was rapidly approaching, they walked with less caution. They knew a town was close at hand, but had not realized how close. They emerged from a grove of trees and found that the road had become a street lined with houses. Should they continue through the town, or seek a way around? Pausing to consider, they saw figures emerge from the shadows of the buildings. They were surrounded before they could turn.

A voice accosted them, "Run now and you run into trouble." The voice, gruff and familiar, startled Salt. Impossible to believe!

The speaker advanced until he was close upon them. Beyond doubt, it was the one-eyed watchman.

The voice was a growl. "I saw you run to the canoe and guessed where you would come ashore. A little waiting—and here you are."

Salt urged: "Let the girl go! Say you have not seen her!"

The watchman waved his words aside. "I know nothing of this. I only come with a message from Tula. I am to give you the names of the towns you will pass through, and the names of clansmen who will provide food and keep you out of sight during the day. You must travel only at night."

The three stood motionless and speechless, trying to understand. Was it a trap? Was One-Eye leading them into an ambush?

"Well?" the one-eyed soldier exploded. "Are you listening?"

The spell broke. Yes, indeed, they listened!

To Salt, the listing of towns and individuals was wasted effort. He could not distinguish one from the other. All names in this strange land were a confusion to him. But he heard Ocelot and Quail murmuring the words, fastening them in their memories.

Salt still groped for understanding. "This is strange. The girl was demanded by the temple. Tula's family will be destroyed if he withholds the girl. . ."

"You are foolish, man from the north. Why did he tell you about the girl? He could not keep her back himself, but if you steal her, how can he help it? Only, I warn you, if you are caught, you will go to the sacrificial stone with the girl. That is my message, and now you have not seen me."

Salt had to ask, "Did you see us leave, then?"

Even suggesting that he might not have seen them was

an insult to One-Eye's vigilance. "Nothing happens at Tula's house that I do not see!" The watchman turned at that and went back into the shadows, and the shadowy forms with him were no more.

Now that they could travel with some security, Salt should have carried a light heart, but as they plodded through the nights that followed, sadness overwhelmed him. He had failed his people. He had been chosen from all the men of his village to find the secret that would save his people. He had found no secret, and in his concern to rescue the slave girl, he had not even gathered the corn that grew in this land. He was empty-handed.

During the daylight hours, while they rested at the home of one of Tula's clansmen, Salt would lie and stare at thatched roof or sky, whichever happened to be over-head, when he should have slept. Not only was he troubled by his failure to find a word or a sign that would protect his people, but more seriously was he troubled by a grow-ing sense that such a secret sign or word did not exist in the world. He remembered, when he asked what he could do to save his village, how Tula had turned the question back on him. Surely if there was a way for men to live without destroying each other, the people of Culhuacan should have found it. With their rich clothes and orna-ments, their abundance of food, their marching armies, their courts and their judges, their towering pyramids and smoking temples—surely they should have found how men may live together in peace and support each other.

Was it possible, as Tula suggested, that in a more ancient

time men had lived in peace, had paid for the gift of life with orderliness and decency, and had been overwhelmed by ruder men and ruder ideas?

He asked Ocelot: "Do your people live in fear of your temples? Are your priests smeared with people's blood?"

And Ocelot replied: "We fear only the people in the land where we have just been. They would destroy us, if they could, demand our crops and our men. My father tells me this, and that is why he feared for our going. We keep a guard on our border, as you shall see."

Salt felt that his question had not been answered, but he did not pursue it further. Perhaps the other had never reflected on the questions that bothered him.

Not many days later, they reached an outpost such as Ocelot had mentioned—a square stone building on the edge of a low bluff that overlooked a narrow mountain pass. Below it were stone barracks for the guards. Salt remembered it from the previous spring, but now the outpost took on a new meaning.

For now, at last, they could travel openly in the daylight, without fear. They were beyond the reach of the soldiers of Culhuacan!

A great valley opened out, bounded by rising mountains, timbered and green, while in the middle distance sharp cones rose up, timbered over also, which once had spilled molten rock and burning ash over the countryside. A scene of peace, with cornfields far below, a stream that curved upon itself, and a family of crows moving on the wing.

It was the moment that Salt had been waiting for, the moment when they should have passed beyond danger. He

turned to Quail and saw that her eyes were filled with the
peace that lay before them. Even her nostrils seemed to
quiver, taking it in. Up to then, she had walked wearily,
in tattered garments, never falling behind, but never
exulting.

Now they were here, beyond the threat of death, and
he asked her: "We said we would not speak of this again
until we came to safety. This is Ocelot's green country.
Soon we will come to his lake. What have you thought?
Will you stay here, where they will make a place for you?
Or will you continue with me to my people, where the land
is poor, where the rains seem to come no more, and where
we live without peace?"

The girl still looked lingeringly at the far-off green
mountains, then turned her gaze on Salt. He stood a head
taller. His expression, she had come to know, was always
serious. He was thinner than he should be, but his strength
was tireless. He seemed ready to go on forever, searching
for whatever it was that his spirit needed.

She watched him a moment, then said: "I have thought
about this ever since we left the lake shore. Indeed, I
thought about it as I left my bed in Tula's house. You
asked me to come with you, and I will go wherever you
go."

Ocelot was not displeased. "This boy from the north
will never be frightened. I never expected to survive that
night, but he would not turn back. It is best that you go
with him. We will rest in my father's house first. With
permission, I will go with you as far as the salt water,
where our boundaries lie."

Chapter 18

Village of the White Rocks

SALT would have hurried on, without resting, if that had been possible. From the time they came in sight of the salt water and said their farewells to Ocelot, Salt thought only of home. He would push out of mind the images of flood-swollen rivers, of thorny brush, of waterless deserts and days of hunger. He would think of nothing but the village in the canyon. Who had died? Who was in power? How did the crops grow?

Before they had traveled far up the coast, they met the

first of many delays. It was the season of summer rains, and the rivers were in flood again. He remembered the long plain that ran along the coast, where the people built their houses on mounds of earth. Now he understood why. The road had disappeared under water, and every village, every house, was an island to itself. He scouted up and down the swampy shore, trying to find a roadway.

Here the mountains rose abruptly only a short distance back from the salt water; their sides were covered with an impassable tangle of thorny growth. After days, while Salt's despair mounted, a single canoeman came within shouting distance, and the boy negotiated by many signs and useless words. The Indian in the dugout canoe, dubious at first, agreed to ferry them across the water and set them on their way. But at parting, he talked volubly, pointing northward.

Two days later they understood what the canoeman meant. The road disappeared under a second flooded area.

The first several weeks passed in that manner. Even when he and Quail traveled on high ground, the drenching rains fell each afternoon and left them floundering in mud. When the rains swept on down the coast, the sun burned away the sodden clouds and they gasped for breath in the hot steam.

Delays and discomforts only made Salt drive the harder. He built canoes or rafts, stole them when that was possible, and negotiated when he had to.

When they came to Culiacan, Salt walked warily through the streets, hoping he would not meet the judge-priest or Yucca Flower Woman. Hospitality would require a feast, and a delay that could grow into many days. Yet he needed to visit the market, since Quail's and his sandals and clothing were falling apart. Also, he remembered the fluted brown pottery in the market and thought of his mother. She would be happy with such a gift. He traded cacao beans, since these were as much relished at Culiacan as they were in the country of the lakes.

Now they traveled inland away from the sea. The country grew drier and more forbidding. The road narrowed to a track; a desolation of impenetrable brush crept upon the trail from either side.

In the long march that followed, across swollen rivers and intervening stretches of waterless rough country, Salt learned a deeper appreciation of the girl who followed. In his driving desire to cover ground, to surmount obstacles, forever to be moving forward, he would often forget her. He never once slowed for her convenience, and rarely did he think to ask if she needed rest. However hard he drove, she was never far behind.

When they stopped to prepare a meal, he might say: "We still have far to go. We must hurry."

She would answer: "I know you are hungry for home. Go as hard as you can. I will follow."

He had left the Village of the White Rocks in the first days of summer. A second summer had passed, and now the time of the winter rains was approaching when Salt and the girl found the headwaters of the north-flowing river that would take them to the land of the big fields.

They spent two days at that place, because Salt wanted
to see again how the ditches were dug to lead water from
the river. He ran the soil through his fingers and fed his
eyes on the spaciousness of the flat valley. The corn was
gone from the fields and meadow grass lay brown, but
even so the land did not look dead. Cool air descending
from the mountains lay in a pleasant haze over the countryside.

To Quail he said: "Here could dwell a great people,
with abundant harvests, such as we left down there in the
Valley of the Lakes. But here a people could live in peace,
as well, and not be burdened with temples crying for
blood."

Quail's face had thinned, the cheekbones showing
sharply, and her eyes in this thinness looked larger. Turning to her, Salt saw in her eyes the same look of peace that
glowed in them when, from a mountaintop, they looked
down into the green valley bordering Ocelot's country. He
had been troubled back there, believing that she had found
in that pleasant country the world of her desire, and that
he would lose her.

Now she saw what he saw—the standing fields, the
flashing water, the crowned cottonwood trees struck golden.
She turned to him, the same pleasant longing shining from
her eyes.

She echoed the very thought that lay in his mind.
"Here," she said, "*your* people could grow strong. And
you would have peace."

A true thing, if he had not come empty-handed from
the Red Land of the South.

He explained: "Our Holy One could not tell me what to bring. I was to use my eyes. But failing all else, I should have brought new corn to replace our tired seed. I waited too long, always thinking I would find something hidden. So I left with nothing in my hands."

Quail smiled, for the first time, he thought, since they talked in Tula's house; a weak smile, burdened by fatigue and the dust of traveling.

"You are not empty-handed," she said. "See, I brought this—"

As she spoke, she unfastened a small leather pouch from her belt, the pouch she had drawn from under the pallet as she rose to follow Salt. In all this journey it had remained unopened.

"You spoke once of this very thing—and I gathered these few kernels from each of the strong corns that grow in the Valley of the Lakes. Who would believe that I myself would carry them to your country!"

On her outspread skirt, she spilled the pouch of corn— and Salt was astonished. Until then he had known only yellow corn. But here were kernels of red, blue, and black corn, and a yellow kernel larger than any he had ever seen. They sparkled, as if alive, in the haze-blurred sun.

Truly he had learned at last to appreciate this girl who had followed so faithfully.

They rose then, crossed the river, and went up into the mountains.

On a day when frost weighed heavily upon dead meadow grass and strands of snow clouds flew like ribbons around

mountain peaks, Salt and Quail came to the valley of his
people. And when, in the gray light of a dying day, they
saw the new village in the bottom of the canyon, it seemed
indeed a cramped and narrow place.

Salt turned to Quail: "Perhaps you will regret that you
came. You see how small it is."

And she answered: "You saw how I lived in a world
that was big. Who knows but what a lesser place will have
more room for me."

Word had gone on ahead, and the Holy One came out
to meet them. Yes, the Holy One still lived! Salt saw the
old man at the head of all the villagers, his white hair
gleaming in the deepening dusk. He came, hurrying a
little, his legs showing unsteadiness. His hands hung low,
palms outward, and as he came near he half raised them
in a sign of wonder.

Salt and Quail then stood side by side.

The Holy One looked first at the boy, then at the girl.
He spoke the first words.

"You may bring gifts of power from the south; you may
bring gifts of peace for our people. We will ask of that
in due time. Whatever else, truly you have brought a gift
of beauty in this girl. We will be happy in her."

And it seemed to be even so.

Salt's mother looked at the girl, and was happy. The
people took her up to the village, into the warmth of the
fires, and whoever looked at her felt a pleasure and a
happiness. They murmured, in quietness away from her
hearing, "The mark of the sun is upon her, there on her
forehead. Have you seen it?"

Salt thought to speak of this. He turned to the Holy One, forming the words in his mind. Then he looked at the girl who was called Young-Quail-Who-Disappears-in-Prairie-Grass-and-Whose-Crest-Stands-Above-the-Grass. She stood with the firelight upon her. Her eyes had never been so full of longing as they were then. Never had the vision of peace so filled them.

The words he would have uttered, explaining the slave mark, dissolved and were gone. The mark itself—the little circle, with parallel lines running to the four directions— glowed brightly as the girl stood before the firelight. And the people spoke in wonder.

Weariness fell away from Salt's limbs, and from his heart as well. The disappointment which had been building so steadily since he left Tula's house, tasting so bitter, was fading like a dream at waking time.

People began to come forward, out of the shadows beyond the fire. Shield, thin as always, his eyes deep in their sockets, placed his hand on Salt's shoulder.

"Our grandson is indeed a man among us. We rejoice in you."

Then Trailing Cloud, the ancient Sun Watcher, came leaning on a younger arm. He too reached out to touch Salt.

"My eyes have lasted until now—and for that I am thankful—that I may see once more our clansman. We will grow great again in your lifetime. Our people will survive in you."

Then out of the crowd came one, the sight of whom made Salt's heart leap up. Day Singer was before him—

an eye destroyed, an angry red scar slashing down his face
from hairline to chin. His graying hair, as always, was
bound in a twist of red cotton cloth. Their hands met.

"The circle is complete, grandson." It was an old-
fashioned way of expressing happiness.

Salt murmured: "I can see how the circle almost ended
for you, in the kiva of the Spider Clan."

"Almost. For Turtle, that was the end."

The note of sorrow burned for a moment, and still
smoldered as others came forward, expressing happiness.

While the joy of reunion mounted to fullness, a strange
thing happened. Who first called out, was not known.
Simply a voice beyond the firelight.

"Take guard! A stranger approaches!"

Talking broke off. All turned to look.

What they saw, at the farthest reach of the firelight,
was startling.

A man stood there, just visible in the darkness. A man
they first took to be in death-mourning. His long hair,
loosened from its binding cloth, fell wildly over face and
shoulders. All ornaments had been stripped from his body;
he walked barefooted, his only garment a breechclout.

He approached within view, then waited to be asked to
come forward.

The Holy One must have suspected at once. He stood
away from the others and cried out:

"Whoever you are, here you are welcome."

The shadowy one advanced, and a gasp went up like a
burst of wind through a pine grove.

Dark Dealer stood there among them, head bowed, waiting to be invited to speak.

"Do you come in friendship?" the Holy One asked, hardness in his voice.

The reply was long in emerging, then: "A second winter is upon us. Our food will soon be gone. Let our women and children come to you. Our men you may wish to punish for striking you. Me, you may feed to the vultures. I am ready."

Voices rose, murmuring, then in loud anger.

"This is a trick!"

"Who can believe him?"

"Send him back to his den of coyotes!"

The Holy One held up his hands, asking silence. But he did not give the answer to Dark Dealer. Instead, he turned to Salt.

"This night, and our future, belong to our grandson. Let him say what we are to do."

The words lighted a glow in the boy's eyes, like sunlight bursting upon a dark morning. Often on a lonely night he had dreamed of the time when he would be asked, as a man, to speak for his people. Now the time had come, on the heels of failure too! Joy could be no sweeter! But, as he prepared to speak, he thought again of the man Tula, and it was as if a tempering hand rested on his shoulder.

"It is not for us to say whether any man has lived his life well," he ventured, and as he spoke his voice grew stronger. "Each man can answer only for himself. If Dark Dealer finds in his heart that he has not done well, and asks us to take him back, we cannot refuse. We cannot deny him his chance to make the gift which will fulfil his life. I say, bring them all back, and make our people whole again."

Dark Dealer, wordless, dropped to his knees before Salt. His right hand moved, scooping dirt. With head on knees, he poured dust on his matted hair. It was the supreme submission.

The people watched, awed into silence. Never had they expected to see Dark Dealer at their feet.

Crane Woman, the bold speaker, voiced the wonder and doubt they felt.

"What has brought this about? Not hunger alone. This man was proud beyond the reach of hunger. Yet, here he is, in the dust. I cannot understand it."

Bold speaking was proper in Crane Woman at last, since she was now called Eldest Woman, taking her place in her generation.

"I think understanding is here among us," the Holy One spoke, when no one else offered. He had been standing back; now he came forward to Salt's shoulder. The firelight caught in his eyes, where it burned brightly.

"We sent this boy out at a time when we were troubled. Murder had occurred. We were thrown out of our village. I, your leader, had failed. Now this boy returns, and at almost that moment our enemy comes with bowed head. Did he watch from the mesa top and plan his return to be with us in our moment of our rejoicing, when we might be expected to relent? I find it impossible to believe."

The old man searched the faces before him, turning

slowly. He stood slightly lower than Salt and had to reach up to place his hand on the boy's shoulder.

"It is not strange, I think, for our enemy to seek us out at this time. The power in this boy has pulled him—"

The Holy One was looking directly at Salt, studying his face, his high, thin nose, his quiet eyes.

"Power is here. The power to restore peace in a bad heart. The very power needed by our people."

The Holy One turned again, his hand still on Salt's shoulder, but his eyes seeking the girl Quail.

"If we ask ourselves how this power comes to this boy, I find that answer not strange either. Here is this girl, bearing some sign, perhaps of the sun, on her brow. Bring her here, where we can look upon her."

Quail, standing among the women, her fingers locked together, would have protested. She felt herself still to be the girl who had gone to sleep in the women's quarters at Tula's house, who had been awakened in the dark, and had risen to follow the boy from the north. If greatness existed, it was in him, as he pushed on among enemies, in strange desert lands. All this she would have protested, but the Holy One was calling her forward, giving her no occasion to speak.

Presently she stood beside Salt; and the people, gazing upon her, saw the mark upon her brow, and the wide, longing look in her eyes.

Then they drew closer, as if pulling sheltering walls around her.

The Holy One was saying: "We will call her Red Corn Woman, honoring the south, which sent her to us. With this name we make her one of us, and her strength will be ours."

"This is true," the people answered. "She will be one of us. We feel her strength entering into us."

Salt, looking across space, saw the slave girl vanish, and beauty stand before him. His smile shone back from her eyes.

Then he spoke for her, since in all that time she had not raised her voice: "You honor yourselves in letting this girl come among you. She will never fall behind. She will never weary. Her devotion is as a river coming down from the mountains. All this is her power, and it will help us to grow great. But if more is needed—why, only look at what she carries in this little pouch tied to her belt."

Quail would still have protested, but when Salt stretched out his hand, her agitation was calmed.

"These few seeds—" she said, breaking her silence. She looked up then, and when she saw how warmly the people held her in their eyes, her heart was overwhelmed. She could not speak again.

This was the manner of Salt's return to his village. The people were reunited, but those who had built houses in the canyon did not return to their dwellings in the cliff. The canyon bottom sheltered them against the high winds of winter, and the women discovered that their lives were less burdened when they did not have to carry water jars up a steep trail.

But the people did not remain for long in the Canyon

of the White Rocks. They planted the corn, the "few seeds" which Quail brought with her, murmuring their astonishment at the color and plumpness of the seed. And it flourished, giving them more food than they had known in many seasons.

It came too late, however. The years had been growing drier in Salt's lifetime, and there came a succession of seasons when no rain fell, the spring ceased to flow at summer's peak, and they almost lost even the precious new seed.

Salt, at last, made the decision which changed the lives of his people. He was then Village Chief, succeeding the Holy One, who named him as he lay dying, on a day in winter when the sun stood frozen in a thin cloud.

The memory of green fields, crowned cottonwoods, and running water had remained with Salt. When he called the people together and asked if they would follow him, they lamented the choice, but agreed.

"After all," he reminded them, "our Red Corn Woman saw this land with me. The wonder of it is still in her eyes."

It softened the blow of removal, knowing that she would be with them. For she had grown close to the people, caring for the aged, speaking softly to the young.

So they left the Canyon of the White Rocks, which today stands tenantless and soundless. They traveled southward, down from the mountains, into the valley of the big fields. Land was set aside for them by those who were there first, and the new corn, when planted and watered abundantly, produced such harvests as had never been known. In their rejoicing the people performed a new ceremony, which they called Red Corn Dance. In time they built a great village of adobe walls, and dug canals to lead water from the river to their planted fields.

There they lived in peace and supported one another.

LAND OF THE FREE

EL SABOR
DE LA INOCENCIA

Amor y Aventura

EL SABOR
DE LA INOCENCIA

Stephanie Laurens

Traducción de María José Losada Rey
y Rufina Moreno Ceballos

VERGARA
GRUPO ZETA

Barcelona • Bogotá • Buenos Aires • Caracas • Madrid • México D.F. • Montevideo • Quito • Santiago de Chile

Título original: *The Taste of Innocence*

Traducción: María José Losada Rey y Rufina Moreno Ceballos

1.ª edición: septiembre 2010

© 2007 by Savdek Management Proprietory Ltd.
© Ediciones B, S. A., 2010
   para el sello Vergara
   Consell de Cent 425-427 - 08009 Barcelona (España)
   www.edicionesb.com
Publicado por acuerdo con Avon, un sello de HarperCollins Publishers

Printed in Spain
ISBN: 978-84-666-4305-4
Depósito legal: B. 20.049-2010

Impreso por LIMPERGRAF, S.L.
Mogoda, 29-31 Polígon Can Salvatella
08210 - Barberà del Vallès (Barcelona)

Árbol genealógico de la Quinta de los Cynster

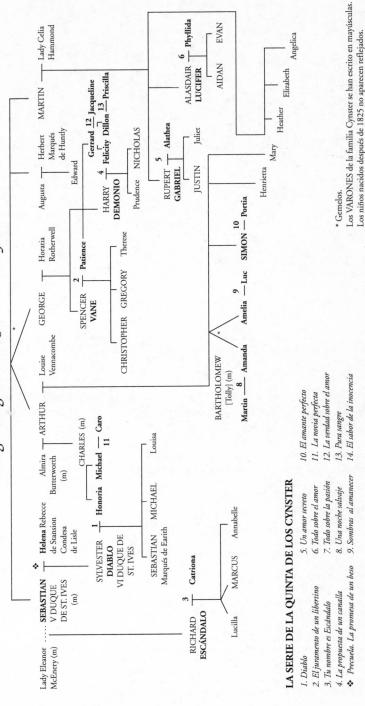

LA SERIE DE LA QUINTA DE LOS CYNSTER

1. *Diablo*
2. *El juramento de un libertino*
3. *Tu nombre es Escándalo*
4. *La propuesta de un canalla*
❖ *Precuela. La promesa de un beso*
5. *Un amor secreto*
6. *Todo sobre el amor*
7. *Todo sobre la pasión*
8. *Una noche salvaje*
9. *Sombras al amanecer*
10. *El amante perfecto*
11. *La novia perfecta*
12. *La verdad sobre el amor*
13. *Para sangre*
14. *El sabor de la inocencia*

* Gemelos.
Los VARONES de la familia Cynster se han escrito en mayúsculas.
Los niños nacidos después de 1825 no aparecen reflejados.

1

Febrero de 1833
Noroeste de Combe Florey. Somerset

Tenía que casarse y lo haría.

Bajo sus condiciones.

Estas últimas palabras resonaron en la mente de Charlie Morwellan al compás del ruido sordo de los cascos de su caballo mientras se dirigía a medio galope hacia el norte. El día era frío y despejado. Cerca de él, las exuberantes colinas verdes al pie de la cara occidental de los montes Quantocks se ondulaban suavemente. Había nacido en ese lugar, en Morwellan Park, su hogar, que ahora se encontraba a un par de kilómetros detrás de él. Con todo, prestaba muy poca atención al impresionante paisaje que lo rodeaba, pues su mente implacable se hallaba enfocada en otros asuntos.

Era el dueño y señor de los campos que lo rodeaban, del valle que había entre los Quantocks al este y los montes Brendon al oeste. Sus tierras se extendían hacia el sur y colindaban con las de su cuñado, Gabriel Cynster. El límite norte se extendía ante él, más allá de la colina. Cuando su castrado moteado gris, *Tormenta*, coronó la cima, Charlie tiró de las riendas y se detuvo, mirando hacia delante pero sin ver en realidad.

El aire frío le acarició las mejillas. Con la mandíbula tensa y la expresión impasible, volvió a pensar en las razones que lo habían conducido hasta allí.

Había heredado el condado de Meredith tras la muerte de su padre varios años atrás. Esa fecha había marcado un antes y un después en la vida de Charlie. A partir de entonces había tenido que capear los infructuosos intentos de las damas para echarle el guante. A los treinta años era un rico conde soltero que hacía babear a las implacables casamenteras. Pero tras una década alternando con la flor y nata de la sociedad, se conocía todos los trucos. Una y otra vez escapaba de las redes que las damas le tendían, algo que, además, disfrutaba haciendo.

Pero incluso para lord Charles Morwellan, octavo conde de Meredith, el matrimonio era un destino del que no podía escapar.

Aunque no había sido eso lo que finalmente le había hecho tomar una decisión.

Hacía casi dos años que sus mejores amigos, Gerrard Debbington y Dillon Caxton, se habían casado. Ninguno de los dos había estado buscando esposa, ni habían necesitado casarse urgentemente, pero el destino había jugado sus cartas y los dos habían acabado frente al altar. El propio Charlie había estado allí con ellos y sabía que sus amigos habían estado felices de casarse.

Ahora, tanto Gerrard como Dillon eran padres.

Tormenta se removió inquieto. Charlie le palmeó el cuello con aire distraído.

Vinculados al poderoso clan Cynster, Gerrard y Dillon junto a sus esposas, Jacqueline y Priscilla, y él mismo se habían reunido como siempre habían hecho después de Nochebuena en Somersham Place, la residencia principal de los duques de St. Ives y hogar ancestral de los Cynster. La numerosa familia Cynster y sus muchas amistades se reunían allí dos veces al año: en agosto en la llamada «Celebración de verano» y de nuevo en las vacaciones de Navidad, cuando se juntaban con ocasión de dichas fiestas.

Charlie siempre había disfrutado de la cálida atmósfera de esas reuniones, pero no en esta ocasión. Y no había sido por la presencia de los hijos de Gerrard y Dillon, sino por lo que éstos representaban. De los tres, amigos durante más de una década, él era el único que tenía la obligación de casarse y tener un heredero. Aunque en teoría podía dejar el deber de procrear la siguiente generación de Morwellan a su hermano Jeremy, que ahora tenía veintitrés años, hacía mucho tiempo que Charlie había aceptado que no podría escabullirse de aquel deber familiar en particular. Cargar sobre los hombros de Jeremy una de las principales responsabilidades vinculadas al título de conde no era algo que pudieran permitirle su conciencia, su naturaleza ni su sentido del deber.

Por esa razón se dirigía a Conningham Manor.

Continuar tentando al destino, dejar que esa peligrosa deidad fuera la que le organizara la vida y le buscara esposa, igual que había hecho con Gerrard y Dillon, sería una completa estupidez, por lo que ya iba siendo hora de escoger a su prometida. Ahora, antes de que comenzara la temporada, así podría elegir a la dama que mejor le conviniera, sin dejar ningún cabo suelto, antes de que la sociedad tuviera noticias de ello.

Antes de que el destino tuviera la oportunidad de poner el amor en su camino.

Tenía que actuar con rapidez para tener un absoluto y completo control sobre su destino, algo que él consideraba una necesidad y no una opción.

Tormenta se encabritó, transmitiendo a Charlie parte de su impaciencia. Controlando al poderoso castrado, Charlie centró la atención en el paisaje que tenía ante sí. A un par de kilómetros, en lo más profundo del valle, se veían los tejados de pizarra de Conningham Manor por encima de las ramas desnudas de los árboles. Los débiles rayos del sol naciente se reflejaban en las ventanas del edificio; una brisa fresca arrastraba el humo que emergía de las altas chimeneas isabelinas, disolviéndolo con rapidez. Conningham en el Manor había existido casi tanto tiempo como Morwellan en el Park.

Charlie se quedó mirando la mansión durante otro minuto, luego salió de su ensimismamiento, aflojó las riendas de *Tormenta* y bajó la colina al galope.

—A pesar de todo, Sarah, Clary y yo creemos firmemente que eres tú quién debe casarse primero.

Sentada de cara a la ventana mirador de la salita de atrás de Conningham Manor, propiedad indiscutible de las hijas de la casa, Sarah Conningham clavó los ojos en su hermana Gloria, de dieciséis años, que le lanzaba una mirada feroz desde su asiento en la ventana.

—Antes que nosotras. —La resuelta aclaración provenía de Clara, Clary para la familia, de diecisiete años, que, sentada al lado de Gloria y con la mirada también fija en su hermana mayor, la urgía a que se lanzara a la implacable búsqueda de marido.

Reprimiendo un suspiro, Sarah bajó la vista al ribete que estaba descosiendo del escote de su nueva chaqueta y con calma volvió a exponer sus razones.

—Sabéis que eso no es cierto. Ya os lo he dicho, Twitters os lo ha dicho y mamá también os lo ha dicho. Que me case o no no os afecta. —Descosió una última puntada y arrancó el ribete, luego sacudió la chaqueta—. Clary será presentada en sociedad la próxima temporada, y tú, Gloria, al año siguiente.

—Sí, pero eso no viene al caso. —Clary miró a Sarah con el ceño fruncido—. Estamos hablando de cómo van a ser las cosas esta vez.

Cuando Sarah la miró arqueando la ceja inquisitivamente, Clary se sonrojó y continuó:

—No cumples con las expectativas, Sarah. Mamá y papá te llevarán a Londres dentro de unas semanas para tu cuarta temporada. Es evidente que todavía esperan que atraigas la atención del caballero adecuado. Después de todo, tanto Maria como Angela aceptaron proposiciones de matrimonio en su segunda temporada.

Maria y Angela eran sus hermanas mayores, de veintiocho y veintiséis años respectivamente. Se habían casado y vivían con sus maridos y sus hijos en las distantes haciendas de sus esposos. A diferencia de Sarah, Maria y Angela habían estado dispuestas a casarse con caballeros de su entorno con quienes se sentían cómodas, dado que dichos hombres poseían grandes fortunas y propiedades adecuadas.

Ambos matrimonios habían sido muy convencionales. Ninguna de sus hermanas mayores había considerado otra alternativa ni mucho menos soñado con ella.

Y, por lo que Sarah sabía, tampoco lo habían hecho Clary o Gloria. Al menos todavía no.

Contuvo otro suspiro.

—Te aseguro que aceptaré encantada la propuesta de un caballero si éste es de mi agrado. Sin embargo, esa feliz circunstancia me parece muy poco probable. —Sarah agradeció para sus adentros que ni Clary ni Gloria supieran la cantidad de propuestas matrimoniales que había recibido y rechazado en los últimos tres años—. Os aseguro que me he resignado a ser una solterona.

Eso era una exageración, por supuesto, pero... Sarah desvió la mirada a la cuarta ocupante de la habitación, la que antaño había sido su institutriz, la señorita Twitterton, conocida cariñosamente como Twitters.* Estaba sentada en un sillón a un lado del ventanal. Tenía la cabeza canosa inclinada sobre su labor y no daba señales de seguir la discusión familiar.

Si no podía imaginar una vida feliz como la de Maria o Angela, mucho menos podía imaginar siendo feliz con una vida como la de Twitters.

Gloria lanzó un bufido. Clary pareció disgustada. Las dos jóvenes intercambiaron miradas antes de lanzarse a una diatriba verbal de lo que consideraban las cualidades más importantes en un caballero, alguien que Sarah vería con buenos ojos y con quien podría casarse.

Sarah sonrió con aire distante mientras doblaba su chaquetilla nueva y el ribete de color escarlata que había descartado. Dejó que sus hermanas siguieran divagando. Realmente quería a sus hermanas menores, pero había una brecha entre los veintitrés años que ella tenía y las edades de Gloria y Clary, algo que, en el curso de la presente discusión, suponía un abismo significativo.

Las jóvenes consideraban ingenuamente que el matrimonio consistía en escoger entre una larga lista de atributos adecuados, pero Sarah había vivido lo suficiente para darse cuenta de que el resultado final solía ser muy poco satisfactorio. La mayor parte de los matrimonios de su círculo se basaban en tales criterios, sin que hubiera nada más intenso que un simple afecto, degenerando luego en unas relaciones vacías que ambas partes mantenían vivas sólo por comodidad.

Pero el amor...

Sólo el amor podía ser suficiente en tales circunstancias. Cualquier otra cosa sería algo barato y vulgar.

Ella misma se había planteado el matrimonio con la mente y los ojos bien abiertos. Nadie la había considerado nunca una rebelde, pero jamás había seguido a ciegas los dictámenes de los demás, en especial los de carácter personal. Así que había estudiado ese tema en profundidad.

* *Twitters* en inglés significa «gorjeos». *(N. de las T.)*

Creía que el matrimonio era algo más importante de lo que las normas convencionales dictaban. Algo más hermoso, un ideal y no un compromiso impuesto, un estado glorioso que llenaba el corazón de necesidad y anhelo y de plena satisfacción; un matrimonio basado en el amor honraría los votos de esa institución.

Y lo había visto. No en el matrimonio de sus padres —que, aunque había sido una unión convencional pero exitosa, no estaba basada en la pasión sino en el afecto, el deber y la comodidad—, sino un poco más al sur de Morwellan Park, en Casleigh. La casa de lord Martin y lady Celia Cynster, y ahora también la casa de su hijo mayor, Gabriel, y su esposa, lady Alathea, de soltera Morwellan.

Sarah conocía a Alathea, a Gabriel y a los padres de éste de toda la vida. Alathea y Gabriel se habían casado por amor; Alathea había tenido que esperar hasta los veintinueve años antes de que Gabriel entrara en razón y le pidiera ser su esposa. En cuanto a Martin y Celia, se habían fugado para casarse hacía mucho tiempo poseídos por una pasión que nadie ponía en duda.

Sarah había visitado con frecuencia a ambas parejas. Desear una boda por amor, a falta de un nombre mejor, era un objetivo digno al que aspirar tras haber observado lo que había entre Gabriel y Alathea, y en la relación madura, y de alguna manera más profunda e intensa, que existía entre Martin y Celia.

Ella no conocía el amor, lo que una pareja sentía ante esa clase de emoción, aunque había visto la prueba de su existencia en la calidez de una sonrisa, en un cruce de miradas, en un simple roce de manos; muestras de afecto inocentes pero cargadas de significado.

Cuando el amor existía, iluminaba tales momentos. Cuando no existía...

Pero ¿qué definía ese amor?

¿Aparecía misteriosamente o era necesario buscarlo? ¿Cómo surgía?

No tenía respuestas, ni siquiera la más mínima pista, y de ahí que aún siguiera estando soltera. A pesar de la mordacidad de sus hermanas, Sarah no se sentía obligada a casarse. Si la propuesta matrimonial no venía acompañada de la emoción que caracterizaba a los matrimonios de los Cynster, entonces dudaba que cualquier hombre, no importaba lo rico, guapo o encantador que fuera, pudiera tentarla a entregarle su mano.

En lo que a ella concernía, el matrimonio sin amor no tenía sentido. No tenía necesidad de una unión carente de ese glorioso sentimiento, sin pasión, deseo y satisfacción. No tenía razones para aceptar una unión inferior a ésa.

—Prometes hacerlo, ¿verdad?

Sarah levantó la mirada hacia Gloria, que se había inclinado hacia delante y la miraba con las cejas arqueadas.

—Quiero decir de la manera apropiada.

—Y que alentarás a cualquier caballero dispuesto y considerarás seriamente cualquier propuesta matrimonial —añadió Clary.

Sarah parpadeó, luego se rio y se puso en pie con la chaquetilla en las manos.

—No, no lo prometo. Sois unas jovencitas muy impertinentes, y estoy segura de que Twitters piensa lo mismo.

Miró a Twitters para encontrarse con que la institutriz, cuyos oídos solían ser muy afilados, miraba con ojos miopes por la ventana, hacia el camino de acceso.

—Me pregunto quién será. —Twitters miró de reojo a Clary, que se había girado para mirar también por la ventana, y luego a Gloria—. No cabe duda de que es un caballero que viene a hablar con vuestro padre.

Sarah también miró. Bendecida con una vista excelente, reconoció al instante al hombre que venía cabalgando por el camino de acceso, pero la sorpresa y el desconcertante escalofrío que le recorrió la espalda —las mismas sensaciones que sentía cada vez que lo veía— le impidieron decir nada.

—Es Charlie Morwellan —dijo Gloria—. Me pregunto a qué habrá venido.

Clary se encogió de hombros.

—Lo más probable es que quiera hablar con papá de la cacería.

—Pero nunca viene a la cacería —señaló Gloria—. Suele pasar esos días en Londres. Augusta dice que apenas lo ven.

—Puede que este año haya decidido quedarse en el campo —dijo Clary—. Oí cómo lady Castleton le decía a mamá que esta temporada sería perseguido sin cuartel en cuanto regresara a Londres.

Sarah había oído lo mismo, pero conocía lo suficiente a Charlie para predecir que no sería presa fácil. Lo observó tirar de las riendas y bajar con agilidad de su caballo castrado al llegar al patio.

15

La brisa agitaba los mechones dorados del cabello de Charlie. La chaqueta marrón era de buena calidad, sin duda obra del mejor sastre londinense, y se le ceñía a los anchos hombros antes de ajustarse a la delgada cintura y estrechas caderas. La camisa era de lino blanco; el chaleco, que sólo podía vislumbrar cuando se movía, era de color castaño oscuro. Los pantalones de cuero, que le moldeaban las largas y musculosas piernas antes de desaparecer en las lustrosas botas Hessians, completaban una estampa que podría haberse titulado «La última moda en el campo».

Sarah se removió molesta mientras se recreaba en la imagen de él. Consideraba que la apariencia de Charlie —y el ridículo efecto que tenía sobre ella— era de lo más injusta. Él sabía que Sarah existía, pero más allá de eso... Desde aquella distancia, la joven no podía ver los rasgos masculinos con claridad, pero su encandilada memoria completó los detalles: clásicas líneas patricias en frente, nariz y barbilla, ángulos y planos aristocráticos, pestañas largas y espesas, grandes y exuberantes ojos azules y una boca sensual y atrevida que hacía que su expresión cambiara de fascinante y encantadora a cruel y dominante en un abrir y cerrar de ojos.

Sarah había estudiado esa cara —y a él— durante años. No tenía dudas de quién era: un aristócrata rico descendiente de los normandos con una pizca de sangre vikinga en sus venas. A pesar de esa aura de férreo control, de haber nacido para imponer sus propias normas, aún acechaba bajo la superficie un indicio de implacable guerrero.

Vio cómo le entregaba las riendas a un mozo de cuadra mientras le dirigía unas pocas palabras. Cuando se giró hacia la puerta principal y desapareció de la vista en dirección al ala central, Clary y Gloria suspiraron al unísono y se volvieron de cara a la estancia.

—Es absolutamente maravilloso, ¿verdad?

Sarah sabía que aquélla era una pregunta retórica.

—Gertrude Riordan dijo que en la ciudad conduce el par de caballos grises más impresionante que ha visto en su vida —dijo Gloria con los ojos brillantes—. Me pregunto si los habrá traído a casa. Es posible que lo haya hecho, ¿verdad?

Mientras sus hermanas discutían la mejor manera de averiguar si Charlie había trasladado a aquel par de caballos a Morwellan Park, Sarah observó cómo el mozo de cuadra conducía al castrado de Charlie a los establos en vez de hacerle dar vueltas por el patio. Fuera cual fuese la razón de la visita de Charlie, esperaba quedarse un buen rato.

Las voces de sus hermanas resonaron en los oídos de Sarah. Sus anteriores comentarios giraron como un calidoscopio en su mente hasta que bruscamente adquirieron una forma inesperada. Algo que la condujo a un sorprendente pensamiento.

Un escalofrío diferente y más intenso que el anterior se deslizó por la espalda de Sarah.

—Bueno, muchacho... —Lord Conningham se interrumpió entre risas y le hizo una mueca a Charlie—. Ya sé que no debería llamarte así, pero es fácil olvidar cuando hace tanto tiempo que te conozco.

Sentado en la silla frente al escritorio en el estudio de su anfitrión, Charlie sonrió y le quitó importancia al comentario con un gesto de la mano. Lord Conningham era un hombre franco y afable con quien Charlie se sentía muy a gusto.

—En nombre propio y en el de lady Conningham —continuó lord Conningham—, puedo decirte sin reserva alguna lo honrados y felices que nos sentimos por tu propuesta. Sin embargo, como padre de cinco hijas, dos de ellas ya casadas, tengo que advertirte que ese tipo de decisiones le corresponde a ella. Tendrás que obtener la aprobación de Sarah, pero que yo sepa no hay nada que se interponga en tu camino.

—¿Sarah no ha mostrado interés en algún otro caballero? —inquirió Charlie tras un segundo de vacilación.

—No. —Lord Conningham esbozó una amplia sonrisa—. Y créeme, me había dado cuenta si lo hubiera hecho. Sarah jamás ha podido ocultarnos nada. Si algún caballero hubiera llamado su atención, su madre y yo lo sabríamos.

La puerta se abrió y lord Conningham levantó la mirada.

—Ah, eres tú, querida. No necesito presentarte a Charlie. Tiene algo que decirnos.

Con una sonrisa, Charlie se levantó para saludar a lady Conningham, una mujer sensata y bien educada a la que no le importaría tener como suegra.

Diez minutos después, con la cabeza hecha un lío, Sarah abandonó su dormitorio y se dirigió a las escaleras. Un lacayo le había entregado el recado de que debía reunirse con su madre en el vestíbulo principal. Se había detenido en el tocador para asegurarse de que su fino vestido de lana en tonos aguamarina no estaba arrugado, de que llevaba bien puesto el escote y de que su pelo castaño claro estaba convenientemente recogido en la nuca sin que se le hubieran escapado demasiados mechones.

En realidad, sí se le habían escapado unos cuantos, pero no tenía tiempo de soltarse el pelo y volver a peinárselo. Además, sólo quería asegurarse de que estaba lo suficientemente arreglada para pasar el visto bueno de Charlie en el caso de cruzarse con él. Era demasiado temprano para que su vecino se quedara a almorzar y no había ninguna razón para imaginar que la llamada de su madre estuviera relacionada con su visita... Ahuyentó la ridícula sospecha que había surgido en su mente y que le había acelerado el corazón. Al llegar a las escaleras comenzó a bajarlas con el estómago revuelto y los nervios de punta.

Todo para nada, se recriminó a sí misma. Era una suposición de lo más absurda.

Sus zapatillas golpearon los escalones. Su madre apareció en el pasillo al lado de las escaleras. La mirada de Sarah voló hacia ella. Estaba deseando saber por qué quería verla y así aliviar sus nervios.

Pero observó que el semblante de su madre, ya iluminado con una sonrisa radiante, se iluminó todavía más al verla.

—Bien, veo que te has arreglado un poco. —Su madre la examinó detenidamente de pies a cabeza y luego la tomó del brazo.

Completamente perdida y con los ojos cargados de preguntas, Sarah permitió que su madre la condujera por el pasillo hasta una pequeña estancia bajo las escaleras.

Después de soltarle el brazo, le cogió la mano y se la apretó.

—Bien, querida, al parecer Charlie Morwellan ha venido a pedir tu mano en matrimonio.

Sarah parpadeó. Por un instante, la habitación le dio vueltas, literalmente.

Su madre sonrió sin mostrar la más mínima compasión.

—No puedo negar que es una auténtica sorpresa, aunque bien sabe Dios que no es la primera vez que rechazas una propuesta de matrimonio. Como siempre, la decisión es tuya, y tu padre y yo te apoyaremos sea cual sea. —Su madre hizo una pausa—. Sin embargo, en este caso, tanto tu padre como yo queremos pedirte que consideres la oferta con mucho cuidado. Cualquier propuesta matrimonial hecha por un conde requiere mucha atención, pero siendo como es del octavo conde de Meredith creemos que merece una mayor reflexión.

Sarah clavó la mirada en los ojos oscuros de su madre. A pesar del evidente placer que su madre sentía por la propuesta de Charlie, se había mostrado seria al darle ese consejo.

—Querida, conoces de sobra la riqueza de Charlie. Conoces su casa, su posición... lo conoces a él, aunque no tan profundamente como deberías. Pero conoces a su familia.

Volvió a tomarle las manos y a estrechárselas ligeramente, llena de excitación.

—Con ningún otro caballero tendrás una relación tan cercana, una base tan buena como cualquier otra para consolidar un buen matrimonio. Es una oportunidad totalmente inesperada, cierto, pero aun así única.

Su madre buscó la mirada de Sarah, intentando leer la reacción de la joven. Sarah sabía que sólo vería confusión.

—Bien. —Lady Conningham esbozó una pequeña sonrisa y continuó hablando en tono más enérgico—. Debes escuchar su propuesta. Escuchar atentamente todo lo que tiene que decir, y luego tomar la decisión adecuada.

Soltándole las manos, su madre dio un paso atrás, y le alisó el escote. Luego asintió.

—Muy bien. Entra... está esperándote en la salita. Como ya te he dicho, tu padre y yo aceptaremos la decisión que tomes. Pero, por favor, valora la propuesta de Charlie en su justa medida.

Sarah asintió con la cabeza, sintiéndose entumecida. Apenas podía respirar. Se apartó de su madre y se dirigió lentamente a la puerta de la salita.

Charlie oyó unos pasos suaves en el pasillo. Se apartó de la ventana cuando vio cómo se abría la puerta y entraba la mujer que había elegido como esposa.

19

Era de estatura media, aunque su delgadez la hacía parecer más alta de lo que era. Tenía la cara en forma de corazón, enmarcada por los suaves mechones sueltos de un hermoso cabello castaño claro, los rasgos delicados, el cutis perfecto —incluidas las diminutas pecas que le salpicaban el puente de la nariz—, la frente ancha y la nariz recta. Las arqueadas y delicadas cejas castañas y las largas pestañas junto con aquellas mejillas sonrojadas y la barbilla suavemente curvada creaban una imagen de tranquila belleza.

Sarah poseía una mirada inusualmente franca. Charlie esperó a que se moviera, sabiendo que lo haría con una gracia innata.

Con la mano en la manilla de la puerta, ella se detuvo y escudriñó la estancia.

Entrecerró los ojos levemente. Incluso a través de la distancia, Charlie percibió la incertidumbre de la joven, pero cuando sus miradas se cruzaron ella vaciló un segundo antes de apartarla, cerrar la puerta y acercarse a él.

Parecía serena, pero aun así había entrelazado las manos delante de ella.

Sarah no podía haberse esperado aquello. Charlie nunca le había dado ningún indicio de que quisiera casarse con ella. La última vez que se habían visto había sido en el baile de los Hunt el pasado noviembre, cuando habían bailado el vals y conversado durante al menos un cuarto de hora, intercambiando los cumplidos de rigor. Eso había sido todo.

Había sido algo deliberado por parte de Charlie. Había sabido —durante años si se detenía a pensar en ello— que ella lo miraba de una manera especial. Que hubiera sido muy fácil, quizá con sólo una sonrisa y algunas palabras, hacer que la joven se enamorara de él, que se sintiera fascinada por él. No es que ella hubiera mostrado nunca el más mínimo interés en él, pero Charlie, desde luego, conocía a las mujeres y sabía que había algo más en Sarah que la serena y fría fachada que mostraba al mundo. Hacía muchos años que él había tomado una decisión y ni una sola vez había dudado en su propósito de no pisar ese terreno. Ella era, después de todo, la dulce Sarah, la hija de unos vecinos que conocía de toda la vida.

Por ese motivo había contenido lo que sus instintos le apremiaban a hacer y la había tratado como a cualquier otra joven dama de la sociedad.

Pero, cuando por fin había decidido elegir esposa, la cara de Sarah se le había aparecido como por ensalmo en la mente. Ni siquiera había tenido que pensárselo dos veces. Sencillamente había sabido que ella era la mejor elección.

Y después, por supuesto, había sopesado y valorado los numerosos criterios que un hombre como él tenía que considerar a la hora de seleccionar una esposa. Aquel ejercicio mental sólo le había confirmado que Sarah Conningham era la candidata perfecta.

Sarah se detuvo ante él, y sus rostros quedaron a menos de medio metro. Los ojos de la joven, de un delicado color azul pálido, estaban ensombrecidos por la preocupación cuando buscaron los de él.

—Charlie. —Le saludó con una inclinación de cabeza. Para sorpresa del hombre, la voz de ella era suave y tranquila—. Mi madre me ha dicho que deseabas hablar conmigo.

Sarah esperó con la cabeza alzada; era la única manera de que ella pudiera mirarle a los ojos, pues la coronilla de la joven apenas le llegaba a la barbilla.

Charlie curvó los labios de manera espontánea. Nada de gritos, ni agitaciones, ni siquiera un «lord Charles». Ninguno de los dos había usado jamás esas formalidades, lo que en esas circunstancias era algo de agradecer.

A pesar de su calma exterior, Charlie sintió la frágil tensión expectante que embargaba a la joven y que la hacía contener la respiración. Sintió un profundo e inesperado respeto por ella. Pero ¿realmente le sorprendía que mostrara más agallas de lo normal?

No; y eso era, en parte, la razón de que él estuviera allí.

Deseó alargar el brazo y pasarle la punta de los dedos por la clavícula sólo para comprobar si aquella piel de alabastro era tan suave como parecía. Jugueteó con la idea durante un momento, pero la descartó. Tal gesto no era apropiado dada la naturaleza de lo que iba a decir, del tono de conversación que deseaba mantener.

—Como tu madre te ha dicho, le he pedido permiso a tu padre para hablar contigo. Me gustaría que me concedieras el honor de ser mi esposa.

Podría haber adornado aquellas sencillas palabras con un montón de perogrulladas, pero ¿con qué fin? Se conocían bien, quizá no tan íntimamente como cabría esperar, pero sus hermanas y las de ella eran amigas. Dudaba que hubiera algún aspecto de su vida que Sarah desconociera.

Y no había nada en la actitud de la joven que sugiriera que había dicho algo inadecuado, aunque, tras unos breves momentos, ella frunció el ceño.

—¿Por qué?

Ahora era él quien se sentía confuso.

—¿Por qué yo? —aclaró ella apretando los labios.

«¿Por qué ahora? ¿Por qué después de tantos años te has dignado finalmente a algo más que a sonreírme?» Sarah tenía esas palabras en la punta de la lengua, pero al levantar la mirada hacia la expresión impasible de Charlie, sintió un deseo casi abrumador de pasarse las manos por la cabeza, deshaciendo los tirabuzones tan pulcramente peinados, y pasear de arriba abajo por la estancia mientras intentaba entender lo que pasaba.

No recordaba un tiempo en el que no hubiera fijado su mirada en él sin que se quedara paralizada, aunque sólo fuera por un segundo y se le cortara la respiración. Después de que hubiera pasado el momento y de que recuperara el aliento que su presencia le había robado, luchaba por no hacer ninguna tontería que desvelara su secreta fascinación por él.

Eran sólo disparates que no conducían a nada, salvo a empeorar las cosas, lo que no habría sido nada bueno para su cordura. Había llegado a la conclusión de que sólo reaccionaba al adonis vikingo y normando que había en él y había admitido a regañadientes que tal reacción no era culpa de ella. Ni de él. Que era normal, que ella había nacido así y que, simplemente, tenía que enfrentarse a ello.

Y allí estaba él, que, con una sonrisa como única advertencia, le había pedido en matrimonio.

Quería casarse con ella.

¿Cómo era posible? Se pellizcó el pulgar sólo para asegurarse, pero él seguía allí, sólido y auténtico, envolviéndola con una fuerza cálida que para Sarah no era más que pura tentación masculina, aunque ahora él también tenía el ceño fruncido.

Y los labios apretados. Había desaparecido la encantadora sonrisa que solía suavizarlos.

—Porque creo que nos llevaremos excepcionalmente bien. —Vaciló y luego continuó—: Podría contarte con todo lujo de detalles lo que sé sobre nuestros familiares, nuestros amigos, nuestras vidas, pero conoces los aspectos más importantes tan bien como yo. Y... —agudizó la mirada— estoy seguro de que sabes de sobra que necesito una condesa. —Hizo una pausa y luego volvió a esbozar una sonrisa—. ¿Serás la mía?

Educadamente ambiguo.

Sarah se quedó mirando sus ojos azul grisáceo, de un azul más sombrío que los de ella, y de nuevo recordó las palabras de su madre: «Debes escuchar su propuesta. Escuchar atentamente todo lo que tiene que decir, y luego tomar la decisión adecuada.»

Sarah buscó la mirada de Charlie, y aceptó que tenía que hacerlo, que esa vez tenía que pensarse la respuesta. Había perdido la cuenta de las veces que había tenido que enfrentarse a un caballero como él y responder a su propuesta matrimonial. Sabía que había muchas respuestas diferentes. Pero nunca había tenido que pensar la respuesta, sólo las palabras con las que darla.

Pero en esa ocasión se trataba de Charlie...

Sin dejar de mirarle a los ojos, Sarah apretó los labios, tomó aire profundamente y lo soltó.

—Si lo que quieres es una respuesta sincera, entonces te diré que no puedo responderte todavía.

Las pestañas doradas de Charlie, increíblemente espesas, ocultaron sus ojos por un instante. Cuando volvió a mirarla tenía el ceño fruncido de nuevo.

—¿Qué quieres decir? ¿Cuándo me responderás?

Sarah se sintió intimidada. Él se estaba conteniendo, cierto, pero definitivamente la estaba intimidando. No la sorprendía. Sabía que el sutil encanto de Charlie no era más que pura apariencia, bajo la cual él era terco, incluso cruel. Sarah le estudió e inesperadamente obtuvo respuestas a dos de las muchas preguntas que le rondaban por la cabeza. Realmente la quería a ella —justo a ella— como esposa. Y quería que lo fuera ya.

Con respecto a las preguntas planteadas por Charlie, no estaba segura de nada. Ni siquiera sabía cuál sería su respuesta.

Era consciente de que él esperaba que ella retrocediera ante el reto que le había lanzado, que, de una manera u otra, se echaría atrás. Le dirigió una sonrisa tensa y alzó la barbilla.

—En respuesta a tu primera pregunta, sabes perfectamente bien que no me esperaba tu propuesta matrimonial. No sabía que tuvieras tales intenciones y me has cogido totalmente desprevenida. Por otra parte no puedes ignorar el hecho de que no te conozco demasiado bien... —Sarah levantó una mano—, a pesar de nuestra larga amistad, y no finjas que no sabes a qué me refiero. Simplemente no puedes esperar que te conteste con un sí o un no.

Sarah hizo una pausa, esperando a ver si discutía. Cuando él se limitó a esperar, con los labios todavía apretados y la mirada afilada clavada en ella, la joven continuó:

—Con respecto a la segunda pregunta, podré responderte en cuanto te conozca un poco mejor y sepa cuál es la respuesta que debo darte.

Él la escrutó con la mirada durante un buen rato.

—Quieres que te corteje —le dijo finalmente en tono resignado, aunque Sarah no había esperado otra cosa.

—No exactamente. Pero necesito pasar más tiempo contigo para poder conocerte mejor. —Hizo una pausa y lo miró a los ojos—. Y para que tú puedas conocerme a mí.

Esto último le sorprendió. Le sostuvo la mirada, luego curvó los labios y asintió con la cabeza.

—De acuerdo. —Charlie había bajado la voz. Ahora hablaba con ella, con Sarah, no con un objetivo formal e impersonal. Su tono se había vuelto más profundo, más íntimo, casi susurrante.

Ella contuvo un escalofrío. Esa voz ronca y masculina resonó en su cuerpo. Hacía varios minutos que quería poner distancia entre ellos, pero había algo en aquellos ojos, en la manera en que le sostenía la mirada, que la hizo vacilar, como si dar un paso atrás equivaliera a admitir su debilidad.

Como huir de un depredador. Una invitación a... Se le secó la boca de golpe.

Charlie ladeó la cabeza y estudió la cara de la joven.

—¿Cuánto tiempo crees que tardaremos en llegar a conocernos mejor?

Había un destello de luz en sus ojos, como si una idea hubiera germinado en las profundidades de su mente, lo que provocó que ella frunciera el ceño interiormente. Quería dejarle claro que no iba a dejarse influenciar por la indudable, incuestionable y completa experiencia sexual que él tenía, pero hacer tal cosa no era en absoluto aconsejable. Lo más probable es que él considerara aquella declaración como un reto categórico.

Y ése era, ciertamente, un reto que ella no podía permitirse.

Por un momento, no fue capaz de apartar su mirada de la de él.

—Un par de meses deberían ser suficientes.

Charlie endureció el gesto.

—Una semana.

Sarah entrecerró los ojos.

—Eso es imposible. Cuatro semanas.

Él frunció el ceño.

—Dos.

La palabra contenía un tono definitivo que Sarah deseó poder desafiar. Apretando los labios, la joven asintió con la cabeza.

—Muy bien —dijo lacónicamente—. Dos semanas... y entonces te responderé con un sí o un no.

Charlie le sostuvo la mirada. Aunque no se movió, Sarah tuvo la impresión de que se había acercado a ella un poco más.

—Tengo una condición. —Aunque había bajado ligeramente la mirada, apartando sus ojos de los de ella, su voz seguía siendo profunda e hipnótica—. A cambio de que acepte estas dos semanas de cortejo, no pondrás objeciones, en el caso de que aceptes mi propuesta matrimonial —volvió a mirarla a los ojos—, a que nos casemos con una licencia especial una semana después.

Sarah se humedeció los labios resecos y comenzó a formular las palabras «por qué».

Él se acercó aún más.

—¿De acuerdo?

A pesar de estar atrapada por la mirada y la cercanía de Charlie, Sarah logró tomar aire para responder.

—De acuerdo. Si acepto casarme contigo, nos casaremos con una licencia especial.

Él sonrió y de repente Sarah decidió que, sin importar cómo se lo tomase Charlie, escapar era una idea excelente. Se tensó y se dispuso a dar un paso atrás.

Pero Charlie la rodeó con un brazo rápidamente y la atrajo hacia su cuerpo.

25

Capturó su mirada con la suya mientras la envolvía suave pero inexorablemente entre sus brazos.

—Nuestras dos semanas de cortejo... ¿recuerdas?

Sarah apoyó las manos en los brazos de él y echó la cabeza hacia atrás para mirarle a los ojos. Sintió que se mareaba al verse envuelta por la fuerza de ese hombre.

—¿Qué quieres decir?

Él curvó los labios en una sonrisa absolutamente masculina.

—Que empiezan ahora —dijo.

Luego inclinó la cabeza y la besó.

2

A Sarah la habían besado muchas veces, pero ningún beso podía compararse con aquél.

Nunca antes le había dado vueltas la cabeza. Nunca antes había perdido el hilo de sus pensamientos. Ahora simplemente estaba bloqueada.

No se planteó si aquello estaba bien o no, no podía pensar lo suficiente para hacerlo. No podía liberar su mente de la pecaminosa tentación que suponía el roce de los labios de Charlie en los suyos, de la astuta y provocativa presión que él aplicaba, de la calidez que parecía penetrarle hasta los huesos... No era un beso cualquiera, ni mucho menos inocente.

Era un beso con el que Charlie pretendía robarle la cordura.

Sarah lo sabía, lo entendía, pero aun así estaba demasiado intrigada y cautivada para negarse.

Charlie lo sabía. Sabía que ella estaba fascinada, que estaba dispuesta a que él le enseñara un poco más.

Que era, precisamente, lo que él deseaba hacer.

Ya era suficiente. Se suponía que sólo era un beso y nada más. Pero para sorpresa de Charlie le llevó su tiempo convencerse de qué era lo que debía hacer y no ceder al sutil deseo de ella. Tuvo que obligarse a romper el beso, a alejarse de aquellos labios rosados que habían resultado ser más deliciosos y tentadores de lo que él había imaginado. Frescos y delicados.

Cuando levantó la cabeza y cogió aire, él se preguntó si sería ése el sabor de la inocencia. Y si había sido ese elixir tan poco familiar para él o los nervios subyacentes de Sarah lo que había enardecido inexplicablemente su deseo.

A pesar de todo, al escrutar los ojos de la joven mientras ella parpadeaba y le devolvía la mirada deslumbrada, Charlie no pudo evitar sentir una intensa satisfacción interior. Sarah era cálida, suave y deseable entre sus brazos, pero él la apartó lentamente y curvó los labios en una encantadora e inocente sonrisa.

—Te veré esta noche en casa de lady Finsbury. —Profundizó la sonrisa—. Allí podremos seguir conociéndonos mejor.

Ella entrecerró los ojos.

Charlie alargó la mano y le rozó la mejilla con un dedo, luego dio un paso atrás, le hizo una reverencia y se marchó.

Antes de que pudiera sentirse tentado a hacer nada más.

Sarah Conningham había resultado ser, definitivamente, la elección correcta.

Sarah se quedó mirando a su potencial prometido cuando éste entró en la sala de lady Finsbury esa misma noche. Alto y apuesto, exudaba una elegancia disoluta con una chaqueta de color nuez, un chaleco entallado de rayas doradas y una camisa de inmaculado tono marfil. Lo vio inclinarse sobre la mano de la dueña de la casa con una indescriptible gracia. Sarah observó cómo la elogiaba con una sonrisa encantadora y cómo comenzaba a moverse por la estancia.

Cuando la había dejado esa tarde, ella había aclarado sus vertiginosos pensamientos y había acudido al estudio de su padre. Sus padres la habían estado esperando. Sin más dilación les había explicado el acuerdo al que había llegado con Charlie. A pesar de no ser lo que habían esperado, se habían mostrado satisfechos. Aunque Sarah no había dicho que sí a la propuesta matrimonial, tampoco había dicho que no, y a sus padres se les había iluminado la cara en cuanto llegaron a esa conclusión. Estaba claro que confiaban en que cuando conociera a Charlie un poco mejor se daría cuenta de la buena oportunidad que se le había presentado.

A Sarah no le había sorprendido aquel optimismo.

Observó cómo Charlie se movía entre los invitados —todos vecinos de la zona y por consiguiente conocidos de ambos—, saludando a unos y otros, mientras se dirigía inexorablemente hacia ella, y tuvo que admitir que era difícil encontrar algún defecto en su porte que pudiera desagradarle.

Pero ella no había insistido en tener un período de cortejo para evaluar aspectos tan físicos y convencionales. Necesitaba confirmar que poseía el único aspecto que ella consideraba totalmente imprescindible para su futura felicidad conyugal, y que era una parte de lo que él estaba ofreciéndole, ya fuera consciente o inconscientemente. Se lo debía a sí misma, a sus sueños, a su futuro y a todos los caballeros cuyas propuestas matrimoniales había rechazado al darse cuenta de que eso no formaba parte de sus intenciones. Tenía que encontrar pruebas evidentes de que él le proporcionaría ese algo de tan vital importancia, de que eso formaría parte integral de su matrimonio.

Una unión por amor o nada; ése era su objetivo, lo que ella necesitaba para aceptar casarse con él.

El interludio de esa mañana no sólo le había aclarado la dirección a tomar, había reforzado su determinación. Si él quería casarse con ella, tendría que ofrecerle su amor a cambio.

Mientras intentaba escuchar los comentarios de las damas y caballeros con los que se encontraba junto a la ventana, observó por el rabillo del ojo cómo se acercaba Charlie. Él sorteó con habilidad a un grupito de jóvenes damas, pero no pudo impedir que una, con un vestido rosa y verde, lo abordara.

Sarah contuvo el aliento, luego recordó que Clary no sabía nada de la propuesta de Charlie ni de su acuerdo; le había pedido a sus padres que mantuvieran el asunto en secreto. Sólo tenía dos semanas para averiguar lo que quería saber, para asegurarse de que Charlie y lo que él le ofrecía eran lo que ella deseaba. Que Clary o Gloria se inmiscuyeran sería una pesadilla.

Charlie se apartó de Clary con una sonrisa. Menos de medio minuto después se había detenido ante Sarah y se había inclinado sobre su mano sin dejar de mirarla a los ojos.

La joven sintió que se le ponían los nervios de punta; un escalofrío de anticipación le recorrió la espalda.

—Buenas noches, Charlie. —Permanecieron de pie uno frente al otro durante un buen rato. Sarah no había pensado jamás en él como «milord». Mirando fijamente aquellos ojos azul grisáceo, le habló con voz queda—: Me atrevería a decir que lady Finsbury sigue sin creerse su buena suerte.

La curva de los labios masculinos se hizo más pronunciada. Le apretó suavemente los dedos antes de soltarle la mano.

—En ocasiones asisto a este tipo de acontecimientos. Y esta noche la fiesta de lady Finsbury tenía un cierto atractivo.

«Ella.» Sarah ladeó la cabeza y esperó con fingida paciencia a que él saludara a los demás y a que intercambiara comentarios sarcásticos y sobre eventos deportivos con otros caballeros.

Pero ya había cambiado algo entre ellos. Aquel extraño sofoco que la había invadido antes volvía a invadirla cada vez que sus miradas se cruzaban, algo que no había sucedido hasta ese momento. Quizá se debiera a que Sarah sólo lo había estado estudiando y evaluando cuando él había llegado a la fiesta y, por tanto, no le había afectado su presencia hasta que Charlie había estado lo suficientemente cerca para mirarla directamente a los ojos y cogerle la mano.

Ése había sido el momento en el que aquella sensación, más fuerte e intensa si cabe, se había apoderado de ella. Pero, para cuando él le dio la espalda, Sarah ya se había controlado.

Tras un rato, él reclamó su atención y la apartó del grupo con disimulo.

Antes de que Charlie pudiera hablar, lo hizo ella mirando por encima de su hombro.

—Dime, ¿conoce tu familia tus... intenciones?

Charlie siguió la dirección de su mirada y vio a su madre, Serena, a su hermana Augusta y a su hermano Jeremy, que acababan de entrar y saludaban a la anfitriona.

—No. —Girándose hacia ella, la miró a los ojos—. Esta decisión me corresponde sólo a mí. Hacerles ver mi interés sólo hará que las cosas resulten más difíciles. —Esbozó una sonrisa—. Pero debo decir que no están ciegos, no tardarán en darse cuenta de mis intenciones. Supongo que tus hermanas no lo saben todavía, ¿no?

—Si así fuera, Clary estaría colgada de tu brazo.

—En ese caso, recemos para que sigan en la ignorancia. —Charlie miró por encima del mar de cabezas—. Parece que va a empezar el primer baile, ¿quieres bailar?

Charlie le ofreció el brazo cuando comenzaron los primeros acordes de un cotillón. Él habría preferido un vals, pero no estaba dispuesto a quedarse a un lado y observar cómo Sarah bailaba con otro caballero. Aceptando la invitación con una inclinación de cabeza, ella le puso la mano en la manga. Mientras la guiaba entre los invitados que se dirigían al comedor, del que habían retirado los muebles para celebrar allí el baile, Charlie fue consciente de que sus expectativas no se estaban cumpliendo, pero pensó que, simplemente, tendría que adaptarse a las circunstancias.

Era ella, Sarah, quien lo desequilibraba todo, quien no se había ceñido a sus planes originales.

Esa tarde había tenido que aceptar su petición de que hubiera un período de cortejo. Después de llegar a casa se había dado cuenta de cuánto había trastocado aquello sus planes. A esas horas esperaba ser ya un hombre comprometido. Sin duda alguna había esperado que ella aceptara su propuesta matrimonial sin rechistar.

Pero, en vez de eso, se había encontrado con algo que no había previsto. Algo lo suficientemente importante como para tener que rehacer sus planes. Mientras la hacía girar y la situaba en la posición correcta, con los brazos alzados y los dedos entrelazados, Charlie fue consciente de una gran fuerza en ella, una cualidad que sería una insensatez ignorar. Sin embargo...

Comenzó a sonar la música, y los dos se movieron formando las figuras del cotillón; girándose, balanceándose, juntándose y separándose. Charlie centró su atención en ella, en su cara, en su graciosa figura, y fue consciente de lo mucho que le atraía, ella y sus esbeltas curvas... incluso aunque estuvieran ocultas. ¿O sería precisamente por eso?

Sarah hizo un giro; sus miradas se encontraron, y se movieron al unísono, luego frente a frente para volver a deslizarse uno junto al otro, rozándose los brazos. Los sentidos de Charlie reaccionaron, excitándose.

Conocerse, intimar. «Aguanta —se ordenó a sí mismo—, aguanta por esos ojos azul ciano.» Charlie sintió cómo la intangible caricia del deseo se deslizaba entre ellos, retorciéndose y girando como la música que los conducía a través de esos intrincados pasos. Cuando volvió a coger la mano de Sarah y a entrelazar sus dedos con los de ella, al tiempo que sus miradas se encontraban, él notó que se le aceleraban los latidos del corazón al ver el deseo en los ojos de la joven.

Apartó la vista bruscamente y respiró hondo. Con rapidez, recuperó el sentido común y la fuerza de voluntad.

Se había sentido más atraído por ella de lo que había esperado;

no podía negarlo. La inesperada resistencia de la joven a darle el sí había atraído su atención de una manera imprevista.

No era otra cosa, se dijo a sí mismo, que el aroma de la persecución, provocada por el encantador sabor de la inocencia... algo que, por otra parte, estaba deseoso de saborear otra vez. No había ninguna duda de que, cuando se hubiera ganado la aprobación de Sarah, su mano y a ella, aquella floreciente fascinación se desvanecería.

Pero ese momento todavía no había llegado.

El baile concluyó. Charlie aceptó la reverencia de la joven; el movimiento los dejó más cerca de lo que habían estado hasta entonces.

Más cerca de lo que habían estado desde aquel momento en la salita de sus padres, cuando la había besado.

Los ojos de Sarah buscaron los suyos. Charlie le sostuvo la mirada y sintió el impulso de volver a besarla, esta vez con más fuerza e intensidad. Por un momento pareció como si sólo estuvieran ellos dos en la habitación. Él bajó la vista a los labios femeninos y ella los abrió involuntariamente.

Estaban en el centro de la pista de baile rodeados por una multitud que, sin duda alguna, se sentiría fascinada al percibir cualquier indicio de conexión entre ellos.

Charlie inspiró bruscamente y apretó los dientes mentalmente, obligándose a dar un paso atrás para romper el hechizo. Sarah parpadeó, bajó la vista y se apartó a su vez.

Sin soltarle la mano, Charlie alzó la cabeza y escudriñó la estancia, pero no había posibilidad de desaparecer, de encontrar un lugar tranquilo en el cual seguir con sus planes, si no mutuos, por lo menos parejos. Ella también quería conocerle mejor. Él quería volver a besarla, saborearla plenamente.

Pero Finsbury Hall era demasiado pequeño y fuera estaba lloviendo.

Charlie la miró con los labios apretados y el ceño fruncido.

—Este lugar no es adecuado para nuestros propósitos. ¿Estarás libre mañana?

Ella lo pensó antes de asentir con la cabeza.

—Sí.

—Bien. —Colocándole la mano en su manga, se giró con ella hacia la salita—. Podemos pasar el día juntos y, entonces, ya veremos.

Charlie fue a buscarla a la mañana siguiente conduciendo sus dos impresionantes castrados. Para gran alivio de Sarah, Clary y Gloria no estaban en casa. Habían ido a dar un paseo con Twitters y no verían cómo Charlie la recogía y la ayudaba a subir al cabriolé. Después de que su acompañante tomara las riendas y azuzara a los caballos, se alejaron de allí como alma que lleva el diablo.

Bien abrigada en una capa de color verde oscuro, Sarah se acomodó al lado de Charlie al tiempo que reflexionaba sobre la necesidad de huir de las restricciones de sus familias y de las, a veces sofocantes, reglas de la sociedad local. Al llegar al final del camino de acceso, él hizo girar los caballos hacia el norte. Sarah lo recorrió con la mirada, contenta de no haberse puesto sombrero. Por supuesto, él estaba impresionantemente guapo con aquel abrigo con capucha, agitando el látigo y tirando de las riendas con dedos ágiles y distraídos.

—¿Adónde nos dirigimos?

—A Watchet. —La miró brevemente—. Tengo negocios allí, en el puerto y en los almacenes que hay detrás. Necesito hablar con mi agente, pero no tardaré mucho. He pensado que después podríamos dar un paseo, almorzar en la posada y... —volvió a mirarla—, salir a navegar si continúa el buen tiempo y el viento lo permite.

Sarah abrió mucho los ojos, aunque él no se dio cuenta pues estaba mirando los caballos.

—¿Te gusta navegar?

—Tengo un velero de un mástil. Cuando puedo, navego solo, pero pueden ir tres personas cómodamente. Está fondeado en el puerto de Watchet.

Sarah se imaginó navegando a solas entre las olas, surcando los vientos que batían la bahía de Bridgwater. Watchet era uno de los muchos puertos que poblaban las costas del sur de Inglaterra.

—Hace años que no navego, desde que era niña. Me encantará. —Le miró—. Sé algo de navegación.

Él sonrió.

—Bien. Así podrás ayudarme a tripularlo.

Charlie refrenó los caballos al acercarse a Crowcombe y atravesaron el pueblo a paso lento. Al dejar atrás la última casa, volvió a espolear a los caballos, que rápidamente adquirieron velocidad.

—¿Qué haces en Londres? —le preguntó Sarah—. Supongo que por las noches irás de baile en baile y de fiesta en fiesta, pero ¿y por el día? Alathea me comentó una vez que Gabriel y tú compartís los mismos intereses.

Sin apartar los ojos de los caballos que con tanta habilidad guiaba por el camino, Charlie asintió con la cabeza.

—Cuando se casaron, Gabriel me puso en contacto con el mundo de las finanzas. Me resultó estimulante y desafiante, y a Gabriel no le importó enseñarme todo lo que hay que saber sobre el negocio. Así que más o menos me dedico a eso. Estos días...

Charlie se sorprendió de lo fácil que le resultó describir su afición por las altas finanzas, particularmente por las inversiones, las innovaciones y el desarrollo de proyectos que contribuían a mejoras de toda índole. Quizá fuera porque sabía que Sarah no se lo había preguntado por simple cortesía, sino porque tenía un interés especial y las ocasionales preguntas que le hacía demostraban que comprendía la complicada tarea.

—En este momento, me interesan las infraestructuras. Merece la pena hacer inversiones con vistas al futuro. La mayor parte de los fondos que manejo, míos y de mi familia, están en bonos y acciones sólidos, pero cualquier tipo de inversión requiere ingenio y paciencia. Son las nuevas empresas las que más me atraen. Invertir en ese terreno exige mucha más perspicacia, pero el éxito es más satisfactorio, tanto en términos personales como monetarios.

—Porque con los bonos y acciones sólidos no corres ningún riesgo, mientras que el resto de las inversiones no sólo te suponen un reto más profundo sino un riesgo mayor, ¿me equivoco?

Charlie la miró. Ella le sostuvo la mirada, arqueando las cejas inquisitivamente. El hombre asintió con la cabeza y volvió a mirar los caballos, un poco desconcertado de que ella lo hubiera comprendido con tanta facilidad.

Pero, si Sarah acababa siendo su esposa, tal comprensión sería de agradecer.

Atravesaron Williton a toda velocidad. Un poco más adelante, él tiró de las riendas en una curva del camino y bajaron la mirada al puerto de Watchet.

Era un pueblo pequeño y animado, con casas en los alrededores de los muelles, que eran el punto neurálgico del pueblo. Había muelles que se adentraban en el mar, que recorrían la costa conectados entre sí. Justo detrás de ellos estaban los almacenes, que se encontraban en perfecto estado a pesar del tiempo que llevaban construidos.

Más al oeste del pueblo, entre las últimas casas y los acantilados que se alzaban sobre el mar, estaban excavando y nivelando un trozo de tierra.

—Has dicho que tenías negocios en esos almacenes. —Sarah levantó la vista hacia él—. ¿Qué tipo de inversiones son? ¿Seguras y aburridas o desafiantes y arriesgadas?

Charlie sonrió ampliamente.

—Un poco de todo. Al haberse expandido las industrias y los molinos de Taunton y Wellington, el futuro crecimiento de Watchet como puerto está asegurado. El más cercano es Minehead. —Señaló con la cabeza hacia el oeste—. Junto a esos altos acantilados. —Charlie bajó la mirada al puerto que tenían a sus pies, a las velas de los barcos anclados, a las olas verdes de la bahía y al Canal de Bristol mar adentro—. Sin duda alguna Watchet se expandirá. La única cuestión es saber cómo y cuándo. El riesgo consiste en invertir cuando no se sabe el tiempo que pasará antes de obtener beneficios.

Los castrados grises se removieron, impacientes por continuar su camino. La carretera que llevaba abajo estaba en buen estado, sin demasiadas curvas pronunciadas, ideal para las pesadas carretas que iban a los muelles, ya fuera para llevar tela o lana a los barcos, o para cargar los barriles de vino y la madera que traían los buques.

Charlie comprobó que ninguna carreta estuviera subiendo por el camino, luego agitó las riendas y condujo a los caballos cuesta abajo.

Entraron con rapidez en el pueblo, y Charlie detuvo el cabriolé delante de la posada La Campana. Dejaron los caballos al cuidado del mozo de cuadra, que conocía bien a Charlie. Apoyando la mano en el brazo de Charlie, Sarah caminó a su lado por la calle principal.

Se dirigieron a atender los negocios de Charlie en el puerto de Watchet. El hombre de Charlie en el pueblo no sólo era agente marítimo sino también el agente encargado de examinar el espacio disponible en los almacenes donde se guardaban las mercancías que iban y venían de los muelles.

Sarah se sentó en una silla al lado de Charlie y escuchó cómo el señor Jones revisaba la disposición de las cargas en los almacenes que Charlie poseía. Casi todos estaban llenos, algo que se ganó la aprobación de Charlie.

—Así están ahora. —Jones se inclinó hacia delante para enseñarles un papel con varios esquemas—. Éstas son las disposiciones que quería conocer con vistas a adquirir un nuevo almacén. Creo que resultará rentable dentro de un año.

Charlie cogió el papel y estudió el contenido con rapidez, luego comenzó a hacerle preguntas a Jones.

Sarah los escuchó con atención; Charlie le había explicado lo suficiente para que la joven siguiera la conversación y pudiera apreciar el riesgo y la potencial recompensa.

Cuando diez minutos después se despidieron de Jones, sonrió y le ofreció la mano a Charlie, consciente de las especulaciones que su presencia al lado del hombre suscitaba.

Desde la oficina de Jones caminaron hacia el oeste por el muelle principal, sintiendo la brisa salada en la cara y oyendo los ásperos chillidos de las gaviotas. Al final del muelle, Charlie la cogió por el codo y la hizo girar hacia una calle empedrada. Tras pasar entre dos viejos almacenes, llegaron a un promontorio rocoso por encima de los acantilados.

Había una rudimentaria barandilla de cuerdas con estacas clavadas en tierra. Charlie la guio hasta un pequeño repecho donde se detuvieron y miraron hacia el mar. El pueblo y los almacenes quedaban a la derecha. Frente a ellos se encontraba el moderno muelle del oeste, que se extendía entre las agitadas aguas de la bahía.

—Mi intención es construir aquí otro almacén. —Charlie se volvió hacia ella—. ¿Qué te parece?

Levantando las manos para recogerse el pelo que el viento le había alborotado, Sarah miró el almacén más próximo y reflexionó sobre lo que Jones había dicho.

—En mi opinión, construiría dos, o al menos uno con el doble de tamaño. No soy muy hábil haciendo cálculos, pero me da la impresión de que el comercio floreciente de Watchet no sólo llenaría dos, sino tres almacenes.

Charlie sonrió ampliamente.

—O incluso cuatro o más. Tienes razón. —Miró hacia el muelle y luego escudriñó el área donde se habían detenido—. Creo que dos implican un riesgo pequeño. El volumen de mercancía que prevemos los llenará fácilmente. No es necesario ser avariciosos... con dos bastará. Pero esa idea de hacer uno con el doble de tamaño...

—hizo una breve pausa y luego añadió—: podría ser una idea excelente.

Sarah se felicitó interiormente.

—¿De quién es el terreno?

Volviéndola a tomar del brazo, Charlie se volvió en dirección al pueblo.

—Mío. Lo compré hace años.

Ella arqueó las cejas.

—¿Una inversión especulativa?

—Una que está a punto de dar sus frutos.

Sin prisas, volvieron caminando a la posada, observando los diversos buques atracados en los muelles y las mercancías que estaban siendo descargadas. El muelle central estaba rebosante de actividad. Charlie la ayudó a sortear las cuerdas y las cajas de madera que se amontonaban por doquier, hasta que doblaron la esquina de la posada.

El dueño los saludó en cuanto cruzaron la puerta. Les conocía a los dos, pero el que atrajo toda su atención fue Charlie, el conde. Les condujo a una mesa en un rincón apartado con un ventanal desde donde podía verse el puerto.

La comida fue excelente. Sarah había esperado que la conversación decayera y diera paso al silencio, pero Charlie le preguntó sobre temas locales y el tiempo pasó volando. Fue al abandonar la posada cuando Sarah se dio cuenta de que Charlie la había utilizado para refrescar la memoria. Casi todas sus preguntas habían girando en torno a lo acontecido en los últimos diez años, años que él había pasado en su mayor parte en Londres.

Deteniéndose en el porche de la posada, observaron el mar. El viento había amainado hasta convertirse en una ligera brisa costera, y las olas eran suaves ahora. El sol se había colado entre las nubes y brillaba entre ellas, cubriéndoles con sus rayos dorados y haciendo desaparecer el frío.

Charlie la miró.

—¿Te apetece navegar?

Ella le miró a su vez y sonrió.

—¿Dónde tienes el velero?

Él la condujo por el puerto, dejando atrás los muelles comerciales y dirigiéndose a los que eran más pequeños y privados. El velero de Charlie estaba anclado al final de uno de ellos. Una mirada a la brillante pintura del casco y a la cubierta limpia y reluciente fue suficiente para que Sarah supiera que estaba en un estado excelente.

La mirada chispeante de Charlie mientras lo ayudaba a soltar amarras y a desplegar las velas, le indicó a Sarah que era un apasionado de la navegación. Su pericia al cambiar el rumbo, alejándose con rapidez del muelle y poniendo proa al mar abierto, le dijo que además era una pasión por la que se había dejado llevar con frecuencia en otros tiempos. No creía que hubiera tenido tiempo de navegar mucho en los últimos años.

Sarah se sentó tras él y lo observó manejar el timón. Se fijó en cómo el viento le revolvía los rizos dorados. No quería pensar en cuán alborotado estaría su propio pelo.

—¿Echas de menos navegar cuando estás en Londres?

Los ojos de Charlie, totalmente grises ahora que estaba en el mar, volaron al rostro de Sarah.

—Sí. —El viento se llevó la palabra. Charlie se acercó a ella, inclinándose ligeramente mientras cambiaba el rumbo. Sarah también se acercó a él para oírle mejor—. Siempre me ha encantado la sensación de volar con el viento, cuando la vela se hincha y el casco surca el mar. Se puede sentir el poder, no es algo que puedas dominar o controlar. Es una bendición poder estar aquí en un día tan espléndido. —La miró a los ojos—. Es como si los dioses nos estuvieran sonriendo.

Sarah le sostuvo la mirada, sujetándose el pelo que se le había soltado mientras viraban en dirección este. Entonces comenzaron a surcar el mar a toda velocidad, cada vez más rápido. Ella se reclinó contra el casco y se rio, observando las nubes que pasaban vertiginosamente sobre ellos, y conteniendo la respiración cuando los alcanzó una ola que hizo balancear el velero antes de que comenzara a volar de nuevo.

Los dioses continuaron sonriéndoles durante la hora siguiente. Sarah se encontró mirando a Charlie más de una vez con una sonrisa tonta en los labios, prendada de la imagen que presentaba: el pelo revuelto por el viento, los ojos grises entrecerrados, los anchos y firmes hombros, los musculosos brazos mientras manejaba el timón. Jamás había visto antes la parte vikinga de Charlie. Una y otra vez contenía sus ensoñaciones y apartaba la mirada, sólo para que sus ojos regresaran a él una vez más.

Al principio Sarah pensó que era algo unilateral, hasta que se dio cuenta de que, cada vez que se movía para ayudarle con la vela, Charlie la seguía con la mirada, demorándose en sus pechos, en sus caderas, en sus piernas cuando se estiraba y cambiaba de posición. Aquella mirada era dura y posesiva. Se dijo a sí misma que era su descontrolada imaginación, que no hacía más que pensar en vikingos y saqueos, pero no podía contener el escalofrío que la recorría cada vez que la miraba de esa manera. No podía evitar estar a la expectativa cada vez que le daba una orden.

Por fortuna, él no sabía nada de eso, así que Sarah se sintió libre de dejar que sus nervios y sus sentidos vagaran libremente mientras consideraba las implicaciones de todo aquello.

Cayeron en una cómoda camaradería; Sarah recordaba lo suficiente de navegación para echarle una mano, agachándose a tiempo cuando la botavara pasaba por su lado y tirando con habilidad de los cabos correctos.

Cuando Charlie regresó al muelle, se sentía cansada pero alborozada. Aunque habían hablado poco, Sarah había descubierto más de lo que esperaba. Aquel día había revelado aspectos de él que ella desconocía.

El pequeño velero ya se deslizaba hacia el muelle con la vela replegada cuando, mientras estaba recostada contra el casco contemplando el pueblo, Sarah observó a un caballero acompañado de otro hombre en el lugar donde Charlie se había planteado construir el nuevo almacén. Protegiéndose los ojos del sol, los miró con atención.

—Hay unos hombres en tu parcela.

Charlie siguió la dirección de su mirada y frunció el ceño.

—¿Quién es el caballero? ¿Lo conoces?

Sarah los miró fijamente, luego meneó la cabeza.

—No es de por aquí. Pero el que está con él es Skilling, el corredor de fincas.

Charlie se vio forzado a desviar su atención hacia el muelle al que se acercaban con rapidez.

—Ese terreno lo compré por mediación de Skilling. Sabe que me pertenece.

—¿Es posible que ese caballero quiera construir más almacenes?

Charlie dirigió una mirada entornada al misterioso caballero. Skilling y él se alejaban ahora de la parcela camino, no de los muelles, sino del pueblo.

—Puede.

Mientras guiaba el velero hacia el muelle, Charlie tomó nota mental de preguntarle a Skilling quién era aquel caballero. Si Sarah no lo conocía, definitivamente no era de la zona, y si un caballero desconocido mostraba interés por las tierras o los almacenes de Watchet, era alguien a quien él tenía que conocer.

Por desgracia, ahora no tenía tiempo de hablar con Skilling; el sol comenzaba a declinar. Tenía que llevar a Sarah a casa antes de que anocheciera.

Saltó al muelle y amarró la embarcación. Sarah terminó de plegar la vela y luego le tendió las manos. Charlie la alzó con facilidad, sosteniéndola hasta que la joven recuperó el equilibrio, apretando sus suaves curvas contra él.

El deseo hizo su aparición.

Charlie notó cómo lo recorría de pies a cabeza, instándolo a estrecharla entre sus brazos, a inclinar la cabeza, apoderarse de sus labios... y besarla. La fuerza de aquel impulso lo estremeció. La pasión lo dejó totalmente abrumado.

Ignorante de todo aquello, Sarah se rio. Charlie forzó una sonrisa ante aquel sonido musical. La miró directamente a los ojos, que resplandecían de alegría y maldijo mentalmente aquel estúpido impulso de besarla delante de todo el mundo cuando eso era algo que no podía permitirse.

Apretando los dientes e ignorando tenazmente el deseo y la necesidad acuciante y compulsiva de besarla de nuevo, dio un paso atrás.

—Vamos —dijo en voz baja. Inspirando bruscamente la cogió de la mano—. Será mejor que regresemos a tu casa.

Al día siguiente era domingo. Como solía hacer cuando estaba en el campo, Charlie asistió al servicio religioso en la iglesia de Combe Florey con los miembros de su familia que residían en Morwellan Park; en esta ocasión acudió acompañado de su madre, su hermano y su hermana más pequeña, Augusta.

Sus otras tres hermanas —Alathea, la mayor, Mary y Alice— estaban casadas y vivían en lugares distintos. Aunque Alathea, casada con Gabriel Cynster, vivía cerca de él, su residencia, Casleigh, quedaba un poco más al sur y asistía a los servicios religiosos con los Cynster en una iglesia cercana a Casleigh.

Lo que Charlie agradecía. Alathea era muy perspicaz, en especial en lo que a él se refería. Como hermana mayor había protegido los intereses de Charlie con sumo celo durante toda su infancia, y había preservado la hacienda que él había heredado. Algo que jamás podría agradecerle lo suficiente, pero que demostraba el profundo interés que su hermana tenía en la vida de Charlie —en el bienestar del condado y en él como conde—, y tal atención lo hacía ser cauteloso.

Y, en este momento, no quería atraer la atención de nadie sobre Sarah y él.

Se sentó en el banco de la familia Morwellan, una pieza elaboradamente tallada situada en la parte delantera de la iglesia a la izquierda del pasillo, y escuchó el sermón a medias. Por el rabillo del ojo podía ver la brillante cabeza de Sarah sentada en el banco de la familia Conningham, al otro lado del pasillo.

Le había sonreído cuando él había recorrido el pasillo detrás de su madre para tomar asiento y él le había correspondido con otra sonrisa, muy consciente de que el gesto era sólo una máscara. Por dentro no sentía ganas de sonreír.

Conseguir pasar tiempo a solas con ella estaba resultando ser muy difícil. Y sabía que sólo de esa manera conseguiría avanzar hacia su objetivo. Puede que la intención de Sarah fuera que se conocieran poco a poco, pero él quería una mayor intimidad de la que había podido conseguir hasta el momento.

Cuando habían vuelto a casa de Sarah el día anterior había esperado tener un momento a solas con ella al llegar a la puerta, momento que hubiera aprovechado para besarla de nuevo. Pero las hermanas de la joven habían salido corriendo de la casa y prácticamente habían asaltado el cabriolé, incluso antes de que ellos bajaran de él. Por lo que Charlie había podido entender, las hermanas estaban impacientes por ver a su pareja de castrados grises. Lo habían acribillado a preguntas, muchas de ellas ridículas, pero no le habían pasado desapercibidas las avispadas miradas que les habían dirigido a Sarah y a él.

Clary y Gloria estaban intrigadas. Y ésa, sin duda, era una situación peligrosa. Respecto a esas dos jovencitas, él compartía todas las reservas de Sarah.

El servicio religioso terminó por fin. Charlie se levantó y acompañó a su madre por el pasillo mientras el resto de la congregación los seguía, con los Conningham al frente.

El instinto impulsaba a Charlie a darse la vuelta y brindarle una sonrisa a Sarah; estaba casi detrás de él, con sólo sus padres interponiéndose entre ambos, pero Clary y Gloria también la acompañaban. Apretó los labios y se obligó a esperar. Podrían hablar en cuanto salieran de la iglesia.

Pero la iglesia de Combe Florey era una de las más concurridas. Casi todos los feligreses, aristocráticos y burgueses, asistían a ella, y su madre y él no tardaron en verse rodeados de gente. Como Charlie no solía ir demasiado al campo, había muchas personas deseosas de hablar con él.

Contuvo la impaciencia, pues sabía que Sarah y su familia irían a almorzar a Morwellan Park, y se obligó a comportarse de una manera socialmente correcta y a charlar con sir Walter Criscombe sobre la caza del zorro, y con Henry Wallace sobre el estado de las carreteras.

Incluso mientras discutía sobre las distintas calidades del macadán, fue muy consciente de la cercanía de Sarah, que estaba un par de metros detrás de él. Aguzó el oído y captó trozos de la conversación de la joven con la señora Duncliffe, la esposa del vicario.

A tenor de esa conversación, sobre el orfanato de Crowcombe, Charlie recordó la impresión que había tenido en casa de los Finsbury; había observado bailar a Sarah mientras él charlaba con otras personas y se había dado cuenta de que la joven era respetada por todos y, por los comentarios de algunos caballeros solteros y algunas señoritas de su círculo, era admirada por su tranquila seguridad.

Del tono de la señora Duncliffe, de una generación mayor que ella, dedujo que Sarah ocupaba un estatus superior al que le correspondería por su edad. Sarah tenía veintitrés años, pero parecía haberse hecho un hueco en la comunidad local en esos últimos años, algo inaudito para una joven soltera como ella.

Ése era precisamente el estatus que, como su condesa, tendría que ocupar. No había pensado en tales aspectos al elegirla como esposa, pero sabía que tales cualidades eran de vital importancia.

Por fin, Henry Wallace pareció quedar satisfecho y se marchó. Con creciente expectación, Charlie se volvió hacia Sarah, pero sólo para descubrir que el padre de la joven había reunido a la familia y se dirigían hacia el carruaje.

Conningham sonrió y le saludó con la cabeza.

—Hasta dentro de un rato, Charlie.

Él apretó los dientes, pero se las arregló para forzar una sonrisa. Captó la mirada de Sarah y observó el gesto comprensivo de sus labios. La saludó brevemente con la cabeza y, con expresión impasible, se dio la vuelta antes de reunirse con su propia familia para dirigirse a Morwellan Park.

Sarah se relajó en un confortable sillón en la salita del Park y en silencio agradeció que ni Clary, ni Gloria, ni Augusta, ni Jeremy conocieran todavía las intenciones de Charlie. Se había preguntado si ese almuerzo sería terriblemente incómodo, pero la comida había sido tan distendida y amena como tantos otros almuerzos dominicales.

La invitación había llegado el día anterior mientras ella estaba en Watchet con Charlie, pero avisar con tan poca antelación no era inusual. Los Morwellan y los Conningham comían juntos cada pocos meses desde que ella podía recordar. Su madre y la de Charlie eran de la misma edad, y las edades de sus hijos también coincidían. Había sido natural que ambas familias, establecidas en la zona desde hacía tanto tiempo y con propiedades limítrofes, acabaran intimando.

Sarah observó a sus padres y a la madre de Charlie, Serena, reunidos en torno a la chimenea, hablando sobre algún escándalo de la sociedad, y estuvo segura de que Serena, al menos, conocía la propuesta matrimonial de su hijo. Quizá lo había adivinado. Había habido un indicio de esperanza no expresada en la manera en que Serena le apretó la mano y le sonrió cuando llegaron. Serena aprobaba la elección de Charlie y le daría la bienvenida como nuera. Se lo había dicho sin palabras. Pero, aunque su aceptación fuera reconfortante, aquella cuestión todavía estaba sujeta a discusión. Sarah seguía sin saber lo que necesitaba saber.

Era cierto que conocía un poco más a Charlie, pero no las cosas realmente importantes. Sobre ese punto en cuestión había hecho muy pocos progresos.

—¡Sarah! —la llamó Clary desde la puertaventana—. Nos vamos a dar un paseo alrededor del lago. ¿Quieres venir con nosotras?

Ella sonrió y negó con la cabeza, despidiéndose con la mano de sus hermanas y de Augusta, que era un año mayor que Clary y que estaba preparándose para su primera temporada. Jeremy, que había llevado a Charlie al otro lado de la habitación, esbozó una amplia sonrisa en cuanto vio a las tres chicas salir, y después de decirle algo a su hermano se dio la vuelta y salió a hurtadillas por la otra puerta, escapándose mientras podía.

La puerta se cerró silenciosamente. Sarah desplazó la mirada a donde Charlie se encontraba. Él miró a sus padres, absortos en su debate, y luego atravesó la habitación hacia ella.

Se detuvo ante Sarah y le tendió la mano. Sus ojos grises capturaron los de ella.

—Ven. Demos una vuelta también.

Sarah le observó con atención. Estaba totalmente segura de que él no tenía intención de unirse a sus hermanas. Llena de anticipación, le cogió la mano y permitió que la ayudara a ponerse en pie.

—¿Adónde vamos? —preguntó como si sólo estuviera vagamente interesada.

Charlie señaló la puertaventana.

—Empecemos con la terraza.

Sin mirar atrás —no quería percibir las miradas esperanzadas de sus padres—, permitió que la condujera fuera. Charlie esperó mientras ella se ajustaba el chal en los hombros, y luego le ofreció el brazo. Sarah se apoyó en él y recorrieron juntos la terraza.

Sus hermanas eran ahora tres pequeñas figuras en la lejanía que seguían el camino que bordeaba el lago artificial.

—Reza para que no nos vean y vengan a buscarnos.

Sarah levantó la mirada; Charlie entrecerró los ojos y las observó. Sonriendo, ella meneó la cabeza.

—Están hablando de la temporada de Augusta. Sólo algo verdaderamente sorprendente llamaría su atención.

—Cierto —masculló él. La miró mientras seguían avanzando por la terraza—. Tú no pareces demasiado entusiasmada por esa manía femenina de las temporadas.

Sarah se encogió de hombros.

—Disfruté de mis temporadas en su tiempo, pero, una vez que pasa la emoción del primer momento, los bailes son sólo bailes y las fiestas no dejan de ser fiestas un poco más chispeantes que las que tenemos aquí. Si tuviese alguna razón para estar allí, supongo que sería diferente, pero a la postre todo ese glamour me resultó algo vano o, si lo prefieres, carente de propósito.

Él arqueó las cejas, pero no respondió.

Llegaron al final de la terraza. En lugar de dar la vuelta, él la guio hacia la esquina donde la terraza continuaba hacia el lado sur de la casa.

Charlie miró la fachada que se alzaba ante ellos.

—Debes de conocer esta casa tan bien como yo.

—Dudo que alguien la conozca tan bien como tú. Quizá Jeremy... —Sarah negó con la cabeza—. No, ni siquiera él. Tú has crecido aquí. Es tu casa y siempre has sabido que la heredarías algún día. Puede que sea el hogar de Jeremy, pero no es suyo. Apuesto lo que sea a que has explorado hasta el último rincón. —La joven ladeó la cabeza y lo miró a los ojos.

Charlie esbozó una sonrisa.

—Tienes razón. Lo he hecho... y sí, siempre supe que sería mía.

Deteniéndose ante otra puertaventana, Charlie la abrió, y retrocediendo un paso la invitó a entrar.

—La biblioteca. Hace años que no entro. —Sarah miró a su alrededor tras atravesar el umbral—. La has redecorado.

Charlie asintió con la cabeza.

—Eran los dominios de Alathea hasta que se casó, luego pasaron a ser míos. Por alguna extraña razón, mi padre apenas venía aquí.

Sarah describió un círculo a su alrededor, fijándose en los cambios hechos en la estancia. Ahora tenía un aire más masculino debido a los sillones acolchados de cuero oscuro, las cortinas de terciopelo de color verde oscuro que enmarcaban las ventanas y la ausencia de lámparas y floreros; adornos que estaba acostumbrada a ver por todos los rincones de la estancia cuando la biblioteca era el refugio de Alathea. Pero la sensación de lujo, de riqueza, seguía presente, realzada por el retrato de uno de sus antepasados que colgaba encima de la chimenea, las líneas limpias de la licorera de cristal o la enorme y antigua librería con puertas de vidrio.

—El escritorio es el mismo. —Sarah estudió la pieza de un tallado exquisito, que se encontraba en un extremo de la estancia. La superficie estaba pulida, pero los papeles apilados, las plumas y los lápices eran mudos testigos de que aquel espacio era muy utilizado.

Charlie había cerrado la puertaventana para impedir la entrada del aire frío. El fuego brincaba y crepitaba bajo la antigua repisa de la chimenea, iluminando la nueva alfombra Aubusson de intensos tonos verdes y castaños. La luz del fuego titilaba sobre las encuadernaciones de piel de los innumerables volúmenes que atestaban las librerías de las paredes y arrancaba destellos de los títulos en relieve dorado.

Sarah se fijó en todo, luego miró a Charlie, que se había detenido en medio de las tres puertasventanas que daban a la terraza, los jardines del sur y a una parte del lago. Estaba observando sus propiedades. La joven se acercó para contemplar las vistas con él.

Girando la cabeza, él capturó sus ojos, sosteniéndole la mirada por un momento, y luego le preguntó con voz profunda y tranquila:

—¿No te gustaría ser la dueña de todo esto?

Charlie se refería a la casa, a los campos, a la hacienda. A su hogar. Pero Sarah, ciertamente, quería ser la dueña de algo más.

Sarah le devolvió la mirada con firmeza. Por dentro, se había estremecido ante el tono del conde y su pregunta. La respuesta estaba clara en su mente, pero ¿cómo expresarla?

—Sí. —Alzando la cabeza, se obligó a no dejarse tentar por lo que él le ofrecía—. Pero... no es suficiente.

Charlie frunció el ceño.

—¿Qué?

—Lo que quiero... —Sarah parpadeó. De repente había encontrado una manera de explicarlo—. Cuando consideras tus inversiones, valoras tanto el riesgo como el desafío que suponen, así como la seguridad y la satisfacción que conseguirás al alcanzar tus propósitos. Pues es lo mismo que yo quiero en un matrimonio. —Le sostuvo la mirada—. No sólo quiero lo convencional, lo mundano, la seguridad, sino que además...

Sarah se quedó sin palabras. En realidad, no había una manera sencilla de explicarlo. Al final, simplemente añadió:

—Quiero la excitación, la emoción, aceptar el riesgo y alcanzar la satisfacción. Quiero experimentar esa gloria.

Fue gracias a los años de práctica en mantener una expresión inescrutable durante las negociaciones mercantiles que Charlie no dejó asomar la sorpresa a su rostro. Sarah era una joven de veintitrés años, virgen. Pondría la mano en el fuego por ello. Pero, a menos que no hubiese oído bien, ella acababa de decirle que, si se casaba con él, la única manera en que se sentiría satisfecha sería con un matrimonio apasionado.

Por lo tanto la razón por la que había deseado conocerle mejor había sido evaluar si un enlace entre ellos daría como fruto la pasión y la gloria que ella buscaba.

Charlie no había esperado tal cosa, pero ciertamente no estaba dispuesto a discutirlo. Curvó los labios.

—No veo ningún impedimento a eso.

Ella frunció el ceño.

—¿No?

Charlie supuso que la pregunta provenía de una falta de confianza en sí misma, de que no creía que ella —precisamente ella— podía provocar unas pasiones de tal índole.

Teniendo en cuenta la reputación de Charlie, y todo lo que ello implicaba, ésa no era, después de todo, una duda tan absurda.

Aunque sí era —y él lo sabía a ciencia cierta— absolutamente infundada.

Estiró los brazos hacia ella, evitando abrazarla para no ponerla nerviosa, y le deslizó las manos por la cintura para instalarla a acercarse un poco más a él.

Sarah se acercó con vacilación. Parecía como... Los instintos de Charlie le decían que era como una potrilla, nerviosa e indomable, que no había sido domada por la mano de un hombre. Virgen en más de un sentido. Y él la deseaba con una pasión intensa, única en su fuerza.

Charlie se reprimió, aplastando e ignorando tal sentimiento mientras le sostenía la mirada.

—Cualquier cosa que quieras en ese aspecto estoy dispuesto a dártela.

Ella lo miró a los ojos y se humedeció los labios.

—Yo...

—Pero está claro que quieres profundizar en ello antes de decidirte. —Charlie se obligó a no bajar la vista a los insolentes labios de la joven.

Sarah abrió mucho los ojos y el alivio que sintió fue casi palpable.

—Sí.

Sonriendo, Charlie inclinó la cabeza.

—Como ya he dicho, no veo ningún impedimento. Ninguno en absoluto. —Pronunció esas últimas palabras justo cuando le rozaba los labios.

Las pestañas de Sarah revolotearon y luego cayeron. Él le acarició los labios suave y tentadoramente con los suyos. Luego se apoderó de ellos con una larga caricia sensual pensada para aplacar los temores de la joven.

Charlie la tentaba y ella respondía, indecisa pero dispuesta. Tras un rato él profundizó el beso. Los labios de Sarah eran tan flexibles y delicados como Charlie recordaba. Contuvo el aliento mientras con la punta de la lengua lamía el labio inferior de la joven, instándola suavemente a que lo abriera para él. Sarah separó los labios con un suspiro y le dejó entrar.

Él penetró en el cálido refugio que era la boca de Sarah, buscando y rozando su lengua con la suya.

Tentándola, fascinándola, cautivándola.

Sí, a ella, pero también a él. A pesar de su experiencia Charlie no era inmune a lo que estaba ocurriendo y no pudo evitar un escalofrío de excitación cuando ella le devolvió las caricias tímidamente.

A Sarah le daba vueltas la cabeza, su mente bailaba al son de un vals fogoso y decadente, lleno de placer. Se excitó e inflamó, deseando aún más a medida que él profundizaba el beso y su magia seductora se le metía bajo la piel.

Los sentidos de Sarah ronronearon de placer.

El sabor de Charlie era peligroso y adictivo. Sintió sus cálidos labios mientras le devolvía los besos, cada vez más atrevida y más segura de sí misma.

Cada vez más convencida de que encontraría la respuesta.

Quería levantar los brazos, rodearle el cuello y acercarse más a él. Quería tocarle y apretar su cuerpo contra el suyo, pero de repente él rompió el beso.

Y no porque deseara hacerlo. Cuando Sarah abrió los pesados párpados, vio que él parecía alerta mientras miraba a través de la ventana por encima de su cabeza.

Entonces le vio apretar aquellos labios tan atrayentes al tiempo que maldecía por lo bajo.

Charlie la miró a los ojos.

—Nuestras hermanas —dijo con disgusto.

Sarah miró hacia el lago e hizo una mueca, sintiéndose igual de frustrada que él. Tras haber bordeado el lago, las tres chicas se dirigían directas a la terraza de la biblioteca. En cualquier momento los verían y...

—Vamos. —Charlie la soltó.

Sarah se sintió extrañamente desolada.

Cogiendo a la joven por el codo, la guio hasta la puerta de la biblioteca.

—Tenemos que regresar.

Salieron al pasillo. Por un instante, ella consideró la idea de quedarse un poco más allí, pero al final desistió con un suspiro.

—Tienes razón. Si no lo hacemos, vendrán a buscarnos.

3

Con un traje de montar de color verde manzana, Sarah cabalgaba por el camino de acceso de la mansión a lomos de su caballo castaño *Blacktail*, llamado así por la cola negra que meneaba con orgullo, mientras lo hacía atravesar los portones antes de tomar dirección norte.

Hacía un día estupendo. El sol brillaba débilmente aunque el aire era todavía frío. Estaba a punto de poner a *Blacktail* a medio galope cuando un sonido de cascos provenientes del sur llegó hasta ella. Y luego oyó su nombre.

—¡Sarah!

Tirando de las riendas, hizo girar a la montura. Sonrió a Charlie mientras éste se acercaba a toda velocidad, de nuevo a lomos de su castrado gris. El ancho pecho del caballo y los pesados cuartos traseros hacían que *Blacktail*, de menor tamaño, pareciera casi diminuto. Como siempre, Charlie guiaba al poderoso castrado con gran destreza y en cuestión de segundos estuvo al lado de Sarah.

Charlie le recorrió la cara con la mirada, demorándose en sus labios un instante, luego volvió a posarla en sus ojos.

—Perfecto... Pensaba ir a caballo hasta el puente de la cascada. Me preguntaba si te gustaría venir conmigo.

«Para pasar tiempo a solas conmigo», adivinó Sarah; el puente de la cascada estaba en Will's Neck, el punto más alto de los montes Quantocks, un mirador popular en la localidad. Sarah hizo una mueca.

—Sólo puedo acompañarte parte del camino, pues el lunes es el día en que visito el orfanato. Es allí adonde me dirijo ahora. Tengo que asistir a la reunión del comité a las diez.

Sarah azuzó a su caballo con los talones y *Blacktail* se puso al trote. El castrado gris de Charlie se ajustó a su paso mientras éste fruncía el ceño.

—¿El orfanato de Crowcombe? —Charlie recordó los retazos de conversación que había oído sin querer entre la señora Duncliffe y Sarah a la salida de la iglesia. Hizo memoria—. La granja Quilley, ¿no? —preguntó mirándola a la cara.

La joven asintió con la cabeza.

—Sí. Soy la propietaria de la granja y de la tierra.

Charlie frunció aún más el ceño. Debería haber prestado más atención a lo que sucedía en la localidad esos últimos años.

—Pero... ¿no es propiedad de lady Cricklade?

Sarah sonrió.

—Lo era. Ella era mi madrina. Murió hace tres años y me dejó el orfanato, la casa y las tierras, así como algunos fondos junto con la responsabilidad de mantener el lugar en funcionamiento tal y como ella hubiera hecho. —Agitó las riendas—. Tengo que apresurarme o llegaré tarde.

Charlie puso a *Tormenta* a medio galope y la siguió.

—¿Te importa que te acompañe? —Miró a Sarah intentando leer su expresión—. Debería interesarme por el orfanato.

Ella le miró a su vez, observándole atentamente, luego asintió con la cabeza.

—Como quieras. —Sarah apretó el paso y se adelantó.

Tormenta se adaptó con facilidad a la zancada del castaño.

—¿Quién más compone ese comité?

—Aparte de mí y de mi madre, a pesar de que casi nunca asiste a las reuniones, están el señor Skeggs, el notario de Crowcombe, y el señor Duncliffe. La señora Duncliffe, el señor Skeggs y yo presidimos el comité y nos encargamos de supervisarlo todo. El señor Handley, alcalde de Watchet, y el señor Kempset, secretario municipal de Taunton, asisten al comité una vez al final del año, o siempre que es necesario.

Charlie asintió con la cabeza.

—¿Cuántos niños hay en el orfanato?

—Ahora mismo hay treinta y uno, desde bebés hasta niños de trece años. En cuanto cumplen los catorce, les buscamos trabajo en Watchet o en Taunton. —Sarah lo miró—. Casi todos son de uno de esos dos pueblos. Cuantas más fábricas hay en Taunton, más accidentes laborales se producen, y es por eso que hay tantos niños sin padres. Además hay madres que se mueren de hambre o por enfermedad. Y con respecto a Watchet acogemos a huérfanos de los pescadores o de los marineros que se pierden en el mar.

—¿Así que has estado ocupándote del orfanato durante los tres últimos años?

—En realidad, desde mucho antes. Lady Cricklade era una de las mejores amigas de mi madre. Su marido murió poco después de casarse y no tuvieron hijos. Mi madre y ella fundaron el orfanato hace ya muchos años. Lady Cricklade siempre tuvo la intención de dejarme a mí la granja Quilley, así que mi madre y ella se aseguraron de que aprendiera todo lo que había que saber del lugar. Voy a la granja Quilley todos los lunes desde que puedo recordar.

Los primeros tejados de Crowcombe aparecieron delante de ellos. Poco antes de llegar a la primera casa del pueblo, tomaron un desvío que conducía a la granja Quilley y que era lo suficientemente ancho como para poder cabalgar uno junto al otro, hasta que alcanzaron la explanada donde estaba ubicado el orfanato.

—¿Qué extensión tiene la granja? —preguntó Charlie.

Ya en terreno llano, hicieron trotar a los caballos hacia la casa que se erguía ante ellos. Edificada con arenisca local de color rojo, ahora de un tono rosado por el paso de los años, su fachada principal daba al valle que se extendía al pie de los Quantocks. Tenía dos plantas de piedra y el ático de madera. El tejado era de pizarra gris, muy común en aquella zona. La estructura parecía vieja pero sólida, como si con el transcurrir de los años sus cimientos hubieran arraigado en la tierra bajo el peso de los gruesos muros de piedra. Delante de la casa había un espacio amplio, cubierto de grava. Los campos se extendían a ambos lados.

—Por el sur, la granja se extiende hasta ese arroyo. —Sarah señaló una ladera donde una línea de árboles marcaba el paso de un riachuelo—. Pero el límite norte no queda tan lejos, llega justo hasta los campos del terrateniente Mack, dos cercas más allá.

Sarah hizo un gesto con la mano hacia la cima de una ladera rocosa que se alzaba detrás de la casa y que formaba parte de las colinas Brendon.

—En la parte trasera hay tres alas, aunque por desgracia no son tan sólidas como la casa principal. Tenemos un huerto y un pequeño terreno donde los animales pueden pastar.

Al abrigo de un pequeño porche, se encontraba la puerta principal, situada en el centro de la fachada de la casa. A cada lado, había ventanas con contraventanas de madera en perfecta simetría. Sarah y Charlie desmontaron y ataron las riendas al poste que había junto al porche. La joven señaló con la cabeza un cabriolé, con una tranquila yegua dormitando entre las varas, atado en un lado del patio.

—La señora Duncliffe ya ha llegado.

Sarah se dirigió a la puerta al tiempo que se quitaba los guantes. Charlie echó un vistazo alrededor, al pueblo de Crowcombe, que estaba unos treinta metros más abajo, en la ladera este de los Quantocks. Desde esa pequeña elevación con el valle a sus pies, los montes parecían estar incluso más cerca.

Sarah giró el picaporte y abrió la puerta. Charlie entró detrás de ella y de repente se encontró en... Babel.

Porque eso era justo lo que parecía aquel lugar. Ocho niños de corta edad atravesaban el vestíbulo en una fila más o menos ordenada hasta que vieron a Sarah, lo que provocó un inmenso alboroto. Los niños se arremolinaron en torno a ella, con una brillante sonrisa iluminándoles la cara mientras se ponían a hablar todos al mismo tiempo.

Charlie, que también había quedado atrapado en el barullo que se había formado a la altura de sus rodillas, tardó un momento en acostumbrarse a aquel murmullo agudo, pero Sarah reaccionó con aplomo. Le vio dar una palmadita en dos cabezas y preguntarle a un niño si se le había caído un diente, aunque la respuesta se hizo evidente en cuanto éste sonrió. Luego, la observó agitar los brazos y restablecer el orden con eficacia, enviando a los niños con la delgada mujer que los había estado guiando.

La mujer sonrió a Sarah, pero abrió mucho los ojos cuando vio a Charlie. Con rapidez se dio la vuelta e instó a sus pupilos a seguir avanzando por uno de los pasillos.

—Los demás están esperando en el despacho —le dijo a Sarah al pasar por su lado.

—Gracias, Jeannie. —Sarah se despidió con la mano de los niños y luego se dirigió a la puerta de la derecha. Mientras alargaba la mano hacia el picaporte, miró a Charlie—. ¿Quieres asistir a la reunión o —señaló la fila de niños con la cabeza— prefieres echar un vistazo a los alrededores?

Charlie la miró fijamente.

—Si no te importa, me gustaría asistir a la reunión. Puedo echar un vistazo después.

Ella sonrió.

—Claro que no me importa. —Frunció los labios—. Puede que incluso aprendas algo.

Mientras la seguía al interior de la habitación, Charlie se preguntó cómo debería haberse tomado ese comentario, pero la verdad es que él ya se había impuesto la obligación de aprender más sobre el orfanato. Aunque estaba lejos de sus propiedades, él era sin duda el aristócrata de más alcurnia de la zona. En cierto modo aquel lugar formaba parte de sus responsabilidades, aunque sabía muy poco sobre él. No tenía ni idea de cómo funcionaba el orfanato, quién lo dirigía, cómo se financiaba y muchas otras cuestiones. Cosas que debería saber.

Que el orfanato fuera legalmente de Sarah, y que ella se hubiera responsabilizado de él, hacía que su desconocimiento del tema fuera incluso menos aceptable.

El despacho estaba bien amueblado con dos escritorios de distinto tamaño y varias sillas y gabinetes. En el centro de la habitación se hallaba una mesa redonda ante la cual estaban sentados la señora Duncliffe y el señor Skeggs. Cuando Sarah entró, interrumpieron lo que parecía ser una conversación banal para darle la bienvenida.

Cuando se percataron de su presencia detrás de Sarah, agrandaron los ojos con sorpresa, pero no interrumpieron sus saludos.

Charlie los conocía a los dos. Les saludó y les estrechó las manos. Después ayudó a Sarah a tomar asiento. Cuando ella se sentó, él cogió otra silla y la puso al lado de la de ella, aunque un poco más alejado de la mesa.

—Espero que no les importe, pero me gustaría saber cómo funciona el orfanato —dijo, dirigiéndoles una sonrisa a Skeggs y a la señora Duncliffe.

Ambos le aseguraron que no tenían ningún inconveniente en informarle; resultó evidente que la señora Duncliffe se preguntaba cuáles serían sus motivos y que Skeggs parecía encantado.

—Cuanta más gente de la localidad comparta nuestros esfuerzos, mejor. —El pequeño notario sonrió. Enderezó un montón de documentos delante de él y se ajustó el monóculo sobre la delgada nariz—. Ahora...

Charlie se reclinó en la silla y escuchó cómo los tres discutían sobre los diversos aspectos cotidianos del orfanato. Se enteró de que compraban la mayoría de los productos perecederos en Watchet, que un par de veces a la semana enviaban la carreta para comprar las verduras, los cereales, la carne y el pescado. Que los productos manufacturados provenían de Taunton; Sarah consultó una lista y declaró que no había nada que necesitaran con tanta urgencia como para enviar la carreta al sur.

La reunión continuó; Charlie se fijó en que, cuando se trataba de artículos para los niños —ropa, zapatos, libros y demás—, no ponían límite de gastos, pero sí lo hacían cuando se trataba de hacer mejoras en el orfanato.

—Ahora —dijo Sarah—, Kennett ha encontrado goteras en el ala sur. Dice que hay que renovar la paja del tejado. Tendremos que llamar a los techadores para que vengan a arreglarlo. —Hizo una mueca.

La señora Duncliffe lanzó un suspiro.

—Ojalá tuviéramos tejados más resistentes para las alas. Ésta es la tercera vez que tenemos que llamar a los techadores en un año; ese tejado ya no aguanta más.

Sarah captó la mirada de Charlie y le explicó:

—El tejado de las tres alas es de paja. Le pedimos un presupuesto a Hendricks, el techador local, para cambiarlo por tejado de pizarra, pero nos dijo que habría que reemplazar todo el conjunto, incluidas las vigas de madera y los brochales, para que puedan soportar el peso de la pizarra, pero entonces los muros no aguantarían la carga extra. En las alas, los muros son en su mayor parte de yeso y paneles, sólo los cimientos son de piedra.

Charlie asintió con la cabeza.

—Ésa es la razón por la que tantas casas de campo siguen teniendo el tejado de paja. No existe manera de reemplazar el tejado sin sustituir también los muros y las vigas... lo que acarrearía cambiar las casas de arriba abajo.

Skeggs lanzó un gruñido.

—Entonces —apuntó—, avisaré a los techadores.

—Entretanto —rogó Sarah—, recemos para que no llueva.

La reunión siguió su curso; Charlie escuchó y aprendió. Cuando el comité concluyó, ya tenía unos conocimientos básicos del funcionamiento del orfanato. Se levantó y siguió a los miembros del comité fuera del despacho. Sarah se despidió de ellos en el vestíbulo. Después de despedirse de Charlie con una inclinación de cabeza, la señora Duncliffe y Skeggs se fueron; la señora Duncliffe llevaría al menudo hombrecillo a su despacho en Crowcombe antes de seguir rumbo al sur, hacia la vicaría en Combe Florey.

Cuando la puerta se cerró tras ellos, Sarah se volvió hacia Charlie.

—Ya es casi la hora del almuerzo. Por lo general paso aquí el resto del día porque siempre hay cosas que hacer y me da la oportunidad de hablar con el personal y también con los niños.

Sarah intentó leer la expresión de Charlie, pero, como de costumbre, su rostro no revelaba cuáles eran sus pensamientos. En el vestíbulo oscuro, los ojos del hombre estaban en sombras; ella, sin embargo, podía sentir su mirada en la cara.

—¿Te importa si me quedo contigo? —Había una leve timidez en su voz, como si temiese que la joven creyera que se estaba extralimitando.

Aquella prueba de sensibilidad la reconfortó. Sonrió.

—Si estás dispuesto a sufrir un almuerzo con una tribu de niños ruidosos, por mí no hay inconveniente. Pero después de comer debo ocuparme de algunas cosas y pasarán horas antes de que me vaya de aquí.

Él se encogió de hombros y esbozó una sonrisa.

—Estoy seguro de que encontraré algo con lo que entretenerme. —Su sonrisa se hizo más amplia mientras tomaban el pasillo que conducía al comedor—. De esa manera —le murmuró cuando casi habían llegado a la puerta abierta— esperaré con impaciencia la vuelta a casa contigo. Solos tú y yo.

Charlie capturó su mirada cuando ella levantó la vista hacia él. Sarah se dio cuenta entonces de lo cerca que estaban el uno del otro. Por un instante, a pesar del ruido que retumbaba en sus oídos, sólo fue consciente de él: de su fuerza, poderosa y palpable —como demostraba la mano que le sostenía la puerta—, de su masculinidad y del calor que emitía su cuerpo a tan sólo unos centímetros del de ella.

Se quedó sin respiración, pero se las arregló para esbozar una suave y ligera sonrisa en respuesta e inclinar la cabeza en agradecimiento a su caballerosidad mientras atravesaba el umbral.

La señora Carter —Katy—, gobernanta además de cocinera, vio a Charlie y agregó con rapidez un servicio más a la mesa principal, que ocupaba el lateral de la estancia. Katy era una matrona de mediana edad que se había quedado sola cuando su marido, marinero de profesión, se había perdido en el mar. La mujer no tenía hijos y había sido elegida por lady Cricklade para llevar el orfanato. Con el paso de los años, Sarah había tenido razones de sobra para bendecir el buen juicio de su madrina.

Sarah condujo a Charlie a la mesa principal, indicándole que tomara asiento junto a ella, luego le presentó a los miembros del personal uno por uno, después los niños irrumpieron en la habitación y fueron ocupando las largas filas de mesas que llenaban el comedor.

La señorita Emma Quince, a la que todos llamaban simplemente Quince, miró a Charlie con gravedad, saludándolo con un renuente gesto de cabeza mientras Sarah explicaba que era ella quien llevaba el libro de cuentas y supervisaba todas las reparaciones de la casa, los muebles y el resto de los enseres.

—Lo que en un centro como éste —añadió Sarah— supone una tarea muy absorbente.

Quince sonrió débilmente, aunque inmediatamente bajó la cabeza y dirigió su mirada al plato.

—También se encarga de los bebés —continuó Sarah—, con la ayuda de Lily.

Lily Posset, una joven vivaracha e inteligente que antaño había sido una de las niñas del orfanato, le dirigió una sonrisa radiante a Charlie, apreciando claramente su elegante manera de vestir. Él le respondió con otra sonrisa y la saludó con un gesto de cabeza. Aunque Charlie apartó la mirada de ella, Lily siguió lanzándole miraditas de reojo. Sarah fingió no darse cuenta.

Jeannie se unió a ellos y tomó asiento después de saludarlos. La seguía un hombre de andar pesado que se hundió en una silla a su lado.

Sarah lo presentó como Kennett, el hombre para todo, un tipo enorme, fuerte y musculoso, que escondía un corazón de oro tras un perpetuo ceño fruncido que no engañaba a nadie y, mucho menos, a los niños.

—Kennett también se encarga de los animales.

Charlie arqueó las cejas en dirección a Kennett.

—¿Qué animales?

—Los habituales —gruñó Kennett—. Tenemos vacas, cabras y ovejas, con lo que disponemos de leche, carne y lana. No tenemos espacio para ninguno más. Utilizamos el terreno para plantar cereales y verduras, y así tener reservas para el invierno.

—Y éste es Jim —interrumpió Sarah, señalando a un joven que se había sentado junto a Kennett—. Es el chico de los recados. Ayuda a todo el mundo en todo y también se encarga de alimentar a los animales.

Jim sonrió a Sarah y saludó a Charlie con la cabeza, luego prestó atención al sabroso estofado que la señora Carter le había servido en el plato.

El último miembro del personal que se unió a ellos fue Joseph Tiller. Sarah le sonrió y él le devolvió la sonrisa. Después de saludar con la cabeza a Charlie, se sentó en su asiento de costumbre junto a Katy. De pelo oscuro y piel pálida, Joseph era un hombre apuesto y discreto. A pesar de su carácter reservado y tranquilo, Katy, Sarah, Jeannie y Quince estaban convencidas de que Joseph sentía algo por Lily. Todas esperaban que en algún momento se armase de valor para pedirle a la joven que, como mínimo, le acompañara cuando llevaba a los niños a la iglesia.

—Joseph Tiller... Lord Meredith. —Sarah esperó mientras Joseph, tras un segundo de vacilación, extendía la mano por encima de la mesa y estrechaba la mano tendida de Charlie. Sarah no tenía muy claro cómo Charlie había sabido que Joseph era un caballero, pero...—. Joseph ha sido enviado por el Obispado de Wells. El orfanato funciona bajo los auspicios del obispo. Joseph da clases a los niños, especialmente a los mayores.

Charlie le brindó una sonrisa comprensiva.

—Supongo que no será una tarea fácil.

Joseph esbozó una sonrisa mientras se sentaba.

—Por lo general no, pero tiene sus compensaciones.

La señora Carter golpeó la tapa de la cacerola con el cucharón y todos los niños guardaron silencio. Joseph inclinó la cabeza y bendijo la mesa con voz firme y segura.

En cuanto dijo «amén» estalló el alboroto. Un ruido ensordecedor se extendió por el comedor. Charlie arqueó las cejas mientras cogía un tenedor.

Joseph observó su gesto y sonrió.

—Siempre ocurre lo mismo.

La comida discurrió con normalidad, aunque diversos miembros del personal tuvieron que levantarse para mediar en varias disputas entre los vociferantes huérfanos. Pero no había reproches ni castigos. No había tensión, sólo alegría y diversión.

Cada lunes, cuando Sara comía en el orfanato, la envolvía una sensación de paz en esa atmósfera solidaria. Era por eso por lo que su madrina había fundado el orfanato, y por lo que ella continuaba dedicándole tanto tiempo.

Tras tomar hasta la última gota de crema de su taza, Charlie se volvió hacia Sarah y le dirigió una amplia sonrisa.

—Son entrañables. Me recuerdan a una enorme familia.

Sarah le devolvió la sonrisa y luego se limpió la boca con una servilleta y la dejó sobre la mesa.

—Ése es exactamente el propósito al que dirigimos todos nuestros esfuerzos. —A la joven no le sorprendió que Charlie se hubiera dado cuenta de ello; al igual que ella, provenía de una familia numerosa.

La mayoría de los niños y parte del personal ya habían abandonado el comedor. Sarah se levantó y Charlie la imitó.

—Tengo que hablar con Quince. Tenemos que hacer el inventario de ropa blanca. Nos llevará algunas horas.

Él se encogió de hombros.

—Daré una vuelta mientras te espero.

Joseph se levantó. Miró a Sarah y a Charlie respectivamente.

—He prometido organizar un partido de *bat & ball* para los chicos mayores en cuanto acaben la clase de aritmética. Será dentro de media hora. Si tiene tiempo, quizá le gustaría unirse a nosotros.

Charlie esbozó una amplia sonrisa.

—¿Por qué no?

Sarah se excusó y se marchó. Le costaba imaginar a Charlie, siempre tan correcto y elegante, jugando al *bat & ball*, al menos de la manera en que jugaban los chicos del orfanato. Los chicos siempre parecían haberse arrastrado por el campo cuando volvían de los partidos. Incluso Joseph acababa con la ropa sucia y arrugada.

Pero pensó que Charlie podría cuidar de sí mismo.

Con aire resuelto, la joven subió las escaleras que conducían al ático. No le cabía ninguna duda de que Quince habría sacado un buen montón de ropa blanca usada para examinar.

Durante la hora siguiente, Quince y ella revisaron y clasificaron montones de ropa. Siempre realizaban aquellas tareas en el enorme ático que también era la habitación de los bebés. Las cunas de los niños que se encontraban bajo la tutela de Quince estaban dispuestas en un lado. Había seis —más de lo habitual—, pero aun así había espacio de sobra entre las cunas y la cama donde Quince pasaba las noches.

Aunque Quince —una mujer seria y huesuda que siempre llevaba el pelo recogido en un moño severo— podía resultar una extraña elección como niñera, Sarah había sido testigo infinidad de veces de cómo a la joven se le suavizaban los rasgos cuando mecía tiernamente a alguno de los bebés. Los pequeños aceptaban encantados sus mimos, con lo que dejaban claro que no había nadie mejor que ella para cuidarlos.

En la tranquilidad de la habitación infantil, Quince y ella se sentaron y ordenaron la ropa.

Más tarde se les unieron Katy y Jeannie. La ropa blanca no sólo incluía las sábanas, sino también las toallas, manteles y servilletas. Tenían que examinarlas todas, apilar a un lado las que hubiera que zurcir y al otro las que hubiera que meter en lejía. La ropa que estuviera inservible la utilizarían como trapos.

Pero la pila de la ropa destinada a zurcir era abrumadora.

—¿Jeannie? —la voz de Lily le llegó desde las escaleras—. Tus niños se están despertando.

—¡Voy! —Jeannie dejó a un lado la toalla que estaba doblando y salió a toda prisa. Se encargaba de los pequeños que empezaban a andar y que hasta ese momento habían estado echando la siesta. Lily, que se encargaba de las chicas mayores, había estado pendiente de ellos.

—Será mejor que me vaya también. —Katy se levantó del viejo sillón en donde se había arrellanado—. Va siendo hora de que empiece a hacer la cena.

Sarah la miró desde el montón de ropa destinada a ser remendada y sonrió.

—Yo me iré en cuanto acabe de ordenar esto. Le pediré a Jim que mañana me traiga la ropa a casa para encargarme de ella.

—Sí. —Katy asintió con la cabeza. Al dirigirse a las escaleras, echó un vistazo por la ventana y se detuvo—. Bueno, menuda vista.

Sarah se levantó y se unió a ella. Siguió la dirección de la mirada de Katy hasta donde los niños mayores, algunos no tanto, y dos definitivamente mucho más mayores, jugaban a la pelota en el patio.

—Por lo general, juegan detrás de la casa —murmuró.

—Hoy son demasiados. —Quince se puso al lado de Sarah—. Parece como si hubieran formado equipos.

Sarah observó cómo Charlie lanzaba la pelota y cómo Maggs, que sostenía el bate, la golpeaba. Hubo risas y vítores mientras el resto de los jugadores salía corriendo detrás de la pelota. Maggs lanzó el bate al suelo, lo rodeó y corrió para tocar la estaca cercana al lugar donde había bateado.

Tras recuperar la pelota, Toby, otro de los chicos mayores, se la lanzó a Charlie. Fue un tiro alto y Charlie tuvo que dar un gran salto para atraparla en el aire. Fulminó a Maggs con la mirada, pero éste sonrió ampliamente. Después de decirle algo al chico, Charlie volvió a lanzar la pelota.

Katy se despidió y con una sonrisa en la cara bajó las escaleras. Uno de los bebés comenzó a llorar y Quince se acercó a cogerlo. Sarah continuó mirando por la ventana. La habitación de los bebés estaba justo bajo el alero y las ventanas quedaban sombreadas por el saliente. Ninguno de los que estaban en el patio podía verla y ella podía observar a placer. Y maravillarse.

Lo que estaba viendo no era algo que se le hubiera ocurrido evaluar como parte de su decisión de casarse con Charlie. Pero Sarah quería tener hijos —era algo que tenía muy claro—, y que su marido fuera capaz de participar en aquellos sencillos juegos infantiles, como Charlie hacía con esos niños, era un punto que debería considerar.

De hecho, no sólo estaba participando en el juego, compartiendo aquel momento con los niños y con Joseph —al que por primera vez veía sonreír de oreja a oreja—, sino que, además, había sacrificado su elegancia sin dudarlo un instante.

Charlie se había quitado la chaqueta, el chaleco y el pañuelo y se había arremangado la camisa —que llevaba fuera del pantalón— hasta los codos.

Y fue un Charlie sumamente desarreglado quien lanzó la siguiente pelota, quien saltó en el aire y quien animó a Toby a que corriera más rápido cuando Maggs acertó a golpear la bola que el chico había lanzado. Sarah observó cómo los niños se apiñaban a su alrededor y cómo él despeinaba a Toby y felicitaba a Maggs, que enrojeció de placer mientras le entregaba el bate a Toby.

Sarah los observó durante diez minutos más. Su mirada era reflexiva cuando finalmente se apartó de la ventana para terminar de doblar la ropa blanca.

Salieron del orfanato media hora después. El partido ya había terminado cuando Sarah bajó las escaleras. Se encontró a Charlie hablando con Joseph, que vigilaba a los niños que estaban terminando sus tareas en el huerto.

Joseph todavía seguía desarreglado, pero Charlie se había esforzado por recuperar su habitual elegancia. Aunque el nudo del pañuelo jamás recibiría un aprobado en ninguna fiesta de la sociedad, no sería reprochable en una excursión campestre. Por los húmedos mechones de su pelo, Sarah dedujo que se había aseado. No cabía duda de que se había esforzado en domar sus desgreñados cabellos.

La joven contuvo las ganas de pasar los dedos entre los húmedos mechones y despeinarlo de nuevo.

Pero se limitó a sonreír, a despedirse de Joseph y de los niños, y a rodear la casa hacia donde les esperaban sus caballos.

Antes de que Sarah pudiera guiar a *Blacktail* al apeadero, Charlie cogió las riendas de su mano enguantada y, rodeándole la cintura con las manos, la subió a la silla de montar.

Ella se quedó sin aliento. Bajó la mirada y metió la bota en el estribo. Luego levantó la vista, esbozó una débil sonrisa y tomó las riendas que él le tendía.

Para cuando él hubo desatado a su castrado gris y subido a la grupa, Sarah ya había recobrado la compostura, y señaló con la mano en dirección sur.

—Por lo general regreso a casa campo a través, es mucho más rápido.

Entrecerrando los ojos, Charlie siguió con la vista la suave línea que marcaba el camino de herradura que conducía al riachuelo.

—Hay un punto donde podemos atravesar la corriente de un salto. —Sarah hizo girar a *Blacktail* hacia su casa y clavó los talones con suavidad—. Vamos.

Sarah se puso en marcha y Charlie la siguió. Cuando llegaron al punto por donde debían atravesar la corriente, él se puso a su lado y saltaron juntos.

Los dos caballos salvaron con agilidad la distancia. Sarah se rio, presa de un inesperado deleite, luego hizo girar a su caballo hacia el oeste, al abrigo de las colinas Brendon, siguiendo el camino de herradura que rodeaba algunos campos de labor y que atravesaba el valle que tenían a la derecha.

Sarah mantuvo a *Blacktail* a un paso constante. El castrado gris de Charlie galopaba a su lado, ajustándose a su ritmo. Sarah miró a Charlie de reojo.

—Es un camino seguro, no hay ni raíces ni baches.

Él asintió con la cabeza.

La tarde caía y comenzaba a oscurecer. Pero aún no había anochecido. A ese paso llegarían a casa de Sarah antes de que se pusiera el sol, pero Charlie tendría que recorrer otros cuatro kilómetros antes de llegar al Park.

Cabalgaron codo con codo siempre que el camino lo permitía. El sonido de los cascos resonaba en las venas de Sarah con un ritmo vibrante; le palpitaba en los oídos, en la yema de los dedos mientras el viento le azotaba las mejillas, que habían adquirido un matiz rosado.

No era la primera vez que la joven montaba de esa manera, algunas veces había galopado incluso más rápido. No sólo era la velocidad lo que alimentaba aquella innegable euforia que crecía en su interior.

Zancada a zancada, recorrieron el camino y llegaron a otro que conducía al patio trasero de la casa. Entraron con gran estrépito en el patio del establo, con los cascos de los caballos resonando en la grava y un peculiar deleite burbujeando en las venas de la joven.

Sarah se sentía eufórica. No podía dejar de sonreír.

Charlie se apeó de un salto y se acercó a ella para ayudarla a bajar. Por un instante la sostuvo en el aire, apoyada contra su cuerpo, mientras los caballos los rodeaban. Luego llegaron los mozos de cuadra para atender a los caballos.

—Haz que dé un par de vueltas por el patio —le indicó Charlie al mozo que había cogido las riendas del castrado gris—. Vuelvo enseguida.

Había dado la orden sin apartar la mirada de la cara de Sarah. La retiró y la cogió de la mano.

—Te acompañaré a casa.

Ella asintió incapaz de saber lo que significaba el brillo de los ojos de Charlie ni la tensión que sentía en la mano que sostenía la suya.

Los mozos se alejaron con los caballos. Charlie se encaminó a la entrada del establo, arrastrándola consigo. Se detuvo bajo el umbral, mirando la extensión de césped sombreado por los grandes árboles que separaba la casa de los establos.

Desconcertada, Sarah siguió la dirección de su mirada preguntándose qué era lo que había visto.

Charlie masculló un juramento por lo bajo y la condujo bruscamente por la parte delantera de los establos hasta doblar la esquina. Se detuvo bajo las ramas de un abeto, se volvió hacia ella y tomándola entre sus brazos, la besó.

Vorazmente.

El placer triunfante que burbujeaba en las venas de Sarah le atravesó la cabeza y le robó el sentido, dejando en su lugar una sensación de excitante certeza.

Los labios de Charlie eran duros y exigentes. Sarah los conocía y respondía a sus exigencias con toda la excitación que sentía.

Pero él quería más, la deseaba con frenesí, con un deseo salvaje. La deseaba con todo su ser.

Sarah nunca había imaginado algo como aquello, nunca había soñado con ese deseo, con que él la deseara de esa manera, pero ahora no era el momento de reflexionar, sino de aplacar la avidez de Charlie y la suya propia.

Sarah separó los labios voluntariamente, él se aprovechó al instante para reclamar su boca por completo. La joven sintió sus caricias exigentes mientras él la empujaba contra la pared de ladrillos del establo y la tomaba de la nuca para profundizar más el beso.

Sarah sintió que se le encogían los dedos de los pies, cuando él le estrechó la cintura.

Se aferró a los hombros masculinos y se pegó a su cuerpo, devolviéndole el beso con una pasión idéntica a la de él.

Unos segundos después, las cosas cambiaron. El ritmo del beso decayó, se suavizó, como si Charlie estuviera haciendo un gran esfuerzo por contenerse, por contenerlos a ambos, como si lo que acababa de suceder entre ellos ya hubiera satisfecho aquel deseo voraz y quisiera saborearla después de que aquel frenesí desesperado hubiera desaparecido.

Lo comprendió; podía profundizar el beso o podía recrearse.

Charlie no la soltó, sino que la sostuvo con más firmeza. Continuó besándola y satisfaciendo el deseo de ambos con largas y tiernas caricias.

Sin duda, la deseaba.

Sarah lo vio en cuanto él levantó la cabeza y suspiró. Le pasó el pulgar por el labio inferior y luego le soltó la cintura. Dio un paso atrás y le cogió la mano.

No sonrió.

—Ven. Te acompañaré a la puerta.

Ella compuso una sonrisa vacilante y permitió que la llevara de vuelta al mundo real. Volvieron a pasar bajo las ramas del abeto y atravesaron el césped. Cuando llegaron a la puerta lateral, Charlie la abrió y dio un paso atrás. Ella cruzó el umbral y se giró hacia él.

Charlie se inclinó sobre su mano en una graciosa reverencia antes de soltársela. Buscó su mirada brevemente.

—Nos veremos mañana por la tarde —dijo a modo de despedida.

Apenas esperó el gesto de asentimiento de la joven antes de darse la vuelta y regresar a grandes zancadas a los establos.

Sarah permaneció en la puerta, observándolo alejarse. Y reflexionó sobre las revelaciones que había tenido ese día. Había muchas cosas que tenía que considerar cuidadosamente.

4

Casleigh, la casa de lord Martin Cynster, era una mansión enorme, una laberíntica casa de campo llena de antigüedades y muebles exquisitos. El martes por la noche, Charlie se movía entre los invitados reunidos en el salón sin fijarse en ninguna de las maravillas que lo rodeaban.

Había pasado casi todo el lunes intentando aclarar sus ideas y reflexionar sobre cómo discurriría su vida una vez que Sarah aceptara casarse con él. Había pensado que pasaría algunos meses en Londres dedicándose a las mismas tareas de siempre, desplazándose al campo de vez en cuando para ver cómo iban el Park y la hacienda. Pero se había dado cuenta de la gran devoción que Sarah sentía por el orfanato y no sabía cómo este hecho encajaría en sus planes. Había reflexionado mucho sobre ello y al final había decidido encarar el problema más adelante.

Después de que Sarah hubiera aceptado ser su esposa.

La impaciencia de Charlie crecía por momentos.

Mientras se detenía a charlar con aquellos invitados que reclamaban su atención esbozando su habitual sonrisa, buscó a Sarah entre la multitud. Sabía que estaba allí, entre la gente. En la cena habían estado sentados uno al lado del otro, pero antes no habían podido estar juntos, ni siquiera cuando ella había llegado con su familia y se habían reunido en la salita habían tenido ocasión de intercambiar una palabra en privado.

Ni cualquier otra cosa.

Aquel beso detrás del establo —un beso provocado por la frustración que él sentía— sólo había servido para fomentar un deseo que no necesitaba ser espoleado.

La oyó reírse. Sin detenerse siquiera a pensar cómo era posible que hubiera reconocido la risa de Sarah en medio de una multitud, siguió la dirección del melodioso sonido hasta que la vio. Estaba parada a un lado de la habitación y le sonreía con dulzura a un caballero que él no conocía.

Se detuvo en seco. Apartándose de los invitados que le rodeaban, Charlie se apoyó en la pared de enfrente y estudió al caballero por encima del mar de cabezas. El hombre le estaba contando algo a Sarah que esa noche iba ataviada con un vestido del mismo color azul que sus ojos. Ella escuchaba al caballero con mucha atención, pero incluso a esa distancia Charlie podía ver que sólo estaba siendo educada y cordial.

Entonces Sarah lo vio.

Charlie no tenía por qué sentirse celoso, gracias a Dios, pero en otras circunstancias se habría puesto en guardia contra aquel caballero. Era... A Charlie le llevó un minuto darse cuenta de que estaba ante un hombre que se parecía muchísimo a él.

Alto, ancho de hombros y con el pecho un poco más musculoso. Aunque aquel hombre era algunos años mayor. Charlie tenía treinta y tres mientras que el hombre debía de rondar los cuarenta. Tenía el pelo un poco más claro y liso, en vez de ondulado como el de Charlie, pero con el mismo matiz dorado.

Sus modales eran, asimismo, confiados, pero parecía más reservado y distante, sin el aire de arrogancia que caracterizaba a la nobleza. Parecía incapaz de mostrar el encanto y la elocuencia de los que Charlie hacía gala.

—¡Aquí estás!

Charlie volvió la cabeza y vio a su hermana mayor —hermanastra para ser más exactos— envuelta en un radiante vestido de seda color ámbar.

Alathea le puso la mano en el brazo, sonrió y, colocándose a su lado, observó la estancia.

—Tengo que hablar contigo —le dijo.

Charlie se puso rígido.

—No te envares. Tengo un par de consejos para ti que no te vendría mal escuchar. Si luego me quieres hacer caso o no, es cosa tuya.

Charlie suspiró para sus adentros. Alathea le llevaba diez años y, casi siempre, era mucho más alarmante hablar con ella que con su madre. Serena era una mujer plácida, mientras que Alathea era todo lo contrario. Pero Charlie jamás podría agradecer todo lo que su hermana había hecho por él en el pasado, algo de lo que ella se aprovechaba cada vez que él se ponía difícil.

—Tú dirás.

—Como parece que por fin te has decidido a escoger esposa, he pensado ahorrarte tiempo y sufrimiento indicándote algunas cuestiones que tú, como hombre que eres, pasarás por alto con esa seguridad que tienes de que el mundo se rige a tu manera.

Charlie se contuvo de fruncir el ceño. Discutir con ella sólo prolongaría su sermón.

—Así me gusta —murmuró Alathea sin apartar la vista de su cara.

Por el rabillo del ojo, Charlie vio que su hermana había arqueado las cejas con arrogancia, como si le hubiera leído el pensamiento. Lo más probable es que lo hubiera hecho. Alathea estaba casada con Gabriel, y Gabriel y él rara vez diferían... salvo en el tema que ella quería discutir.

Charlie se aprestó para la lucha y no dijo nada.

Entrecerrando los ojos, Alathea volvió a mirar a la multitud y continuó hablando:

—Sé que ahora no está de moda, pero en nuestra familia sólo ha habido matrimonios por amor. Y no, no me refiero a los Cynster, a pesar de que a ellos les sucede lo mismo.

Charlie se dio cuenta de que la mirada de su hermana se había clavado en su marido, Gabriel Cynster, que acababa de unirse a Sarah y al caballero desconocido. Resultaba evidente que Gabriel sí conocía al hombre.

—Los hombres de nuestra familia —continuó Alathea— llevan muchos siglos casándose sólo por amor y harías bien en intentar considerar los pros y los contras antes de seguir adelante y romper tal tradición.

Charlie, con la atención fija al otro lado de la habitación, tardó un rato en darse cuenta de que Alathea esperaba una respuesta de su parte.

—Sí, de acuerdo.

Incluso sin mirarla, sabía que su hermana le estaba mirando furiosa.

Charlie la ignoró y le preguntó:

—¿Quién es el caballero que está hablando con Gabriel?

Alathea seguía furiosa, pero siguió la dirección de su mirada y luego se volvió hacia él.

—Es un inversor al que ha invitado Rupert, un tal señor Sinclair. Al parecer piensa invertir en la zona.

Charlie se quedó mirando al grupo formado por Gabriel, Sinclair y Sarah. Prestó especial atención a la sincera sonrisa de Sarah. Desde que Gabriel se había unido a ellos, la joven se había relajado. Charlie entrecerró los ojos.

—¿De veras?

Alathea paseó la mirada del grupo a su hermano. Él seguía sin mirarla; alzó la mano que su hermana le había colocado en la manga y, con un suave apretón, la soltó.

—Discúlpame.

Charlie se abrió paso entre la multitud con determinación.

Alathea lo vio alejarse. Observó cómo rodeaba el grupo para ponerse al lado de Sarah, justo entre Sinclair y ella, separándola de manera deliberada del hombre. Alathea continuó mirando a su hermano mientras Gabriel le presentaba a Sinclair, que le estrechó la mano. Después, Charlie le ofreció el brazo a Sarah, y Alathea estudió con atención la expresión de la joven cuando lo aceptó y la expresión de Charlie cuando, con la mano de Sarah en su brazo, se volvió hacia Sinclair.

Al otro lado de la habitación, Alathea sonrió.

—Vaya, vaya, hermanito. Parece que después de todo no necesitabas mis consejos.

Satisfecha, regresó a sus deberes de anfitriona.

Entretanto, Charlie estaba tan intrigado como parecía estarlo Gabriel con su nuevo vecino. La presentación de su cuñado de «este caballero es el señor Malcolm Sinclair, un inversor del nuevo ferrocarril» había sido suficiente para captar la atención de Charlie. Al parecer, Sinclair había alquilado Finley House, justo a las afueras de Crowcombe, y estaba considerando establecerse de forma permanente en la zona.

—Este lugar me resulta muy tranquilo —dijo Sinclair—. Con esas colinas suaves, los verdes valles y el mar tan cerca.

—Es muy bonito en primavera, cuando los árboles y los setos florecen —dijo Sarah.

—He visto que hay un orfanato en Crowcombe, la granja Quilley, si no me equivoco. —Los ojos color avellana de Sinclair se posaron en la cara de Sarah—. Tengo entendido que es de su propiedad, señorita Conningham.

—Sí —respondió Sarah—. Lo heredé de mi difunta madrina. Tenía gran interés en esa obra.

Sinclair esbozó una sonrisa educada y distante, y cambió de tema. Charlie se sentía más tranquilo ahora que estaba cerca; Sinclair parecía un hombre aburrido, por lo menos para las damas.

Las inversiones, sin embargo, eran otro tema.

Llamó la atención de Sinclair.

—Creo haberlo visto en Watchet en compañía de Skilling, el corredor de fincas.

Sinclair curvó sus delgados labios antes de contestar.

—Ah, sí. Estaba interesado en una parcela, pero Skilling me dijo que usted se me había adelantado.

Charlie sonrió ampliamente. Al indagar en la mirada del otro hombre no encontró nada en su expresión que sugiriera irritación. Dada la reputación de Sinclair como inversor en los nuevos ferrocarriles, sin duda sería interesante saber cuál era su opinión como inversor de la zona.

Naturalmente, Charlie le preguntó al respecto.

—¿Cree que esta zona tiene potencial para nuevas inversiones?

—Como estoy seguro de que ya sabe —dijo Sinclair—, hay muchas probabilidades de que se produzca un incremento sustancial en el mercado de Watchet. La aparición de nuevas fábricas en Taunton y...

Con una sonrisa y una inclinación de cabeza, Gabriel se alejó. Más tarde podría preguntarle a Charlie sobre el tema.

Éste continuó hablando con Sinclair sobre el futuro mercantil de la zona, siempre en términos generales, como suelen hacer los inversores, sin mencionar los proyectos específicos en los que estaba involucrado. No tenía sentido dar información gratuita a la posible competencia. Luego siguieron debatiendo sobre el desarrollo en todo el país. Charlie era consciente de que tenía que averiguar algo más sobre la evolución del ferrocarril, un tema sobre el que Sinclair tenía amplios conocimientos y del que estaba dispuesto a hablar. Aquella conversación, sin embargo, no era del interés de Sarah, que muy pronto dejó de prestar atención.

A pesar de lo mucho que le gustaba disertar con Sinclair, Charlie no podía evitar ser consciente de la presencia de Sarah a su lado. Tenía que centrarse en su cortejo, que seguía sin progresar tal y como él quería.

Si deseaba conseguir algo esa noche, tenía que actuar ya.

Le brindó a Sinclair una amplia sonrisa.

—Me encantaría escuchar más cosas acerca de su experiencia en el mundo del ferrocarril. Creo que tendremos más oportunidades de hablar del tema, ahora que está usted en la zona.

Sinclair ladeó la cabeza.

—Será un placer escuchar su opinión sobre la economía local en cualquier momento. —Desplazó la mirada de Charlie a Sarah e hizo una reverencia—. Señorita Conningham.

Sarah sonrió y se alejaron de Sinclair.

Charlie la condujo a través del salón. Ella le lanzó una mirada llena de curiosidad.

—¿Vamos a alguna parte?

—Sí. —Él bajó la cabeza y le murmuró al oído—: He pensado que deberíamos pasar algún tiempo a solas para seguir conociéndonos.

—Ah. —Ella asintió con la cabeza mientras volvía la mirada al frente. Su tono indicaba que estaba muy dispuesta. La guio a una de las puertas laterales de la sala—. ¿Adónde vamos?

—Ahora lo verás. —El único lugar que les proporcionaría total intimidad era el mirador que había en el jardín, pero aún estaban a finales de febrero y el chal de Sarah era demasiado fino para resguardarla del frío, así que optó por llevarla a una de las salas de la parte trasera de la casa.

Cuando él abrió la puerta, la estancia estaba a oscuras y vacía. Charlie dio un paso atrás para dejar pasar a Sarah, que entró en la sala con decisión. La luz de la luna invernal, fría y plateada, entraba por las ventanas sin cortinas y no tuvieron ningún problema en sortear los muebles.

Sarah se detuvo en medio de la estancia cuando oyó que la puerta se cerraba suavemente a sus espaldas.

—¿De qué te gustaría hablar?

Se dio la vuelta y se encontró entre los brazos de Charlie, que la atrajo hacia su cuerpo. Sin titubear, alzó la cara hacia él al tiempo que Charlie bajaba la cabeza y sus bocas se encontraban a medio camino.

Se rozaron, se acariciaron y luego se fundieron. Sarah abrió los labios y él se aprovechó al instante. Asumió el control y le devoró la boca, si bien la joven no opuso resistencia al beso, sino que, por el contrario, se entregó por completo a aquel apasionado intercambio.

Un beso cada vez más apasionado. Estaba claro que conversar era lo último que Charlie tenía en mente, por lo menos en ese momento.

La exploración de los labios masculinos era diferente ahora. Una comunicación a otro nivel.

Y lo cierto era que ella estaba tan ansiosa como él por saber, aprender y experimentar. Por probar, tentar, sentir y saborear las sutiles complejidades de ese beso, ese increíble frenesí que se apoderaba de ellos cuando se besaban. Cuando ella le ofreció su boca, él la aceptó, la reclamó, profundizando aún más el beso.

Si ella quería conocerlo, saber todo lo que él quería de ella, entonces tenía que aceptar todo esto.

Charlie la sostuvo entre sus brazos y la parte más primitiva de él sintió una oculta satisfacción, se deleitó con todo eso: con ella, con su suavidad, con su fresca inocencia, con su cuerpo flexible y aquellas curvas sensuales que pronto serían suyas. Toda suya.

Unas voces agudas y unas risas burbujeantes los arrancaron de aquel embeleso. Él levantó la cabeza, parpadeó y se apresuró a soltar a Sarah al mismo tiempo que se oía el clic del picaporte y se abría la puerta.

Tres niños entraron corriendo en la salita. Charlie apenas logró contener una maldición.

Clavó los ojos en Sarah y, en medio de la penumbra provocada por la luz de la luna, la vio esbozar una sonrisa.

Aunque los niños le devolvieron la sonrisa, pues todos conocían a Sarah, se detuvieron en seco.

—¡Tío Charlie! —El más pequeño, Henry, de siete años, lo miró con reproche mientras su hermano mayor, Justin, que ya había cumplido los doce, cerraba la puerta—. No has venido a saludarnos, así que hemos estado buscándote por todos lados.

Henry se arrojó sobre Charlie y, rodeándole la cintura con los brazos, le dio un abrazo feroz.

Juliet, de diez años, se puso a dar saltos sobre el sofá.

—La verdad es que te hemos visto escapar del salón y hemos decidido venir a hablar contigo. —Arrugó la nariz y miró a Sarah como si fuera a compartir un gran descubrimiento con ella—: ¡Hay tanto ruido allí dentro que no sé cómo la gente mayor puede pensar siquiera!

Sarah sonrió a la niña e intercambió una mirada con Charlie. Al parecer ninguno de ellos entraba en la categoría de «gente mayor».

Justin cogió una de las manos de Charlie.

—Has traído contigo a ese par de caballos grises, ¿verdad? —dijo clavando los ojos grises en la cara de Charlie—. Jeremy dijo que creía que lo harías. ¿Nos dejarás guiarlos?

Charlie bajó la mirada a las caras respingonas de sus sobrinos; Henry también le miraba con los ojos redondos y suplicantes.

—No. —Les dio tiempo para que asimilaran la rotunda respuesta y luego les prometió—: Pero si sois buenos, puede que os lleve conmigo a dar un paseo en el cabriolé.

—¡Sí! ¡Oh, sí! —Ambos niños, cada uno agarrado de una mano de Charlie, comenzaron a saltar, alborozados.

—¡Yo también quiero! —Juliet dio aún más saltos en el sofá.

—Muy bien. —Charlie intentó retomar las riendas de la conversación—. Ahora...

—¿Adónde iremos? —preguntó Justin.

—¡A Watchet! —suplicó Henry.

—No... a la cascada —dijo Juliet—. Es más bonito.

—¿Por qué no a Taunton? —sugirió Justin—. Podríamos ver las vías del ferrocarril que llegan hasta Londres.

Se desarrolló entonces un animado debate sobre cuál era la mejor sugerencia de todas. Charlie intentó intervenir, ejercer algún tipo de autoridad, pero le resultó imposible.

Miró a Sarah. La joven se había sentado en el brazo del sofá y los observaba a él y a sus tres acosadores. Bajo la tenue luz de la estancia, Charlie no podía verle los ojos, pero por su expresión sabía que se estaba divirtiendo.

En sus labios, de un rosa suave bajo la luz de la luna, asomaba una sonrisa.

Charlie se los quedó mirando, y sintió un abrumador deseo de besarla.

Volviendo a prestar atención a los niños, Charlie levantó las manos.

—¡Basta! Os prometo que traeré mis caballos grises y os llevaré a dar un paseo antes de que regrese a Londres, pero no será hasta la semana que viene, así que mientras tanto podéis decidir adónde queréis ir. —Los condujo hacia la puerta. Los niños habían conseguido su propósito, así que no opusieron ninguna resistencia.

Charlie abrió la puerta y los empujó al pasillo. Justin y Henry salieron sin demora, hablando todavía de caballos. Charlie agradeció para sus adentros que aún fueran demasiado jóvenes para preguntarse qué habían estado haciendo Sarah y él en la salita a solas, pero Juliet captó su atención cuando pasó por su lado.

Los ojos de su sobrina chispearon mientras le dirigía una sonrisa burlona.

Charlie contuvo el aliento, pero la niña salió detrás de sus hermanos después de brindarle esa engreída sonrisa, típicamente femenina.

Charlie lanzó un suspiro y comenzó a cerrar la puerta mientras oía los inconfundibles sonidos de los niños, que se dirigían al vestíbulo principal.

Tras cerrarla, se quedó mirando el panel de madera. Gracias a sus sobrinos y a su pícara sobrina, Sarah y él se habían quedado sin tiempo.

Se dio la vuelta y se la encontró a su lado.

A través de la penumbra la vio sonreír, relajada y segura.

—Deberíamos regresar.

Aunque oyó las palabras, sólo pudo prestar atención a los seductores y tentadores labios de la joven. No podía volver a la fiesta sin saborearlos una vez más.

Charlie le enmarcó la cara entre las manos. No confiaba en sí mismo; sabía que si la tomaba entre sus brazos no se conformaría con un simple beso. Alzando la cara de Sarah la miró directamente a los ojos.

La mirada de la joven era serena cuando él inclinó la cabeza y la saboreó con un beso que era un vivo reflejo de adónde quería llegar; un beso que le estremecía los huesos y le hacía perder el control.

Automáticamente, dio un paso atrás y se obligó a soltarle la cara.

Esperó a que ella enfocara la mirada y recuperara la respiración antes de girar el picaporte.

—Sí. Tenemos que regresar.

La frustración tenía garras afiladas.

Le había arañado antes, pero no hasta el punto de desgarrarle las entrañas.

Esa misma noche, Charlie se paseaba de arriba abajo por la biblioteca en penumbra de Morwellan Park, con una copa de brandy en la mano y la cabeza cargada de preguntas. ¿Cuánto tiempo más podría aguantar antes de reclamar a Sarah? ¿A cuántas reuniones sociales más tendría que asistir? ¿Cuántas interrupciones imprevistas tendría que soportar?

Aún no había comenzado la temporada social y, a falta de algo mejor, las anfitrionas locales se dedicaban a organizar una fiesta tras otra. A Charlie siempre le había parecido una buena costumbre, una prueba para las jóvenes debutantes antes de que fueran presentadas en sociedad.

Y, sin duda, seguía pensándolo, pero eso suponía tener que aceptar un montón de invitaciones a bailes, cenas y fiestas adonde Sarah y él tendrían que asistir por separado.

En la ciudad, Charlie consideraría tales acontecimientos como perfectas oportunidades para alcanzar su objetivo. En el campo, sin embargo, no servirían para nada más que para perder el tiempo. Las casas eran demasiado pequeñas, y los invitados, escasos. Sarah y él no podían esfumarse más tiempo del debido sin faltar al decoro. Sólo había que ver lo que había pasado en Casleigh. A pesar de ser la mansión más grande del distrito, no había podido robar más que unos insignificantes minutos.

Deteniéndose ante la chimenea, clavó la mirada en las ascuas.

Quería que Sarah se casara con él. Y quería que lo hiciera tan pronto como fuera posible. No le gustaba tener que perder el tiempo, incluso aunque hubiera aceptado un período de cortejo.

Ella era la mujer indicada, no tenía ninguna duda al respecto. Tenía que idear un plan, si quería que Sarah aceptara de una vez su propuesta, y por qué no, en menos de una semana.

Tomó un sorbo de brandy y clavó la mirada en las diminutas llamas mientras una idea comenzaba a germinar en su cabeza. La determinación se reflejó en su rostro.

Sarah aceptaría casarse con él antes de la noche del martes siguiente.

Era un reto.

Y si algo tenía claro Charlie es que siempre había disfrutado con los retos.

El tiempo y el lugar eran los primeros obstáculos que debía sortear, pensó Charlie mientras se despedía de lady Conningham, Sarah, Clary y Gloria. Había sido una visita más que correcta. Se había pasado media hora charlando con ellas sobre problemas locales.

—¿Podría —le preguntó a lady Conningham después de lanzarle una mirada a su hija mayor— dejar que Sarah me acompañe a los establos?

Y lady Conningham, por supuesto, consintió. Sonriendo, Charlie tomó la mano de Sarah. La joven lo acompañó de buena gana con una mirada ansiosa en la cara.

Al sostenerle la puerta para que pasara, Charlie lanzó una mirada por encima del hombro a las hermanas de Sarah. Hizo una mueca para sus adentros. Clary y Gloria se habían dado cuenta. Tenían los ojos muy abiertos y cargados de preguntas, pero no dijeron nada.

Cerrando la puerta a esas miradas ávidas e inquisitivas, Charlie se dijo que despertar la curiosidad de las hermanas de Sarah había sido inevitable desde el principio. Al menos esperaba que lady Conningham ejerciera la autoridad suficiente para mantenerlas a raya.

Sarah lo condujo a una puerta lateral y salieron al césped. El sol de la tarde se reflejaba en los establos.

Al caminar hacia ellos, Charlie la cogió del brazo.

—¿Te gustaría dar un paseo más largo?

Ella sonrió con deleite; él acababa de contestar a una pregunta no formulada.

—Sí, por supuesto. —Echó un vistazo a su alrededor—. ¿Adónde vamos? Mi madre no podrá contener a Clary y a Gloria por mucho tiempo.

—En ese caso, será mejor que desaparezcamos. —Charlie le señaló el camino que conducía al riachuelo que discurría a corta distancia.

Sarah asintió. Él le ofreció el brazo y ella enlazó la mano en su codo. Cruzaron el césped hacia el camino lleno de rododendros y muy pronto perdieron la casa de vista.

Al llegar a la primera curva, continuaron avanzando por el camino, siguiendo el curso de la corriente.

—Supongo que asistirás a la cena de lady Cruikshank esta noche, ¿no? —Sarah lo miró—. Habrá mucha gente.

—En efecto. —Charlie miró al frente. Si no le fallaba la memoria, justo un poco más allá de la siguiente curva, el riachuelo desembocaba en una presa, bordeada por el camino. En el centro había un cenador de madera pintado de blanco, justo al abrigo de una loma. Lo recordaba de su niñez, cuando su madre y la de Sarah se habían sentado en el cenador para observar a sus hijos jugar en el agua poco profunda del embalse o, en su caso, pescar—. Y, por supuesto, estaré allí esta noche.

Un grupo de árboles y arbustos bloqueaban el paisaje delante de ellos. Vieron el cenador al doblar la siguiente curva.

Charlie sonrió y condujo a Sarah hacia allí.

—Pero como ya hemos comprobado, intentar pasar un tiempo a solas para llegar a conocernos mejor no resulta fácil en esta época del año.

—En especial para ti. —Cuando Charlie le dirigió una mirada ligeramente ceñuda, Sarah sonrió y miró hacia delante—. Ahora eres el conde. Las obligaciones del heredero del título no son las mismas que las del propio conde... Ahora no podrás evitar algunas reuniones. Por lo menos no podrás hacerlo mientras no te cases, ni mientras el resto de los caballeros no conozcan tu opinión sobre diversos temas.

Él hizo una mueca.

—Cierto. —Aunque era conde desde hacía tres años, no había pasado demasiado tiempo en el campo; para muchos de los hacendados del distrito, él era un completo desconocido.

—En cualquier caso... —Charlie miró hacia delante—, eso nos lleva al tema del que quería hablar.

Subieron por los escalones del cenador.

Charlie miró a su alrededor y se relajó. Aquel lugar era perfecto. Las contraventanas de madera, de cara a la loma y los árboles, estaban cerradas y bloqueaban la vista del interior. Los arcos abovedados se abrían a la presa, donde el agua reflejaba el color grisáceo de las nubes. En verano se podía disfrutar de una brisa fresca, mientras que, en invierno, el cenador quedaba protegido del viento por la colina y los árboles que lo rodeaban. Ahora, sin embargo, el aire era cálido y suave, gracias al sol de la tarde.

Sarah se soltó de su brazo y caminó hasta el sofá de mimbre con un cojín acolchado a juego con los de los sillones que tenía a ambos lados, todos de cara al paisaje.

Para Charlie no había un lugar más íntimo que ése. Estaba oculto de la casa por los jardines, y en esa época del año era poco probable que alguien se acercara hasta allí.

Charlie siguió a Sarah al interior del cenador y observó que todo estaba limpio y cuidado. No había hojarasca en el suelo ni telarañas en el techo.

Sarah se había detenido justo delante del sofá y examinaba el paisaje. Charlie se paró a su lado, mirándola a la cara. Tras un momento, la joven giró la cabeza y lo miró a los ojos, luego arqueó una ceja inquisitivamente.

Charlie la giró hacia él y la rodeó con los brazos. Ella se dejó abrazar, sin dudas ni vacilaciones. Bajó la mirada a su rostro y la observó durante un momento, entonces inclinó la cabeza y la besó.

Fue un beso largo y profundo. Mientras pasaban los minutos, Charlie permitió que el deseo creciera para aplacar la curiosidad de la joven. Luego, con un gran esfuerzo, se obligó a interrumpir el beso, levantó la cabeza y murmuró:

—No nos van a quitar el ojo de encima. Todas las matronas y las jovencitas... incluso los caballeros. Al igual que tus hermanas, empiezan a sospechar algo y, al no haber hecho ningún anuncio por nuestra parte, seguirán con avidez cada uno de nuestros movimientos.

Sarah aceptó a regañadientes que él no volvería a besarla, al menos por el momento. Abrió los ojos y buscó la suave mirada azul que tantas veces le había ocultado sus pensamientos. No era fácil saber lo que Charlie pensaba.

—Me pediste un período de cortejo —continuó él—, para llegar a conocernos mejor, pero nuestros compromisos sociales nos tienen realmente atados.

Por un instante, Sarah se preguntó si él iba a pedirle que tomara una decisión en ese mismo momento, antes de que terminaran las dos semanas de gracia, pero antes de que pudiera sentirse presa del pánico, pues seguía sin saber qué le iba a responder, él continuó hablando:

—Podemos aceptar esas restricciones o podemos sortearlas.

El alivio de Sarah fue evidente.

—¿Y cómo lo hacemos? —Incluso ella notó la ansiedad en sus palabras.

Charlie sonrió.

—Muy sencillo. Nos reuniremos aquí. —Señaló el lugar que les rodeaba y luego bajó la mirada a los labios de la joven—. Todas las noches. Después de la fiesta a la que hayamos asistido, vendremos al cenador para pasar algún tiempo los dos solos. Los dos queremos, necesitamos, llegar a conocernos mejor, y sólo podremos hacerlo en la intimidad de este lugar, por la noche... si tú quieres.

Él la miró a los ojos.

—¿Vendrás? ¿Querrás reunirte aquí conmigo todas las noches, hasta que me conozcas lo suficientemente bien para darme una respuesta? —Ella parpadeó y él continuó hablando—: ¿Vendrás esta noche después de la cena de lady Cruikshank?

—Sí. —Sarah no tenía ninguna duda. Para dejarlo claro, añadió—: Vendré esta noche después de la cena de lady Cruikshank, y todas las noches, hasta que pueda darte mi respuesta.

La sonrisa de Charlie fue ligeramente triunfal. Sarah lo notó, pero entonces él la estrechó entre sus brazos y la besó de nuevo.

Otro beso adictivo, excitante y placentero, aunque extrañamente incompleto. Cuando él lo interrumpió, Sarah tuvo que contenerse para no agarrarlo y atraerlo de nuevo hacia sí, para exigirle algo que desconocía. Lo que seguía a aquel beso, pero ¿qué era?

Ésa era una de las cosas indefinibles que necesitaba saber.

Charlie la miró a los ojos y pareció satisfecho con lo que vio en ellos.

—Tenemos que regresar a los establos o tus hermanas comenzarán a buscarnos. —La soltó, pero le cogió una mano y se la llevó a los labios—. Hasta esta noche —dijo esbozando una sonrisa.

—Hasta entonces —respondió ella con otra sonrisa.

5

Esa misma noche, Charlie ató a *Tormenta* en el límite de los jardines de Conningham Manor, luego avanzó resueltamente por un estrecho sendero que conectaba con el camino que seguía el riachuelo. Las nubes atravesaban con rapidez el cielo, y la luna asomaba entre ellas intermitentemente, brillando un momento para desaparecer al siguiente, dejando el camino sumido en profundas sombras.

Consciente de la creciente tensión y de la crispación que atribuía a la impaciencia por conducir el cortejo en la dirección que quería, Charlie rezó con la intención de que Sarah no se asustara de la oscuridad y no se dejara disuadir por las sombras cambiantes.

Charlie llegó al cenador, subió las escaleras... y la vio. Sarah le estaba esperando, otra vez, delante del sofá. Debía de haberle visto llegar, pues no se sorprendió cuando se acercó a ella, sino que sonrió y le tendió las manos.

Él se las cogió, notando la suavidad de su piel y la delicadeza de sus huesos entre los dedos. Luego le puso las manos en sus propios hombros y deslizó las suyas a la cintura de la joven para atraerla hacia sí, abrazándola, aunque sin llegar a estrecharla contra su cuerpo. Bajó la cabeza y le cubrió los labios con los suyos, saboreando la sorpresa de la joven ante aquel primer estremecimiento sensual que provocaban sus cuerpos al tocarse desde el pecho hasta las caderas y los muslos.

Sarah recobró el aliento física y mentalmente. Se sentía mareada y le daba vueltas la cabeza, pero tenía que evitar abandonarse a esas sensaciones; si quería aprender todo lo que necesitaba saber de ese encuentro, tenía que recuperar el sentido.

Aprendería de ése y de los siguientes encuentros. Del beso de Charlie, esa comunión de bocas que ya no era ni remotamente inocente; de su abrazo, diferente esa noche, pues, aunque él dejó las manos en su cintura, podía sentir la fuerza masculina que le rodeaba, intensa y tentadoramente peligrosa.

Sarah le deslizó las manos por los hombros. Al sentir los marcados músculos bajo las palmas, tensó los dedos, deleitándose con aquella cálida dureza. Luego continuó deslizando las manos por la firme columna de su cuello y le acarició la nuca. Extendió los dedos y se los pasó por el pelo.

Fascinada, tocó los espesos mechones, estremeciéndose ante la sedosa textura y la manera en que él reaccionaba a su contacto. Continuó disfrutando del beso y de él, enardecida por su propio atrevimiento.

Sarah sabía lo que quería, y quería más. Quería que él le enseñara todo, que le permitiera ver qué había más allá de aquel deseo que era tan nuevo para ella. Así que le devolvió el beso con firmeza, exigiéndole, invitándolo a una mayor exploración. Charlie vaciló un instante antes de aceptar el reto, de volver a tomar las riendas y hacerse con el control.

La arrastró hacia algo más cálido y urgente.

La besó larga, profunda e insinuantemente hasta que el calor la abrumó, amenazando con derretirle los huesos y hacerle perder el sentido. Hasta que no pudo pensar, hasta que se le enrojeció la piel y sintió el cuerpo insoportablemente lánguido e indescriptiblemente tenso a la vez.

Expectante.

Aunque sin saber qué esperaba.

Charlie se recordó a sí mismo que Sarah era inocente, en todo el sentido de la palabra. No sabía qué ansiaba, ni a lo que lo invitaba cuando le acariciaba la lengua atrevidamente con la suya una y otra vez.

Todas las respuestas de la joven por tentadoras que fueran eran instintivas, poseían ese toque de frescura tan adictivo que él asociaba ahora con ella. Sarah era diferente a cualquier mujer que él hubiera conocido, distinta a todas aquellas con las que había adquirido su experiencia. Y es que, a diferencia de todas las demás, ella poseía el sabor de la inocencia.

Charlie jamás había esperado encontrar ese sabor tan adictivo y excitante.

Tan intensamente atrayente que tenía que luchar —con todas sus fuerzas— contra sus deseos, contra el fuerte instinto de tomarla entre sus brazos, tenderla sobre el sofá y...

Pero no era ése su objetivo, al menos, no esa noche. Se repitió a sí mismo que esa noche, y las siguientes, tenía que dedicarlas a un largo asedio. Tácticas y estrategias que inclinaran la balanza a su favor. Sarah tenía algo que él quería y esa noche le estaba mostrando lo que estaba dispuesto a pagar por ello.

Así que, inteligentemente, se limitó a sujetarla por la cintura en vez de dejarse tentar para tomarla entre sus brazos; esa noche no pretendía estrecharla contra su cuerpo... todavía no. No hasta que ella estuviera preparada, no hasta que Sarah anhelara el contacto con un deseo superior al suyo.

Continuó besándola provocativamente, con tal firmeza y pasión que Sarah se vio obligada a aferrarse a sus hombros, a hundirle los dedos en el pelo, hasta que su cuerpo estuvo cálido, flexible y anhelante.

Charlie puso fin al beso. Si bien tuvo que recurrir a toda su fuerza de voluntad, se mantuvo firme en su propósito y se apartó de los labios de Sarah. Sintió el aliento femenino sobre el suyo y luchó contra el deseo de volver a hundirse en aquella deliciosa boca y saborearla de nuevo.

Maldijo para sus adentros. Lo haría pronto, pero no esa noche. Esa noche...

Charlie se obligó a levantar la cabeza.

—Es suficiente.

No estuvo seguro de a quién se lo decía, si a ella o a sí mismo. Esperó a que Sarah abriera los párpados y a que la aturdida neblina se desvaneciera de sus ojos. La joven parpadeó y enfocó la vista en la cara de él. Lo observó intentando leerle el pensamiento. Charlie hubiera sonreído para tranquilizarla, pero tenía los rasgos tensos.

—Es tarde. —Apartó las manos de la cintura de Sarah y, a regañadientes, renunció a la sensación que provocaba el suave y flexible cuerpo de la joven contra sus palmas—. Vamos. Te acompañaré de vuelta a casa.

A Sarah le resultó difícil concentrarse al día siguiente, sobre todo por la noche, pues era complicado estar con Charlie y sentir su impaciencia ante el próximo encuentro en el cenador, ya que eso alimentaba la propia impaciencia de la joven.

La velada pareció alargarse eternamente mientras el padre de Sarah ejercía de anfitrión para los hacendados de la zona, a los que había invitado a cenar para hablar sobre las cacerías locales. Cuando los caballeros se reunieron finalmente con las damas en la salita, la frustración de Sarah había alcanzado límites insoportables. Mientras sus vecinos hablaban a su alrededor, la joven mantuvo una sonrisa dulce en la cara y se las arregló para charlar educadamente cuando todo lo que sentía era una molesta irritación.

Al final se fueron todos, incluido Charlie. Al estar rodeados de gente en el momento de la despedida, Sarah no tuvo oportunidad de preguntarle si tenía intención de ir a su casa y regresar luego o si, por el contrario, guiaría al par de castrados grises hasta el embalse, campo a través. Cuando subió las escaleras detrás de su madre, Sarah sopesó el tiempo y la distancia en el caso de que él dejara sus preciosos caballos en un campo, pero no estaba segura de a qué hora debía esperarlo o cuándo llegaría él al cenador.

De lo que sí estaba segura era de que iría. Sabía que él acudiría en algún momento de la noche y que ella podría seguir aprendiendo, si no todo, sí un poco más.

Al llegar a su dormitorio, Sarah envió a su doncella, Gwen, a dormir, y se quitó con pesar su bonito traje de seda sustituyéndolo por un viejo y sencillo vestido. Si por casualidad alguien la descubría en los jardines a altas horas de la noche, podría alegar que había sido incapaz de conciliar el sueño y que había decidido dar un corto paseo.

Cogió un chal de lana a juego y sopló la vela antes de sentarse ante la lumbre a esperar a que sus padres se fueran a la cama y la casa se quedara en silencio.

Media hora después, se levantó y salió a hurtadillas de la habitación sin que nadie se diera cuenta. Bajó por las escaleras de servicio y salió por la puerta lateral de la casa. Cruzó el césped con sigilo, refugiándose entre las sombras.

En cuanto llegó al camino y estuvo fuera de la vista de la casa, Sarah apretó el paso. Se acomodó el chal sobre los hombros y se permitió pensar en la noche que la aguardaba.

Literal y figuradamente.

Después de la noche anterior, Sarah había regresado a su habitación, se había metido en la cama y, contrariamente a lo que esperaba, se había sumido en un profundo sueño. Pero había tenido todo el día para reflexionar sobre las acciones de Charlie y el plan que éste había trazado. Parecía evidente que él pensaba tentarla con el deseo para que aceptara casarse con él, prometiéndole pasión y todo lo que eso conllevaba.

¿Por qué si no se había detenido cuando la había besado? ¿Por qué si no había establecido un límite antes de llegar a un punto revelador? Sarah había notado cómo Charlie se contenía, la implacable fuerza de voluntad que había utilizado para detenerse cuando lo había hecho. Él no había interrumpido aquel beso porque hubiera querido, sino porque era lo que se había propuesto.

Puede que ella no estuviera de acuerdo por completo con ese plan, pero tampoco le disgustaba.

No era tan inocente como para no darse cuenta de que él podía hacerla desear la urgente necesidad de experimentar el placer final hasta el punto de aceptar casarse con él sin saber si la amaba o no. Sabía que corría un gran riesgo al someterse a los planes de Charlie, pero aun así merecía la pena arriesgarse con tal de aprender todo lo que necesitaba saber. El plan de Charlie —que en esencia consistía en seducirla para que se casara con él— la ayudaría a obtener lo que quería: saber por qué él estaba tan empeñado en casarse con ella y no con otra.

Sarah se lo había preguntado, pero en realidad él no le había respondido. Se había limitado a darle todas las razones convencionales, pero éstas no eran suficientes para ella y, lo que era aún más importante, estaba segura de que no eran esas razones lo que le había impulsado a pedirla en matrimonio.

Charlie podía haber elegido a la mujer que quisiera, a cualquier joven debutante de la sociedad, pero la había elegido a ella. Y a pesar de la renuencia de la joven, de su insistencia en ser cortejada —negándose a seguir dócilmente los planes originales del conde—, él seguía en sus trece, más decidido que nunca a casarse con ella.

Lo que podía ser un buen augurio o una prueba contundente de la costumbre que tenía Charlie de imponer su santa voluntad.

De una manera u otra, si seguía el plan de Charlie, Sarah descubriría la verdad: por qué la deseaba a ella.

Al doblar la curva del camino, vio que Charlie la estaba esperando en el cenador.

Percibió su alta figura moviéndose entre las sombras, apartándose de la columna tallada contra la que había estado apoyado. Inspirando profundamente, la joven se cogió las faldas y subió los escalones.

De nuevo se encontraron ante el sofá. Él le tendió la mano para que se acercara. Sarah la tomó y fue consciente de la fuerza con la que la asía.

La atrajo hacia sí con suavidad. Le alzó la mano y le besó suavemente el dorso de los dedos. Luego, capturando la mirada de la joven con la suya, le giró la mano y le posó los labios en el interior de la muñeca.

A Sarah le dio un brinco el corazón.

No había necesidad de hablar, los dos sabían por qué estaban allí.

Los cálidos labios de Charlie recorrieron la cara interior del desnudo antebrazo de Sarah, provocando una miríada de sensaciones que no eran más que un preludio, una advertencia sensual. Luego él le alzó la mano a su propio hombro y la acercó a su cuerpo.

Pero a diferencia de la noche anterior, la rodeó con su brazo, manteniéndola presa mientras inclinaba la cabeza. Sarah alzó la cara con ansia y buscó los labios de Charlie con los suyos.

La joven sonrió para sus adentros, saboreando la firme presión de los labios masculinos, y cedió a la clara exigencia, ofreciéndole su boca. Se dejó llevar por los sentidos, notando la creciente llamarada de deseo, en sí misma y en él.

Habían bailado un vals juntos sólo una vez, hacía muchos meses; éste era un vals diferente, donde los sentidos de ambos giraban a un ritmo frenético al compás de las sensaciones: el profundo roce de la lengua de Charlie contra la suya, los estremecimientos de ella, el redoblar creciente de sus corazones.

Notando la tensión de los dedos de Charlie en su espalda, Sarah supo que le costaba mantener el control.

Totalmente embelesada, la joven saboreó la sensual y familiar pasión de su beso, y se dejó llevar por él.

Sarah era totalmente consciente de Charlie, de los labios, las manos y el cuerpo masculino; de la flagrante promesa que conllevaba aquel abrazo, pero se había vuelto insensible al mundo que les rodeaba, a las profundas sombras más allá de sus brazos, a los suaves sonidos de la noche más allá del cenador, al murmullo distante del agua en el embalse.

Aquí y ahora, con él, el mundo se había reducido a los sentidos. A la siguiente fase del plan.

Sarah se estremeció presa de una agitada y fría expectación, de un creciente anhelo que ahora sabía que era deseo.

Charlie aceptó la respuesta de Sarah mientras se hundía en los sensuales placeres de su boca. Sintió su delicado y tembloroso suspiro cuando le deslizó la mano bajo el chal, subiéndola desde la cintura hasta la curva exterior de un pecho.

Sarah sintió un escalofrío, una respuesta que incitaba e invitaba a Charlie a tocarla y acariciarla, y eso hizo. La acarició suavemente, rozando las curvas plenas de la joven hasta que ella ardió y deseó más. Sólo entonces él se apoderó de su pecho, curvando la mano sobre el firme montículo y apretándolo con suavidad antes de comenzar a amasarlo provocadoramente.

Sarah profundizó aún más el beso. Una vez más le agarró la cabeza y le enredó los dedos en el pelo, arqueándose contra el brazo con el que Charlie la sujetaba, presionando su pecho contra la mano masculina, ofreciéndoselo e invitándolo, incluso exigiéndole más atenciones. El movimiento provocó que las caderas de la joven se apretaran contra los muslos masculinos.

Un movimiento que lo pilló desprevenido, haciéndolo arder cuando todavía no quería arder. Por un momento, Charlie dudó, luego volvió a zambullirse en el beso, conteniendo a sus recién despertados demonios el tiempo suficiente para capturar el aliento de la joven.

¿Desde cuándo una joven inocente podía doblegar su voluntad, conduciéndolo a un mundo húmedo y ardiente que sólo conocían las mujeres más experimentadas de la sociedad? La parte más racional de Charlie se burló ante su falta de confianza, que volvió a centrarse en los deleites de aquella deliciosa boca. La estrechó con más fuerza contra su cuerpo, resuelto a retomar el control y a seguir adelante con su plan.

Respondiendo a la clara invitación de Sarah, describió círculos con los dedos sobre su pecho, hasta llegar a rozarle suavemente el pezón, que se irguió y tensó todavía más. Charlie lo oprimió, provocando que la joven jadeara y se aferrara a él, no sólo física sino mentalmente, atrapada por las redes del deseo y el placer.

Pero aquello no era suficiente. La parte racional de Charlie volvió a entrometerse, recordándole que ella no había resultado ser tan maleable como él había esperado. Si quería tener éxito, conducirla a una pasión más profunda y adictiva, aquello no era demasiado sensato.

Pero dado que pensaba ganar —obtener su mano y casarse con ella—, no había razón, ni social ni moral, que le prohibiera mostrarle un poco más.

Mientras seguía esa línea de razonamiento, Charlie era consciente —más que consciente— de que el primitivo impulso de tocarla no era por el bien de Sarah, sino por el suyo propio.

No era para deleitar los sentidos anhelantes de ella, sino los de él.

Cuando sus dedos encontraron los botones del corpiño, no podía pensar en otra cosa que no fuera la apremiante necesidad de tocarla y de satisfacer su propia necesidad.

La distrajo sumergiéndola en un beso más acalorado, en un breve duelo de lenguas que les hizo perder la cabeza a los dos. El vestido de la joven estaba muy usado y los botones se abrieron con facilidad.

Cuando el corpiño estuvo totalmente abierto, él apartó la tela e introdujo la mano debajo.

Ella se quedó sin aliento ante aquel ardiente beso, pero entonces él colocó la palma sobre la fina seda de la camisola que cubría la cálida piel aún más sedosa de la joven. Sarah se quedó paralizada. Se estremeció. Se tensó bajo la caricia suave pero insistente, hasta que él encontró la cinta que buscaba y tiró de ella.

La cinta se desató.

Con un experto movimiento, él bajó la camisola sobre el tenso pezón y, de repente, el seno de Sarah le llenó la mano.

Piel contra piel. Provocando una sensación cálida y ardiente.

Una dulce sensación los desbordó a ambos. Guiado por el instinto, Charlie cerró la mano suave pero posesivamente sobre su anhelante seno.

Una pasión voraz se apoderó de sus sentidos.

Una pasión ardiente que también atravesó a Sarah, que sentía que se derretía al ser asaltada por dos frentes: la caricia en el pecho y aquel beso embriagador.

Se hundió contra él con total abandono, con una promesa y una flagrante invitación.

Sarah lo deseaba tanto como él la deseaba a ella. Cada instintiva respuesta de la joven se lo gritaba a su inservible y chamuscado cerebro.

El pecho de Sarah, pesado e hinchado, le quemaba la palma y el pezón se erguía como un cálido abalorio, uno que su boca se moría por saborear.

Charlie se sentía mareado, borracho de sensaciones. La joven era suave y seductora, cálida y maleable entre sus brazos. Era casi como si estuviera abrazando una llama ardiente, una criatura sensual y elemental que lo embrujaba con su pasión.

Que lo sumergía en ella.

Charlie bebía del fuego de Sarah, lo sorbía gustosamente de sus labios hambrientos. Cuando ella se arqueó contra él, sintió que lo envolvían las llamas, que se extendían rápida y ávidamente por su cuerpo, por debajo de su piel, uniéndose a su propio fuego interior.

Tensó el brazo con el que rodeaba la espalda de Sarah para alzarla y tenderla sobre el sofá que tenía a su espalda, pero, finalmente, su parte racional recuperó el sentido común, y se detuvo.

No se enfrió. Todavía ardía, muerto de deseo por ella. Algo en el interior de Charlie se enfureció contra el control que estaba ejerciendo, pero seguir adelante no formaba parte de su plan.

Casi había descarrilado; como una de esas nuevas locomotoras a las que pensaba seguir la pista. Y como una locomotora desbocada, tuvo que hacer un gran esfuerzo para dar marcha atrás y recapacitar.

Si quería ceñirse a su plan, tenía que ponerle fin a todo aquello en ese mismo momento.

Antes de que la pasión de ella amenazara con abrumarlo de nuevo.

Se obligó a quitar la mano del pecho de Sarah. Y aunque no pudo ocultar su renuencia, intentó disimularla bajo su acostumbrado control, como si retirarse fuera lo que realmente quisiera hacer.

Arrancada de las fogosas profundidades que habían estado explorando —en perfecta armonía, según ella—, Sarah parpadeó mentalmente, pero cuando Charlie apartó la mano de su pecho, cuando la liberó de su abrazo, se dio cuenta de que él no tenía intención de que siguieran estando en perfecta sintonía.

La analogía era acertada; Sarah se sentía infeliz y decepcionada, como si le hubieran puesto un pastel delante de las narices, y luego se lo hubieran quitado de las manos.

Sarah sintió que una extraña rabia crecía en su interior cuando él —aunque fuera con evidente renuencia— levantó la cabeza y rompió el beso, y mientras, ella se pasaba la lengua por los labios, abría los ojos y observaba la cara en sombras de Charlie.

Estudió el rostro masculino. Charlie tenía la mirada baja mientras le abrochaba los botones del corpiño. No se movió para ayudarle, pero examinó los planos angulosos de sus mejillas y de su frente, la línea firme de su mandíbula.

Cada uno de sus rasgos parecía más duro, más agudo. La respiración de Charlie, aunque no era tan agitada como la suya, tampoco era regular.

Sarah no lo hubiera imaginado. Charlie había estado tan excitado como ella, tan estremecido de placer como ella, pero, por supuesto, había sido él quien se había retirado.

Ése era el plan de Charlie. Sarah resistió el impulso de mirarle con los ojos entrecerrados. Se mordió la lengua para no decirle que sabía lo que pretendía hacer. Se tranquilizó mientras él le abrochaba el último botón y dejaba caer las manos lentamente. Se aseguró a sí misma que lo mejor era dejar que siguiera con su plan, mientras ella urdía el suyo propio.

Había surgido algo entre ellos que, durante al menos un momento, le había arrebatado el control. Saberlo la hizo sonreír con suficiencia justo cuando él levantaba la mirada hacia los ojos de la joven.

—Eso ha sido... —Para sorpresa de la propia Sarah la voz le salió demasiado ronca. Había estado afónica en alguna ocasión, pero jamás había oído semejante tono en su voz. Se aclaró la garganta y alzó la barbilla—. Iba a decir que ha sido placentero, pero hubiera sido una descripción tan pobre que quizás es mejor no decir nada.

Él sonrió ampliamente, pareciendo más joven de lo que era, y de repente se vieron envueltos por una brisa fresca. Charlie miró el embalse detrás de ella. Sarah se volvió y sintió la brisa nocturna como nunca antes la había sentido, unos dedos fríos que le rozaban la cálida piel.

La sensación le trajo recuerdos. Se estremeció más por el placer evocador que por el frío.

—Vamos —dijo él a su espalda—. Te acompañaré a casa.

Le subió el chal desde los codos hasta los hombros. Con una inclinación de la cabeza, ella se lo ajustó y luego le dio la mano.

Él cerró los dedos en torno a los de ella, engulléndole la mano.

Sin una palabra más, caminaron de regreso a la casa.

Para su sorpresa, Sarah volvió a dormir como un tronco.

Se despertó tarde y luego tuvo que darse prisa. Debido al apuro con el que tuvo que arreglarse y dirigirse al almuerzo de lady Farthingale en Gilmore, no tuvo tiempo para meditar sobre lo que había sucedido la noche anterior antes de entrar en la salita de lady Farthingale y ver a Charlie.

Cuando ella llegó, él ya estaba charlando con la señora Considine al lado de la chimenea. No había imaginado que él estaría allí, no en aquella reunión, y Sarah tuvo que obligarse a no mirarlo fijamente.

El hecho de que las matronas asistentes y sus hijas la miraran con avidez fue de mucha ayuda. Resultaba evidente que todos suponían que Charlie la estaba cortejando, aunque no hubiera habido ningún anuncio oficial.

Junto a la chimenea, Charlie notó la expectación que se había creado a su alrededor y se giró. Las miradas de ambos se encontraron, pero los dos mantuvieron las formas, luego, él curvó los labios dándole la bienvenida y le tendió la mano.

Abandonando a su madre y a sus hermanas para que se unieran al grupo que eligieran, Sarah se acercó a él, rezando para que el sobresalto de sus sentidos no fuera tan evidente.

Charlie le tomó la mano y le hizo una educada reverencia. El roce de sus dedos provocó que a Sarah se le disparara el corazón. Él le sostuvo la mirada mientras se enderezaba, luego colocó la mano de la joven sobre su manga y se volvió hacia la mujer con la que había estado hablando.

—La señora Considine me ha estado hablando sobre la nueva raza de ovejas que su hijo está criando.

Aunque todo el distrito había sido invadido por esos animales, Sarah sabía muy poco de ellos: la crianza, el pastoreo y el esquileo. Sin embargo, la joven sí sabía bastante sobre hilandería y tejeduría.

Consciente de ese hecho, la señora Considine le dirigió una mirada inquisitiva.

—Esta nueva raza produce una lana diferente, querida. Es más fina de lo habitual. Si fuera tuya, ¿a qué hilandería la enviarías?

Sarah consideró la pregunta, consciente del interés de Charlie tanto por la razón por la que la señora Considine le hubiera pedido su opinión como por cuál sería su respuesta.

—Si como ha dicho la lana es más delicada, la enviaría a Corrigan en Wellington. Es una hilandería pequeña pero la mejor equipada para trabajar en algo que requiere un especial cuidado. En las demás sólo se dedicarían a someterla al proceso habitual en vez de intentar sacar el mejor partido de ella.

—A Corrigan, ¿eh? —La señora Considine asintió con la cabeza—. Se lo diré a Jeffrey, se sentirá encantado de conocer tu opinión.

Después de recomendarle a Charlie que invirtiera en esa nueva raza, la señora Considine los dejó solos.

Sarah se giró hacia Charlie y lo miró directamente a los ojos.

—¿Qué estás haciendo aquí?

La expresión de Charlie se tornó sombría, pero el efecto sólo se notó en su mirada, que únicamente podía ver ella, en vez de en sus rasgos, visibles para todas aquellas damas que lo estaban observando de cerca.

—No me di cuenta de que era esta clase de reunión. —Lanzó una mirada a su alrededor; sólo Sarah estaba lo suficientemente cerca de él para percibir algo que se parecía mucho a la desesperación—. Pensé que no sería el único caballero presente.

Obviamente se estaba refiriendo a caballeros como él. Sarah se abstuvo de señalar que había pocos caballeros de la categoría de Charlie en la localidad.

—Hay siete hombres presentes, y todos son caballeros.

—Dos más viejos que Matusalén y cinco jovenzuelos que aún no han salido del cascarón —gruñó él—. Empiezo a sentirme como un fenómeno de feria.

Ella sofocó una risita.

—Bueno, entonces, ¿por qué has venido?

Charlie la miró fijamente pero no dijo nada. Ella conocía la respuesta, percibía una exasperada frustración en sus ojos. La joven contuvo el aliento. Por un instante se preguntó si él le respondería.

—Ya sabes por qué he venido —dijo él en voz baja para que sólo lo oyera ella—. Pensé... —Hizo una mueca—. Está claro que calculé mal.

Sabía lo que él quería decir. Sarah sentía lo mismo, aquella urgente necesidad de tocar, de besarse y abrazarse, y notó que se le aceleraba la respiración.

—En cualquier caso, ya estás aquí, y no puedes marcharte. Tendrás que sacar el mejor partido de la situación.

—Ésa ha sido, exactamente, mi conclusión. —Charlie volvió a cogerle la mano y a colocarla sobre el antebrazo, situándose a su lado y paseando la mirada por encima de la interesada concurrencia—. Además, no existe ninguna razón por la que debamos fingir una educada indiferencia.

—Eso parece.

—¿Cómo es que sabes tanto sobre el procesamiento de la lana? —Charlie comenzó a pasear lentamente por la estancia; Sarah supuso que era para evitar que a alguien se le ocurriera unirse a ellos.

—Ya te he contado que cuando los niños del orfanato cumplen catorce años les buscamos trabajo en los pueblos de los alrededores. Seguimos con interés los negocios a los que enviamos a nuestros niños, así que sabemos qué tipo de trabajo están desempeñando. Eso significa conocer todos los detalles del proceso. —Lo miró—. Conozco a fondo el funcionamiento de las hilanderías y de las fábricas de Taunton y Wellington.

Él asintió, meditabundo.

—¿También tienes conocimientos de los almacenes y los muelles de Watchet?

—No tan profundos. Es el señor Skeggs quien se encarga de eso.

—Tengo que acordarme de visitar a Skeggs. —Sostuvo la mirada de la joven—. Quizá podría charlar con él en el orfanato.

Ella sonrió ampliamente.

—Después de ese partido, siempre te darán la bienvenida.

Él sonrió y miró hacia delante.

A pesar de la expectación que suscitaban. Charlie se mantuvo a su lado, mientras se detenían a charlar con las matronas que los abordaban y, cuando se anunció el almuerzo, sostuvo el plato de Sarah mientras la joven se servía salmón antes de acompañarla por el resto de la mesa, donde se sirvió un poco de cada plato con aire despreocupado y abstraído.

Se sentaron a comer en una mesa pequeña. Clary y Gloria se unieron a ellos; Sarah observó con diversión cómo Charlie, resignado, respondía a sus ocurrencias con una educada paciencia que finalmente obtuvo el efecto deseado. Sus hermanas se dirigieron a buscar el postre y se quedaron con sus amigas en vez de regresar con ellos.

La mayoría de los asistentes acabaron haciendo lo mismo. Todavía captaban alguna que otra mirada, pero no el implacable seguimiento al que se habían visto sometidos al principio. Por primera vez, Sarah fue capaz de respirar con normalidad.

De manera inesperada, la mirada de la joven se desplazó hacia Charlie. Estaba sentado a su lado y miraba el plato vacío con la cabeza en otro sitio.

De pronto, él centró toda su atención en ella. No se movió, no cambió de posición ni un dedo, pero ella sabía que lo había envuelto una extraña quietud.

En ese momento Charlie levantó la cabeza y sus ojos se encontraron. El fuego ardía en las profundidades de sus ojos azules, algo que atraía a la joven y la hizo responder de inmediato.

El cuerpo de la joven se calentó y cobró vida. Se le erizó la piel, se le tensaron los nervios. Sus pezones se contrajeron al máximo.

Sarah inspiró bruscamente y apartó la mirada de él. Se dijo que aquello era una locura. Comenzó a sentirse mareada.

Con sólo una mirada, Sarah podía recordar el tacto de los labios de Charlie en los suyos, de su mano sobre el pecho. Y por lo que podía ver él también lo recordaba.

A la joven le palpitaron los labios.

Charlie estaba allí, a su lado, y sus traidores sentidos lo sabían muy bien, y querían más. Ahora. Que las personas que los rodeaban lo hicieran imposible no tenía la más mínima importancia.

Incapaz de contenerse, volvió a mirarlo. Charlie volvía a tener la vista clavada en la mesa sin saber lo que miraba. Él sintió que ella lo observaba de nuevo. La miró, entonces se levantó de la silla bruscamente y le tendió la mano.

—Ven. —Señaló con la cabeza a los otros invitados que también se había levantado y la guio hacia la puerta—. Al parecer hemos sido subyugados por una especie de música.

El tono de Charlie dejaba claro que le parecía una tortura. Pero, con sinceridad, ella no podía hacer nada. Dándole la mano, Sarah se puso en pie.

La fuerza con la que le tomó la mano, la manera en que se había levantado, revelaba la completa frustración que sentía Charlie. Una tensión igual o mayor que la de ella.

Aunque Sarah no sabía, por lo menos no en la práctica, lo que vendría a continuación si seguían el plan de Charlie, él sí lo sabía. Probablemente fuera eso lo que estuviera alimentando su mal humor, lo que le daba un filo acerado a su voz.

La llevó con los demás que salían en fila del comedor y se dirigieron a la salita de música, quedándose siempre detrás del resto.

Sarah tenía los nervios de punta, respiró hondo y expulsó de su mente cualquier pensamiento perturbador. Sin embargo, sintió una pequeña satisfacción al pensar que, en ese momento, él estaba tan alterado como ella.

Todos los invitados entraron en la sala de música y durante un momento se quedaron solos en el pasillo. Él inclinó la cabeza y le murmuró al oído:

—¿Vendrás esta noche?

Sarah lo miró a los ojos. Estuvo a punto de decir «por supuesto» en un tono sorprendido que habría hecho reflexionar a Charlie. Que habría levantado sus sospechas.

Al escrutar su mirada, confirmó que él no se imaginaba que ella sabía lo que él estaba haciendo, que conocía su plan. Sarah abrió la boca, tentada a ser sincera, pero se limitó a decirle:

—Sí, de acuerdo.

Como si tuviera que preguntarle. O recordárselo.

Charlie asintió con la cabeza y la acompañó a la salita. Encontró dos sillas junto a la pared. Sentada a su lado, Sarah reflexionó sobre que había una significativa diferencia entre ser inocente y ser ingenua, algo que Charlie —que no era nada inocente, pero sí un poco ingenuo— no percibía.

Sarah podía ser inocente, pero ciertamente no era ingenua.

Él se daría cuenta de eso muy pronto. De noche, mientras se reunían en el cenador, donde cada uno de ellos llevaría a cabo sus propios planes.

Esa noche fue ella quien esperó en el cenador. Ambos corrieron al encuentro del otro. Charlie le tomó la cara entre las manos mientras sus labios se unían y se entregaban a un beso apasionado y ardiente, al tiempo que sus cuerpos se estrechaban el uno contra el otro, ansiando el contacto y deseando aún más.

La pasión estalló entre ellos. En unos segundos, quedaron atrapados en una vorágine incontrolable, una expresión tempestuosa de su deseo mutuo.

Del uno por el otro. Y eso era lo que lo hacía maravilloso, el nivel de urgencia que los dos experimentaban, las crecientes sensaciones que se apoderaban de sus mentes, borrando cualquier tipo de pensamiento. ¿Cómo podía haber algo más fascinante que eso?

¿Algo más excitante y cautivador?

Charlie la deseaba, y mucho, no podía negarlo. No podía ocultárselo ni siquiera a ella, a pesar de lo inocente que era.

El deseo se percibía en sus acciones, en los duros labios que devastaban los de ella, en cada roce profundo y provocador de su lengua. En la dureza del torso masculino, en la fuerza de los brazos que la estrechaban contra sí.

En la audacia de su mano, que con pericia desabrochaba los botones del corpiño.

Sarah se preparó para sentir cómo la mano de Charlie se cerraba sobre su pecho.

Pero en lugar de eso, él se inclinó, la cogió en brazos y, dándose media vuelta, se sentó en el sofá con ella en el regazo.

Entonces sí que le deslizó la mano debajo del corpiño y le cubrió el pecho. Los labios que le devoraban la boca se bebieron el jadeo de Sarah.

Charlie la acunó entre sus brazos mientras anulaba los sentidos de la joven, mientras la hacía girar y arquearse invitadoramente para disfrutar del placer que le ofrecía.

Pero no era suficiente. Sarah quería más.

Tenía que experimentar más para aprender a llevar a Charlie a donde quería.

Estirándose, Sarah le rodeó el cuello con los brazos y le devolvió el beso. Con total lascivia, con labios y lengua, retorciéndose entre sus brazos, invitándole a un contacto sin restricciones.

Sarah no esperaba que él se negara, y no lo hizo. Pero tampoco había previsto lo que él haría. No había tenido ni la más leve idea, así que se sorprendió un poco cuando él le soltó el seno, le puso la mano en el hombro y le deslizó el vestido hasta que el pecho quedó desnudo, expuesto al aire de la noche, a los cálidos y duros dedos masculinos, a las caricias sensuales de Charlie.

Sarah saboreó cada segundo. Cerró los ojos y echó la cabeza hacia atrás, arqueándose cuando él cerró los dedos sobre el pecho y le pellizcó el pezón suavemente. Charlie deslizó los labios por la barbilla de Sarah, por la larga curva de la garganta hasta la base del cuello, depositando un beso ardiente con la boca abierta en el lugar donde palpitaba el pulso de la joven.

Sarah contuvo la respiración mientras sentía los labios masculinos recorriéndole la piel, demorándose en la curva superior del pecho desnudo antes de bajar todavía más.

Charlie bañó el pezón con su cálido aliento, luego abrió los labios para darle un delicado beso que hizo estremecer a Sarah de pies a cabeza.

La joven jadeó y se arqueó cuando él volvió a repetir la caricia con más suavidad.

Charlie abrió la boca y tomó el pezón en ella.

Sarah gritó cuando sintió que la atravesaba una húmeda y ardiente sensación. Sofocó otro grito cuando él comenzó a succionar con suavidad. Con el corazón galopando, la joven intentó encontrar algún punto de apoyo, intentó comprender, ver... pero en aquel momento estaba ciega.

Cegada por la pasión, por el placer y el deseo.

Charlie sabía lo que estaba haciendo. La despojaba de cualquier pensamiento racional, tentándola a ser todavía más lasciva que antes. Incluso más descarada.

Por voluntad propia, Sarah alzó las manos para cogerle la cabeza. Enredó los dedos en el cabello de Charlie para atraerlo más hacia sí, instándolo a que continuara con aquella tierna tortura mientras se arqueaba contra su cuerpo y le exigía más.

Entonces oyó —o más bien sintió— una risita ahogada. Se habría sentido ofendida si el sonido no hubiera estado tan cargado de tensión. Sumido en la pasión, Charlie parecía tan jadeante y ansioso como ella.

En ese momento, él accedió a sus silenciosas súplicas.

Durante un buen rato, Sarah no fue consciente de nada más que de aquellas dulces y absorbentes sensaciones. Pasaron los minutos mientras ella saboreaba el placer lascivo que él le daba, que ella quería que le diera. Estaba segura de que él se deleitaba con sus súplicas; lo sentía en sus caricias, en los besos que él compartía con ella en medio de esa adoración a sus pechos, en la suave enseñanza de sus sentidos.

En su deseo.

Saber lo que él estaba haciendo, lo que pretendía hacer, le daba fuerzas a Sarah para observar, para ver más de lo que él tenía intención de revelar.

Al observar la cara de Charlie, perfilada por la débil luz de la luna, y sentir el roce sensual de sus dedos y el afilado mordisco del deseo que le provocaba, vio que el mismo deseo también estaba grabado a fuego en los marcados rasgos masculinos, sintió cómo flaqueaba el control de Charlie cuando él bajó la mirada a la mano que deslizaba por su piel desnuda.

Sarah alargó la mano y acercó la cabeza de Charlie a la suya, atrayendo sus labios a los de ella, y le abrazó. Le dieron la bienvenida al deseo, a la necesidad, a la pasión, y se dejaron envolver por ellos en un intento por estrechar aún más sus cuerpos.

Cuando él le devolvió el beso, Sarah creyó sentirlo estremecer como si estuviera refrenando su necesidad, intentando ocultársela a ella, lo que a su vez le provocaba una dolorosa sensación.

Al mismo tiempo, otra necesidad fluyó y atravesó a Sarah, sorprendiéndola por su intensidad.

Lo obligó a seguir besándola, tentándolo y camelándolo, desafiándolo, jugando con él de la manera que había aprendido que más le excitaba. Apartando una mano de la nuca de Charlie, se la deslizó bajo la chaqueta y le desabrochó el chaleco con rapidez.

Sarah apartó la tela de terciopelo a un lado y puso la mano sobre el pecho de Charlie, sintiendo la dureza de los músculos bajo la fina camisa. Luego le colocó la mano sobre el corazón y saboreó el pesado y resonante latido.

Un latido que alcanzó una parte primitiva de Sarah y la animó a ser más descarada, a deslizar la mano más abajo, con la palma abierta, entre ambos, sobre el plano abdomen, sobre la tensa cintura y el vientre, para acariciar la dura cordillera de su erección.

Él se quedó inmóvil. Era la inmovilidad de un depredador que le recordó a ella bruscamente que estaba entre los brazos de alguien más fuerte que ella.

En ese momento él rompió el beso y soltó una maldición por lo bajo, agarró la muñeca errante de Sarah con fuerza y le apartó la mano.

La puso de nuevo sobre su hombro, e inclinó la cabeza con la evidente intención de reanudar el beso. Antes de que pudiera apoderarse de sus labios, Sarah se echó hacia atrás.

—¿Por qué no puedo?

—Todavía no. —Charlie apretó los dientes.

—Pero yo...

La besó con dureza, crueldad y determinación.

Ella lo supo, y con la misma determinación, dejó que barriera sus sentidos durante unos minutos, luego intentó imponer su voluntad de nuevo.

Lo suficiente para hacer que él rompiera el beso a regañadientes.

Ella se encontró con los ojos de Charlie a un par de centímetros de los suyos. Entonces bajó la mirada a la boca masculina y se pasó la punta de la lengua por el hinchado labio inferior.

—Quizá —Sarah respiró hondo y lo miró a los ojos— ya hemos llegado lo suficientemente lejos por esta noche.

Charlie la miró desconcertado. Un momento después, parpadeó y bajó la vista a sus pechos desnudos, hinchados, sonrojados y erguidos.

El esfuerzo con el que a Charlie le costó recobrar el control y acceder a su sugerencia fue evidente, pero se relajó y asintió con renuencia.

—Sí, tienes razón. Es suficiente por esta noche —dijo con voz tensa.

Sarah permitió que le colocara la ropa, estudiándole, maravillándose de la tensión en su cara, del inflexible control que él había impuesto sobre el deseo. A pesar de todo, de la renuencia de Charlie, del hecho de que una parte de él no quisiera parar incluso aunque eso significara someterse a las caricias de Sarah, le dijo que su atrevimiento había valido la pena.

Charlie no habló mientras la acompañaba de regreso a casa a través de los jardines envueltos en las sombras de la noche, pero ella caminó satisfecha a su lado.

Él quería que ella le acariciara, pero no quería arriesgarse.

¿Por qué?

Mientras se separaban ante la puerta y lo observaba alejarse con paso airado, Sarah pensó que ésa era una pregunta muy interesante.

6

El día siguiente era sábado. A media mañana, Charlie se encontraba galopando hacia el sur por la carretera que conducía a Taunton, guiando a *Tormenta* tras el castaño de Sarah y maldiciendo para sus adentros. ¿Cómo era posible que hubiera accedido a esto?

Habían salido de excursión para visitar la feria ambulante que había acampado a las afueras de Taunton. En la fiesta de lady Finsbury, Charlie había sido invitado a unirse al grupo de damas y caballeros que había decidido ir a la feria a pasar un buen rato. Charlie había aceptado, pues en aquel momento la excursión le pareció la ocasión perfecta para conocer mejor —y de una manera completamente inocente— a su futura esposa.

Pero eso había sido entonces; ahora tenía una opinión diferente.

Las excursiones inocentes, en particular con Sarah, y más especialmente después de lo sucedido la noche anterior, no eran algo que le apeteciera demasiado hacer. Ya no veía tales encuentros con imparcialidad, ni mucho menos con comodidad.

Después de la noche anterior, tener a Sarah cerca, incluso verla, era suficiente para que su cuerpo la anhelara sin tener en cuenta las instrucciones previas de su cerebro. Montar a caballo cuando estaba medio excitado nunca había sido su idea de la diversión.

Pero allí estaba, sintiendo una incomodidad si no dolorosa, sí lo suficientemente molesta para tener que pasar el día con Sarah en público. Peor todavía, entre los otros seis participantes de la excursión, había tres señoritas que parecían sentir mucha curiosidad por un supuesto romance entre Sarah y él. Charlie tendría que aguantarse, tendría que apretar los dientes y contenerse, aunque eso no le hiciera feliz, sobre todo si tenía que pasar el tiempo con Sarah, sin poder hacer otra cosa que charlar y ser sociable con los demás.

No podía imaginar ninguna actividad peor para su estado de ánimo.

Después de la noche anterior, había llegado a una situación en que lo único que deseaba era estar a solas con Sarah para enseñarle mucho más de la sensualidad, para hacerla sentir un deseo tan profundo que al final ella se rindiera y aceptara casarse con él sin demora. Sin embargo, en su fuero interno, a un nivel más intelectual, sabía que actuar con prudencia sería lo más sabio.

Sarah lo había sorprendido. Casi lo había despojado del control con una simple e inocente caricia. No era algo que ella debiera poder hacer, y menos con tanta facilidad. Por lo tanto, Charlie se había repetido a sí mismo que debía mantener un férreo control en todos sus futuros encuentros con ella.

Un inquebrantable control.

Perder el control en cualquier aspecto no era algo que él contemplara con comodidad, así que ni se imaginaba consentirlo. No tener el mando era para un Morwellan, como él bien sabía, el camino hacia la perdición.

Los tejados de Taunton aparecieron a lo lejos, materializándose entre la niebla y el humo que la ligera brisa y el débil brillo del sol hacían dispersarse. Charlie examinó el paisaje y luego a quienes iban delante de él: las cuatro señoritas que galopaban en parejas; Sarah montaba al lado de Betsy Kennedy, y Lizzie Mortimer y Margaret Cruikshank iban delante de ellas. Sarah vestía un traje de montar de color verde pálido y un sombrerito con una brillante pluma a juego.

Las jóvenes, por supuesto, iban charlando; el sonido de sus suaves voces llegaba hasta sus acompañantes, que las seguían montando también en parejas. Tras intercambiar algunos saludos después de reunirse con ellos en Crowcombe, y tras algunos comentarios intrascendentes, los caballeros habían cerrado la boca y se habían dedicado a disfrutar del paseo y las vistas, ambos bucólicos y femeninos.

Detrás de Charlie montaba su hermano Jeremy, otro observador al que hubiera preferido evitar.

Todos refrenaron las monturas cuando se aproximaron a las primeras casas. Al llegar al puente de adoquines, se pusieron al paso. La vía estaba abarrotada, pues además de la feria era día de mercado. Por fortuna no tenían que atravesar el pueblo para llegar a la feria.

Dejaron los caballos en Taunton Arms, una enorme posada justo al lado del puente que luego atravesaron a pie. Bajaron una suave pendiente hacia los brillantes carromatos y tenderetes que se habían instalado sobre un campo en barbecho a orillas del río Tone.

En la otra orilla, los altos muros de piedra del castillo normando se cernían, sombríos, sobre ellos. En contraste, los banderines de ricos colores y el bullicio alegre de la feria eran todo un alivio para la vista.

Era casi mediodía cuando pagaron los peniques que costaba la entrada y accedieron al recinto ferial pasando bajo un arco resplandeciente adornado con brillantes cintas y banderines. El lugar ya estaba abarrotado. Las calles, formadas por los tenderetes y los carromatos, estaban animadas con gente y niños de todas las edades.

En cuanto atravesaron el arco, se detuvieron para planear qué hacer. Jeremy, de pie al lado de Charlie, echó un vistazo a su alrededor y dijo:

—No hay manera de que logremos permanecer juntos. Propongo que nos reunamos aquí a las tres. Tendremos que emprender el camino de vuelta entonces si no queremos cabalgar en la oscuridad.

Todos se mostraron de acuerdo; el reloj de la torre de la iglesia cercana podía verse desde todos los puntos de la feria. Luego, las cuatro jóvenes, con los ojos brillantes y llenos de determinación, se encaminaron hacia los primeros tenderetes, donde se vendían todas las baratijas imaginables. A los caballeros no les quedó más remedio que seguirlas. Ése no era el tipo de lugar donde una joven podía pasear sin acompañante. Había gente de mala calaña entre la multitud y, aunque en la feria reinaba un espíritu festivo y la gente se reía y bromeaba, no había manera de predecir lo que podía ocurrir.

Al principio todas las chicas permanecieron juntas, yendo de un puesto a otro, admirando cintas y abalorios, llamándose las unas a las otras, señalando artículos y pidiéndose opiniones. Pero luego Margaret Cruikshank se entretuvo en un puesto de magia. Jeremy, que también parecía interesado en la mercancía, se quedó con ella mientras los demás seguían adelante. Margaret y Jeremy eran los más jóvenes del grupo, tenían la misma edad y eran amigos de toda la vida; Charlie sabía que podía confiar en que su hermano pequeño cuidara de Margaret.

Al ser el mayor del grupo, Charlie sentía una cierta responsabilidad hacia los demás, pero eso no quería decir que deseara pasar las siguientes tres horas en su compañía. Una vez que hubieron perdido de vista a Margaret y a Jeremy, sólo quedaba dejar atrás a Lizzie Mortimer y Betsy Kennedy, y a Jon Finsbury y Henry Kilpatrick.

Al final del primer callejón se toparon con un tenderete de brillante color púrpura y dorado con un letrero que anunciaba a «La gran madame Garnaut, la extraordinaria adivina». Lizzie y Betsy comenzaron a dar saltitos entusiasmadas, un entusiasmo que Sarah no compartía, aunque al final se dejó convencer por sus amigas y, después de pagar los seis peniques que costaba la consulta, esperaron a ser llamadas a la presencia de madame Garnaut.

Charlie había acompañado a muchas mujeres a ferias y reuniones similares, así que suspiró y se dispuso a esperar frente al tenderete, desde donde podría vigilar la entrada con adornos coloridos del tenderete de madame Garnaut. Jon y Henry, mucho más jóvenes que él, protestaron, sin embargo se dispusieron a esperar también pacientemente mientras discutían si tendrían tiempo para ver los despliegues pugilísticos que tenían lugar en unas pistas al otro lado del campo.

Charlie escuchó el debate en el que los jóvenes lo incluyeron educadamente, aunque contribuyó poco al mismo. Tenían cinco o seis años menos que él, por lo que solían mirarlo con cierto temor reverencial. Durante un rato le dio vueltas a la cabeza sobre cuál sería la mejor manera de conseguir que Sarah y él pudieran perder de vista a los otros cuatro.

El destino le sonrió y, primero Betsy y luego Lizzie, las dos nerviosas y sonrojadas, salieron del tenderete de madame Garnaut. Sarah fue la última en entrar por la colorida puerta de tela. Cuando la joven dejó caer la tela, Lizzie le hizo algunas confidencias a Betsy en voz baja, luego cruzaron la calle sin prisa para reunirse con sus acompañantes.

Jon se enderezó y metió las manos en los bolsillos.

—¿Qué os ha dicho madame Garnaut? —les preguntó a ambas chicas.

Lizzie y Betsy intercambiaron una mirada, entonces Lizzie golpeó el brazo de Jon.

—No te importa. Eso es algo que nos compete a nosotras y que tú sólo podrás imaginar.

Las dos chicas miraron hacia el siguiente puesto y se removieron inquietas, impacientes por irse. Volvieron a mirar la tienda de la adivina, la consulta de Sarah estaba durando más tiempo que la suya.

Charlie sonrió para sus adentros. Por fuera hizo una mueca para disimular.

—¿Por qué no seguís adelante? Yo esperaré a Sarah.

Los cuatro jóvenes se miraron en silencio, luego le dirigieron una mirada de agradecimiento y se apresuraron hacia la siguiente atracción, un tenderete donde se vendían cintas y pañuelos.

Charlie les observó alejarse, luego sonrió, y de nuevo se dispuso a esperar.

Dentro del tenderete de color púrpura, Sarah estaba sentada con los ojos clavados en una gran bola de cristal verde. La sostenía entre las palmas de las manos tal y como le había pedido madame Garnaut que hiciera. Antes de eso le había leído las dos palmas, había fruncido el ceño y mientras negaba con la cabeza le había dicho con marcado acento: «es complicado».

No era lo que Sarah había esperado oír. No es que creyera mucho en la adivinación, pero ya que estaba allí, no perdía nada por preguntarle a madame Garnaut si Charlie la amaba o no o si, en caso de que no lo hiciera, llegaría a amarla cuando estuvieran casados. Aquélla era una oportunidad demasiado buena para dejarla pasar. Estaba dispuesta a utilizar cualquier medio a su alcance para descubrir lo que necesitaba saber.

Pero no veía nada en la bola de cristal.

Miró a la adivina, sentada al otro lado de la pequeña mesa redonda con un mantel de terciopelo de color azul profundo. Las manos de la gitana, extrañamente frías, rodeaban las de Sarah. La mujer miraba con los ojos entrecerrados la bola de cristal; una mirada de absoluta concentración que le hacía fruncir el ceño.

El pelo de madame Garnaut, largo y rizado, y tan negro como el ala de un cuervo, parecía sobresalir de su cabeza. En ese momento, cerró los ojos y, echando la cabeza hacia atrás, exhaló lentamente. Comenzó a hablar en medio de una extraña quietud.

—Desea saber si un hombre puede amarla. Es alto, pero no moreno, y muy apuesto. La respuesta a su pregunta es sí, aunque el camino no está claro. Para obtener lo que busca y conocer esa respuesta, tendrá que tomar una decisión. Será decisión suya, no de él.

Pasó un largo rato, luego la adivina soltó un suspiro. Ante las dilatadas pupilas de Sarah, la mujer pareció desinflarse.

Madame Garnaut soltó las manos de Sarah y la miró directamente a los ojos.

—Es todo lo que veo... lo único que puedo decirle. Así que la respuesta es sí, pero... —La mujer se encogió de hombros—. El resto es complicado.

Sarah inspiró bruscamente. Retiró las manos de la bola de cristal y asintió con la cabeza. Apartó la silla de la mesa y se levantó.

—Gracias. —En un impulso, rebuscó en su ridículo, sacó otros seis peniques y los dejó sobre la mesa—. Por las molestias.

La gitana tomó la moneda y asintió con la cabeza.

—Usted es una dama, pero ya lo sabía. —En sus negros ojos sabios asomó un brillo desconcertante—. Le deseo buena suerte. Con él no va a ser fácil.

Girándose, alzó la puerta de tela del tenderete y salió, parpadeando desorientada ante la claridad del día. Vio a Charlie —que estaba solo— esperándola al lado de un puesto cercano. Cruzó la callejuela al tiempo que se colgaba el ridículo del brazo, momento que aprovechó para recobrar la compostura.

«No será fácil. Será decisión suya, no de él.»

Al llegar al lado de Charlie, levantó la mirada.

Él sonreía ampliamente.

—¿Qué te ha dicho? ¿Alto, moreno y guapo?

Ella sonrió con más confianza de la que sentía.

—¿Y tú qué crees?

Él le cogió la mano y la puso sobre su brazo antes de conducirla a la siguiente callejuela.

—Creo que eso demostraría por qué no debes creer en las profecías de las adivinas. No son más que charlatanas.

Era lo que ella había pensado siempre. Ahora ya no estaba tan segura.

Pero él era la última persona con la que deseaba discutir las revelaciones de madame Garnaut. Echó un vistazo a su alrededor mientras paseaban uno al lado del otro, y entonces se dio cuenta de que los demás no estaban a la vista.

—¿Dónde están los demás?

—Han seguido adelante.

Sarah lo miró, esperando que dijera algo, pero él no añadió nada más, ni siquiera sugirió que tuviera intención de buscarlos ni, mucho menos, de volver junto a ellos. La joven se encogió de hombros mentalmente, pensando que aquello también le venía bien a ella.

En especial dadas las revelaciones de madame Garnaut. Si las cosas iban a resultar tan complicadas, si todo dependía de sus propias decisiones, entonces cuanto más supiera de él...

La mirada de la joven cayó sobre una figura corpulenta muy peripuesta, que venía por la calle en dirección a ellos. Sarah se acercó más a Charlie.

—Supongo que estarás enterado de la expansión de la industria en Taunton. ¿Conoces al señor Pommeroy? —Señaló con la cabeza al hombre que se acercaba—. Es el dueño de la nueva fábrica de sidra que se ha establecido en las afueras del pueblo.

—Hacia el oeste, ¿verdad? He oído hablar de ella, pero rara vez paso por allí —Charlie apartó la mirada del señor Pommeroy y la miró a los ojos—. ¿Lo conoces?

Ella asintió con la cabeza.

—Ha contratado a dos de los chicos del orfanato como aprendices. —Sin esperar su respuesta, la joven compuso su mejor sonrisa y se dirigió al señor Pommeroy.

Al verla, él sonrió y se detuvo.

—Señorita Conningham. —Tomó la mano de la joven entre las suyas—. Tengo que decirle que esos dos muchachos que me envió son muy buenos trabajadores. Si tienen a más como ellos, estaremos encantados de que se unan a nosotros.

—¡Excelente! —Recuperando su mano, Sarah señaló a Charlie—. Me gustaría presentarle a lord Meredith.

El señor Pommeroy pareció encantado. Le hizo a Charlie una reverencia.

—Milord.

Charlie, siempre educado y correcto, asintió con la cabeza. El señor Pommeroy les presentó a su esposa, tras lo cual, Charlie se pasó los siguientes cinco minutos hablando de fábricas, rendimientos y transportes. Sarah los escuchó con atención; siempre estaba ojo avizor ante cualquier oportunidad para los chicos del orfanato, como el negocio del transporte, que, por lo que se deducía de la conversación entre Charlie y el señor Pommeroy, iba en alza. Tomó nota mental de hablar con el señor Hallisham, que poseía un negocio de transporte local.

La señora Pommeroy, sin embargo, a pesar de la sonrisa que esbozaba, comenzó a removerse con inquietud. Apiadándose de ella, Sarah tomó cartas en el asunto. Hizo una pregunta de carácter general al tiempo que le pellizcaba el brazo a Charlie. Él la miró, pero aceptó en silencio su decisión de terminar la conversación y se despidieron de los Pommeroy.

Mientras continuaban su camino, ella le murmuró:

—Puedes ir a visitarlo en alguna ocasión cuando no esté su esposa presente.

Charlie arqueó una ceja y luego curvó los labios, asintiendo con la cabeza.

—Supongo.

—¡Señora! ¡Hermosa señora!

Estaban delante de una nueva hilera de tenderetes. Un hombre mayor con la cara ancha y las manos nudosas le hizo señas a Sarah para que se acercara.

—¡Venga! ¡Es perfecto para usted que es tan bonita como un cuadro! —Asintió con la cabeza con una expresión radiante y volvió a hacerle señas para que se acercara. Sarah dio un paso hacia él, llena de curiosidad. El hombre bajó la mirada a su mostrador y rebuscó con sus gruesos dedos entre las mercancías—. Directamente llegados de Londres. Collares de Rusia. Tengo los colores perfectos para usted.

No pasaba nada por echar un vistazo. Sarah arrastró a Charlie hasta el puesto, deteniéndose delante del mostrador.

—¡Mire! —El hombre levantó la vista. Entre sus enormes dedos sostenía un collar con piezas de esmalte de distintas formas unidas entre sí y que estaban decoradas con una mezcla de brillantes colores verdes como la primavera y azules como el verano. El collar parecía ridículamente delicado entre las enormes manos del hombre.

Sarah abrió mucho los ojos. Tenía que tocarlo.

—Venga. —El comerciante salió a toda prisa de detrás del mostrador—. Pruébeselo y mire.

Con destreza, el hombre colocó el collar de esmalte alrededor del cuello de Sarah y lo sostuvo en alto para que lo viera.

Charlie observó el gesto con resignación. Tenía que felicitar al hombre por su destreza. Sabía cómo vender a las damas.

Pero a Sarah, no cabía duda, le encantaba el collar. Charlie ladeó la cabeza y lo examinó, considerando cómo le quedaba, cómo lo examinaba con los dedos, cómo estudiaba su reflejo en un espejo con manchas que el comerciante había sacado de debajo del mostrador.

El efecto era... complejo. El esmalte parecía ser bastante bueno. La pieza era el resultado de combinar una inocente simplicidad y la decadencia de los vibrantes colores.

A Charlie le bastó una mirada a la cara de Sarah para saber que a ella le había gustado tanto como a él. No necesitó mirar al sagaz comerciante para saber que ahora el hombre lo estudiaba de cerca, presto a animarlo para que se lo comprara a su dama.

Charlie estudió el collar de nuevo. La luz parecía arrancarle destellos de colores cada vez que lo iluminaba. A pesar de su arraigada costumbre de no comprar nada que se vendiera en una feria de gitanos, Charlie levantó la mano para tocar los esmaltes. Sarah le miró desde el espejo. Él la vio, pero no le sostuvo la mirada.

Era una pieza delicada tal y como deberían ser los collares de esmalte. Pasó el dedo por una de las piezas y le dio la vuelta.

Se quedó impresionado. El trabajo de remate en el reverso del esmalte era de la misma calidad que en los collares más caros.

A Alathea le gustaban mucho los esmaltes, sobre todo los de origen ruso. Era de ella de quien había aprendido cómo distinguir los collares originales de los falsos. Puede que esa pieza no fuera original, pero sin duda era bastante buena.

Componer su mejor cara de hombre de negocios le resultó muy útil. Miró fijamente al comerciante con una expresión totalmente neutra.

—¿Cuánto?

Sarah le miró de reojo. Charlie se dio cuenta de que había pensado comprárselo ella misma, pero cuando él no le devolvió la mirada y se limitó a regatear con el comerciante, se limitó a mantener la boca cerrada y permitió que se lo comprara.

Una pequeña victoria, casi insignificante, pero que a Charlie le supo a gloria.

Para cuando el comerciante y él se despidieron, y Sarah y Charlie se alejaron del tenderete, había comprado no sólo el collar de esmalte, sino un anillo y tres broches. Uno dorado, rojo y negro para Alathea, y otro para Augusta en sus tonalidades favoritas, púrpura, amatista y malva. Tras alejarse del mostrador, Charlie detuvo a Sarah al lado del puesto y le prendió el tercer broche, de esmaltes azules y verdes, en la solapa del traje de montar.

Sarah curvó los labios suavemente y acarició el broche con la yema de los dedos, luego levantó la cara.

—Gracias, es muy bonito.

Charlie le sostuvo la mirada durante un instante, luego le cogió la mano derecha y después de deslizarle el anillo a juego en el dedo corazón, le puso la mano sobre el pecho para poder admirar las tres piezas juntas.

Charlie sintió una opresión en el pecho. Sabía que estaba mirando los esmaltes, pero no era eso lo que veía en su imaginación.

Alzó la vista y miró a Sarah a los ojos.

—Es sólo hasta que me dejes regalarte algo de más valor. —Esbozó una sonrisa y, antes de que ella pudiera hablar, le preguntó—: ¿Has visto las esmeraldas Morwellan?

Sarah parpadeó, luego le deslizó la mano en el brazo y comenzaron a pasear de nuevo.

—No. —Frunciendo el ceño, ella negó con la cabeza—. No recuerdo haberlas visto.

—De haberlo hecho, te acordarías. Mi madre rara vez se las pone, no le gustan. Son transparentes y perfectas. El juego consta de un collar, unos pendientes, una pulsera y un anillo. Es el juego de esmeraldas más perfecto que se conoce. —Volvió a mirar a la mujer que llevaba del brazo... su futura condesa—. Te gustarán.

Ella levantó la vista y lo miró a los ojos.

—Si me caso contigo.

No existía un «si». El mudo reto en la mirada de Sarah provocó una tormenta en el interior de Charlie que tuvo que contener el impulso de ceder a él y terminar con la resistencia de la joven, de dejarle claro que no habría otro resultado. Tensó el brazo. Con algo parecido al horror, luchó contra el primitivo e intenso deseo de demostrarle a Sarah que la verdad era muy simple e imposible de malinterpretar: ella era suya.

«Suya».

Apretó los dientes y se obligó a aceptar sus palabras —pues la joven tenía derecho a negarse— con una inclinación de cabeza. Luego miró sin ver hacia delante, todavía intentando contener su reacción.

Charlie nunca se había considerado un hombre particularmente posesivo. ¿De dónde provenía tal impulso? ¿Por qué era tan fuerte? ¿Qué significaba?

Pero si cedía a ese impulso, si la dejaba sospechar que de verdad no iba a tener otra alternativa, que ella no había tenido elección desde el momento en que él había hablado con su padre para pedir su mano —por no considerar todo lo que había ocurrido desde entonces—, si le mostraba cualquier indicio de que su destino estaba trazado de antemano sin tener en cuenta lo que ella pensara al respecto, se estrellaría contra un muro de resistencia femenina.

Y eso era algo que sabía muy bien que tenía que evitar. Alathea se defendía de manera similar a la de Sarah, con la voluntad de hierro que caracterizaba a las mujeres Cynster. Ningún hombre en sus cabales provocaba tal cosa.

Había batallas que era más sabio no luchar.

Se repitió todos esos argumentos hasta que logró calmarse. Hasta que la bestia que ella había provocado se avino a observar y esperar.

Sarah paseó a su lado fingiendo no notar la tensión que había embargado a Charlie, la que él había doblegado y controlado. Gradualmente, el brazo sobre el que reposaba la mano de la joven, se relajó.

Poco a poco, Charlie anduvo con menor rigidez hasta alcanzar su agilidad y gracia acostumbradas.

Entonces, Sarah respiró más tranquila. Era evidente que a Charlie no le gustaba que ella sugiriera que no se casaría con él. Lo que la llevaba de vuelta a la cuestión que tanto le preocupaba: por qué estaba tan empeñado en casarse con ella.

Si en respuesta a esa pregunta a Charlie se le ocurría decir que la vida —la de los dos— sería considerablemente más sencilla, entonces quedaría claro que no la conocía. Así que ella tendría que seguir presionando, ciñéndose a su plan, hasta que lo conociera lo suficiente para entenderlo.

—¡Señorita Conningham!

—¡Eh, señorita!

Sarah se detuvo y se dio la vuelta. La joven observó sonriente cómo tres muchachos —o más bien tres jóvenes adultos— se abrían camino entre la multitud. Al llegar hasta ella, los tres le hicieron una reverencia y le sonrieron con descaro.

—Dígame, señorita —dijo Bobby Simpson—, ¿ha visto a la mujer barbuda? Está en aquel puesto de allí.

—Es realmente asombroso, señorita, nadie sabe si es un hombre o una mujer —aseguró Johnny Wilson.

Naturalmente, aquellos jóvenes pensaban que ésa era la atracción más excitante de todas. Sarah contuvo la risa.

—¿Qué más me recomendáis?

Los tres estuvieron encantados de contarle que había una muestra de dulces de Carnaval en el perímetro de la feria. La conocían de sus años en el orfanato y era por eso que ninguno se sentía cohibido con ella, así que con gran entusiasmo expresaron sus puntos de vista masculinos. Habían observado que estaba acompañada de Charlie, ¿cómo no iban a hacerlo? Era imposible no ver la mano que ella había apoyado en la manga de su acompañante, pero tras unas rápidas e inseguras miradas, ninguno de los tres le había reconocido.

Finalmente, los jóvenes acabaron de contarle sus descubrimientos.

—Gracias. Ahora ya sé que no debo perdérmelo. —Señaló a Charlie—. Éste es lord Meredith.

Los tres arquearon las cejas de inmediato; conocían muy bien el título.

—Ahora contadme —continuó Sarah con suavidad—. ¿Qué tal os va en la curtiduría?

Se lo contaron, pero estaba claro que aquello no les resultaba tan fascinante como la feria. Sonriendo, Sarah se despidió de ellos. Tras unas rápidas reverencias, los jóvenes se perdieron en la multitud. Charlie los observó desaparecer.

—Por aquí debe de haber bastantes personas a las que conoces del orfanato. —Comenzaron a pasearse de nuevo—. ¿A cuántos jóvenes les encontráis trabajo cada año?

—Depende. Y también están las chicas. Ellas acaban en casas de la localidad, a menudo como criadas, a veces como aprendices de cocineras.

Continuaron recorriendo las calles de la feria, observando los puestos, evitando dejarse tentar y probar las mercancías, y mirando las numerosas atracciones. Había muchos niños viendo la función de marionetas. Se detuvieron allí durante un rato para observar el espectáculo, más divertidos por los niños y sus reacciones que por la propia función; luego siguieron su camino.

Sarah agradeció que no ocurriera nada más que provocara otro conflicto de voluntades. No le veía ningún beneficio a insistir sobre un punto sobre el cual conocía la reacción de Charlie.

Era una extraña costumbre, cruel e implacable, que él quisiera salirse siempre con la suya, sobre todo teniendo en cuenta su encanto y su carácter jovial, algo que caracterizaba a las mujeres de la familia Morwellan, a las que Sarah conocía muy bien. Sin embargo, él nunca había tratado de embelesarla. Una decisión sensata; el encanto fácil nunca había funcionado con ella y, en el caso de Charlie, ella sabía que esa capa de barniz civilizado era tan fina como una tela de araña.

Sabía lo que él era, lo que había debajo del glamour. Cuanto más se conocían, cuanto más tiempo pasaban juntos, Sarah se daba cuenta de que había ciertos aspectos en él que jamás había notado antes. Aparentemente, Charlie era tan transparente y perfecto como las esmeraldas de su familia. Pero ella siempre había percibido algo en él que no había podido explicar.

Y dado que ella aún no había respondido a su propuesta matrimonial, y a tenor de las afiladas miradas de reojo que él le lanzaba, Sarah sabía que Charlie estaba estudiando la manera de arrancarle una respuesta afirmativa, pues era indudable que había una cuestión sin resolver entre ellos.

Pero esa noche sería demasiado pronto para hablar del tema.

Fiel reflejo de los pensamientos de la joven. Sin embargo, los nervios y los sentidos de Sarah no estaban en absoluto disciplinados. Ni tranquilos ni fríos.

Ella deseaba que lo estuvieran. Esperaba que sus sentidos no dieran un brinco cada vez que la multitud los obligaba a acercarse, que sus nervios no la hicieran estremecerse cuando, por un repentino empujón, el brazo de Charlie le rozaba el pecho.

Según transcurría la tarde y la multitud era cada vez más densa, todas las dudas de Charlie sobre aquella pequeña excursión se vieron confirmadas. Por desgracia, no le alegraba haber acertado en sus predicciones. Ni tampoco le alegraba tener la certeza de que Sarah era igual de susceptible que él, ni de verla dar un brinco cada vez que le ponía la mano en la espalda, ni que contuviera el aliento cuando la multitud de cuerpos hacía que se rozara contra su muslo.

En ese momento, un grupo de jóvenes pendencieros apareció cantando y saltando por la calle y obligó a los demás viandantes a echarse a un lado para dejarles pasar.

Aquel repentino movimiento de la multitud amenazó con arrojar al suelo a los que paseaban por el borde de la calle.

Charlie reaccionó instintivamente. Rodeando a Sarah con un brazo y, protegiéndola con su cuerpo, la sacó medio en volandas del peligro, llevándola hasta el estrecho hueco que había entre dos puestos.

La oleada de empujones humanos atravesó la multitud y pasó de largo. El sonido de las canciones y los enardecidos jóvenes desaparecieron, dejando que el gentío se sacudiera el polvo y reanudara su paseo de manera más tranquila.

Dejando a Charlie y a Sarah pegados el uno al otro.

Después de observar cómo los jóvenes desaparecían, Charlie volvió la cabeza hacia Sarah y sintió que un estremecimiento de anticipación sexual le recorría desde los hombros hasta las rodillas. Ella sintió la ardiente, voraz e insaciable reacción de Charlie —era imposible de ocultar—, incluso antes de que los ojos de él coincidieran con los suyos.

Charlie sabía que su necesidad, su incontrolable deseo, también estaba reflejado en aquellos ojos azul ciano.

Ella separó los labios y contuvo el aliento; tenía las manos alzadas entre sus cuerpos, suspendidas justo a la altura de su torso. No sabía dónde ponerlas y, aunque Sarah sabía que no debía tocarle, deseaba hacerlo.

Y eso era más que evidente para Charlie, que pudo sentir su caricia sin contacto y cómo su propio deseo crecía como una ola, como un gato arqueándose contra esa caricia fantasma. Y quiso más.

Por un instante, él se tambaleó a punto de rendirse a su deseo y al de ella. Bastaba sólo un momento para que la pasión se desbordara entre ellos, pero ése no era el lugar adecuado.

Charlie inspiró hondo antes de retroceder; romper el hechizo era la cosa más difícil que había tenido que hacer en la vida, pero logró hacerlo. Algo que fue muy doloroso para los dos.

Tomó a Sarah de la mano y la arrastró sin que ella ofreciera resistencia alguna fuera del estrecho hueco, de vuelta a la calle. Con los brazos enlazados, se dieron la vuelta. Tras un instante de vacilación, volvieron a pasear.

Pasaron unos minutos antes de que los dos pudieran respirar con normalidad.

Charlie suspiró profundamente: su respiración aún no era demasiado serena. Mirando hacia delante, le dijo:

—Esta noche.

Era una afirmación, no una pregunta. Sintió que ella lo miraba a la cara brevemente y por el rabillo del ojo la vio asentir con la cabeza.

Sarah miró también hacia delante.

—Sí. Esta noche.

Esa noche se ocuparían del deseo que ardía entre ellos.

Pero ahora...

—Aquí hay demasiada gente —dijo, aunque era más que evidente—. Quizá deberíamos dirigirnos al punto de encuentro.

Ella miró al reloj de la torre. Marcaba las dos y media, pero asintió con la cabeza.

—Puede que allí haya menos gente.

Para alivio de los dos, resultó ser cierto. Incluso tuvieron más suerte, pues los demás también habían pensado que la multitud era agobiante y en menos de diez minutos todos se habían reunido donde habían acordado.

—¿Tomamos un té rápido en la posada antes de subirnos a los caballos? —propuso Jon.

Todos asintieron. Caminaron de regreso al Arms Inn. Tras refrescarse, se montaron en los caballos y tomaron el camino del norte hacia sus casas.

Sarah cabalgó al lado de Charlie intentando dejar la mente en blanco. Intentando no pensar en aquel momento cargado de tensión entre los tenderetes ni en la cita de esa noche. Ya tendría tiempo suficiente de pensar en ello luego. Hasta que estuvieran solos, no podía hacer nada.

Nada que aliviara el deseo que los embargaba o que acallara el insistente palpitar de sus venas.

7

Él no estaba allí cuando Sarah llegó al cenador sumido en la quietud de la noche. Aguzó el oído, pero no oyó ningún ruido de pasos acercándose sino solamente el suave discurrir del agua en el embalse.

Sarah entrelazó las manos y se obligó a calmarse, inspirando profundamente e intentando aclarar sus pensamientos a pesar del nudo de anticipación y ansiedad que la envolvía. La joven intentó pensar, razonar, centrarse con firmeza, recordándose a sí misma cuál era su objetivo y cómo tenía intención de conseguir sus propósitos.

Cómo pretendía obligar a Charlie a enseñarle lo que había más allá de su deseo por ella.

Estaba pensando en ello cuando el sonido de una bota resonó en la grava del camino, y de repente lo vio, subiendo los tres escalones de un salto, una elegante figura masculina que cruzó el suelo de madera con unas largas y rápidas zancadas.

Al instante Sarah se vio envuelta entre sus brazos, rodeada por su fuerza, antes de que él tomara posesión de su boca y la besara. Se sintió devastada, consumida por un fuego que sólo podía ser alimentado por aquel deseo mutuo.

Un deseo que cada noche se hacía más ardiente, que cada día abrasaba los sentidos de ambos; un deseo que se veían obligados a contener hasta caer la noche, con lo que sólo conseguían atizar todavía más las llamas de la pasión.

Hasta que el deseo se volvía casi insoportable.

Hasta que el día daba paso a la noche y, al fin, podían aliviar el fuerte latir de sus venas, satisfacer la pasión tanto tiempo contenida.

Por lo cual, Sarah no puso objeción alguna cuando él invadió su boca y devastó sus sentidos, cuando la estrechó contra su cuerpo y le pasó la mano en una suave caricia por la curva de la cadera y el trasero, acariciándola luego con más firmeza, amasándole la carne provocativamente.

Sarah contuvo el aliento cuando él la moldeó contra sí, y sus sentidos amenazaron con explotar cuando la dura cordillera de la erección de Charlie se apretó contra su vientre. El fuego siguió creciendo cada vez con más fuerza, como una ardiente caldera que provocaba un doloroso vacío en lo más profundo de su interior.

Y entonces Charlie la arrastró consigo sobre el sofá, dejando a la joven sin respiración; Sarah aterrizó de costado debajo de él, y los dos quedaron con las piernas enredadas y las manos entrelazadas.

Charlie le abrió el corpiño con un ágil movimiento. Ella le abrió la chaqueta y le deslizó las manos por los hombros para quitársela. Él masculló una maldición y se apartó lo suficiente para que ella pudiera despojarle de la prenda. Entonces Sarah bajó las manos a los botones del chaleco; Charlie masculló otra maldición.

Pero la besó de nuevo y la apretó contra el sofá, deshaciéndose con rapidez del corpiño y la camisola de la joven. Luego le ahuecó un pecho desnudo con la mano y Sarah jadeó de nuevo, con más fuerza esta vez, sintiendo una opresión en los pulmones. Se quedó sin aliento cuando notó que él deslizaba la palma de la mano sobre el seno, acariciándoselo, luego cerró los dedos cuando comenzó a juguetear con el pezón, agudizando las sensaciones de la joven, provocándole un placer abrasador que la atravesó por completo. Era una tentación envolvente, una llamada al deleite. Sarah dejó que el placer fluyera por su cuerpo, hasta que logró recuperar el sentido.

Hasta que logró hacerse dueña de sus actos y recobrar parte del control mientras le devolvía el beso. Entonces, levantó una mano y ahuecó la cara de Charlie, buscando su lengua con la de ella con la intención de distraerle un poco.

El tiempo suficiente para poder desabrocharle los botones de la camisa y deslizar la mano bajo la prenda para tocarle a placer.

La reacción de Charlie fue instantánea. Dejó de besarla y tomó aliento. Se le endurecieron los músculos y se quedó inmóvil. Pero no se apartó. En medio de la oscuridad, Sarah no podía ver su expresión, pero sí que tenía los ojos cerrados y la mandíbula tensa. Parecía como si la mano de ella le quemara, como si su caricia fuera algo que le provocara una dolorosa e intensa agonía, pero era el propio Charlie quien estaba en llamas.

La piel masculina era como lava ardiente sobre roca sólida, suave, casi fluida, aunque él seguía permaneciendo inmóvil.

Decidida a aprender, a saber, Sarah siguió acariciándolo. Tras un rato, cedió a sus sentidos y le exploró los poderosos músculos del pecho con ambas manos, luego las deslizó por el abdomen tenso hasta más abajo y las metió bajo la cinturilla del pantalón para poder sentir la piel desnuda y ardiente bajo las palmas.

Por un instante, Sarah se deleitó en él, recreándose en su perfección, luego él interrumpió su exploración. La apretó contra los cojines del sofá, se inclinó sobre ella y volvió a capturarle la boca, vaciando la mente de la joven de cualquier pensamiento.

Sin voluntad para pensar, Sarah se dejó llevar por las sensaciones, por su reacción a las acciones de Charlie, inmersa en un nivel diferente de ávido deseo.

Era una necesidad más explícita, más aguda, menos controlada. Maravillada, se abandonó a ella. Cautivada y fascinada dejó que aquel intenso deseo fluyera por su cuerpo.

Eso era lo que quería aprender, saber, y luego analizar. Eso —el deseo de Charlie— era lo que necesitaba explorar.

Charlie la mantuvo presionada contra el sofá sin dejar de besarla, arrebatándole el sentido mientras él se enfrentaba a un enigma que jamás había encarado antes, no en esa lid ni con ninguna otra mujer. Se encontraba sometido a unas contradictorias compulsiones, cada una de ellas implacable y exigente, y sentía un instintivo deseo de aplacar la pasión de la joven, de satisfacer de buena gana el deseo ardiente que la consumía y enseñarle todo lo que ella quería saber, de animarla a llegar todavía más lejos. Pero sus planes le dictaban otra cosa. Le exigían seguir una línea de ataque diferente.

. Las pequeñas manos de Sarah se habían deslizado por su espalda debajo de la camisa. Le arañaba y acariciaba la piel. Con urgencia, con necesidad.

Un toque inocente que le hacía arder, que lo reclamaba con voracidad, despertando a la bestia hambrienta que ella tanto deseaba y necesitaba conocer.

Cada instinto de Charlie lo instaba a reclamarla, a poseerla, a terminar con aquel extraño cortejo que habían seguido hasta ese momento, pero si le mostraba todo el misterio, si se unía a ella esa noche, ¿estaría Sarah lo suficientemente encandilada por los placeres de la carne para aceptar ser suya para siempre?

Si se unía a ella esa noche, ¿estaría dispuesta a casarse con él al día siguiente? Con cualquier otra dama no hubiera tenido ninguna duda de que la respuesta sería sí, pero Sarah no era como las demás mujeres y ya le había sorprendido en múltiples ocasiones.

No. Por ahora era mejor ajustarse al plan original y utilizar su tiempo y su experiencia para que ella pudiera apreciar el deseo en todo su esplendor. Para que aprendiera a saborear los placeres en los que él se proponía introducirla y, por consiguiente, gozar con ella durante el resto de sus vidas.

¿Cómo iba a valorarlo Sarah si realmente no lo conocía? Si no entendía cuáles eran los elementos del placer.

Enseñarle, introducirla en el deseo paso a paso como había planeado desde el principio, era lo más seguro. La manera inequívoca de convencerla de que aceptara su propuesta y consintiera ser su esposa.

A pesar de lo atrayente que pudiera parecerle el cuerpo flexible y suave que se extendía debajo de él —sin duda, la quintaesencia de la feminidad—, a pesar de lo caprichoso de su beso, de la manera en que ella se rendía a su boca, de cómo salía a su encuentro y lo desafiaba, tentándolo y jugueteando con él, no era Sarah quien mandaba allí, sino él, y tenía que acordarse de hacer lo que era más sabio. No podía permitirse el lujo de olvidarlo.

Por encima de todo quería que ella estuviera ansiosa y dispuesta a ser su esposa.

Así que Charlie refrenó su deseo, reprimió implacablemente sus instintos y se resistió a la lujuria de Sarah, a la manifiesta invitación que ella tan tentadoramente le ofrecía. Centró sus pensamientos en eso y dejó de besarla, deslizando sus labios más abajo, trazando un sendero de besos por la garganta femenina.

Continuó por la clavícula de la joven y, abriendo el corpiño del todo, accedió a las rosadas puntas de sus senos. Luego se dispuso a mostrarle a Sarah lo que era el placer. O, por lo menos, una parte de él.

Las respuestas de la joven eran compulsivas y vertiginosas, cada noche más intensas que la noche anterior, acrecentadas por la frustración del día. Bien. Charlie se centró en ella, en sus reacciones, mientras con labios, boca, dientes y lengua se concentraba en sumergir los sentidos de la joven en un deleite adictivo y cegador.

Como siempre, el sabor del despertar de Sarah provocaba en él una profunda admiración. Cada pizca del placer que él le daba era correspondida por la joven de una manera que Charlie jamás hubiera imaginado.

Ella se contorsionó debajo de él, envuelta en el placer que le proporcionaban sus experimentadas caricias, el toque firme de sus manos, el húmedo calor de su boca, el roce de su lengua mientras le arrancaba un jadeo tras otro a aquellos labios deliciosamente hinchados. Cuando la oyó gritar, después de que él bajara la cabeza y capturara un pezón tenso y dolorido con su boca, sintió que lo invadía una cálida sensación de orgullo. No sólo porque él fuera el hombre afortunado que la iniciaba en los placeres de la sensualidad, su mentor sexual, el único que educaría los sentidos de la joven en ese campo, sino porque era ella quien lo había invitado. Era a él a quien ella había escogido.

Y aunque realmente fuera él quien la hubiera elegido como esposa, una parte desconocida de su razonamiento le decía que él era a quien ella había estado esperando, que si Sarah hubiera tenido oportunidad, le habría escogido como esposo.

Y allí, en ese ruedo, lo había hecho.

Charlie había descubierto que era un honor inesperado ser elegido por ella, un honor concedido por el deseo que ella mostraba. No había sabido que tal cosa pudiera significar tanto para él, que a pesar de sus frustradas necesidades, disfrutaría de esos instantes. Jamás podrían volver a vivir ese momento en el que él estaba abriendo los ojos de Sarah a la pasión.

A pesar de sentirse embelesada, casi absorbida por las sensaciones, Sarah era consciente del paso del tiempo. En algún momento, él pondría fin a la cita, y ella seguiría sin haber hecho ningún progreso real. Sólo habría tenido un breve vislumbre antes de que él hubiera cerrado de golpe la puerta de su deseo. Pero ella necesitaba más.

Mucho más.

Aunque la única manera de conseguirlo era haciéndose de nuevo con el control.

Obtener la fuerza de voluntad necesaria para hacerlo requirió un esfuerzo supremo pero, finalmente, logró recuperar el suficiente sentido común para que las placenteras sensaciones que la atravesaban revirtieran en él.

Le deslizó las manos por la espalda, intentando llegar más abajo, pero descubrió que no alcanzaba más allá de la cintura. Apretándole los costados, lo urgió a subir un poco más, pero Charlie ignoró sus suaves demandas.

Intentó distraerla succionando su pecho con más fuerza; Sarah tuvo que detenerse e inspirar profundamente para, a duras penas, mantener el raciocinio ante la aguda y poderosa sensación que amenazaba con arrebatárselo. Y tuvo éxito, contuvo el aliento mentalmente y, con más determinación, lo intentó de nuevo.

Apartando una mano del cálido torso de Charlie, le ahuecó la mandíbula y, suave pero insistentemente, tiró de él hasta que por fin alzó la cabeza y llevó sus labios a los de ella.

Sarah estaba preparada para recibirlos, permitió que sus bocas se unieran, que sus lenguas se batieran en un duelo. Luego ella se retorció y se deslizó debajo de él de manera que sus cabezas quedaran a la misma altura. En ese mismo movimiento, la joven retiró la mano de la espalda y la introdujo entre sus cuerpos, buscando su erección dura y rígida bajo los pantalones.

Lo acarició con atrevimiento, luego cerró la mano en torno a él para explorarlo.

La reacción de Charlie fue inmediata. A pesar de que la otra mano de Sarah todavía le sostenía la mandíbula, interrumpió el beso y soltó una maldición. Medio incorporándose sobre ella, le cogió la muñeca con la fuerza de un torno y apartó la mano femenina de su carne excitada.

—No. —Levantó la mano de Sarah por encima de su cabeza y

la apretó contra los cojines del sofá. Entrecerrando los párpados, la miró directamente a los ojos.

Ella le lanzó una mirada feroz.

—¿Por qué?

—Porque...

Charlie se interrumpió con un siseo cuando ella se retorció bajo su cuerpo y logró acariciar su parte más sensible —e útil para los propósitos femeninos— con el muslo. Él cerró los ojos, pero apretó los dientes con fuerza. Maldiciendo de nuevo, agarró la otra mano de Sarah y la sostuvo junto a la anterior por encima de su cabeza mientras cambiaba de posición y se inclinaba sobre ella con todo su peso, atrapándola con su cuerpo.

Inmovilizándola debajo de él.

A Sarah le llevó sólo un segundo darse cuenta de que eso no era necesariamente algo malo. Charlie había colocado una pierna entre las de ella y su rodilla se hundía en los mullidos cojines, de tal manera que el músculo duro del muslo se apretaba contra el lugar más sensible de la joven.

Eso la hizo perder momentáneamente el hilo de sus pensamientos.

Pero luego recordó.

—¿Por qué? —exigió saber con los ojos entrecerrados.

Charlie le tenía apresadas las dos manos con una de las suyas y se las apretaba contra los cojines, con un brazo a cada lado de su cabeza. Tenían las caras muy cerca. Él la miró directamente a los ojos.

—Porque no estás preparada para esto —escupió las palabras con sombría frustración.

Sarah consideró todo lo que aún tenía que aprender, lo que podía sentir en el duro, tenso y definitivamente excitado cuerpo masculino que tenía encima.

—¿Por qué no?

Era más una pregunta sincera que una exigencia desafiante y no pudo evitar que algo de su nerviosismo se le reflejara en la voz.

Charlie estudió su mirada y luego su expresión. Pasó un rato en el que sus cuerpos ardientes no se enfriaron ni una pizca, en el que la pasión que crepitaba en el aire no disminuyó en lo más mínimo; después él curvó los labios y esbozó una mueca de resignación.

Un extraño pensamiento inundó la mente de Sarah; estaba convencida de que tal resignación no era real. ¿Charlie rindiéndose? No parecía probable.

—No puedes... No debes dejarte llevar sin más. No deberías considerarlo como un acto simple, sino como un arte. No sólo importa la ejecución, sino también el placer que se alcanza. Y eso es algo que necesitas aprender paso a paso.

Aunque podía verle los ojos a través de la penumbra, no podía leer en ellos. Pero Sarah no era tonta, Charlie quería tener el control de cada uno de esos pasos. Era evidente. Se movió un poco bajo él, sólo un poco, pero fue suficiente para que la atención del hombre se centrara en los desnudos, hinchados y firmes pechos.

—Entonces, ¿cuál es el paso siguiente?

Una vez más, la voz de Sarah tenía un tono seductor.

Charlie le sostuvo la mirada un instante, luego inclinó la cabeza, susurrando la respuesta a su desafío sobre sus labios.

—¿Crees que estás preparada?

Ella le miró a los ojos.

—Oh, sí —dijo, y luego le besó, ¿o fue él quien la besó a ella? Daba lo mismo. Lo único que realmente importaba era que sus labios se sellaron de nuevo y que, al instante, resurgieron unas chispas de deseo que volvieron a avivar las llamas de la pasión que ambos habían creído tener bajo control mientras hablaban.

Ahora esas llamas ardieron con más fuerza, impulsándolos, apremiándolos a satisfacer el deseo.

«¿Cuál era el paso siguiente?» La pregunta parpadeó en la mente de Sarah mientras la invadía la urgente necesidad de aprender más. Sin dejar de besarla, Charlie le alzó aún más los brazos y le sujetó ambas manos con una de las suyas. Se movió de manera que su muslo quedara entre los suyos, pero sin echar todo el peso de su cuerpo sobre ella. Sarah sintió cómo él alargaba la mano libre y le subía el vestido por encima de las rodillas.

Luego metió la mano debajo, deslizando la dura palma por el suave muslo femenino.

Sarah se estremeció.

Él se detuvo un instante. Dejó la mano quieta, aunque ella pudo sentir el esfuerzo que tuvo que hacer para detenerse, justo antes de dar el paso siguiente.

Charlie suavizó el beso, pero antes de que él pudiera dejar de besarla y hablar —para preguntarle si estaba segura una vez más—, Sarah se arqueó y le besó con ferocidad, respondiendo de esa manera a la pregunta no formulada.

La mano con la que le sujetaba el muslo se aflojó, la caricia se volvió al instante más seductora, más peligrosa. La lengua de Charlie tanteó inquisitivamente la de ella, luego se retiró. Con sólo la presión de los labios masculinos distrayéndola, los sentidos de Sarah se centraron en aquella mano. Charlie deslizó los dedos más arriba, provocando unas envolventes sensaciones en la ingle. Trazó esa línea fina con un dedo, luego retrocedió de nuevo. Sarah estaba completamente atrapada, apenas podía respirar, esperando ansiosa ver qué hacía él a continuación.

Necesitaba saber más.

Charlie deslizó la palma por su cadera, entonces tomó impulso y rodó a un lado, llevándola consigo. Le soltó las manos. Sin pensar, Sarah las posó en sus hombros, aspirando sobresaltada cuando sintió que él deslizaba la mano por su trasero desnudo. Con la mano libre, la tomó de la nuca, haciendo que acercara la boca hacia la suya, adueñándose lánguidamente de su voluntad mientras que con la otra mano seguía explorando por debajo de sus faldas.

Sarah se vio sometida a la voluntad de Charlie. Bajo su completo y absoluto control.

A pesar de las apremiantes y absorbentes sensaciones que la embargaban, del hechizo al que eran sometidos sus sentidos, de la oleada de estremecimientos cada vez más intensos que la atravesaban y que la hacían temblar de anticipación, Sarah era consciente de la intensa concentración de Charlie. De la firme contención que ejercía sobre sí mismo en ese momento. Un compromiso no sólo de mantener un férreo control —su baluarte y defensa— sino el de ella, de darle placer para, como le había dicho, educarla en ese arte.

Para educar sus sentidos, para enseñarle qué se sentía mientras aquella mano masculina le acariciaba sin prisa el trasero desnudo, trazando con sus dedos la hendidura entre los tensos hemisferios gemelos para luego juguetear íntimamente con el nicho entre sus muslos.

Sarah se estremeció y se apretó contra él. Removiéndose sobre el cuerpo de Charlie le deslizó la mano en la nuca y le pidió más a través del beso.

Él vaciló, luego sus dedos abandonaron aquella zona tan sensible y bajaron por la parte trasera de los muslos de Sarah hasta alcanzar su rodilla. Se la agarró y la alzó, doblándole la pierna para que le rodeara la cadera con ella. Por un breve momento le acarició la rodilla, luego trazó suavemente la línea del muslo, hacia donde estaba abierta y expuesta, para que sus dedos acariciaran la delicada carne de su entrepierna.

Sarah se estremeció de nuevo, pero él no se detuvo. La tocó, rozándole ligeramente los rizos, dibujando figuras concéntricas sobre ellos. Luego se acomodó para explorarla más profundamente, delineando el contorno de su sexo. Las suaves caricias de Charlie hicieron que las terminaciones nerviosas de Sarah se erizaran de expectación, provocando que ella siguiera mentalmente sus movimientos, que rastreara cada caricia hasta el final, pero cada una de ellas la dejaba anhelante, deseosa de más.

Deseosa de que satisficiera con su tacto algo que ahora sabía que era deseo. Le calentó la carne hasta que ésta empezó a palpitar. Se sintió embargada por una extraña inquietud. El anhelo de que la tocara más íntimamente floreció y creció.

Hasta que se vio consumida por un deseo ardiente.

Charlie pareció saber el momento exacto en el que ella estaba a punto de rendirse y pedir más. Dejó de besarla y deslizó los labios por la mandíbula de Sarah hacia su oreja.

—Cuando nos casemos, te abrirás a mí de esta manera, separarás las piernas y me rodearás la cintura con ellas, y yo te llenaré con mi carne —le murmuró al oído.

Las palabras —y la imagen que éstas conjuraron— estremecieron a Sarah. En medio de la oscuridad, enfocó la atención en la cara y los labios de Charlie, tan cerca de los suyos, en sus ojos entornados. Se humedeció los labios con la lengua, un gesto que capturó la mirada de él.

La voz masculina estaba llena de pasión, de un deseo incontrolable.

—Colmaré ese extraño vacío que sientes en tu interior —le dijo lentamente, pronunciando las audaces palabras con una cadencia deliberada—. Te penetraré, repetidas veces, y tú me suplicarás que siga haciéndolo, pues para entonces habrás perdido la razón.

Charlie regresó a sus labios, lamiéndolos durante un buen rato.

—Como tanto necesitas y deseas. Así será.

«Mía.»

Charlie oyó la palabra resonándole en la cabeza, pero no la repitió en voz alta. Había luchado y había logrado que la inesperada insistencia de Sarah se convirtiera en una ventaja. Pero ya era suficiente. Antes de que ella pudiera liberarse de la neblina de sensualidad en que la había envuelto, retiró la mano de debajo de la falda, le tomó la cara y la besó profundamente. Tan profundamente como la deseaba.

—Por esta noche es suficiente. —El gruñido con el que habló era un fiel reflejo de que no era eso lo que su cuerpo deseaba, ni tampoco el de ella. Sin embargo, su mente, se mantuvo firme.

Ella lo miró con el ceño fruncido.

—¿Por qué?

Las palabras favoritas de Sarah. Charlie consiguió no devolverle el ceño.

—Porque si nos permitimos desbocarnos, iremos demasiado rápido y te perderás un montón de cosas. —Selló esas palabras tan lógicas con una declaración que resultó imposible de refutar—: Y los dos queremos que todo salga bien porque sólo hay una primera vez.

A la tarde siguiente, Charlie se encontraba de pie en una esquina del alto vallado que bordeaba el césped de la vicaría sosteniendo una taza de té entre sus manos y considerando, con la expresión más impasible que podía adoptar si tenía en cuenta que su futura esposa estaba sentada tomando otro té en la esquina opuesta, lo lejos que estaban el uno del otro.

¿Quién habría pensado que aquello saldría tan mal? Charlie maldijo el impulso que le había hecho aceptar una invitación para el té dominical que cada mes se ofrecía en la vicaría. Había oído que la señora Duncliffe iba a invitar al señor Sinclair, y pensó que podría distraerse departiendo con él sobre inversiones sin tener que perder a Sarah de vista.

Por desgracia, Sinclair tenía otros compromisos. Y para mayor infortunio, Charlie había subestimado el efecto acumulativo de las citas nocturnas con Sarah, y dicho efecto había hecho su aparición en el momento en el que la joven y él habían estado lo suficientemente cerca para tocarse.

Sólo una mirada, un roce de manos, y los dos habían sentido la irritante sacudida, el profundo estremecimiento. La abrumadora y poderosa necesidad de estar juntos en el sentido físico de la palabra.

Buscando seguridad, ambos se habían retirado a las esquinas contrarias del césped para así poder mantener una fachada de respetabilidad y no correr el riesgo de escandalizar a los presentes, casi todos vecinos de la zona además de sus respectivas madres, cediendo a alguna acción atrevida, imposible de malinterpretar.

Charlie se había refugiado con Jon, Henry y un grupo de caballeros. Y Sarah estaba rodeada de otras señoritas, aunque la mayoría de los ojos femeninos, tanto jóvenes como viejos, estaban puestos en ellos, preguntándose por esa repentina separación, en especial ahora que todo el mundo suponía por dónde iban los tiros.

Sin tener en cuenta tales especulaciones, estar juntos en público ya no era inteligente.

¿Qué era lo más difícil de aceptar para él? Que jamás en su vida se había visto afectado hasta ese punto por una mujer. Por conseguir a una mujer. En ese momento se parecía más a un adolescente babeante ante su primer amor, que al afable, gallardo y sofisticado hombre de mundo que era. ¡Por el amor de Dios, tenía treinta y tres años! Un caballero de su clase, de su edad y experiencia, no debía sentirse como si su vida dependiera de introducir una erección demasiado activa en el cálido refugio de un cuerpo femenino en concreto.

No debería sentirse como si poseer a Sarah lo fuera todo para él, el objetivo final de su existencia.

Pero le gustase o no, era así como se sentía.

Aceptó otra pasta de té del platito que le tendían y la mordisqueó mientras volvía a posar la mirada en Sarah, preguntándose pensativamente por qué se torturaba de esa manera. Estaban en la vicaría y no había ninguna posibilidad de que pudiera aliviar aquella picazón ardiente mientras siguiera allí. Desvió la vista a la rosaleda de la señora Duncliffe mientras volvía a revivir los acontecimientos de la noche anterior.

Había abandonado el cenador aliviado y satisfecho. Aliviado porque había superado el reto, satisfecho porque la batalla que había disputado con Sarah no sólo no le había hecho perder el control, sino que había logrado establecer una base, una justificación razonada que ella comprendía, para seguir adelante con su plan.

Si bien el alivio había desaparecido, no había dudas de que seguía satisfecho.

Lo que suponía una pequeña victoria.

Pero sin importar cómo tergiversara los hechos, lo que él no podía comprender o explicar, ni mucho menos negar, era que, mientras había estado seduciendo a Sarah —con éxito, todo hay que decirlo—, había acabado siendo seducido a su vez.

No podía echarle la culpa a ella. Dadas las diferencias de edad y experiencia, sencillamente no cabía la posibilidad de que ella pudiera seducirle. Pero, una y otra vez, se había encontrado con que perdía el control. Y una y otra vez había tenido que adaptarse y cambiar de táctica. En cuanto trazaba una línea decidido a no traspasarla, ella le presionaba y él se encontraba teniendo que reajustar sus planes.

Puede que hubiera sido ella quien había planteado sus exigencias, pero había sido él quien había accedido a ellas.

Sarah no podía ser capaz de controlarle, y no había nada ni nadie más involucrado, así que tenía que ser él, algo en su interior, que por alguna extraña razón lo empujaba, seduciéndole, instándole a hacer cosas que hacían que ese cortejo fuese mucho más duro todavía. No lo comprendía, pero estaba resuelto a ganar. Y lo haría.

Volvió a mirar a Sarah. Ella lo percibió y, por un instante, le sostuvo la mirada desde el otro lado del césped; luego le dio la espalda. La vio levantar la taza y dar un sorbo; le temblaba la mano cuando dejó la taza sobre el platito. Charlie apartó los ojos.

El tiempo que se había propuesto para llevar a cabo su plan finalizaba el martes por la noche. Hasta esa noche la tomaría un poco más, la tentaría, pero sin dejar de estar en guardia a cada paso del camino.

Contra lo que fuera que estuviera invadiéndole la mente.

La luna relucía sobre el embalse cuando Sarah acudió a la cita de esa noche. Charlie y ella estaban hambrientos, demasiado hambrientos, algo implícito en el beso que se dieron con voracidad y que precedería a muchos más.

Muchísimos más.

Sarah ardía de deseo, pero no eran sólo los placeres físicos los que ella buscaba. Quería saber por qué, y si bien comenzaba a entender que no eran unas razones frías y lógicas lo que había detrás del evidente deseo de Charlie, se le escapaban los motivos reales que lo provocaban.

Y aun así, aquel efímero deseo físico estaba ligado a esos motivos y era consecuencia de ellos. Si llegaba a saber la razón de uno, comprendería los otros.

El plan de la joven se había reducido a eso. A permitir que él le mostrara lo que haría, y luego instarle a que le mostrara aún más. Hasta que ella aprendiera y finalmente entendiera.

Y si se estremecía cuando Charlie cerraba la boca sobre su pecho, si gritaba, con un gemido primitivo cuando él comenzaba a chuparle el pezón con ferocidad, si se le derretían las extremidades y se le erizaban las terminaciones nerviosas cuando él le levantaba las faldas y la acariciaba, tocándola y ahuecándola, explorando ligeramente aquella parte de su feminidad hasta que las llamas le bajaban por la columna y le inundaban el vientre con un fuego hirviente, entonces, se dijo a sí misma, era necesario hacer un intercambio.

Si quería aprender más de él, tenía que entregar más de sí misma.

Cuánto estaba dispuesta a ofrecer no lo supo hasta que una vez más estuvieron echados en el sofá con las extremidades enredadas, apasionados y ardientes, hambrientos y deseosos. Hasta que hundió las manos en el sedoso pelo de Charlie, totalmente cautivada, con los labios separados, sensuales y ansiosos bajo los de él, con la lengua entrelazándose con la suya, desafiándolo y jugueteando, exigiéndole todavía más. Hasta que sintió las manos masculinas cubriendo su cuerpo, rozándole con los dedos la unión de los muslos, acariciándole una y otra vez la carne hinchada de su entrada secreta.

Sarah necesitaba más. Ahora, no más tarde. Necesitaba lo que venía a continuación más de lo que necesitaba respirar. Necesitaba... No estaba segura de qué necesitaba, pero sí de que él lo sabía.

Cuando Charlie intentó mantenerse firme en la línea invisible que había trazado y le negó más intimidad, ella le rogó en silencio, con sus labios y su lengua, con sus manos y su cuerpo, que la traspasara.

Charlie descubrió que no era capaz de resistirse a aquella súplica sensual. Si ella deseaba, él le ofrecía. Alguna parte incontrolable de su mente había hecho de esa máxima su lema y la había grabado a fuego en su cerebro. Sin importar lo dispuesto que estuviera a mantener un absoluto control y a dictar cada caricia, cada súplica, cada deleite que ella descubría, no podía reprimirse de aplacar la explícita necesidad de Sarah.

No podía negarse a disfrutar de ese placer.

Guiado por esa pasión que él seguía sin reconocer del todo, por esa necesidad para la que no tenía nombre, le rodeó la entrada resbaladiza con la punta del dedo. Luego, cuando ella le imploró más, él presionó en su interior sólo un centímetro. Pero cuando Sarah lo recibió cálida y ansiosa, arqueándose contra su mano, invitándolo, tentándolo, Charlie se rindió y le dio lo que deseaba.

Sintió sobre su boca cómo ella contenía el aliento cuando deslizó el dedo profundamente en esa apretada funda. Notó la tensión de aquella carne virgen que se contraía en torno a su dedo, bañándolo con sus fluidos ardientes. Estudió su respuesta, esperando a que ella asimilara la primera sacudida para comenzar a acariciarla con una lentitud deliberada al principio, permitiendo que los vertiginosos sentidos de la joven absorbieran el impacto de aquella primera e íntima penetración. Luego el deseo de ambos se fue incrementando gradualmente, palpitando con más rapidez, con más fuerza, hasta que adoptó el ritmo de sus corazones, el correr de la sangre por sus venas.

Sarah se retorció, se removió debajo de él, alzando las caderas de una manera instintiva hacia aquella íntima caricia. Guiado por ella y por su propia necesidad compulsiva, Charlie capturó la boca de Sarah, y entonces se reacomodó para sentir la escalada y la innegable pasión de la joven.

La guio hasta la cima, cada vez más rápido, hasta que ella alcanzó el pico más alto, se tensó y clavó los dedos en el brazo de Charlie, hasta que estalló en miles de fragmentos y se deshizo entre sus brazos.

La oleada fulgurante que había atravesado a Sarah murió, se desvaneció y la abandonó, dejándola sin fuerzas. La joven se relajó bajo él con el cuerpo totalmente laxo. Charlie retiró la mano de su cuerpo, dejando caer la falda. Esperaba que Sarah hubiera quedado satisfecha.

Luego interrumpió el beso, que en el último momento se había vuelto más suave, levantó la cabeza y la miró a la cara, pálida a la luz de la luna. Era la cara de un ángel, uno que escondía una voluntad semejante a la suya.

«Ésa es una de las razones por las que la deseo.»

Aquel pensamiento irrumpió en su mente, luego desapareció. Sarah parpadeó y abrió los ojos. Lo miró y frunció el ceño.

—Te quiero dentro de mí —se quejó ella de manera provocativa. Aunque no llegó a hacer un puchero, parecía estar a punto de hacerlo.

Charlie suspiró y se echó hacia atrás. Se obligó a cerrar la puerta a sus demonios internos, muerto de deseo por ella, preparado y dispuesto a seguir tal sugerencia.

—Todavía no. —Su voz sonó entrecortada y tensa.

Se obligó a enderezarse. Tomó entre sus brazos el cuerpo laxo de la joven y la acomodó en su regazo.

La cadera de Sarah presionaba contra su erección, pero él no pudo hacer otra cosa que apretar los dientes y aguantar. Y negarse a escuchar sus más bajos instintos, que le decían que estaba tan duro que se arriesgaba a sufrir una lesión permanente.

Tenía que pensar, pero con ella en sus brazos, aquello parecía una tarea demasiado difícil. Intentó concentrarse con todas sus fuerzas, pero lo único que llenaba su mente, lo único de lo que era consciente, era del tacto de aquella mejilla contra su pecho desnudo.

Sarah había logrado despojarlo del abrigo y el chaleco, le había vuelto a abrir la camisa para deslizar las manos por su torso desnudo, piel contra piel. Quizá fuera ese gesto lo que le había arrebatado la capacidad de pensar, aunque no podía imaginar cómo había llegado a ocurrir tal cosa. Jamás había sido susceptible a algo parecido con ninguna otra mujer, pero con ella... susceptible se había convertido en su segundo nombre.

Cerró los brazos en torno a ella, abrazándola. Acunándola.

De repente, Sarah soltó una risita seca y ligeramente cínica.

—Después de nuestra representación en la vicaría, mi madre me ha preguntado si nos había pasado algo.

La madre de Charlie no había preguntado, aunque lo había mirado intrigada.

—¿Qué le has dicho? —preguntó con curiosidad.

—Que nos parece demasiado desconcertante ser el centro de atención de todo el mundo.

A pesar de todo, Charlie sonrió.

—Una respuesta perfecta. Y además se ajusta a la verdad. —Tomó nota mental por si tenía que recurrir a ella más tarde.

Siguieron sentados en el sofá mientras la luna se deslizaba por el cielo y una acogedora oscuridad los rodeaba.

Un momento después ella se removió. Levantando la cabeza, Sarah le tomó la mejilla con una mano.

—Charlie...

—No. —Él capturó los dedos de la joven, se los llevó a los labios y le sostuvo la mirada mientras se los besaba. Por fin había recuperado la cordura. Había comenzado a darse cuenta de que había ocurrido de nuevo—. Todavía no —murmuró—, tenemos que ir paso a paso.

Paso a paso.

Que Dios le ayudara.

A la mañana siguiente, Charlie se encontraba sentado en el escritorio de la biblioteca con la barbilla apoyada en una mano, mirando ensimismado la alfombra Aubusson, sin ser capaz de comprender cómo había podido llegar hasta ese punto.

Su plan había estado claro desde el principio y lo había ejecutado con gran precisión, pero de alguna manera la continua interacción con Sarah y la intención de ésta de ir más allá con rapidez habían minado su voluntad y se había visto incapaz de parar.

Y aunque sabía muy bien que tenía que poner freno a aquel aprendizaje sensual, una parte de él —una parte muy poderosa— no quería más que dejarse llevar. Quería zambullirse en la pasión que ardía entre ellos, quería atiborrarse de aquella creciente lujuria, saciarse y luego deleitarse y recrearse en ella.

A pesar de la caminata en la fría noche después de haber acompañado a Sarah a casa, a pesar de la larga cabalgada entre los campos desolados por el invierno, apenas había logrado pegar ojo la noche anterior, incapaz de liberar la mente y los sentidos de la promesa de pasión que ella representaba.

Por su experiencia sabía que podía hacerlo, pero no sabía qué ganaría con ello.

Era aquel elusivo y tentador sabor de la inocencia.

Era eso, decidió, lo que había invadido sus pensamientos, lo que lo había convertido en un adicto. El sabor de la inocencia. Y las adicciones, como las obsesiones, podían llevar a los hombres a hacer cosas que normalmente no harían, a comportarse de manera ilógica. Pero las adicciones, gracias a Dios, podían vencerse. Como acabaría sucediendo con ésta.

En cuanto ella hubiera aceptado casarse con él y fuera suya para siempre. Una vez que estuvieran casados, aquella inocencia se desvanecería gradualmente. En unas semanas —un mes a lo sumo— aquella curiosa fascinación que Sarah ejercía sobre él quedaría saciada, y se disiparía por sí sola.

Así que no tenía de qué preocuparse. Ésta no era una obsesión, como sí podía serlo el amor. Sólo era un adictivo encaprichamiento.

Reflexionó sobre esa conclusión y no encontró nada en ella que pudiera rebatir. Por lo tanto no había ningún problema para seguir adelante con su plan.

Pero era lunes, el día que Sarah pasaba en el orfanato.

A pesar de la auténtica compulsión que sentía de ensillar a *Tormenta* y cabalgar hasta la granja Quilley, y de las indudables oportunidades que surgirían ese día de aliviar la picazón de abrazarla, besarla, tocarla, mientras disimulaba sus reacciones ante todos los demás, bastaba con imaginar la cantidad de veces que tendría que apretar los dientes y los puños para aplacar a los demonios que lo inundaban, para mantenerse quieto en la silla.

Y ese pensamiento hizo que finalmente se centrara en los diversos documentos de la hacienda que tenía delante. Haciendo una mueca, recogió una pluma y se obligó a tratar de resolver todos los asuntos legales durante el día, y dejar los auténticos retos para la noche.

—Ha venido a verla un caballero, señorita.

Sarah levantó la vista hacia Maggs, que había asomado la cabeza por la puerta. La joven había estado doblando y ordenando la ropa recién lavada de la guardería del orfanato, una manera perfecta de evitar que su mente se fuera por otros derroteros infinitamente más divertidos.

—La señora Carter me ha dicho que le diga que lo ha hecho pasar al despacho y que si puede bajar a hablar con él. —El muchacho esbozó una amplia sonrisa—. Parece el vivo retrato de Shylock.*

—Ya veo. —Sarah acabó de doblar un par de calcetines rosa de lana y se dirigió a la puerta—. Gracias por el mensaje, regresa a tus clases... y no te entretengas por el camino.

Maggs le lanzó una mirada ofendida que Sarah le sostuvo con firmeza y que hizo que el chico soltara un suspiro.

—De acuerdo. Iré directo a clase.

Sarah le siguió escaleras abajo. Observó cómo Maggs se encaminaba cabizbajo al pasillo que conducía a la habitación donde Joseph daba sus clases y sonrió ante la evidente renuencia del adolescente; luego se dirigió al despacho.

Joseph había estado enseñándole a los chicos mayores la obra de Shakespeare. Aunque dudaba mucho que algún prestamista hubiera ido a verla, no la sorprendió abrir la puerta del estudio y descubrir a un caballero delgado y de facciones angulosas vestido de negro riguroso. Tenía los ojos pequeños, hundidos y oscuros, y la nariz aguileña, algo que respondía claramente a la imagen que Maggs tendría de Shylock.

Ocultó su diversión tras una sonrisa de bienvenida.

—Buenas tardes. Soy la señorita Conningham.

El hombre, que se había levantado de la silla que había frente al escritorio cuando ella entró, le hizo una educada reverencia.

—El señor Milton Haynes para servirla, señorita. Soy un abogado de Taunton y he venido a hacerle una oferta en nombre de uno de mis clientes.

* Shylock es uno de los personajes de *El mercader de Venecia*, de William Shakespeare; representa el estereotipo de un avaricioso prestamista judío. *(N. de las T.)*

Sarah le hizo un gesto con la mano para que volviera a sentarse en la silla mientras ella se dirigía al otro lado del escritorio y tomaba asiento.

—¿Una oferta?

—Así es, señorita. —El señor Haynes levantó una cartera de piel sobre su regazo, la abrió y extrajo un documento doblado—. ¿Me permite? —Ante el asentimiento de Sarah, puso la cartera en el suelo y, con gran teatralidad, extendió el documento encima del escritorio—. Como voy a mostrarle a continuación, señorita Conningham, mi cliente quiere hacerle una generosa oferta por la casa y las tierras que se conocen como granja Quilley por la suma que puede ver aquí. —Señaló el importe con una uña pulcra—. Ahora, si me permite aconsejarle...

Con el ceño fruncido, Sarah cogió el papel y lo deslizó bajo el dedo del abogado. El hombre pareció renuente, pero al final levantó el dedo y dejó que cogiera el documento.

Aunque Sarah estaba poco familiarizada con tales documentos, una rápida ojeada a las complejas frases legales bastó para confirmar que alguien le estaba haciendo una oferta por la granja Quilley, por las tierras y la casa, y que la cifra era lo suficientemente grande como para hacerla parpadear.

El señor Haynes se aclaró la garganta.

—Como acabo de decirle, esta oferta es muy generosa, sin duda más elevada de lo que podría esperar en el mercado inmobiliario de la zona, pero mi cliente está muy interesado en esta propiedad, por lo que está dispuesto a pagar una cantidad mayor a la de su valor en el mercado. —Se inclinó hacia delante—. En efectivo, debo añadir. Todo legal, se lo puedo asegurar.

Sarah levantó la mirada a la cara de Haynes.

—¿Quién es su cliente? —Según los documentos, la oferta había sido hecha a través de las oficinas de Haynes.

El hombrecillo se reclinó en la silla, con expresión remilgada.

—Me temo que no puedo decirle su nombre. Es un hombre un tanto excéntrico, y prefiere conservar su intimidad.

Sarah arqueó las cejas.

—¿De veras? —Ella no tenía ni idea de qué hacer con eso. ¿Eran habituales tales transacciones anónimas? De cualquier manera, no era algo en lo que estuviera interesada—. Me temo, señor Haynes, que su cliente ha sido mal informado. —Se puso en pie, dobló la hoja y se la tendió a Haynes, que, con cara larga, se vio obligado a levantarse también—. No tengo ningún interés o intención de vender la granja Quilley.

La sorpresa asomó a los angulosos rasgos de Haynes. Algo comprensible dada la cantidad de dinero que ofrecía su cliente, así que Sarah añadió:

—En realidad, la granja es un orfanato y me fue legada con la condición de que siguiera como tal. No puedo romper la confianza que se ha depositado en mí.

Haynes abrió la boca y la cerró.

—Oh —dijo tras un momento.

Desanimado, dejó que Sarah lo acompañara fuera del despacho hasta la puerta principal.

Una vez allí se volvió hacia ella.

—Por supuesto, le comunicaré su decisión a mi cliente. Supongo que no existe ninguna posibilidad de que cambie de opinión, ¿verdad?

Sarah sonrió y le aseguró que tal posibilidad no existía. Con los hombros hundidos, Haynes se montó en la jaca que había dejado atada frente a la puerta y se alejó al trote por el camino de acceso.

Cruzando los brazos, Sarah se apoyó contra el marco de la puerta y lo observó alejarse. El abogado desapareció durante un momento entre las casas de Crowcombe para reaparecer un momento después al girar hacia el sur, por el camino que conducía a Taunton.

Sarah oyó pasos a su espalda y giró la cabeza. Katy Carter apareció en el vestíbulo y se detuvo junto a ella en el umbral. Secándose las manos en el delantal, miró en la dirección por la que había desaparecido la figura del abogado.

—Me dijo que tenía una oferta para ti que no podrías rechazar —le dijo Katy, lanzándole una mirada inquisitiva.

—En eso se equivocaba —le respondió con una amplia sonrisa—. Era una oferta para comprar la granja, la casa y las tierras, pero ya le he dicho que no estaba interesada en vender.

Katy asintió con la cabeza y se volvió hacia la casa.

—Sí, bueno, sabía que no lo harías. La vieja lady Cricklade se habría revuelto en su tumba.

Sarah se rio entre dientes mientras meneaba la cabeza.

—Sin duda habría salido de la tumba para rondarme. —Acabó sonriendo ante el recuerdo de la figura flaca y autoritaria de su madrina, que, sin embargo, había sido muy cariñosa con todo el mundo.

»!Katy, si viene alguien más queriendo comprar la granja, déjale bien claro que no está en venta! —le gritó mientras Katy se dirigía a la cocina.

Katy le lanzó una sonrisa confiada.

—Descuida, así lo haré.

Sarah permaneció en la puerta y volvió a mirar el valle que se extendía a los pies de los Quantocks. A su espalda el orfanato bullía de vida y esperanza. Había sido escogida por su madrina y por su madre para ser la guardiana de aquel lugar, pero si ejercía aquel papel era porque deseaba hacerlo y porque el orfanato también le aportaba algo.

Mientras el sol declinaba lentamente, surgiendo bajo las nubes e iluminando el otro lado del valle, aún sumido en el monótono invierno, Sarah intentó definir qué era ese algo. Después de un momento, concluyó que el orfanato ocupaba un lugar importante en su vida, un lugar donde ella desempeñaba un papel que la satisfacía y que era una parte vital de su existencia.

Sin embargo, aquel lugar sólo representaba un aspecto de su vida, una pieza más del rompecabezas. Un puzle que todavía estaba por definir, al que todavía le faltaban piezas por colocar antes de poder ver el resultado final.

Su vida.

Ese pensamiento le hizo recordar el tema que la había estado consumiendo durante toda la semana anterior. Charlie y su propuesta de matrimonio. Dos asuntos, dos piezas, pero ambas inseparables. Si quería una, tenía que aceptar la otra. Durante incontables horas había estado reflexionando sobre la auténtica pregunta a la que se había enfrentado: ¿eran Charlie y la posición que le ofrecía una parte esencial de su vida?

¿Debería aferrarse gustosa a lo que él le ofrecía, aceptarlo y encajarlo dentro de su rompecabezas?

¿Lograría encajar en él?

Ése era el quid de la cuestión, y aunque todavía no conocía la respuesta, sabía mucho más ahora que cuando él le había pedido tan inesperadamente que fuera su prometida.

Como le había dicho él, compartían una trayectoria común desde su nacimiento. Sus encuentros habían confirmado que eso ofrecía cierta comodidad digna de tomar en cuenta. Además, si vivía en casa de Charlie, aún estaría rodeada de personas a las que conocía. Aunque él tenía amigos y conocidos en Londres y más allá del valle que ella no conocía, aquí, en casa, compartían prácticamente todas las amistades.

Gran parte de sus vidas seguían el mismo camino.

En definitiva, no había nada en él a lo que pudiera poner reparos, ni como hombre ni como persona, por no hablar de todas sus posesiones.

En lo que concernía a preocupaciones menos tangibles, como lo que él sentía o podía llegar a sentir por ella, Sarah ya había descubierto que la proposición matrimonial de Charlie no había sido guiada sólo por la lógica y las razones convencionales. Había sido influenciada por otra emoción, ya que era evidente que una o más de las emociones que ella quería descubrir —pasión, deseo o incluso amor— habían jugado un papel fundamental. Y aunque el amor aún estaba por verse, parecía que lo que él sentía por ella podía ser todo lo que Sarah deseaba.

La joven reflexionó sobre eso y lo que él le hacía sentir, y si bien sospechaba, dada la forma en que él respondía a ella, que lo dos sentían lo mismo el uno por el otro, lamentaba no haber podido averiguar aún a su completa satisfacción qué sentía ella por él, si era verdad o no que lo amaba.

Estaba fascinada y sumida en una especie de abandono sensual, sí, pero ¿era eso amor?

Tras un momento, decidió dejar aparcado el tema, aún por resolver, y continuó con su reflexión. ¿Qué más había aprendido? Evidentemente, que a él le gustaban los niños, que le hacían disfrutar y que podía y quería jugar con ellos, y eso era un punto a su favor.

Repasó su lista mental y le sorprendió descubrir que ya había marcado muchas cosas a su favor. Miró al camino y, al ver pasar a otro viajero, recordó la oferta del cliente de Haynes.

Lentamente se enderezó y sintió una opresión en el pecho.

Si se casaba con Charlie, ¿qué ocurriría con el orfanato? Era suyo, cierto, pero sus propiedades, al casarse, pasarían a ser legalmente de su marido.

Siguió allí de pie mirando sin ver las colinas ondulantes hasta que, al cabo de un rato, se rodeó con los brazos, se dio la vuelta y entró.

Tenía que hablar con Charlie.

8

Esa noche el cielo estaba claro y sin nubes. La luz de la luna llena arrojaba un brillo sombrío sobre las colinas, teñía de plata las ondas en la superficie del embalse y entraba a raudales en el cenador, donde Charlie esperaba a Sarah.

Dado que esa tarde no había habido ninguna reunión social, Charlie había acudido temprano al cenador esperando que Sarah hiciera lo mismo. De todas maneras, prefería esperar allí, cerca de ella y de la promesa de esa cita nocturna, que en los confines de Morwellan Park bajo la atenta mirada de su perspicaz familia.

Paseó lentamente de un lado para otro, cada vez más consciente de la fuerte anticipación y del agudo deseo. Un rato después vio a Sarah acercarse por el camino y de inmediato supo que había pasado algo.

La joven tenía los brazos cruzados y se ceñía el chal con firmeza. Caminaba con brío, pero no miraba el cenador, sino el camino que tenía delante.

Su atención no estaba puesta en él y en lo que iba a acontecer esa noche, por el contrario estaba absorta en algún otro asunto que parecía tenerla preocupada.

Si se hubiese tratado de otra mujer, a Charlie le habría irritado no ser el centro de atención y perderse todas esas cosas que había previsto hacer. Pero tratándose de Sarah, la anticipación, el deseo y el pálpito de su corazón ante la simple visión de la joven se transformaron al instante en algo más.

La estaba esperando cuando Sarah subió los escalones del cenador y entró en la penumbra que arrojaba sombras sobre el lugar.

—¿Qué sucede?

Ella levantó la cabeza. Se acercó y parpadeó ante la pregunta. Luego imaginó que él había notado su ensimismamiento y le respondió:

—Hoy he estado en el orfanato y... —Se detuvo ante él, escudriñándole la cara iluminada por la luz de la luna. Luego alzó la barbilla con firmeza y continuó—: Si acepto tu oferta y me caso contigo, el orfanato pasará a tus manos.

Ahora fue Charlie quien parpadeó. No había considerado tal cosa, pero lo que acababa de decir Sarah era cierto.

Entrelazando las manos, Sarah se volvió y caminó por el cenador.

—Lo que tú no sabes es que para mí el orfanato es mucho más que una simple propiedad. Como ya te he mencionado, lo heredé de lady Cricklade, mi madrina, por quien sentía un profundo aprecio y, desde que yo era muy joven, tanto ella como mi madre me alentaron a interesarme vivamente por el lugar, no sólo a supervisarlo desde lejos.

Deteniéndose bajo uno de los arcos, Sarah levantó la mirada y observó el embalse.

—Llevo varios años encargándome del orfanato. —Se dio la vuelta y lo miró a través de las sombras—. Es algo que requiere tiempo, esfuerzo y cuidado, pero a cambio el orfanato me ofrece satisfacción a muchos niveles. —Hizo una pausa antes de continuar—: Si me caso contigo, o con cualquier otro, dudo que pueda ceder alegremente todo eso... no sólo por la obligación que siento ante el legado que me hizo lady Cricklade, sino por el interés y la satisfacción que me produce. Ciertamente no es algo que haría de manera voluntaria.

Charlie se unió a ella bajo el arco. Sarah miró aquellos rasgos iluminados por la luz de la luna.

—No existe ninguna razón para que tengas que renunciar a todo eso. Es una cuestión muy simple. —La miró directamente a los ojos, pensando a toda velocidad y sopesando las distintas soluciones—. Tienes razón al pensar que cuando nos casemos la granja Quilley pasará a ser mía, pero podemos dejar estipulado, como parte de los acuerdos matrimoniales, que la propiedad vuelva a ser tuya en caso de viudedad. Podemos disponer que el título de propiedad más una suma adecuada para los gastos de mantenimiento del lugar sean destinados para tu uso exclusivo desde el día de nuestra boda hasta incluso después de mi muerte, y que a la tuya la granja pase a ser de nuestros herederos. —Charlie hizo una pausa y la miró arqueando una ceja—. ¿Tiene eso tu aprobación?

Su aprobación y mucho más. Sarah asintió con la cabeza.

—Sí. —Había sabido que él no se casaba con ella por dinero ni por cualquier otra propiedad que ella pudiera poseer, pero no había esperado un acuerdo semejante—. ¿Invertirías una suma en...?

Charlie curvó los labios.

—Considéralo un regalo de bodas, uno cuyos beneficios recogeré cuando te cases contigo.

Sarah sonrió. Charlie era incorregible, en especial cuando tenía un objetivo en mente, aunque ella jamás había dudado de su determinación. Aun así, no había podido negar su sorpresa por el hecho de que él hubiera adivinado sus afligidos pensamientos antes de decir una sola palabra o de mirarla siquiera a los ojos, ni por haber mostrado una actitud al respecto que no tenía nada que ver con el depredador sensual al que la había acostumbrado en sus citas. Por el contrario, había sido la encarnación de un caballero de brillante armadura dispuesto a matar los dragones que se cruzaran en el camino de Sarah.

Un pensamiento soñador. No obstante, mientras lo estudiaba a través de la penumbra, aquella imagen que había aparecido en su mente no se desvaneció. Sarah se movió hacia él envuelta en las sombras proyectadas por la luz de la luna. Alzó las manos al torso de Charlie y las deslizó lentamente hasta sus hombros mientras se acercaba un paso más.

Con descaro se estrechó contra su cuerpo, se puso de puntillas y le rozó los labios con los suyos.

—Gracias —dijo, y luego se echó hacia atrás, lo justo para verle la cara, para observar los cambios que el deseo había producido en sus rasgos. El tono que Charlie había empleado para hablar del orfanato: enérgico, serio, de hombre de negocios, la había tranquilizado incluso más que sus palabras. Ahora sabía todo lo que necesitaba saber en el plano material. Sólo quedaba una pregunta por hacer.

Y Sarah no era reacia a aprovechar aquella inesperada oportunidad, y utilizarla en su propio beneficio, para obtener la respuesta a esa última cuestión.

—Es muy generoso por tu parte —dijo bajando la mirada a los labios de Charlie. Con las manos en sus hombros lo empujó hacia atrás. Él vaciló un instante, luego cedió y permitió que ella lo dirigiera hasta que sus corvas tropezaron con el sofá y cayó sobre los cojines cuando Sarah le dio un último empujón.

Ella continuó. Apartando una mano de su hombro, la joven se subió las faldas descaradamente y levantando primero una rodilla y luego la otra, las apoyó sobre los cojines a ambos lados de los muslos de Charlie. El chal de Sarah cayó al suelo cuando ella se sentó a horcajadas sobre él. Luego se deslizó lentamente por los duros muslos masculinos e inclinándose sobre aquel ancho pecho, lo besó.

Seduciéndolo manifiesta y audazmente.

Estaba segura de que no hacía falta explicarle que ésa era la manera que ella había elegido para agradecérselo. Cuando ambos abrieron los labios y se fundieron en un beso ardiente, cuando sus lenguas se encontraron y se batieron en un duelo, cuando él cerró las manos firmemente en su cintura, Sarah pensó que ciertamente no había necesidad de aclarar qué era lo que quería hacer a continuación.

Esa vez, sin embargo, tenía intención de llegar hasta el final.

Charlie se recostó, satisfecho de que ella hubiera tomado la iniciativa de besarle. La dejó seguir adelante con aquel asalto sensual y que llevara la delantera por el momento, permitiendo que el sabor de la inocencia de la joven le inundara el cerebro.

Charlie le abrió el corpiño dejándole los pechos expuestos para su completo deleite y luego cerró las manos sobre ellos. Oyó el suspiro de Sarah, sintió la cálida y firme carne bajo las palmas de las manos y sonrió. Ella tenía los labios curvados en un gesto de burlón desafío. Jactándose para sus adentros, Charlie le rodeó las caderas con un brazo y la atrajo hacia sí. Luego posó sus labios en la ruborizada piel de la joven y oyó cómo ella soltaba un jadeo.

Charlie comenzó a orquestar una sinfonía a costa de ella, repleta de gemidos sensuales y apasionados, de suspiros y jadeos, hasta que consiguió arrancarle sollozos suplicantes. Cada uno de esos sonidos repercutía intensamente en él, alimentando y provocando su deseo voraz, dejándolo sin aliento y haciendo que se esforzara todavía más para controlarse, para saborearla y saciarse de ella. Más profunda y completamente que nunca.

Esta vez, aunque lo sabía sólo por instinto, estaba completamente seguro de que iba a ser así.

Pero ir más allá no formaba parte de sus planes para esa noche. Esa noche lo único que quería era estrechar todavía más el cerco de la tensión sensual, lo suficiente como para volver loca de deseo a la joven para que se decidiera a ser suya.

Pronto. Tenía que decidirse ya.

Ése era el único pensamiento que tenía Charlie en la cabeza mientras se deleitaba con aquellos pechos ruborizados, con los suaves gemidos de placer que la joven dejaba caer en sus oídos mientras sentía cómo le enredaba los dedos en su pelo. Sarah era receptiva a sus caricias y no lo ocultaba, no hacía ningún esfuerzo por esconder todo lo que él la hacía sentir.

Los ojos de Sarah chispeaban bajo sus párpados cuando él levantó la cabeza lo suficiente para mirar aquellos montículos rosados que había capturado con sus manos y recrearse en su belleza, lo suficiente para sentir una aguda satisfacción ante aquellas hinchadas redondeces, aquel peso sensual, aquellos pezones tensos y erectos que hacía rodar entre las puntas de sus dedos.

Sarah soltó un suspiro tortuoso. Tensó los dedos enterrados en el pelo de Charlie y luego cerró los puños. Tiró con fuerza y le hizo levantar la cabeza para poder besarlo de nuevo. Él alzó una mano y le ahuecó la cara, hundiéndose en el delicioso refugio de su boca para volver a disfrutar de su sabor.

Y así lo hizo, pero de repente sintió que perdía la cabeza. Ella había metido la mano entre sus cuerpos, buscándolo y encontrándolo duro como el acero, rígido como el hierro. La joven lo tocó, apretando la palma de su mano contra el dolorido miembro, acariciándolo con atrevimiento por encima de la tela de los pantalones.

Y Charlie perdió el control. Se sintió inundado por un creciente calor sensual, por una enorme oleada de deseo ardiente.

Antes de poder recobrar el aliento, antes de poder recuperar la razón, o la voluntad, para atrapar la mano de Sarah y apartarla, la joven se dejó caer sobre él, apretando sus pechos desnudos contra su torso desnudo. ¿Cuándo había ocurrido eso?

—¿Por qué me quieres a mí? —murmuró ella con una voz sensual y provocativa, como una sirena en la noche.

Charlie no podía pensar, así que no contestó.

Sarah movió la mano, deslizando un dedo arriba y abajo. Charlie cerró los ojos e intentó recuperar la cordura, intentó acordarse de cuál era su plan —porque tenía un plan, ¿verdad?— y ceñirse a él.

—No quieres casarte conmigo por dinero. Yo no soy rica y tú sí.

Sarah vertía las palabras suavemente sobre sus labios sin dejar de sorbérselos y lamérselos, luego deslizó los labios hacia la mandíbula de Charlie. Y durante todo el rato la joven no dejó de mover los dedos sobre el miembro masculino. Él tensó los dedos en su espalda. Deslizó las manos a los costados de la joven y la sujetó con fuerza. Debería apartarla, por lo menos lo suficiente para volver a recuperar el juicio, pero Sarah no dejaba de contonearse, restregándose contra él, y el roce de sus pechos desnudos contra su torso era demasiado tentador. Charlie vaciló, pues no quería poner fin a aquellas sensaciones, todavía no, no hasta que sus sentidos sedientos se hubieran saciado por completo.

—Tampoco te casas conmigo por mi linaje —ronroneó ella en su oído mientras cerraba la mano sobre su miembro para volver a abrirla al momento—. Mi familia no es tan importante. Es más, los Conningham no tienen la categoría suficiente para formar una alianza con los condes de Meredith.

Las palabras de Sarah atravesaron suavemente la marea de deseo que envolvía a Charlie. Pero discutir estaba más allá de sus posibilidades, y más teniendo en cuenta que lo que ella decía era cierto.

—Y desde luego no quieres casarte conmigo por ninguna distinción personal que yo pudiera darte... no soy un «diamante de primera clase», ni poseo una belleza espectacular, ni destaco en la sociedad. —Levantó la cabeza y lo miró a la cara—. No soy ni nunca seré un trofeo que ganar.

Charlie intentó fruncir el ceño. En eso se equivocaba. Puede que aún no la hubiera visto desnuda, pero sin duda sabía apreciar la belleza femenina y ella era toda una belleza; cuando finalmente la tuviera desnuda entre sus brazos, sería una diosa con la piel perlada, encantadoras curvas, puras líneas creadas sólo para él, pensadas para saciar sus sentidos.

—Yo...

Ella le puso un dedo en los labios.

—Tú me deseas. —Lo siguió acariciando; no había discusión en ese punto—. Pero ¿por qué? —Sarah ladeó la cabeza y bajo la luz de la luna buscó su rostro, sus ojos—. ¿Por qué quieres casarte conmigo?

Sarah esperó su respuesta. Y Charlie se dio cuenta de que tendría que responder. Pero con aquella cálida y pequeña mano, intensamente femenina, acunando su enorme erección, con la cabeza dándole vueltas y su deseo a flor de piel, no le cabía otra alternativa. Ya no poseía fuerzas para negar la respuesta, para esquivar sus directas y francas preguntas.

Tampoco podía mentirle, no aquí y ahora con el calor de la pasión envolviéndolos por completo. Sintió cómo las llamas del deseo le lamían la piel mientras se las ingeniaba para tomar aire y decir:

—Porque eres tú. —Su voz sonó ronca, áspera, llena de deseo al responder a la llamada de su ardiente sirena. La miró a los ojos y luego bajó la vista a sus labios. Se lamió los suyos y confesó—: Porque tú eres lo que deseo.

No encontraba palabras para expresar lo que Sarah le hacía sentir, lo que sentía por ella. Por ella y sólo por ella. La deseaba más de lo que había deseado nunca a ninguna mujer. Sarah le había obligado a replantearse unos sentimientos que le eran extraños. Muy distintos a los sencillos deseos que un hombre sentía por una mujer y que él encontraba totalmente familiares. Esto era diferente y, si era sincero consigo mismo, siempre lo había sido. Se había dicho más de una vez que era porque Sarah era la mujer que había elegido para ser su esposa, pero eso le conducía a la pregunta que Sarah le había planteado. ¿Qué era lo que él sentía?

Todo lo que sabía es que era un sentimiento más fuerte, que era una pasión más ardiente, un deseo más profundo e intenso que ningún otro.

Algo que le había asombrado continuamente y que ahora, allí sentado entre las sombras que proyectaba la luna con Sarah en su regazo, tan increíblemente seductora, con sus intenciones asomando de una manera tan clara en sus ojos, Charlie descubrió que lo que sentía por ella era incluso más fuerte de lo que había pensado.

Y no estaba alimentado sólo por su deseo sino también por el de ella, y juntos, combinados, tenían la fuerza suficiente para hacerle perder la cabeza.

Sarah no había dicho nada, pero le había estudiado el rostro; y ahora esbozaba aquella sonrisa de sirena que tanto le fascinaba, como si le hubiera encantado su respuesta. Aquella suave y encendida sonrisa dejaba claro que ella estaba, si no completamente aliviada, sí bastante satisfecha. Y que por supuesto quería seguir adelante y aprender más, mucho más. De él, y de ella. De los dos juntos.

Contoneándose seductoramente sobre él, le ofreció su boca y él la tomó. Con avidez y codicia, Charlie los zambulló de nuevo en la ardiente pasión que no había llegado a desaparecer del todo. Tomándole la cabeza con una mano, la besó con más audacia y ella le devolvió el beso, hasta que un calor abrasador los engulló y los devoró.

Hasta que las llamas los envolvieron y los impulsaron más allá.

La mano que Sarah tenía entre sus cuerpos desabrochó los botones del pantalón, luego se deslizó bajo la tela y lo buscó.

Charlie aspiró sobresaltado ante aquella caricia inocente. Su control se tambaleó cuando la joven lo agarró con firmeza. Luego soltó un gruñido al sentir cómo aflojaba un poco los dedos y lo acariciaba.

Charlie le soltó la cintura y con un rápido movimiento le levantó las faldas y rebuscó debajo de ella. Encontró la carne tierna entre los muslos femeninos y la acarició, luego indagó suavemente con los dedos.

Sarah se estremeció, contuvo el aliento y rozó tentadoramente el rígido miembro. Cerró la mano en torno a la carne turgente y la apretó suave y firmemente.

El significado de ese gesto no podía ser más claro.

Y esa vez, él no tenía ni la habilidad ni el juicio necesarios para negarse.

Con sólo moverla un poco podría hacerla bajar sobre su cuerpo y enfundar su erección en aquella tierna carne resbaladiza. A pesar del fuerte impulso que tenía de hacerlo, Charlie sabía que por ahora no podría ser de esa manera. No con ella. No la primera vez. Él era demasiado grande y grueso para que ella lo tomara con holgura en esa posición. Podría intentarlo, pero sería muy difícil continuar...

En un hábil movimiento, él la hizo girar y la tumbó sobre los cojines. Sarah se dejó llevar y se aseguró de que él se moviera con ella; Charlie no opuso resistencia a la pequeña mano que se aferraba a su hombro. Se acomodó entre sus muslos, que extendió a ambos lados de sus caderas y, con los dedos aún enterrados en la funda femenina, le acunó la cabeza con la otra mano, sin dejar de besarla.

Él no había querido que la primera vez de Sarah fuera de esa manera, en un sofá en el cenador, envueltos en la noche oscura y en las capas de ropa que los separaban. Charlie habría preferido estar desnudo, y que ella estuviera desnuda también, pero hacía demasiado frío para desvestirse. Aunque en el calor de la pasión Charlie había dejado expuestos los senos de Sarah y, aunque todavía no supiera cómo, ella le había dejado el torso desnudo, la noche era demasiado fría para prescindir de más ropa.

Debajo de las faldas, Sarah guio la erección a su entrada. Charlie sacó los dedos de la funda femenina, tan caliente, mojada y preparada para él, y capturando la mano de la joven, entrelazando sus dedos con los de él, la apartó de su miembro.

Luego se hundió lenta y suavemente en aquel calor hirviente.

Sarah se quedó sin respiración. Se tensó, pero aspiró el aliento de Charlie a través del beso y se relajó. Sus dedos se agarraron con firmeza a los de él. Charlie empujó en su interior, con seguridad y firmeza, no demasiado rápido pero tampoco tan despacio que ella tuviera tiempo de reaccionar. Entonces alcanzó la barrera de su virginidad y, con un fuerte envite, se abrió paso penetrando profundamente en su cuerpo.

Ella soltó un grito, un sonido que él amortiguó con sus labios, y se puso tensa. Charlie se quedó inmóvil, dándole tiempo para que se ajustara a él.

Dándose tiempo a sí mismo para aquietar sus vertiginosos sentidos. Para asimilar la sensación del terciopelo ardiente que lo ceñía con fuerza. Para apretar los dientes y contener el intenso y abrumador deseo de montarla con fuerza y rapidez. Como una parte de él llevaba queriendo hacer tanto tiempo.

Él le había dicho que sería así, que le separaría las piernas y que ella le rodearía la cintura con ellas, que su cuerpo se abriría bajo el suyo, que se hundiría en ella, llenándola por completo.

Los sentidos de Charlie continuaron dando vueltas, más afectados de lo que él hubiera imaginado que podían estar. Hilvanar un solo pensamiento racional quedaba fuera de sus posibilidades, pero a veces aparecía algún retazo suelto en su mente. Era débilmente consciente de que ése no era su plan, que satisfacer los deseos de Sarah iba contra el objetivo que se había propuesto en un primer momento. Pero sus planes habían dejado de tener importancia. Ahora sólo quería aliviarla, satisfacer aquel deseo que había crecido en el interior de la joven, ese que él mismo había provocado y alimentado. No había nada que importara más que responder a la ancestral llamada femenina y darle todo lo que deseaba.

Porque Sarah lo deseaba con un deseo intenso, agudo y definido, y él quería feroz, casi compulsivamente, satisfacer su necesidad, mostrarle el éxtasis y compartir su deleite.

El placer de Sarah podría ser suyo. Lo sabía sin pensar. La había reclamado. Tenía derecho a sumergirla en el más absoluto gozo, poseyéndola y llenándola, y mostrándole la dorada gloria del paraíso terrenal.

Con un suave y provocador suspiro, ella le ofreció su cuerpo, aceptándolo. Instintivamente contrajo los músculos de su apretada funda y lo sintió allí; se estremeció.

Apretando los dientes ante el inevitable impacto de esa caricia, Charlie se retiró un poco, y luego se hundió de nuevo, llenándola por completo. Ella contuvo el aliento y luego soltó el aire, aferrándose a él con brazos y piernas. Charlie se retiró de nuevo y volvió a llenarla. Los pulmones de Sarah se ensancharon cuando aspiró profundamente y comenzó a seguirle el ritmo.

Charlie marcó el paso, lento y constante, y sólo fue aumentándolo gradualmente cuando sintió la respuesta de Sarah, cuando el deseo creció, fresco y urgente, y los fuegos de la pasión los reclamaron conduciéndolos a un éxtasis cegador.

Y a más, mucho más de lo que aquel acto había sido nunca, alcanzando una parte de Charlie que nadie más había alcanzado antes, con una rendición íntima y una posesión absoluta. Sarah se rindió a Charlie y él se rindió a ella. Charlie la poseyó y ella lo poseyó a él. Aquélla no era una unión sencilla, un placer normal, sino algo más intrincado y complejo, más significativo, que se enroscaba y mezclaba con los sentimientos y emociones que nunca había tenido antes, al menos en esas lides.

Sólo con la mujer que tenía debajo y que tan atrevidamente lo había aceptado en su interior.

Como si en realidad ella fuera su diosa, la guardiana de su alma, y él no pudiera más que rendirle culto.

Sarah cabalgó con él, sintiendo el placer que Charlie le daba, notando cómo sus alocados sentidos cantaban de puro gozo. Era muy consciente de aquella abrumadora e íntima unión. Tenía los ojos cerrados, no oía nada, su mundo se limitaba sólo a ellos dos, a otro universo que cobró vida en torno a ellos, un paisaje cargado de sentimientos, de calor y deseo, de intensas sensaciones, y de la promesa del éxtasis.

Charlie se movió dentro de ella y ella respondió a cada envite, saliéndole al encuentro, dándole la bienvenida para luego soltarle a regañadientes otra vez.

El placer y el deleite florecieron, fluyeron, se adueñaron de Sarah. El momentáneo dolor se había desvanecido con tanta rapidez que sólo era un recuerdo nebuloso, arrollado por la sólida realidad del duro, fuerte y elemental hombre que se unía profunda e inexorablemente a ella.

Charlie le soltó los dedos y le deslizó la mano por la cintura para agarrar una de sus nalgas. Le inclinó las caderas, y Sarah se quedó sin aliento cuando la nueva posición permitió que la penetrara más profundamente todavía.

La potencia contenida de cada envite provocaba en la joven una emoción excitante. Una primitiva sensación de peligro, un reconocimiento de su vulnerabilidad. Charlie era mucho más fuerte que ella, su cuerpo era más duro, mucho más poderoso que el suyo.

Pero Charlie estaba siendo muy cuidadoso. Ella lo sabía, pero no pudo centrarse lo suficiente en ese pensamiento, pues el calor de la pasión subió un grado más y la reclamó.

La ardiente y voraz necesidad que corría por sus venas la hizo contorsionarse y jadear. Se dejó llevar inexorablemente por el intenso deseo de su cuerpo, hasta que se quemó y ardió.

Hasta que estalló en llamas, y éstas se unieron y concentraron, haciéndola arder con más calor y ferocidad. Hasta que sollozó y se aferró desesperada a él, incitándole a más, y Charlie la montó más rápido, más duro, más profundo.

Hasta que de repente todo fue calor y Sarah tuvo que aferrarse a ese vertiginoso pico final. Sintió que él embestía una última vez y el horno que él había encendido y alimentado explotó, haciéndola alcanzar un éxtasis que le hizo arder la sangre.

Y que la atravesó por completo.

La cabeza de Sarah dio vueltas y más vueltas, y en medio de esa acalorada dicha, se le quedó la mente en blanco. Oyó débilmente cómo Charlie gemía, un sonido largo y gutural, y apenas fue consciente de que, unido íntimamente a ella, él se había quedado rígido entre sus brazos. De manera distante, sintió cómo él derramaba su cálida semilla en su interior.

Flotando en medio de ese arrebatador éxtasis dorado, Sarah sonrió.

Sarah ya había encontrado la respuesta que buscaba. De hecho, había encontrado varias respuestas.

Cuando pudo pensar otra vez, se sintió bastante satisfecha. No sólo había tenido éxito en la consecución de su plan, sino que el placer que había encontrado en los brazos de Charlie había probado ser todavía más delicioso de lo que había imaginado.

Sin embargo, aquello, relativamente hablando, era algo accidental. Había tenido un objetivo principal al tomar ese camino, una pregunta cuya respuesta quería conocer y, si bien él no le había dado esa respuesta con palabras claras y sencillas, se la había mostrado. Sarah había captado la verdad sin problemas. Las acciones, después de todo, decían mucho más que las palabras. En especial si se trataba de caballeros, o eso había oído siempre.

Quizás él estuviera en lo cierto; contestar con palabras no era fácil. Incluso ahora a Sarah le resultaba difícil describir, aun para sí misma, lo que había sentido. Un poder intangible, esquivo pero intenso, una emoción imperativa, una fuerza capaz de invalidar la voluntad racional, de dirigir el comportamiento para satisfacer sus propios objetivos, pero aquellos objetivos se enfocaban en otro.

Ese poder parecía existir sólo en términos ajenos.

Ella se había entregado a él, pero el objetivo de Charlie había sido darle placer a ella, y hasta que no lo había alcanzado, él no había buscado su propio placer.

Por el contrario, el objetivo de Sarah había sido él. Muchas de sus acciones habían respondido a la instintiva necesidad de saciar el deseo que provocaba en él. De darle placer.

A cambio de casarse con él, quería el amor y todas las emociones que conllevaba. Y era amor lo que ella había sentido por él, en especial en ese impulso de dar y colmar al otro por completo.

Ahora, Sarah sabía que sentía eso por Charlie. Tras lo sucedido en la última hora, aceptaba lo que había hecho, que cuando estaban juntos y lejos del mundo, él, sus deseos y necesidades se convertían en el único objetivo de su existencia. Ahora sabía de qué manera ese sentimiento, ese poder, la instaban a actuar, y que las acciones de Charlie se correspondían con las suyas.

El amor podía ser difícil de describir, pero sus síntomas eran muy claros.

Si lo que Sarah sentía por él era amor, entonces era de suponer que él sintiera lo mismo, ya que quería casarse con ella y sólo con ella.

Sarah llegó a esa conclusión mientras Charlie se cambiaba de posición. Aquel movimiento la trajo de vuelta al mundo. Abrió los ojos para orientarse. En algún momento Charlie los había acomodado. Ahora él estaba sentado en el sofá con ella en su regazo, rodeándola con sus brazos. La cabeza de la joven descansaba sobre su pecho y tenía la palma de la mano extendida sobre su corazón. El calor de la piel de Charlie que la rodeaba y el fuerte latido de su corazón bajo su mano la reconfortaban sobremanera. No había en ese momento ningún otro lugar en el mundo en el que se sintiera más a gusto.

La conciencia sensual envolvía su cuerpo. Se sentía diferente, satisfecha y más viva de lo que se había sentido nunca.

«Entonces te sentirás completa.» Eso le había dicho Charlie, y ahora lo entendía. Con él, estaba completa. Él era una pieza fundamental en el puzle de su vida. No podía imaginar sentirse así —comportarse de esa manera— con ningún otro hombre.

Charlie tensó el brazo, inclinó la cabeza y le dio un suave beso en la sien.

—¿Estás bien?

Charlie notó que la preocupación le teñía la voz. Era lo que sentía en su interior. Sabía que ella seguía despierta, pero se había mantenido quieta y en silencio. ¿Habría sentido demasiado dolor? ¿El placer había sido demasiado sorprendente?

Él apenas era capaz de formar un pensamiento coherente, y tenía mucha más experiencia que ella. Aquella especie de enajenación mental no era normal en él. Aún seguía sin comprender cómo había podido ocurrir algo así con Sarah, había tenido centenares de encuentros con otras mujeres, y nunca, jamás, habían sido como ése.

Para alivio de Charlie, Sarah asintió con la cabeza y le dio un beso en el pecho. Una caricia que lo excitó profundamente.

—Sí. Ha sido... precioso.

El tono de la joven, el suspiro con el que pronunció la palabra «precioso» halagó el ego de Charlie. El trémulo asombro que teñía la palabra expresaba algo que él también había sentido.

A pesar de todo, Charlie tenía que reajustar su plan... una vez más. Y esta vez haría un cambio radical. Había pensado que en cuanto hubieran satisfecho el deseo que surgía entre ellos, ella ya no le resultaría tan atractiva, al menos desde un punto de vista sensual, pero, dada la intensidad de lo acontecido, puede que ése no fuera el caso. Ciertamente seguía estando interesado en ella, más interesado de lo que había estado nunca. Si volvían a hacerlo otra vez, ¿sería igual de glorioso? ¿Volverían a sentir unas sensaciones tan intensas y profundas? ¿Tan fascinantes?

¿Se estaría haciendo ella esas mismas preguntas? A diferencia de él, Sarah no tenía con qué comparar lo que había sucedido entre ellos.

No sabía si ella pensaba en tales términos, y no se sentía lo suficientemente confiado para basar sus estrategias en ese punto.

Lo que le dejaba considerando el insistente soniquete que su parte más primitiva repetía en su mente.

«Tienes que casarte conmigo.»

Sabía que era mejor no pronunciar esas palabras en voz alta. Tenía cuatro hermanas, tres de ellas casadas y la menor, Augusta, tenía dieciocho años. Una declaración como ésa sólo provocaría desprecio y risas, y *a posteriori*, una firme resistencia, aunque fuera cierta. Pero no pensaba dejarla ir. Si de algo estaba seguro era de que ella no se casaría con ningún otro hombre.

Aun así, ¿había alguna manera de que él pudiera aprovechar aquella intimidad para inclinar la balanza a su favor? Para que Sarah no se resistiera y mostrara su beneplácito.

Su mente se plantó. Bufó para sus adentros. ¿De qué le valía tener una labia fácil y ser tan encantador si no era capaz de convencer a la mujer que yacía dulce y completamente saciada entre sus brazos de que se casara con él?

—He tomado una decisión.

Aquellas suaves palabras lo pillaron desprevenido. Bajó la mirada.

Sarah levantó la cabeza, lo miró y sonrió. La somnolienta saciedad del placer todavía asomaba en sus ojos.

—Me casaré contigo. —Ladeó la cabeza y lo miró directamente a los ojos—. En cuanto tú quieras.

Sarah había recordado la profecía de la gitana. Aquélla era una decisión suya, no de él. Si quería amor, tenía que tomar una decisión, aceptar el riesgo y aferrarse a las posibilidades. Tenía que seguir adelante.

Había entendido que, a pesar de todo, siempre había un riesgo —aunque podía haber interpretado mal la situación—, pero si quería amor, tenía que aceptar la oportunidad que se le ofrecía y esperar tener éxito.

Y eso es lo que haría.

Charlie había abierto mucho los ojos, pero tenía una expresión neutra... como si ella le hubiera sorprendido de verdad. Entonces parpadeó y ella notó que estaba intentando recuperar el habla. Al final, sostuvo la mirada de la joven, tomó aire y, apretando la mandíbula, asintió con la cabeza.

—Bien.

Si se hubieran casado cuando Charlie quería hacerlo, la boda habría tenido lugar al día siguiente. Por desgracia, en cuanto informaron a sus madres de su decisión de casarse, ambas demostraron tener unas ideas muy diferentes a las de ellos.

—El martes de la semana que viene —declaró Serena, con una mirada firme.

Desde su posición ante la chimenea, Charlie le devolvió la mirada con dureza.

Estaban en la sala del Park. Esa misma mañana, Charlie se había dirigido a casa de Sarah para hablar con sus padres. Tras las esperadas y emocionadas felicitaciones, todos se habían trasladado a Morwellan Park para reunirse con Serena.

—Sarah necesita tiempo para organizar su ajuar, y lord Conningham y yo tendremos que supervisar multitud de arreglos. La boda del conde de Meredith será, como es natural, todo un acontecimiento —aclaró Serena, interpretando correctamente el desacuerdo no expresado que ocultaba el semblante rígido e impasible de su hijo.

La mirada de Serena le advertía que cualquier resistencia sería inútil. Era su hijo mayor, y ella no estaba dispuesta a que se celebrara aquel matrimonio sin la pompa debida. De todas maneras, había accedido a mucho más de lo que él hubiera esperado. No había insistido en que Sarah y él se casaran en St. George, en Hannover Square.

—De acuerdo. —Apretó los dientes, pero intentó mantener un tono suave para no estropear el ambiente festivo. Asintió con la cabeza en dirección a Serena y lady Conningham—. El martes que viene.

Siete días. Con sus noches.

—¡Excelente! —Lady Conningham, que estaba sentada en uno de los sillones frente a la chimenea, miró a Sarah—. Nos marcharemos mañana a primera hora de la mañana, querida. Necesitamos todas las horas de que dispongamos en Bath, pues también tendremos que elegir los vestidos de tus hermanas. Y, por supuesto, todo lo demás. —La madre de Sarah fue levantando sus dedos uno a uno, como si estuviera contando mentalmente—. Querida... creo que no estaremos de regreso hasta el lunes —concluyó sin mirar ni a Sarah ni a Charlie, sino a Serena, que descartó su muda pregunta con un gesto.

—Estoy segura —dijo Serena— de que Frederick y yo podremos ocuparnos de todos los detalles que surjan aquí. Y, por supuesto, Alathea nos ayudará.

Ése fue el principio de un ávido debate que abarcó «todos los detalles». Charlie sólo lo escuchó a medias. Su mente estaba perdida en las siete noches de abstinencia obligada y no en qué carruaje se marcharían de la iglesia cuando ya estuvieran felizmente casados.

Miró a su futura esposa, sentada en la *chaise* al lado de su madre. Sarah parecía prestar atención, pues intervenía con rapidez para declarar su preferencia ante cualquier sugerencia. Mejor que fuera ella quien se encargara de todo eso. Había sido muy sabio por su parte hacerlo así. Contuvo un estremecimiento cuando Sarah se negó a que un montón de niños con flores la precedieran en la iglesia. Con tales horrores potenciales amenazándolos, intentó no distraerla y esperó pacientemente a que el debate llegase al final.

Para entonces, ya se hablaba de las invitaciones que se enviarían para la cena en la que se anunciaría el compromiso y que se celebraría en el Park esa misma noche.

—¡Es todo muy apresurado! —declaró lady Conningham—. Pero es así como tiene que ser.

Serena le lanzó una mirada de advertencia, pero Charlie sólo sonrió y se reservó su opinión.

Se sirvió de su encanto cuando tuvo que acompañar a sus futuros suegros y a su prometida al carruaje. Aprovechó el momento en el que lord Conningham ayudaba a su esposa a subir al carruaje para agarrar a Sarah del brazo y susurrarle al oído:

—Hasta esta noche. Como siempre.

Ella le sostuvo la mirada, vaciló y luego asintió con la cabeza.

—De acuerdo, pero puede que me retrase. Van a querer hablar durante horas.

Charlie hizo una mueca, pero asintió con la cabeza. La mirada de Sarah era compasiva. Cuando la ayudó a subir al carruaje, ella volvió a mirarle a los ojos. Le apretó los dedos y él le devolvió el apretón. Luego la soltó y dio un paso atrás.

El cochero cerró la puerta del carruaje. Charlie se despidió con la mano y vio cómo Sarah volvía la mirada hacia él y sonreía.

A pesar de la resignación que sentía, aquella imagen hizo que se relajara un poco.

9

Irritado. Así se sintió Charlie cuando por fin llegó al cenador y descubrió que Sarah todavía no estaba allí.

En la penumbra, maldijo entre dientes, luego paseó de un lado a otro y esperó.

La tarde había sido demasiado estresante. Celia y Martin Cynster habían llegado al Park con Alathea, Gabriel y sus hijos. Además, en la pequeña reunión familiar en la que lord Conningham había anunciado el compromiso de su hija con lord Charles Morwellan, octavo conde de Meredith, habían estado presentes las hermanas y los padres de Sarah y sus propios hermanos, Jeremy y Augusta.

También habían asistido el vicario, el señor Duncliffe, que oficiaría la ceremonia el martes siguiente, su esposa, y lady Finsbury y lady Cruikshank con sus respectivos maridos, entre otras personalidades de la localidad, para que fueran testigos del enlace. Dadas las inclinaciones de tales damas al cotilleo, Charlie no dudaba que las noticias de su compromiso no tardarían en ser difundidas a lo largo y ancho de la sociedad.

Por supuesto su madre, Celia y Alathea también harían su parte.

La reunión había transcurrido en un tono jovial, feliz y relajado. Charlie no podía negar que todo había resultado mejor de lo que él había esperado, pero aun así Charlie había sido muy consciente de su creciente impaciencia.

En los negocios jamás había tenido ese problema, no había sentido esa necesidad constante de contenerse, como si una parte primitiva y poderosa de sí mismo no pudiera evitar quebrantar las normas del decoro. Por otro lado, no había ninguna razón para sentirse de esa manera ahora que Sarah había aceptado ser su esposa. La lógica se lo decía, pero aquella imperiosa necesidad de controlarse no había cedido ni un ápice.

Al contrario, cada vez se había hecho más pronunciada.

Sólo podía atribuirla al inusual y profundo deseo que sentía por Sarah y que no había saciado por completo. Lo más probable es que cuando ella fuera realmente suya, cuando se hubiera entregado a él unas cuantas veces más, aquella compulsiva necesidad se desvaneciera.

Deseaba poder creer eso, que aquel impulso era sólo físico, sólo la consecuencia de un deseo no saciado. Se decía a sí mismo que no podía ser otra cosa, pero...

Un leve sonido de pasos hizo que se diera la vuelta.

Sarah venía corriendo por el camino. Subió apresurada los escalones y se acercó a él con rapidez.

—Lo siento... Como te dije, querían...

Charlie la estrechó con fuerza entre sus brazos.

Sarah se tragó las siguientes palabras mientras él la besaba de una manera voraz y exigente. Cualquier pensamiento sobre disculparse desapareció de la cabeza de la joven, sobrecogida por la necesidad de aliviar y saciar aquel deseo feroz, de darle a Charlie todo lo que quería.

Y resultaba evidente que él no quería hablar.

Al cabo de lo que parecieron unos pocos segundos, yacía debajo de Charlie en el sofá con el corpiño abierto hasta la cintura y los senos hinchados bajo las caricias experimentadas de una de las manos de su prometido, mientras que, con la otra, le agarraba la falda y la deslizaba hacia arriba.

El fuego ya había comenzado a arder entre ellos; Charlie buscó con los dedos su entrada ya húmeda y resbaladiza, y comenzó a acariciarla, sondeando, hasta que el fuego se hizo más intenso.

Habiendo capeado una vez ese temporal, Sarah lo aceptó y se dejó llevar por el placer, excitada ante el hecho de ser deseada con tal afán inquebrantable, con tal intensidad y concentración, con tal adoración. A pesar de la pasión que Charlie parecía sentir por ella y del deseo que le endurecía el cuerpo, le acariciaba con una cuidadosa suavidad que jamás vacilaba.

Una cautela que le hacía contenerse, que hacía que respirara tan entrecortadamente como ella. Su beso contuvo una pizca de desesperación hasta que sus experimentados dedos hicieron que Sarah perdiera el contacto con la realidad e inundaran los sentidos de la joven de un indescriptible placer.

Sólo entonces él se movió, manteniéndola inmóvil bajo él para penetrarla.

Sarah se quedó sin aliento, se arqueó bajo él y gimió al tiempo que Charlie aprovechaba aquella instintiva invitación para hundirse más profundamente en aquel cuerpo que se había rendido por completo a él. La joven se cerró en torno a Charlie y éste se detuvo, apretó los párpados tensando cada músculo, al borde del éxtasis. Luego tomó aire, se retiró y empujó en ella de nuevo hasta que Sarah perdió el contacto con el mundo.

Y una vez más todo lo que ella sintió fue fuego y la constante e implacable posesión de Charlie. Un vertiginoso y delicioso placer que la atravesaba de los pies a la cabeza y que era la prueba del amor de él.

Estaba presente en la entrecortada respiración masculina cuando ella se removió, alzándose y arqueándose hacia él, provocando que el áspero vello del pecho masculino se rozara contra sus sensibles pezones.

Estaba presente en la manera en que él se contenía, en cómo le cogía la mano que ella le había puesto en la espalda para que no se apresurara y alcanzara el placer demasiado pronto, en cómo capturaba su aliento sensual y unía sus bocas en una primitiva y evocadora danza. En el controlado ritmo, más contenido que la primera vez. Más devorador, más absorbente. Más íntimo.

El amor de Charlie estaba presente en los guturales susurros con los que la animaba cuando Sarah inició de nuevo aquella escalada inexorable hacia la cúspide, cuando sintió el clamor de la pasión y de repente se encontró al borde del más puro e intenso éxtasis.

En la manera en cómo la acunaba y abrazaba, en cómo se movía firme e implacablemente dentro de ella, atizando las llamas, haciendo que los sentidos de la joven giraran vertiginosamente.

Y estaba allí cuando la reclamó el éxtasis y él la estrechó contra su cuerpo, y cuando, sin dejar de abrazarla, los músculos de Charlie se estremecieron prolongando el placer, haciendo que ella gimiera de puro gozo.

Y en aquel sublime momento final, cuando Charlie se perdió en ella.

Sarah se puso en camino a la mañana siguiente con su madre, Twitters, Clara y Gloria para pasar cinco días en Bath, somnolienta pero feliz y convencida de haber tomado la decisión correcta.

No sabía si Charlie era consciente o no, si era amor en toda la extensión de la palabra o sólo los primeros brotes de algo que tardaría toda una vida en florecer. Pero la posibilidad estaba allí, no cabía duda, y eso era todo lo que ella necesitaba saber.

Con un suspiro, cerró los ojos, apoyó la cabeza en el respaldo y volvió a recordar una vez más los acontecimientos de la noche anterior.

¿Qué había pasado con su control? ¿Por qué cuando estaba con ella simplemente se desvanecía?

Ésa y otras preguntas similares atravesaban la mente de Charlie dos días después, mientras conducía su par de castrados grises hacia Watchet.

Desde que Sarah se había marchado, pasaba el tiempo inmerso en sus negocios, no sólo en lo que a la hacienda y su fortuna concernía, sino también en el acuerdo matrimonial. Lord Conningham y él habían aceptado los términos del matrimonio y sólo faltaba redactarlo. A su futuro suegro le había sorprendido lo que Charlie había estipulado con respecto a la granja Quilley, y había comentado su generosidad y comprensión. Charlie había permanecido callado, pero hubiera deseado admitir que la generosidad había tenido poco que ver con ello, que había sido la propia Sarah la que le había querido dejar aquel asunto resuelto.

La granja Quilley había sido un pequeño precio a pagar con tal de que ella fuera suya.

Lo que le llevaba de vuelta a la molesta pregunta acerca de su pasión por ella, su futura esposa. Sin experiencia previa que la guiara, ella no podía saber —y con suerte, jamás lo adivinaría— que aquel deseo... desesperado —no se le ocurría otra manera mejor de definirlo— que él sentía cuando estaba con ella no era normal, que esas cosas no les sucedían a los caballeros como él.

Jamás se había dejado llevar antes por una pasión como ésa, no de esa manera. No hasta el punto en que cuando estaba con Sarah, conduciéndola al éxtasis, sobre todo cuando estaba profundamente enterrado en lo más hondo de su interior y, por lo tanto, disfrutando con ella, su único objetivo en la vida era hacerla alcanzar el placer más absoluto.

Era algo extraño y chocante. Incluso angustioso. Tal conexión no era lo que él había esperado, no con la dulce e inocente Sarah.

Aquella dulce inocencia parecía ser una droga sensual para él, pero ¿cómo podía estar seguro?

El arco de la posada La Campana apareció ante él. Refrenando a los castrados grises, se dijo a sí mismo lo que se había dicho cientos de veces durante las últimas cuarenta y ocho horas: su reacción ante ella era una adicción y, una vez saciada, esa adicción se desvanecería.

Sencillamente tenía que saciarla, y eso, sin duda, tampoco estaba mal. Tras un mes o menos casados, todo volvería a su cauce. Sólo tenía que aguantar hasta el final.

Dejó los castrados grises en la posada y se acercó a la parcela donde tenía intención de construir su nuevo almacén. Sarah tenía razón. Un almacén de doble tamaño sería una mejor inversión que dos de tamaño normal. El constructor local al que solía contratar, Carruthers, le estaba esperando. Hablaron del proyecto durante un buen rato, luego Carruthers se marchó para reunirse con el delineante que se encargaría de hacer los planos y de calcular los costes; mientras Charlie se dirigía a los muelles y, en concreto, a la oficina de Jones.

El agente marítimo se alegró de verle.

—No sé qué flota en el aire —dijo Jones—, pero hay mucha gente husmeando por aquí.

Charlie arqueó las cejas.

—¿Sinclair?

—Sin duda, pero hay alguien más. No es un caballero y trabaja para un tercero. —Jones sonrió ampliamente—. Y si los últimos rumores de la compañía marítima son ciertos, la suerte está de nuestra parte.

Con lo que Jones quería decir que el tráfico marítimo a través de Watchet iba en aumento. Charlie le devolvió la sonrisa.

—Ésas son excelentes noticias, pues ya he decidido construir un nuevo almacén. —Puso a Jones al corriente de su decisión. La idea de construir una estructura de doble tamaño pareció interesar al agente marítimo.

Tras intercambiar opiniones sobre cuándo podría estar disponible el nuevo almacén, y discutir sobre el tráfico de mercancías y con qué comerciantes debería ponerse en contacto Jones, Charlie abandonó la oficina y regresó a la calle Mayor.

Se detuvo en medio de la estrecha acera y volvió la mirada hacia el puerto.

—Lord Meredith. Me alegro de verle.

Charlie se dio la vuelta. Sonriendo, le tendió la mano.

—Sinclair. Llámeme Charlie, por favor.

Devolviéndole la sonrisa, Malcolm Sinclair le estrechó la mano.

—Malcolm —dijo a su vez—. Estaba a punto de dirigirme a La Campana para almorzar. ¿Te gustaría acompañarme?

—Me encantaría.

Cruzaron la calle empedrada y entraron en la posada. La llegada de tales clientes, los dos altos, bien plantados y elegantemente vestidos, atrajo la atención del dueño del local, Matthews, que se acercó a ellos corriendo. Les hizo una reverencia y los condujo a la misma mesa que Sarah y Charlie habían compartido la vez anterior, situada en un rincón con vistas al puerto.

Malcolm señaló con la cabeza los buques de carga que se balanceaban sobre las olas.

—He visto muchos puertos pequeños en la costa, pero en éste nunca falta el trabajo.

—Es una excelente alternativa a Bristol, en especial para ciertas cargas. —Se sentaron y Matthews se apresuró a servirles un primer plato de sopa y pan recién hecho.

Cuando el tabernero se retiró, Charlie miró a Malcolm.

—¿Tienes intención de establecerte en esta zona?

—Definitivamente espero establecerme aquí —admitió Malcolm después de probar la sopa.

—¿No tienes una residencia en algún otro sitio?

Mientras tomaban la sopa, Malcolm le explicó:

—Me quedé huérfano y sin parientes cercanos a una edad muy temprana. Por lo tanto, he vivido en Eton, Oxford y finalmente en Londres. Londres es el hogar de cualquier inglés que se precie, por lo que jamás establecí vínculos en ninguna otra parte. Ahora, sin embargo, necesito encontrar un lugar donde retirarme, y de todos los sitios que he visitado, ésta es la zona que más me atrae. —Malcolm lo miró directamente a los ojos—. Puede que tú no lo percibas por haber nacido aquí, pero el paisaje es muy bonito a la vez que tranquilo. Quizá no sea espectacular pero sí relajante. Estoy buscando la casa adecuada.

Charlie sonrió.

—Si me entero de alguna que esté en venta, te lo haré saber.

—Hazlo —dijo Malcolm—. Me gustaría hacerte una pregunta. Dado que tanto a ti, como a mí nos gustan las inversiones de alto nivel, ¿cómo son las negociaciones por aquí? ¿Cómo son las comunicaciones con Londres durante el invierno? ¿Se cortan en esa época del año? Y si es así ¿durante cuánto tiempo?

—En eso tenemos suerte. —Charlie se recostó en la silla mientras retiraban los platos de sopa, luego explicó a grandes rasgos los diferentes modos de comunicación con la capital, dejando claro que rara vez se interrumpían. Después se enzarzaron en un debate sobre inversiones, los plazos más favorables y cuáles eran sus intereses personales en ese momento.

Aunque los dos evitaron mencionar ningún proyecto específico, Malcolm dejó caer los suficientes datos para que Charlie se diera cuenta de que era tan cuidadoso como Gabriel o él mismo; a ninguno de ellos les gustaba perder dinero. Sin embargo, Malcolm le comentó abiertamente que se había metido en algunas inversiones arriesgadas que le reportarían grandes beneficios en caso de tener éxito, por lo que bien merecía la pena correr el riesgo.

Aquello intrigó a Charlie. Aunque nunca había tenido dificultades en resistirse al atractivo de ciertas inversiones arriesgadas, pero sin haber obtenido tales éxitos —y por lo tanto grandes beneficios—, era algo que le atraía irremisiblemente. Lo mismo que a Gabriel.

—Hago muchas de mis inversiones a través de los fondos Cynster, bajo la dirección de Gabriel Cynster. —Haciendo girar una copa de vino entre los dedos, Charlie hizo una mueca—. Pero tengo que admitir que vamos a lo seguro y que la mayoría de los fondos casi siempre revierten en las propias inversiones y financiación de proyectos en vez de en el desarrollo directo de nuevas empresas.

Malcolm asintió con la cabeza.

—Estuve charlando un rato con Cynster la semana pasada. Por supuesto, todo el mundo sabe que los fondos Cynster han tenido un enorme éxito con el paso del tiempo. Sin embargo, la inversión a largo plazo, y no es que la critique, carece de la excitación que supone seguir la trayectoria de los nuevos negocios.

—Exacto. —Charlie sonrió ampliamente—. Estoy de acuerdo en que las inversiones a largo plazo, si bien son seguras, son un tanto aburridas. Aunque es muy agradable ver los números positivos en los libros de cuentas, rara vez inspiran el placer de la victoria.

Hicieron una pausa mientras les servían el plato principal a base de rosbif. Cogieron sus cubiertos y el silencio reinó entre ellos durante algunos minutos.

—Dime, ¿cómo es que te involucraste en el negocio del ferrocarril? —preguntó Charlie finalmente.

Ésa era una pregunta que a Malcolm le habían hecho con frecuencia.

—Fue cuestión de suerte. Yo tenía casi veinte años cuando Stephenson intentaba despertar el interés de los patrocinadores para que invirtieran en la línea Stockton-Darlington. Aunque todos estaban interesados, la mayoría de los inversores prefirieron no arriesgarse y esperar a ver si el negocio funcionaba. En ese momento yo contaba con suficiente dinero en efectivo y, dado que sólo se trataba de un tramo corto, no creía que supusiera un gran riesgo. Así que invertí. Éramos muy pocos y, una vez que la línea de ferrocarril se inauguró con éxito, los primeros inversores siempre teníamos preferencia para invertir en cada nuevo tramo. Fue así como invertí en el tramo Liverpool-Manchester, y también en la extensión hasta Londres.

—Así que has prosperado por las inversiones en el ferrocarril. —Charlie se limpió los labios con la servilleta y apartó el plato a un lado.

—Sí. —Malcolm frunció el ceño—. Pero no he participado en la inversión de todos los tramos que me ofrecieron, que fueron muchos.

—Ah, ¿sí? ¿Por qué?

—Porque para empezar es muy difícil elegir bien. Todo el mundo piensa que todos los tramos van a tener éxito, pero lo cierto es que hay propuestas de lo más descabelladas. Está claro que unir Londres con Manchester y Liverpool tiene un sentido comercial. Pero no estoy del todo seguro de la viabilidad, hablando en términos físicos, del tramo Newcastle-Carlisle, aunque ya han comenzado a construirlo. También sé que la línea Londres-Bristol se ha puesto en marcha, y aunque en este caso sí me parece factible, no estoy del todo convencido de que el dinero que se invierta en ella sea recuperado con la rapidez suficiente para que el negocio pueda ser considerado un éxito. Es por esa misma razón por la que he rechazado la mayoría de las propuestas.

Charlie entendió lo que quería decir.

—Quieres decir que tardará en dar beneficios.

Malcolm asintió con la cabeza.

—Considera el tramo Stockton-Darlington. Invertimos a principios de 1821. Se empezó a construir de inmediato y los primeros beneficios comenzaron a llegar en 1825 de manera más o menos regular. Un tiempo prudente para una inversión. El tramo Liverpool-Manchester se construyó entre 1827 y 1830, de nuevo un tiempo prudencial. La extensión a Londres, sin embargo, llevará bastante más tiempo completarla. Desde que me di cuenta de eso, he sido más cauteloso y, francamente, ninguna de las propuestas actuales verá beneficios hasta dentro de una década.

Reclinándose en la silla, Malcolm sostuvo la mirada de Charlie.

—No es el tipo de proyecto que me gusta. —Levantó una mano—. No me interpretes mal, estoy seguro de que las líneas de ferrocarril serán siempre un negocio rentable. Pero el largo tiempo invertido es algo que no juega a nuestro favor.

Hizo una pausa, como si considerara algo y luego añadió:

—Además, demasiadas de esas propuestas vienen avaladas por el mismo grupito de inversores. Necesitan que participe más gente en esos proyectos, pero son demasiado estirados, financieramente hablando, para ceder la iniciativa a otros. No me sorprendería demasiado que para la próxima década haya un gran número de sociedades entre los fundadores.

—Es un caso claro de intentar abarcar demasiado —dijo Charlie entrecerrando los ojos—, demasiado rápido, y además invirtiendo poco dinero para los beneficios que se espera recoger a cambio.

Malcolm asintió con la cabeza.

—También están prestando poca atención a las dificultades que entraña la construcción de algunos tramos. Otra razón más para alejarse del negocio de los ferrocarriles, por lo menos en términos de inversiones.

Charlie arqueó las cejas.

—¡Efectivamente!

Terminaron de comer, apartaron las sillas de la mesa y se levantaron. Después de pagar la cuenta al posadero, salieron a la calle. Charlie se volvió hacia Malcolm.

—Gracias por compartir conmigo un tema tan fascinante.

—De nada. —Malcolm le tendió la mano y Charlie se la estrechó—. Ha sido un placer hablar con alguien que comparte mis mismos intereses.

Charlie opinaba lo mismo.

—Debemos reunirnos en alguna otra ocasión, y compartir estas aficiones nuestras con más profundidad.

Malcolm asintió con la cabeza y se separaron, los dos muy satisfechos.

Charlie bajó la mirada al puerto. El viento había aumentado, batiendo las espumosas olas hacia la orilla. No hacía buen tiempo para navegar en el velero. Y la última vez que había salido a la mar, Sarah le había acompañado...

Girando sobre sus talones, se dirigió al patio de la posada. Mejor volver a casa y encontrar otra cosa con la que ocupar la mente.

Los preparativos de la boda avanzaron deprisa bajo la dirección de la madre de Charlie y lord Conningham; no había mucho que Charlie pudiera hacer. Todo el mundo era de la opinión de que él debía mantenerse al margen de todo. Por ese motivo, dos tardes después, tras haberse pasado el día conduciendo a los castrados por el condado con Jason, Juliet y Henry, se refugió en la biblioteca para leer el periódico, buscando alguna noticia que lo interesara lo suficiente para entretenerse el resto de la tarde cuando Crisp, su mayordomo, llamó a la puerta.

—Milord, ha llegado el señor Adair.

Charlie parpadeó, se incorporó y dejó a un lado el periódico.

—Hazle pasar, Crisp.

Con suma curiosidad se preguntó qué estaría haciendo Barnaby por allí, y más a esas horas. Tenía que haber ocurrido algo.

Una sola mirada a Barnaby mientras el mayordomo lo hacía pasar a la estancia confirmó sus sospechas. Su amigo tenía una expresión seria, los rizos rubios despeinados y la corbata torcida. Todavía era el caballero guapo y bien vestido que encandilaba a la sociedad, pero claramente parecía fatigado por el viaje.

Charlie se levantó. Le dio la bienvenida estrechándole la mano y palmeándole el hombro antes de invitarlo a sentarse en uno de los sillones que había frente al acogedor fuego de la chimenea.

—Siéntate y entra en calor. —Barnaby tenía las manos heladas—. ¿Has cenado?

Barnaby negó con la cabeza.

—Vengo directamente desde la ciudad.

Charlie arqueó las cejas.

—Te quedarás aquí, ¿verdad?

Dejándose caer en el sillón, Barnaby frunció los labios.

—Si tienes alguna habitación libre...

Con una sonrisa irónica —el Park era enorme—, Charlie se volvió hacia Crisp y ordenó que trajeran una cena sustanciosa y que prepararan una habitación para Barnaby. Crisp se apresuró a cumplir sus órdenes. Charlie se acercó a la licorera.

—¿Brandy?

—Por favor. —Barnaby se reclinó en el sillón—. Ahí fuera hace un frío de mil demonios.

Charlie recorrió a su amigo con la mirada. No sólo era el clima lo que había afectado a Barnaby. Tenía una expresión inusualmente sombría y resuelta, como si hubiera algo que le preocupara desde hacía días.

Charlie le sirvió una copa de brandy francés, se la entregó y se sentó en el sillón de enfrente. Tomó un trago de su propia copa, observando cómo se relajaba la tensión en el rostro de su amigo mientras éste tomaba un sorbo de la ardiente bebida. Charlie se arrellanó en el sillón.

—¿Qué ha ocurrido?

—Al parecer se están produciendo una serie de actividades ilícitas por parte de un tipo especialmente hábil.

Charlie esperó a que continuara.

—Mi padre y la comisión han solicitado mis servicios, de manera oficial pero discreta, para investigar y, si es posible, llevar ante la justicia a quien esté detrás de varios casos de especulación de tierras —dijo Barnaby finalmente.

El padre de Barnaby era uno de los pares que supervisaba al recientemente instituido cuerpo de policía de Londres. Charlie frunció el ceño.

—¿Varios casos?

Barnaby tomó otro sorbo de su copa y asintió con la cabeza.

—Un asunto muy feo. De vez en cuando existen casos de usura menor que no sorprenden a nadie y que, de hecho, no se consideran un delito. Pero estos casos en concreto, y ahora te explico cuál es la diferencia, se han estado dando a lo largo y ancho del país durante años. Casi una década, en realidad. No ha sido nada agradable descubrir el tiempo que lleva produciéndose esta clase de actividades delictivas, y delante de nuestras propias narices además, pues todos los casos están diseminados por la geografía nacional y nadie se había dado cuenta hasta ahora.

Barnaby se detuvo a beber otro sorbo de brandy y continuó:

—Hasta hace poco, no había ninguna autoridad a la que comunicar tales delitos. —Carraspeó—. Llevo una semana y pico recorriendo el país de arriba abajo consultando todos los casos con los magistrados, sheriffs y representantes de la Corona.

Barnaby suspiró. Se reclinó en el sillón y cerró los ojos.

—Me detuve en Newmarket de vuelta a la ciudad y me quedé con Dillon y Pris. Cuando le conté lo que sucedía, Dillon avisó a Demonio y los tres hablamos sobre todo lo que habíamos averiguado del asunto. Hemos llegado a la conclusión de que la situación es seria y muy difícil de destapar.

El ceño de Charlie se hizo más profundo.

—No he oído ningún rumor de especulación de tierras por aquí, ni en ninguna otra parte. Y estoy seguro de que Gabriel tampoco.

Barnaby agitó su copa con un gesto cansado.

—Eso es lo que sucede con la especulación. Nadie se entera de nada hasta mucho después de que el daño esté hecho. Y eso si sale a la luz. Como con estos casos en particular, de los que hemos tenido constancia gracias a que algunas de esas nuevas compañías del ferrocarril tienen inversores comunes que se han mostrado descontentos, por no decir enfurecidos, ante los precios abusivos que sus compañías se han visto y se ven obligadas a pagar por ciertas parcelas. Han enviado a la policía una lista con las propiedades por las que sus compañías han pagado enormes cantidades de dinero, para que lo investiguen. Por eso me ha avisado mi padre.

—Ah. —Una cínica comprensión teñía la voz de Charlie—. Ya entiendo. —Muchos de esos inversores eran nobles o tipos acaudalados, de esos a los que las autoridades deseaban contentar—. Quieren hacerles la pelota, ¿no?

—Por así decirlo. —Barnaby hizo una pausa, luego continuó—: De Newmarket fui a Londres, donde me entrevisté con mi padre y nuestro viejo amigo el inspector Stokes. En resumidas cuentas, ellos pensaban que nuestra mejor opción era contar también con tu ayuda y la de Gabriel.

Charlie arqueó las cejas.

—No entiendo cómo podemos ayudaros, pero tienes toda mi atención.

Barnaby esbozó una sonrisa fugaz.

—Primero te explicaré por qué estos casos son diferentes. —Se interrumpió cuando Crisp regresó cargado con una bandeja.

Charlie bebió de su brandy y esperó mientras colocaban la bandeja en una mesita frente a Barnaby y su famélico amigo daba cuenta de la comida.

En cuanto Crisp cerró la puerta, Barnaby continuó con su explicación entre bocados de rosbif.

—En todos los casos que hemos investigado se ha visto involucrada una parcela de tierra en particular. En cada caso, esa parcela ha sido imprescindible para la terminación de un canal, una nueva carretera de peaje o, en los últimos años, las vías del nuevo ferrocarril.

—¿Cómo de imprescindible?

Barnaby masticó y tragó sin apartar la mirada del plato.

—En el caso del ferrocarril es más fácil de explicar. Las locomotoras de vapor no pueden subir o bajar pendientes empinadas. Cuando es necesario salvar grandes desniveles, las vías deben sortearlos con una serie de curvas para mantener una pendiente constante. Las parcelas en torno a esas cuestas empinadas son de vital importancia para la construcción de la vía. A menudo no hay alternativa. Hay otros lugares, como un paso natural entre altas colinas, en los que el problema se resuelve con túneles o puentes, pero resultan más caros. Y en todos los casos que he investigado, no ha habido más remedio que comprar esa parcela.

—Así que esos terrenos han sido elegidos deliberadamente, según tu opinión, por alguien que sabe mucho de la construcción de canales, carreteras de peaje y ferrocarriles.

Barnaby asintió con la cabeza.

—Además, quienquiera que sea tiene conocimiento de las futuras rutas de canales, de las carreteras de peaje y de las líneas del ferrocarril mucho antes de que salga a la luz el proyecto. En algunos casos esas tierras se han comprado años antes de que se propusieran dichas rutas, incluso antes de que fueran estudiadas por cualquier entidad privada.

Charlie arqueó las cejas.

—¿Cuáles son tus sospechas?

—Ojalá tuviera alguna, pero no se me ocurre nada. Cada caso que he investigado... bueno, si fuera el villano de la historia, diría que cada terreno investigado ha sido una joya. Una parcela perfectamente escogida para especular con ella. Cada una de ellas... No puedo creer que alguien tenga tan buen ojo.

—¿De cuántos casos estamos hablando?

—De veintitrés hasta el momento.

—Has dicho que son varios casos. Supongo que todos siguen un mismo patrón en el que a los propietarios originales del terreno, ignorantes del valor potencial del mismo, se les hace una oferta demasiado buena para rechazarla. Aceptan e ingresan su dinero felizmente en el banco. Luego, más tarde, años en la mayoría de los casos, el nuevo dueño vende a una compañía en desarrollo esa misma tierra a un precio elevado, al borde de la extorsión. —Cuando Barnaby asintió con la cabeza, Charlie le preguntó—: ¿Por qué razón piensas que estos veintitrés casos son obra de un mismo villano?

—O villanos. —La mirada de Barnaby se oscureció—. Lo creo así por las medidas de persuasión utilizadas.

Charlie parpadeó.

—¿Las medidas de persuasión? ¿Para vender?

Barnaby asintió.

—Siempre comienza de una manera inocente. Una oferta por los terrenos realizada a través de un abogado local. Si los dueños aceptan, llegan a un acuerdo y no hay ningún tipo de delito. Todo va rodado. Los dueños originales no ganan el dinero que podrían haber ganado y las compañías en desarrollo acaban pagando un dineral por unas tierras que podrían haber adquirido a buen precio, pero, al menos hasta ahora, se consideraba un riesgo del negocio.

»Sin embargo, en dieciséis de los veintitrés casos denunciados por nuestros inversores, los dueños originales rechazaron esa primera oferta y también una segunda aún más generosa. Entonces era cuando comenzaba el acoso. Al principio de manera suave, en forma de ganado extraviado en el caso de una granja, o de cercas derribadas. Ya te lo puedes imaginar. Provocaciones anónimas pero cada vez más irritantes. Entonces aparecía una tercera oferta todavía más alta.

Barnaby cogió su copa.

—El acoso era cada vez mayor, cada vez más agresivo, acompañado de ofertas más altas, aunque ambas cosas no parecían tener conexión alguna. De hecho, en algunos casos, las nuevas ofertas parecían ser hechas a medida para ayudar a resolver los problemas. A menudo los dueños cedían y vendían. Sin embargo, existen al menos siete casos donde la coacción se convirtió en un ataque directo. Y al menos en tres de ellos, los ataques resultaron ser insuficientes para obligar a los propietarios a vender, así que el acoso se llevó al último extremo. —Barnaby miró a Charlie directamente a los ojos—. La muerte.

Charlie le sostuvo la mirada durante un buen rato. Un leño crepitó detrás de la reja de la chimenea.

—¿Quiénes son esas personas?

—Eso es lo que Stokes, mi padre y yo queremos descubrir. Lo que estamos resueltos a averiguar. La razón de la oferta por esas tierras nunca fue obvia hasta mucho más tarde, incluso los ataques y las muertes, supuestamente accidentales, no se habían relacionado con los compradores de las tierras hasta este momento. Todos los casos que hay en mi lista se deben a la ira de los inversores en las compañías del ferrocarril, y los delitos sólo fueron evidentes una vez que investigué la serie de acontecimientos.

»Y no es una investigación normal donde se pueda seguir fácilmente el rastro de los implicados. Puede que pienses que los nuevos propietarios son fáciles de localizar, pero lo he intentado y no he tardado en verme envuelto en una horrible trama de abogados, empresas y más empresas. —Barnaby dejó la copa vacía en el suelo—. Sólo Gabriel podría arrojar alguna luz en medio de este laberinto. Sin embargo, no es ésa la razón principal por la que he venido a verte.

—¿Cómo podemos ayudarte? —Tan sombrío ahora como Barnaby, Charlie se terminó la copa de un trago.

Barnaby le estudió la cara.

—Lo único que se me ha ocurrido para atrapar a esos delincuentes y acusarlos de algún delito es pillarlos mientras coaccionan a alguien para que venda una parcela. La coacción criminal es el único delito legislado que cometen. Pero para sorprenderlos en un acto deshonesto de esa clase, tenemos que encontrar...

—Una zona donde ese desarrollo aún no se haya producido, pero que sin duda lo hará en la próxima década. —La mirada de Charlie se volvió distante por un momento, luego la enfocó en la cara de Barnaby—. Supongo que estás pensando en la línea de ferrocarril que en algún momento se construirá entre Bristol y Taunton y que, desde allí, probablemente se extenderá a Exeter y Plymouth.

Barnaby asintió con la cabeza.

—He hablado con alguno de los directores de la compañía del ferrocarril. Taunton podría ser el punto de partida de una nueva línea dentro de unos años. —Arrellanándose de nuevo en el sillón, estudió la cara de Charlie—. Esta zona es tu hogar, y el de Gabriel. ¿Qué probabilidades hay de que llegue a vuestros oídos algo de este tipo?

Charlie lo pensó un momento y luego hizo una mueca.

—No tantas como puedes pensar. La gente no suele hablar de las ofertas que se hacen por sus propiedades, no hasta después de venderlas. A menos que crean que hay algo turbio detrás. Y como has dicho, a veces ni entonces. Nuestro villano particular no ha pujado por ninguna parcela de un hacendado importante, y si lo ha hecho, se ha preocupado por no presionarlos demasiado, y los agricultores no suelen airear sus asuntos. No creo que Gabriel o yo oigamos nada hasta que sea demasiado tarde y lo más probable es que para entonces nos enteremos por medio de las habladurías.

Barnaby suspiró.

—Temía que me dijeras eso.

Charlie levantó una mano.

—Pero puede que haya otra manera de averiguar algo más de esos malhechores. Si tienes razón con respecto a esta zona, existen muchas colinas en los alrededores que podrían ser un objetivo. Si averiguamos más sobre el modus operandi de estos individuos, podríamos ampliar la búsqueda y saber qué lugares de esta zona serían una buena apuesta para ellos.

Miró a Barnaby.

—Tenemos que hablar con Gabriel... y los demás. —Parpadeó—. Te envié una carta... Una invitación. ¿La has recibido?

Barnaby negó con la cabeza.

—Entre mi reunión con mi padre y todo esto, no he estado localizable. ¿Por qué? ¿Qué se celebra?

Charlie sonrió ampliamente.

—Me caso. Dentro de tres días. Estás invitado. Y también los demás.

Barnaby esbozó una sonrisa sincera y algo burlona.

—¡Felicidades! Primero Gerrard, luego Dillon y ahora tú. Me ha tocado bailar en vuestras bodas.

Charlie arqueó una ceja.

—¿No piensas seguir nuestros pasos?

—De eso nada. Tengo cosas más interesantes que hacer, como perseguir malhechores.

—Cierto. Al menos asistir a mi boda te ayudará en tus investigaciones. No sólo vendrán Gabriel y Diablo sino también Vane y todos los demás, incluidos Demonio y Dillon. Será la oportunidad perfecta para hacer una lista colectiva y elaborar un plan. Entre todos encontraremos la manera de dar con tus villanos.

—Amén —respondió Barnaby—. Otra cosa... no comentes el asunto con nadie más. No tenemos ni idea de quién puede estar detrás de todo esto.

Sarah regresó a Conningham Manor en el carruaje con su madre, sus hermanas y Twitters a primera hora de la tarde del lunes.

El largo viaje había sido una dura prueba para ella, sometida a las inocentes, pero innecesarias, especulaciones de Clary y Gloria sobre lo que ocurriría al día siguiente. En cuanto entraron en la casa y saludaron a los amigos y familiares que habían llegado para la boda, se escabulló poniendo el orfanato como excusa.

Mientras galopaba hacia el norte a lomos de *Blacktail*, Sarah inspiró hondo, sintiéndose libre por primera vez en días. Galopaba a toda velocidad, consciente de que tenía muy poco tiempo, no más de una hora para hacer todo lo que normalmente hacía a lo largo de un día.

A partir de ese día, el camino para llegar a la granja sería más largo. Tendría que salir más temprano de lo habitual desde el Park, que estaba tres kilómetros más al sur. Esperaba que ése fuera el único cambio que se produciría a partir de ese día, que todo permanecería más o menos igual.

Al llegar a la granja, ató a *Blacktail* frente a la puerta, sonrió y saludó a los niños que jugaban en el patio, y entró a toda prisa en la casa. Se dirigió directamente al despacho para echarles un vistazo a los libros de cuentas y arreglar algunos pagos y pedidos urgentes. Katy la encontró allí y con su laconismo habitual la puso al corriente de las actividades de aquel pequeño mundo.

Sarah descubrió que casi todo estaba al día y que sólo faltaban por comprobar unas cuentas y aprobar las decisiones que habían tomado esa mañana Skeggs y la señora Duncliffe.

—¡Gracias! —Le lanzó una sonrisa de agradecimiento a Katy cuando cerró el libro de cuentas.

—Sí, bueno, todos pensamos que deberías empezar tu vida de casada sin que nada perturbara tu mente. —Katy sonrió ampliamente.

Quince apareció en la puerta. Miró primero a Katy y luego a Sarah.

—Queremos que veas algo.

—¿Sí? —Levantándose del escritorio, Sarah se unió a Katy y a Quince y las siguió al vestíbulo.

—¡Felicidades, señorita! —Todos los residentes del orfanato se habían congregado allí y se habían colocado en filas ordenadas en el vestíbulo para corear aquel mensaje de felicitación con unas enormes sonrisas en sus rostros.

Ginny, la mayor de las chicas, dio un paso al frente con un paquete envuelto en papel de estraza entre las manos. Con una sonrisa radiante, hizo una reverencia y le ofreció el paquete a Sarah.

—Para usted, señorita. ¡Esperamos que su boda sea impresionante!

Sarah volvió a mirar a aquella multitud de caras brillantes. Había recibido muchas felicitaciones durante los últimos días, pero aquélla era, con diferencia, la más conmovedora de todas.

—Gracias. —Parpadeó con rapidez, sonrió y cogió el paquete. Era sólido y pesado.

Los niños, con una sonrisa de expectación en la cara, se removieron con inquietud, esperando que ella abriera el regalo. Sarah notó que Maggs estaba inusualmente serio y se mordisqueaba el labio inferior.

Sarah bajó la mirada y rasgó el papel. Entre sus manos apareció un gnomo de unos treinta centímetros con una rana a sus pies.

—Es precioso. —Y realmente lo era. Había cierta sabiduría en la expresión del gnomo mientras miraba a la rana. La figura demostraba una notable atención a los detalles.

Maggs avanzó despacio hacia ella, mirándola a la cara. Lo que allí vio debió de tranquilizarlo.

—Lo he hecho yo —confesó—. Lo cocimos en el horno del alfarero camino de Stogumber y lo pintó Ginny. Pensamos que podría llevárselo a su nuevo hogar y ponerlo en el jardín y así pensaría en nosotros cada vez que lo viera.

Sarah sonrió y le abrazó brevemente, luego abrazó a Ginny.

—Eso haré. Es perfecto. —Tomó nota mental para averiguar si entre los alfareros de la localidad había alguno que quisiera tomar a Maggs como aprendiz cuando tuviera edad para ello. Miró al resto de los niños—. Siempre conservaré como un tesoro al... señor Quilley.

Sarah sostuvo al gnomo en alto como si fuera un trofeo y los niños mayores prorrumpieron en vítores, encantados con el nombre que ella le había puesto a la figura. Los más pequeños miraron a su alrededor y dieron saltos de incontenible alegría. Era la hora del té. El personal condujo al grupo hasta el comedor, donde se había servido un té especial en honor a la boda de la señorita Conningham.

Sarah pasó la media hora siguiente celebrando su compromiso con los niños y el personal. Cuando los niños regresaron a regañadientes a sus clases, ella les dio unas calurosas gracias al personal, aceptando sus felicitaciones. Luego ató al señor Quilley a la silla de *Blacktail* y regresó a su casa.

Aún quedaba tanto por hacer que deliberadamente apartó de su mente cualquier cosa relacionada con vestidos, flores, lazos y ligueros, y se centró en el paisaje que la rodeaba mientras cabalgaba, dejando que los verdes campos la tranquilizaran como siempre habían hecho, al tiempo que ponía en orden sus pensamientos y se concentraba sólo en las cosas que consideraba más importantes.

Durante los tres últimos días se había sentido corroída por la incertidumbre. ¿Había tomado la decisión correcta? Mientras estaba con Charlie, se había sentido segura, convencida de que casarse con él era lo más acertado, que ser su esposa era el camino que debía tomar. Que cuando se casara con él el amor estaría presente en sus vidas; sería la piedra angular de su unión.

El amor había sido el precio que ella había puesto y él la había convencido de que era amor lo que había entre ellos, mejor dicho, ella se había convencido a sí misma de ello, y ésa era, precisamente, la causa principal de su actual estado de ánimo.

¿Y si todo era cosa suya? ¿Y si simplemente se había convencido de que lo que había visto en esa relación era lo que había querido ver, la promesa de amor en las caricias y el cariño de Charlie? ¿Y si todo lo que había visto no era más que un producto de su imaginación?

Charlie no le había dicho que la quería, pero tampoco lo había hecho ella, y no lo haría, no antes de que él lo hiciera. Su futuro marido no era el tipo de caballero dado a las frases floridas, a la poesía o cosas por el estilo; decir apasionadamente «te amo» en voz alta, simplemente, no iba con él.

Sabiendo eso, Sarah había buscado otras señales —en sus gestos, en sus reacciones— y las había encontrado. O eso creía.

Durante los últimos días, lejos de la presencia de Charlie y mortificada por la incertidumbre, había vuelto a revivir los momentos que habían compartido en el cenador y en otros sitios, todo lo que había observado y aprendido de él, y seguía sin estar segura. Lo único que había conseguido con todo aquello era un terrible dolor de cabeza y que se le revolviera el estómago.

Pero ahora no podía echarse atrás. Había aceptado casarse con él, había aceptado convertirse en su esposa y todos lo sabían.

Y casarse con él era lo único que podía hacer. ¿Serían sus dudas con respecto a aquella decisión el motivo por el cual madame Garnaut había descrito su futuro como «complicado»?

El Manor apareció a la vista; Sarah miró a la casa y suspiró. Mañana dejaría de ser su hogar.

¿Era normal que todas las novias tuvieran dudas antes de casarse?

10

Como era de esperar, Sarah no pudo dormir esa noche. Ataviada con un viejo vestido de diario, salió a hurtadillas de la casa, pero esta vez la excusa que tenía preparada por si alguien la pillaba —que era incapaz de dormir y había decidido dar un paseo por los jardines— era cierta. Charlie y ella no habían concertado una cita esa noche. La tradición dictaba que no deberían volver a verse hasta que se reunieran frente al altar al día siguiente.

Al mediodía se habría convertido en la condesa de Meredith. Una sofocante sensación de incertidumbre la abrumó. Intentó apartar el tema de sus pensamientos, concentrándose en el aquí y ahora, en los jardines envueltos en la oscuridad, en la brisa fresca de la noche, en las sombras que parecían más densas y más oscuras a la débil luz de la luna menguante, pero sus pies la guiaron, sin que ella opusiera resistencia, hacia el camino que llevaba al riachuelo, al embalse y al cenador.

La estructura blanca parecía fuerte y sólida contra el oscuro telón de fondo de la arboleda. Puede que allí encontrara algún sosiego, algún rastro palpable de lo que había ocurrido entre Charlie y ella en ese lugar, y que todavía estaba presente en sus pensamientos.

Subió los escalones y se adentró en la penumbra. Entonces lo vio. Estaba sentado en el sofá, inclinado hacia delante, con los codos apoyados en los muslos y las manos colgando entre las rodillas. La miró a través de las sombras. Sarah sintió su mirada, anhelante y ardiente, clavada en ella y, al instante, se encendió.

Se detuvo un momento, luego se acercó a él con deliberada lentitud.

Charlie se enderezó mientras Sarah se aproximaba. No la había esperado. Por un momento, cuando ella se había detenido en el umbral bajo la débil luz de la luna, él se había preguntado si su mente le estaría jugando una mala pasada y lo que estaba viendo era un fantasma, un producto de su imaginación.

Pero no fue un espectro lo que se detuvo ante él. Sin apartar la mirada del rostro de Sarah, Charlie le cogió la mano y sintió sus delicados huesos entre los dedos.

En la penumbra, la joven lo miró directamente a los ojos. Charlie comenzó a levantarse, pero ella lo detuvo poniéndole la mano libre en el hombro, luego se inclinó para besarlo.

Él le devolvió el beso, no con la voracidad que deseaba sino como presentía que ella quería. Con avidez pero sin prisas, tomándose su tiempo para explorarle y saborearle la boca. Durante un buen rato sólo se comunicaron con los labios y con sus lenguas acariciándose, con un anhelo ardiente que reconocían abiertamente, pero que por el momento mantenían a raya.

Familiar pero diferente. El deseo, la necesidad y la pasión estaban allí, a punto de estallar, y aun así parecía que eso no era todo lo que tenían que compartir.

Sarah lo empujó con la mano que le agarraba el hombro. Obedientemente, él se echó hacia atrás hasta que sus hombros chocaron con el respaldo del sofá. Ella le siguió sin interrumpir el beso, luego le soltó el hombro y se levantó las faldas para poder colocar primero una rodilla y luego la otra a ambos lados de los muslos de Charlie, acercándose todavía más. Luego le soltó los dedos y se puso lenta y descaradamente a horcajadas sobre él.

Ella ya había estado así antes, pero esta vez era diferente. Esta vez, cuando él levantó las manos y las cerró en los costados de Sarah, curvando los dedos índices en la espalda flexible de la joven para volver a sentir el cuerpo femenino entre sus manos, tan vivo, tan suyo, sintió otra emoción a la que ni siquiera él podía dar nombre. Algo que lo atravesaba, que lo reclamaba, que lo sumergía en un deseo diferente: la necesidad de volcarse total y completamente en ella.

En los deseos de Sarah, que ella le transmitía libremente a través de aquel lento, minucioso y resuelto beso.

Charlie se recostó, conteniéndose para dejar que fuera ella quien tomara el control, aunque no del todo —jamás podría ceder por completo ante ella—, sólo lo necesario para dejar que fuera la joven la que escribiera el guión de esa escena. Ella ya no era tan inocente, algo que resultaba bastante evidente. Cuando deslizó las manos entre ellos y le desabrochó los botones de la camisa, Sarah dejó muy claro lo que quería.

En cuanto le abrió la prenda y le puso las manos en el pecho, sus pequeñas palmas sobre su piel caliente, el único pensamiento de Charlie fue complacerla, darle todo lo que quería, sin reservarse nada.

Así que dejó que Sarah jugara con él tal como ella quería, dejó que le acariciara el torso mientras intentaba mantener su intensa y primitiva reacción bajo control, incluso cuando ella descubrió sus tetillas bajo el vello que le cubría el pecho y se las pellizcó.

Charlie se estremeció, sentía como si Sarah hubiera afinado cada terminación sexual que poseía. Incluso mientras le seguía besando podía percibir su sonrisa contra los labios y la satisfacción que la embargaba. Apretó los dientes mentalmente, reprimiendo el instinto que le impulsaba a reaccionar, a hacérselo pagar y volver a recuperar el control, pero esperó.

Sarah le deslizó las manos sobre el pecho y más abajo. A través del beso, él notó la respuesta de la joven. Concentrado totalmente en ella, sintió que Sarah se recreaba en él, y una parte oscura de su ser se regocijó con ello.

Charlie siguió la lenta e inexorable escalada del deseo de Sarah. Por una vez no hacía nada para provocarla, para encenderla. Se limitó a observar fascinado cómo la pasión de la joven florecía y crecía, sólo por estar allí, entre sus brazos, y a dejar que lo hiciera suyo.

Sólo cuando ella se removió inquieta y llena de deseo, alzó Charlie las manos y las cerró sobre los senos de la joven. Sarah se quedó sin aliento, pero se arqueó y se removió para provocarlo, cerrando una de sus manos sobre la espalda de él, instándole a seguir adelante. Sonriendo contra sus labios, él aceptó su demanda, le desabrochó los botones del corpiño, tan familiares ahora, y lo abrió lo suficiente para meter la mano y, con un rápido tirón, prescindir de la camisola para ahuecarle el seno hinchado con la mano.

Aquel simple toque lo hizo sufrir.

A Sarah la hizo arder. Puede que las sensaciones de la joven no fueran tan frenéticas como lo habían sido antes, pero ahora era plenamente consciente de la fiereza de su deseo. De su fuerza, de la pasión que la embargaba, de las llamas de deseo que le hacían hervir la sangre.

Charlie movió los dedos, acunándole los pechos con ambas manos, encontrando y apretando aquellos picos doloridos. Sarah interrumpió el beso con un jadeo, se aferró a los hombros de Charlie para mantener el equilibrio mientras echaba la cabeza hacia atrás y aspiraba profundamente a la vez que absorbía, saboreaba y gozaba el placer que él le proporcionaba.

Sin ninguna reserva.

Sarah sintió cómo sus sentidos se descontrolaban y se dejó llevar, disfrutando del delicioso gozo que le provocó Charlie cuando inclinó la cabeza y posó los labios en su sensible carne. La joven se estremeció cuando él lamió y torturó uno de sus rígidos pezones. Cuando lo tomó en su boca y succionó, ella gimió.

Sarah ahuecó la cabeza de Charlie con los dedos extendidos y le acarició el pelo mientras él le encendía los sentidos. Como ella quería, como ella deseaba.

Hasta que ardió de una manera tan intensa y apasionada que su yo más íntimo no le negó nada.

La joven le asió la cara y le alzó la cabeza, se inclinó sobre él y lo besó, apoderándose de sus labios, entrelazando su lengua con la suya y acariciándole una y otra vez.

Y entonces sintió la oleada de puro deseo que recorrió a Charlie por debajo de la piel, tensándolo, excitándolo; un hambre voraz que hizo que sus músculos se pusieran rígidos como el acero. Por debajo de esa fiebre ardiente, de esas llamas tentadoras que lo envolvían, Sarah sintió lo intensa y poderosa que era la pasión que él contenía con mano firme. El control estaba allí, inquebrantable y absoluto, pero era ella y no él quien lo tenía. Era ella quien sujetaba las riendas.

Sarah se llenó de júbilo, una emoción exultante que la dejaba mentalmente sin aliento y que hacía que su corazón palpitara con fuerza. Con los labios en los de él, la boca de Charlie cubriendo la suya, Sarah metió la mano entre sus cuerpos y asió los botones del pantalón. Charlie la ayudó cambiando de posición bajo ella, pero no se hizo cargo de la tarea. Dejó que ella lo liberara, que ella cerrara su mano en torno a su miembro y lo acariciara.

Haciéndolo estremecer.

Sarah curvó los dedos a su alrededor tal y como deseaba hacerlo y buscó la manera de conseguir que Charlie le suplicara. Experimentó sin prisas, disfrutando de unos segundos de poder antes de que él volviera a tomar el mando y le sujetara la mano, enseñándole a acariciarlo. Entonces sintió cómo él empezaba a perder el control.

Pero Sarah no se detuvo, sino que siguió provocándole, presionándole hasta que notó que él jadeaba, luchando, intentando con todas sus fuerzas no perder la razón. Cerrando los dedos en torno a aquel rígido miembro que parecía acero cubierto de cálida seda, la joven movió las rodillas sobre los cojines y se alzó sobre las caderas masculinas. Levantándose por completo la falda, se colocó sobre el cuerpo de Charlie con la intención de guiarlo a su interior.

Llevado hasta un punto de desesperación sensual que jamás había experimentado antes, Charlie se tambaleó mentalmente y le soltó los pechos; cerró las manos sobre las rodillas de Sarah y las deslizó por sus largos muslos hasta sujetarla por las caderas. Al instante sintió la ardiente humedad de la joven rozar la hinchada punta de su erección.

Sintió cómo las pasiones que estaba reprimiendo atronaban en su interior.

La atrajo hacia sí, buscando la apretada funda femenina, clavándole los dedos en las caderas y...

Sarah interrumpió el beso con un jadeo, levantó la cabeza y arqueó la espalda.

—¡No! ¡Déjame a mí!

Fue una exclamación apasionada, tan suave e intensamente femenina que estremeció el corazón de Charlie. Tensó los dedos, clavándoselos en la carne. Apretó los dientes. Resultaba una agonía luchar por contener el deseo casi incontrolable de bajarla hacia su erección mientras él empujaba hacia arriba para empalarla.

Charlie ya no estaba seguro de si estaba aún o no en este mundo. No podía concentrarse, ni pensar en nada que no fuera la intensa necesidad de estar dentro de ella. Pero entonces Sarah le acarició la mejilla, se inclinó sobre él y lo besó suavemente. Con la otra mano, le rodeó una muñeca; usándola como punto de apoyo se dejó caer sobre él.

Y Charlie descubrió que aquello sí era realmente hacer el amor, nada comparado con lo que había experimentado antes.

En vez de tomarla él, era ella quien se le ofrecía, y aquello era lo más cercano al paraíso en la tierra.

Poco a poco, centímetro a centímetro, Sarah lo introdujo en su cuerpo, hundiéndose lentamente en él, mostrándole un nuevo camino al edén.

Charlie sintió una opresión en el pecho. Apenas podía respirar cuando ella se hundió hasta el último centímetro, tomándolo por completo. Luego se detuvo. Con sumo cuidado, tanteando, Charlie aflojó el tenso control con el que había contenido a su yo más salvaje, y descubrió que se disolvía.

En el placer.

Listo para dejarse llevar y permitir que ella lo deslumbrara.

Sarah seguía experimentando, descubriendo, aprendiendo lo mismo que él. A través del beso, la joven parecía sentir el asombro de Charlie y su deseo aún por saciar. Cuando él aflojó un poco la fuerza con que la agarraba, Sarah se relajó levemente, luego se levantó unos centímetros antes de hundirse de nuevo en él.

Charlie permitió que su prometida marcara el ritmo durante el tiempo suficiente para recobrar el aliento. Luego, cuando ella se empaló de nuevo en él, Charlie se arqueó hacia arriba y la llenó por completo.

Sarah contuvo el aliento y se quedó inmóvil un momento, saboreando la plenitud con la que la llenaba, la realidad física de tenerle enterrado profundamente en su interior. Después se alzó de nuevo y utilizó la unión íntima de sus cuerpos para darle placer, a él y a sí misma.

El vínculo entre ellos era más fuerte ahora. Sarah lo sentía en cada caricia de sus manos, en cada beso, suave o apasionado. Estaba presente en la manera en la que él se obligaba a sí mismo a aceptar el ritmo lento que ella establecía para que la joven pudiera saborear cada matiz de esa unión a la vez que él disfrutaba del placer y el deseo de ella. Estaba en la manera en que él permanecía firme ante sus propios deseos aunque cada músculo de su cuerpo le pedía a gritos una liberación activa e inmediata.

Charlie luchó para no ceder a ese impulso, para darle a Sarah lo que deseaba.

Fue consciente de cada segundo de esa batalla, y supo que Sarah también era consciente de ello. Que percibía esa lucha interna y lo entendía, que se daba cuenta de la devoción que él sentía hacia las necesidades de ella, y que apreciaba cada pizca de fuerza que ejercía sobre su control para satisfacerla.

Sólo por eso merecía la pena contenerse. Convertía aquel momento en algo glorioso, y gracias a ello reunió la fuerza necesaria para mantenerse firme incluso cuando la pasión creció en su interior hasta límites insoportables.

Era una batalla que valía la pena librar por oír los incesantes jadeos de Sarah, por sentir la desesperación que la atravesaba y saber que no era él quien la conducía, no era él quien orquestaba y controlaba lo que ella sentía.

Mientras se movían juntos, ella cabalgándole y él empujando lo justo para aliviarles a ambos, dejando que la pasión fluyera sin trabas, que aquel familiar deleite sexual floreciera entre ellos, que la pasión los atravesara y los atrapara en sus redes, Charlie fue ligeramente consciente de lo diferentes que eran aquellas familiares sensaciones.

Mucho más cargadas de sentimientos, de significado. De emoción.

El final, cuando llegó, fue una explosión de sensaciones, más placenteras, más envolventes y más profundas de lo que lo habían sido nunca.

Sarah se desplomó en los brazos de Charlie con un grito agudo, triunfal y muy femenino. Las contracciones de aquella funda apretada lo atraparon, lo capturaron. Él llegó al clímax y gimió su nombre, abrazándola con fuerza mientras se estremecía bajo ella.

Sarah se relajó en sus brazos. Él la estrechó contra su cuerpo, cerró los ojos y apoyó la mejilla contra su pelo. Dio gracias a Dios por haber experimentado el profundo placer que ella acababa de mostrarle y por la pasión que acababan de compartir.

Diferente. Con ella siempre era diferente, pero aun así tan familiar que lo desconcertaba.

Desplomado en el sofá con Sarah hecha un cálido y saciado ovillo femenino sobre su pecho, Charlie clavó los ojos en el techo oscuro del cenador y regresó lentamente al mundo real.

Un mundo donde, gracias a ella, el paisaje había cambiado. Otra vez.

Charlie sopesó el motivo por el cual aquella unión había sido muy diferente a la de la última vez. Puede que se debiera a que ella había tomado la decisión de ser suya, y que como él ya había obtenido lo que quería, no tenía ninguna razón para controlarse y no disfrutar de ello.

Sin duda tenía que ser eso. Charlie no había acudido al cenador esperando encontrar allí a Sarah; había vuelto sólo por una extraña y nebulosa sensación que le había dicho que, puesto que no podía dormir, su lugar era ése, donde debía esperar por si acaso ella aparecía.

Por si acaso ella lo necesitaba.

Y al final Sarah había acudido, lo había buscado; para qué, no lo sabía, pero había ido. Y le había necesitado.

A él. Algo que sólo él podía darle.

Incluso ahora, Charlie no estaba seguro de qué era ese algo. Pero había sentido que ella lo necesitaba y había respondido a esa llamada. Una parte de él había reclamado el derecho, el honor, de darle todo lo que ella quería, y eso había hecho. Sarah había querido seguir un camino sensual que Charlie no sabía que existía, uno que había exigido mucho de él, pero en el que parte del placer, parte del reto, había sido darle a la joven esa satisfacción que tanto deseaba, haciendo un sacrificio sensual que jamás había hecho antes.

Sarah se removió entre sus brazos. Charlie la besó suavemente en la sien y ella se relajó de nuevo, incapaz de volver al mundo real todavía. Sonrió satisfecho. Estaba seguro de que, cuando la joven se fuera a la cama, dormiría profundamente.

Apoyó la cabeza en el respaldo del sofá y pensó en lo que les esperaba al día siguiente... a la noche siguiente. Por fin tendría a Sarah desnuda entre sus brazos. Esa visión... No podía dejar de pensar que sería una diosa... su diosa.

De hecho, ya lo era.

En lo más profundo de su ser, sabía que eso era cierto. Había algo en Sarah que hacía que la adorara, que la reverenciara; se le había colado sigilosamente bajo la piel, haciendo que cambiara su visión de ella. En parte se debía al placer que él había sentido durante aquella unión física. Algo que alimentaba el impulso indomable de satisfacer los deseos y exigencias de Sarah. Y eran los deseos y necesidades de la joven los que ahora gobernaban la vida de Charlie. Creyó que se estremecería ante tal pensamiento, pero sólo se sintió optimista, como si una parte de él, sin duda la parte más primitiva, supiera que eso era lo correcto.

Era curioso, pero era así como se sentía.

Puede que sólo fuera un síntoma más de su adicción al sabor de la inocencia.

Una adicción que Charlie había creído que se desvanecería gradualmente.

Pensar en esa adicción hizo que su mente regresara a ella, a ese cálido cuerpo femenino que todavía lo retenía en su interior.

Charlie enfocó los sentidos. Se dio cuenta de que debían de haber perdido la noción del tiempo, de que Sarah volvía a recuperar la conciencia, las sensaciones, el control de sus extremidades y pensamientos. Luego se contrajo en torno a él y Charlie ya no tuvo que pensar más.

Se movió y, medio alzándola, la tumbó de espaldas sobre el sofá, sin romper su unión, reacomodando las largas piernas femeninas bajo las faldas arrugadas para que le rodeara las caderas con ellas.

Entonces la penetró de nuevo.

Y al instante sintió la respuesta de la joven. Vio cómo sus ojos chispeaban bajo los párpados cuando se arqueó debajo de él.

Charlie se inclinó sobre ella, agarrándole las caderas para inmovilizarla, atrapándola bajo su cuerpo.

—Es mi turno —murmuró.

Sarah curvó los labios, hinchados y brillantes. Sonriendo como un gato satisfecho, la joven le ofreció aquella boca deliciosa, alargó las manos y le rodeó el cuello con los brazos, invitándolo en silencio a tomar lo que deseaba.

Charlie no estaba seguro de cuál de los dos estaba más cansado, saciado y dispuesto a dormirse cuando una hora después acompañó a Sarah a la puerta lateral del Manor. Quedaban pocas horas antes de que tuvieran que levantarse y hundirse en el caos del día de su boda, pero dudaba de que a cualquiera de los dos le importara mucho.

Con la mano en el picaporte, Sarah volvió la mirada hacia él, le acarició la mejilla con la mano libre y le brindó su sonrisa de *madonna*.

—Gracias.

Charlie se inclinó y la besó.

—Te aseguro que el placer ha sido todo mío. —La miró directamente a los ojos mientras daba un paso atrás—. Te veré en el altar,

Después de que ella retirara la mano de su rostro, Charlie se despidió con la cabeza, se dio la vuelta y se perdió en la noche.

Al mediodía siguiente, Sarah recorrió la nave de la pequeña iglesia de Combe Florey abrumada por la felicidad. Sus ojos estaban fijos en Charlie, que la esperaba en los escalones frente al altar y sintió que aquella alegría radiante que su madre, sus hermanas y todos los demás habían visto en ella esa mañana se incrementaba todavía más.

Provenía de lo más profundo de su interior, y era alimentada por la absoluta certeza de que Charlie la amaba como ella lo amaba a él. Puede que ese día sólo fuera el comienzo de ese amor, pero no había dudas de que ese sentimiento estaba allí presente.

La noche anterior había sido más que una confirmación. Había sido una promesa de consagración.

Cuando llegó a los escalones frente al altar, Sarah le tendió la mano a Charlie y se puso a su lado.

Al poco rato estaban casados; su unión había sido oficiada por el señor Duncliffe ante la mirada de sus parientes, cercanos y lejanos. Clary, Gloria y Augusta habían acompañado a Sarah por el pasillo central; Jeremy estaba situado al otro lado de Charlie junto a dos caballeros que la joven no conocía.

Sarah era consciente de que detrás de ellos la iglesia estaba a rebosar. El resto de su conciencia estaba centrada en la ceremonia, en los votos que había pronunciado y en los que Charlie le había respondido.

«Honrar y obedecer. Honrar y querer.»

Charlie le puso una alianza de oro en el dedo y se besaron para sellar el pacto, una caricia que se alargó más de lo que era apropiado. Apartaron los labios y sus miradas se encontraron. Fue un instante que sólo les perteneció a ellos y a su propia dicha, luego la realidad se inmiscuyó y se separaron con una sonrisa resignada. De nuevo volvieron a adoptar al papel que les correspondía interpretar ese día.

Recorrieron el pasillo cogidos del brazo, riéndose y sonriendo, aceptando las felicitaciones de todos los que abarrotaban la pequeña iglesia. Una vez fuera les recibieron con una lluvia de arroz, pero en vez de correr para refugiarse en el carruaje, se detuvieron bajo el brillante sol para recibir las felicitaciones de la gente del pueblo que se había reunido allí para verles; las mujeres alabaron las exquisitas perlas de Bruselas y los abalorios que adornaban el vestido blanco de seda de Sarah mientras los hombres estrecharon la mano de Charlie y le saludaron con respetuosas inclinaciones de cabeza.

Todo el mundo sonreía encantado. Parecía el final feliz de un cuento de hadas.

Los dos eran de la localidad. Habían vivido la mayor parte de sus vidas —toda la vida en el caso de Sarah— a pocos kilómetros de esa iglesia. No había nadie que no les deseara lo mejor, y la joven no recordaba un momento más emotivo en su vida.

Había esperado que Charlie se removiera con inquietud a su lado y que quizá se dirigiera a donde sus padrinos esperaban junto al engalanado carruaje. Pero en vez de eso, permaneció a su lado con el brazo enlazado con el de ella y desplegando su irresistible encanto con todo aquel que se acercaba a saludarle, dejando a todo el mundo satisfecho.

El señor Sinclair apareció entre la multitud y se inclinó sobre la mano de la joven.

—Enhorabuena, condesa. —Le brindó una atractiva y sincera sonrisa. Luego se volvió sonriente hacia Charlie y le tendió la mano—. Eres un hombre afortunado, milord.

—Sin duda alguna —murmuró mientras le estrechaba la mano y asentía con la cabeza sin apartar la mirada de Sarah— soy un hombre muy afortunado.

Sarah notó que se sonrojaba. Sin saber cómo, supo exactamente lo que Charlie estaba pensando. Se separaron de Sinclair y la joven miró a su alrededor para distraerse. A un lado de la multitud vio la cabeza color zanahoria de Maggs y se dio cuenta de que Lily y Joseph habían traído a los niños mayores a la ceremonia. Se volvió hacia Charlie, pero él ya había seguido la dirección de su mirada.

Capturó la atención de Sarah y sonrió.

—Venga. Vamos a saludarlos.

Sarah leyó la resignación en los ojos de Charlie, pero había algo más en ellos, algo que lo hacía aceptar todas las exigencias sociales de ese día. Sarah no sabía qué era ese algo, pero sonrió y le dejó guiarla hasta los niños.

Después de charlar con el grupo y de que todas las niñas alabaran su vestido de novia, se acercó Jeremy para decirles que tenían que marcharse.

—Os veré la semana que viene —les prometió Sarah a los niños. Y se despidió de ellos con la mano mientras su marido la alejaba de allí.

En cuanto llegaron al carruaje abierto, Charlie la ayudó a subir y al sentarse junto a ella se vieron asaltados por silbidos y vítores de «¡Viva Meredith!». La pareja sonrió y se despidió con un gesto de la mano mientras el cochero agitaba las riendas y el vehículo atravesaba el pueblo, alejándose de la iglesia. Con un suspiro se recostaron en los asientos. Minutos después cruzaron los impresionantes portones que conducían al largo camino de acceso a Morwellan Park.

Sarah aspiró profundamente captando la esencia de los árboles en flor en la suave brisa. La primavera estaba a la vuelta de la esquina, y la joven se sintió inundada por la sensación fresca y jovial.

Pronto llegaría a su nuevo hogar. Hoy era el principio del resto de su vida.

A su lado, Charlie le cogió la mano, consciente, como tantas veces antes cuando estaban juntos, de que ese día se estaba desarrollando de un modo diferente a como había imaginado.

En realidad, Charlie no había esperado disfrutar de la boda, pero en el mismo instante en que había puesto los ojos sobre Sarah, una visión radiante que se deslizaba por el pasillo central de la iglesia hacia él, había sentido como si el sol hubiera aparecido de pronto y desde entonces estuviera brillando sólo para él. Para ellos.

Ahora Sarah era suya y, aunque una parte de Charlie se sentía aliviada, otra parte, sin embargo, sentía orgullo. Estaba orgulloso de ella, y de haber conseguido que fuera su esposa. Hasta ese momento no se había dado cuenta de lo afortunado que había sido al pedir su mano. Había pensado que Sarah era una candidata excelente para ser su condesa, pero hasta hoy no había sabido cuán acertado había sido su juicio.

Al verla en medio de la multitud que había fuera de la iglesia, sonriente y sabiendo exactamente qué decir en todo momento ya fuera a alguien de rango, a la esposa del molinero o a los huérfanos del orfanato, supo que era la mujer perfecta para ser su esposa. Se relacionaba con facilidad con gente de todos los niveles sociales, igual que él hacía, pero no era una habilidad que tuvieran todas las mujeres. Muchas habrían considerado aquello como un simple deber, y habrían confiado en él para que las guiara. Sarah, sin embargo, sentía un verdadero interés por todos los que vivían en la zona. Había sido ella quien había llevado el peso de la conversación, dejando que él desempeñara el papel relativamente fácil de novio orgulloso y aristócrata de la localidad.

Bajó la mirada hacia ella y vio cómo, sonriendo con los ojos cerrados, ella alzaba la cara hacia los rayos del sol. Se la veía radiante, y era suya. Una cálida sensación de placer le inundó el pecho.

Era un sentimiento muy agradable y reconfortante.

Muchos de los invitados al almuerzo de bodas habían llegado antes que ellos; una multitud les estaba esperando en la salita para recibirlos con aplausos. Después de eso, Sarah y Charlie tuvieron que separarse, reclamados por amigos y familiares. Charlie se quedó sorprendido al darse cuenta de lo consciente que era de la ausencia de Sarah a su lado, pero había asistido a las suficientes bodas para seguir desempeñando su papel de manera automática. Dieron vueltas por la estancia, cada uno por su lado, charlando con todo el mundo hasta que Crisp les pidió que se dirigieran al salón de baile para tomar el almuerzo.

Se sentaron en las largas mesas adornadas con manteles blancos. Los rayos del sol que entraban por la ventana arrancaban destellos a los cubiertos de plata y a las copas alargadas de champán dispuestas en su lugar. Debería haber sido el padre de Charlie quien hiciera el primer brindis, pero ya había muerto. Gabriel Cynster era el pariente masculino más cercano de Charlie, pero en deferencia a su título, fue Diablo Cynster, duque de St. Ives, quien se levantó y propuso el primer brindis por la feliz pareja, dándole la bienvenida a su gran familia.

Todos se levantaron y alzaron las copas, coreando «por Charlie y Sarah» antes de beber. Charlie cubrió la mano de Sarah mientras se sentaba a su lado y sonrió a todos los presentes antes de volver a mirarla. En ese momento sintió que la extraña sensación que le oprimía el pecho se intensificaba.

Sarah parecía tan feliz que casi dolía mirarla. La imagen le hizo parpadear varias veces y sentirse humilde.

Luego, todos volvieron a sentarse de nuevo y, en medio de las conversaciones y la risa, se sirvió la comida. Todo el mundo hablaba. La mayoría de los invitados estaban emparentados de alguna manera u otra. Al no haberse iniciado aún la temporada social y haber pasado más de dos meses desde Navidad, había mucho de lo que ponerse al día. Había murmullos por todos lados, pero era un sonido agradable y envolvente, el de la felicidad compartida.

La hora siguiente transcurrió sin incidentes. Se hicieron los brindis acostumbrados; algunos de ellos, como era de esperar, provocaron hilaridad. El buen humor y el alborozo eran palpables en todos los invitados cuando se pusieron en pie y comenzaron a circular por la estancia.

Cuando se giró para charlar con lord Martin Cynster, Charlie observó que Alathea había pillado a Sarah. Estaban sentadas juntas en una mesa cercana, enfrascadas en una conversación. Quizá debería acercarse y escuchar qué clase de «sabiduría» le estaba impartiendo su hermana mayor. Pero se quedó donde estaba estudiando la cara de su esposa. La felicidad que irradiaba la joven era evidente.

Aquel resplandor que inundaba su piel fina parecía iluminarla desde dentro, haciendo brillar aquellos ojos azul ciano. Unos ojos que parecían más brillantes que nunca.

Por un instante, perdido en aquel resplandor, Charlie se preguntó qué era lo que estaba sintiendo, por qué la imagen de ella avivaba algo tan intenso y profundo en su interior. Por qué su propia respuesta a lo que veía era tan fuerte y poderosa que le dejaba momentáneamente sin respiración.

Y también mareado.

Levantó la copa y tomó un sorbo de champán. Recordó cuáles habían sido sus razones para casarse. Recordó los comentarios de Sinclair y los demás. Realmente era un hombre afortunado. Estudió la cara de Sarah y revivió en su mente los votos que había hecho: «honrar y querer».

De manera inesperada su mente hizo otro voto, uno que formuló en silencio mientras observaba a su esposa. Haría todo lo que estuviera en su mano por defender y proteger la felicidad que veía brillar en los ojos de Sarah.

Haría todo lo que pudiera para hacer realidad el deseo de felicidad que veía en la cara de su mujer.

—¡Aquí estás!

Charlie parpadeó y se giró para ver a Jeremy, que parecía algo agobiado, detenerse a su lado.

—¿Quién habría imaginado que casar a mi hermano mayor resultaría una dura prueba? —preguntó Jeremy con resignación, aunque con una mirada ligeramente mordaz—. Músicos. Recuerdas que tenemos músicos, ¿verdad? Están esperando, no sin cierta impaciencia, a que les des la señal para tocar el primer vals.

—Ah. —Charlie se acabó la copa y se la dio a Jeremy—. En ese caso, considera que ya he dado la señal.

Jeremy puso los ojos en blanco, lanzó un suspiro y les hizo una señal a los músicos situados en el otro lado de la estancia.

Cuando sonaron los primeros acordes, Charlie se acercó a Sarah y le cogió la mano. Mirándola a los ojos, sonrió y la hizo ponerse de pie.

—Creo que éste es nuestro baile.

Ella sonrió visiblemente feliz.

Charlie la guio al centro de la pista de baile, donde habían retirado las mesas, y sintió que los dedos de la joven temblaban entre los suyos. La tomó entre sus brazos, la miró directamente a los ojos y murmuró:

—En este momento al menos, somos sólo tú y yo.

Sarah le sostuvo la mirada, mientras la hacía girar por la pista. Un momento después notó que ella se relajaba, dejando a un lado el nerviosismo que la había asaltado al ser de pronto el centro de atención de todos. Sarah lo siguió por la pista sin titubear; sus faldas se rozaban contra las piernas de él mientras giraban sin parar. Charlie sonrió y la estrechó aún más contra su cuerpo al tiempo que la hacía girar completando una vuelta entera por la estancia.

—Ya está —murmuró él, sonriendo y manteniéndola cerca de

él después de que hubieran completado la vuelta de honor. Entonces, Alathea y Gabriel, seguidos de Dillon y Pris, y Gerrard y Jacqueline, saltaron a la pista de baile. Después los acompañaron otras parejas.

Sonriendo a su vez, Sarah suspiró. Buscó la mirada de Charlie.

—Todo ha salido perfecto, ¿verdad?

Charlie sintió que su sonrisa se hacía más profunda.

—Sí. —Y el día no había acabado aún. No pronunció las palabras, pero la dirección que habían tomado sus pensamientos debió de asomar a su mirada, porque ella se sonrojó y apartó la vista.

Sonriendo para sus adentros, Charlie miró a su alrededor y observó a las ahora numerosas parejas que giraban cerca de ellos. Martin y Celia pasaron riéndose por su lado. Charlie había visto cómo Diablo arrastraba a su duquesa, Honoria, a la pista; pasaron por su lado mientras Honoria le decía algo a Diablo. Evidentemente, se trataba de alguna clase de sermón, pues la expresión de la apuesta cara de Diablo era de suma diversión.

Charlie se preguntó si Sarah y él serían igual que ellos después de llevar años casados. Observó la cara de su esposa y, una vez más, sintió una profunda calidez en su interior ante lo que vio allí.

La música cesó y los bailarines se reunieron en grupitos para charlar. Sarah no se soltó del brazo de Charlie; no parecía dispuesta a alejarse de él.

La joven dirigió la mirada a un rincón de la estancia donde las matronas se habían sentado en unos sofás.

—Deberíamos... —Señaló a las damas de más edad con la mano—. ¿No crees?

Charlie no lo creía.

—Hemos hablado antes con todas en la salita. —Lady Osbaldestone estaba entre aquellas damas y no quería tener que escuchar los punzantes comentarios de la anciana, que sólo se habían hecho más afilados con los años. Sentadas con ella estaban Helena, la duquesa viuda de St. Ives; lady Horatia Cynster, la marquesa de Huntly y otras grandes damas. Todas ellas tenían algo en común: veían demasiado (como la inesperada respuesta de Charlie a la felicidad de Sarah tras haberse convertido en su esposa) y no había poder sobre la tierra que impidiera que comentaran lo que les viniera en gana.

»No tenemos por qué saludarlas de nuevo. —Charlie hizo girar a su esposa hacia invitados menos desconcertantes—. Allí están las gemelas, Amanda y Amelia. Las conoces, ¿verdad?

—Sí, por supuesto. —A Sarah le agradó mucho unirse al grupo donde brillaban las dos cabezas rubias de sus amigas.

Les saludaron con deleite y luego el grupo se dividió en dos. El que estaba compuesto por Amanda, condesa de Dexter, su hermana gemela Amelia, vizcondesa de Calverton, y Sarah, ahora condesa de Meredith, comenzó un fascinante debate sobre niños —las gemelas tenían tres cada una y al parecer habían decidido poner fin a su involuntaria rivalidad— que luego derivó en la próxima temporada social y en la probabilidad de que volvieran a reunirse en Londres en breve.

El grupo compuesto por Charlie, el marido de Amanda, Martin, conde de Dexter, y el marido de Amelia, Luc, vizconde de Calverton, intercambiaron miradas de resignación y entablaron una conversación sobre temas políticos. Los tres estaban emparentados con Diablo y Gyles Rawlings, conde de Chillingworth, que habían actuado como patrocinadores y mentores de cada uno de ellos cuando les tocó ocupar sus asientos en la Cámara de los Lores, y que les habían guiado por el, a veces confuso, mundo de la política.

La política era un aspecto de la vida que los cinco —Charlie, Luc, Martin, Diablo y Gyles— compartían como pares del reino, preocupándose por las vicisitudes que atravesaba el país. Todos se aseguraban de estar en Londres para votar cuando era necesario, si bien ninguno albergaba aspiraciones políticas más profundas.

No obstante, todos habían aceptado sus responsabilidades políticas. Eran algo inherente a su posición y habían crecido preparándose para asumirlas.

Sin embargo, como el Parlamento no había abierto todavía sus sesiones y no había agitaciones a la vista, tenían poco que discutir, a diferencia de sus mujeres. Aunque antes de que se les acabara la conversación se les acercaron Barnaby por un lado y, por otro, Reggie Carmarthen, un viejo amigo de Amanda y Amelia, y su esposa Anne, hermana de Luc, también se unió a ellos acompañada de Penelope, la más joven de las hermanas de Luc.

Sarah saludó con alegría a los recién llegados. Gracias a que Alathea estaba emparentada con el clan Cynster, y la familia de Sarah había sido invitada a todas las reuniones importantes en el Park y en Casleigh, la residencia de los Gabriel y Alathea Cynster, ya conocía a esas damas de antes. Nadie había imaginado que ella se casaría con Charlie, y ahora que lo había hecho, Amanda, Amelia y todas las demás estaban dispuestas a recibirla con los brazos abiertos y a darle la bienvenida a ese grupo tan cálido y acogedor.

El interés y la promesa de futuras amistades añadieron otra capa de alegría a un día repleto de ellas.

Barnaby Adair era un caballero al que ella no conocía, pero cuando Charlie se lo presentó, él le sonrió y la elogió. Rubio, muy apuesto y sofisticado, estaba claro que formaba parte de ese grupo, quizá más por amistad que por parentesco.

Charlie también presentó a Barnaby y a Penelope, otra joven a la que el hombre no conocía. La chica le lanzó una seria mirada desde detrás de las gafas y le tendió la mano.

—Eres el que investiga todos esos delitos, ¿verdad?

Tomando su mano, Barnaby admitió que así era, pero hábilmente cambió de conversación hacia otro tema menos sensacionalista. Penelope entrecerró los ojos y, tras recuperar su mano, se volvió hacia Sarah y las demás damas.

Mientras permanecía a un lado del salón, hablando de multitud de temas con aquel agradable grupo, e iluminados por los brillantes rayos del sol que entraban a raudales por la ventana, la incertidumbre que había invadido a Sarah sobre si sería capaz de manejar la casa de Charlie en Londres y todo lo que su posición conllevaba se evaporó. Con amigos así, no había nada que temer.

Amanda y Amelia insistieron en que acudiera a ellas si necesitaba cualquier tipo de ayuda.

—Ya hemos pasado por esto antes —dijo Amanda—, y sabemos que resulta muy abrumador al principio.

—Así es nuestro mundo —añadió Amelia—, una vez que sobrevivas a tu primer baile social como anfitriona, serás capaz de hacer cualquier cosa.

Todas se rieron, luego Amelia y Amanda se reunieron con sus esposos, que se alejaron con ellas sin oponer resistencia.

Charlie, Reggie y Barnaby reanudaron su discusión sobre caballos. Sarah se volvió hacia Anne y Penelope, que no habían hablado mucho.

Penelope clavó los ojos en Sarah de manera directa y audaz. A diferencia de las otras hermanas de Luc —la suave y femenina Anne, la mayor de todas, Emily, y la atractiva e intimidante Portia—, Penelope parecía una joven seria, con el espeso pelo oscuro recogido en un moño tirante y aquellas gafas sobre su pequeña nariz recta. También hablaba de una manera muy franca.

—Mi madre me ha dicho —dijo— que diriges un orfanato.

Sarah sonrió.

—Así es. Cuando lo heredé de mi madrina, ya era una institución establecida. —La mirada de Penelope era claramente inquisitiva. Sarah miró a Anne y vio que también parecía interesada. De una manera escueta esbozó el funcionamiento del orfanato y su objetivo de ofrecerles a los niños una ocupación en el futuro.

—¡Ajá! —Penelope asintió con la cabeza—. Eso es justo lo que necesito saber. Verás, junto con Anne, Portia y otras damas, dirijo una Casa de Acogida en Londres. Nos enfrentamos a las mismas dificultades que tú aquí, pero nos hace falta desarrollar un sistema para ayudar a los niños una vez que son lo suficientemente mayores para irse. —Penelope echó un vistazo a los invitados a la boda, pero eso no pareció disuadirla de seguir interrogando a Sarah—. ¿Te importaría dedicarme un poco de tiempo y explicarme cómo funciona vuestro sistema?

—No, claro que no. El orfanato es uno de mis principales intereses. —Sarah hizo una pausa y añadió—: Después de mi nuevo marido, por supuesto.

—Sé que Portia anda por aquí. Debería oír tu explicación también. —Poniéndose de puntillas, Penelope escudriñó la habitación—. ¿Veis a Simon Cynster?

—¿Por qué? —preguntó Anne mirando también a su alrededor—. ¿Está con ella?

Penelope soltó un bufido.

—No, pero si le ves, hay muchas posibilidades de que la esté mirando con el ceño fruncido. —Cuando Sarah la miró inquisitivamente, Penelope se encogió de hombros—. Es lo que suele hacer en las reuniones de este tipo.

En ese momento, Charlie captó la mirada de Sarah y arqueó una ceja. La joven decidió que quizá sería más prudente no enfrascarse en una discusión sobre el orfanato y se volvió hacia Anne y Penelope.

—Creo que es mejor que te presente a la señora Duncliffe, la esposa del vicario. Forma parte del comité del orfanato y aún sabe más que yo sobre cómo encontrar una ocupación a nuestros niños.

Penelope prestó de inmediato mucha más atención.

—¿La señora Duncliffe? ¿Quién es?

Por fortuna, la señora Duncliffe estaba sentada en un sofá no muy lejos de ellas. Sarah guio a ambas hermanas hasta allí y las presentó. Luego se alejó, dejando que las tres compartieran sus experiencias.

Volvió al lado de Charlie cuando los primeros acordes de otro vals resonaron en la estancia.

—Bien. —Charlie le cogió la mano y se la llevó a los labios para besarla—. Te he echado de menos.

Murmuró las palabras sólo para ella. Sarah sintió que la calentaban y la hacían flotar, luego se encontró entre los brazos de su marido, dando vueltas por el salón, y durante unos minutos nada más tuvo importancia.

Nada más tenía cabida en la mente de la joven cuando estaba rodeada por los fuertes brazos de su marido, no cuando giraba vertiginosamente con la mirada perdida en sus ojos.

—Uno de los beneficios del matrimonio —dijo él finalmente— es que podemos bailar el vals las veces que queramos.

Ella sonrió.

—No hay nadie más con quien quiera bailar un vals, sólo contigo —respondió.

A Charlie se le dilataron las pupilas. Sarah tuvo la impresión de que le había sorprendido de alguna manera, pero lo que acababa de decir era cierto. Charlie le escrutó los ojos y Sarah sonrió profundamente, dejando traslucir sus sentimientos.

Charlie tomó aire, luego levantó la vista y la hizo girar en sus brazos. No dijeron nada más hasta que la música cesó y se detuvieron en medio de la pista.

—¿Y ahora qué? —murmuró ella.

Charlie cerró la mano sobre la de ella con fuerza y luego se obligó a soltarla. Aún le quedaban muchas horas por delante antes de poder relajarse, antes de que pudiera explorar y saborear aquella fascinante ternura que él había vislumbrado en los ojos de su esposa.

—Ven. —La miró—. Quiero presentarte a mis mejores amigos.

Sarah había conocido a Gerrard y a Dillon en la iglesia, pero no a sus esposas. Desde el momento en que Charlie le presentó a Jacqueline y a Pris resultó evidente para Dillon, Gerrard y él que la única preocupación que tendrían de ahora en adelante sería cómo separarlas a las tres. Parecía que existía una enorme variedad de temas sobre los que sus esposas tenían que discutir e intercambiar opiniones.

Algunos de esos temas, como los bailes y cenas que cada una de ellas pensaba dar para la próxima temporada, eran de poco interés para sus maridos, que prefirieron retirarse a un lado y dejar a las tres jóvenes hablando solas

—Se acabó tu libertad —le dijo Dillon a Charlie con gran satisfacción—. Recuerdo mi boda, en la que presumías de ser el último hombre soltero. —Sonrió pícaramente—. ¿Cómo te sientes ahora que finalmente eres un hombre casado?

Charlie le devolvió una amplia sonrisa, sin pizca de arrepentimiento.

—En realidad, es menos estresante y mucho más placentero de lo que había imaginado.

Gerrard enarcó una ceja.

—Ver para creer. Ahora tienes que recuperar el tiempo perdido. Nosotros ya tenemos un heredero, así que tendrás que apresurarte en tener uno.

Charlie se rio entre dientes. Le guiñó el ojo a Gerrard.

—Lo tendré en cuenta.

Habían bajado la voz, pero aun así, comprobaron que sus esposas no les habían oído.

Los tres se las quedaron mirando durante largo rato. Al final, Charlie se obligó a apartar la mirada de la animada cara de Sarah y notó que tanto Dillon como Gerrard también se habían quedado mirando a sus esposas.

Había una expresión tierna en la mirada normalmente dura de sus amigos que Charlie jamás les había visto antes a no ser que estuvieran mirando a sus esposas o sus hijos.

Volvió a mirar a Sarah y finalmente lo entendió. Sintió de nuevo aquella sensación cálida y fluida, y sí, extrañamente tierna, que florecía en su interior cuando la miraba. Una sensación que sólo se hacía más profunda e intensa al pensar en verla con un hijo suyo entre los brazos.

Tomó aire y se dio la vuelta, un tanto mareado por la fuerza de aquel sentimiento. Pero viendo a Gerrard y a Dillon, aquello no parecía de extrañar...

Charlie frunció el ceño mentalmente. Ciertamente, su situación y la de ellos era diferente.

Antes de poder continuar con aquel perturbador pensamiento, Barnaby se acercó a ellos. Miró a las tres mujeres.

—¿No crees —le murmuró Gerrard en tono provocador— que ha llegado el momento de lanzarte y unirte a nosotros?

Barnaby observó cómo miraban a sus esposas y esbozó una sonrisa encantadora.

—Creo que no. Ahora mismo estoy interesado en otras cosas.

Dillon se rio.

—Eso era lo que pensábamos nosotros hasta que nos dimos cuenta de que estábamos equivocados.

La sonrisa fácil de Barnaby no flaqueó.

—Sospecho que estoy hecho de otra pasta. Seré para vuestros hijos el excéntrico tío Barnaby. Todos los niños merecen tener un tío excéntrico, ¿no creéis?

—¿Por qué piensas que estás hecho de otra pasta? —preguntó Charlie.

Barnaby lo miró directamente a los ojos y luego hizo una mueca.

—¿De veras crees que alguna dama podría comprender lo que yo hago? ¿A qué dedico mi tiempo? ¿Que alguna joven vería con buenos ojos que prefiera comprometerme con una investigación criminal antes que acudir a fiestas sociales?

Los demás intercambiaron unas miradas y luego hicieron una mueca.

Pero Gerrard negó con la cabeza.

—Sea como sea, no se me ocurriría tentar al destino pensando que no te casarás nunca.

—Sea como sea —repuso Barnaby mirando a Charlie—, parece que ha llegado el momento perfecto para que tengamos nuestra pequeña reunión.

Recordando lo que habían planeado, Charlie echó un vistazo a su alrededor.

—Cierto —dijo. La fiesta todavía estaba en su apogeo. Las mujeres aún charlarían durante horas, e incluso los caballeros tenían temas de sobra sobre los que hablar. Se volvió hacia Gerrard y Dillon—. Barnaby anda detrás de unos desagradables criminales y quizá podamos ayudarle de alguna manera. —Inclinó la cabeza hacia Dillon—. Tú ya has oído hablar del asunto, pero Barnaby y yo pensamos que hoy es la oportunidad perfecta para explicaros a todos lo que sospechamos. ¿Por qué no nos esperáis en la biblioteca —dijo mirando a Barnaby— mientras reunimos a los demás?

Dillon y Gerrard abrieron mucho los ojos antes de asentir con la cabeza. Lanzaron una rápida mirada a sus esposas, confirmando que todavía estaban absortas en la conversación, y luego salieron del salón de baile.

Charlie miró a Barnaby.

—Ve por ese lado y yo iré por éste.

Barnaby asintió con la cabeza y se separaron. Sin prisas, dieron una vuelta por el salón, buscando a los demás entre los invitados.

11

Cuando Charlie se dirigió con Gabriel a la biblioteca, los demás ya estaban allí.

Diablo se había sentado frente al escritorio, dejando para Charlie la silla que había detrás del mismo. Vane Cynster, primo de Diablo, estaba recostado contra una de las librerías. El hermano de Vane, Harry, conocido como Demonio, y Alasdair Cynster, hermano de Gabriel y al que todos llamaban Lucifer, habían cogido el sofá del otro lado de la estancia y lo habían acercado al escritorio.

Gyles, conde de Chillingworth, amigo y Cynster honorario, había colocado una silla junto a la de Diablo, mientras que Simon Cynster, el más joven de los presentes, y soltero como Barnaby, se había apoyado con elegancia en el respaldo del sofá.

Dillon, Gerrard y Barnaby habían cogido las sillas libres y se habían sentado entre los demás, mientras que Luc y Martin se habían apoyado en otra de las librerías, uno junto al otro, con las largas piernas cruzadas y las manos en los bolsillos.

Todos ellos tenían en sus rostros, duros y atractivos, una expresión seria y expectante. Gabriel se sentó entre Lucifer y Demonio en el sofá. Charlie sintió todas las miradas fijas en él mientras se dirigía a la silla detrás del escritorio.

Tomó asiento y miró a su alrededor, sosteniendo brevemente la mirada de cada uno de los presentes.

—Gracias por venir. Barnaby necesita nuestra ayuda en una misión.

Después miró a Barnaby, que explicó a grandes rasgos el motivo de la investigación.

Durante ese tiempo nadie se movió ni cambió de posición. Charlie estaba seguro de que incluso podría haber oído caer un alfiler sobre la alfombra Aubusson. Nadie interrumpió ni carraspeó.

—Aunque mi padre y otros pares están supervisándolo todo con ayuda de algunos altos cargos de la policía, quieren que resuelva este asunto ya. Dado que hay mucha gente rica, parlamentarios y caballeros influyentes, involucrada en las compañías del ferrocarril, cualquier investigación que llevemos a cabo deberá realizarse con suma discreción —concluyó finalmente Barnaby.

Luego guardó silencio. Los demás comenzaron a removerse y a intercambiar miradas. Como grupo eran poderosos de muchas maneras; ricos e influyentes, la mayoría tenían un título y habían nacido en el seno de la elite.

—Todos los aquí presentes —murmuró Gabriel— hemos hecho algunas inversiones financieras en compañías que pueden ser un objetivo de este... llamémosle extorsionista. Por lo tanto somos víctimas potenciales, aunque no vaya a perjudicarnos de una manera directa. Pero esta clase de actividad delictiva bien podría dar como resultado la bancarrota de algunas compañías y, por lo tanto, una pérdida de confianza en todo el sector financiero que a largo plazo afectaría a nuestras inversiones.

Diablo se removió en su asiento. Intercambió una mirada con Chillingworth antes de tomar la palabra.

—Existe un problema de fondo en todo esto que no sólo perjudica a nuestras inversiones individuales. —Lanzó una mirada a su alrededor—. Todos sabemos que el futuro de este país depende del éxito de las inversiones en infraestructuras, en especial las del ferrocarril. Los canales que se han construido durante los últimos decenios son de menor interés comparados con los ferrocarriles, algo que es de vital importancia para la próxima generación. Si se hace público que invertir dinero en una compañía de ferrocarril acarrea un riesgo pues dicha compañía puede ser objeto de extorsión y, en consecuencia, acabar en bancarrota, los pequeños inversores, esenciales para financiar el proyecto, se echarán atrás. A ninguno de ellos le gusta correr riesgos.

—Y mucho menos asumirlos —apostilló Lucifer.

Diablo asintió con la cabeza.

—En efecto. Y todavía más, si se da a conocer que un determinado lugar que está cerca de una ruta propuesta para el ferrocarril puede llegar a ser objeto de las tácticas disuasorias a las que nuestros extorsionistas someten a los agricultores, podría tener lugar un amotinamiento en esa zona, pues nadie permitiría que el ferrocarril cruzara por sus tierras.

—El hecho de que sólo perjudique a parcelas específicas no supondrá ninguna diferencia —dijo Chillingworth—. El pánico no se rige por la lógica.

La mirada de Barnaby se había vuelto distante. Había palidecido al darse cuenta del panorama que le pintaban.

—Santo Dios —dijo con voz débil—. No creo que mi padre y los demás se hayan planteado nada parecido.

Diablo hizo una mueca.

—Probablemente lo hayan hecho, pero no han visto ninguna razón para entrar en detalles. Aunque saben que serás discreto.

Barnaby parecía muy afectado.

—Cierto. Pero tales perspectivas hacen incluso más imperativo que identifiquemos y detengamos a este extorsionista.

—¿Estás seguro de que siempre es el mismo hombre o grupo quien está detrás de esas extorsiones? —preguntó Martin.

Barnaby asintió con la cabeza.

—Llegué a esa conclusión cuando intenté rastrear las ganancias exorbitantes de las ventas de algunas parcelas. Deduje que los beneficios debían volver finalmente a las manos de quien está detrás de todo esto, pero cada propiedad es comprada por una compañía distinta, y vendida por la misma. Después de cada venta, la compañía original es disuelta, y sus ganancias, el dinero de la venta, transferidas a otras compañías, que a su vez pagan a otras empresas. Al intentar avanzar en mi investigación descubrí que no había más que una red de compañías que se disolvían en la nada.

»Y esa misma situación se repetía siempre que intentaba rastrear el dinero de la venta de una parcela. La compañía original conducía a otras y, aunque todas son diferentes, la estrategia es exactamente la misma. Es tan complejo y efectivo que me cuesta creer que esto haya sido planeado por dos personas diferentes.

Vane miró a Gabriel.

—¿Existe alguna manera de seguir el rastro en medio de tal laberinto?

—Debería haberla —respondió Gabriel—, pero si el extorsionista ha sido lo suficientemente listo para montar una red de compañías que sirva a sus intereses, entonces es muy probable que acabemos dando palos de ciego. Hasta que el gobierno apruebe una ley que obligue al registro de los dueños de las compañías, y me refiero a los propietarios legales, y todavía más importante, a los que reciben los beneficios que éstas producen, en especial cuando han sido creadas para encubrir la identidad del propietario en el que revierten las ganancias, todo será una pérdida de tiempo.

Gabriel miró las caras que le rodeaban.

—Recomiendo que reservemos nuestros esfuerzos para investigar por otro lado.

Hubo muecas de disgusto por parte de todos ellos, y durante un buen rato reinó el silencio.

—Muy bien. —Luc miró a Barnaby—. Nuestras haciendas se extienden por todo el país. Deberemos mantenernos atentos ante cualquier indicio de extorsión que surja en cualquiera de las áreas que mejor conocemos.

Barnaby asintió con aire sombrío.

—Todos conocéis las zonas donde se piensa construir vías de ferrocarril con desniveles. Avisadme en cuanto escuchéis algo sobre ofertas de venta a los propietarios de las tierras colindantes. He pasado los últimos días examinando los terrenos entre Bristol y Taunton, y un poco más al oeste. Dada la topografía, es probable que nuestro extorsionador intente actuar en esta región, por lo que mantendremos vigilada esta área.

Suspiró y se reclinó en la silla.

—Parece que es todo lo que podemos hacer por el momento.

—En realidad —dijo Charlie, tamborileando con los dedos sobre el papel secante y mirando a Gabriel—, creo que hemos pasado por alto otro camino a seguir. Y es muy probable que nuestro malhechor también lo haya pasado por alto.

Gabriel sostuvo la mirada de Charlie durante un momento, pero luego, con un amago de sonrisa, sacudió la cabeza.

—No creo que tenga que ver con las finanzas. ¿A qué te refieres entonces?

—No estoy del todo seguro, pero... —Charlie miró a su alrededor y luego clavó los ojos en Gabriel—. Nuestro extorsionista ha sido muy hábil ocultando adónde va el dinero. Pero ¿ha sido igual de hábil ocultando la procedencia de ese dinero?

Todos los demás se pusieron en alerta. La tensión en la estancia se incrementó bruscamente. Se intercambiaron varias miradas mientras todos comprendían adónde quería llegar Charlie, luego clavaron los ojos en Gabriel.

Éste asintió con la cabeza lentamente sin apartar la mirada de Charlie.

—Una pregunta interesante. —En la voz arrastrada de Gabriel había un toque depredador.

Charlie sonrió ampliamente, una sonrisa que reflejaba el aire depredador de su cuñado.

—Sin importar de dónde salga ese dinero, al final, las ganancias regresarán a su lugar de procedencia. Es la ley de las finanzas.

—Oh, sí —convino Gabriel—, y aunque nuestro hombre haya creado una red de compañías para ocultar los movimientos de las ganancias, si buscamos en la otra dirección, de dónde ha salido ese dinero para comprar las tierras, incluso aunque nuestro hombre vuelva a usar una red de compañías, podremos averiguar en qué momento han entrado esos fondos en la red.

—Los fondos que entran en la red... desde la fuente. Nuestro extorsionador. —Diablo arqueó una ceja en dirección a Gabriel—. ¿Es difícil rastrear los fondos que son el capital inicial de una compañía?

Gabriel no respondió de inmediato.

—No será fácil —dijo finalmente. Todos los presentes sabían que con ese «no será fácil» Gabriel había querido decir que sería muy difícil—, pero podemos intentarlo.

—Podríamos encontrarnos involucrados en una trama similar —dijo Charlie—, pero si nos concentramos en una sola empresa, y buscamos sólo el origen de la financiación, incluso aunque nuestro hombre se haya movido por varias compañías, todavía podremos dar con un rastro. Una suma identificable. Es poco probable que se le haya ocurrido pagar la suma inicial en cantidades más pequeñas.

—Además, el capital inicial habrá llegado por alguna ruta alternativa. —Gabriel asintió con la cabeza—. Es algo que merece la pena investigar. —Miró a Barnaby—. Necesitaremos conocer todos los detalles que tengas de la compañía que haya comprado la parcela más cara de la que hayas tenido noticia. Cuanto mayor sea la suma invertida, más fácil será rastrearla. Podemos —Gabriel miró a Diablo— decirle a Montague que se centre en esa compañía, que averigüe todo lo que pueda de ella. Que busque el capital inicial a través de los movimientos bancarios. Con algo de suerte, debería ser capaz de seguir el rastro hasta las cuentas de nuestro extorsionador.

Diablo asintió con la cabeza.

—¿Le dirás qué debe buscar?

—Preferiría que lo hicieras tú. —Gabriel miró a Barnaby, luego a Charlie—. Estoy de acuerdo, tal y como ha dicho Barnaby, en que esta zona, de entre todas las regiones de Inglaterra, es donde probablemente invertirá nuestro hombre. Creo que seré más útil aquí, donde pueda vigilarlo de cerca.

La reunión terminó. Los caballeros regresaron al salón de baile en grupos de dos o tres, un número apropiado para ocultar el hecho de que había tenido lugar aquel encuentro. Y tuvieron éxito. Ninguna de sus madres, hermanas o esposas pareció haber notado su colectiva ausencia entre el todavía considerable gentío.

Aliviados por no tener que rendir cuentas a nadie, cada uno regresó con su respectiva esposa o, en el caso de Simon, con su eterna irritación hacia Portia Ashford. Charlie encontró a Sarah charlando con dicha señorita sobre el orfanato. Saludó a Portia con la cabeza, tomó a Sarah del brazo y esperó a su lado.

Al regresar al salón de baile, Charlie les había indicado a los músicos que las sonatas que les había ordenado tocar mientras él estaba recluido en la biblioteca ya no eran necesarias y que podían volver a los valses.

Durante todo el día había contenido el inevitable efecto de la noche anterior, reprimiendo su impaciencia por probar su hipótesis y asegurarse de que su adicción a Sarah disminuiría una vez que fuera legalmente suya. Había actuado como se requería que actuara un aristócrata en el día de su boda, y él, ellos, se habían comportado como era debido. Pero la impaciencia de Charlie, ligeramente aplacada por la reunión en la biblioteca, había regresado con mayor ímpetu.

Dos minutos después, las notas de un vals inundaron la estancia. Charlie susurró algo al oído de Sarah y, después de pedirle a una sonriente Portia que los disculpara, guio a su esposa a la pista de baile.

—¿Dónde te habías metido? —le preguntó Sarah en cuanto comenzaron a bailar.

Charlie bajó la vista hacia ella, luego miró por encima de su cabeza mientras la hacía girar por la pista.

—He estado hablando con los demás sobre negocios. Preferimos irnos a un lugar más tranquilo.

—Oh. —A Sarah pareció sorprenderle que él pudiera dedicar un solo pensamiento a los negocios en ese momento.

Como si él hubiera adivinado sus pensamientos, capturó la mirada de la joven y sonrió; fue su sonrisa más íntima y sincera, desprovista del sofisticado encanto que mostraba hacia los demás.

—Intentaba pasar el tiempo.

Ladeando la cabeza, Sarah le estudió, intentando descifrar qué había querido decir con eso.

—¿Pasar el tiempo?

—Hasta que... —La hizo girar otra vez mientras la guiaba entre la multitud de bailarines. Se detuvo en un rincón del salón donde un aparador elaboradamente tallado los ocultaba de la vista de todos.

Tomándola de la mano, buscó la mirada de Sarah.

—Hasta que podamos hacer esto. —Alargando la mano, hizo girar una manilla del mueble y una puerta oculta se abrió de pronto con un silencioso clic—. Y fugarnos.

El corazón de Sarah —y todas sus terminaciones nerviosas— dio un brinco, pero se limitó a lanzar una rápida mirada a los invitados que giraban en la pista.

—No te preocupes —murmuró él—. La mayoría se sorprendería más si nos quedáramos. —Rodeándole la cintura con un brazo la instó a cruzar la puerta. Sin mostrar una auténtica resistencia, la joven atravesó el umbral hacia un estrecho corredor de servicio.

Charlie la siguió y cerró la puerta. Volviendo a cogerle la mano, se la puso en el brazo y le indicó el camino.

Sarah levantó la mirada hacia su cara.

—¿Por qué esperan que nos vayamos tan subrepticiamente?

—Para que evitemos una salida mucho más embarazosa, en especial la «despedida» que Jeremy, Augusta, Clary y Gloria habían planeado para nosotros durante los últimos días. —Arqueó una ceja—. ¿O de verdad quieres saber qué tenían planeado?

Sarah se rio y negó con la cabeza.

—Creo que viviré mucho más tranquila si no me lo cuentas.

—Gracias a Dios. Estaba seguro de que lo entenderías.

La joven percibió una auténtica nota de alivio en la voz de su esposo y sonrió para sus adentros. Luego recordó adónde se dirigían. Y para qué. Y se sintió dominada por un extraño nerviosismo. Sarah miró a su alrededor intentando orientarse mientras él la hacía tomar un pasillo que conducía a un estrecho tramo de escaleras.

Charlie abrió una puerta, y recorrió a Sarah con la mirada mientras la guiaba.

—¿Has estado antes en esta ala?

Entraron en un pasillo ancho y lujosamente decorado que evidentemente era uno de los pasillos principales de la casa. Sarah miró a su alrededor y luego a través de la ventana para orientarse. Los sonidos del salón de baile se habían desvanecido y ahora los rodeaba un denso silencio.

—No. Estamos en el ala oeste, ¿verdad?

Asintiendo con la cabeza, Charlie volvió a tomarla de la mano, engulléndola en la suya.

—Los aposentos del conde están en esta ala. Llegarás hasta aquí subiendo por las escaleras principales. —Señaló con la mano detrás de ellos mientras la guiaba hacia delante.

Sarah comenzó a tener dificultades para respirar.

Se dijo a sí misma que era una tontería sentirse así, como si Charlie y ella jamás hubieran estado juntos. Pero eso había sido en el cenador, en el profundo silencio de la noche, y no allí. Aquello era muy diferente.

El pasillo acababa en una antesala circular. Había una brillante mesa redonda en el centro con un florero chino de talle alto que contenía un ramo de flores del invernadero de la casa. Al entrar en la estancia, Charlie le soltó la mano y se volvió hacia ella. Alzando la mirada, Sarah parpadeó. Luego avanzó lentamente con la mirada fija en el enorme tragaluz circular que se abría por encima de la mesa.

Oyó un sonido a su espalda y se dio la vuelta. Vio a Charlie asegurando con unos pernos las enormes puertas dobles que separaban aquella antesala del pasillo.

Charlie dio un paso atrás y examinó su trabajo.

—Eso debería contenerlos.

Se volvió hacia ella y sonrió, luego acortó la distancia que había entre ellos. Charlie la miró a los ojos y vio el repentino nerviosismo que embargaba a la joven. Le brindó una sonrisa más suave, más íntima y tranquilizadora.

Alargó el brazo y le cogió la mano, pasándole el pulgar por los nudillos.

—No quiero que nadie nos interrumpa —dijo con total sinceridad.

Sin dejar de mirarla a los ojos, levantó la otra mano y le ahuecó la cara. Lentamente, le alzó la barbilla y, con la misma deliberada lentitud, inclinó la cabeza y la besó.

Fue un beso ligero, suave, que no exigía nada más que la respuesta instintiva de la joven. Una respuesta que Sarah le ofreció sin pensárselo dos veces.

Los labios de Charlie eran firmes, y ella se rindió a ellos, abrió los suyos y esperó. Cuando la lengua de su esposo encontró y acarició la suya, Sarah suspiró.

Durante un buen rato la boca de Charlie se movió sobre la de ella, entrelazando la lengua con la suya en una exploración lenta y sensual, reclamando aquello que era suyo. Le acarició la barbilla, deslizando los dedos más abajo, por la garganta, mientras le inclinaba la cara con el pulgar y ponía en práctica su considerable experiencia para atraerla hacia sí. Luego llevó la otra mano a la cintura de su esposa y la estrechó contra su cuerpo.

Era suya.

Cuando levantó la cabeza y la miró directamente a los ojos, estudiándole la cara, Sarah ya estaba sumergida en una red de placeres sensuales que sabía que se intensificaría en cuestión de minutos.

Que era lo que él quería.

Charlie curvó débilmente los labios; en su rostro había aparecido la expresión sensual que Sarah conocía tan bien. Él le liberó la cara y, tomándola de la mano, la hizo volverse hacia la puerta de su habitación.

Mientras la conducía a los aposentos del conde, Sarah se dio cuenta de que lo que había pasado entre ellos en el cenador nunca podría compararse con eso. Con lo que iba a suceder a continuación.

Sarah era ahora su esposa... ésa era la diferencia.

Charlie abrió la puerta y la hizo pasar a la habitación. Con las pupilas dilatadas y los nervios de punta, Sarah se detuvo y miró a su alrededor. Oyó cómo se cerraba la puerta a su espalda. Los labios le palpitaban un poco por el beso compartido, y su respiración era superficial cuando contempló la enorme cama de cuatro postes elaboradamente tallados, con cortinajes de seda azules y la colcha del mismo color.

Sarah sintió la mirada de Charlie en su cara. Él se detuvo, observando cómo la joven miraba los ostentosos muebles, el dosel con cordones dorados que sostenía los cortinajes de la cama y las cortinas de terciopelo azul de las ventanas. Toda la habitación estaba decorada en tonos azules, incluso las flores de lis del empapelado blanco de la pared eran azules. En contraste, los lujosos muebles de madera dorada resplandecían: la cama, los altos armarios alineados contra las paredes, el tocador con un espejo oval situado entre dos ventanas y el confortable sillón de orejas que había al lado y que estaba tapizado en tonos azules. Sin embargo, el resultado final no era recargado.

Sarah bajó la mirada al suelo y vio que en las alfombras persas que cubrían el suelo de madera pulido se repetía el mismo patrón; una rica mezcla de tonos azules, marfiles y dorados.

Cada objeto donde posaba la vista era elegante, caro pero no recargado. Las lámparas, los candelabros de la pared, incluso los platos decorativos parecían formar parte del conjunto, de tal manera que uno no encajaría bien sin el otro.

Encantada, Sarah se acercó al tocador, donde habían colocado sus cepillos. La imagen hizo que se estremeciera, aunque no pudo explicarse por qué.

Se movió para asomarse a las ventanas. Daban al sur, al jardín que rodeaba el lago artificial. Los árboles bordeaban el césped con las ramas todavía desnudas, aunque ya comenzaban a surgir los primeros brotes verdes.

Era media tarde. El día llegaba a su fin y el sol comenzaba su declive, aunque aún había luz suficiente para ver con claridad. Charlie se situó junto a ella en la ventana y Sarah aspiró profundamente antes de volverse hacia él y mirarle a la cara.

Charlie estaba a menos de treinta centímetros de ella y la miró a los ojos. El deseo estaba grabado en cada ángulo y plano de su rostro, volviéndolo más afilado, un rasgo que ella conocía muy bien. Los ojos azules de Charlie eran resueltos; le estudiaba la mirada, la expresión intentando leerle el pensamiento.

Sarah esperaba que tuviera suerte; ella no podría haberle dicho lo que sentía en ese momento, sencillamente no encontraba palabras para expresar tal cúmulo de sentimientos.

—Sólo podía imaginarte rodeada de azul. Espero que te guste, pero si no es así puedes cambiarlo todo —dijo Charlie, rompiendo el silencio.

Tenía la voz ronca, cargada de deseo.

Ahora que lo miraba a los ojos, Sarah supo instintivamente qué era lo que la había hecho estremecerse. Charlie había decorado ese lugar para ella; allí, en esa habitación, ella sería su esposa de la manera más íntima y elemental.

Haciéndose eco de sus pensamientos, Charlie le tomó las manos entre las suyas. Clavando sus ojos en los de ella, alzó primero una mano y luego la otra a sus labios y le besó los sensibles nudillos.

—Todo lo que ves —murmuró Charlie— forma parte de tus dominios. Ahora eres dueña y señora de este lugar.

Sarah le miró y sintió que el poder que los había envuelto a los dos en el cenador volvía a rodearlos con una fuerza intrínseca, constante y real.

Pero allí, en esa habitación, crecía y ardía con más intensidad.

Sarah liberó su mano de las suyas y alargó el brazo para tomarle de la nuca. Luego se puso de puntillas y lo besó, ofreciéndose a él, al poder que los unía.

Charlie la rodeó con sus brazos y la estrechó contra su cuerpo. Respondió a los labios de la joven y sin ningún esfuerzo asumió el control del beso, haciéndolos girar en medio de las llamas.

Como si estuvieran bailando un vals sensual.

El retumbar de sus corazones, el ritmo creciente y alentador de la pasión en cada latido; el beso, cada vez más ardiente y desenfrenado, alimentaba esa sensación y hacía que los sentidos de ambos giraran sin parar, dejándolos mareados.

Los dos se turnaron para deshacerse de la ropa. Ella le despojó del pañuelo del cuello mientras él abría los diminutos botones de perla de la espalda del vestido. Había docenas de ellos. La joven lo interrumpió para forcejear con la chaqueta ceñida de Charlie y aprovechó para quitarle también el chaleco.

Charlie volvió a rodearla con sus brazos y a estrecharla contra su cuerpo, sin dejar de besarla con insistencia y exigencia, excitándola cada vez más.

La familiar sensación de fuego volvió a fluir entre ellos, atravesándolos a toda velocidad mientras ella luchaba para abrirle, con las manos atrapadas entre sus cuerpos, los botones de la camisa. Al mismo tiempo él le desabrochó el último botón de perla y con un gruñido de frustración la soltó para deshacerse del pesado vestido de seda.

Sarah sacó los brazos de las ceñidas mangas al tiempo que Charlie le deslizaba el corpiño hasta la cintura, luego las faldas cayeron al suelo con un suave frufrú. Él le tomó la mano para sostenerla mientras ella obedientemente, casi ansiosamente, se levantaba las enaguas y daba un paso adelante para liberarse por completo de las faldas.

Un paso que la alejó de la ventana pero que la acercó más a la cama.

Consciente de eso, del intenso ardor que brillaba en los ojos azules de Charlie, Sarah permitió que la abrazara de nuevo, pero levantó las manos y le deslizó la camisa abierta por los hombros y los brazos.

Todavía tenía los puños abrochados.

Charlie masculló un juramento y la rodeó con los brazos para forcejear con los botones detrás de la espalda de Sarah mientras la estrechaba contra su cuerpo e inclinaba la cabeza para besarla; un beso, de eso no cabía la menor duda, que pretendía dejarla sin sentido, pero Sarah no pensaba consentirlo. Colocó las palmas de sus manos sobre el pecho masculino y lo empujó ligeramente, apartándolo lo suficiente para hacer lo que deseaba.

Después de todo, él era parte de sus dominios.

Uno que quería poseer en ese momento.

Por completo.

Más completamente de lo que había podido hacer en el restringido espacio del cenador. Ahora, bajo la tenue luz del día invernal, Sarah podría apreciar el ancho y musculoso pecho de Charlie, cada banda de músculo esculpido y la fuerza que contenía. Extendió los dedos y lo exploró, apretando las palmas de las manos sobre la cálida piel, suave como el acero candente. Una fina capa de vello castaño y rizado le cubría el torso, y Sarah enredó los dedos en ella. Bajo aquel vello, sus dedos indagadores descubrieron los discos planos de las tetillas y se los acarició con atrevimiento.

Charlie se quedó inmóvil, conteniendo el aliento, tensando los músculos. Encantada y fascinada, Sarah siguió acariciándolo. Instintivamente sabía que a él le gustaba lo que estaba viendo, que también se sentía fascinado por lo que ella estaba haciendo.

Pero ¿hasta dónde llegaría esa fascinación? ¿Hasta dónde le tentaría? Levantando la vista del pecho de Charlie, Sarah lo miró a los ojos mientras deslizaba las manos por el plano abdomen, recreándose en los músculos que se tensaban bajo su tacto. Luego las bajó a la bragueta para desabrocharle los botones del pantalón.

Los ángulos y planos del rostro de Charlie se hicieron más afilados y duros, más definidos. Apretó los dientes cuando Sarah le abrió los botones, pero la dejó hacer sin dejar de mirarla a los ojos.

Permitió que le desvistiera hasta quedar desnudo ante ella, hasta que no hubo ninguna prenda sobre su cuerpo que ocultara su belleza masculina.

Con los pulmones constreñidos y la boca seca, Sarah lo contempló totalmente asombrada. Era todavía más hermoso, más elegante y masculino sin ropa que con ella. La joven deseó dar un paso atrás, varios en realidad, para tener una mejor perspectiva, pero instintivamente sabía que él no se lo permitiría. Permanecer quieto y sostener la mirada fascinada de su esposa lo estaba llevando casi al límite del control.

Un límite que ella tenía intención de hacerle traspasar, aunque todavía no.

Inspirando profundamente, Sarah alargó el brazo y le puso la mano en la cintura. Luego la movió lentamente, rozándole el estómago con la yema de los dedos, deslizándoselos por las caderas mientras giraba alrededor de él.

Cuando pasó junto al hombro de su marido, vio que éste cerraba los ojos, que apretaba los dientes. Que cerraba los puños. Pero, al sentir la cálida mano de Sarah contra su piel, permitió que ella se acercara y lo rodeara lentamente. La joven lo hizo, maravillándose de las líneas largas y definidas de su cuerpo, de los suaves planos y los duros ángulos, de los poderosos y flexibles músculos de sus hombros y espalda, de las fuertes piernas.

Podría haber sido el modelo de un escultor. Cada línea de su cuerpo parecía haber sido modelada por los dioses.

Sarah se detuvo detrás de él, le puso los dedos en el hueco de la espalda y sintió la tensión que lo atravesaba en reacción a su caricia, a su mirada.

La joven continuó avanzando sin dejar de mirarle, recreándose en su imagen mientras lo rodeaba. Charlie abrió los ojos cuando ella completó el círculo. En el mismo momento en que Sarah se detuvo delante de él, antes incluso de que tuviera la posibilidad de alzar la mirada, él alargó el brazo y la agarró de la cintura, haciéndola girar para poder desatarle con rapidez las cintas que le aseguraban las enaguas.

Sarah sintió la violencia en los rápidos e impacientes tirones. Después de todos los pasos que habían dado, ahora estaban enfrente del tocador. Sarah vio el reflejo de Charlie en el espejo; estaba detrás de ella con la cabeza inclinada y la atención puesta en desatar los nudos.

En desnudarla.

Sarah no pudo contener una risita seductora. Charlie levantó la cabeza y sus ojos se encontraron en el espejo; el fuego que ardía en la mirada masculina abrumó a la joven.

Lo que vio en sus ojos le robó el aliento.

La privó de cualquier pensamiento, mejor dicho, centró cada uno de ellos, y todos sus sentidos, en él, en ellos dos.

Sarah estaba completamente cautivada cuando él bajó la mirada y con un último tirón le soltó las cintas. Bruscamente, Charlie le deslizó las enaguas por las piernas hasta que cayeron en un charco a sus pies.

Ahora sólo llevaba puestos la camisola, las medias, los ligueros y los escarpines de boda. Para esa ocasión, la camisola era de la seda más fina, casi transparente. Charlie le puso la mano en la cintura y la tela no supuso una barrera más sólida que una tela de araña entre su piel y la de él.

La piel de la joven se calentó bajo la mano dura. Charlie levantó la vista y capturó la mirada de Sarah en el espejo.

—Me toca.

La voz de su marido era baja y ronca, cargada de una emoción masculina que ella desconocía. Deslizó la mirada por su cuerpo envuelto en seda. Sarah abrió mucho los ojos y esperó, conteniendo el aliento, a ver qué haría él a continuación.

Charlie se inclinó y cogió el taburete del tocador para colocarlo delante de Sarah.

Se irguió de nuevo, muy cerca de ella; el calor que emitía su cuerpo se extendió por su espalda mientras le ponía una mano en la cintura para sujetarla. Buscó la mirada de la joven en el espejo.

—Pon un pie en el taburete y quítate la media.

Las terminaciones nerviosas de Sarah se tensaron y anudaron. Tomó aire e hizo lo que le decía. Sacó el pie del escarpín de raso y lo apoyó en el taburete. Cuando los dedos del pie tocaron el terciopelo, la camisola se abrió, revelando el liguero antiguo que sujetaba la media.

Sarah tocó el liguero bordado al tiempo que él le ponía la mano en la parte de atrás del muslo, con lo que la pierna de la joven quedaba completamente expuesta. Él la acarició lentamente, haciéndole contener la respiración. Mareada, agarró el liguero mientras con dedos firmes él la ayudaba a bajárselo. Charlie siguió el recorrido de la media hasta la rodilla, acariciándole el sensible hueco de las corvas; luego, lenta y provocativamente, subió la mano de nuevo hasta el muslo al tiempo que ella se quitaba la media y el liguero antes de poner de nuevo el pie en el suelo.

Sarah cogió fuerzas para repetir todo el proceso con la otra pierna. Sabiendo como sabía lo que vendría después, trató de ganar tiempo.

—Los ligueros eran de tu madre, ¿lo sabías? —dijo jadeante, esperando distraerlo y ganar otro minuto para calmar sus nervios—. Eran algo prestado.

—¿De veras? —repuso él con un gruñido. Le apretó la cintura con los dedos—. La otra pierna.

Sarah tomó aliento e hizo lo que le decía, aunque esta vez fue incapaz de contener un estremecimiento cuando él la acarició, pues una vez que se deshizo de la media Charlie subió la mano por el muslo hasta acariciarle las nalgas.

A la joven se le debilitaron las rodillas y casi se tambaleó.

Charlie apartó lentamente la mano y se acercó un paso más.

Le rozó los hombros con el pecho y ella pudo sentir la dura erección contra la espalda antes de rodearle la cintura con las manos. Sarah volvió a mirar el espejo, preguntándose qué estaría planeando su marido pero, aunque él también miraba su reflejo, no la miraba a los ojos.

Él subió lentamente las manos por los costados. Con los pulgares le rozó —oh, tan suavemente, tan tentadoramente— la parte inferior de los pechos ya tensos. Un estremecimiento sensual atravesó a Sarah. Desde debajo de sus párpados repentinamente pesados, Sarah vio que Charlie curvaba ligeramente los labios.

Desplazó las manos más arriba y le ahuecó los pechos, cerrando los dedos sobre ellos de una manera casi posesiva. Luego inclinó la cabeza y le rozó la oreja con los labios.

—Ahora nos desharemos de esto —murmuró.

Tiró de la cinta que anudaba la camisola, desatando el lazo que anidaba entre sus pechos. Tomó la tela entre los dedos y la deslizó lentamente hasta la cintura, dejándole los pechos al descubierto. Luego hizo un movimiento de muñeca y la fina seda flotó alrededor de sus piernas hasta caer al suelo.

Dejándola tan desnuda como estaba él.

Sarah no sabía qué estaría viendo Charlie, o qué habría esperado ver. Tuvo que luchar para continuar respirando, calmar sus vertiginosos pensamientos y encontrar el valor suficiente para levantar la mirada al espejo y buscar la mirada de él en el reflejo, para ver tatuada en sus rasgos... la misma fascinación que sentía ella ante el cuerpo desnudo de su marido.

El placer que sintió fue como una droga que arrasó sus sentidos mientras le observaba deslizar los ojos por su cuerpo, mientras le veía alzar de nuevo aquella cálida y devoradora mirada hacia su rostro.

Sus ojos se encontraron en el espejo, y Sarah dejó que leyera en ellos la alegría que sentía al saber que la encontraba tan deseable como ella a él. Luego la mirada de Charlie bajó a sus labios.

Sarah se tensó para darse la vuelta, pero él le aferró la cintura con las manos y la inmovilizó.

—No. Espera. —Con los ojos clavados en el cuerpo de ella, Charlie la soltó y dio un paso atrás. Sarah se sintió acalorada cuando él deslizó la mirada por su espalda como si fuera una caricia, un toque que también notó en las nalgas y en la parte posterior de las piernas. Entonces Charlie alargó el brazo y le cogió la mano, haciéndola girar muy lentamente.

El calor que embargaba a Sarah se convirtió en un fuego potente cuando se detuvo frente a él. Charlie le miraba los pies.

Su marido fue subiendo la vista muy lentamente. Fascinado pero resuelto, Charlie recorrió cada centímetro de su piel.

Sarah luchó para contener los estremecimientos que la atravesaban cuando los ojos de Charlie alcanzaron finalmente los suyos. Impulsivamente dio un paso hacia delante, pero él la detuvo con la mano todavía en su espalda.

—No. Todavía no —dijo Charlie, exhalando tan bruscamente como ella. Su voz era un murmullo áspero y ronco, en la que claramente se reflejaba que intentaba mantener el control—. No tienes ni idea de cuánto tiempo he esperado para poder verte así.

El tono de su voz, su cadencia, se filtró en la mente de la joven con un mensaje mucho más profundo, más primitivo y evocador que sus palabras. Sarah se retorció, pero él la inmovilizó con más fuerza.

Después alzó la otra mano y, con la más leve de las caricias, le rozó el pecho con el dorso de los dedos, luego lo rodeó y le acarició la parte inferior.

Sarah se estremeció y cerró los ojos.

—Esperando esto. —Las palabras provocaron el mismo efecto en Sarah que su tono ronco—. Esperando para tomarte. Ansiando tomarte.

Los dedos de Charlie le recorrieron la piel, dibujando intrincados patrones sobre ella.

Sarah sintió que ardía con cada roce, con cada provocativa caricia.

Charlie llevó las manos al pelo de la joven, buscando y retirando las horquillas que sujetaban la pesada melena de color castaño dorado. De una manera lenta él le deshizo las trenzas y las extendió sobre sus hombros.

Se acercó a ella.

Sarah sintió su aliento en la mejilla y percibió el embeleso de su esposo cuando dijo:

—Eres una diosa y una ofrenda, las dos cosas a la vez. Eres la mujer que adoro, la mujer que debo tener. La mujer que tomaré y que a su vez me tomará a mí.

Charlie no sabía de dónde habían salido esas palabras, sólo sabía que eran ciertas; podía sentir cómo resonaban profundamente en su interior. Un lugar adonde sólo ella, la dulce e inocente Sarah, había llegado.

Esas palabras contenían la verdad, la verdad de los dos y de lo que había crecido entre ellos; la verdad que los rodeaba ahora y que los envolvería siempre. Adorarla era una pasión que él demostraba abiertamente con sus manos, sus labios, su boca y su cuerpo.

La sujetó allí, desnuda ante él, mientras le acariciaba cada curva, cada línea del cuerpo delgado. Mientras la sumergía en las más íntimas delicias, disfrutando del placer de tocar sin ser tocado. En sus anteriores encuentros sexuales, Charlie había aprendido qué era lo que más enardecía los deseos de Sarah, lo sensible que era la parte inferior de sus pechos o cuánto le excitaba que la acariciara las nalgas. De una manera lenta y firme aplicó sus conocimientos, incitándola a una pasión que rivalizaba con la suya.

Charlie se tomó su tiempo. Implacable en su necesidad de adorarla, pasó varios minutos saciando su curiosa voracidad; sólo la tomó en sus brazos y la estrechó contra su cuerpo cuando Sarah fue incapaz de seguir en pie.

Se unieron, piel con piel, carne ardiente con carne ardiente. Sarah se quedó sin aliento y él contuvo un largo estremecimiento. Luego ella se movió contra él, acariciando con sus sedosas piernas las más duras y velludas de él, acunando la dolorida erección en su vientre. Charlie hundió una mano en el cabello brillante de la joven y agarrándolo la hizo ladear la cabeza mientras inclinaba la suya para besarla de manera dura, implacable y exigente.

Charlie estaba resuelto a tener todo el control esta vez, a no debilitarse ni ceder ante ella en ningún momento. En vista de lo ocurrido anteriormente entre ellos, reducirla a un estado de puro deseo parecía una idea sabia.

Había niveles de fuego, grados de llamas sensuales. Bajo las experimentadas caricias de Charlie, cada vez más duras y urgentes, más encaminadas a un objetivo inquebrantable, Sarah se calentó, pasando lenta pero segura de un nivel al siguiente, de un ardiente grado de anhelo a unas llamas cada vez más profundas.

Charlie la acompañó, pero él estaba más acostumbrado al calor de la pasión, a su latido, a resistir el impulso que crecía en su interior.

Hasta que el incendio sensual los capturó a los dos, tanto a él como a ella. Hasta que los envolvió en un abrazo tan ardiente que incineró cualquier pensamiento racional y sólo los dejó concientes del intenso deseo de unirse.

El deseo ardió en llamas cada vez más candentes. La pasión rugió a través de esas llamas.

Charlie se inclinó, la cogió en sus brazos y la llevó a la cama. La dejó sobre la colcha de raso que tenía el mismo color de los ojos de Sarah, extendiendo su pelo, un velo brillante, sobre las almohadas, mientras ella se contorsionaba y trataba de abrazarle, ardiente y lasciva, casi muerta de deseo. Charlie se detuvo un segundo saboreando la imagen de la joven desnuda, excitada, y toda suya, sintiendo, mientras se movía para unirse a ella, una chispa de algo parecido al triunfo oscurecido por la tormenta de deseo que le atravesaba todo el cuerpo.

Ese momento de lucidez fue suficiente para que Charlie volviera a tomar las riendas, y mientras se acostaba al lado de ella en la cama considerara cuánto más allá podría presionarla, cuánto más alto podría llevar la pasión que la envolvía antes de permitir que traspasara el límite.

Cuanto más alto, cuánto más placer, para ella y para él.

Charlie le cogió la mano que Sarah alargaba hacia él y se inclinó sobre ella haciendo que su torso le rozara los tensos picos de los pechos mientras la besaba profunda y desenfrenadamente, haciéndola saber de qué manera tan salvaje llenaba ella sus sentidos con aquel provocativo sabor.

El sabor de la pasión y de la dulce inocencia.

La combinación era una mezcla adictiva, pero ahora su mente se ceñía a un plan, la ejecución no requería más pensamientos.

Sólo acción.

Sujetándola sobre los cojines de la cama, la besó y la acarició provocativamente hasta que ella se arqueó, rogándole con su cuerpo que la complaciera. Interrumpió el beso para deslizar los labios por la línea tensa de la garganta de Sarah y la curva cremosa de sus pechos, dándole la primera lección que le había pedido.

Charlie se recreó en los pechos de su esposa, sin dejar ni un centímetro sin lamer, chupar y succionar mientras ella se contorsionaba y jadeaba bajo él, mientras le tomaba la cabeza entre las manos al tiempo que él extraía hasta el último aliento y gemido que ella podía darle.

Se deslizó luego por la cintura de Sarah, deteniéndose un momento para homenajear el hueco sensible del ombligo antes de seguir su camino hacia abajo.

Atrapando una de las largas piernas de Sarah bajo las suyas, la alzó e inmovilizó sobre su hombro, depositando un beso ardiente en los rizos que protegían el sexo femenino.

Charlie la oyó jadear y sintió cómo se estremecía, tensa y envuelta en el placer. Alzando la mirada hacia ella, vio cómo el intenso azul ciano de sus ojos ardía bajo los párpados, cómo los labios, hinchados y húmedos por sus besos, se abrían con incrédula sorpresa. Lentamente, él se inclinó más abajo y puso los labios sobre la carne resbaladiza e hinchada entre sus muslos.

Sarah se retorció y gimió. Charlie la lamió y ella gritó. La joven alargó la mano hacia él, pero sólo pudo tocarle la cabeza. Enredó los dedos en sus cabellos y tiró con fuerza, pero él la lamió otra vez de una manera lenta e indagadora y ella dejó de moverse.

Esperó jadeando, con los ojos cerrados.

Jactándose interiormente, Charlie decidió adorarla de esa manera también, saboreándola, llenando sus sentidos con ella, y los de ella con él.

Sarah le dejó hacer, permitió que la saboreara tal y como deseaba, dejó que la probara con la lengua y la volviera loca.

Él tanteó y ella se rindió. Él tomó y ella entregó. A cambio, Charlie le dio placer con una inquebrantable devoción que la hizo sollozar y gemir su nombre.

Charlie se incorporó y la hizo rodar sobre la espalda. Trazó un sendero de besos ardientes por el vientre y los pechos mientras se deslizaba sobre ella, separándole los muslos y acomodándose entre ellos. Apoyándose en los brazos mientras la besaba, saboreó el deseo desesperado en los labios de Sarah. Entonces, con un único y fuerte envite, se unió a ella.

Sarah se ciñó en torno a él como un guante y él se quedó sin aliento. Como la diosa que había nombrado antes, ella le dio la bienvenida a su templo y lo acogió en él.

Charlie se movió y ella respondió con total fluidez mientras se abandonaban a un baile familiar. Charlie perdió su capacidad de raciocinio cuando se vio envuelto en un torbellino de sensaciones que lo hizo volar, girar y caer.

Y ya no hubo nada parecido al control, ninguna clase de contención una vez que los dos soltaron las riendas. Sólo existían él y ella, y el violento placer que los atravesaba buscando una liberación que se habían negado durante demasiado tiempo.

A través de la tempestad de sus pasiones, a través de la salvaje y turbulenta cabalgada, Sarah sólo fue consciente de las sensaciones que le asaltaban y abrumaban la mente grabándose a fuego en su conciencia. A pesar del calor y del placer suplicante que provocaba el cuerpo que se movía sobre el de ella, a pesar de los poderosos envites y de la imposible y clamorosa urgencia que la hacía inclinar las caderas para tomarle aún más profundamente, que la impulsaba a arquear la espalda instándole desesperadamente a que la montara con más fuerza, el único elemento que brillaba a través del rugiente velo de la pasión era el deseo que Charlie sentía por ella. Igual de profundo, poderoso y exigente que su deseo por él.

No... más.

Por él, en él, ese deseo era tan intenso, tan profundamente arraigado, que Sarah no dudaba de que Charlie daría hasta el último aliento por saciarlo, por consumarlo, que daría la vida por ella allí en su cama. Ese deseo que lo controlaba, que lo guiaba, también arrastró a Sarah dentro de aquel torbellino que lo envolvía hasta que estuvo tan desesperada como él por encontrar la manera de aplacarlo, de saciarlo, de rendir culto en su templo y sacrificarse a sí misma en el altar.

Y por fin, en el momento final, cuando ella rasgó con las uñas el velo sensual, vio claramente el poder del deseo, vio, sintió lo que sus propios sentidos habían sospechado que era.

Incuestionablemente, sin lugar a dudas.

En ese momento él empujó una última vez y con un grito ella se desintegró; con un sollozo perdió el contacto con la realidad y cayó. Ingrávida durante unos segundos, se dejó caer pesadamente en el suave mar del placer satisfecho.

El éxtasis la envolvió, la inundó, la elevó, dejándole las piernas laxas, eliminando hasta la última pizca de tensión. Luego el resplandor se hizo más intenso y llameó al tiempo que con un gemido gutural él se tensaba entre sus brazos.

Sarah lo miró con los ojos entrecerrados, captando el momento en que los rasgos de Charlie quedaron desprovistos de toda sofisticación, de todos los velos y máscaras. En el instante en el que él se perdió en ella, cuando se estremeció y finalizó de una manera tormentosa, sólo había una emoción grabada en su rostro.

Una que Sarah estaba segura de reconocer en su corazón.

Charlie cayó sobre su cuerpo, tan débil como ella. La joven cerró los ojos mientras curvaba los labios. Recordó las palabras de su marido. Y supo que allí, en esa habitación, en sus dominios, él era suyo.

Pero si bien regía en aquella dimensión física, también quería regir en otra dimensión, en otro mundo dominado por el amor.

El de él y el de ella. Sarah lo había sentido en ella; lo había sentido y visto en él.

Sin lugar a dudas.

Charlie se incorporó y cayó pesadamente a su lado. Luego la atrajo hacia sus brazos y ella acudió gustosa; la complacía y la hacía más feliz de lo que jamás había soñado.

Allí, con Charlie, estaban su vida, su futuro, el camino correcto para ella. Con él encontraba la satisfacción que buscaba. Con él todo estaba bien.

Había tomado la decisión correcta.

Sus pensamientos iban a la deriva, su mente estaba abrumada por el placer.

—Te amo —susurró segura entre los brazos de Charlie con la mejilla apoyada sobre su pecho.

Si bien ya comenzaba a dormirse, oyó la leve sorpresa en su propio tono de voz y sonrió.

—Y sé que tú me amas también.

Se durmió entre sus brazos, y se sumergió en unos sueños colmados de dicha.

Tumbado sobre su espalda, con los suspiros casi etéreos de Sarah en su cabeza, Charlie yacía bajo el suave peso de su mujer, rodeándola con los brazos, con su cuerpo demasiado saciado para tensarse.

Clavó la vista en el dosel de seda del mismo color que los ojos de su esposa.

Y se preguntó qué era lo que había resultado mal en su maravilloso plan.

Charlie se despertó cuando el sol comenzaba a despuntar en el cielo. Mientras una rosada claridad salpicaba el horizonte, hundió los dedos en la hinchada y lujuriosa suavidad de Sarah; dormía a su lado y la acarició suavemente hasta que, con la misma lentitud del sol naciente, ella suspiró, y sonrió cuando él se deslizó en su cuerpo.

La penetró lentamente, sin perder ni una pizca de control, estudiándola con rigidez, desesperado por convencerse de que su adicción y su rugiente deseo por ella se habían acallado. De que el poderoso impulso que lo guiaba, que alimentaba su incontrolable necesidad y crecía inexorablemente en su interior hasta apoderarse de él, hasta hacerle perder el control y arrastrarlo fuera de este mundo, había menguado.

Pero no lo había hecho. En lo más mínimo.

De hecho, parecía que sólo había aumentado.

Abrazó a Sarah hasta que volvió a quedarse dormida, luego Charlie se tumbó de espaldas y clavó una mirada ciega en el techo, enfrentándose a la dura realidad mientras un frío amanecer se alzaba sobre sus tierras.

Alathea había tenido razón. Antes que él, el amor había capturado invariablemente a todos los hombres de la familia Morwellan. Había atrapado a su padre hasta que se había convertido en una obsesión para él; había sido el amor lo que había impulsado a su progenitor a correr riesgos que casi habían destruido a su familia, el condado y todo lo que le importaba.

Con ese ejemplo grabado en su mente, Charlie había elegido un camino diferente. Había concertado un matrimonio de conveniencia con la intención de excluir el amor y tener un control absoluto de su vida, a salvo de esa peligrosa emoción.

Pero el destino había jugado sus cartas, y Charlie había apostado con arrogancia sin pensar que éste le haría trampa.

Se había casado con la dulce e inocente Sarah y ahora se veía enfrentado a todo lo que había combatido, algo que jamás había planeado ni esperado.

Estaba enamorado de su esposa.

Y no, ya no podía fingir lo contrario. No cuando ese poder aún se aferraba a su pecho, aún tenía las garras hundidas en su corazón. No tenía sentido negar más la existencia de esa emoción, por lo menos ante sí mismo.

Debería haberlo previsto... pero no lo había hecho. Quizá debería haber adivinado que era eso lo que había hecho a Sarah diferente, distinta a todas las demás mujeres a las que había conocido, pero Charlie no había tenido experiencia para juzgar eso. Ni siquiera se le había pasado por la cabeza la idea de que ella estaba allí sólo porque él la amaba.

La amaba, de eso no había dudas. Había caído víctima de esa ingobernable emoción y ahora estaba unido a su mujer para siempre por esa fuerza irresistible, por ese poder que podía convertirse con facilidad en una obsesión.

Ese poder que había conducido a su padre al borde de la ruina.

En lugar de convertirse en el baluarte que él había pretendido, en la salvación que buscaba, su matrimonio se había convertido en su peor pesadilla.

¿Cómo demonios iba a manejar todo aquello? ¿Qué podía hacer?

12

A Sarah la despertó el sonido de una puerta cerrándose seguido por el de unos pasos vacilantes. Parpadeó y miró a su alrededor, entonces recordó dónde estaba. Se incorporó apoyándose en un codo. A su lado las sábanas estaban arrugadas, pero la cama estaba vacía.

Los cálidos y brillantes rayos del sol entraban a raudales por las ventanas, pero no vio a Charlie por ninguna parte.

Sólo a Gwen, que se había trasladado con ella al Park y había colocado una jarra con agua caliente en el tocador. Su doncella se dirigía hacia la puerta cuando miró hacia la cama. Al ver que Sarah estaba despierta le brindó una amplia sonrisa.

—He pensado que sería mejor que la despertara, señorita... digo milady. Le he traído agua caliente para su aseo. —Abrió una puerta y señaló el interior con la cabeza—. Su vestidor está aquí, ¿lo ha visto?

—Oh, no. —Sarah se retiró el pelo de la cara. No había visto nada más que la cama desde que Charlie la había depositado en ella. Estaba a punto de retirar las sábanas cuando se dio cuenta de que estaba desnuda. Se sonrojó.

—Verteré el agua en la palangana y le traeré la bata —dijo la doncella sonrojándose también.

Sarah miró a un lado de la cama y vio su precioso vestido de novia caído en el suelo. Recordó la mirada que le había dirigido Charlie cuando se lo había quitado, y sonrió ampliamente. En ese momento Gwen se acercó con la bata y Sarah se la puso. Dejó a su doncella recogiendo la ropa y entró en el vestidor, que, al igual que el dormitorio, estaba decorado en tonos azules y dorados.

Se aseó con rapidez.

—Gwen, ¿qué hora es? ¿Ha pasado ya la hora del desayuno? —Para su sorpresa estaba muerta de hambre.

—Acaban de dar las once —dijo Gwen desde el dormitorio—. Pero el desayuno se ha retrasado, y acaban de reunirse todos en el comedor.

—Oh, bien. —Sarah le hizo una mueca a su reflejo en el espejo. Su primer día como dueña de la casa y era la última en bajar a desayunar. De hecho, tendría que enfrentarse a varias miradas de curiosidad y comportarse como si aquel fuera sólo otro día más, pero con Charlie en la misma habitación.

Ante esa perspectiva lo menos que podía sentir era un nudo en el estómago, pero, para su sorpresa, se dio cuenta de que todavía estaba demasiado relajada para ello, demasiado lánguida después de las apasionadas atenciones de Charlie, y la tensión no supondría ningún problema por ahora.

Considerando con cuidado las inesperadas ramificaciones de sus deberes de esposa, abandonó las habitaciones del conde y recorrió el corredor hacia la galería y las escaleras. Al bajarlas, llegó al vestíbulo delantero y otras áreas de la casa que le eran familiares.

El comedor del desayuno era soleado y estaba al lado del invernadero. En el centro de la estancia había una mesa rectangular con sillas dispuestas todo a lo largo. Vio un pesado aparador contra una de las paredes sobre el cual había diversas fuentes y platos calientes. Tanto en la mesa como en el aparador había jarrones con flores blancas del día anterior que otorgaban a la estancia un toque encantador.

En cuanto Sarah apareció en el umbral, todos echaron la silla hacia atrás y se pusieron en pie para saludarla. Sarah vaciló y sonrió, aunque no estaba segura de qué hacer a continuación; Serena, a la que conocía de toda la vida y que ahora era su suegra, se apresuró hacia ella con una sonrisa en la cara.

—Aquí estás, querida. —Serena le dio un caluroso abrazo, rozándole las mejillas con las suyas; luego la condujo a la silla de la cabecera de la mesa—. Éste es ahora tu lugar. Por supuesto, ya nos conoces a todos. —Con un gesto señaló a sus hijas y a sus respectivos esposos. Le indicó a Sarah que tomara asiento antes de sentarse en la única silla vacía que había a su lado—. Estamos verdaderamente encantados de verte ocupar ese asiento.

—Gracias. —Sarah se acomodó en la silla elaboradamente tallada.

Paseó la mirada alrededor de la mesa, saludando con la cabeza a las sonrientes Mary y Alice, las hermanas de Charlie, y a sus respectivos maridos, Alec y George, y a Augusta y a Jeremy. A todos parecía complacerles su presencia y lo acontecido el día anterior.

Alice se inclinó hacia delante y, con una amplia sonrisa, continuó con una anécdota sobre uno de los invitados a la boda que había estado contando antes de la llegada de Sarah. Todos prestaban atención a Alice, todos salvo Charlie. Él estaba sentado enfrente de Sarah en el otro extremo de la mesa, con una taza de café en la mano y un periódico en la otra, pero su mirada no estaba clavada en las noticias, sino en ella.

Sarah le sostuvo la mirada y sonrió, sólo para él. Aliviada y feliz, la joven usó el gesto para expresarle lo bien que se sentía.

Charlie, no obstante, mantuvo la expresión impasible. A esa distancia, con las ventanas detrás de él y el sol brillando fuera, Sarah no podía leerle los ojos. Pero entonces él la saludó con la cabeza, levantó la taza para tomar un sorbo de café y volvió a concentrarse en el periódico.

Sarah frunció el ceño interiormente. Se quedó mirándole, perpleja al ver que no sonreía. Puede que fuera debido a la presencia de la familia, pero Charlie no parecía relajado. Ni por asomo parecía estar tan relajado como ella.

—¿Té, milady?

Pasó un segundo antes de que Sarah se diera cuenta de que la pregunta iba dirigida a ella. Levantó la mirada hacia Crisp, que se había detenido a su lado.

—¡Oh, sí! Gracias, Crisp. Té y... —Miró al aparador.

Crisp siguió la dirección de su mirada y se puso detrás de ella para apartarle la silla.

—Milady, permítame que le sugiera los huevos rellenos; son excelentes. Una especialidad de la cocinera.

Sarah le brindó una sonrisa mientras se levantaba.

—Entonces debo probarlos.

Durante los quince minutos siguientes, Sarah bebió y comió, rellenó de nuevo su plato y comió algo más, rodeada por la calidez de aquella enorme familia feliz.

—Los demás invitados se fueron anoche o esta mañana temprano —le dijo Serena al margen de la conversación general—. De hecho, si no fuera porque viajaremos con Mary, Alice y su prole, ya nos habríamos ido nosotros también. Todos los recién casados necesitan pasar unas semanas a solas para adaptarse el uno al otro y a la vida juntos.

Sarah abrió mucho los ojos; no había pensado en eso.

—Oh, no es necesario que os marchéis. Ésta es tu casa, ni se me ocurriría ocupar tu lugar.

Los ojos color avellana de Serena rebosaban comprensión cuando le palmeó la mano.

—Pero tú eres ahora la condesa, querida, y créeme cuando te digo que estoy encantada de confiar el cuidado de esta casa a tus jóvenes manos. Nos quedaremos el tiempo suficiente para explicarte lo que necesitas saber, luego nos iremos a Lincoln con Mary y Alec, y desde allí, Augusta y yo pensamos visitar a varios familiares a los que no hemos visto desde hace años; nos reuniremos con Charlie y contigo en Londres, una vez que comience la temporada.

Serena la estudió, luego alargó a mano y le colocó un mechón de pelo detrás de la oreja. Sonrió levemente.

—Créeme, querida, todo saldrá bien.

Sarah no estaba segura de qué abarcaba «todo», pero por lo que dedujo de las palabras de Serena, debía de referirse a temas relacionados con la gerencia de la casa.

Al otro lado de la mesa, Charlie, que antes se había enfrascado en un debate sobre el precio del maíz con Alec y George, observaba cómo Sarah, sin alboroto ni fanfarrias, comenzaba a asumir la posición de condesa. Había imaginado que le resultaría fácil, dado que conocía a su familia, pero no sólo era la familiaridad lo que hacía que Crisp revoloteara a su alrededor, o que Serena y Augusta le explicaran todo lo que necesitaba saber de la casa.

Sarah, simplemente, encajaba. Era, como él había previsto, la mujer idónea para ocupar esa posición.

El hecho de haber sido tan perspicaz y haber acertado en su elección, sólo sirvió para que se incrementara su inquietud por lo que no había previsto y comprendido en su arrogancia.

Los sonidos que lo rodeaban, las voces de sus hermanas, las profundas carcajadas de sus cuñados y su hermano, la confortable cacofonía que disfrutaba normalmente a la hora del desayuno, no hicieron nada para aliviar su alma.

De hecho consiguieron todo lo contrario.

En ese momento, Alec comenzó a describir las travesuras de su hijo, que ya era lo suficientemente mayor para montar su primer poni, y la anécdota sirvió para aumentar las preocupaciones de Charlie.

Con una expresión neutra, se puso en pie.

—Si me disculpáis, tengo que ocuparme de algunos asuntos.

Alec y George levantaron la mirada y sonrieron, luego continuaron charlando. Charlie se alejó de la mesa; Jeremy lo miró brevemente y continuó bromeando con Alice.

Tras cruzar la estancia, todas las mujeres interrumpieron su conversación y lo miraron expectantes.

Él saludó a su madre con la cabeza y luego a Sarah.

—Te veré más tarde.

Sarah sonrió, evidentemente feliz, pero escrutó la mirada de su marido.

Con paso relajado, Charlie pasó junto a ella y continuó hacia la puerta, seguro de que ella no había podido leerle el pensamiento. Poseer un enorme control de sus expresiones faciales había resultado ser una inesperada bendición.

Nunca había imaginado tener que emplear tal escudo con su esposa.

La noche cayó. Envuelta en un provocativo conjunto de bata y camisón de seda con encajes, otra prenda de su ajuar, Sarah se paseaba ante el fuego de la chimenea que chisporroteaba en el dormitorio del conde, preguntándose dónde estaba su marido.

Las cortinas de terciopelo estaban descorridas. Fuera, caía la lluvia mientras el viento agitaba las ramas desnudas de los árboles cercanos. Las velas que había sobre la repisa de la chimenea y las mesillas que flanqueaban la cama contribuían con su resplandor a la acogedora calidez que envolvía la estancia.

Sarah había tenido un día ocupado. Desde que se había levantado de la mesa del desayuno había dedicado cada minuto de su tiempo a informarse de los innumerables detalles sobre cómo administrar Morwellan Park y las numerosas tareas que recaerían sobre ella ahora que era la condesa de Charlie.

Ninguno de esos detalles o tareas había sido una sorpresa, pero había tenido que concentrarse en ellos; Serena y Augusta se ausentarían durante semanas y no estarían presentes para poder consultarles las dudas que le surgieran, así que necesitaba enterarse de todo ahora para no encontrarse luego con no saber qué hacer.

La tarea la había distraído de la actitud distante que había mostrado Charlie. Un distanciamiento que él parecía querer establecer entre ellos para convertir su matrimonio en una relación formal y fría. El comportamiento de su esposo en la sala de desayuno había sido sólo el comienzo. Se había comportado de la misma manera a la hora del almuerzo, y su actitud distante había sido todavía más acusada durante la cena y el poco tiempo que había pasado luego en la salita antes de que Jeremy, Alec, George y él se hubieran ido a jugar al billar.

Era cierto que ella había estado todo ese tiempo con su madre y sus hermanas, casi siempre enfrascada en una absorbente conversación en la que le habían dado muchos consejos e informado de todo lo que ella necesitaba saber. Pero aun así...

Sarah hizo una mueca. Quizás aquella inesperada actitud reservada de Charlie sólo había sido una simple reacción al estar sometido al escrutinio de su familia, que observaba cada gesto que ellos hacían. A pesar de su natural encanto, Charlie era un hombre reservado, y los miembros de su familia eran, sin duda alguna, unos expertos observadores capaces de leer su expresión y sus reacciones con más facilidad.

Puede que sólo estuviera pensando en cómo admitir públicamente el estrecho vínculo que había entre ellos, o que estuviera, dado lo reciente de su unión, inseguro sobre ella.

Lo cierto es que Sarah aún no sabía cómo relacionarse con él cuando había más gente presente; quizás a él le pasara lo mismo. Quizá también anduviera a tientas.

Se detuvo ante la chimenea y cruzó los brazos bajo los pechos, mirando sin ver las llamas. En ese momento el reloj de la repisa de la chimenea dio la hora. Sarah lo miró y frunció el ceño. Las once. ¿Dónde estaría Charlie?

Justo entonces, como si fuera una respuesta a su pregunta, oyó pasos en la antecámara, una zancada familiar. Bajó los brazos y levantó la cabeza, girándose para observar cómo Charlie abría la puerta y entraba.

Él la vio y vaciló un momento, luego cerró la puerta y se acercó a ella.

Sarah le estudió la cara, buscó su mirada mientras él se acercaba y notó una vacilación, una incertidumbre similar a la que ella sentía en su corazón.

También vio con claridad meridiana la caída de la extraña barrera que había habido entre ambos a lo largo del día. Observó que el interés había reemplazado a la impasibilidad en sus ojos, notó el deseo que crecía y afilaba sus rasgos.

Cuando se detuvo ante ella, la luz del fuego iluminó su perfil, arrancando destellos a las ondas doradas de su pelo. A Sarah no le cupo la menor duda de que, al menos allí, en aquella habitación, no había cambiado nada entre ellos, que todo seguía como ella había pensado.

Charlie clavó la mirada en el rostro de Sarah durante un rato. Parecía buscar algo en ella. Luego bajó la vista por sus hombros, casi desnudos bajo la diáfana seda, y siguió bajando la mirada lentamente por sus pechos, por la estrecha cintura, por sus caderas y muslos, envueltos tentadoramente en encaje y seda color marfil; luego cerró los ojos.

Charlie tomó aire y levantó la cabeza.

—Eres tan deseable que me duele mirarte —murmuró con los ojos cerrados y la mandíbula tensa.

Las palabras le salieron entrecortadas, como si le hubiera costado un esfuerzo decirlas. Sarah sonrió.

—Entonces no abras los ojos —repuso ella acercándose a él. Tenía la voz ronca como cada vez que respondía a él, cuando el evidente deseo de Charlie despertaba el de ella—. No abras los ojos y deja que yo te guíe.

Lentamente Sarah apoyó las manos en el pecho de su marido, se puso de puntillas y le besó. Por un momento, él se lo permitió, luego comenzó a responder, inclinando la cabeza hacia ella y levantando los brazos para acercarla a su cuerpo. La estrechó contra sí mientras se alimentaba de su boca, mientras la saboreaba y dejaba que ella le

233

saboreara a él. Sarah suspiró para sus adentros y se relajó contra él; alargó una mano y le tomó la nuca, luego deslizó los dedos en su sedoso cabello y tiró de él, provocándolo. Durante largos minutos, Sarah saboreó el juego, el confiado toma y daca, segura de su poder; luego echó la cabeza hacia atrás e interrumpió el beso.

—No abras los ojos —susurró contra sus labios. Dio un paso atrás y vio que él fruncía la boca. Sonriendo, procedió a despojarlo de su ropa.

Aunque Charlie mantuvo los ojos cerrados obedientemente, con los altos pómulos ensombrecidos por las largas pestañas, no se quedó quieto. Mientras ella forcejeaba con la chaqueta, el chaleco y la camisa, recorrió con sus manos el cuerpo envuelto en seda de la joven, tocándolo aquí y allá, acariciándola tentadoramente, provocando que sus terminaciones nerviosas se tensaran y brincaran de anticipación. En respuesta, Sarah dio rienda suelta a su fascinación, moviendo las manos por la tensa piel del torso musculoso de su marido que había dejado al descubierto, recreándose en los fuertes músculos de sus hombros, en las líneas tensas y planas de su abdomen. Sus caricias se convirtieron en un juego sensual que incrementó las sensaciones y que les dejó a los dos sin respiración, pero conservando todavía el control.

Excitados y absortos.

Charlie trató de agarrar la mano de Sarah otra vez cuando los dedos de ella encontraron los botones de sus pantalones. Sarah se puso de puntillas y volvió a cubrirle los labios con los suyos. El beso fue más ardiente esta vez, el deseo más fuerte, la pasión más intensa. La joven sintió que el calor se extendía bajo su piel, sintió las llamas del deseo arder profundamente en su interior, pero por una vez tenía claro cuál era su objetivo.

Interrumpió el beso.

—No lo olvides... los ojos cerrados.

Charlie se movió, apretando los labios y tensando los dedos en la espalda de Sarah, pero no protestó. Tuvo que soltarla y dejar que ella se apartara de sus brazos. La joven lo besó suavemente en el pecho, se agachó y tironeó de sus pantalones hacia abajo; después se ocupó de las medias y los zapatos. Se deshizo de todo con rapidez y aprovechó la oportunidad que se le brindaba.

Sarah había oído sin querer algunos comentarios de Maria y

234

Angela, sus hermanas casadas. Había comprendido lo suficiente como para hacerse preguntas. Ahora, tenía a su propio marido y sentía mucha curiosidad con respecto a su cuerpo y lo que podía gustarle.

Sólo había una manera de averiguarlo. Apoyando las manos en los músculos tensos de los muslos de Charlie, se arrodilló ante él y deslizó las manos hacia arriba por la marcada musculatura de sus piernas, hacia donde su erección se erguía orgullosa, sobresaliendo rígida del nido de rizos como si suplicara su atención.

Incluso antes de que ella cerrara los dedos en torno a su miembro, Charlie adivinó sus intenciones e inspiró bruscamente. Pero justo entonces Sarah curvó los dedos sobre su carne rígida y él se estremeció. Le costaba respirar.

—¿Sarah?

La palabra sonó débil, una mezcla de conmoción, perplejidad y duda.

—No mires, recuérdalo. —Apoyando los antebrazos en los muslos duros como una piedra, Sarah se detuvo un segundo para estudiar lo que sostenía entre sus manos, luego inclinó la cabeza, abrió los labios y los deslizó suave y lentamente sobre la cálida y sedosa vara encerrada entre sus dedos.

Charlie gimió. Se le tensaron todos los músculos del cuerpo mientras ella recordaba las palabras de sus hermanas y utilizaba la imaginación para interpretarlas. Libremente.

Charlie siseó y apretó los dientes. Puso la mano en la cabeza de Sarah y enredó los dedos en sus cabellos. Por un momento, la joven se preguntó si la apartaría, pero entonces sintió cómo tensaba los dedos. Unos segundos después se dio cuenta de que él la estaba dirigiendo, enseñándole lo que le gustaba.

La inundó una felicidad vertiginosa, y entusiasmada se dedicó a aprender cuál era la mejor manera de conseguir que él suplicara. Una breve mirada hacia arriba le reveló que él mantenía la cabeza alzada y los rasgos tensos con una súplica apremiante. Ninguna otra imagen podría haberla complacido más.

Encantada, Sarah dedicó toda su atención a sus acciones, a aprender todo lo que pudiera de él.

Aquello último quedó demostrado cuando se alargaron los minutos y Charlie se aferró mentalmente con uñas y dientes a lo poco que le quedaba de control. ¿Cómo? ¿Dónde? No le importaba. No le interesaba saber cómo ella sabía eso, sino absorber con avidez y codicia cada pizca de placer que Sarah le brindaba de una manera tan inesperada.

La húmeda calidez de la boca de Sarah, su suave succión, cada vez más atrevida, los roces tentadores de su lengua, la leve caricia del pelo de la joven contra sus muslos mientras movía la cabeza provocativa y sensualmente, lo despojaron de cualquier pensamiento. Era su cautivo sensual, estaba total y completamente atrapado por ella.

Pero si bien Charlie mantenía los ojos cerrados y sentía una dolorosa opresión en los pulmones, estar a merced de Sarah no era lo que provocaba su reacción física o que se le hubiera tensado cada uno de sus músculos. El impacto mental de las acciones de su esposa era infinitamente más devastador. El hecho de que ella se hubiera puesto de rodillas porque quisiera, que lo hubiera tomado en su boca por voluntad propia y que deleitara sus sentidos tan patentemente, que interpretara los deseos más oscuros de él, haciéndolos realidad, le excitaba profundamente.

Eran ella y su poder, el poder que ahora esgrimía, el que la poseía, lo que más lo seducía. Por completo. Todo lo que Sarah hacía le excitaba tanto que se sentía indefenso para combatirlo, para levantar sus defensas contra ella. Contra todo lo que Sarah y la unión de los dos le hacían sentir.

Charlie ya había conocido la pasión y el deseo antes, pero con ella ambas cosas se intensificaban, se infundían de ese poder y eran, por consiguiente, más potentes e infinitamente más intensas. Más adictivas.

Y mezclado con todo ello, se arremolinaba en torno a él una posesividad cada vez mayor. Charlie jamás había sentido nada semejante, no con ninguna de las incontables mujeres con las que se había acostado, pero con ella, con su esposa, la posesividad no era un simple remolino, era un mar embravecido.

Hasta esa noche... Hasta que había entrado en el dormitorio, Charlie no había sabido cómo se comportaría, cómo se desarrollaría su encuentro, ni a qué nivel.

Una parte de él había esperado —había rezado— poder contener su reacción esa noche, dar un paso atrás, trazar una línea y mantenerse firme en ella, continuar el proceso que había empezado esa mañana de mantener su relación dentro de las directrices de un matrimonio de conveniencia.

Había logrado mantenerse alejado de ella durante todo el día, pero la visión de Sarah esperándole ante la chimenea, con las llamas titilando sobre ella, revelando la figura femenina bajo el traslúcido camisón, había sido suficiente para acabar con su determinación y destruir la coraza que había esperado conservar.

Pero esto...

Sentía cómo el pecho se le oprimía mientras ella lo apresaba con sus labios firmemente y le deslizaba la mano por el muslo, cómo le palpitaba la erección cada vez que se hundía en la mojada calidez de la boca de su esposa.

Charlie aspiró profundamente y abrió los ojos. Bajó la mirada y la vio de rodillas ante él, con aquella gloriosa melena, dorada bajo la luz del fuego, ondeando sobre sus hombros, meciéndose cuando movía la cabeza para darle placer. Vio sus propios dedos hundidos en esos cabellos mientras sentía que ella lo tomaba por completo en su boca, que le rodeaba la base del pene con los dedos y apretaba.

Por un instante, Charlie permitió que sus sentidos absorbieran todo aquello, dejó que su yo interior, que rara vez liberaba, se perdiera en la gloria de ella y su devoción. Luego tomó aliento e intentó recuperar el control.

Lo que no fue nada fácil. Sentía que le daba vueltas la cabeza cuando recurrió a todas sus fuerzas para apartar la mano del sedoso pelo dorado y seguir la línea de la mandíbula. Luego deslizó los dedos bajo aquel velo dorado para levantarle la barbilla.

—Basta —dijo débilmente. Ella accedió más por la presión de sus dedos que porque se lo hubiera ordenado.

Le soltó y se sentó sobre los talones. Apoyando las manos sobre los muslos de su marido, deslizó la mirada por su cuerpo hasta llegar a sus ojos.

La expresión de Sarah, el resplandor de sus ojos y su cara, hizo que Charlie contuviera la respiración. ¿Había visto alguna vez una *madonna* tan satisfecha? Alargó los brazos hacia ella, la agarró por la parte superior de los brazos y la hizo ponerse en pie.

—Has abierto los ojos —murmuró ella.

Charlie le sostuvo la mirada durante un instante, luego la estrechó contra su cuerpo.

—Me toca —dijo, inclinando la cabeza.

La besó. No como antes, no con velos o corazas entre ellos, la besó con la muda voracidad que ella provocaba en él, con aquella tambaleante mezcla de pasión, deseo y necesidad... La necesidad de poseerla.

Completa y absolutamente.

Quería poseer su cuerpo y su alma, como ella poseía los suyos.

Eso era lo que Sarah y el poder que tenía exigían.

Pues que así fuera.

Sarah aceptó de buena gana la pasión que se desbordaba en el beso, pero jadeó interiormente cuando él profundizó la caricia, domándola implacablemente, indagando con la lengua y luego retirándose, sólo para regresar y retomar la posesión que ella sabía que llegaría.

Las sensaciones se perdieron en un ardiente remolino y Sarah se estremeció cuando Charlie le deslizó las manos por los hombros, soltándola para agarrar los bordes de la bata de seda y encaje. Se la arrancó y dejó que cayera al suelo. Con dos rápidos tirones, deshizo los lazos de los hombros del camisón a juego. La prenda se deslizó susurrante por el cuerpo de Sarah hasta formar un charco a sus pies.

Charlie le deslizó las manos por la cintura y la agarró, apretándola con fuerza contra su desnuda longitud. Ardiente, duro, masculino, la promesa de su cuerpo encendió el de ella como una llama, haciéndola derretirse, fusionarse y arder de nuevo. Conduciendo el fuego de las venas de Sarah hasta su vientre, alimentando su deseo y provocando que el dolorido vacío que la joven sentía en su interior creciera todavía más.

Charlie la tenía atrapada en el beso, pero ella quería tocarle, extender la mano para acariciar aquella parte de él que deseaba sentir en su interior, llenándola, estirándola, colmando ese doloroso vacío y satisfaciendo el palpitante deseo que corría por sus venas. Pero cuando él la tomó entre sus brazos, Sarah se había aferrado a sus hombros, y cuando la estrechó con fuerza contra su cuerpo, deslizando las manos por su espalda y amoldándola a él, no pudo encontrar la fuerza o la voluntad necesarias para apartarlo y meter las manos entre ellos.

Luego, él la hizo arquearse hacia atrás y buscó con los dedos los rizos que cubrían su montículo para acariciarla. Lenta y provocativamente. Sus caricias fueron cada vez más intensas y profundas. Presionó un poco más en su sexo y encontró la carne entre sus muslos ya hinchada y mojada. Se la acarició con más exigencia, con más intimidad, con una posesividad que la excitó todavía más.

Charlie la privó de cualquier pensamiento amoldando sus labios a los de ella, metió una rodilla entre los muslos y deslizó primero uno y luego dos dedos dentro de la apretada funda de Sarah. La joven sintió que un ardiente fuego le recorría la piel cuando Charlie movió la mano entre sus muslos, atizando la conflagración interior.

El cuerpo de Sarah ya no le pertenecía a ella, sino a él, Charlie le había arrebatado el sentido, la había atrapado en ese momento. En el deseo que crecía continuamente, en la tensión que aumentaba con el fuego y la atenazaba.

En ese instante, él enterró sus dedos dentro de ella y Sarah se desintegró. Jadeó en medio del beso, pero él la presionó. En lugar de caer ingrávida en el familiar vacío, Sarah se encontró remontando una oleada de pasión incendiaria que la hizo subir cada vez más alto, luego Charlie retiró los dedos, la agarró por la cintura y la alzó contra sí.

Sarah interrumpió el beso. Con los ojos entrecerrados y los pechos hinchados, se agarró a los hombros de su marido y bajó la mirada a su cara, ladeando la cabeza.

La expresión de Charlie era una máscara de puro deseo.

—Rodéame con las piernas.

Ella apenas pudo obedecer aquella áspera orden. Tardó un momento en darse cuenta de que él había deslizado las manos bajo sus nalgas, sosteniendo su peso. Con esfuerzo, Sarah obligó a los músculos de sus piernas a obedecerle.

En cuanto lo rodeó con los muslos, él le bajó las caderas y Sarah notó su punzante erección contra la estrecha entrada de su cuerpo. Luego ella se hundió sobre su miembro.

Mientras él se impulsaba hacia arriba.

Sarah echó la cabeza hacia atrás y jadeó cuando la empaló, cuando la sensación de sentirlo duro en su interior engulló y envolvió sus sentidos.

Arrastrándola a un remolino de hirviente deseo, a una pasión abrasadora, a una necesidad tan fogosa que le derritió los huesos. Charlie la alzó y la bajó de nuevo, empujando hacia arriba a la vez, y cada terminación nerviosa que Sarah poseía se estremeció de placer.

Con una necesidad que él comprendía. Afianzando las piernas, Charlie la sujetó entre sus brazos delante de la chimenea, con las cálidas llamas bailando sobre la piel ruborizada de la joven mientras le agarraba las nalgas y la bajaba una vez más, sosteniendo su cuerpo contra el suyo y colmándola de nuevo una y otra vez.

Sarah le rodeó el cuello con los brazos y se aferró a él, con los sentidos estirados más allá de lo soportable, con el placer sensual rugiendo en su mente. Luego inclinó la cabeza mientras él alzaba la suya, y sus labios se encontraron.

Y el hambre rugió con furia.

No la de ella, ni la de él, sino la de ellos. Una fuerza más potente que cualquiera de los dos, capaz de someterlos a ambos. Una fuerza tan poderosa como para sumirlos en un estado sin sentido, en una necesidad vertiginosa... Una intimidad imparable donde nada más importaba, sólo la búsqueda desesperada del placer mutuo.

Hasta que alcanzaron el éxtasis. Hasta que los envolvió una ola ardiente, los hizo pedazos, los atrapó y los fundió.

Los destruyó.

Los disolvió.

Los refundió y los completó.

Cuando la tormenta pasó y regresaron al mundo, se encontraron con las piernas enredadas, sobre la alfombra ante el fuego.

Sarah tomó aire y le acarició la cara, iluminada por las brasas, con una mano mientras él la contemplaba y ella se maravilló nuevamente de lo que veía allí. La pasión, el deseo y la necesidad habían desaparecido, dejando en su lugar una emoción inconfundible, la única que guiaba aquellas otras emociones, que les daba una intensa vitalidad.

Abrumada, ella le sonrió. No había necesidad de palabras.

Charlie la miró a los ojos, inclinó la cabeza y la besó suavemente; la más sencilla de las bendiciones.

Luego se apartó, la alzó en brazos, se levantó y la llevó a la cama.

Abrigado, saciado por completo, Charlie permanecía tumbado al lado de Sarah, escuchando la respiración regular de su esposa y el viento que soplaba furioso tras las ventanas.

Los dos sonidos reflejaban a la perfección lo que ambos sentían; Sarah había aceptado lo que había crecido y florecido entre ellos sin ningún titubeo mientras que él no había sido capaz de hacerlo.

La ardiente pasión que le había reclamado, que todavía lo embargaba a pesar de sus inquietos pensamientos, jamás había sido tan intensa, tan profunda y satisfactoria. No podía fingir lo contrario, no podía negar la intensa sensación de triunfo que había sentido cuando, finalmente, Sarah se había derrumbado entre sus brazos, cuando el último vestigio de control de su esposa se había evaporado y le había entregado su cuerpo para ayudarle a alcanzar su propia liberación. Tampoco podía negar su satisfacción al compartir aquellos efímeros e indescriptibles momentos posteriores con ella.

Sarah era diferente y siempre lo sería. Y no importaba cuánto deseara que fuera de otra manera, no pensaba alejarse de todo lo que ella representaba. De todo lo que ella le daba.

Sarah era su pareja de una manera elemental, de una manera primitiva y posesiva que Charlie jamás había imaginado que pudiera aplicarse a él. Era suya. La había reclamado y ella se había entregado voluntariamente. Sería la madre de sus herederos.

De dónde habían salido esa agresividad, posesividad y arrogancia no lo sabía. Lo único que sabía era que aquello era una parte intrínseca de él, que era Sarah quien lo provocaba y que sólo ella podía satisfacerlo. Así de simple. Y eso, ese poder absurdo y potencialmente obsesivo lo había conducido hasta la situación a la que debía enfrentarse ahora.

Cuando estaba allí, a solas con ella en esa habitación, no había nada que él pudiera hacer —ni mucho menos imaginar— para evitar u ocultar esa verdad, lo que en realidad sentía por ella y cómo se sentía con ella. Cuando estaba allí, a solas con Sarah, la necesidad de poseerla era, simplemente, demasiado poderosa. Un doloroso e inesperado placer. Tomarla ya no era un simple deseo, si es que alguna vez había sido sólo eso; él se sentía impulsado no sólo a deleitarla sexualmente, sino a enseñarle, y aún más, a cuidarla y protegerla por encima de todo. Era un impulso irresistible. E incontrolable.

Era un deber.

Pero su deber, a fin de cuentas, no sólo la incluía a ella. No cabía duda de que se había casado porque se había sometido a un deber mayor. Un deber que se regía por su lealtad, su devoción y su honor. Por su cautela.

Charlie era el defensor y el protector de su título, de sus tierras, de su gente. Su deber era velar por todo, garantizar tanto la seguridad como el futuro del condado. Era una parte indivisible de él, su derecho de nacimiento y por tanto un deber inalienable, uno que no podía arriesgar ni siquiera por ella.

Ni por sí mismo, ni por su propio placer.

Dos deberes, ambos importantes. No eran precisamente contradictorios —para ningún hombre supondría una dificultad cumplir con ambos—, pero no dejaba de ser un motivo de preocupación, un serio y potencial problema. No obstante, Charlie iba a tener que conciliar ambos; ese poder que ardía entre Sarah y él, y su obligación de controlar todas sus decisiones y no permitir que el amor lo controlara a él. No podía dejar que el amor se convirtiera en una obsesión capaz de regir su razón.

Entrecerrando los ojos miró fijamente la habitación en penumbra y reflexionó sobre el día anterior y la noche que había seguido.

A fin de cuentas, nunca tomaba decisiones en la cama.

Ideó un nuevo plan y lo estudió desde todos los ángulos.

Podía ser difícil, pero no imposible.

Y además era lo que tenía que hacer.

Sarah comenzó su segundo día de casada con más decisión, con más confianza en sí misma, que el día anterior. Aunque Charlie permaneció claramente distante en el desayuno y más tarde en el almuerzo, después de las revelaciones de la noche, la joven no albergaba ninguna duda sobre la naturaleza de su matrimonio.

La familia de Charlie todavía seguía allí, y su distanciamiento se hizo más que evidente durante todo el día. Estaba claro que la presencia de sus familiares hacía vacilar a su marido. Que le costara tomarse las cosas con más tranquilidad, adaptarse al matrimonio y aprender a relacionarse con su esposa. Aunque tenía como ejemplo los matrimonios de sus hermanas, sobre todo el de Alathea y Gabriel, y mucho antes el de Serena y su padre, Charlie era, después de todo, un hombre. No se habría molestado en prestar atención a cómo interactuaban esos caballeros con sus esposas.

Pero su marido era muy inteligente. Aprendería con rapidez. Y tiempo era algo que les sobraba, de hecho tenían el resto de sus vidas.

Así que Sarah emprendió el día con una sonrisa en la cara, sin preocupaciones que le nublaran la mente y llena de anticipación.

Tras el almuerzo, Charlie, Alec y Jeremy fueron a dar un paseo a caballo. Dejaron a Serena y a sus hijas recogiendo la sala que había sido el dominio de Serena años atrás. Sarah por su parte estaba instalando sus cosas en la salita que había elegido para ella.

Al parecer todas las condesas debían tener una salita privada. Serena le había mostrado esa mañana las salas de visita que existían en la casa, muchas de las cuales ni siquiera se usaban.

—Esta casa es tan grande —había dicho Serena— que no hay razón para verte obligada a usar la estancia que yo elegí cuando llegué aquí. Ésta ha sido tradicionalmente la sala de la condesa —le había explicado Serena cuando llegaron a una salita al fondo del ala oeste, justo debajo de los aposentos del conde—. Pertenecía a la primera esposa del padre de Charlie. Aunque fue años antes de que yo me casase con él, no me parecía correcto usar esta habitación. Alathea todavía era una niña y no quise que creyera que estaba intentando suplantar a su madre o, lo que era peor, borrar sus recuerdos.

Sarah había examinado detenidamente esa salita, observando las altas ventanas y la puertaventana que se abría a la terraza que daba al sur. La luz era maravillosa. Era una estancia de gran tamaño como todas las de esa ala, y estaba decorada como correspondería a la salita de una condesa, con damascos y brocados en tonos dorados, marrones, verdes y marfil.

—¿Crees que a Alathea le importará que utilice esta sala? —le había preguntado Sarah a Serena volviéndose hacia ella.

Serena sonrió con placer.

—Oh, no... todo lo contrario. Creo que a ella le gustaría que te instalases en esta salita.

Y eso había hecho. Sarah había informado a Figgs, la temible ama de llaves, de su decisión. Figgs había ordenado al instante que una cuadrilla de criadas limpiara la habitación a fondo.

—Milady, la sala estará lista para después del almuerzo. Le diré a Crisp que avise a los lacayos para que traigan sus cosas y pueda instalarse.

Por la tarde, con el sol entrando a raudales por las altas ventanas, Sarah permanecía a solas en la silenciosa sala y más contenta de lo que había estado nunca.

Además de los cómodos sofás y sillones, la estancia estaba bien surtida de librerías, mesitas y un escritorio con una silla a juego que habían colocado contra una de las paredes. Con el olor a cera de abeja flotando en el aire, Sarah había dejado abierta la puerta de dos hojas que daba al pasillo y la puertaventana de la terraza.

Finalmente terminó de desempaquetar las tres cajas de libros y de colocar los volúmenes bien ordenados en los estantes, pero se quedó con un libro delgado en la mano. Lo estudió y le dio la vuelta. Examinó las cubiertas plateadas de la portada y contraportada bajo los inclinados rayos del sol. Había una espiral plateada grabada en el lomo. Sonriendo con cariño, trazó con la yema del dedo los grabados que cubrían todo el libro y luego acarició la gran amatista que había estampada en la portada.

Una sombra se interpuso entre ella y los rayos del sol.

Sarah levantó la mirada y el corazón le dio un brinco. Por un instante, pensó que era Charlie el que estaba en el umbral de la puertaventana, con su silueta recortada por la luz del sol, pero luego vio las diferencias. Charlie tenía el pelo más claro, el pecho más ancho y los rasgos diferentes.

La instintiva sonrisa de placer de la joven se había desvanecido. Había sido reemplazada por un saludo formal.

—Señor Sinclair. Qué amable de su parte venir a visitarnos.

Parecía como si el hombre se hubiese quedado paralizado, pero dado que tenía el sol a sus espaldas y el rostro en sombras, Sarah no podía asegurarlo. Quizás estaba tan sorprendido de verla como ella de verlo a él.

Sin embargo, las palabras de Sarah lo sacaron de su ensimismamiento.

—Lady Meredith —dijo él sonriendo, relajándose visiblemente.

Entró en la salita y ella le ofreció su mano. Él se inclinó sobre ella, haciéndole una pequeña reverencia, y luego le soltó la mano.

—Estaba buscando a su marido. —Llevaba entre las manos lo

que parecía un boletín informativo—. Le dije que le traería esto. Es un boletín sobre los inversores del ferrocarril.

—Ah, ya veo. —Sarah no tenía ni idea de que Charlie estuviera interesado en el ferrocarril, pero sabía que le gustaba invertir—. Se ha ido hace rato. Debe de estar a punto de llegar.

—Lo sé —repuso Sinclair con una leve sonrisa—, por eso me he acercado hasta aquí. El mozo de cuadra me dijo que ya había regresado. Vi la puerta abierta y pensé que esta estancia era la biblioteca.

—La biblioteca está aquí al lado. En esta misma ala.

—Ah. —Sinclair bajó la mirada al diario con las cubiertas plateadas que ella todavía sostenía en las manos. Una vez más pareció quedarse extrañamente paralizado. Luego parpadeó—. Ese libro parece inusual. ¿Hay muchos así?

—¿Se refiere a éste? —Sarah lo levantó, mostrándole la portada con la amatista—. Imagino que habrá muchos parecidos. Es un recuerdo de mi difunta tía, la hermana mayor de mi madre. Tenía un montón de ellos, cada uno con una piedra diferente en la portada. Cuando murió, cada una de sus sobrinas heredó uno como recuerdo suyo.

Sarah miró el libro con cariño, hojeando algunas páginas.

—Debo admitir que todavía no lo he leído, pero tía Edith era única para las recetas y consejos útiles. Como ahora estoy a cargo de esta casa, quizá pueda encontrar algo en él que me sea de utilidad.

—Me lo imagino.

La joven frunció el ceño interiormente ante el tono forzado de Sinclair. Entonces se oyó ruido de pasos en el pasillo. Sinclair y ella se dieron la vuelta cuando Charlie apareció en el umbral.

—Oh, ya has llegado. —La joven sonrió, pero Charlie había clavado los ojos en su inesperada visita. La mirada de su marido era dura y extrañamente... ¿desafiante? Sarah se apresuró a añadir—: El señor Sinclair te ha traído algunos papeles.

Sinclair sonrió. Se acercó a Charlie rezumando seguridad por cada poro de su cuerpo.

—Son los informes de inversión de los que te hablé —dijo, blandiendo las hojas.

La extraña tensión de Charlie desapareció.

—Ah, gracias. —Sonrió—. ¿Por qué no me acompañas a la biblioteca y los comentamos? —Apartó la mirada de Sinclair y la observó a ella—. ¿Nos disculpas, cariño?

Era una pregunta retórica. Sarah esbozó una dulce sonrisa y asintió cortésmente ante la reverencia de Sinclair y el gesto de cabeza de Charlie. Cuando se fueron, atravesó la estancia, abrió la tapa del escritorio y guardó allí el diario.

Luego cerró la tapa y se quedó mirando el escritorio, refunfuñando para sus adentros. Se dio la vuelta y observó la estancia. La sutil elegancia y la suntuosidad del lugar estaban revestidas con un toque personal.

Era una habitación preciosa y, ahora, le pertenecía.

Maldito Sinclair. Sarah había querido que la primera visita de Charlie a su salita privada acabara de otra manera.

De todas maneras, podría mostrársela cuando estuvieran solos esa noche. Y quizá podría pensar en alguna manera original de expresar su gratitud.

Sarah sonrió al imaginárselo y se acercó a cerrar la puertaventana.

La familia de Charlie —Serena, Augusta, Jeremy y sus otras dos hermanas con sus respectivos maridos— se fue al día siguiente. Todos se reunieron en el patio delantero a media mañana para despedirse de ellos.

Entre risas y sonrisas, las damas se hicieron recomendaciones unas a otras mientras los lacayos y criadas se apresuraban de un lado para otro con cajas y baúles. Finalmente, todos se metieron en los tres carruajes donde los caballos pateaban el suelo con impaciencia.

Sarah permaneció en el porche delantero mientras se despedía con la mano. Lamentaba verlos partir, pero a la vez se sentía agradecida. Serena tenía razón. Todos los recién casados necesitaban unas semanas a solas para adaptarse a la vida en común.

La última en abandonar la casa fue Serena, que envolvió a Sarah en un cálido abrazo.

—Ten paciencia, querida, y todo saldrá perfectamente —le susurró al oído.

246

Sarah le devolvió el abrazo y luego dio un paso atrás. Buscó la sabia mirada de su suegra y sonrió, tranquila y feliz.

—Así lo haré. —No sabía si Serena se refería a Charlie o al cuidado de la casa, pero estaba segura de que todo saldría bien.

Serena se volvió hacia Charlie. Tendiéndole la mano para que la ayudara a bajar las escaleras, permitió que la condujera hasta el carruaje.

Se detuvo en medio del patio y lo miró.

Charlie le devolvió la mirada y vio, como había esperado, que tenía el ceño levemente fruncido. Su madre lo estudió durante un rato, luego levantó la mano enguantada y la posó en su mejilla.

—Es la mujer perfecta para ti. Cuídala. —Serena tenía una expresión seria y tierna, pero luego esbozó una sonrisa—. Y cuídate tú también.

Charlie le brindó una sonrisa cariñosa.

«Cuídate» era lo que Serena le decía cada vez que se separaban desde que él era pequeño.

Su madre le dio una palmadita en la mejilla, bajó la mano y se volvió a la puerta abierta del carruaje. Charlie la ayudó a subir las escalerillas, luego dio un paso atrás mientras un lacayo cerraba la portezuela.

Se despidió de Serena y Augusta con la mano y le hizo un gesto con la cabeza a Jeremy, que había preferido viajar en el pescante, al lado del cochero. Luego se dirigió al porche y se colocó al lado de Sarah para despedirse de los ocupantes de los tres vehículos por última vez. Cuando el último carruaje se puso en marcha, Charlie fue consciente de la calidez que desprendía Sarah a su lado. Era necesario retirarse mentalmente y dio un paso atrás.

Sarah se volvió hacia él con los ojos brillantes de felicidad.

—He pensado que, como aún no has ido a montar esta mañana, quizá podríamos cabalgar juntos. Hace días que no salgo con *Blacktail*.

Charlie la miró, más que tentado a aceptar su oferta, barajando la posibilidad de relajarse con ella, de cabalgar y reír para celebrar el hecho de que estaban juntos y solos, pero...

Charlie luchó contra esa tentación y logró mostrar una expresión impasible.

—Lo siento, pero tengo negocios que atender. —Se volvió hacia la casa. Luego, recordando las palabras de Serena, volvió la mirada atrás—. Si sales, que te acompañe un mozo.

Con una ambigua inclinación de cabeza, y sin atreverse a mirarla a los ojos, entró en la casa y se dirigió a la biblioteca.

Sarah permaneció de pie en el porche y lo observó marcharse. La felicidad que había brillado en sus ojos había sido reemplazada por un ceño.

13

Sarah se dijo a sí misma que aquello no era un rechazo, que Charlie estaba realmente preocupado por sus negocios. Cuando en lugar de reunirse con ella para almorzar en el comedor, ordenó que le llevaran un plato con fiambre a la biblioteca, se recordó que tal comportamiento era perfectamente normal entre los matrimonios de su círculo social.

Los esposos no vivían pendientes el uno del otro. No obstante, ella había esperado que...

Frunciendo el ceño interiormente, Sarah abandonó el comedor. Algo decepcionada, se dirigió a su salita privada y se pasó la tarde redactando la larga lista de notas de agradecimiento que tenía pendiente.

Por lo visto Charlie tenía costumbre de salir a montar a caballo por la hacienda justo después de desayunar, como también tenía costumbre de dejarla deliciosamente exhausta en la cama por la mañana. Pero cuando ella se despertó y se levantó, él ya había desayunado y se había ido.

Al día siguiente Sarah se armó de paciencia y fue recompensada cuando, al regresar del paseo a caballo, Charlie se reunió con ella para comer. Parecía feliz al contarle voluntariamente dónde había estado y lo que había visto, hablando de los asuntos de la hacienda de los que se había estado ocupando.

Justo como debía ser.

Sarah le escuchó, aprendió y respondió con acierto a todo lo que él le planteó.

La tarde anterior, su primera tarde solos, la habían pasado hablando animadamente en la mesa del comedor y luego habían ido a la salita. La noche que había seguido, una vez que estuvieron a solas en el dormitorio, sólo había vuelto a confirmar de manera patente que no había nada extraño entre ellos. Que los dos estaban hechos el uno para el otro.

Aliviada, esperó a que terminaran de almorzar y salieran al pasillo para sugerirle:

—Quizá podríamos salir a montar esta tarde, ¿te parece bien? —Era sábado, sin duda alguna él podría pasar algunas horas alejado de sus negocios.

Sarah se detuvo y se volvió hacia él, mirándolo con un brillo anhelante en los ojos.

La máscara impasible de Charlie estaba de nuevo en su lugar. Él le sostuvo la mirada un breve instante, luego miró hacia delante y negó con la cabeza.

—Me temo que no puedo. Tengo que ocuparme de algunos asuntos. —Vaciló un segundo, luego inclinó la cabeza—. ¿Me disculpas?

Charlie no esperó su respuesta, y se dirigió a grandes zancadas hacia la biblioteca.

Sarah se quedó allí viéndole marchar, con los ojos entrecerrados clavados en su espalda y los labios apretados en una línea tensa.

Comenzaba a odiar con todas sus fuerzas esa biblioteca.

Por la tarde, Sarah ya había controlado su temperamento. Después de pasarse horas reflexionando en el ambiente acogedor de su nueva salita, había llegado a la conclusión de que quizás esa incómoda diferencia de actitudes que parecía existir entre ellos durante las horas diurnas era simplemente el resultado de las expectativas más convencionales que Charlie tenía sobre cómo pasarían los días.

Por mucho que Sarah quisiera que fuera de otra manera, no podía negar que esa explicación del comportamiento de Charlie tenía sentido. Si quería que las cosas fueran diferentes, era tarea de ella hacerle cambiar de idea.

Conociendo su temperamento, Sarah sabía que eso no sería nada fácil, pero, dada la intimidad que existía entre ellos cuando estaban en el dormitorio —momento en el que ella podía ver cómo Charlie se relajaba y cómo desaparecía la barrera distante que él erigía entre ellos durante el día—, la joven tenía esperanzas de lograrlo.

Al día siguiente era domingo, con lo cual fueron a la iglesia. A Sarah le resultó extraño sentarse a la izquierda del pasillo en vez de a la derecha, donde estaban sus padres y sus hermanas, Clary y Gloria, que la miraban con una sonrisa radiante en la cara.

Se alegró especialmente de ver a sus hermanas. Sarah no las había vuelto a ver desde la boda y tenía una ligera sospecha de qué pensamientos cruzaban por sus mentes mientras fingían escuchar el sermón del señor Duncliffe.

Al finalizar el servicio religioso, Charlie la tomó de la mano y la ayudó a ponerse en pie. La guio por el pasillo central hacia el señor Duncliffe, que esperaba en la escalera de la iglesia para saludar a los feligreses. Dada la posición que Sarah ocupaba ahora, le tocaba ser la primera en dar la mano al señor Duncliffe.

El reverendo le brindó una brillante sonrisa.

—¡Mi querida condesa! —Le estrechó una mano entre las suyas y luego miró a Charlie por encima del hombro de la joven—. Qué día más feliz, milord. Me alegro de verle aquí con su nueva esposa.

—Gracias. —Charlie le tendió la mano, haciendo que el señor Duncliffe soltara las de ella.

—¿Y su madre y su hermana? —preguntó el señor Duncliffe.

—Han ido a pasar algún tiempo con lady Mary en Lincoln.

—¡Excelente! ¡Excelente!

Antes de que el señor Duncliffe pudiera hacer más preguntas, Charlie cogió a Sarah por el codo, sonrió, saludó al reverendo con una inclinación de cabeza y siguió adelante.

Ella contuvo una risita mientras recorrían lentamente el camino.

—Parece tan complacido por habernos casado, que nos habría retenido en las escaleras un buen rato con tal de seguir disfrutando del recuerdo.

—Probablemente.

Se detuvieron en medio del césped y esperaron a que la familia de Sarah se acercara. Durante los minutos siguientes, Charlie y su suegro charlaron sobre algunos asuntos del condado mientras Sarah satisfacía la curiosidad de su madre, que deseaba saber cómo le iba la vida de casada. El resto de la congregación pasó por el lado de la joven, saludándola con la cabeza, levantando el sombrero o esbozando tímidas sonrisas. Su madre y ella devolvieron las sonrisas sin dejar de hablar. Las hermanas mayores de Sarah, Maria y Angela, y sus maridos sólo habían ido a la boda y se habían marchado al día siguiente, por lo que su madre le dio recuerdos de su parte. A su vez, Sarah se los dio de parte de Mary y Alice, y también le transmitió el deseo de Serena de que se reunieran en Londres en unas semanas.

Sarah no hizo nada por aplacar la curiosidad de Clary y Gloria, sin importarle lo mucho que resplandecieran sus ojos.

Tras lanzar una mirada de advertencia a sus hijas menores, la madre de Sarah se reunió con su esposo.

Clary se quedó atrás con Sarah sin apartar los ojos de la espalda de su madre.

—¿Podemos ir a visitarte?

Sarah contuvo una amplia sonrisa.

—Mamá os traerá cuando sea apropiado. —Lo que no ocurriría hasta dentro de una semana o más—. Después, podréis venir a verme cuando queráis.

Clary formó una O con los labios, luego asintió con la cabeza y se apresuró a seguir a su madre.

Charlie se volvió hacia Sarah enarcando las cejas.

Su esposa enlazó el brazo con el suyo mientras le brindaba una sonrisa. Decirle la razón que había detrás del deseo de Clary y Gloria de ir a visitarlos no ayudaría a sus propósitos.

—Quizá —dijo la joven mientras se dirigían hacia su carruaje— podríamos dar·un paseo cuando regresemos. Hace muchos años que no visito los jardines del Park, y tú los conoces mejor que nadie.

Sarah le miró de reojo y casi pudo ver cómo Charlie volvía a erigir a su alrededor aquel muro impenetrable.

El rostro de su marido no revelaba nada cuando llegaron al portón del recinto de la iglesia y él lo sostuvo para que ella pasara.

—Será mejor que sea el jefe de jardineros quien te enseñe el lugar.

«¿Mejor para quién?» Mientras atravesaba el portón, Sarah se volvió para mirarlo a los ojos.

Charlie la siguió fuera, rehuyendo su mirada.

—Sé que Harris está deseando mostrarte sus dominios y discutir contigo sobre los parterres y los árboles frutales. Lo harás mejor si yo no estoy presente.

Puede que tuviera razón. Los jardines eran después de todo parte de sus dominios, su responsabilidad, y Harris podía sentirse confundido por la presencia de su amo, pero...

—Meredith, qué placer volver a verte...

Sarah se dio la vuelta cuando Malcolm Sinclair abrió el portón y se unió a ellos.

Él sonrió y se inclinó elegantemente sobre su mano, saludándola con deferencia. Luego se volvió hacia Charlie y le estrechó la mano.

—He recibido noticias de Londres —le dijo al conde—. Ven a visitarme cuando quieras y te pondré al corriente.

Sarah hubiera jurado que el hombre había intentado quitarse el sombrero y seguir adelante, pero Charlie tardó en soltarle la mano. Observó que su marido había clavado su afilada mirada en la cara de Sinclair y luego la miró a ella, con la misma expresión ilegible de siempre.

Entonces miró de nuevo a Sinclair con una leve sonrisa.

—¿Por qué no vienes a almorzar? Podemos hablar entonces. Me gustaría conocer tu opinión con respecto a algunas ideas que he tenido sobre la próxima conexión entre Bristol y Taunton.

—Bueno... —Sinclair miró a Sarah.

Charlie la miró también, y ella notó algo en sus ojos que hizo que se sintiera como si la estuviera poniendo a prueba. Forzando una sonrisa educada, la joven se volvió hacia Sinclair.

—Por favor, señor Sinclair, acompáñenos. Su presencia animará la comida. —Volvió a mirar a Charlie fijamente—. Ahora solemos guardar silencio.

Sinclair paseó la mirada de uno a otro, pero cuando Charlie arqueó una ceja expectante aceptó la invitación. Sarah no podía criticar los modales de Sinclair.

Los de su marido, sin embargo, eran otra cuestión.

Sarah no estaba de buen humor, pero una tarde explorando los extensos jardines con Harris, escuchándole exponer su punto de vista sobre las complejidades de los arbustos y las pérgolas, intercambiando opiniones sobre los colores más apropiados para los parterres que adornaban el césped y encontrar un lugar adecuado para el señor Quilley, el gnomo que le habían regalado, tuvo un efecto tranquilizador en ella. Consiguió recobrar su acostumbrado equilibrio, el suficiente para pensar con determinación y no dejarse llevar por su mal genio.

Charlie estaba poniéndose difícil, pero ella sabía lo que quería: lograr que el amor fuera la base de su matrimonio tanto de día como de noche; por el bien de los dos.

Durante la tranquila cena y la hora que pasaron en la salita, Charlie leyendo una novela mientras ella bordaba —la viva estampa de un matrimonio convencional—, Sarah lo observó disimuladamente, sin encontrar ninguna pista a la extraña actitud de su marido ni a su casi sempiterno rostro impenetrable.

No sabía por qué él se estaba comportando de esa manera, ni por qué se retraía tanto sin mostrar ningún indicio de aprecio fuera del dormitorio, pero si ella actuaba sabiamente, sabía que con un poco de perseverancia él pasaría finalmente por el aro.

Por consiguiente, tras otra ardiente noche de frío invierno en su habitación, durante la cual ella no encontró nada reprochable en la actitud de su marido, Sarah se obligó a sí misma a levantarse a una hora temprana, a asearse con rapidez y a ponerse el traje de montar antes de bajar corriendo las escaleras. Entonces se topó con él —literalmente— cuando abandonaba el comedor del desayuno.

—¡Oh! —dijo ella rebotando hacia atrás.

Charlie la cogió por los codos, la ayudó a recuperar el equilibrio y luego la soltó.

Sarah le brindó una sonrisa.

—Te pillé. Quería preguntarte si te apetecía cabalgar conmigo hasta el orfanato. Algunos de los niños me han preguntado si...

—Lo siento. —Charlie dio un paso atrás con expresión pétrea—. Voy a casa de Sinclair. Necesito que me enseñe unos documentos.

—Oh. —Ella no pudo ocultar su desencanto; pudo sentir cómo su felicidad se esfumaba junto con su sonrisa. Pero tomó aire con rapidez, conteniendo su mal humor, y se recordó a sí misma que debía ser perseverante—. Bueno —se obligó a mostrarse alegre—, como la casa del señor Sinclair está en Crowcombe, Finley House, ¿no?, podremos cabalgar juntos hasta allí.

Charlie la miró brevemente, luego se alejó de ella.

—Antes tengo que escribir unas cartas. No sé si estaré preparado antes de que salgas. Tu reunión es a las diez, ¿verdad?

Charlie miró por encima de la cabeza de Sarah el reloj que había en la repisa de la chimenea de la salita; ella siguió la dirección de su mirada... eran casi las nueve.

—Tendrás que darte prisa. —La voz de su marido estaba desprovista de cualquier tipo de emoción. Ella sintió que la miraba por un momento, luego él retrocedió y le hizo una reverencia—. Si me disculpas, dejaré que desayunes.

Ella se quedó allí de pie, en la puerta, con los ojos fijos en el reloj mientras oía los pasos de Charlie alejándose por el pasillo.

Charlie no había concertado ninguna cita con Malcolm Sinclair, pero sin duda podía ir a visitarlo alegando cualquier excusa. En realidad, dado que a su nuevo amigo y a él les gustaba hablar sobre las compañías del ferrocarril y su financiación, cualquier excusa para verse de nuevo sería bien recibida. Charlie podía empezar un debate con sólo proponérselo.

Llegó a Crowcombe a las once, una hora aceptable para que un caballero visitara a otro. Finley House, una mansión clásica de estilo georgiano, quedaba cerca de la carretera que conducía a Watchet, justo al pasar Crowcombe.

Desmontó delante de la verja y guio a *Tormenta*, ahora dócil tras la cabalgada, a través de la estrecha franja de hierba que separaba la casa del camino. Se acercó a un árbol con frondosas ramas, ya que no había un lugar mejor que ése para atar al castrado, luego recorrió el camino de losas hacia el porche.

Imaginó que la puerta principal y el vestíbulo estaban flanqueados por dos habitaciones de gran tamaño. Charlie aguzó el oído, preguntándose si Sinclair le había visto llegar. Al no oír ningún sonido dentro, alzó la mano y golpeó la puerta. Y esperó.

Había considerado hablarle a Sinclair sobre sus investigaciones.

Después de todo era un renombrado inversor en el ferrocarril, uno de los mayores, aunque no estuviera entre los que habían acudido a las autoridades, y se había visto perjudicado por el extorsionador. Pero aunque Charlie suponía que Sinclair no tenía nada que ver con el especulador, sabía muy bien lo rápido que se propagaba ese tipo de rumores entre los inversores. Si le contaba algo a Sinclair, incluso aunque le pidiera que no dijera nada, Sinclair se sentiría en su perfecto derecho de contárselo a alguien de confianza, que a su vez haría lo mismo y así sucesivamente, hasta que esa información secreta fuera del dominio público y llegara a oídos del especulador.

Así que ignoró aquellos principios morales que le impelían a contárselo todo a Sinclair.

Oyó ruido de pasos proveniente de la parte trasera de la casa. Un momento después Malcolm Sinclair abrió la puerta.

—Charlie. —Sonrió.

Charlie le devolvió la sonrisa.

—Malcolm. —Se estrecharon la mano y Sinclair le invitó a pasar.

Lo condujo a una biblioteca que dedicaba a estudio situada en un rincón de la parte trasera de la casa.

—Aunque no sea gran cosa, éste es mi santuario.

Charlie entró y recorrió con la mirada las librerías que cubrían las paredes repletas de volúmenes con lomo de piel que no habían sido leídos en años, un ordenado escritorio y unas sillas, un sillón y una mesa auxiliar delante de la chimenea y la puertaventana que daba a un pequeño patio. Malcolm lo invitó a sentarse y Charlie se sentó en una silla frente al escritorio mientras su anfitrión se sentaba detrás.

—Bien. —Malcolm le sostuvo la mirada—. ¿A qué debo este honor?

Charlie sonrió y le expuso el tema que le había llevado hasta allí. Sinclair caviló sobre sus palabras y respondió en consecuencia. Pronto estuvieron enzarzados en una animada discusión sobre el proyecto original que había sido financiado por Stockton Darlington y sobre cómo, en opinión de Sinclair, podía incrementarse el capital, tanto desde el punto de vista de los inversores como desde el propio proyecto.

Le llevó muy poco esfuerzo, ya fuera sutil o no, conseguir que Malcolm le hablara sobre ese tema. Después de que hubieran conversado durante algún tiempo, Charlie miró el reloj de la repisa de la chimenea y le sorprendió descubrir que había pasado más de una hora.

Parpadeó y se enderezó.

—Tengo que irme... no tenía ni idea de que te hubiera robado tanto tiempo.

Malcolm siguió su mirada hacia el reloj. Enarcó las cejas con evidente sorpresa. Luego sonrió, un gesto educado que Charlie reconoció instintivamente como más sincero que los suyos. Aunque aquella sonrisa parecía un tanto oxidada.

—Se me ha pasado el tiempo volando. No me había pasado nunca y... —Malcolm hizo una pausa y luego buscó la mirada de Charlie— debo reconocer que jamás había conocido a nadie con intereses similares a los míos. —Curvó los labios—. Nadie que tuviera mi misma facilidad para comprender las finanzas y sus ramificaciones.

La sonrisa se hizo más profunda cuando Charlie se puso en pie.

—Disfruto enormemente con nuestras conversaciones. Por favor, ven a visitarme cuando quieras.

Charlie se acercó a la puertaventana y se detuvo ante ella. Sabía lo que había querido decir Malcolm. Durante la última hora habían disfrutado mucho intercambiando opiniones típicamente masculinas mientras debatían sobre las finanzas. Un intercambio sincero. Él jamás lo había hecho, ni lo habría hecho Malcolm a menos que, como en ese caso, aceptara la confianza que le ofrecía un hombre tan parecido a él. Un mayor grado de empatía de la que se solía encontrar.

Charlie no podía fingir que no le alegraba aquella inesperada amistad. Le dirigió a Malcolm una breve mirada. Éste aún estaba sentado tras el escritorio, observándole, luego se volvió hacia a la ventana.

—Lo recordaré.

Se produjo un dilatado silencio.

—¿Qué tal te va con tu nueva condesa? —preguntó entonces Malcolm.

Charlie se puso rígido por dentro, pero mostró una fachada relajada, con las manos en los bolsillos mientras miraba por la ventana el jardín que había más allá del patio. La pregunta había sido expresada de una manera tímida. Sería perfectamente aceptable que él le respondiera con una frase al uso y dejar así las cosas.

—Las mujeres tienen, en su mayoría, una idea de la vida matrimonial a menudo diferente de la que tenemos los caballeros —dijo finalmente.

—Ah. —Malcolm no dijo nada más, pero la simpatía, la empatía y la comprensión estaban incluidas en esa única sílaba.

Charlie cambió el peso a la otra pierna, con la mirada clavada en los arbustos de fuera.

—Lo único que puedo hacer es mantenerme firme en mi postura. Algo que ella acabará por aceptar finalmente.

O eso creía.

Tras un momento, Malcolm volvió a hablar en ese tono apocado e indiferente.

—Parece una mujer sensata. La señora Duncliffe me dijo que ella, Sarah, ha vivido en esta zona toda su vida y tiene diversos intereses.

La expresión de Charlie se volvió sombría.

—El orfanato. —Señaló con la cabeza hacia la parte delantera de la casa, en dirección al orfanato. Y sintió que se le encogía el estómago.

Esa mañana, su primera reacción a la entusiasmada y decidida invitación de Sarah para que lo acompañara al orfanato había sido aceptar con una sonrisa. Se había contenido justo a tiempo. La mención de los niños le había ayudado. A Charlie le gustaban los niños de todas las edades. Se encontraba a gusto con ellos y ellos con él. Pero los niños siempre sabían cuando uno estaba fingiendo. Si estaba rodeado de ellos, y Sarah estaba presente, jamás podría ocultar lo que sentía por ella.

Y sólo pensar en verla rodeada por ellos, colgados de sus faldas, con su cara de *madonna* encendida mientras intentaba tranquilizarlos...

No. No podría volver con ella al orfanato nunca más.

—Bueno —murmuró Malcolm—, supongo que, una vez que tenga su propia prole, su interés por el orfanato decrecerá.

Charlie pensó en Sarah con un hijo suyo en los brazos y sintió que se le aflojaban las rodillas, que su decisión, simplemente, se disolvía. ¡Santo Dios! ¿Cómo se enfrentaría a eso?

Tomó aliento y enderezó la espalda. Tenía un año, por lo menos nueve meses, para averiguar cómo enfrentarse a tal eventualidad.

Cómo tratar con su esposa al tiempo que mantenía el amor que sentía por ella bajo llave.

—Será mejor que regrese. —Se dio la vuelta y, sosteniendo la mirada algo preocupada de Malcolm, sonrió. Se acercó al escritorio y le tendió la mano—. Supongo que son los nervios de cualquier recién casado. Estoy seguro de que se me pasará con el tiempo.

La seguridad de sus palabras y su sonrisa hacían que pareciera más confiado de lo que en realidad se sentía, pero sirvieron para tranquilizar a Malcolm, que se levantó y estrechó la mano de Charlie. Juntos atravesaron la casa.

Charlie se detuvo en el porche delantero y alzó la mirada donde el orfanato se elevaba sobre el pueblo. Volvió la mirada hacia Malcolm.

—Mañana espero recibir algunos informes bancarios desde Londres con noticias de los últimos acontecimientos financieros. ¿Por qué no vienes a almorzar y los comentamos entonces?

Malcolm arqueó una ceja.

—¿Es así como te mantienes al corriente de todo a pesar de estar enterrado en el campo?

Charlie asintió con la cabeza.

—En efecto. ¿Te espero al mediodía?

Malcolm vaciló. Clavó sus ojos color avellana en la cara de Charlie y luego asintió con la cabeza.

—Muy bien. Gracias. Te veré entonces.

Tras despedirse con una sonrisa, Charlie se dirigió hacia *Tormenta*; desató las riendas y condujo al poderoso caballo gris por la vereda. Al llegar al final, se subió a la silla de montar y, saludando con la mano a Malcolm, se alejó cabalgando.

Malcolm Sinclair permanecía de pie en la puerta abierta, con los ojos entornados mientras seguía a Charlie con la mirada. Luego alzó la vista hacia el orfanato. Después de un buen rato, entró en la casa y cerró la puerta.

A la mañana siguiente, Sarah consideró los acontecimientos del día anterior mientras se aseaba y se vestía. Cada vez estaba más confundida. Era casi como si estuviera casada con dos hombres diferentes; el hombre cálido y cariñoso con el que compartía cama, y el noble distante y frío con el que se encontraba por los pasillos de la casa.

Pero ni siquiera eso describía adecuadamente cómo se había sentido.

El día anterior, cuando Charlie había rechazado su invitación, evitando pasar una sola hora en su compañía, se había sentido herida. Se había negado incluso a acompañarla durante seis kilómetros. ¡Montados a caballo, por el amor de Dios! Ni siquiera hubiera sido en un carruaje, donde habrían estado muy cerca el uno del otro.

¿Qué era lo que le ocurría a Charlie?

Sarah había sentido que se inflamaba su temperamento, pero se había visto obligada a reprimir su enfado al llegar al orfanato. Charlie y su irracional comportamiento podrían desquiciarla, pero Sarah no pensaba dejar que eso afectara a sus relaciones con los demás, en especial con los niños.

Aquel ejercicio de contención había sido de gran ayuda. Al regresar a casa al atardecer, estaba perfectamente controlada.

No obstante, durante toda la tarde, su temperamento había estado ardiendo a fuego lento, en espera de que él lo avivara con algún acto o palabra. Pero Charlie se había mostrado tranquilo. No cálido y cariñoso, sino más bien frío y distante. Durante la hora y media que habían estado juntos, no en la sala formal de la casa, sino en la acogedora salita de Sarah, había sentido la mirada de Charlie sobre ella infinidad de veces, pero cada vez que había levantado los ojos de su labor de bordado, lo había visto leyendo el libro.

¿Qué significaban aquellas miradas subrepticias? ¿Estaría debilitándose la resolución de su marido de conducirlos a aquel estúpido estado en el que estaba tan resuelto a llevarlos?

Preguntándose qué pasaría aquel día, Sarah bajó las escaleras.

Como había esperado, el comedor del desayuno estaba vacío, sin ningún conde a la vista. Charlie ya había salido a cabalgar. Como siempre, se había mostrado muy atento antes de abandonar la cama, y como siempre Sarah se había levantado demasiado tarde. O para ser más exactos, se había levantado mucho más tarde de lo que solía hacerlo antes de casarse. Últimamente se estaba acostumbrando a desayunar a las diez.

Algo que podría remediar con facilidad. Pero el resto...

Se tomó una tostada y bebió el té mientras miraba con los ojos entrecerrados la silla de la cabecera de la mesa, afianzando su resolución.

Pensó en cómo desearía que fueran las cosas. Aunque sabía a ciencia cierta que un caballero como Charlie jamás pondría su corazón en una bandeja, que en público siempre sería más reservado que en casa, no había razón para que insistiera en seguir con aquella actitud distante.

Eso se tenía que acabar. De hecho tenía suficientes ejemplos de matrimonios que se amaban de los que aprender. A su desayuno de bodas había asistido un montón de parejas Cynster, sin mencionar los mejores amigos de Charlie y sus esposas. No le cabía duda de que ésa era la clase de matrimonio que quería para ellos.

Su problema, sin embargo, era cómo convencer a Charlie de ello. De lo bien que les irían así las cosas.

Al levantarse y dirigirse a la salita para terminar de escribir las notas de agradecimiento, decidió que el mejor camino a seguir era comportarse sencillamente con constancia y firmeza. Si desempeñaba el papel de amante esposa con diligencia, en algún momento él se rendiría y prescindiría de aquella absurda actitud, y sería por fin el marido que ella quería que fuera.

El cariñoso marido que realmente era.

El matrimonio era como un baile en el que la pareja tenía que moverse al mismo compás, adaptarse el uno al otro para hacer que funcionara. Charlie sólo tenía que aprender los pasos.

Sarah se concentró en escribir las notas de agradecimiento. Cuando llevaba la mitad de la lista, se recostó en la silla ante el escritorio y enderezó la espalda. Estaba a punto de volver a dedicarse a la tarea cuando oyó un golpe lejano.

Aguzó el oído y oyó los pesados pasos de Crisp cruzando el vestíbulo. Un momento después le llegó el eco de unas voces. Echó un vistazo al reloj y confirmó que ya era mediodía. Preguntándose quién habría llegado, se levantó y se dirigió al vestíbulo.

Al entrar vio al señor Sinclair tendiéndole el sombrero y los guantes a Crisp. Sarah avanzó hacia él forzando una sonrisa.

—Buenos días, señor Sinclair. ¿Está buscando a su señoría?

Sinclair tomó la mano que ella le ofrecía y se inclinó elegantemente sobre ella.

—Así es, lady Meredith. —Él vaciló, escudriñándole la cara—. Su señoría me invitó a venir —añadió luego.

Sarah parpadeó y se dio cuenta de lo que Sinclair, con suma delicadeza, le acababa de decir. Era mediodía y él había venido en respuesta a una invitación.

Se giró hacia Crisp.

—El señor Sinclair se quedará a comer, Crisp.

El mayordomo hizo una reverencia y se retiró.

Conteniendo la creciente furia que la invadió ante aquella nueva inconveniencia, esbozó una suave sonrisa. Sinclair no tenía la culpa de aquello. Con un gesto de la mano lo invitó a seguirla a la salita.

—Como Crisp sin duda le ha informado, Charlie debe de estar a punto de regresar de su paseo matutino y...

Las palabras de Sarah se desvanecieron cuando oyó unos pasos —concretamente el sonido de unas botas— en el pasillo en dirección a ellos. Sarah enderezó la espalda, entrelazando las manos en un gesto educado. Podía mantener la expresión imperturbable, pero no podría hacer nada con el brillo de su mirada. Si su enfado se reflejaba en sus ojos, él se lo había buscado.

Con calma esperó ante la puerta de la salita. Sinclair y ella se giraron cuando Charlie apareció por el pasillo que conducía a la puerta lateral y a los establos.

Tenía el pelo dorado despeinado por el viento. Llevaba una chaqueta de color aceituna, un pañuelo en el cuello y un chaleco marrón sobre una camisa blanca que había remetido en unos ceñidos pantalones de piel. Las botas de montar eran de color marrón.

Sarah absorbió su imagen, hasta el último detalle, absorbió el gran impacto que la presencia de su marido provocaba en sus sentidos con una rápida mirada. Y se preguntó por qué no se había fijado en cómo vestía Sinclair, con el que llevaba hablando un buen rato. Ni siquiera sabía si iba vestido como un caballero.

Dada la situación, esa sensibilidad a su marido era más una irritación que otra cosa.

Charlie mantuvo la vista baja mientras se quitaba los guantes. Cuando levantó la cabeza y los vio, detuvo sus zancadas. Pero luego se acercó a ellos con una fría y despreocupada máscara en su rostro y aquella sonrisa educada que solía curvarle los labios.

Sarah se sorprendió de haber pensado alguna vez que tenía una sonrisa encantadora.

—Malcolm. —Charlie le tendió la mano y Sinclair se la estrechó—. Lamento el retraso, estaba con uno de mis arrendatarios.

Con la sonrisa grabada en la cara, Charlie se volvió hacia Sarah.

—Cariño, Malcolm y yo tenemos mucho que discutir. Me temo que te aburrirías en nuestra compañía. ¿Puedes ordenar que nos traigan el almuerzo a la biblioteca?

Se despidió de ella con un gesto de cabeza y se dio la vuelta, indicándole a Sinclair que le acompañara.

Pero Sinclair no lo hizo de inmediato. Se volvió hacia Sarah y la miró, haciéndole una reverencia.

—Gracias por su tiempo, lady Meredith.

Sarah tomó aire y asintió educadamente con la cabeza. Mientras Sinclair se enderezaba, la joven observó una inesperada comprensión y un poco de compasión en aquellos ojos color avellana. También percibió cómo Charlie fruncía de repente el ceño cuando advirtió la mirada que habían intercambiado Sinclair y ella.

Mientras Malcolm se giraba, Sarah sostuvo la mirada de su marido por un breve instante, luego se dio la vuelta y se encaminó a la salita, sin mirar cómo Sinclair y Charlie se alejaban por el pasillo.

Se detuvo en medio de la estancia y tomó una larga bocanada de aire.

No, definitivamente, no iba a perder la calma delante de Sinclair.

Dos noches más tarde, Sarah estaba en su lado de la cama, de cara a las ventanas, con las mantas echadas sobre los hombros y las velas apagadas cuando Charlie entró en la habitación.

Era tarde, el viento rugía detrás de los cristales.

La joven permaneció inmóvil, mordiéndose los labios para contener las imprudentes palabras que tenía en la punta de la lengua. Quería decirle lo que pensaba de su actitud. Lo que sentía en su interior. Quería insultarlo por comportarse de una manera tan estúpida. Pero ¿qué lograría con eso?

Pasara lo que pasase, no pensaba suplicar.

Esa mañana, al llegar a la mesa del desayuno, había encontrado una nota sobre su plato. Era de Charlie. Al parecer había hecho planes para pasar el día en Watchet con el señor Sinclair y compartir sus últimos conocimientos de los cargamentos marítimos y negocios de almacenes.

Sarah se había sentado, clavando los ojos en la nota durante todo un minuto mientras se preguntaba por qué él había evitado mencionar su cita con Sinclair la noche anterior. La noche anterior, cuando ella se había tragado su ira y había respondido con honesta calidez y un genuino deseo cuando Charlie se había reunido con ella en la cama, Sarah había querido provocar el amor y cariño de su marido para que dejara aquel distante comportamiento fuera de las paredes del dormitorio.

Finalmente, dejó la nota a un lado mientras hacía una mueca. Luego emprendió su jornada diaria a solas tal y como su marido quería.

Hasta que la señora Duncliffe se acercó a visitarla esa tarde. Era sólo una visita de cortesía, pero dada la sagacidad de la mujer combinada con el hecho de que, aunque no fuera dada a murmuraciones, era muy amiga de su madre, Sarah se había visto obligada a interpretar el papel de recién casada feliz. Para cuando la señora Duncliffe se fue, Sarah tenía dolor de cabeza.

Por fortuna, era muy poco probable que cualquier otra mujer de la comunidad fuera a visitarla hasta la semana siguiente, pues era la costumbre general. La posición como esposa del vicario otorgaba a la señora Duncliffe una dispensa especial.

Sintiéndose un poco indispuesta, Sarah se había retirado a echar una siesta. Fue consciente de que la fuerza del viento se aplacaba a lo largo de la tarde; luego había oído los pasos de Charlie en la terraza bajo las ventanas del dormitorio. Resultaba evidente que acababa de regresar. Se había preguntado entre sueños si él iría a buscarla al no encontrarla en la salita. Si subiría a verla.

Por supuesto, no lo hizo.

Charlie se había retirado a la biblioteca, de donde no salió hasta la hora de la cena. El ritual de la noche fue el mismo de siempre. Sarah le había preguntado y él le había contado lo que había hecho en Watchet, le había descrito que Sinclair y él se habían reunido con diversos comerciantes y agentes marítimos, y también con algunos concejales para discutir sobre el futuro del pueblo. Más tarde, ella había bordado y él había leído. Luego, la joven se había retirado y había subido a su habitación para dormir.

Sarah sentía una enorme opresión en el pecho, y apenas podía respirar. Charlie parecía decidido a negar lo que ella sabía que era cierto. Si él seguía negando ese amor durante mucho más tiempo, ¿acabaría ella por rendirse y darle la razón?

Lo escuchó cruzar el vestidor, y cómo se movía de un lado para otro mientras se desvestía. Entretanto, Sarah intentó buscar una salida, una manera de reclamar el amor que sabía que existía entre ellos, de obligarle a admitirlo ante ella.

Jamás lo había hecho.

La joven clavó la mirada en la oscuridad suavizada por la luz de la lumbre y repasó con rapidez sus recuerdos, confirmando que Charlie nunca, ni una sola vez, le había dicho que la amaba.

Ella se lo había dicho en una ocasión, y él había aceptado sus palabras.

Pero jamás había admitido que él sintiera lo mismo por ella.

Charlie salió del vestidor. Sarah escuchó el susurro de la bata cuando él la dejó caer. Luego la cama se hundió cuando se acostó a su lado.

Sarah no pudo evitar tensarse ni que el nudo que sentía en el pecho se apretara aún más. Aun así sus traidores sentidos reaccionaron de inmediato a él. Permaneció inmóvil. Charlie se acercó más y, a través de la oscuridad, Sarah captó el olor a mar.

Su marido había estado navegando. Mientras estaba en Watchet, había salido con Sinclair en su pequeño velero. A ella no se le había ocurrido preguntar, pero él tampoco lo había mencionado.

El nudo que tenía en el pecho se congeló y se hizo más profundo.

Por primera vez desde que se habían casado, Sarah no estaba dispuesta a recibirlo entre sus brazos. Fingió estar profundamente dormida hasta que él se dio la vuelta y se acomodó para dormirse.

La joven siguió sin moverse, con la mirada fija en la oscuridad de la noche.

Fuera aullaba el viento, como si hubiera regresado el invierno.

A la mañana siguiente, Charlie sintió una opresión en el pecho mientras dejaba otra nota en el plato de Sarah sobre la mesa del desayuno.

Apretó los labios, giró sobre sus talones y salió de la estancia. Se dirigió a los establos, montó a lomos de *Tormenta* y guio a su caballo en dirección sur, donde le dio rienda suelta.

Se dirigía a Casleigh; Gabriel estaba allí con Barnaby, quien había elegido la casa de su cuñado, que se encontraba algo más al sur que la suya, como base de operaciones temporal mientras Gabriel y él investigaban con discreción las especulaciones y extorsiones que podían darse en las distintas rutas del ferrocarril entre Bristol y Taunton.

Había llegado el momento de saber a qué conclusiones habían llegado los dos hombres y, además, era la manera perfecta de pasar otro día alejado de Sarah.

Se obligó a aflojar la fuerza con la que sostenía las riendas, pero ni el resonar de los cascos de *Tormenta* ni el aire que le azotaba la cara podían distraerle de los inquietos pensamientos que le daban vueltas en la cabeza.

Durante los últimos días, se había esmerado en hacer lo que estaba seguro que era lo mejor para Sarah y él. Cada noche había experimentado el poder que surgía entre ellos y lo fuerte que éste era, tanto que podía llegar a dominarle. Y no podía consentirlo. No podía permitir que le afectara y entrara en su vida durante el día y no sólo en las horas que pasaban juntos en la cama.

Y a pesar de todo, su plan parecía funcionar perfectamente, al menos en el sentido de que ella parecía haber aceptado que durante el día, fuera del dormitorio, siempre habría un muro entre ellos.

Pero la noche anterior...

Intentó convencerse a sí mismo de que Sarah había estado profundamente dormida antes de que él llegara, pero su parte más primitiva, su instinto, sabía que había estado despierta. Que su esposa se había apartado de él.

Esa parte primitiva de sí mismo había protestado y rugido, herida y lastimada. Pero eso era lo que él había querido, ¿no? Al menos durante el día.

Quería que hubiera una distancia entre ellos, quería que Sarah comprendiera y aceptara eso. ¿Qué derecho tenía él a quejarse si ella llevaba las cosas un poco más lejos?

Pero no era eso lo que él quería. No ahora. Ahora que el amor le había alcanzado, ahora que lo había probado, no podía soportar perderlo por completo.

El viento frío traspasó la tela de su chaqueta y le acarició el pecho con dedos gélidos. Pero el frío helado que sentía en su interior no tenía nada que ver con los elementos.

Tenía que construir un muro más alto y más grueso entre ellos. Puede que entonces dejara de sentir ese doloroso frío.

Contener el amor una vez que se había probado era muchísimo más difícil de lo que él había pensado.

14

Sarah se sentía traicionada.

Reconocía que su caso no era como el de otras mujeres que se habían casado con un mujeriego, pero aun así no podía evitar sentirse profundamente traicionada.

Engañada.

Charlie la había engañado de manera deliberada y absurda.

A la mañana siguiente, la joven continuó con la tarea de escribir las notas de agradecimiento a todos aquellos que le habían enviado sus felicitaciones formales por la boda. Hizo un pulcro montoncito con las notas y les puso la dirección; luego, con los labios apretados, las llevó a la biblioteca y las depositó sobre el papel secante de Charlie.

Como siempre, él había salido a montar. Sarah dio un paso atrás y observó durante un momento el tambaleante montón; luego se dio la vuelta y se marchó, dejándole las notas para que las franqueara él.

Regresó a su salita. Sin ninguna ocupación inmediata que pudiera distraerla, comenzó a sentirse inquieta. Miró por la ventana para ver qué tiempo hacía. El clima se había vuelto inestable. Algunos rayos de sol brillaban entre las nubes, pero el cielo parecía estar lo suficientemente claro para arriesgarse a dar una vuelta por los jardines.

Salió a la terraza por la puertaventana, bajó los escalones y caminó con brío por la rosaleda, un área entre los arbustos y el lago con los caminos pavimentados y bordeada por parterres. Harris se enorgullecía particularmente de sus rosales, así que los caminos estaban siempre bien cuidados. Incluso durante el invierno, cuando se habían cortado las rosas y sólo quedaban los troncos recién podados, era el lugar perfecto para que pasearan las damas.

Sarah recorrió los senderos, observando los troncos cortados y las varillas de sujeción con el corazón en un puño.

El dolor que sentía en su interior era cada vez más intenso.

No había querido que su matrimonio careciera de amor. Si había aceptado casarse con Charlie era porque sabía que él la amaba, aunque no se lo hubiera dicho expresamente. De otra manera no habría aceptado. No había sido tan idiota como para creerse las promesas de un caballero. Había esperado a comprobar que él la amaba.

Y Charlie lo hacía.

Todavía la amaba.

Se había asegurado de ello. Lo que ella no había sabido era que, a pesar de amarla, Charlie no había tenido intención de permitir que ese amor fuera la piedra angular de su matrimonio. Que a pesar de sus votos sagrados, de saber que la amaba, él se negaría a permitir que ese amor floreciera, que diera rienda suelta a sus vidas, que fuera la fuerza y el sostén en el que ambos se apoyaran como ella sabía instintivamente que podía ser, que debía ser.

Con el ceño fruncido y cruzando las manos en la espalda, caminó hasta el final del sendero; luego, se giró con un revuelo de faldas para emprender el camino de vuelta.

Charlie le había mostrado su amor, pero jamás había tenido intención de compartirlo, de vivir de acuerdo con aquella antigua y tácita promesa del amor. La traición y el engaño ensombrecían los pensamientos de la joven, pero lo que realmente inflamaba su temperamento, lo que la enfadaba hasta el punto de tener que apretar los dientes para contener un grito de frustración, era no saber por qué.

Porque no había ninguna razón para ello.

Ninguna que fuera lógica. Ninguna que pudiera comprender.

Él había tomado un inflexible y determinado camino, seguro de salirse con la suya simplemente porque... ¿pensaba que era así como debían ser las cosas?

Sarah no lo sabía, pero desde luego no había nada que pudiera excusar tal comportamiento.

El dolor y la ira pugnaban en su interior, pero, de las dos, la ira era más fuerte. Lejos de querer retirarse para lamer sus heridas, quería agarrar a Charlie por los hombros y sacudirle hasta que espabilara y viera a lo que tan tontamente estaba dando la espalda.

Si ella fuera un hombre... pero desde luego no lo era. Era una mujer, de los pies a la cabeza.

Parpadeó. Se detuvo y clavó la mirada en un arbusto inerte. Era una mujer, por lo tanto Charlie, su descerebrado marido, había asumido que era más débil, menos fuerte y, lo más importante, menos terca que él.

Sarah dejó de fruncir el ceño; sus labios, hasta entonces apretados en una línea tensa, esbozaron una sonrisa. Charlie suponía que si él se mantenía firme en su postura, ella acataría su dictamen sin luchar y que dejaría que su matrimonio se convirtiera en la entidad vacía que él deseaba que fuera, sin amor en el corazón. Pero no había ninguna razón por la que ella tuviera que aceptar todo eso sin más.

No había ningún motivo por el que ella no pudiera luchar por lo que quería, un matrimonio basado en la sólida fuerza del amor.

Parada en medio de los troncos podados, Sarah saboreó la perspectiva de tal batalla. Una que, necesariamente, tendría que librar con acciones y no con palabras, y que resultaba mucho más aceptable que rendirse sin más. Si conseguía que Charlie cambiara de opinión, si podía obligarlo a ver el futuro a través de sus ojos, sería él quien desearía unirse a ella para hacerlo realidad. No sabía cómo lo haría, pero sin duda, ése sería su objetivo.

Oyó pasos a su espalda y se dio la vuelta con rapidez. El corazón le dio un brinco, pero enseguida se tranquilizó. Una vez más no era su errante marido el que se dirigía hacia ella. Tomó aire, se obligó a esbozar una sonrisa y extendió la mano.

—Señor Sinclair.

—Condesa. —Él le tomó la mano y se inclinó educadamente sobre ella, antes de soltarla. Echó un vistazo a los parterres inertes—. La vi dirigirse hacia aquí.

—Estaba tomando el aire. —Sarah señaló el camino con la mano—. El césped está algo mojado, es más seguro caminar por aquí. —Observó los papeles que él llevaba en la mano—. ¿Le espera el conde?

Sinclair le sostuvo la mirada y levantó los papeles.

—Su marido quería verlos... Me han llegado esta mañana de Londres.

Sarah suspiró para sus adentros. Resultaba evidente que no iba a poder luchar contra Charlie ni en el almuerzo ni durante el resto de la tarde.

—Me temo que ha salido a cabalgar, pero debería estar de vuelta de un momento a otro.

Sinclair vaciló.

—En ese caso —dijo, buscando su mirada—, si no le importa, pasearé con usted.

Sarah se quedó sorprendida, pero tenía claro cuál era su deber de anfitriona. Con una suave sonrisa, ladeó la cabeza y se giró para emprender el camino.

Para Sarah fue fácil entablar una conversación banal, preguntarle cómo le iban las cosas en Crowcombe y en su casa alquilada o qué pensaba sobre las bucólicas costumbres de la localidad.

—El puente que cruza la cascada de Will's Neck es el mejor lugar para ver los Quantocks. —Le miró a la cara—. ¿Ha estado allí?

—No. —Sinclair le sostuvo la mirada—. ¿Cómo se llega?

Sarah sonrió y se lo dijo. Mientras caminaba, la joven fue consciente de la estatura de su acompañante. Era tan alto como Charlie pero un poco más robusto y, si bien no poseía una belleza clásica, sin duda era elegante y educado. Aunque en muchos aspectos parecía una versión más madura de Charlie, Sinclair no excitaba sus sentidos de ninguna manera.

Pero sus sentidos sí dieron un brinco cuando otros fuertes pasos resonaron en el camino detrás de ellos. Sarah se giró con su habitual sonrisa en los labios. Sin importar cuál fuera la situación entre ellos, la joven no creía que su cálido e instintivo saludo hacia Charlie pudiera cambiar en algún momento. Su marido le lanzó a Sinclair una mirada dura y claramente desafiante.

Por un breve instante, Sarah vio a Charlie como un caballero armado presto a presentar batalla.

Luego parpadeó, y Sinclair, sonriendo y sin verse afectado por la amenaza que ella creía que pendía sobre su cabeza, dio un paso adelante.

—Meredith. —Le tendió la mano.

Charlie parpadeó y luego, moviéndose con más lentitud de la habitual, se la estrechó.

—Sinclair. —La mirada de Charlie pasó del caballero a ella, pero Sarah no pudo leer la expresión en sus ojos. Llevaba puesta su habitual máscara impasible.

—La condesa ha sido muy amable haciéndome compañía hasta que llegases. —Sinclair blandió los papeles—. He traído esos informes que querías ver.

Charlie bajó la mirada hasta los papeles. Tras un instante, asintió con la cabeza.

—Excelente. —Miró a Sarah—. Si nos disculpas, cariño, estaremos en la biblioteca.

«Por supuesto.» Con su nuevo propósito en mente, ella se obligó a sonreír.

—Ordenaré que os lleven el almuerzo allí —dijo.

Charlie no estaba seguro de qué responder a eso.

—Gracias.

Con un gesto de cabeza y una reverencia, los dos hombres se alejaron de ella. Sarah los observó dirigirse hacia la terraza y desaparecer en la biblioteca.

Se permitió el placer de esbozar un mohín de disgusto. La mirada de la joven cayó sobre uno de los rosales más antiguos, un tronco nudoso tan grueso como su brazo. Pensó en la extraña reacción de Charlie al verla con Sinclair, y revivió de nuevo aquella breve impresión.

¿Se había sentido celoso?

¿Sería ésa la razón por la que había adoptado una actitud tan rígida y amenazadora? Había sido sólo un instante, hasta que Sinclair le había dicho por qué estaba allí... recordándole sutilmente a su marido que no tenía pensado seducir a su esposa.

Sarah entrecerró los ojos y aguzó la mirada que tenía clavada en el rosal. Observó unas leves protuberancias, las primeras señales de brotes que más adelante formarían nuevas ramas.

Quizá su matrimonio fuera como aquel rosal inerte, que, con la cantidad adecuada de luz, volvería a llenarse de rosas. No había dudas de que, con la atención suficiente, florecería. ¿Quizás era eso lo que acababa de vislumbrar en su marido? ¿El primer indicio de un brote? ¿Una señal de que, sin importar la imagen que él se esforzaba por proyectar, ella podía salir victoriosa y conseguir todo lo que quería?

Mantuvo los ojos clavados en el rosal durante algunos minutos más, luego se volvió y se encaminó hacia la casa.

No perdía la esperanza de tener el matrimonio que quería.

Charlie tardó unos minutos en perder la rigidez y dejar de tener erizado el pelo de la nuca. Sólo podía agradecer que Malcolm no hubiera dado indicios de haberse percatado de ello, aunque, por supuesto, tendría que haberlo hecho. No le gustaba la idea de haber reaccionado como un hombre primitivo, revelando cuánto le había molestado ver a Malcolm al lado de Sarah. Tan rápido como había surgido, apartó ese pensamiento de su mente.

Condujo a Malcolm a la biblioteca y tomaron asiento para echar un vistazo a los informes de los inversores que Malcolm había llevado. Hicieron una pausa en la conversación, cuando Crisp apareció con dos bandejas llenas de comida, y continuaron discutiendo sobre el flujo de fondos en varios proyectos mientras daban cuenta de unas rebanadas de pan con fiambre y rosbif frío.

Después de que un lacayo retirara las bandejas del escritorio, Sinclair extendió los informes sobre la ancha superficie para examinarlos.

Charlie se había reclinado en la silla y escuchaba la explicación de Malcolm sobre los fondos que se habían utilizado para hacer operativa la línea entre Liverpool y Manchester, cuando Crisp entró inesperadamente con una bandejita de plata.

—Ha llegado un abogado de Taunton para verle, milord. Le he informado de que estaba ocupado, pero ha solicitado que le entregue su tarjeta y le diga que tiene una propuesta de negocios para usted.

Crisp le ofreció la bandeja. Charlie recogió la tarjeta.

—Thomas Riley, de Riley y Ferguson, abogados, con despacho en la calle Mayor de Taunton. —Levantando la mirada, arqueó las cejas en dirección a Malcolm—. Confieso que no tengo ni idea de qué se trata. ¿Te importa si lo hago pasar?

—Por supuesto que no. —Y Malcolm hizo ademán de levantarse.

Charlie le indicó con la mano que no se moviera.

—Quédate, por favor. Al menos hasta que sepa de qué va el asunto. —Miró a Crisp—. Haz pasar al señor Riley.

Riley resultó ser un típico abogado de provincias. Modesto y con tendencia a hablar en voz baja, se expresaba con frases complejas.

Charlie interrumpió su larga presentación y lo invitó a coger una silla y a sentarse. Malcolm se había retirado hasta una de las ventanas y miraba los jardines de fuera.

—Bien, señor Riley. —Charlie se inclinó hacia delante, apoyando los codos en el escritorio y entrelazando las manos—. Le agradecería que me dijera cuál es el motivo por el que ha venido a verme.

Riley, que vestía de manera descuidada con un polvoriento traje oscuro, tragó saliva.

—Por supuesto, milord. Soy consciente de que...

—¿Podría ir al grano, señor Riley?

—Ah, tengo un cliente que desea hacerle una oferta por unas tierras de su propiedad. —Riley metió la mano en la desgastada cartera de piel que balanceaba sobre las rodillas y extrajo un fajo de papeles, junto con un binóculo que se puso sobre la nariz. Repasó los documentos y luego miró a Charlie—. Es la propiedad Quilley, en las afueras de Crowcombe.

Charlie no disimuló su sorpresa.

Riley continuó de una manera apresurada.

—Mi cliente desea agregar la granja Quilley a las innumerables propiedades que posee en la zona y, dado que la granja está muy alejada del resto de sus tierras, esperaba que estuviera dispuesto a considerar su oferta.

La curiosidad llevó a Charlie a preguntarse cuál era la oferta y quién la hacía, pero en cualquier caso eso carecía de importancia. Se reclinó en la silla.

—Lo siento, señor Riley, pero no puedo vender esa propiedad.

Riley abrió mucho los ojos, como quien teme ver volatizarse sus honorarios.

—Pero mi cliente está dispuesto a ser más que razonable...

—No es por eso —lo interrumpió Charlie. No había razón para prolongar la visita del abogado; de hecho estaba impaciente por continuar su debate con Malcolm—. No puedo vender esa propiedad por la sencilla razón de que no es mía. Señor Riley, me temo que le han informado mal.

—Pero... —las dilatadas pupilas de Riley le hacían parecer una ardilla. Una ardilla consternada— la granja pertenecía a la señorita Conningham, y ella se ha casado con usted.

—Cierto. —Charlie hizo una breve pausa para que el abogado captara su tono duro y desalentador—. La señorita Conningham se ha convertido en mi condesa y la propiedad de la granja ha pasado a mis manos. Aun así, ya no dispongo de ella.

Los labios de Riley formaron una O de sorpresa que resultó casi cómica.

Charlie caviló si decirle o no quién era ahora la dueña de la granja Quilley, pero Sarah era su esposa y era su deber protegerla de la innecesaria presión de otros abogados como Riley y de su cliente, quienquiera que fuera éste. No ganaba nada hablándole a Sarah de Riley. Charlie conocía cuál sería su respuesta a cualquier oferta de compra por la granja Quilley.

—Bueno... quizás usted podría decirme quién es el nuevo dueño de la granja.

Charlie negó con la cabeza.

—Pero sí que puede decirle a su cliente que el nuevo propietario no necesita fondos, y por consiguiente es improbable que quiera vender esas tierras sin importar el dinero que le den por ellas.

Riley pareció desinflarse. Su expresión se tornó sombría mientras guardaba sus documentos en la cartera. Luego se levantó, le hizo una reverencia a Charlie y se despidió. Crisp, que había permanecido al lado de la puerta, lo acompañó fuera de la estancia.

—Interesante. —Malcolm se giró para observar al abogado marcharse. Regresó a su silla frente al escritorio y arqueó las cejas—. La venta de la granja ha sido muy rápida. No sabía que el orfanato tenía un nuevo dueño.

Charlie hizo una mueca.

—No tan rápida como crees, porque la verdad es que ni siquiera ha cambiado de manos. El título de propiedad sigue siendo de Sarah mediante los acuerdos matrimoniales. —Se encogió de hombros—. Siente un profundo interés por el orfanato.

Quizá debería haber presionado a Riley para saber quién era su cliente, aunque estaba seguro de que el abogado no le habría revelado el nombre. Pero...

«Mi cliente desea agregar la granja Quilley a las innumerables propiedades que posee en la zona.»

—Sospecho que su cliente será uno de los agricultores de la zona —pensó en voz alta, antes de asentir con la cabeza—. Supongo que a cualquiera de ellos le gustaría hacerse con la propiedad.

—Es posible. —Inclinándose hacia delante, Malcolm cogió uno de los informes financieros que había traído—. ¿Por dónde íbamos?

—Por la estructura financiera que está detrás de los fondos otorgados a la línea entre Liverpool y Manchester.

—La granja ha vuelto a manos de la condesa, así que es ella con quien tenemos que hablar.

—¿Todavía quiere la propiedad?

—Oh, sí. Claro que sí. Es una de las mejores que haya encontrado nunca.

—Si ése es el caso, seguiré en ello.

—Por supuesto. Pero debes ser discreto, puedo esperar.

Hubo unos segundos de silencio.

—¿Por qué? —preguntó perplejo más que desafiante.

La respuesta requirió un momento de reflexión, y aun así, resultó claramente renuente.

—Porque ahora existe una leve tensión entre los condes. No por culpa de ella, que parece estar muy... triste.

—Es posible que ahora sea más receptiva a la venta, ¿no?

—No... Lo más probable es que se aferre a lo que ya conoce. Algo que es suyo. Sin embargo, el conde no es precisamente tonto. Estoy seguro de que, con algo de tiempo, recobrará la cordura. En cuanto lo haga, el humor de la condesa mejorará, se distraerá con otras cosas y... sí, no cabe duda. Aceptará vender entonces.

Transcurrió otro minuto.

—¿Está diciéndome que espere a que el conde vuelva a hacer feliz a la condesa?

Una risa sorda inundó la estancia.

—Oh, no. Puede que aprecie la perspicacia del conde, pero no pienso someter mis planes a su antojo. Puedes proceder cuando quieras, pero, como ya te he dicho, debes ser precavido y tener paciencia. De una manera u otra, la granja Quilley será nuestra a su debido tiempo.

Sarah siguió tenazmente con su plan. Si se comportaba como si el amor fluyera entre ellos y se negaba a vacilar, sin importar la actitud formal y distante de Charlie, entonces finalmente, con el tiempo, él tendría que admitir que estar rodeado por su amor era demasiado gratificante para negarlo.

Dada la obstinación de Charlie, tal plan era como utilizar agua para picar piedra, pero con perseverancia esperaba salir victoriosa.

El domingo, cuando salió de la iglesia del brazo de su marido, Sarah se felicitó para sus adentros por su creíble interpretación de una mujer enamorada; una que sentía tanta confianza en sí misma que había superado el escrutinio de Clary y Gloria, e incluso el de Twitters, que obviamente era una romántica empedernida, cuando Charlie la informó de que Malcolm Sinclair iría a visitarlos después del almuerzo. Otra vez.

Sarah contuvo un ácido comentario al recordar sus planes.

—El señor Sinclair parece un caballero interesante —dijo arqueando las cejas.

Por el rabillo del ojo, Sarah vio que su marido fruncía el ceño; una pequeña victoria. Por el momento, sólo había conseguido pequeñas victorias como ésa, pero sabía ser paciente.

Resignada a pasar la tarde sola cuando, después del almuerzo, Charlie se fue a la biblioteca para estudiar algunos documentos con Sinclair, Sarah se retiró a su salita.

Fuera hacía frío. La joven miró por las ventanas y luego se paseó por la estancia. Quería seguir adelante con su campaña, pero en ese momento no podía hacer nada más.

Con un suspiro de frustración, se sentó en el sofá y cogió la cesta de ropa para remendar que había traído del orfanato. El personal hacía todo lo que podía, y Twitters solía ayudarla. En ocasiones incluso lograba convencer a Clary y a Gloria para que echaran una mano, pero aun así siempre había mucha ropa que zurcir.

Se había puesto a la tarea cuando oyó pasos en el pasillo. Como siempre, había dejado las puertas abiertas. Levantó la vista justo cuando el señor Sinclair echó un vistazo dentro. Evidentemente iba camino de la biblioteca, pero al verla se detuvo y entró, sonriendo, a saludarla.

Devolviéndole la sonrisa, Sarah le tendió la mano. Sinclair no tenía la culpa de que Charlie lo utilizara como escudo, y no había nada en sus modales ni en su persona que provocara la desaprobación de la joven.

—Buenas tardes, señor. Por favor, perdone que no me levante, pero como puede ver estoy atrapada.

Bajó la manta que estaba zurciendo.

Sinclair se inclinó sobre su mano, pero cuando se enderezó se fijó en la manta. Ella casi podía oír su muda pregunta de por qué la condesa de Meredith zurcía una manta vieja.

—Es del orfanato —le explicó—. Ayudo en lo que puedo.

—Ah. —Se le aclaró la expresión. Echó un breve vistazo a su alrededor, observando la estancia—. Ha conseguido darle a este lugar un toque muy acogedor.

—Gracias.

Sinclair miró de nuevo la cesta de ropa para zurcir.

—Había escuchado que estaba involucrada con el orfanato. —Indicó con la cabeza un sillón cercano. Intrigada, Sarah le invitó a sentarse.

Tras hundirse con gracia en el sillón, continuó:

—He visto la granja Quilley; en realidad puedo verla desde mi casa. Como ya sabe, pienso establecerme en esta zona. Jamás he vivido fuera de Londres y... bueno, he pensado que, si me intereso por algo como el orfanato, sería una buena manera de pasar algunas horas y establecer contacto con la gente de la localidad.

Si no hubiera añadido eso último, Sarah habría sospechado que intentaba coquetear con ella, pero, por el contrario, sólo vio sinceridad en sus ojos.

Sinclair se inclinó hacia delante con atención.

—¿Podría contarme algo sobre el lugar?

Sarah sonrió y le complació. Las palabras acudieron con facilidad a sus labios. Como en otras ocasiones, siempre era un placer hablar de la institución que su madrina había establecido.

Pero sabía que era mejor no explayarse sobre ese tema demasiado tiempo.

—Dado el número de fábricas que surgen en Taunton y el incremento del tráfico de mercancías, por mucho que deseemos lo contrario, lo más probable es que haya muchos más niños huérfanos a raíz de distintos accidentes y tragedias —concluyó.

Sinclair, que la había estado escuchando con atención, asintió con la cabeza.

—Ya veo. —Sonrió brevemente, como disponiéndose a hacer una confidencia—. Estaba presente cuando su señoría rechazó la oferta por el orfanato el viernes. Ahora sé por qué dijo que usted nunca estaría interesada en vender.

Sarah parpadeó. La sangre se le heló en las venas.

—¿Oferta? ¿Vender el orfanato?

Sinclair clavó sus ojos en los de ella. Con rapidez, casi con incredulidad, buscó una salida. Un leve rubor le tiñó las pálidas mejillas.

—Lo siento... Había asumido que su marido le habría mencionado el tema.

Sarah sintió cómo se le endurecían los rasgos y restó importancia a las palabras avergonzadas de Sinclair con un gesto de la mano.

—No es necesario que se disculpe.

Sinclair se levantó.

—No obstante, espero que me perdone.

El tono de su voz —como si estuviera irritado, pero no con ella— hizo que guardara silencio mientras lo observaba.

Él le sostuvo la mirada por un segundo, luego bajó los párpados ocultando sus ojos color avellana y se despidió con una inclinación de cabeza.

—Si me disculpa, tengo que reunirme con Meredith en la biblioteca. Creo que me está esperando.

—Por supuesto —convino Sarah, en un tono menos rudo de lo que podría haber sido. No era culpa de Sinclair que ella se sintiera así.

Sin embargo, poco podía hacer con su expresión. Su cara parecía de piedra cuando le despidió con un gesto de la cabeza. Sinclair se dio la vuelta y se fue. Ella lo observó desaparecer en el pasillo.

El ruido de pasos se desvaneció, luego oyó cerrarse una puerta.

Sarah se quedó inmóvil durante un minuto, luego cogió la manta de su regazo y continuó con su labor.

No quería pensar en nada más hasta que se enfriara su temperamento.

Hasta un soltero empedernido como Sinclair sabía que Charlie debería habérselo contado.

Hora y media después, Sarah cruzó el césped hacia los caminos pavimentados de la rosaleda. Caminaba a paso vivo con los brazos alrededor del cuerpo. Apretaba con fuerza la mandíbula para que no le castañearan los dientes, pero el frío que sentía en los huesos no tenía nada que ver con el clima.

¿Cómo podía entablar batalla con él, rebatir aquellas estúpidas ideas, cuando Charlie continuaba apartándola de él? ¿Cuando incluso se negaba a hablar con ella de los temas que la concernían y prefería levantar un muro entre los dos, una pared que cada día era más alta, gruesa y sólida?

Por lo menos, Charlie había rechazado la oferta. En eso, ciertamente, había cumplido su promesa.

Pero cumplir lo prometido con respecto a su matrimonio, a su amor, era otro tema muy distinto. Simplemente se negaba a hacerlo.

Aunque Sarah había logrado tranquilizarse un poco, apenas podía contener los gritos de frustración.

Caminaba con paso furioso de un lado a otro del camino. Los rosales a punto de florecer ya no la distraían como lo había hecho antes. En ese momento su mente no estaba de humor para buscar alentadoras analogías. Hoy estaba tan absorta y fría que se sentía como un carámbano.

Se sentía increíblemente sola.

Se había criado bajo el cuidado de Twitters y rodeada de cuatro hermanas. Rara era la ocasión en que había pasado un momento a solas. Pero ahora que vivía en su nuevo hogar con su marido, la joven sentía, por primera vez en su vida, el pellizco de la soledad.

Se sentía vacía.

Conteniendo un escalofrío, Sarah se dio la vuelta y se encaminó hacia la casa. Escuchó un leve sonido y levantó la mirada.

Vio a Sinclair en la terraza. Charlie estaba despidiéndose de él desde la puertaventana de la biblioteca. Sinclair se había quedado menos tiempo que en otras ocasiones. Incluso a esa distancia, la joven detectó una cierta rigidez en la postura de Charlie, en cómo inclinaba la cabeza para despedirse de Sinclair. Sarah no podía verle la expresión, pero parecía que su marido no estaba precisamente contento.

Sinclair se giró y recorrió la terraza, pasando ante la salita de Sarah en dirección a los establos. Charlie se retiró y cerró la puertaventana.

Sinclair caminaba a buen paso hasta que la vio. Se detuvo vacilante en medio de la terraza, volviendo la mirada hacia las ventanas de la biblioteca; luego bajó con rapidez las escaleras y se encaminó hacia ella.

Sorprendida, Sarah se detuvo y lo esperó. Sinclair, al igual que Charlie, tenía una expresión normalmente ilegible. Era raro que su rostro mostrara algún indicio de sus pensamientos y, mucho menos, de sus sentimientos; pero ella ya estaba acostumbrada a tratar con Charlie. Se había vuelto toda una experta en buscar pequeños indicios.

Cuando el inversor se reunió con ella, la joven no pudo evitar quedarse perpleja. Él parecía estar conteniendo una intensa irritación.

—Lady Meredith. Quería informarla de que, después de mi metedura de pata con usted, me sentí impulsado a mencionarle mi indiscreción a su señoría.

Sarah arqueó las cejas. No se lo había esperado.

—Aunque él parece haber reaccionado de manera indiferente, yo... —Sinclair hizo una pausa y cogió aliento. Apretó aún más los labios—. En resumen, su falta de consideración al no haberla informado de la oferta recibida por el orfanato me ha decepcionado.

Con brusquedad, Sinclair clavó los ojos en la cara de Sarah. Su afilada mirada avellana buscó la de ella. La joven intentó descifrar la emoción que teñía los ojos y la voz del hombre, y se sorprendió al descubrir que era preocupación.

Una preocupación absolutamente genuina.

—Me he dado cuenta, querida, de que no tengo experiencia en tales asuntos. Siempre he vivido solo. —El tono de su voz parecía ahora más tranquilo, pero no dejaba de tener un cierto aire sombrío—. No es mi intención meterme en lo que no me importa, pero he notado que existen algunas tiranteces entre Charlie y usted. Puede que sea algo normal dado que se han casado hace poco, pero en cualquier caso le ruego que me disculpe si de alguna manera he contribuido a tal tensión. Le aseguro que no era mi intención.

Ella le sostuvo la mirada y saboreó la sinceridad de sus palabras, luego asintió con la cabeza.

—Gracias. —Sarah vaciló, luego miró por encima del hombro de Sinclair hacia la casa—. Sería inapropiado añadir nada más, pero le agradezco sinceramente su preocupación.

Ninguno de los dos se movió durante un momento.

—Él... se parece mucho a mí —dijo entonces Sinclair en tono más suave y tranquilo—. En muchos aspectos me recuerda a una versión más joven de mí mismo, cuando comenzó mi fascinación por las finanzas y las inversiones.

Ella le miró. Sinclair tenía los ojos fijos en la biblioteca. Curvó los labios en un gesto de pesar.

—Como ya le he mencionado, he vivido toda mi vida solo. Lo suficiente para desear, por el bien de su señoría, que recobre la cordura. —Volvió a mirarla directamente a los ojos—. Que se dé cuenta de la suerte que tiene de estar casado con usted.

A Sarah le sorprendió que le hubiera hecho un comentario tan personal; aquello excedía sin duda los límites de una conversación educada.

Pero antes de que pudiera recobrarse lo suficiente para responder, él le hizo una reverencia.

—Adiós, mi querida condesa. Le deseo lo mejor. Hasta que volvamos a vernos.

Dicho eso, se dio la vuelta y atravesó el césped con grandes zancadas. Al llegar a la terraza, subió las escaleras y se dirigió a los establos.

Con una extraña sensación de consuelo, Sarah volvió a rodearse con los brazos. Le dio la espalda a la casa y se encaminó a lo más profundo del jardín.

Habiéndose sentido reconfortada por el inesperado apoyo de Sinclair, consideró entrar y desafiar a su marido, pero si ella se había dado cuenta de la desaprobación del inversor, Charlie también lo habría hecho. Por su rígida despedida de Sinclair resultaba evidente que no estaba de buen humor para hablar de ese asunto y mucho menos con ella.

Con la mirada perdida en el camino que se extendía ante ella, Sarah esbozó una mueca. Puede que Sinclair hubiera tenido buenas intenciones, pero Charlie era Charlie, masculino, arrogante y, probablemente, tan inflexible como el acero si le presionaban. No creía que aguijonearle en ese momento fuera algo bueno para su causa.

La sensación de soledad de Sarah y aquel vacío, que se habían visto aligerados por el inesperado apoyo de Sinclair, volvieron a caer sobre sus hombros. Un escalofrío demasiado intenso para contenerlo la hizo mirar a su alrededor. La soledad volvió a atraparla con más fuerza y emprendió el camino a casa.

Regresó a su salita a través de la terraza. Acababa de cerrar la puertaventana mientras el día languidecía cuando apareció Crisp con una vela que ahuyentó la penumbra reinante.

El mayordomo también llevaba una bandejita.

—Ha recibido una nota, milady —le dijo.

Sarah cogió el papel doblado.

—Gracias, Crisp. —La abrió, leyó con rapidez las líneas escritas y frunció el ceño.

—¿Algún problema, milady?

La pregunta de Crisp la sacó de su ensimismamiento. Miró al mayordomo.

—En realidad no estoy segura. —Volvió a mirar la nota—. La señora Carter me ha escrito diciéndome que anoche hubo un extraño suceso en el orfanato, pero no explica qué ocurrió. —Observó la nota y se obligó a esbozar una sonrisa despreocupada—. Dice que me contará los detalles cuando vaya allí mañana y, dado que la señora Carter no pide mi ayuda, sospecho que sólo me ha enviado la nota para mantenerme informada.

—Sin duda, milady. Como debe ser.

Tardó un momento en comprender la última frase de Crisp. Lo miró, pero con su habitual máscara de impasibilidad, el mayordomo se dispuso a encender las velas que Sarah había colocado por toda la estancia, así que no podía ver la expresión de sus ojos.

El mayordomo se inclinó para encender la lámpara de la mesa auxiliar. En cuanto prendió la mecha y la ajustó, se volvió hacia ella y le hizo una reverencia. Luego se enderezó y habló mirando algún punto por encima de la cabeza de Sarah.

—La señora Figgs y yo… Bueno, nos hemos dado cuenta de que, por una u otra razón, no hemos tenido tiempo de recibirla de la manera en que se recibe tradicionalmente a una nueva condesa en el Park. Sé que presentarle al personal habría sido una redundancia, pues usted ya nos conoce a todos. Sin embargo… —Crisp se irguió en toda su estatura— la señora Figgs y yo, y el resto del personal, queremos transmitirle nuestra más cariñosa bienvenida y la esperanza de poder servirla fielmente durante muchos años.

Sarah tuvo que parpadear para contener las lágrimas.

—Gracias, Crisp. —Con voz suave, añadió—: Por favor, transmite mi agradecimiento a la señora Figgs y al resto del personal por sus deseos y su buena voluntad de servirnos.

—Eso haré, milady. —Crisp hizo una profunda reverencia, giró sobre sus talones y se marchó.

Sarah tomó una gran bocanada de aire, luego se hundió en la *chaise*. Ahí tenía una segunda e inesperada declaración de apoyo. Recordó que Crisp llevaba días lanzándole miradas de preocupación, igual que Figgs. ¿Habrían detectado lo mismo que Sinclair? Sí, podían palpar la tensión entre Charlie y ella.

Debería haber sospechado que el personal se daría cuenta, pero parecía que ellos también se habían puesto de su parte. Que también apreciaban lo que ella le ofrecía a Charlie, la promesa de amor y el poder que llevaba implícito.

Parecía que el único que no lo hacía era Charlie.

Su primer impulso fue coger el toro por los cuernos, pero conocía a su marido demasiado bien. Insistir no serviría a sus propósitos, no esa tarde.

Apretó los puños. La nota de Katy crujió entre sus dedos atrayendo su mirada hacia ella. Era enigmática y preocupante, pero Katy era una mujer experimentada y competente. De haber necesitado su ayuda esa noche, se la habría pedido.

Al día siguiente era lunes. Como siempre, Sarah cabalgaría hasta el orfanato. Pensaba pasar allí el día entero.

Mejor ir allí que quedarse sola en casa.

El reloj dio la hora. Sarah lo miró y se levantó; se dirigió al escritorio. Había adquirido la costumbre de dejar la tapa bajada. Después de todo, aquella era su salita privada. Dobló la nota y la puso en el casillero donde guardaba todos los papeles relacionados con el orfanato. Volvió a mirar a su alrededor y luego con un suspiro se dirigió a las escaleras. Sin duda, tomar un largo baño caliente la ayudaría.

El diario de tía Edith había desaparecido.

Algo más tarde, Sarah estaba ante el escritorio abierto con la mirada fija en el hueco vacío donde había estado el diario. Después de una cena silenciosa, algo que se había convertido en una costumbre entre ellos, su marido la había acompañado a la salita. Charlie se había acomodado en el sillón junto a la chimenea y parecía absorto en alguna clase de texto sobre ingeniería. Cansada de zurcir y bordar, Sarah había decidido leer un poco más las divertidas observaciones de su tía, algunas incluso podrían serle de utilidad. Pero no había nada en el lugar donde había guardado el diario. Rebuscó por los casilleros del escritorio, pero no había ningún volumen con cubiertas plateadas.

—Pero... —frunció el ceño y pasó los dedos por el hueco vacío— sé que lo dejé aquí.

Lo había puesto allí el día que habían llevado sus pertenencias a la salita y no lo había vuelto a coger desde entonces.

—¿Cómo demonios ha desaparecido?

¿Y dónde podía estar? Puede que las criadas lo hubieran cambiado de lugar. Buscó en los cajones del escritorio, pero no encontró nada; luego echó un vistazo a su alrededor y se acercó a la mesita auxiliar. El pequeño cajón contenía velas, pero ningún diario.

Rebuscó por toda la estancia, en todos los lugares donde podía haberlo puesto. Cada vez más frenética, no pudo negar la creciente convicción de que el diario no iba a aparecer, de que se lo habían robado. Durante la última semana Sarah había dejado con frecuencia la puertaventana de la terraza abierta. Pero aquella era la casa de un conde, y no era fácil que alguien pudiera entrar en ella.

Percatándose de los movimientos de Sarah, Charlie levantó la mirada. Ella sintió los ojos de su esposo fijos en ella, pero no se giró para mirarle. Aunque su agitación era más que evidente notó que él vacilaba, que en realidad debatía consigo mismo si debía preguntarle o no, pero al final lo hizo.

—¿Qué pasa?

De espaldas a él, Sarah apretó los labios durante un segundo para contener la rabia y las palabras airadas que tenía en la punta de la lengua; luego habló con calma.

—El diario de mi tía Edith. Lo dejé en el escritorio, pero ya no está —dijo, con algo parecido a la desesperación tiñendo su voz.

De repente, Sarah quiso que la envolviera entre sus brazos, que la abrazara y le dijera que todo iría bien. Sintió que Charlie se tensaba como si fuera a ponerse en pie y acercarse a ella, pero luego vaciló. Cuando ella le miró, vio que volvía a colocarse el libro en las rodillas.

—Sin duda lo habrás perdido. —Las palabras sonaron despectivas y distantes. Ni siquiera se molestó en mirarla, sino que retomó la lectura.

Por un momento, Sarah se lo quedó mirando aturdida y perpleja por la bofetada emocional.

Luego respiró hondo, apretó los dientes y se dio la vuelta. «¡No es cierto!», le gritó mentalmente, pero se negó a dar rienda suelta a la furia... se negó a rebajarse de esa manera. Por el momento.

Se aferró a lo que consideraba más importante, y volvió a sentir la convicción interior de que el diario había desaparecido de verdad. Pensó en cómo podía haber sucedido. Volvió a respirar hondo e, ignorando a Charlie por completo, se dirigió con fría calma hacia el cordón de la campanilla que colgaba al lado de la repisa de la chimenea.

Tiró con fuerza y luego esperó con las manos entrelazadas.

Crisp respondió a la llamada. Llegó con una bandeja con una tetera de plata y un juego de tazas de porcelana china. Al ver la postura que había adoptado Sarah, dejó con rapidez la bandeja en la mesita auxiliar junto a la *chaise* y se acercó a ella.

—¿Sí, milady?

Con la cabeza erguida, Sarah buscó su mirada.

—Dejé el diario de mi tía en el escritorio, Crisp, pero no está allí.

Crisp miró hacia el escritorio con el ceño fruncido.

—¿Uno con cubiertas plateadas, milady? Mandy, la criada que quita el polvo me habló de él.

—Es un diseño inusual, probablemente único. —Sarah hizo una pausa, luego, retorciendo los dedos mientras intentaba contener con todas sus fuerzas sus revueltas emociones, dijo—: Quería mucho a mi tía, y le tengo muchísimo cariño a ese diario... es un recuerdo de ella. ¿Podrías preguntarle al servicio si lo han visto en algún otro lugar de la casa?

La mirada de Crisp se desvió hacia la puertaventana, luego a Charlie, que seguía enfrascado en su libro, aparentemente ajeno al tema. Cuando volvió a mirar a Sarah, su simpatía era evidente.

—Por supuesto, milady. Lo buscaremos. Le preguntaré a Mandy cuándo fue la última vez que vio el libro. Creo que anteayer quitó el polvo de esta sala.

Su resuelta respuesta proporcionó a Sarah un poco de alivio. Al menos no tardaría en saber si habían cambiado el diario de lugar. Asintió con la cabeza.

—Gracias, Crisp. Por favor, mantenme informada de lo que te diga Mandy, y pregúntale si el diario seguía en el mismo lugar la última vez que estuvo aquí.

—Por supuesto, señora. —Tras lanzarle otra rápida mirada a Charlie, que seguía con la mirada impertérrita en el libro, hizo una reverencia y se fue.

Los ojos de Sarah cayeron sobre la tetera. Después de un rato, se acercó a la mesa auxiliar sin mirar a Charlie y se sirvió una taza. Su marido jamás tomaba té a esa hora si podía evitarlo. Cogiendo la taza y el platito de la bandeja, se sentó con cuidado y tomó un sorbo; luego centró su atención en la cesta de ropa para zurcir.

Siguiendo un impulso, cogió la cesta y rebuscó entre las mantas, sábanas y toallas, pero no había ningún libro con cubiertas plateadas entre las telas.

Esa noche, Sarah apagó de un soplo la vela que tenía en la mesilla al lado de la cama. Se acurrucó bajo las mantas y tiró de la colcha para cubrirse los hombros. Entonces intentó relajarse. Intentó dormirse, pero con tanta rabia y dolor acumulados en su interior, supo que pasarían horas antes de lograr calmarse.

Charlie. ¿Qué iba a hacer con él? No había dejado de notar la instintiva respuesta de su marido a su desasosiego, igual que había percibido su deliberada contención. Sí, la amaba, pero lo negaba... ¡se lo negaba a sí mismo! Se negaba a demostrarle ese amor.

Sarah habría dejado pasar su comportamiento, lo habría ignorado como otro ejemplo más de su terca actitud, de lo que podía esperar de él mientras no se rindiera y dejara de negar su amor, pero es que era el diario de tía Edith lo que había perdido.

Sarah sentía esa pérdida como una herida en el corazón. Edith había sido mucho más que su tía. Había sido alguien muy especial, alguien que la había comprendido, que le había enseñado muchas cosas, que había compartido con ella su sabiduría y sus consejos. Había sido Edith quien había educado su mente y le había abierto los ojos a la vida... y al amor.

Sus errantes pensamientos se detuvieron en ese punto. Si no hubiera sido por Edith y sus profundas reflexiones, ¿se habría casado con Charlie? ¿O habría seguido el mismo camino de su madre y sus hermanas mayores, aceptando una unión sencilla que no exigiera nada por su parte?

Curvó los labios ante la ironía.

Fuera, el viento rugía, como una criatura famélica que descargara su furia contra los enormes árboles, sacudiendo las ramas unas contra otras y golpeando las ventanas con fuerza.

Sarah se estremeció, se acurrucó más bajo las mantas y cerró los ojos. Trató de no pensar en la opresión que sentía en el pecho. Igual que el clima inclemente, la vida parecía haberse vuelto inesperadamente cruel.

Se dijo a sí misma que aquello pasaría, que la tormenta desaparecería y que muy pronto volvería a brillar la luz del sol. Pero con el corazón ya herido, la inesperada pérdida del diario sólo había conseguido profundizar aún más la herida. Oyó cómo se abría la puerta y los pasos de Charlie al entrar en la habitación. Se quedó inmóvil, fingiéndose dormida.

Diez minutos después la cama se hundió a sus espaldas y su marido se acostó a su lado bajo las mantas. Sarah mantuvo los miembros relajados y la respiración lenta y regular mientras intentaba contener la rabia que amenazaba con abrumarla.

Como se atreviera a abrazarla, como intentara tocarla, comenzaría a pegarle.

Charlie se limitó a apoyarse sobre un codo y a observarla. Sarah podía sentir el peso de su mirada. El silencio se alargó, siguiendo el ritmo marcado por el lento tictac del reloj de la repisa de la chimenea.

Luego él cambió de posición y se apartó, tendiéndose de espaldas. Sarah creyó oírle suspirar. Entonces comenzó a respirar de manera más profunda y regular y la joven estuvo segura de que se había quedado dormido.

Bufando mentalmente, se prometió hacer lo mismo.

Con la mirada fija en el dosel en penumbra Charlie se preguntaba qué diablos iba a hacer. Sabía que ella no estaba dormida, pero tal y como estaban las cosas entre ellos —con aquel duro y frío silencio envolviendo la cama— se sentía impotente para cambiar la situación. Incapaz de actuar, inseguro de cómo proceder.

Vulnerable.

Quería consolarla, pero ya no sabía cómo hacerlo.

O, quizá, ya no estaba seguro de tener derecho a eso.

Y, a pesar de todo, cada uno de sus instintos, los mismos instintos que había tenido que contener y mantener a raya en la salita cuando se había dado cuenta de la consternación de Sarah, los mismos instintos que le habían retorcido las entrañas cuando Sinclair había mencionado la oferta por el orfanato —un tema que él había esperado sacar a colación esa tarde— le instaban a abrazarla y aliviar cualquier daño que su error hubiera podido causarle, pero, una vez más, no sabía cómo hacerlo, no después de haber contenido y combatido con furia esos impulsos primitivos. Ese tenso control que insistía en mantener fuera de esa habitación y que, ahora, tenía que mantener también dentro.

Charlie quería aflojar las riendas de ese control, al menos allí, en la segura oscuridad de su lecho, pero ya no estaba seguro de si sería prudente hacerlo.

Jamás se había sentido tan desgarrado en toda su vida, tan roto y vapuleado, como si una parte primitiva de él, una parte esencial, hubiera declarado la guerra a su parte racional, a esos rasgos más precavidos que le impulsaban a protegerse y que definían los patrones de su comportamiento y que le decían que no debía dejarse llevar por los instintos sino por el intelecto.

No veía una salida. No había ningún medio, ningún camino, ninguna medida que tomar que pusiera fin a ese conflicto de una manera aceptable.

No para ella.

Ni para él.

Sabía que a Sarah no le gustaba su actitud, que de ningún modo aprobaba la decisión que él había tomado, su forma de encarar su vida matrimonial. Pero no veía otra alternativa. Si encontrara una, la aceptaría.

Porque a él ya no le gustaba, ni aprobaba —ni ciertamente disfrutaba— lo que estaba ocurriendo entre ellos. En su camino había surgido un pantano de dolor que había emponzoñado sus vidas.

15

La conciencia de Sarah se abrió paso entre los velos del sueño, despertando su mente. La joven se resistía a volver a la realidad. Puede que hubiera amanecido, pero aún era temprano y se encontraba tan cómoda y abrigada en la cama con la mejilla descansando sobre una piel firme y elástica, sobre un montículo de duros músculos cubiertos por un ligero vello rizado y acunada por un par de brazos fuertes que...

Abrió los ojos de golpe y respiró lenta y profundamente. Estaba tumbada de manera desgarbada sobre Charlie, que la envolvía con firmeza entre sus brazos. Su marido estaba tendido de espaldas totalmente desnudo. A ella se le había subido el fino camisón de seda hasta la cintura; tenía las piernas desnudas y enredadas con las de él bajo las mantas.

Una mirada a su lado de la cama le confirmó que eso no había sido obra de Charlie, sino de ella, pues él ni siquiera se había movido.

Sarah maldijo para sus adentros. Por la respiración lenta y regular de su marido, Sarah pensó que todavía estaba dormido, pero a juzgar por la tenue luz matutina que entraba en la habitación, la joven supuso que no tardaría mucho en despertarse, si no lo había hecho ya.

Sarah cogió aire lentamente y, conteniendo la respiración, intentó apartarse de sus brazos.

Charlie se tensó.

—No. —Pasaron un par de segundos—. Déjame abrazarte.

El tono de su voz la hizo parpadear. Ése no era el Charlie arrogante que conocía, sino un Charlie vulnerable, un ser con el que no se había tropezado antes. No podía verle la cara sin tener que apartarle el brazo y alzar la cabeza y, por la fuerza con que la sujetaba, tendría que forcejear con él si quería liberarse de su abrazo, algo que, estaba segura, no consentiría. No antes de que se hubiera puesto la máscara de impasibilidad. Con curiosidad, se permitió relajar los músculos, hundiéndose sobre el cuerpo de su marido, esperando con los sentidos encendidos.

Él movió la cabeza y presionó los labios contra su pelo.

—Lamento lo del diario de tu tía. La querías mucho, ¿verdad?

Ella se miró la mano que descansaba al lado de su cara, con los dedos extendidos sobre el pecho de Charlie; sobre su corazón.

—Sí. —Él no dijo nada más, como si esperara a que ella continuara hablando, así que añadió—: Era muy especial para mí y ese libro es el único recuerdo que tengo de ella. Sólo había leído las primeras páginas... Empieza en enero de 1816, por lo que supongo que cubre todo ese año. No solía escribir en el diario todos los días, sólo cuando tenía algo que contar. La entrada que leí describía una fiesta en la mansión de lord Wragg, y a continuación una receta de carne con membrillo que había conseguido sonsacar al ama de llaves de Wragg.

—La vida diaria. Las grandes y pequeñas cosas de cada día.

Ella asintió con la cabeza, frotando la mejilla contra su pecho; se sentía reconfortada por la simple cercanía. Por ese momento de intimidad.

—Tenía intención de leerlo cuando tuviera tiempo... O cuando estuviera de humor. —En ese momento, la mente de Sarah estaba demasiado ocupada en sus pensamientos como para prestar atención a nada más. Suspiró—. Pero ahora ha desaparecido y ya nunca podré hacerlo... Nunca volveré a sentirla cerca de mí. Tengo la sensación de haber perdido el último vínculo que tenía con ella.

Nunca más, se dijo, se sentiría conectada con el alma de su tía a través de esas páginas.

—Eso no es cierto. —El tono de Charlie era suave y tranquilizador. Volvió a rozarle el pelo con los labios—. Tú la querías y ella te quería a ti... El diario era sólo un símbolo de eso, pero el amor permanece. Eso no lo has perdido. ¿No es ése el verdadero vínculo?

Sarah parpadeó. Qué ironía que él, tan empeñado en ignorar su amor por ella, pudiera ver eso y expresarlo con las palabras adecuadas.

Apretó los labios. Si de algo le había hablado Edith era de personas y emociones, de símbolos, palabras y acciones. Y de todo eso, eran las acciones las que hablaban con más claridad, las que más importancia tenían.

Sarah presionó la palma de la mano contra el pecho de Charlie para poder alzar la cabeza y mirarle. Lo suficiente como para buscar su mirada y ver si hablaba con sinceridad o no.

Y pudo confirmar que la vulnerabilidad que había percibido en él era real. Que aquello por lo que había estado luchando, lo que existía entre ellos, no se había perdido. Que sin importar cuánto lo intentaran, ni ella ni él podían evitarlo.

Retorciéndose para liberar sus brazos, alargó las manos y le enmarcó la cara.

—Sí. Tienes razón. —Estudió los ojos azules de su marido durante un instante más y luego alzó el rostro y le besó.

Con toda la pasión contenida en su alma. No tenía intención de guardarse nada, ni de intentarlo siquiera. Sabía lo que sentía por él y lo que él sentía por ella. Ese conocimiento guiaba sus acciones, cada lánguido barrido de su lengua contra la de él, cada provocativo movimiento mientras se alzaba sobre el cuerpo de su marido para compartir mejor el beso, para dar rienda suelta a su amor e incitar y disfrutar del suyo.

Charlie respondió como ella sabía que lo haría y, si bien a cierto nivel, Sarah se complacía de la respuesta de su marido, de su incapacidad de resistirse a ella y a su amor, también apreciaba cada sutil matiz, cada prueba de su deseo, cada chispa de deleite que sintió cuando le rodeó la cintura con las manos, la alzó y la tendió sobre su cuerpo, atrayendo sus pechos hacia su boca para darle placer.

Hasta que ella dobló las piernas y apoyó las rodillas en la cama a ambos lados de él, sentándose a horcajadas sobre sus caderas. Metió la mano entre sus cuerpos y la deslizó hacia abajo, encontrándole duro y preparado, ardiente y pesado en su mano. El camisón había caído sobre sus caderas, y los dedos de Charlie abandonaron sus pechos para agarrar y levantar el fino tejido, y colarse debajo. Charlie deslizó las manos por los muslos desnudos de su esposa y las curvó sobre sus nalgas. Sarah interrumpió el beso y, apoyando una mano sobre su pecho, levantó las caderas para guiar con la otra mano el rígido miembro de su marido hacia la entrada de su cuerpo.

Lo sintió allí, el engrosado glande le acariciaba la carne con una patente promesa, y se estremeció de anticipación. Con los ojos entrecerrados, Sarah observó la cara de Charlie, su mirada ardiente, mientras se levantaba un poco más y, lentamente, saboreando cada cálido y duro centímetro, se empalaba en su miembro, llenando su cuerpo y sus sentidos con él.

El deseo voraz que se reflejaba en el rostro de Charlie le decía a Sarah todo lo que necesitaba saber. La fuerza casi temblorosa con que la sostenía, controlando sus movimientos, permitiéndole que se moviera, dejándola llevar el control y escribir el guión de esa escena como ella deseaba, era prueba suficiente de su compromiso de amor.

Sarah se inclinó hacia delante mientras entrecerraba los ojos, apoyando ambas manos sobre su pecho, comenzando a montarle. Quería saborearlo por completo, disfrutar de cada pizca de súplica que sabía que vería en su mirada, y darle todo el placer a cambio. Cerró los párpados. Sus sensaciones eran cada vez más intensas mientras se concentraba en la resbaladiza penetración, en la extraña pero bienvenida posesión, en el repetitivo movimiento de su cuerpo sobre el suyo, el rítmico vaivén de sus muslos sobre los de él. La floreciente, creciente y abrumadora intensidad de esa unión.

Charlie había llevado de nuevo las manos a sus pechos, acariciándolos sensualmente, masajeándolos, pellizcando sus pezones hasta convertirlos en brotes tensos. Entonces le abrió el camisón y se irguió bajo ella. Sarah contuvo el aliento cuando la cálida boca de su marido se cerró sobre un dolorido pezón al tiempo que sus experimentados dedos atendían las súplicas del otro, haciendo que ramalazos de placer la recorrieran de los pies a la cabeza, seguidos de oleadas de ardiente deleite que inundaban y atravesaban su cuerpo. Su vientre.

Durante un buen rato, Sarah lo montó con la cabeza echada hacia atrás, dejándose llevar por las sensaciones, dejando que sus vertiginosos sentidos le llenaran la mente. Abrumada por el deleite sensual, por la conciencia de su cuerpo y el intenso placer, más ardiente de lo que había sido nunca, Sarah se contuvo.

Charlie soltó un gruñido, un sonido gutural que despertó una conciencia diferente. Un instante más tarde, incluso antes de que Sarah pudiera abrir los ojos, él rodó, llevándola consigo, envolviéndoles a ambos en una confusión de mantas. Enredados en la cama, Charlie la inmovilizó bajo su cuerpo y empujó con fuerza y dureza. Sarah se arqueó y lanzó un grito. Cuando él embistió de nuevo, incluso con más fuerza aún, ella cogió aire con desesperación. Entonces lo rodeó con sus brazos, levantó las piernas y le envolvió las caderas con ellas, arañándole la espalda con las uñas mientras se unía a él con la misma frenética urgencia con la que él la montaba.

Duro, rápido, desesperado por llegar al clímax, dispuesto a dar lo que fuera por llegar al punto culminante.

Estaban allí, jadeando, deseando, luchando por alcanzar el éxtasis.

Y de repente, éste cayó sobre ellos, envolviéndolos y haciéndolos pedazos. Finalmente, con un profundo gemido gutural, se dejaron llevar por el placer.

Se perdieron en él.

Luego, sonriendo tontamente, mareados por el deleite, riéndose suavemente, se derrumbaron uno en los brazos del otro y se dejaron mecer por el momento.

Casi una hora después, Sarah bajó a toda velocidad la escalinata principal, vestida con su traje de montar se dirigió al comedor del desayuno con la esperanza de pillar a Charlie antes de que se fuera. Su marido y la resistencia que oponía al amor eran agotadores. Había llegado el momento de presionar un poco más, y Sarah ya sabía cómo hacerlo.

Le pediría su ayuda. Charlie siempre respondía cuando alguien le pedía ayuda; era una parte intrínseca e inherente a su naturaleza. Si había algún problema en el orfanato, ¿a quién mejor que él podía recurrir?

Correr por los pasillos con la cola del traje de montar recogida sobre el brazo no era propio de una dama, pero se apresuró tanto como pudo y abrió la puerta del comedor justo cuando él dejaba a un lado la servilleta y se levantaba de la mesa.

Charlie iba con retraso. Saber que él se había quedado más tiempo de lo normal en la cama para abrazarla y consolarla por la pérdida del diario —y para hacerle el amor— le levantaba el ánimo. Con una brillante sonrisa, Sarah lo esperó en el pasillo junto a la puerta del comedor. Charlie respondió a esa sonrisa con su habitual conducta fría, pero Sarah no creía que él hubiera olvidado el motivo por el cual se había retrasado.

—Esperaba que pudieras venir conmigo al orfanato. —Alzando la cabeza, lo miró directamente a los ojos—. Al parecer ha ocurrido algo allí y, aunque no sé cuál es el problema que ha habido, agradecería muchísimo tu opinión.

En la máscara inexpresiva que cubría el rostro de Charlie no había nada de las cálidas sonrisas que habían compartido tan sólo una hora antes.

—No creo que sea acertado.

Sarah parpadeó. Oh, no, no, no... no volverían a eso. No permitiría que mostrara esa fría actitud distante hacia todo lo que tenía que ver con ella. Respiró hondo.

—Charlie...

—Querida, creo que no comprendes la situación.

Su tono la detuvo en seco. Ahora estaba hablando el conde, no Charlie, su marido, el hombre que la amaba aunque no deseara reconocerlo. Y el señor feudal estaba acostumbrado a que lo obedecieran sin titubear.

Charlie continuó hablando con calma, con la voz dura y fría como el acero.

—No estoy interesado en el orfanato. Es tuyo y como tal no va a formar parte de mi vida ni de mis responsabilidades. —Sostuvo la mirada de Sarah, que no pudo ver en sus ojos el suave azul del verano—. No quiero tener ninguna relación con él. No la he tenido en el pasado y desde luego no pienso tenerla en el futuro. —Charlie hizo una pausa, luego añadió suavemente—: Espero que haya quedado claro.

El temperamento de Sarah estalló. Una fría furia se deslizó por sus venas. Alzó la cabeza.

—Clarísimo. —Le sostuvo la mirada, permitiendo que él viera la rabia que sentía.

Sarah se estremecía por la necesidad de dar media vuelta y marcharse para evitar decir algo que lamentaría más tarde, pero esta vez no pensaba ceder tan fácilmente. No pensaba dejarle escapar.

—Lo entiendo perfectamente —dijo, tras tomar aire, en un tono más frío que el de su marido—. Sin embargo, había pensado... —Sus pensamientos la ahogaban; se interrumpió y luego continuó con una voz todavía más helada—: Espero que recuerdes que cuando acepté casarme contigo insistí en que quería un matrimonio apasionado. Y si no recuerdo mal, tu respuesta fue que no veías ningún impedimento a eso. Y yo, como una tonta, te creí. Sinceramente pensé que nuestro matrimonio sería algo más que un cascarón vacío.

Él le sostuvo la mirada, parpadeó una vez y luego tensó la mandíbula todavía más.

Sarah percibió el esfuerzo que le costaba a Charlie mantener ese rígido control. La joven se estremeció deseando añadir algo más, pero había recuperado el suficiente sentido común como para recordarse a sí misma cuál era su plan... su objetivo final.

Apretando los labios, giró sobre los talones y se alejó lentamente con paso regio.

Charlie la observó marcharse y, por primera vez en su vida, comprendió lo que era tener el corazón roto. Le dolía el pecho como si una espada se lo hubiera partido en dos. Se sentía perdido. Se dio cuenta de que Sarah se dirigía a los establos y su única preocupación fue que su esposa no había desayunado y que tenía que comer algo antes de salir a cabalgar, pero ¿qué podía hacer? ¿Llamarla y ordenarle que tomara algo?

Sencillamente, parecía haber renunciado a su derecho de cuidar de ella, o al menos eso era lo que su esposa pensaba.

Oyó ruido de platos a su espalda y comprendió que Crisp estaba en el comedor del desayuno y que sin duda habría oído la discusión. Forzó a sus piernas a que lo llevaran a la biblioteca, abrió la puerta y se encerró allí.

Se vio rodeado por una comodidad familiar, pero eso no alivió sus heridas internas. Sentía como si le hubieran arrancado el corazón del pecho. Sabía —se lo había dicho a sí mismo durante la hora anterior y todas las horas previas a ésta— que tenía que poner orden en su vida para que todo funcionara como debía... Pero una parte fuerte y fundamental de su interior se negaba a aceptarlo. Se negaba a pasar por ello.

Se negaba a que Sarah pasara por ello.

Se detuvo ante los grandes ventanales y miró fuera. Había sabido que ella tenía unas expectativas del matrimonio diferentes a las suyas (expectativas que él había considerado femeninas y floridas).

Pero lo que no había sospechado cuando le dijo a Sarah que no veía ningún impedimento a que su matrimonio fuera apasionado —que estaba preparado para proporcionarle una unión apasionada—, era que para ella eso quería decir una unión donde el amor era libre y abiertamente reconocido.

Charlie lo comprendía ahora. Entonces, cuando ella había hablado de excitación, emociones, riesgos y satisfacción, él había pensado que se refería a la pasión sexual.

Pero incluso aunque él hubiera comprendido el significado de sus palabras por completo —¿y cómo podría haberlo hecho cuando él no sabía en ese momento qué era el amor?—, incluso así, se habría casado con ella. Porque por aquel entonces él ya sabía que Sarah era suya, su esposa, la mujer que quería que fuera su condesa.

Y todavía lo era. Nada había cambiado en ese aspecto. De hecho, su convicción era todavía más fuerte. Su compromiso hacia su esposa era más intenso cada día; sólo había que ver lo difícil que le había resultado contener sus sentimientos por ella durante esos dos últimos días. Esas emociones que sólo ella provocaba eran cada vez más fuertes y poderosas, casi ingobernables.

Pero antes que a ella, se debía al condado. Desde muy pequeño, le habían enseñado que su deber estaba por encima de sus necesidades. Pero ¿qué ocurriría con los votos que había hecho en el altar de la iglesia de Combe Florey?

«Honrar y querer.» O lo que para la mayoría significaba amar y proteger. Por un lado, él había hecho ese voto de mala fe, pues nunca había tenido intención de cumplir con la primera parte. Pero sin tener en cuenta eso, la segunda parte era una promesa que no podía mantener, pero que a su vez era incapaz de incumplir. No podía evitar amarla y, ciertamente, no podía evitar el impulso de protegerla. Antes de casarse con ella, no había comprendido cómo se sentiría y, ahora que era suya, amarla y protegerla eran unos instintos fundamentales que no podía contener de la misma manera que no podía detener el sol.

Soltó un doloroso suspiro de frustración y echó la cabeza hacia atrás mientras clavaba los ojos en el techo pintado. Esa mañana, tras las horas que habían pasado en la cama, se había endurecido para repeler cualquier nuevo esfuerzo que ella hiciera, figuradamente hablando, cuando abriera la puerta del dormitorio y buscara amor en sus encuentros cotidianos. Había sospechado que ella había creído ver, en esas horas que habían pasado juntos, la prueba de que su determinación por mantener una distancia prudencial entre ellos se había debilitado, y así había sido.

Pero el orfanato... De todas las cosas con las que podría haberle abordado, Sarah había escogido ésa. El corazón de Charlie había dado un brinco deseando aceptar la invitación e ir con ella, para encargarse del pequeño problema que había surgido en el orfanato, para verla de nuevo con los niños, para integrarse en el grupo. Pero jamás podría volver a encerrarse en sí mismo si estaba cerca de su esposa en momentos como ése sintiendo lo que sentía por ella.

El esfuerzo por rechazarla —por negar su otro yo— casi lo había matado. Se sentía como si en realidad fuera dos hombres, que Sarah y todo lo que sentía por ella se habían abierto paso en su corazón, en su mente y en su alma, y lo habían dividido en dos. Y sus dos mitades estaban ahora en lucha continua.

No podía seguir así. Dejando a un lado todo lo demás, el equilibrio entre esas dos mitades era variable. La parte que quería el amor de Sarah haría cualquier cosa por entregarle todo a cambio de poseerlo. Pero Charlie ya no sabía qué era lo mejor... por qué debería luchar, qué mitad debería triunfar. Ni siquiera sabía qué mitad quería que ganara.

No podía recordar haberse sentido nunca de esa manera, y no podía recurrir a nadie para pedirle consejo. Estaba perdido.

A la deriva.

Como un náufrago en el mar.

Cuando Sarah llegó al orfanato había logrado controlar su temperamento a base de esfuerzo, junto con todos los sentimientos encontrados que la actitud de Charlie había provocado. Pero las noticias que la aguardaban eran tan extrañas que arrancaron cualquier otro pensamiento de su mente.

—¿¡Fantasmas!?—Sentada en la mesa entre Skeggs y la señora Dunstable, Sarah clavó los ojos en Katy, que hizo una mueca.

—Eso es lo que los niños dijeron. Muchos de ellos lo oyeron y lo vieron, tanto la noche del sábado como la del domingo.

—¿Qué oyeron y vieron? —preguntó Skeggs.

—Gemidos y el rechinar de cadenas. Algunos de los mayores se atrevieron a asomarse. Y dicen que vieron algo blanco y ondulante.

—Lo más probable es que sean los muchachos del pueblo —dijo la señora Dunstable—, con unas cadenas viejas y una sábana.

Katy asintió con la cabeza.

—Sí, eso fue lo que sospeché. Pero los más pequeños tienen miedo, y algunos de ellos no pueden dormir. A otros les da miedo acostarse, pobrecitos, sólo se sienten seguros cuando ya ha amanecido y están con los demás.

—Es una molestia. —Skeggs frunció el ceño—. La pregunta es cómo resolver el problema.

Lo que no era nada fácil. Sarah dejó que los demás discutieran sobre quién creían que podía estar detrás de todo eso para cantarle las cuarenta, mientras ella pensaba en los muchachos del pueblo que conocía y cómo podría desalentarlos.

Cuando los demás concluyeron que no se podría hacer nada sin saber qué muchachos —de Watchet, Taunton, Crowcombe o cualquiera de los pueblos que se extendían por las colinas— estaban involucrados, Sarah golpeó ligeramente la mesa.

—Tengo una idea —dijo, y a continuación expuso su plan.

Katy sonrió ampliamente. Skeggs se rio entre dientes. La señora Dunstable asintió con la cabeza.

—Muy ingenioso, querida. Es casi como ponerle el cascabel al gato.

Tan pronto como dieron por finalizada la reunión, y Skeggs y la señora Dunstable se marcharon, Sarah llamó a Kennett y, junto con Katy, rodearon la casa estudiando las áreas donde el «fantasma» había sido visto, examinando las localizaciones más cercanas a la casa y los árboles y arbustos que había cerca.

Finalmente, Kennett dio un paso atrás y se rascó la cabeza pensativo.

—Sí, creo que funcionará. Un hilo de pescar sería lo más conveniente, y tenemos suficientes cencerros en el cobertizo. Jim y yo nos encargaremos de ello. Si ese tipo regresa esta noche, se llevará una buena sorpresa.

Sarah sonrió. Katy y ella dejaron a Kennett enfrascado en la tarea y se encaminaron de regreso a la casa. Una vez dentro, Sarah se vio engullida por el alboroto de siempre. Estuvo ocupada todo el tiempo, y el almuerzo y la tarde pasaron con rapidez.

Charlie llegó a Finley House a última hora de la tarde. Se había pasado el día tratando de encontrar algo que le distrajera de la helada sensación que se le había alojado en el pecho. Dada la rigidez con la que había concluido su último encuentro, visitar a Sinclair era su último recurso.

Pero los negocios siempre habían sido un interés común y Malcolm le dio la bienvenida sin mostrar ninguna señal de tensión. Se sentaron en su estudio y se enfrascaron en la lectura de los últimos boletines informativos, leyendo los diversos anuncios de negocios. Pero ni siquiera eso tenía el poder de reprimir la inquietud de Charlie. Mientras Malcolm seguía leyendo, dejó a un lado el boletín que había estado estudiando, se puso en pie y se acercó a la ventana.

Al menos el estudio daba a los Quantocks y no a Crowcombe y al orfanato.

Oyó a su espalda el crujido del papel cuando Malcolm dejó a un lado el boletín que había estado examinando con detenimiento. Charlie sintió la mirada de Malcolm en su espalda.

—¿Cómo está la condesa? —le preguntó Sinclair finalmente.

Charlie logró no ponerse rígido. La pregunta había sido planteada en un tono inseguro y cauteloso, como si Malcolm supiera que pisaba terreno peligroso pero aun así se viera impelido a preguntar.

Charlie iba a encogerse de hombros, pero se detuvo. Metiéndose las manos en los bolsillos de los pantalones, clavó la mirada en el paisaje.

—Está bien, pero ha desaparecido un diario que poseía. Un recuerdo de una tía. Le ha afectado mucho, pero yo no puedo hacer nada al respecto. —Aunque deseaba poder hacerlo. Le molestaba la sensación de impotencia, le tocaba una fibra sensible—. Esta mañana ella quería que la acompañase al orfanato... ¡Como si me sobrara el tiempo!

El silencio se extendió entre ellos.

—Quizá sea porque es recién casada y todo eso. Tal vez si pasaras algún tiempo con ella podrías solucionarlo... aunque, por supuesto, no sé mucho de esto. Sin embargo, parece que es así como son las cosas.

Una vez más Sinclair había hablado con precaución, escogiendo las palabras, vigilando su tono. Charlie hizo una mueca.

—Sarah y yo nos conocemos de toda la vida. No necesitamos conocernos el uno al otro de la manera en que necesitan hacerlo otras parejas.

Una vez más se hizo un largo silencio entre ellos, y entonces Malcolm carraspeó y murmuró:

—Puede que tengas razón, pero me refería a lo que todos sabemos que ocurre muy a menudo, cuando una joven atractiva como tu condesa no recibe la atención adecuada de su marido.

Charlie no se movió. No pudo hacerlo. Necesitó hasta el último gramo de su considerable fuerza de voluntad para contener su violenta e instintiva reacción ante el panorama que Malcolm le pintaba. Se dijo a sí mismo que Sarah jamás haría algo parecido a lo que Sinclair sugería.

Pero recordó la cautela que tenía el tono de Malcolm. Había intentado decirle lo que cualquier amigo le habría dicho, lo que el propio Charlie diría si...

Sacándose las manos de los bolsillos, miró a Sinclair.

—Será mejor que me vaya. Pronto anochecerá.

La expresión de Malcolm era tan inescrutable como la suya. Se levantó y lo acompañó a la puerta principal. Se estrecharon la mano y luego Charlie se dirigió con grandes zancadas hacia donde había atado a *Tormenta*. Soltó las riendas y se subió a la silla de montar. Se despidió de Malcolm con un brusco gesto de cabeza y se giró hacia el camino.

Atravesó al trote las calles de Crowcombe. Reuniendo toda su fuerza de voluntad, mantuvo la mirada apartada del orfanato, que se encaramaba en lo alto del pueblo. Aun así, no pudo evitar preguntarse si Sarah ya habría regresado a casa. En cualquier caso, ella iría campo a través. En cuanto dejó atrás las últimas casas de Crowcombe, puso a *Tormenta* al galope. Quería llegar a casa y asegurarse de que Sarah estaba de vuelta, sana y salva, bajo su protección otra vez.

Al día siguiente, Sarah regresó al orfanato para saber si alguien había caído en su trampa durante la noche. Así había sido. Poco antes de la medianoche, habrían repicado los cencerros. Kennett, Jim y Joseph habían salido a toda prisa, pero lo único que habían visto era una figura vestida de blanco que huía campo a través hacia el norte. Luego la habían visto subir de un salto al caballo que la aguardaba y alejarse al galope.

Los niños se sintieron aliviados y felices. Eran muchos los que habían visto cómo el fantasma daba media vuelta y huía. La mayoría veía ahora el incidente como un espectáculo hilarante. No habría más noches en vela.

Después de montar a *Blacktail*, Sarah se dirigió hacia el Park antes de permitir que su mente se concentrara en lo que la esperaba allí. No era feliz, pero las horas pasadas en el orfanato, tanto el día anterior como esa misma jornada, habían calmado su espíritu. El hecho de que la hubiesen necesitado, de que hubiesen agradecido su ayuda y de que el plan que había ideado hubiese tenido éxito, había sido un bálsamo para su alma herida.

Al llegar al Park, entró en los establos; dejó a *Blacktail* con el mozo de cuadra y se dirigió a la casa pensando que había algo en aquel incidente que no encajaba. Habían pensado que los culpables serían los muchachos del pueblo, pero cuando le había preguntado a Kennett, a Jim y, más tarde, a Joseph, le habían descrito la figura de un hombre. Un varón adulto, corpulento y grueso... y no precisamente joven.

¿Por qué un hombre hecho y derecho se dedicaría a rondar el orfanato haciéndose pasar por un fantasma?

Los demás se habían encogido de hombros. Kennett había sugerido que el hombre podía estar «mal de la chaveta». Pero Sarah no lo creía así. La sábana, las cadenas, la sigilosa manera de acercarse a medianoche... todo sugería un plan, lo que no era propio de aquellos que están mal de la cabeza.

Aún seguía desconcertada cuando entró en la casa y se dirigió a la salita. Se quitó los guantes e hizo sonar la campanilla para que le llevaran el té. Lo hicieron de inmediato. Para su inmensa sorpresa, Charlie venía con él.

Ante la mirada fija y aturdida de su esposa, él se sentó en el sillón que ocupaba todas las noches y cogió una taza.

303

Sarah tomó su propia taza de té y el platito y se sentó en la *chaise*. Tomó un sorbo y miró a su marido inquisitivamente.

El lacayo se retiró. Charlie dejó su taza en el platito.

—¿Cómo va todo en el orfanato? —le preguntó sin mirarla.

«Ajá.» A pesar de todo, se sintió tentada a contarle la historia del fantasma, y saber qué pensaba él de que el intruso hubiera resultado ser un hombre en vez de un muchacho, pero las palabras que Charlie le había dicho la mañana anterior todavía le resonaban en la cabeza. Todavía le dolían.

—Bien —respondió clavando los ojos en la taza y encogiéndose de hombros.

Sarah tomó otro sorbo, luego apuró el té de golpe. Dejó la taza a un lado y cogió la cesta de ropa para zurcir. Encontró otra manta con un agujero y la puso sobre su regazo para dedicarse a la tarea.

Charlie la miraba. Sarah podía sentir sus ojos clavados en ella. Pasó un minuto, luego él se terminó su té. Se levantó y dejó la taza y el platito en la bandeja sin decirle nada más.

Con la cabeza inclinada sobre su labor, Sarah escuchó cómo se desvanecían los pasos de su marido en el pasillo. Luego le oyó abrir la puerta de la biblioteca y cerrarla un segundo después.

La mañana del sábado, Sarah acababa de organizar los menús de la semana con Figgs cuando Crisp entró en la salita con una bandejita de plata.

—Ha llegado esta nota del orfanato, milady. El joven Jim está esperando por si usted desea enviar una respuesta.

Sarah cogió la nota, conteniendo un ceño y un instintivo «Oh, ¿y ahora qué pasa?».

Una rápida ojeada a las escuetas líneas que Katy había escrito le confirmó que su instinto no se había equivocado.

—¡Dios mío!

—¿Algún problema, milady?

Sarah levantó la mirada hacia la expresión preocupada de Crisp, que parecía dispuesto a ofrecerle su ayuda.

—Sí. Un canalla ha echado sal en el pozo del orfanato.

Podía pensar en otros nombres por los que llamarle, pero «canalla» tendría que bastar.

—Dios santo. —Crisp frunció el ceño—. Pero ¿por qué?

—Exacto. ¿Por qué? —Sarah dobló la nota y la deslizó en el bolsillo de su vestido—. Parece que alguien intenta causar problemas en el orfanato. Tendré que ir a ver qué ha sucedido. Por favor, dile a Jim que espere. Iré a ponerme mi traje de montar.

Crisp hizo una reverencia mientras ella salía de la estancia. Diez minutos más tarde, *Blacktail* seguía al corpulento jamelgo de Jim en dirección norte. Cuando llegaron al orfanato, Sarah ya había pensado cómo resolver el problema más inmediato.

—Haremos que Wilson traiga barriles de agua —le dijo a Katy mientras ataba las riendas de *Blacktail* en el poste que había frente a la puerta principal del orfanato. Wilson era el carretero de Crowcombe—. Iré a verlo de camino a mi casa. Le diré que también puede sacar agua del pozo del Manor, luego me pasaré por allí y hablaré con mis padres. Seguro que nos les importa ayudarnos; allí hay un montón de barriles, así que al menos tendremos agua para lo más imprescindible.

Katy asintió con la cabeza.

—Sí, como veas. Kennett dice que no es tan malo como podría haber sido, pero sí lo suficiente para perjudicarnos.

Sonriendo tranquilizadoramente a los niños con los que se cruzaban, Sarah siguió a Katy a través de la casa y en dirección al pozo inutilizado que había en la parte posterior del ala septentrional.

Kennett estaba allí parado, dirigiendo su mirada sombría a la boca negra del pozo. Levantó la vista cuando Sarah se reunió con él.

—Han vertido un saco de sal ahí dentro. ¿Lo ves? —Señaló un saco de yute que habían dejado a un lado—. El canalla lo dejó ahí para que lo encontráramos. —Le dio una patada al saco—. Por fortuna, aún hace mucho frío y sigue habiendo nieve en las colinas, con lo cual la capa freática ascenderá. En cuanto comience el deshielo, el nivel del agua subirá, y aunque el pozo sea profundo, habrá muchas filtraciones por los lados, ¿lo ve?

Kennett señaló el muro interior del pozo. Sarah vio que las piedras estaban de hecho mojadas, aunque el nivel del agua no había subido todavía.

—¿Quieres decir que la sal será arrastrada por la corriente subterránea?

—Poco a poco. El agua volverá a ser potable dentro de un mes o así.

Sarah contuvo un suspiro de alivio.

—Podremos arreglárnoslas hasta entonces. —Le explicó su idea de cómo suministrar agua potable desde el Manor.

Kennett asintió con la cabeza.

—Ésa es la fuente más cercana.

Y no tendrían que pagar por el agua. Sarah se encaminó hacia el orfanato.

—Voy a organizarlo todo de inmediato. En lo que respecta a quién ha hecho esto...

—Será el mismo idiota que espantamos la noche del lunes —dijo Kennett—. Seguro que no le gustó que lo pusiéramos en ridículo.

Katy asintió con la cabeza.

—Sí... seguro que fue eso. Ojo por ojo. De hecho, tras este incidente, se habrá acabado su sed de venganza. Dudo mucho que vuelva a molestarnos.

Sarah frunció el ceño. Deseó poder sentirse igual de optimista, pero echar sal a un pozo le parecía un acto de lo más ruin, no un simple incidente. Aunque ¿de qué podría tratarse?

Aquella pregunta le rondó la cabeza durante el resto de la mañana mientras organizaba el suministro de agua al orfanato. Pero cuando se dirigió a casa de sus padres para almorzar, había relegado esa preocupación a lo más profundo de su mente.

La mañana del lunes, Sarah se dirigió a caballo al orfanato y vio el tílburi del doctor Caliburn fuera. Ató a *Blacktail* y se dijo a sí misma que el doctor había ido allí por alguna de las habituales enfermedades infantiles o por uno de esos accidentes sin importancia que solían ocurrir cuando había muchos niños juntos.

—¿Qué ha ocurrido? —le preguntó a la primera persona que vio después de entrar.

Jeannie hizo una mueca.

—Es Quince —le dijo, intentando ocultar su preocupación a los niños que estaban cerca de ellas—. Será mejor que subas y lo veas.

Con los ojos muy abiertos ante la evidente preocupación de Jeannie, Sarah se apresuró a subir las escaleras.

Entró precipitadamente en el ático y se encontró al doctor Caliburn metiendo su instrumental en el maletín. Quince estaba sentada en un sillón con el brazo en cabestrillo.

Katy, al lado de Quince, levantó la mirada e hizo una mueca.

—Las escaleras estaban completamente heladas. Ese tunante ha debido acercarse por la noche para derramar agua sobre los escalones de atrás.

—Salí al amanecer como todos los días para traer la leche de los bebés. —Quince tenía la voz ronca—. Me resbalé. —Se señaló el brazo—. Me lo rompí al caer sobre el camino.

El doctor Caliburn cerró su maletín.

—Es una rotura limpia, pero tardará en sanar. No debe utilizar ese brazo hasta que esté totalmente curado.

Aunque sus palabras iban dirigidas a Quince, le lanzó una mirada significativa a Sarah. La joven se volvió hacia Quince.

—Tendrás que tomártelo con calma, Quince. Tienes que pensar en los bebés, necesitan que te cures pronto, y Lily podrá ser tus manos hasta que te recuperes.

—Sí, bueno, ya les ha dado el biberón esta mañana, y los durmió, pero hay más cosas que hacer, y que limpiar... la pobre chica no puede encargarse de todo.

—Contrataré a alguien del pueblo para que os ayude. Nos arreglaremos. —Intercambió una mirada con Katy antes de girarse y acompañar al doctor a la puerta—. Ahora vuelvo. Idearemos un plan para organizarnos.

El doctor Caliburn esperó a llegar a las escaleras antes de hablar.

—Debe tomárselo con calma. Ya no es joven, y los huesos viejos tardan más en sanar.

—¿Cómo está? —le preguntó Sarah mirándole fijamente.

—Yo diría que conmocionada, y bastante dolorida, aunque no ha querido tomar el láudano que le he sugerido. Me ha dicho que temía no poder despertarse cuando llorara cualquiera de los bebés que están a su cargo.

Sarah asintió con la cabeza.

—Ordenaré que lleven otra cama arriba para Lily, así Quince no tendrá que encargarse sola de los problemas que surjan por la noche.

—Bien. —Al llegar al final de las escaleras, Caliburn se inclinó sobre la mano de Sarah—. Si desean ayuda extra, podrían pedírsela a la señora Cothercombe. Es muy trabajadora y le gustan los niños.

—Gracias. Me pasaré por su casa y le preguntaré si puede echarnos una mano.

Sarah regresó lentamente al Park. Comenzaba a sentirse como un holandés intentando taponar las fugas de un dique. ¿Dónde tendrían la siguiente «fuga»?

Y lo que era más importante aún: ¿quién estaba detrás de todo eso? ¿Se trataba sólo de un simple deseo de venganza? ¿Había sido ése el último incidente o habría más?

Todas esas preguntas le dieron vueltas en la cabeza durante el resto del día.

Charlie no pudo evitar notar el ensimismamiento y la preocupación de Sarah. Pero no sabía qué era lo que la preocupaba. Ni siquiera sabía si estaba relacionado con el orfanato o con alguna otra cosa. Pero el impulso de ayudarla, de preguntarle e intentar arreglar las cosas, le carcomía.

Era, literalmente, como una bestia bajo su piel. No podía ignorarla.

Pero después de haberle dicho que ciertos aspectos de su vida no tenían interés para él —sin duda el comentario más estúpido que había hecho en su vida—, ¿cómo esperaba poder protegerla si no sabía lo que le estaba pasando? No podía hacer nada para aplacar aquella picazón ardiente e incesante. Ya no podía preguntarle sobre esos temas y esperar que le respondiera. Tenía que esperar a que ella se lo contara, si es que volvía a hacerlo.

Había mentido, pero ya no podía retirar las palabras más de lo que podía admitir la mentira. Si lo hacía, abriría las esclusas y no estaba seguro de poder controlar lo que sucedería.

Algo que Sarah le había demostrado repetidas veces era que el amor que había entre ellos era más fuerte que él. Más fuerte que su voluntad, lo suficientemente poderoso para socavar su determinación. Algo que podría hacer sin proponérselo siquiera, y él no podía arriesgarse a que lo controlase.

Así que, mientras caía la tarde, Charlie clavó los ojos en las páginas de su libro e intentó mantener la atención en él en vez de en su esposa, que estaba sentada en la *chaise* remendando una toalla rota con un profundo ceño grabado en su rostro.

El viernes por la mañana, Sarah estaba a punto de morderse las uñas por la ansiedad y la frustración que sentía, preguntándose si volvería a recibir otro mensaje del orfanato anunciando un nuevo desastre.

El miércoles llegaron noticias de que los cercados de los animales y el jardín habían sido destrozados y que el ganado de la granja había pisoteado durante la noche todo lo que habían plantado. Por fortuna, aún era invierno y, salvo algunos sembrados tempranos en el huerto de la cocina, no habían perdido más que coles, algo fácil de reemplazar.

No obstante, Sarah se había dirigido hacia el norte otra vez y se había pasado la mayor parte del día tranquilizando al personal y a los niños, ayudando a arreglar el huerto antes de volver a plantar y organizando con Kennett y Jim la reparación de los vallados.

Aquel gasto imprevisto no era su mayor preocupación. Lo que más le preocupaba era lo que ocurriría a continuación. Vallados y pozos eran una cosa, pero después de que Quince se hubiera roto el brazo, Sarah vivía con el temor constante de que alguien más resultara herido.

Se había pasado horas pensando qué hacer, si es que había algo más que se pudiera hacer. Había consultado con Skeggs y con la señora Duncliffe pero, al igual que ella, no creían que el oficial de policía de Watchet considerara importante ese tipo de «crímenes» ni que les ofreciera ninguna ayuda útil.

Sentada ante el escritorio, tamborileó con el lápiz sobre el papel secante e hizo una mueca. Esperar dócilmente el siguiente golpe no iba con su carácter.

Oyó el sonido de los pasos de Crisp antes de que apareciera en el umbral de la puerta. Llevaba la bandejita de plata, pero para gran alivio de la joven, no contenía una nota, sino una tarjeta de visita.

Crisp se acercó a ella, hizo una reverencia y le ofreció la tarjeta.

—Un abogado de Taunton solicita verla, milady.

Sarah cogió la tarjeta y leyó: «Señor Arnold Switherton, de Switherton y Babcock, abogados. Calle Este. Taunton.» Frunció el ceño. Durante los últimos días, Charlie había notado su preocupación y sus continuos viajes al orfanato y había desarrollado la costumbre de informarle de adónde iba cuando salía. Ese día había ido a visitar a Sinclair. Sarah no podía imaginar qué era lo que quería el señor Switherton. Miró a Crisp.

—¿Este caballero ha solicitado verme a mí o al conde?

—Ha solicitado verla específicamente a usted, milady.

Sarah enarcó las cejas y dejó la tarjeta sobre el escritorio.

—Hazlo pasar.

Crisp hizo una reverencia y se retiró.

La joven consideró levantarse, pero decidió quedarse sentada tras el escritorio. ¿Tendría que ver de nuevo con el orfanato? Pero se trataba de un abogado diferente, y también un bufete diferente.

El hombre al que Crisp condujo a la salita no se parecía al desventurado Haynes. El señor Arnold Switherton tenía una nariz afilada con anchos orificios nasales y su cara anodina mostraba una expresión de eterno disgusto. A Sarah le costó trabajo no sentir aversión hacia él, y su discurso de entrada no hizo nada para ganarse su simpatía.

—Condesa —dijo con una educada reverencia—, estoy aquí para presentarle una oferta por una propiedad cuyo título le pertenece. —Frunció el ceño—. Algo inusual, teniendo en cuenta su reciente matrimonio. Habría preferido hablar de este tema con su marido, sin embargo, me han informado de que es a usted a quien debo dirigirme.

Sarah no lo invitó a sentarse. Esperó, en silencio, mientras él rebuscaba en su cartera de piel y extraía un fajo de documentos.

El abogado los hojeó.

—Sí, está todo en orden. —Le tendió los documentos y ella los cogió.

»Como puede ver —Switherton señaló la parte superior de las hojas con el dedo—, la oferta es por la granja Quilley, casa y terrenos, y ésta es la suma que se ofrece. —Señaló un poco más abajo.

Sarah miró la suma, que había aumentado significativamente desde la oferta de Haynes. Siguió leyendo el resto de los documentos, ignorando el ceño fruncido del abogado. Después de leer la última página, levantó la mirada hacia él.

—¿Quién es su cliente?

—Ah... mi querida condesa, eso no es algo que necesite saber.

—¿De veras? —Su helado desprecio y la fría furia que había detrás hicieron parpadear a Switherton—. Yo no soy su querida, señor Switherton.

Él trago saliva e inclinó la cabeza a modo de disculpa, pero luego se irguió en toda su estatura.

—Mi cliente insiste en mantener un completo anonimato. Comprendo que usted, por supuesto, no tiene experiencia en tales materias, pero es una práctica habitual en la compra de tierras.

—No me sorprende. —Sarah ya había tenido suficiente del señor Switherton—. De todas maneras no tengo interés en vender la granja Quilley. Puede decírselo a su anónimo cliente. —Le tendió los documentos.

Switherton dio un paso atrás, negándose a cogerlos.

—Es una oferta muy generosa, lady Meredith. Le aconsejo que pida consejo a su marido antes de actuar con precipitación y arrepentirse luego. Estoy seguro de que el conde le verá sentido a sacar provecho del capricho de mi cliente al ofrecer una suma tan evidentemente absurda por tal propiedad. Nadie espera que las mujeres comprendan tales cuestiones... así que insisto en que deje este tema en manos de su marido. Él sabrá qué es lo más conveniente para usted.

Sarah dejó pasar un momento de absoluto silencio.

—Señor Switherton —dijo finalmente con voz queda—, si hay algo que me ha quedado realmente claro es que aún no ha comprendido el motivo por el cual el título de la granja Quilley ha quedado en mis manos. Y es para poder rechazar ofertas como ésta. —Le arrojó los documentos al abogado. El señor Switherton soltó una exclamación ahogada y los cogió en el aire, aplastándolos contra su pecho—. Además de evitarle a mi marido, el conde, tener que bregar con importunos abogados como usted. Mi negativa no es impulsiva, es deliberada. La granja Quilley es mía y seguirá siéndolo por razones que no le conciernen. Y eso no cambiará. Le aseguro que por lo único que lamento que el conde no esté aquí es para que le trate de la manera que se merece, algo que, ciertamente, no corresponde a una dama.

Sostuvo la mirada de Switherton durante un minuto cargado de tensión, luego dijo con serenidad:

—Crisp, acompaña al señor Switherton a la puerta.

—Por supuesto, milady. Por aquí, señor.

Sarah ocultó una sonrisa ante el tono de Crisp, uno que transmitía de manera inequívoca que, en ausencia del conde, Crisp estaría encantado de demostrar lo que ella estimaba que Switherton se merecía si éste le daba la más mínima excusa.

Ese pensamiento aplacó el temperamento de Sarah. Miró al escritorio, no tenía nada más que hacer allí. Se levantó y regresó a la *chaise*. Allí le esperaba la costura, como siempre, pero...

Estaba contemplando los jardines cuando Crisp regresó para informarla de la partida de Switherton y preguntarle si, en ausencia del conde y habiendo desayunado poco esa mañana, quería que le llevara el almuerzo allí.

—Gracias, Crisp. Sería maravilloso. —Sonrió cuando él se fue. Crisp y Figgs, y todo el personal, eran muy amables con ella. Atentos, pero no entrometidos. Habían aprendido sus rutinas y las aceptaban, en vez de imponerle las costumbres de la condesa viuda, Serena. Eso había hecho que ocupar la posición como condesa de Charlie fuera mucho más fácil.

Mientras daba cuenta del almuerzo estuvo pensando en todo lo que su posición conllevaba. Después de recuperar las fuerzas con la sucesión de sabrosos platos que le había preparado la cocinera —no había sido capaz de tomar más que té para desayunar durante las últimas semanas— decidió que dar un paseo por la rosaleda no le vendría mal.

Anduvo a lo largo de los caminos de adoquines, sin detenerse a mirar los pequeños brotes que comenzaban a surgir en los rosales. Había apartado de su mente la fastidiosa pregunta de a qué se debían los extraños incidentes en el orfanato y la había reemplazado por la visita de Switherton y su oferta. De repente, una idea horrible surgió en su cabeza y conectó ambas cosas.

—Santo Dios. —Se detuvo y clavó una mirada ciega en el césped. ¿Sería posible?

¿Y si realmente existía esa conexión? Y si después de haberse negado a aceptar aquella primera oferta... No, ya habían sido dos; después de casarse se habían acercado a Charlie con una oferta para comprar la granja, y poco tiempo después habían comenzado los accidentes en el orfanato. ¿Qué ocurriría si el comprador anónimo había decidido crear problemas en el orfanato para irritarla y exasperarla a ella, e incluso a Charlie, para ofrecer luego una oferta «evidentemente absurda» para animarla a lavarse las manos y vender?

No era posible. Se rodeó con los brazos. Su mente comenzaba a jugarle malas pasadas.

Pero una vez que había surgido la idea, no pudo hacerla desaparecer de la mente. Siguió caminando mientras reflexionaba sobre eso. ¿Podría haber una conexión tan atroz entre los accidentes del orfanato y las ofertas? ¿O se trataba sólo de una simple coincidencia? Alguien que no se hubiera informado bien sobre ella podría pensar que, tras unas semanas de feliz matrimonio, perdería el interés por su «pasatiempo» y que estaría dispuesta a vender.

No había, se dijo a sí misma, ninguna razón para vincular los accidentes en el orfanato con las ofertas por la granja.

16

Pero Sarah no pudo expulsar aquella posibilidad de su mente.
La tarde del sábado se dirigió de nuevo a la rosaleda. Era un lugar tranquilo y aislado, sin nadie que pudiera verla paseando de un lado para otro ni la oyera mascullar de vez en cuando. En su salita siempre cabía la posibilidad de que Charlie, Crisp o cualquiera de los lacayos o criadas que pasaban por allí la viera y se preocuparan por ella más de lo que ya lo estaban.

Desde que se le había ocurrido aquella horrible idea el día anterior, había estado distraída, inquieta, intentando convencerse a sí misma de que los accidentes y las ofertas de compra por el orfanato no estaban relacionados. Pero a pesar de todos sus esfuerzos, no había tenido éxito.

Por fin, se había dado por vencida y ahora trataba de decidir qué hacer... a quién podía recurrir para pedirle consejo. ¿A su padre? A pesar de conocerla bien, lo más probable es que pensara —como una parte de ella seguía haciendo— que estaba viendo fantasmas donde no los había y preocupándose sin razón alguna.

¿A Gabriel Cynster? Con su historial en los negocios sin duda aceptaría que algo así pudiera ocurrir, pero él no la conocía muy bien, y cuando le hablara de los accidentes y sus sospechas podría parecerle un poco histérica. Y, ciertamente, se preguntaría por qué hablaba con él y no con Charlie.

Con lo cual sólo había una conclusión y era contárselo todo a su marido. Si no lo había hecho antes era porque pensaba que podía encargarse ella sola del asunto del «fantasma». Desde entonces las cosas habían ido de mal en peor, pero Charlie no había vuelto a preguntarle al respecto, y sus palabras de que no estaba interesado en el orfanato todavía resonaban en la mente de la joven, todavía herían sus sentimientos. Así que Sarah había evitado decirle nada; aunque él sabía que había algo que la preocupaba, no sabía qué era.

Y quería saberlo. De hecho parecía atormentado por no saber qué pasaba.

Sarah hizo una mueca. Con los brazos cruzados, se dio la vuelta y desanduvo el camino. Si entraba en la biblioteca y le pedía su opinión sobre los problemas que habían surgido en el orfanato, tendría de inmediato toda la atención de su marido. Charlie no mencionaría sus anteriores palabras, ni tampoco las de ella. Todo sería terriblemente educado, pero también muy poco satisfactorio.

Aquello era una estupidez. En el dormitorio, no había barreras entre ellos —ni la cuidadosa cautela de Charlie ni la irritación de Sarah—, ninguno de los dos podía negar lo que sucedía allí dentro, no importaban cuáles fueran sus sentimientos, ni las reglas del amor... No importaba nada de eso en absoluto. Pero en cuanto abandonaban la habitación, se levantaba un muro entre ellos, y ella todavía no había encontrado la manera de sortearlo ni de atravesarlo.

Sarah quería derribarlo, sacudir sus cimientos hasta que cediera y se viniera abajo sin que fuera posible para Charlie volver a reconstruirlo. Todavía no sabía cómo lograrlo, pero darle una salida a la creciente actitud protectora de su marido sin que éste reconociera que tal proteccionismo estaba allí, dolorosamente presente, porque él la amaba, le parecía una mala idea. De esa manera nunca conseguiría avanzar en su relación.

Si ella hiciera tal cosa, él se daría cuenta y se aferraría a ello como prueba de que su plan —el impenetrable muro que levantaba cada día— podía funcionar. Y no podía hacerlo, no debía hacerlo, pero él era un hombre y casi tan terco como ella.

No obstante, si no buscaba la ayuda de su marido —ayuda que él debería y podría darle—, ¿qué ocurriría si ella tenía razón? ¿Si los accidentes y las ofertas por el orfanato estaban vinculados?

—¡Maldita sea! —Sarah se detuvo, debatiéndose entre su deber para con el personal y los niños del orfanato y tener que tragarse su orgullo e ir a pedirle ayuda a Charlie ya, ahora, antes de que ocurriera algo más, antes que alguien más resultara herido. Sí, pedirle ayuda perjudicaría sus objetivos personales, pero Sarah era terca, más terca que él incluso y, con el tiempo, conseguiría que Charlie cambiara de actitud.

Apretó los dientes y cogió aire mientras levantaba la cabeza para mirar hacia la biblioteca. Un movimiento en el otro extremo de la terraza, cerca de la salita, captó su atención.

Era Barnaby Adair, que venía de los establos.

Todo lo que ella había escuchado sobre Barnaby cruzó como un relámpago por su mente... Todo lo que Charlie le había dicho, todo lo que Jacqueline, Pris y los demás habían comentado de él. Las preguntas de Penelope. No se dio tiempo a cuestionar su juicio, simplemente le llamó y le hizo señas con las manos.

Él la oyó y luego la vio. Cuando Sarah se recogió las faldas y corrió hacia él atravesando el césped, Barnaby se detuvo y la esperó.

—Sarah. —Le tomó la mano que ella le ofrecía y se inclinó sobre ella.

Haciendo caso omiso de cualquier formalidad, la joven se aferró a su mano.

—Necesito tu opinión sobre un asunto... es algo urgente. ¿Puedes dedicarme unos minutos?

La aguda mirada de Barnaby buscó la de ella.

—Todos los que necesites.

Ella señaló su salita.

—Ven, sentémonos.

Al entrar, Sarah le indicó que tomara asiento en la *chaise*. Ella permaneció de pie delante de la chimenea. Se apretó las manos y cogiendo aire, dijo:

—Soy dueña de una granja, la granja Quilley, a las afueras de Crowcombe, hacia el norte. Sólo consta de una casa y algunos campos, no demasiado grandes, pero suficiente para un orfanato. —Con brevedad, le explicó que la había heredado de su madrina, luego continuó—: A principios del mes pasado, vino a verme al orfanato un abogado con una oferta de un cliente anónimo que quería comprarme la granja, y que yo rechacé. Las cosas parecieron quedarse ahí, pero más tarde, después de casarnos, Charlie recibió una oferta similar. Quienquiera que desee comprar la granja dio por sentado que el título le pertenecía a él en virtud de nuestro matrimonio, pero no es así. Lo recuperé inmediatamente por medio de los acuerdos matrimoniales.

Barnaby seguía con los ojos azules clavados en su rostro y una expresión de absoluta concentración. Asintió con la cabeza a las palabras de la joven con los labios apretados en una línea tensa.

—¿Y qué pasó después?

—Luego... —Sarah respiró hondo— empezaron a ocurrir los accidentes.

Sarah comenzó a pasearse por la estancia, describiéndole concisamente todos los incidentes.

—Y es por ello que las cosas son cada vez más complicadas. No puedo creer, como cree el personal del orfanato, que esos accidentes sean obra de algún perturbado. Después de eso... —Sarah dejó de pasear y clavó la mirada en Barnaby— vino a verme otro abogado ayer por la mañana. Charlie no estaba y él había preguntado específicamente por mí. Traía otra oferta por la granja que era incluso mayor que la primera, tan generosa que él mismo admitió que era absurda. Era un hombre arrogante y despótico, pero antes de rechazar la oferta exigí saber el nombre de su cliente. Me dijo que era información confidencial.

Barnaby había demostrado ser un buen oyente, pero cuando Sarah hizo una pausa y lo estudió, se dio cuenta de que tenía los ojos como platos y se había erguido en el asiento; su mirada azul se había vuelto distante como si estuviera viendo algo que ella no podía.

Entonces él parpadeó y la miró directamente a los ojos.

—Ah, lo siento. Es sólo que... —De nuevo se le nublaron los ojos y se le perdió la mirada—. Has dicho que el orfanato está hacia el norte, ¿verdad? Es decir en el valle entre Watchet y Taunton, ¿no?

Sarah frunció el ceño.

—Sí.

Barnaby se puso repentinamente en pie, tan bruscamente, que ella dio un paso atrás. Él levantó las manos en un gesto tranquilizador.

—Espera un momento.

Sarah se dio cuenta de que estaba poseído por una excitación tan intensa y vibrante, que hasta se le entrecortaba la voz.

—Tengo que comprobar algo con Charlie. No te muevas de aquí... volveré dentro de un momento... Entonces decidiremos qué hacer.

Atónita, Sarah lo vio abandonar la salita a toda prisa. Oyó el resonar de sus pasos en el pasillo, y el abrir y cerrar de la puerta de la biblioteca.

—Bueno. —La joven se quedó mirando la puerta de la salita durante un rato, luego se acercó a la *chaise*. Barnaby le había dicho que no se moviera de allí, pero no que tuviera que esperar de pie.

Sentado en el escritorio de la biblioteca, Charlie clavó los ojos en la pluma que sostenía entre los dedos. La tinta se había secado en la punta. Sobre el papel secante había un sucinto e incompleto resumen de todo lo que había aprendido con Malcolm Sinclair sobre el mundo financiero de las compañías ferroviarias. Había comenzado a escribirlo para hacer algo útil, para distraerse de lo que se veía incapaz de hacer: ayudar a Sarah en lo que fuera que la estuviese preocupando.

El hecho de no poder hacerlo —de seguir en aquella extraña situación sin poder proteger a su esposa como todos sus instintos le impulsaban a hacer— sólo le provocaba una constante inquietud. Su incapacidad de actuar iba contra lo que era, contra el hombre que sabía que debería ser.

Sobre todo, contra el hombre que quería ser.

Lo único que había conseguido apartando a Sarah —y todo lo que sentía por ella— de su lado era que la joven lo hubiera excluido de su vida. Algo que él no había previsto, ni había considerado siquiera. No había pensado que se sentiría aislado de algo que, ahora sabía, era de vital importancia.

Con los dientes apretados, dio golpecitos en la página con la punta de la pluma dejando pequeños puntos emborronados. Eso —su vida tal y como la había planeado— no funcionaba. Se había equivocado por completo, demasiadas emociones pesaban sobre él. Tenía que cambiar las cosas, pero ¿cómo?

No tenía ni idea. En especial cuando, en ese caso, él estaba atado de pies y manos y, pese a todo, era incapaz de permitir que el amor entrara libremente en su vida.

Oyó el sonido de unos pasos apresurados junto a la puerta un segundo antes de que Barnaby entrara bruscamente en la habitación. Un Barnaby transformado. Charlie parpadeó ante el rostro resplandeciente de su amigo mientras se acercaba apresuradamente al escritorio.

—Acabo de hablar con Sarah. Dime, ¿es cierto? —Apoyándose en el escritorio, Barnaby clavó los ojos en Charlie lleno de excitación—. Después de tanto investigar, apenas puedo creer que haya estado delante de nuestras narices todo este tiempo. Jamás podríamos encontrar una oportunidad mejor que ésta para atrapar a nuestro especulador.

Una fría oleada atravesó a Charlie. Miró a Barnaby fijamente sin comprender lo que había querido decir, pero con una certera premonición helándole lentamente la sangre en las venas.

Al ver el desconcierto de su amigo, Barnaby hizo una breve pausa, luego continuó:

—Quizás he sacado una conclusión precipitada. ¿Es esa granja un objetivo? ¿Es crucial para la construcción de la línea del ferrocarril?

«¿Qué granja?» Pero Charlie lo sabía. Lentamente, dejó la pluma en el escritorio.

—La granja Quilley.

Barnaby notó el extraño tono de voz de su amigo; intentó leer su expresión, pero fracasó.

—Sarah acaba de contarme lo de los accidentes. Todo me hace sospechar que nuestro especulador está detrás de ellos, y teniendo en cuenta las ofertas de compra por la propiedad...

—¿Ofertas? ¿En plural?

Barnaby asintió con la cabeza y apretó los labios.

—Pero hay que comprobar si la granja está ubicada en una zona crucial para la futura construcción de la línea del ferrocarril. ¿Es así?

A Charlie le costó trabajo reprimir sus emociones lo suficiente para poder pensar. Respiró hondo. El control que tenía sobre sus sentidos era muy frágil, pero Charlie conocía la zona y su topografía. Tardó sólo un minuto en determinar la ubicación de la granja.

—Sí. —Apretó los labios—. Totalmente. Una vez que esté en marcha la línea entre Bristol y Taunton, sería lógico continuar hasta Watchet; es una mina de oro comercial. Y el valle donde está la granja es... La propiedad incluye una franja de tierra por donde podría pasar el ferrocarril.

Con la cabeza ya en otro sitio, Charlie se levantó, se acercó a una cómoda y abrió el último cajón.

—Échale un vistazo al mapa. Más allá de Crowcombe el terreno asciende bruscamente y no queda espacio para meter curvas. La línea del ferrocarril tendría que comenzar a subir antes, por la ladera anterior a Crowcombe, al sur de la granja, para proseguir por la franja de terreno que te decía, atravesando los campos hacia el norte. Ése sería el mejor recorrido.

Sacó un enorme plano del cajón, lo desenrolló y lo extendió sobre el escritorio.

—Trazando una línea a lo largo del valle, podrías llegar hasta Crowcombe, pero no más allá.

Barnaby alisó el plano y se inclinó sobre él.

—No queda más remedio que comprar la granja.

Charlie no se molestó en asentir con la cabeza. Situó la granja en el mapa.

—Si me perdonas un momento...

No esperó respuesta, no le importaba lo que Barnaby pensara. Lo único que sabía cuando abrió la puerta de la biblioteca era lo que él sentía. Una especie de horror diferente que no podía compararse a nada que hubiera sentido antes, seguido muy de cerca por una furia ciega.

Sentada en la *chaise*, Sarah cavilaba sobre la abrupta salida de Barnaby cuando oyó que se abría la puerta de la biblioteca y, acto seguido, el sonido de pasos apresurados acercándose a la salita.

Reconoció las zancadas de Charlie un instante antes de que éste apareciera en la puerta. Aunque su marido la taladraba con la mirada, la distancia era aún demasiado grande para leerle la expresión. Charlie vaciló, luego se dio la vuelta y, con deliberada lentitud, con todo el control que poseía, cerró la puerta doble.

Una oleada de inquietud recorrió la espalda de Sarah, impulsándola a erguirse en su asiento. Pero en vez de eso, se negó a dejarse intimidar y se reclinó en la *chaise*, observando cómo su marido se acercaba a ella.

Charlie cruzó la estancia con paso lento y deliberado. Se detuvo ante la chimenea y bajó la mirada hacia ella.

Sarah estudió su pálido y rígido rostro; cada línea, cada plano parecía inclemente y duro. Pero su expresión, por una vez, no era impasible; era tensa, casi torturada.

Su mirada atrapó la de ella y la sostuvo. Charlie respiró hondo antes de hablar:

—Acabo de enterarme, por Barnaby, de que ha habido una serie de accidentes en el orfanato. Y de que has recibido más ofertas de compra por la propiedad, ofertas que sospechas que podrían estar relacionadas con los accidentes. —Charlie le sostuvo la mirada con dureza—. En resumen, crees que, como propietaria del orfanato, eres el blanco de un extorsionador que pretende obligarte a vender.

Sarah no dijo nada, sólo le observó.

De repente, los ojos de Charlie llamearon.

—¿Por qué no me lo has dicho? —Aquel grito atormentado le salió del alma—. ¡Eres mi mujer! —continuó gritando mientras caminaba de un lado para otro de la estancia—. Es mi deber protegerte... Hice votos ante Dios para honrarte y defenderte. ¿Cómo voy a hacerlo si ni siquiera me entero cuando alguien te está amenazando?

Charlie le lanzó una mirada furiosa. Ella mantuvo la calma por fuera. Por dentro, su temperamento estaba a punto de estallar, aunque encontraba intrigante el estallido de su marido. Charlie jamás perdía la calma.

—Sabes que esos accidentes son muy serios... llevas semanas preocupada por ellos. Y aun así no me has dicho nada. Te pregunté, pero no, decidiste dejarme a un lado. —Los ojos de Charlie eran un turbulento mar de emociones. Tenía los músculos tensos y sus gestos eran bruscos—. Pero en cuanto viste a Barnaby te faltó tiempo para ir a contarle tus problemas.

Charlie se llevó la mano al pelo y se despeinó su corte elegante mientras soltaba un gruñido. Sarah observó fascinada cómo se agarraba un mechón y tiraba con fuerza antes de soltarlo bruscamente. Su marido se giró con violencia y volvió a caminar, deteniéndose delante de ella con una ardiente mirada llena de emociones desnudas.

—Me has ocultado todo esto a propósito. —La voz de Charlie no había aumentado de volumen, pero sí de fuerza torturada—. Te negaste a decirme lo que tenía derecho a saber. Lo que necesitaba saber.

Charlie se atragantó. Sus ojos relampaguearon.

—¿Por qué?

Era una exigencia furiosa, una súplica torturada.

Mirándolo directamente a los ojos, Sarah comprendió, por fin, lo que Charlie quería decir. El dolor oscurecía sus ojos azules, un dolor provocado por lo que no podía evitar sentir. Era real, a Sarah no le cupo duda.

Pero ella no estaba dispuesta a aceptar ni la más mínima pizca de culpa.

—¿Me preguntas por qué? —Con esfuerzo, Sarah mantuvo el tono neutro con la mirada clavada en los ojos furiosos de su marido—. Porque me dejaste muy claro que el orfanato era sólo asunto mío, que no era responsabilidad tuya, que no estabas interesado ni querías tener ninguna relación con él. Me dejaste bien claro que el orfanato formaba parte de mi vida personal, no de la tuya.

Sarah titubeó, luego continuó hablando:

—¿Acaso no es eso lo que llevas semanas diciéndome... justo desde que nos casamos? Que no querías saber, que no querías que te molestara con nada, que no querías que te incluyera en mi vida. ¿No era eso lo que querías?

Al ver que la mirada de Charlie se vaciaba de toda expresión y al percibir su repentino desconcierto, Sarah se detuvo; luego, sin dejar de mirarlo a los ojos, añadió en voz muy baja:

—No te lo dije porque creí que no querías saberlo.

Charlie no apartó la mirada, no le ocultó lo que ella veía en sus ojos, aunque por la evidente tensión de sus músculos Sarah supo el esfuerzo que eso le costó.

Sin embargo, permaneció quieto, mirándola, y Sarah vio aparecer la primera grieta en el muro que había levantado su marido. La vio crecer. Vio cómo toda la edificación se tambaleaba, se resquebrajaba y caía, hasta que entre ellos dos no hubo barrera alguna.

Por un momento, reinó un silencio absoluto; luego él suspiró profunda y dolorosamente, y acercándose al sillón que había frente a ella se dejó caer sin dejar de mirarla.

Sin barreras, sin escudos.

—He cambiado de idea.

Dijo las palabras en voz baja pero llena de emoción. Sarah sabía que no sólo se estaba refiriendo al orfanato.

Charlie se recostó lentamente en el sillón con la mandíbula tensa, con los ojos aún fijos en ella.

—Sobre todo. Sobre nosotros. Pero ahora debemos concentrarnos en el orfanato. Del resto... hablaremos más tarde.

Era una pregunta. Charlie esperaba su respuesta, su conformidad. Reconociendo que el repentino y radical cambio de su marido lo había dejado conmocionado, inseguro, y a pesar de todo dispuesto a hablar de las emociones que existían entre ellos, y sabiendo que aún era media tarde y que Barnaby estaba en la biblioteca, sin duda impaciente por reunirse con ellos, Sarah asintió con la cabeza.

Charlie soltó el aliento con algo más de calma.

—Háblame de los accidentes. Y de las ofertas.

Ella lo hizo, rápida y concisamente. Charlie estaba más familiarizado con la situación que Barnaby, así que no le llevó demasiado tiempo.

Cuando terminó, Charlie la estudió por un momento antes de decir:

—Lo que tú no sabes es... —Sucintamente, le contó la misión de Barnaby. No tuvo que explicar la conexión, por la mirada entornada de Sarah supo que la había visto de inmediato. Le explicó las distintas opciones que habían barajado, y el detallado resumen de las finanzas del ferrocarril que le había sonsacado a Malcolm mientras Barnaby y Gabriel se concentraban en identificar las parcelas que podrían ser objetivo del extorsionador por su probable ubicación en la futura línea entre Bristol y Taunton.

Al final, concluyó con seriedad:

—Al parecer no íbamos tan desencaminados, sólo que mirábamos en la dirección contraria. —Miró hacia la puerta—. Deberíamos llamar a Barnaby; le he dejado estudiando un mapa en la biblioteca. —Volvió a mirar a Sarah.

Las noticias sobre el especulador y sus pasadas fechorías la habían alarmado. Su esposa había visto la necesidad de centrar la atención en el orfanato, de pensar en cómo protegerlo. Sarah asintió con la cabeza.

—Es la hora del té. Podemos tomar algo mientras hablamos.

Levantándose, Charlie tiró del cordón de la campanilla. Cuando Crisp apareció en la puerta, Sarah ordenó que trajera el té mientras Charlie le pedía a un lacayo que avisara a Barnaby.

—Dile que traiga el plano.

Diez minutos más tarde, los tres estaban sentados alrededor de una mesita baja que colocaron entre la *chaise* y el sillón para extender el plano encima.

Tras confirmar que la granja Quilley sería de vital importancia para cualquier enlace ferroviario entre Taunton y Watchet y que, por consiguiente, su extorsionador estaría con toda seguridad detrás de las ofertas y de los accidentes, Barnaby les habló de las investigaciones que había llevado a cabo hasta la fecha.

—Montague aún no ha descubierto nada, pero le gustó tu sugerencia de buscar el origen del capital... dice que ya sabe cómo obtener algunas respuestas. Gabriel y yo hemos investigado varias propiedades que podrían interesar al especulador entre Bristol y Taunton, pero no encontramos ninguna prueba de que haya extendido sus redes por allí.

Hizo una mueca.

—Al parecer no estábamos siendo tan previsores como deberíamos, pero como la línea entre Londres y Bristol apenas está en proceso y el tramo entre Bristol y Taunton no se construirá hasta mucho después, ¿quién habría imaginado que nuestro hombre estaría interesado en una línea que tardará tanto tiempo en ver la luz?

—Tú lo has dicho. —Charlie bajó su taza—. Es cauteloso. A menos que fueras un transportista local o alguien consciente del crecimiento gradual de la región, no habría ninguna razón para imaginar que se construirá una línea entre Taunton y Watchet. Los imperativos comerciales no son tan evidentes, ni mucho menos.

—Es alguien precavido y listo. Y muy bien informado —refunfuñó Barnaby.

Se recostaron en sus asientos, tomaron el té y discutieron sobre lo que sabían de ese hombre, y cómo podrían averiguar todavía más.

—No creo que los abogados vayan a decirnos quién es.

—Dejadme eso a mí. —Apoyando un pequeño cuaderno de notas en la rodilla, Barnaby anotó los nombres de los tres abogados—. Son todos de Taunton. Es interesante que hiciera cada oferta por medio de un abogado distinto.

—Es menos arriesgado de esa manera que mostrar ante los abogados, que son de la localidad, un inusitado interés por una propiedad sin ningún valor aparente. —Charlie hizo una mueca—. Incluso aunque lograras sonsacarle algo, es muy probable que detrás de cada oferta haya un nombre diferente, incluso el nombre de una compañía en vez de una persona.

—Cierto. —Barnaby levantó la mirada—. Pero alguien tuvo que contratar a los abogados, ya fuera por carta o en persona. Y probablemente han tenido que rendirle cuentas a la misma persona. Eso podría darnos alguna pista.

—Quizás. Entretanto... —Charlie buscó la mirada de Sarah— nosotros nos ocuparemos de la seguridad del orfanato. Y esperaremos el siguiente paso de nuestro especulador.

Cuando Charlie siguió a Sarah al dormitorio esa noche, estaba lejos de sentirse satisfecho con la situación, aunque no podía hacer otra cosa que resignarse, pues sabían que habían hecho todo lo humanamente posible. El rechazo de la última oferta había dejado la pelota en el tejado del extorsionador. Ahora debía ser él quien tomara la iniciativa.

Habían pasado la tarde con Barnaby y, durante la cena y la tertulia posterior, habían considerado qué medidas tomar para proteger el orfanato y a sus ocupantes. No era una tarea sencilla. Cuando Sarah había sugerido diversas acciones, Barnaby se había puesto serio y le había señalado que ésa podía ser su única oportunidad de atrapar al malhechor, alguien que ya había matado varias veces y cuyos planes eran cada vez más arriesgados. Con una apuesta tan alta, no debían dar ningún paso que pudiera advertirle de sus intenciones; si el especulador tenía el más mínimo indicio de que le vigilaban, de que esperaban descubrir su juego, interrumpiría sus planes y desaparecería sin dejar rastro.

A fin de cuentas, había un montón de sitios y una infinidad de líneas de ferrocarril por construir. Si no conseguían atraparlo allí, no había muchas posibilidades de que volvieran a dar con él.

Sarah, cuya principal preocupación eran los niños y el personal del orfanato, había aceptado a regañadientes. Por su parte, Charlie estaba desolado. Permitir que aquellos que él consideraba bajo su protección estuvieran expuestos a ese tipo de riesgos no le sentaba nada bien.

Tras cerrar la puerta del dormitorio y quedar los dos solos,

Charlie se detuvo, observando cómo Sarah se acercaba lentamente, todavía absorta en sus preocupaciones, hasta la única ventana que no tenía las cortinas corridas y por la que se veían el lago y los jardines iluminados por la tenue luz de la luna. Una vela en el tocador y el fuego de la chimenea eran las únicas fuentes de luz de la estancia.

Charlie estudió a través de las sombras danzantes la delgada figura de su esposa, el gesto regio de cabeza, los suaves tirabuzones castaño claro que le caían sobre la nuca. Y una vez más sintió la realidad de que era suya.

Y recordó, vivamente, todo lo que había sentido antes... Todo lo que había tenido que relegar a un rincón de su mente para poder pensar con claridad e idear un plan con Barnaby y con Sarah para atrapar al malhechor y proteger al orfanato. Y lo había conseguido, pero...

Aún se estremecía de horror. Hasta ese momento en la biblioteca, cuando las revelaciones de Barnaby habían desgarrado el velo que le cubría los ojos, no se había dado cuenta de lo tonto que había sido. Se había convencido a sí mismo de que su deber hacia el condado estaba por encima de todo, pero, en realidad, no tenía deber más sagrado, más fundamental en su vida, que el que le debía a Sarah.

Había irrumpido en la salita dominado por tantas emociones que no había sabido cuál de ellas imperaba sobre todas las demás —rabia, miedo, rechazo, dolor—, presa del pánico por haber creado una situación en la que su esposa había corrido peligro sin que él hubiera sido consciente de ello. Cuando ella le había formulado aquella pregunta, «¿No era eso lo que querías?», se había quedado paralizado, enfrentado al resultado de su cobardía emocional. A las emociones que había estado conteniendo.

Pues era eso lo que había estado haciendo, consciente e inconscientemente. Pero ya no podía engañarse por más tiempo.

Sarah era el centro de su vida, de todo lo que quería, de todo lo que necesitaba; ahora lo sabía. Ella era el origen de todo, de la familia, de sus herederos, de la vida familiar que había deseado durante toda su vida y que siempre había dado por sentado que tendría. Por esos motivos y más, ella era la piedra angular de su hogar.

La dueña de su corazón.

Había sido él quien la había puesto ahí y luego había intentado negarlo.

Pero ahora, finalmente, lo entendía. En su mente veía a Alathea sonriendo. Casi podía sentirla dándole una condescendiente palmadita en la mejilla.

Sarah todavía estaba delante de la ventana, con la mirada perdida en la oscuridad. Preocupada por el orfanato y, quizá, preguntándose por ellos. Por él. Charlie había necesitado la tregua que ella le había dado esa tarde para ponerse en pie de nuevo, tiempo para asumir sus vertiginosas y convulsivas emociones y aclararse. Por ese motivo, él le debía... eso.

Charlie se movió y atravesó la estancia lentamente. Se detuvo al lado de ella, hombro con hombro. Deslizó las manos en los bolsillos y se quedó mirando la misma oscuridad que ella.

—Sobre nosotros... y todo lo demás...

Sarah le miró y esperó.

Charlie no le devolvió la mirada, sino que siguió mirando por la ventana; el tenue reflejo de la cara de su esposa se reflejaba en el cristal.

—Sé que cometí un error y que te hice daño, y no tengo palabras para decirte lo mucho que lo siento. Pero lo hecho hecho está, y no puedo reescribir el pasado. Sin embargo, si estás de acuerdo conmigo, si aceptas, me gustaría empezar de nuevo. —Hizo una pausa, apretó los dientes y luego continuó—: Volver a intentarlo.

Ella desvió la mirada de la cara de Charlie al cristal de la ventana, buscando allí sus ojos como si se reflejara en un espejo. Esperó.

Él le estudió la cara y cogió aire.

—Tengo... tengo problemas, dificultades para manejar y acostumbrarme a lo que hay entre nosotros. No me gusta y me resisto a cualquier cosa que pueda hacerme perder el control. Lo que ha crecido entre nosotros... lo que ocurre todas las noches sólo confirma lo poderoso que es lo que siento por ti. Por eso he luchado contra ello.

Charlie hizo una pausa como si buscara las palabras adecuadas para lo que tenía que decir. Sarah le sostuvo la mirada a través del reflejo del cristal. «No más engaños.» Él sintió una opresión en el pecho. Apretó los dientes y siguió:

—Ignorar mis instintos. Darle la espalda a mis temores y aceptar lo que siento por ti... no me resulta fácil. Acostumbrarme a ello será todavía peor, pero reconocerlo abiertamente y dejarme llevar...

—Volvió a coger aire sin dejar de sostener la mirada de su esposa—. Eso será todo un reto. Puedo arreglármelas dentro de esta habitación, pero fuera de aquí...

Sin dejar de mirar los ojos de Sarah, Charlie se obligó a continuar:

—Sé lo que quieres, pero no puedo prometerte que me reforme de inmediato. Lo único que puedo prometerte es que lo intentaré. Y que lo seguiré intentando... siempre y cuando sea eso lo que tú quieres.

Sarah parpadeó varias veces para aclararse los ojos. Jamás había esperado oír tales palabras —tal admisión— por parte de su marido. ¿Había cambiado él o lo había hecho ella? ¿Quizás habían cambiado los dos?

Charlie la estaba observando, esperando. Sin previo aviso las palabras de la gitana resonaron en la mente de Sarah.

«Es complicado.» Por supuesto.

«Será decisión suya, no de él.»

Sarah había pensado que la gran decisión que había tenido que tomar era aceptar o no la propuesta de matrimonio de Charlie, pero quizá fuera ésta la auténtica decisión, ahora que sabía cómo era él, que lo conocía, ahora que habían dejado caer todos los velos y los dos sabían qué era lo que querían el uno del otro, y eran sinceros acerca de lo que ofrecían a cambio.

Sarah tomó aire y asintió con la cabeza sin dejar de mirar su reflejo.

—Sí, eso es lo que quiero... Lo que siempre he querido. Pero... —Él había sido sincero, más de lo que había esperado, y ella tenía que serlo a su vez—. Probablemente te estaré vigilando. No porque espere lo peor, sino porque no estoy segura.

Charlie entrecerró los ojos.

—No confías en mí —dijo tras un momento.

Ella arqueó las cejas.

—Te confío mi vida, pero mi corazón...

Él le sostuvo la mirada durante un largo rato, luego curvó los labios y bajó la vista.

—Quizás... —Esperó a que él volviera a levantar la mirada y buscara sus ojos en el cristal—. Quizás ésa sea la verdadera piedra angular de nuestro matrimonio. La confianza. Que yo confíe en que no volverás a equivocarte, a pesar de algún lapsus ocasional, y no vuelvas a reincidir y dejarme de lado. De que hieras mis sentimientos. Estar segura de que, pase lo que pase, no volverás a comportarte así. Y que tú confíes en que yo nunca utilizaré lo que hay entre nosotros para intentar controlarte, para obligarte a hacer lo que no quieres. Quizás eso es lo que necesitamos, tener confianza el uno en el otro.

Él le sostuvo la mirada durante un largo rato, luego se giró hacia ella.

Sarah hizo lo mismo.

Charlie alargó los brazos y tomándole el rostro suavemente entre las manos, se lo alzó hacia él para mirarla directamente a los ojos.

—Quizá.

Luego bajó la mirada a los labios de Sarah y ésta sintió cómo palpitaban en respuesta. El tiempo de hablar había pasado. Él inclinó la cabeza y ella se puso de puntillas para recibir el beso.

Un beso que fue como pura ambrosía para dos hambrientos. Los dos estaban necesitados, ávidos de obtener una confirmación tras aquella intensa agitación emocional. Los dos se necesitaban el uno al otro más que nada en el mundo.

Dejaron caer la ropa al suelo como pétalos esparcidos a su alrededor, como velos descartados. Se tocaron la piel desnuda. Se rozaron y acariciaron con los labios. Lentamente. Con suaves suspiros que muy pronto se convirtieron en gemidos entrecortados.

La llama de la vela titiló; la pálida luz de la luna se derramó sobre ellos cuando él la alzó en sus brazos, y ella le rodeó la cintura con las piernas, cuando la bajó hacia él y la llenó por completo.

Se movieron juntos con los labios fundidos, con los cuerpos unidos y ese poder que siempre surgía entre ellos, y se rindieron a él.

Se dejaron envolver por él.

Los atravesó y los rodeó.

Charlie la alzó y la bajó lentamente. Sarah se aferró a él y lo soltó, para volver a agarrarlo con más fuerza. Saboreando cada instante como sabía que él hacía. Saboreando el placer de su marido a través del beso y sin ocultar el suyo.

Durante unos momentos se comunicaron sin palabras en la penumbra, él, ella y aquel poder que los embargaba, que los vinculaba, que los unía.

Hasta que el deleite se convirtió en placer, y el placer en pura pasión. Hasta que el deseo los atrapó y los fundió. Hasta que explotaron y cualquier pensamiento racional desapareció de sus mentes.

Hasta que aquella potente explosión creció y los envolvió, los acosó y derribó, los espoleó y, entonces, los destruyó, los hizo pedazos y los rompió, dejándolos expuestos al placer que les atravesaba las venas.

Que llenaba de dicha sus corazones.

Finalmente la oleada cesó. De alguna manera fueron tambaleándose hasta la cama y cayeron sobre ella. Sarah se giró hacia Charlie y apoyó la cabeza en su pecho. Sintió que él tiraba de las mantas y cubría sus cuerpos húmedos; luego la rodeó con sus brazos.

Charlie yacía boca arriba, relajado; los únicos músculos que aún seguían tensos eran aquellos con los que estrechaba a Sarah contra su cuerpo.

Sarah sonrió, besó el cálido músculo que tenía bajo los labios. Estaba a punto de dejarse llevar por el sueño cuando él le dio un beso en el pelo.

—No has comprendido lo que te he dicho. No me preocupa lo que tú puedas hacer, sino lo que yo podría hacer bajo la influencia de un poder que jamás seré capaz de controlar.

17

El siguiente movimiento del extorsionador se produjo dos días más tarde bajo la forma del deán Ferris, enviado por el Obispado de Wells.

Al reconocer el emblema del obispo en la puerta del carruaje, Crisp pidió a un lacayo que avisara a Charlie. Sarah estaba en su salita privada con él. La joven se apresuró hacia la puerta y Charlie la siguió a paso vivo mientras el deán subía lentamente las escaleras de la puerta principal.

—Deán Ferris. —Sarah salió al porche para recibirlo—. Es un placer darle la bienvenida a Morwellan Park, señor.

El deán la conocía desde hacía años. Sonrió y tomó la mano de Sarah entre las suyas.

—Querida, no necesito preguntarte cómo estás, el sol brilla en tus ojos. —Luego le soltó la mano, mostrando un semblante serio—. Por desgracia, estoy aquí por un asunto serio, uno que me temo te resultará muy perturbador.

—¿Sí? —Abriendo mucho los ojos, Sarah se giró hacia Charlie, que se había parado a su lado—. No sé si conoce a mi marido, lord Meredith. —Dirigiéndose a Charlie dijo—: Como sabes, el orfanato funciona bajo los auspicios del Obispado de Wells. El deán Ferris es el primer consejero del obispo.

El deán Ferris no conocía a Charlie. Le estrechó la mano mientras sus sagaces ojos azules tomaban nota de la presencia intimidante del conde y la rápida mirada que éste le lanzó a Sarah.

—Por favor, acompáñenos dentro, señor, y háblenos sobre ese

asunto tan perturbador. —Dando un paso atrás, Charlie hizo un gesto con la mano al deán y a Sarah para que entraran delante de él.

Al darse cuenta de que su marido la había incluido en aquella reunión, Sarah condujo al deán a la salita, luego avisó Crisp y le pidió que les llevara el té. Mientras esperaban a que llegara, el deán les informó que estaba realizando una visita de rutina por las iglesias del distrito, pero que «a raíz de una inesperada información que había recibido el obispo» había decidido pasarse por allí para consultarla con Sarah.

En cuanto llegó el té y lo sirvieron, y Crisp se hubo retirado, el deán se volvió hacia ella.

—Querida, como habrás imaginado, mi visita tiene que ver con el orfanato. El obispo recibió una carta anónima, como suelen ser este tipo de cartas. Pero en vista de la seriedad de las acusaciones vertidas en ella, el obispo resolvió que, en conciencia, deberíamos avisarte de este asunto lo más rápidamente posible.

Sarah dejó la taza en la bandeja.

—¿Qué sucede? ¿Qué acusaciones?

El deán parecía incómodo. Le lanzó una mirada a Charlie.

—En la carta nos comunicaban que el personal del orfanato permitía ciertas costumbres a los muchachos que... En resumen, se los acusa de permitir actos inmorales.

Sarah clavó los ojos en el deán.

—¡Eso es absurdo! Lo sabe de sobra. Tanto usted como el obispo conocen al personal del orfanato. Así que saben muy bien que tales acusaciones son falsas.

—Por supuesto. —El deán Ferris asintió con la cabeza, tanto las palabras como el gesto demostraban determinación—. Es por eso por lo que el obispo y yo nos hemos sentido impulsados a actuar. —Inclinándose hacia delante tomó la mano de Sarah entre las suyas—. Querida, tales acusaciones, a pesar de que los dos sabemos que son falsas, son... bien, espantosas. El obispo y yo creemos que son obra de alguien deseoso de infligir un daño serio al orfanato o a ti. —Miró a Charlie—. Es por eso por lo que no hemos dudado en poner este asunto en tus manos de inmediato.

Sarah cruzó una mirada con Charlie. Supo que él pensaba lo mismo que ella, que aquello era, claramente, la siguiente maniobra del extorsionador.

Charlie miró al deán.

—¿Por casualidad ha traído la carta con usted, señor?

—S... sí. —El deán parecía avergonzado mientras metía la mano en la sotana—. Querida, espero que no lo tomes a mal si insisto que sea sólo lord Meredith quien lea la carta. Mi conciencia no me permite manchar tu mente con este tipo de cosas.

La joven vaciló, pero resultó evidente que el deán hablaba en serio. No tenía sentido contrariarle. Sarah asintió con la cabeza y observó cómo Charlie cogía la misiva, la abría y la leía.

Los rasgos de su marido se endurecieron mientras sus ojos se desplazaban por la hoja. Al leer la segunda página tensó la mandíbula. En cuanto finalizó, alzó las cejas.

—¡Santo Dios! —Con una evidente expresión de aversión en su rostro Charlie dobló de nuevo las hojas—. ¿Le importa que me quede con la carta, señor? Una vez que le expliquemos la razón de todo esto, y vea lo que está ocurriendo, entenderá por qué esta misiva puede serme útil.

El deán se retorció las manos.

—A decir verdad, estaría feliz de deshacerme de ella. Quienquiera que la escribió tiene la mente muy sucia.

—Una mente muy sucia, sin duda. —Reclinándose en el sillón, Charlie le explicó que un desconocido estaba empeñado en comprar el orfanato, que intentaba obligar a Sarah a vender la granja por las buenas o por las malas. Luego le relató la larga serie de crímenes que había cometido el malhechor y la naturaleza de dichos crímenes.

El deán se quedó consternado.

—Santo cielo.

Charlie asintió con la cabeza.

—Por fortuna, en esta ocasión, somos conscientes de lo que está pasando gracias al señor Adair y sus conexiones con el nuevo cuerpo de policía de Londres. Sin embargo, aunque sabemos cuál es el motivo de estos incidentes, nos falta identificar quién está detrás de ellos. Quién es realmente nuestro extorsionador.

—¿Y es el mismo hombre, u hombres —preguntó el deán—, que está detrás de los demás incidentes?

—Creemos que sí. Parece poco probable que haya dos grupos u hombres independientes que sean capaces de tramar algo tan complejo, aunque la esencia del plan sea bastante sencilla. —Charlie miró fijamente al deán—. Se trata de alguien muy cauteloso y listo.

—Y carente de escrúpulos —añadió el deán señalando con la cabeza la carta que Charlie había dejado a un lado—. Difamar a mujeres inocentes que dedican sus vidas a cuidar a los huérfanos es un acto de lo más vil.

—Tenemos una oportunidad única para atraparlo —dijo Charlie—. Espero que nos ayude.

El deán le lanzó una mirada perspicaz.

—Haré todo lo que esté en mi mano para ayudar.

—Excelente. —Charlie miró a Sarah y sonrió débilmente—. Ayer pasamos el día en el orfanato explorando todas las vías posibles para mejorar las medidas de seguridad sin delatar nuestros propósitos. Es muy probable que nuestro hombre esté vigilando el lugar y que espere alguna reacción a esta carta. Si nos acompaña al orfanato hoy, supondrá que lo hace en respuesta a esas acusaciones. —Miró al deán—. Tenemos que representar una charada para que crea que su carta ha logrado el resultado deseado: crear problemas en el orfanato, y a Sarah. Si cree que lo ha conseguido, nos abordará con otra oferta. Y eso es lo que queremos, hacer que caiga en nuestra trampa.

El deán sonrió y dejó la taza en la mesita.

—Hace años que no participo en una charada.

El resto del día siguió las directrices de un cuidadoso guión escrito con la intención de dar gato por liebre al malhechor. Todos adoptaron un semblante grave y serio cuando llegaron al orfanato en el carruaje del obispo, e hicieron lo mismo cuando abandonaron el lugar horas después, tras un agradable y divertido almuerzo con los huérfanos y una seria, pero muy motivadora, charla con el personal.

Al salir, las mujeres que formaban parte del personal del orfanato los acompañaron al porche para representar su papel. Katy Carter había parecido asustada mientras retorcía el delantal con sus manos; Quince había sorbido por la nariz mientras bajaba la cabeza; Jeannie estaba ruborizada —más de indignación que de otra cosa— y algo aturdida; mientras Lily había logrado mostrar una asombrosa combinación de enfado y hosca severidad. El deán, que intentaba en todo momento mantener una expresión condenatoria en su rostro ante tales habilidades histriónicas, se había paseado de un lado a otro del porche, gesticulando y sermoneándolos. En realidad las palabras que había dicho habían sido una bendición.

Charlie había permanecido detrás de ellos, contemplando la función con expresión impasible. Colgada de su brazo, Sarah había adoptado el semblante más inexpresivo que podía, como si aquel episodio hubiera resultado ser demasiado para ella y no pudiera esperar a escaparse de allí.

Charlie había escudriñado con discreción los alrededores, pero con los montes Quantocks enfrente y las colinas Brendon detrás, había muchas posiciones ventajosas desde las que un hombre con un catalejo pudiera vigilar de cerca el lugar. Salvo asegurarse de que el carruaje del obispo estuviera a un lado del camino para que no impidiera la vista de la escena que representaban ante la puerta, poco más podían hacer.

Después del aparente escarmiento al personal del orfanato, se habían subido al carruaje y habían hablado sin parar de regreso al Park.

Llegaron a tiempo para el té de las cinco y recibieron a Gabriel, Alathea y Barnaby, que llegaron a caballo desde Casleigh. Gabriel y Alathea conocían al deán. Todos se acomodaron en la salita y Charlie les explicó el último acontecimiento y cómo se habían ocupado de él.

—Tratar con malhechores siempre debería tener una parte de diversión. —Alathea cogió la taza que le ofrecía Sarah—. Es la única manera de hacer frente a tales horrores.

Sonriendo, el deán la alabó por su sabiduría.

Con su pasado común en mente, Gabriel y Charlie se miraron disimuladamente y pusieron los ojos en blanco.

Barnaby había viajado al sur el día anterior por la mañana para visitar a los tres abogados de Taunton y ver qué información lograba sonsacarles. De camino, se había detenido en Casleigh con intención de reclutar a Gabriel, y se había encontrado con la ayuda no sólo de Gabriel sino de Alathea.

—Me quedé sorprendido —les informó Barnaby—. Los tres consintieron en hablar conmigo.

—Por supuesto. —Alathea cogió una galleta de la bandeja—.

Ejercen la abogacía en la localidad. Perder el favor de los Cynster y los Morwellan sería como suicidarse laboralmente. —Alathea miró a Charlie—. Esgrimí tu título de una manera desvergonzada. —Sonrió ampliamente—. Has sido muy útil a pesar de no estar presente.

Gabriel y Charlie intercambiaron otra mirada.

Barnaby, sin embargo, seguía impresionado.

—Aunque no les contamos ningún detalle, los tres nos dieron voluntariamente toda la información que tenían sobre el cliente que había presentado la oferta de compra por el orfanato. —Miró a Charlie e hizo una mueca—. Como predijiste, los clientes eran compañías con domicilio en Londres.

—Todas parecen sospechosamente direcciones de abogados —apuntó Gabriel—. Todas están cerca de Inns of Court.

Charlie suspiró.

—Por la manera en que nuestro hombre lo tiene todo organizado, sugiero que reprimamos la tentación de investigar esas direcciones.

—Nos encontraríamos ante compañías ficticias —convino Gabriel—, o nos toparíamos con abogados menos dispuestos a colaborar.

Barnaby asintió con la cabeza.

—En especial cuando la comunicación entre los abogados y las compañías no tiene lugar en esas direcciones.

Cuando Charlie le miró con el ceño fruncido, Barnaby le brindó una amplia sonrisa.

—Aunque parezca mentira, nuestro extorsionador utiliza un agente. Un hombre de carne y hueso. Al parecer es de estatura media, con el pelo castaño, aunque medio calvo, y cara redonda; los rasgos comunes de un individuo sencillo y poco llamativo que ronda los treinta y cinco. Utiliza la ropa pulcra de los agentes de comercio. Es cuidadoso con las palabras y, definitivamente, no es un caballero.

Barnaby hizo una pausa, como saboreando una pequeña victoria.

—Los tres abogados nos dieron la misma descripción. En cada caso, nuestro hombre presentó sus credenciales como agente de la compañía pertinente. Discutió los detalles de la oferta y le ofreció a cada abogado una parte de sus honorarios como anticipo. Posteriormente, después de que la oferta hubiera sido rechazada, los abogados habían esperado informar a la empresa en la dirección que les habían dado, pero en las tres ocasiones el agente fue a verlos en persona, en uno de los casos incluso coincidió con el abogado cuando regresaba a Taunton tras hacer la oferta, así que los abogados le dieron la triste noticia directamente al agente.

—Un dato interesante —intervino Gabriel—. Los tres abogados no esperaban recibir el resto del pago convenido, pero se quedaron sorprendidos cuando el agente, al ser informado de su fracaso, les pagó igualmente.

Gabriel miró a Charlie.

—Quienquiera que esté detrás de todo esto no es un tunante de medio pelo, dada su manera de actuar. No intenta robar cada vez que puede... se concentra en un solo objetivo, pero por lo demás se comporta de una manera íntegra.

Charlie recordó a otros malhechores con los que se habían topado y asintió con la cabeza.

—No será fácil de identificar. Nadie le delatará.

—Lo que nos lleva al punto de donde partimos —dijo Barnaby—. La única manera que tenemos de atrapar a este hombre es por medio del orfanato de la granja Quilley.

Quince minutos más tarde, Charlie, Sarah y Barnaby estaban en el porche despidiendo a Gabriel y a Alathea. Volvían cabalgando a casa. Cuando Charlie acompañó a Sarah al interior, sonrió para sus adentros al recordar la mirada que había visto intercambiar a Alathea y a Gabriel, y la risita que habían soltado un instante antes de espolear sus caballos hacia el camino y salir cabalgando como alma que lleva el diablo.

Miró a Sarah y se dio la vuelta cuando Barnaby se excusó y se retiró para reparar los estragos que había sufrido su normalmente impecable persona tras dos días a caballo.

—Yo también tengo que marcharme —dijo el deán sonriendo en medio del vestíbulo. Tomó la mano de Sarah y se la palmeó—. Me siento aliviado, querida, al ver que tanto el orfanato como tú contáis con unos defensores tan buenos. Informaré al obispo de la verdadera naturaleza de los sucesos acaecidos aquí. Nuestras oraciones estarán contigo. —Se despidió de Charlie con un gesto de cabeza—. Y con usted, lord Meredith. Es necesario encontrar y detener a ese malhechor.

Charlie asintió con la cabeza.

—Haremos todo lo posible para atraparle.

Un traqueteo de ruedas en el camino de entrada anunció la llegada del carruaje del obispo. Charlie y Sarah acompañaron al deán al exterior. Cuando subió al vehículo, volvieron al porche y se despidieron de él con la mano mientras el carruaje se alejaba.

Había un hombre a caballo al final del camino. Se echó a un lado y, al observar el emblema del coche, se inclinó respetuosamente mientras pasaba por su lado. Luego, con un movimiento de muñeca agitó las riendas y enfiló hacia el Park.

Charlie se volvió hacia Sarah, que le dirigió una mirada vacilante.

—Es Sinclair. —Hizo una mueca—. Sin duda es de fiar, pero cuantas menos personas conozcan nuestros planes mejor. ¿Te sientes con fuerzas para seguir actuando? Tendrás que mostrarte contrariada, ya que se supone que el deán ha sermoneado al personal del orfanato amenazando con cerrarlo.

Ella dejó caer los hombros.

—Me mostraré cansada, disgustada y sin querer hablar en absoluto del tema. —Apoyándose en el brazo de su marido, alzó la mirada hacia él—. Me quedaré lo suficiente para saludar al señor Sinclair, pues sería extraño que no lo hiciera, pero me retiraré con la excusa de un dolor de cabeza.

Con la mirada clavada en la cara de Sarah, Charlie dudó, luego murmuró:

—Me mostraré irritado y molesto, y diré que ya hablaremos de esto más tarde. En cuanto te hayas ido le contaré la visita del deán al orfanato. Si en realidad hubiésemos creído esas acusaciones, yo insistiría en que vendieras el lugar, que es lo que nuestro hombre espera oír. Malcolm comienza a ser conocido en los alrededores. Aunque no me gusta engañarle y utilizarle, puede ser un buen medio para dar a conocer nuestra reacción ante este último acontecimiento. Cualquiera que oiga una observación de él no imaginará que haya nada raro detrás.

Sarah asintió con la cabeza mientras Malcolm entraba al trote en el patio delantero.

—Sí, me parece una idea estupenda.

Y lo fue, y como Sarah pensó luego, ofrecieron una actuación excelente.

Cuando Sinclair se acercó, la joven esbozó una sonrisa forzada —que ni siquiera le llegó a los ojos ni borró las líneas verticales entre sus cejas— y le tendió la mano.

—Señor Sinclair.

—Condesa. —Él hizo una pequeña reverencia y la miró con preocupación—. ¿Se encuentra bien?

Sarah apretó los labios.

—Me temo que he recibido una... dolorosa noticia —reconoció. La joven le lanzó una mirada de reojo al rígido hombre que había a su lado. Charlie llevaba puesta su habitual máscara de impasibilidad, pero irradiaba desaprobación e irritación—. Yo... eh... —Levantando una mano se frotó la frente—. Si me disculpa, creo que me acostaré un rato. Estoy segura de que mi marido... —dijo lanzando una rápida mirada a su censuradora presencia— apreciará su compañía.

—Por supuesto, querida. —Bajo el tono ronco de Charlie se percibía la dureza del acero—. Sé cuánto te han disgustado las últimas noticias. Hablaremos de ello más tarde.

La última frase parecía contener una promesa que no presagiaba nada bueno. Sarah se despidió de Sinclair con un gesto de cabeza y luego, con los labios apretados y la cabeza y la espalda erguidas, se dirigió a las escaleras.

Mientras la observaba marcharse, Charlie contuvo el impulso de aplaudir. Sarah había interpretado el papel de «mujer ultrajada y frágil» a la perfección. Una mirada al ceño fruncido de Sinclair le confirmó que lo había convencido por completo. Charlie le indicó con la mano el camino a la biblioteca.

Sinclair caminó a su lado.

—Hummm, una visita del clero... ¿Ha sido el obispo el causante del malestar de la condesa?

Charlie reconoció que la pregunta no era demasiado correcta; no era lo que un caballero preguntaría en tales circunstancias. Aunque un poco molesto por que Malcolm hubiera mostrado el suficiente interés en Sarah como para preguntar algo que sin duda era de carácter privado, aprovechó la oportunidad que le ofrecía la pregunta.

Alargó la mano hacia la puerta de la biblioteca mientras fruncía el ceño, luego miró a un lado y otro del pasillo como si comprobara que no había nadie en los alrededores que pudiera escucharle; después invitó a Malcolm a entrar en la estancia antes de seguirlo y cerrar la puerta.

Charlie lo condujo a su escritorio.

—Me temo que la condesa no es consciente de que se está viendo involucrada en una... —apretó los labios y se hundió en la silla— desagradable situación en el orfanato. Por involucrada me refiero a la relación que tiene con el lugar, no a que esté personalmente envuelta en alguna fechoría.

—Por supuesto que no. —Malcolm se sentó en la silla frente al escritorio.

—El consejero del obispo vino a informarnos de un problema, un asunto que llegó a oídos del propio obispo y que involucra al personal del orfanato —continuó Charlie con voz brusca. Recogió una pluma y tamborileó con ella sobre el papel secante—. Creo necesario que la condesa se distancie del lugar y sé que ella estará de acuerdo conmigo una vez haya descansado y recuperado el equilibrio.

Malcolm frunció el ceño. Vaciló, luego dijo tímidamente:

—Según tengo entendido, su relación con el orfanato es de hace mucho tiempo, cuando lo heredó.

Charlie asintió bruscamente.

—Sin embargo, dadas las circunstancias, Sarah no dudará en buscar otra obra benéfica en la que emplear su tiempo y, después de todo, su madrina está muerta. —Intencionadamente, clavó la mirada en el papel doblado que Malcolm había sacado del bolsillo—. ¿Es el boletín informativo sobre el consorcio Newcastle-Carlisle?

Malcolm miró la página parpadeando, como si hubiera olvidado que la llevaba en la mano.

—Ah... sí. Te lo he traído por si querías verlo. —Alargó la mano hacia el escritorio y le tendió la página a Charlie.

Charlie la cogió y la abrió. A partir de ese instante y durante el resto de la visita de Malcolm sólo se dedicaron a hablar de temas financieros.

Cuando Malcolm finalmente se levantó y se marchó, Charlie le siguió con la mirada suspirando para sus adentros. Se pasó la mano por la cara intentando deshacerse de los últimos rastros del desagradable y despreciable papel que le había tocado interpretar: rígido, controlador, despiadado y cruel con tal de proteger su condado y su reputación, y dispuesto a pisotear los sentimientos de su esposa para alcanzar esa meta. Había dejado que Malcolm creyera que él era esa clase de hombre y, si bien todo era fingido, se sentía deshonrado.

Casi culpable por asociación.

Quitándose ese sentimiento de encima, fue en busca de Sarah para asegurarse a sí mismo —y a ella— que él no era esa clase de marido.

Pasaron dos días antes de que sus esfuerzos dieran sus frutos bajo la forma de un abogado. En esta ocasión el hombre provenía de un bufete de Wellington. Sin dilación expuso ante los condes de Meredith lo que creía que era una oferta justa y más que generosa por la compra de la granja Quilley.

Charlie estaba sentado en un sillón de la salita de Sarah, luchando por ocultar una amplia sonrisa mientras observaba a su esposa. Ella estaba sentada en la *chaise* dándole al desventurado empleado del bufete una lección sobre cuál era la manera correcta de hacerle una oferta a una condesa por un terreno que dicha condesa poseía.

Una vez que redujo al empleado a meros balbuceos, cuando prácticamente lo tenía postrado ante sus delicados pies, la joven se dignó coger los documentos con la oferta que él le tendía.

Sarah hojeó las páginas, observando la suma de dinero y la ausencia del nombre del cliente. La joven levantó la mirada y le indicó al abogado que saliera un momento.

—Espéreme en el vestíbulo. Me gustaría hablar de este tema con mi marido.

Aguardó a que Crisp, que estaba esperando en la puerta, acompañara al joven, que no dejaba de hacer reverencias, fuera. Luego le pasó los documentos a Charlie.

—No viene ningún nombre, pero la oferta es mayor que la última vez.

Barnaby, que había estado observando el jardín por la puertaventana, se acercó a ellos y leyó por encima del hombro de Charlie las páginas que su amigo iba pasando.

—Wellington... Está al oeste de Taunton, ¿no es así?

Charlie asintió con la cabeza.

—A unos veinte kilómetros. —Tras acabar de leer la última página, le pasó los documentos—. Salvo por la falta de nombre, es una oferta bastante sencilla. —Levantó la mirada hacia Barnaby—. ¿Qué opinas? ¿Seguimos adelante con tu plan?

Barnaby asintió, levantando la mirada de los documentos. Se habían pasado horas discutiendo sus opciones... o la falta de ellas.

—Yo mismo le daré la respuesta a este abogado. Indudablemente no tendrá más información que los demás, pero si nuestro hombre sigue el mismo patrón de siempre, aparecerá el agente para conocer vuestra respuesta. Cuando lo haga, yo estaré allí. Seguiré al empleado del bufete, dejaré que se adelante por si acaso el agente se acerca a él por el camino.

Charlie estudió la cara de Barnaby.

—Ten cuidado.

Barnaby sonrió con dulzura.

—Lo tendré. —Miró a Sarah—. Tú también tienes que tener cuidado, y seguir fingiendo con respecto al orfanato. Con un tipo de esta calaña, uno que quizá tenga una apariencia perfectamente respetable, nunca se sabe cuándo él o alguien que él conozca te estará vigilando.

Sarah hizo una mueca, pero asintió con la cabeza.

—Si vas hasta Wellington, no podrás estar de regreso esta noche.

La dulce sonrisa de Barnaby se tornó más dura.

—No importa. Me quedaré en Wellington hasta que encuentre al agente.

Esa misma noche, Charlie yacía junto a Sarah en su mullida y cómoda cama, rezando por que Barnaby hubiera tenido éxito. En cuanto pudo se había deshecho de su papel autoritario, para convertirse en el mejor marido del mundo.

Tenía las cálidas piernas de Sarah enredadas con las suyas. La joven, exhausta tras el placer que acababan de compartir, se había acurrucado contra él y había acomodado la cabeza en el hueco de su hombro como si hubiera sido hecho para ella. Charlie la estrechaba entre sus brazos; la satisfacción que sentía era como una droga que le recorría las venas.

El sabor de la inocencia se había transformado en otro sabor más puro y apasionado, incluso más adictivo. Y él quería asegurárselo para siempre, quería saber que siempre sería suyo.

Y haría cualquier cosa, literalmente hablando, para asegurarse de que así era.

Ese impulso —ese compromiso— chocaba de bruces con el papel que actualmente se veía obligado a interpretar.

La sensación de su adormecida esposa descansando confiadamente contra él sólo reforzaba su resistencia a fingir como lo había hecho los últimos días, cada vez que cualquier desconocido estaba presente. Sarah había avisado a la señora Duncliffe y a Skeggs para ponerlos al corriente de la visita del deán y asegurarles que el buen nombre del personal del orfanato permanecía intacto, por si acaso al especulador se le ocurría comenzar una compaña de difamación con la intención de presionarla aún más y conseguir que vendiera. Pero teniendo en cuenta la necesidad de mantener el secreto, no habían podido decirle a la esposa del vicario ni a Skeggs toda la verdad. De hecho, habían tenido que convencerles no con palabras, sino con hechos, de que Charlie insistía en privado en que Sarah se deshiciera del orfanato.

Nada más lejos de la realidad. O lo que era peor, el papel que había asumido Charlie exigía que se comportara de una manera que era totalmente contraria a sus deseos. A como quería, ahora y siempre, comportarse con ella.

A como sabía y aceptaba que tenía que comportarse si quería que su matrimonio funcionara.

Se habían reído juntos después de que la señora Duncliffe y Skeggs se hubieran ido. Como si sintiera la incomodidad de su marido, Sarah había sonreído y bromeado, quitándole importancia al asunto y aliviando las heridas emocionales que la escena les había infligido a los dos. Pero él no podía evitar sentir —de manera ilógica quizá— que incluso aquellos actos forzados traicionaban su amor.

Charlie se estremecía interiormente cada vez que pensaba en esa palabra en relación consigo mismo.

Lo que ilustraba a la perfección su acuciante necesidad de poner fin a esa charada, liberarse de la inesperada influencia de ese malhechor y así poder concentrarse en superar aquella arraigada reacción que le impedía confesarle su amor a Sarah. Poder demostrárselo a su esposa sin tener que tomar en cuenta cuándo y dónde estaban. Luchar contra las ideas que durante años habían prevalecido en su mente no era tarea fácil; todavía persistía la creencia de que el amor era una peligrosa emoción a la que dar rienda suelta.

Pero estaba resuelto a conseguirlo, a vencer y erradicar aquella atrincherada resistencia, y darle a Sarah y a su matrimonio lo que ambos necesitaban, no sólo para sobrevivir sino para prosperar.

Quizá si pudiera decir las palabras... Pero no podía, sabía que no podía. Eso marcaba un objetivo que él debía alcanzar.

Un pequeño objetivo, quizá, pero ¿acaso no decían los filósofos que si alguien se comprometía a algo de palabra tenía que cumplirlo? Eso era algo que valía para los negocios, ¿por qué no para el matrimonio?

Así que necesitaba hacer una declaración, algo real, algo que ella supiera que le salía del corazón.

Palabras, las palabras correctas.

Estaba razonablemente seguro de que éstas no eran «¿estás embarazada?». Si bien él sospechaba que podría estarlo, Sarah no le había dicho ni una palabra al respecto, y él no sabía si tenía derecho a preguntárselo, al menos todavía no. Quizá sería mejor esperar a que ella se lo dijera. Sospechaba que era una de esas cosas de mujeres sobre las que los hombres inteligentes fingían absoluta sorpresa.

Volvió a darle vueltas a la cabeza al tema de las palabras correctas, cavilando una y otra vez hasta que se quedó dormido.

Dos días después, mientras la tarde caía sobre las colinas, Sarah salió del orfanato a lomos de *Blacktail* para regresar a su casa, Morwellan Park. Sonrió al pensar en lo rápido que había comenzado a pensar en el Park, la casa de Charlie, como suya. Desde su primer día como condesa, había sentido que era así, como un guante que se ajustara a la perfección.

Ansiosa por regresar, agitó las riendas de *Blacktail*. Detrás de ella, Hills, el mozo de cuadra que Charlie había insistido en que la acompañara, le seguía el paso.

Había cabalgado hasta el orfanato sólo para ver cómo iban las cosas por allí, y asegurarse de que todos estaban bien y no había habido más accidentes, como así había sido. Todo el mundo lo achacaba al estricto nivel de vigilancia, la mejor manera de estar en guardia contra más ataques.

Charlie había querido acompañarla, pero Malcolm Sinclair había ido a verlo para hablar de algunos informes sobre inversiones que Charlie había prometido compartir con él. Aunque mantenían la charada ante Sinclair, Charlie se había quedado de mala gana. Saltaba a la vista que hubiera preferido mandar a Malcolm a freír espárragos y cabalgar con ella hacia el norte.

Sarah sonrió ampliamente recordando el momento, atesorándolo en su corazón por todo lo que aquel gesto había significado para ella. El viento le echó el pelo hacia atrás; se rio y se inclinó hacia delante para palmear el cuello de *Blacktail*.

Sólo oyó un débil zumbido antes de que una punzada ardiente le atravesara la espalda.

Soltó un grito ahogado al sentirse desgarrada por el dolor. Se puso rígida, intentando respirar, ignorando la agonía creciente.

Escuchó un grito a su espalda... Hills. Las riendas de *Blacktail* se le deslizaron de las manos. El castrado continuó su galope. Algo había impactado en la espalda de la joven. A través del ardiente dolor podía sentir algo allí, clavado en ella, rebotando con cada paso de *Blacktail*. Agarrando con una mano las crines ondeantes del caballo, se aferró con fuerza a él, mientras con la otra mano se tanteaba la espalda, intentando saber qué la había golpeado. Palpó una especie de palo con plumas. El simple hecho de tocarlo hizo que soltara otro jadeo y le diera vueltas la cabeza.

Cuando volvió a abrir los ojos, vio sangre, húmeda y roja, en su guante. ¿Una flecha?

Apenas podía creerlo.

Apresurándose para alcanzarla, Hills se puso a su lado.

—¡Milady!

Con la cara cenicienta, el mozo intentó coger las riendas de *Blacktail*.

—¡No! —gritó Sarah con voz ahogada—. No te detengas. Quienquiera que haya disparado todavía está por aquí.

Si no se hubiera inclinado hacia delante...

—Al Manor —dijo dejándose caer sobre el cuello de *Blacktail*. Tenía la voz débil, pero Hills la escuchó—. Déjale a su aire y me llevará allí.

Le costaba mantener los ojos abiertos, así que los cerró, aunque se obligó mentalmente a seguir el camino del caballo; Sarah había tomado esa ruta cientos de veces y se la conocía como la palma de su mano.

Supo cuándo *Blacktail* viró para coger el sendero que conducía al Manor. Notó el cambio de dirección cuando el caballo se salió del camino de herradura, más arenoso y recorrió los campos de su padre.

Luego llegaron al puente de madera que cruzaba el riachuelo; cada paso del caballo la sacudía. Sarah gritó, casi se desmayó, pero logró conservar la conciencia hasta que los guijarros resonaron bajo los cascos de *Blacktail* y éste se detuvo en el patio de los establos del Manor.

El caballo resopló y echó la testuz hacia atrás.

Sarah oyó gritos, llamadas, una confusión de voces; luego sintió unas manos firmes pero suaves que la bajaban del lomo del caballo.

Suspirando, se dejó llevar y se hundió en una profunda oscuridad.

Repantigado en un sillón ante la chimenea de la biblioteca, Charlie estudió a Malcolm —que estaba sentado en otro sillón frente a la lumbre leyendo los boletines informativos de inversiones bursátiles que Charlie había recibido de Londres— y deseó que se diera prisa en leerlos. Aunque eso era algo que ya no tenía demasiada importancia. Desplazó la mirada a las ventanas y vio que estaba atardeciendo. Sarah volvería pronto. De hecho —frunció el ceño mentalmente— ya debería estar en casa.

¿Habría habido algún problema en el orfanato?

Charlie se removió, mirando de reojo el reloj. Eran casi las cuatro. Sarah ya debería haber regresado. Quizá ya había regresado y no se le había ocurrido pasarse por la biblioteca a saludar.

Frunció aún más el ceño interiormente. Sin duda, Sarah sabría que él querría saber que había vuelto... No podía creer que al menos no se pasara a verle para decirle que todo iba bien.

Lo embargó el impulso de levantarse y averiguar si había llegado a casa, y en caso contrario, ir a buscarla al orfanato y descubrir qué la había retrasado. Pero Malcolm seguía siendo una fuente de información valiosa, y él había prometido explicarle las complejidades de la banca de inversiones a cambio de los profundos conocimientos de Malcolm sobre la financiación del ferrocarril.

Pasaron otros dos minutos en silencio. Charlie preparaba las palabras para excusarse un momento e ir a averiguar si Sarah había vuelto a casa cuando el sonido de unos pasos apresurados resonó en el pasillo fuera de la biblioteca.

Tanto él como Malcolm se volvieron alarmados hacia la puerta cuando ésta se abrió de golpe.

Crisp irrumpió en la estancia, había llegado corriendo por el pasillo; Charlie estaba de pie antes incluso de que el mayordomo empezara a hablar.

—Milord, es lady Sarah. Hills acaba de llegar diciendo que le han disparado cuando regresaba a casa desde el orfanato.

Un frío desolador oprimió el corazón de Charlie.

—¿Le han disparado? —gritó mientras corría hacia la puerta.

Crisp se volvió hacia él.

—Según Hills le han disparado una flecha, milord. Está seguro. La han herido en la espalda. Ocurrió frente al Manor, y es allí donde está. Se desmayó justo cuando llegaron, milord, pero su padre dijo que la herida no es grave.

Charlie ya corría por el pasillo. Entonces recordó, se detuvo y se volvió. Y vio a Malcolm siguiéndole los pasos con la cara pálida y la expresión tan desencajada y horrorizada como la de él.

Malcolm le hizo un gesto brusco para que siguiera.

—¡Vete! No te preocupes por mí.

Charlie no esperó más, se giró y corrió hacia el establo.

A lomos de *Tormenta*, Charlie enfiló hacia el norte campo a través, tomando la ruta más rápida hacia Conningham Manor y Sarah.

Cinco minutos más tarde, Malcolm Sinclair abandonó Morwellan Park por el camino principal. También se dirigía al norte a lomos de su castrado negro, pero sin salirse del camino.

Sarah despertó ante la caricia suave y tranquilizadora de la mano de su madre apartándole el pelo de la frente. El dolor ardiente de la espalda había disminuido, casi desaparecido. Ahora era más parecido al dolor producido por un arañazo.

Abrió los ojos y parpadeó. Estaba tumbada de lado con la cabeza en el regazo de su madre. Levantó el cuello con cuidado y se incorporó lentamente, notando que tenía un vendaje en la espalda por debajo de la blusa.

—Despacio, cariño. —Su madre la ayudó a levantarse. Cuando Sarah finalmente se incorporó y se sentó, la soltó—. Ya está. —Miró al otro lado de la habitación—. Señorita Twitterton, ¿podría pedirle a la cocinera que envíe ahora ese caldo de pollo?

Sarah movió la cabeza y descubrió que ya no le daba vueltas. Sintiéndose lo suficientemente estabilizada en el familiar asiento junto a la ventana de la salita de atrás, Sarah miró a su alrededor y vio desaparecer las faldas de Twitters por la puerta, y a Clary y a Gloria, las dos con los ojos muy abiertos, mirándola impacientes desde el otro lado de la estancia. Parecía como si tuvieran cientos de preguntas en la punta de la lengua. Antes de que decidiesen cuál de las dos preguntaba primero, Sarah miró a su madre.

—¿De verdad me dispararon una flecha?

Su madre asintió con la cabeza mientras apretaba los labios.

—Una flecha de ballesta. Como las de tu padre. Pero no hay ninguna razón para que alguien utilice esa arma fuera de temporada.

Sarah intentó tocarse la espalda, pero hizo una mueca al estirar la piel y el músculo.

—No es necesario que te toques. —Su madre le cogió la mano y se la apartó de la espalda—. Por suerte, el doctor Caliburn estaba aquí hablando con tu padre. Limpió la herida y dijo que no era demasiado profunda. —Le dio una palmadita en la mano, luego la soltó y cogió aire, que expulsó lentamente—. Dijo que habías tenido mucha suerte.

Al oír el temblor contenido en la voz de su madre, Sarah se obligó a esbozar una sonrisa y le apretó la mano.

—Estoy bien, de verdad.

Y lo estaba, siempre y cuando ignorara la punzada dolorosa de su espalda. Desvió la mirada hacia la ventana y vio que estaba anocheciendo.

—¿Qué hora es?

—Poco más de las cuatro. Evidentemente, mandamos a nuestro

mozo de cuadra para que avisara a Charlie. —La madre de Sarah sacudió la chaquetilla y los restos de la blusa que su hija había llevado puesta—. Podemos lavar y arreglar la chaqueta, pero la blusa está inservible. La que llevas puesta es de Clary.

Sarah bajó la mirada hacia la fina blusa que la cubría y luego le brindó a Clary una sonrisa.

—Gracias.

Clary hizo un gesto con la mano para quitarle importancia.

—No tiene importancia. ¿Qué sentiste? Me refiero al clavárse-te la flecha.

—¡Clary! —recriminó lady Conningham mirando a su sanguinaria hija con un ceño severo.

Pero Sarah sonrió ampliamente y dijo:

—Fue como una punzada ardiente.

—Ya basta, chicas. —Lady Conningham interrumpió a Glory cuando intentaba decir algo, frunciendo aún más el ceño. En ese momento Twitters reapareció llevando una bandeja con un tazón de la famosa sopa de pollo reconstituyente de la cocinera.

—Necesitas recuperar fuerzas —le dijo la diminuta gobernanta mientras depositaba la bandeja en la mesita que habían colocado delante de Sarah—. Sin duda el conde llegará dentro de poco y no querrás desmayarte otra vez.

Ocultando una sonrisa ante el ingenio de Twitters, que siempre sabía qué argumento emplear para salirse con la suya, Sarah cogió la cuchara y comenzó a tomar la sopa.

Jamás se había desmayado antes, pero para su sorpresa descubrió que sí necesitaba tomar algo para recuperar las fuerzas.

Justo cuando dejaba la cuchara junto al tazón vacío, el sonido de cascos sobre la grava atrajo la atención de todas hacia el patio, donde vieron a Charlie bajar de un salto de la silla de montar y correr hacia la puerta principal.

Lady Conningham miró a Sarah con el ceño fruncido.

—¿Te encuentras lo suficientemente bien para ponerte en pie?

La joven se puso en pie con cuidado. Twitters se apresuró a apartar la mesa con la bandeja. Salvo una punzada de dolor en la espalda, Sarah no se encontraba mal. No se mareó. Reanimada por la taza de caldo de pollo, se sentía relativamente bien.

—Me encuentro bien.

Y quería irse a casa. Con su madre y Twitters revoloteando a su alrededor como gallinas cluecas, y Clary y Gloria presionándola para que contara cada sangriento detalle, el Manor podía ser confortable pero ya no era su hogar.

Esa certeza cristalizó en su mente mientras la puerta de la salita se abría de golpe, con tal violencia, que casi golpeó a Clary que, con un grito agudo, la consiguió atrapar.

Charlie no pareció oírla. Parado en el umbral, miraba a Sarah con ojos ardientes y ensombrecidos, que le recorrieron el cuerpo, examinando cada mínimo detalle desde la cabeza a los pies. Cuando terminó la miró directamente a los ojos. Con la misma dolorosa intensidad le escrutó la cara, los ojos, la expresión.

—¿Estás bien?

Sorprendida —algo anonadada incluso— de verle tan alterado, de que mostrara abiertamente las crudas y desnudas emociones en su rostro, de que las exhibiera sin tapujos ante su madre, Clary, Gloria y Twitters, Sarah se estremeció mentalmente y se apresuró a brindarle una sonrisa mientras le tendía las manos.

—Tengo una pequeña herida en la espalda y una autoridad competente me ha dicho que es poco más que un arañazo profundo.

Charlie masculló algo que Sarah creyó interpretar como «¡Gracias a Dios!». Luego cruzó la estancia en dos zancadas, la tomó de las manos para acercarla a su cuerpo y la rodeó suavemente con los brazos. Teniendo mucho cuidado de no tocarle la herida, le rozó con los dedos el vendaje que le cubría la espalda bajo la blusa.

—Hills me ha dicho que te dieron debajo del omóplato —le murmuró contra el pelo.

Sarah no podía creer lo reconfortante que era su calidez, cuánto la aliviaba sentir aquella fuerza rodeándola.

Oyeron que alguien se aclaraba la garganta y Charlie alzó la cabeza y se giró, pero sin soltar a Sarah.

—Quizá —dijo su madre— deberíamos trasladarnos a la salita de estar.

Sarah supo exactamente en qué momento Charlie se dio cuenta no sólo de que llevaba el corazón en la mano, sino que lo agitaba para que todo el mundo lo viera. Se puso rígido. Los brazos que la rodeaban se tensaron, pero no se aflojaron; no la soltó ni la apartó de él.

Sarah le cogió de la manga y tiró de ella. Cuando Charlie bajó la mirada, Sarah les habló tanto a él como a su madre.

—En realidad preferiría emprender el viaje de regreso al Park antes de que anochezca.

—No creo que... —dijo su madre.

—Por supuesto. —Charlie interrumpió a la madre de Sarah sin vacilación—. Le pediré prestado el carruaje a tu padre.

Sosteniéndole la mirada, Sarah hizo una ligera mueca.

—Será más cómodo para mí montar a *Blacktail*. Así no tendré que sufrir el traqueteo del carruaje y podremos dirigirnos a casa campo a través y no por los duros caminos.

Charlie frunció el ceño. Por el rabillo del ojo, Sarah vio que su madre volvía a abrir la boca para protestar, pero se detuvo y la cerró a regañadientes.

—Muy bien, sólo si estás segura de que estás lo suficientemente bien para ir a caballo. —Charlie todavía tenía el ceño fruncido, pero su mirada se había vuelto distante. Sarah supo que estaba planificando el regreso, luego centró su atención en ella y asintió con la cabeza—. Pero si vamos a volver a casa a caballo tenemos que salir de inmediato.

Charlie se volvió hacia la madre de Sarah y la tranquilizó con su habitual encanto, asegurándole que su pollito estaría en manos seguras.

Sarah ocultó una amplia sonrisa. A él no le gustaría saber que era su anterior y preocupada reacción por lo sucedido lo que su madre encontraba más tranquilizador, que era eso lo que había hecho que cerrara la boca cuando su padre y ella los acompañaron al patio de los establos.

Charlie subió a Sarah a la silla de montar. No se apartó de su lado hasta asegurarle los estribos y observar cómo la joven se recogía las faldas y tomaba las riendas. Sarah parecía lo suficientemente fuerte, pero se movía con rigidez, y él supo que ella quería irse a casa.

Y eso era algo que él no pensaba discutir.

Charlie se dio la vuelta y le estrechó la mano a lord Conningham, luego se subió a lomos de *Tormenta*. Hizo que el enorme caballo de caza se pusiera al lado de *Blacktail* y se despidió del resto de la familia de Sarah con la cabeza. Cruzaron lentamente el arco de los esta-

blos ante Clary y Gloria, quienes sonreían radiante y alentadora-
mente, y luego tomaron dirección sur.

Al principio fueron al trote, luego Sarah puso a *Blacktail* a medio galope. Charlie le siguió el paso hasta que coronaron la primera colina y quedaron fuera de la vista del Manor.

—Frena. —Charlie observó cómo Sarah, que había permanecido en silencio desde que abandonaron el patio de los establos de su
padre, le obedecía.

Cuando *Blacktail* se detuvo, ella giró la cabeza y lo miró con las
cejas enarcadas.

Él detuvo a *Tormenta* a su lado, luego acercó el enorme caballo
gris al costado de *Blacktail*. Cogió las riendas de la mano de Sarah
y estiró los brazos hacia ella.

—Ven aquí.

Sarah permitió que la tomara por la cintura y la alzara para sen-
tarla delante de él en la silla. Que no emitiera una sola protesta le indicó a Charlie que había tenido razón: la herida no era tan grave
como para no poder montar a caballo, justo lo que ella había dicho.

—Estoy bien —murmuró ella mientras él le acomodaba las piernas y las faldas antes de reclinarla contra su pecho.

—Cierto, pero así te dolerá menos. Apóyate en mí.

Él ató las riendas de *Blacktail* a su silla de montar, luego la rodeó
con un brazo y la estrechó contra su cuerpo. Cogió las riendas de
Tormenta y se pusieron en marcha.

Acunada entre los brazos de su marido, protegida por el cuerpo
de Charlie contra cualquier sacudida o movimiento brusco, Sarah
se fue relajando poco a poco. Con un suspiro apoyó la cabeza contra su hombro.

Charlie relajó la mandíbula, que había mantenido apretada. Algo
en su interior se liberó. Le rozó el pelo con los labios.

—El mozo que envió tu padre me dijo que tu vida no corría peligro, pero no sabía lo grave que era la herida y Hills tampoco supo
decírmelo.

Ella levantó la cabeza y lo miró a los ojos. Luego alzó una mano
y le acarició la mejilla.

—De verdad, estoy bien.

Charlie asintió con la cabeza, luego respiró hondo y dejó salir
el último resto de aquel miedo oscuro que lo había atenazado.

—Cuéntame qué pasó.

Sarah guardó silencio por un momento. Él sintió que tenía el ceño fruncido cuando le respondió:

—En realidad, no lo sé. Iba a caballo, acababa de dejar atrás las colinas. Había cruzado el puente del riachuelo, así que fue un poco después. Me incliné hacia delante, palmeé el cuello de *Blacktail* y entonces... sentí que me golpeaba la flecha.

—Hills me dijo que no vio a nadie, pero que estabais mucho más adelante del punto en que ocurrió cuando miró hacia atrás.

Sarah asintió con la cabeza.

—Yo iba al galope y dejé caer las riendas, así que *Blacktail* siguió al mismo paso.

Charlie no hizo más preguntas. No le gustaba nada la dirección que estaban tomando sus pensamientos. Quería reflexionar sobre ellos antes de compartirlos con nadie. *Tormenta* y *Blacktail* conocían el camino al establo, así que abrazó a Sarah y dejó que su mente y todos sus sentidos se tranquilizaran ante la realidad de que ella estaba sana y salvo, y con él. Todavía con él.

Malcolm Sinclair no tiró de las riendas al llegar a su casa alquilada en Crowcombe, sino que siguió adelante, hacia el norte, a la costa.

Con los labios apretados y el semblante sombrío, urgió a su caballo negro a subir la cuesta a Williton.

—Ten paciencia —masculló con los dientes apretados—. Sé discreto. ¡Y el tonto va e intenta matarla! ¿Qué demonios cree que está haciendo?

No había nadie a su alrededor que pudiera oírle ni, mucho menos, contestarle. Dejándose llevar por la furia que le embargaba, azuzó a su caballo.

18

El mozo de cuadra, Croker, los esperaba cuando llegaron a los establos del Park. Hills también estaba allí, ansioso y preocupado. Sarah se fijó en que había más sirvientes detrás y casi pudo sentir el alivio de todos cuando la vieron capaz de sentarse y sonreír, aunque débilmente.

Tanto Croker como Hills le dirigieron una amplia sonrisa mientras sujetaban las riendas de los caballos. Charlie se apeó, dejándola en la silla de montar mientras lo hacía, luego la ayudó a bajar. Permitió que sus pies tocaran el suelo sólo el tiempo suficiente para girarla y alzarla entre sus brazos teniendo cuidado de no presionarle la herida.

Sarah continuó sonriendo. Charlie la llevó fuera del patio de los establos y atravesó el césped. Ella esperó a estar a medio camino de la casa y que no los oyera nadie para mirarle a la cara y decirle:

—Puedo caminar, ya lo sabes.

Él la miró brevemente, luego clavó la mirada hacia delante. Tenía los dientes apretados.

—Limítate a seguirme la corriente.

Era una pequeña petición, algo que Sarah estaba dispuesta a conceder con facilidad.

La habría dejado en el suelo para abrir la puerta lateral, pero cuando se acercaron a ella, ésta se abrió. Barnaby estaba detrás, sosteniéndola para que pasaran.

Charlie le gruñó su agradecimiento y giró a Sarah mientras atravesaban el umbral; luego volvió a acomodarla entre sus brazos. Bajó la mirada hacia ella.

—¿Adónde me dirijo?

—A mi salita. Aún falta una hora para la cena.

Charlie recorrió el pasillo con Barnaby a su lado.

—Si no os importa, me gustaría que me dijerais qué ha sucedido.

Al igual que Charlie, Barnaby tenía la cara pálida y una expresión muy seria. La sonrisa de Sarah se desvaneció un poco.

—Sí... deberías saberlo.

No cabía ninguna duda ni para él, ni para Charlie, ni para ella, una vez que les contó los detalles, que su «accidente» podía ser obra del especulador.

Envuelta en la acogedora calidez de su salita, Sarah narró los hechos de nuevo, luego Charlie añadió las observaciones de Hills.

Barnaby apoyó la cabeza en el respaldo del sillón en el que se había dejado caer.

—No me imaginé que deseara la propiedad hasta tal punto.

Parado delante de la chimenea, Charlie le miró con el ceño fruncido.

—¿A qué te refieres?

Barnaby giró la cabeza y lo miró directamente a los ojos.

—Si Sarah muere sin dejar descendencia, la propiedad pasará a ser tuya y, dado que hemos proyectado la imagen de que estás en contra del orfanato, sería razonable suponer que si Sarah muriese, en especial si es por algún motivo relacionado con el lugar, y después de guardar el debido luto, tú estarías dispuesto a deshacerte por completo de la granja Quilley. No está vinculada a las tierras Morwellan, es una propiedad pequeña e improductiva, poco atractiva para un hacendado como tú.

Charlie suspiró y cerró los ojos.

—Tienes razón. Y como resulta evidente que nuestro malhechor no tiene prisa por asegurarse la propiedad puede seguir jugando al gato y al ratón indefinidamente. —Abrió los ojos y miró a Sarah, luego sostuvo la mirada azul de Barnaby—. Cuando todo esto haya acabado y podamos echarle el guante, tengo la intención de hacerle pagar por todo el daño que ha hecho.

Barnaby curvó los labios en una fiera sonrisa.

—Yo te sostendré la chaqueta.

Sarah sacudió la cabeza mentalmente. Estudió a Barnaby. Había estado ausente desde que había partido hacia el sur siguiendo al empleado del bufete.

—¿Has averiguado algo sobre el agente?

La expresión de Barnaby se ensombreció.

—No, salvo que es muy hábil. —Miró a Charlie—. Seguí de lejos al empleado hasta Wellington, pero en los caminos abiertos antes y después de Taunton, es probable que el agente me viera y decidiera proceder de una manera más segura. No lo sé. En cualquier caso, seguí al empleado hasta una casa de huéspedes, luego, como era tarde, busqué habitación para esa noche.

»A la mañana siguiente, hablé con el abogado y le persuadí para que nos ayudara. La descripción que me dio del agente era la misma que la de los otros abogados, por lo que al parecer es siempre el mismo hombre. En este caso, el abogado, Riggs, estaba seguro de que el agente no era de la zona. Lo cual —Barnaby levantó un dedo— nos facilita las cosas si queremos buscarle. Los lugareños detectan enseguida a los extraños.

Barnaby apretó los labios.

—Por desgracia, cuando llegó el empleado del bufete, me enteré de que el agente se había tropezado casualmente con él en la taberna en la que suele refugiarse por las tardes para evitar a su mujer. Si lo hubiera sabido, me habría quedado a mirar, pero... —Barnaby hizo una mueca— al parecer el abogado le dijo al agente que un amigo de la familia, por supuesto yo, estaría en Wellington al día siguiente para hablar de la oferta por la granja Quilley con él. El agente puso mala cara y dijo que la oferta final era ésa, que la tomábamos o la dejábamos, pero que desde luego no estaba interesado en discutirla. Dijo que su cliente tomaba la falta de aceptación inmediata como una negativa y le ofreció al abogado un sobre con el resto del pago acordado.

Charlie maldijo por lo bajo.

—Exacto. —Barnaby parecía sombrío—. Hay que encontrar a ese agente. Centraré mis pesquisas en él y rastrearé la zona. Alguien lo habrá visto y se habrá dado cuenta de que no es un lugareño. Lleva semanas por aquí y es imposible que haya podido permanecer oculto todo el rato. —Entrecerró los ojos y endureció el tono de voz—. Cuando lo encuentre, voy a persuadirlo para que nos conduzca hasta su cliente.

Mirándole, Charlie enarcó ligeramente las cejas.

—Me alegro de que hayas dicho «nos».

Decidiendo que no vendría mal la civilizadora influencia de una buena cena, Sarah se levantó y se sacudió las faldas arrugadas.

—Voy a cambiarme de ropa para cenar. Nos vemos en media hora, caballeros.

Charlie la observó con la mirada afilada de un halcón mientras se dirigía a la puerta; consciente de su mirada, Sarah se giró y le brindó una tranquilizadora sonrisa antes de abrir la puerta y dirigirse a sus habitaciones.

Charlie se apoyó en el respaldo de la cama y observó el rayo de luna que entraba por la ventana del dormitorio. Sarah estaba tumbada a su lado, saciada y dormida. Durante la cena habían hablado de todo lo que sabían del extorsionador, concluyendo que todavía estaban muy lejos de poder identificarle.

En lugar de quedarse en el comedor para tomar el oporto, Barnaby y él habían trasladado la reunión a la salita de Sarah. Charlie comenzaba a sentirse tan a gusto en esa estancia, con ella, como lo estaba en la biblioteca. Habían barajado los mejores lugares para que Barnaby comenzara la búsqueda; después habían revisado de nuevo las medidas de seguridad del orfanato, aceptando a regañadientes que era demasiado arriesgado poner vigilantes en las colinas circundantes. Corrían el riesgo de que el malhechor los viera y desapareciera.

Hablar con Barnaby le había recordado a Charlie todas las implicaciones del plan del especulador, pero ahora sus instintos le decían que era necesario capturar y desenmascarar al hombre por una cuestión puramente personal.

Los acontecimientos de la tarde regresaron a su mente junto con las revelaciones que habían traído consigo. El helado terror del que fue Charlie presa cuando oyó que Sarah estaba herida no era algo que fuera a olvidar nunca, todavía le afectaba, le perturbaba; el alivio —puro, profundo y revitalizador— le había inundado en cuanto vio a su esposa, de pie junto a su madre, herida, pero todavía viva.

Mientras la parte cuerda, lógica, racional y arrogante de él estaba dispuesta a pasar por alto dicho temor, la desesperación y la desolación que acechaban detrás y que lo impulsaban a reclamarla como ella había hecho con él —un precio a pagar durante el resto de su vida por dejar que el amor le reclamara—, otra parte de él, la parte que Charlie apenas empezaba a conocer, sólo podía sonreír y regocijarse en el placer de su alivio, en la calidez y alegría que sentía al cuidarla, al preocuparse de ella, al consentirla como nunca se había consentido a sí mismo... De hecho comenzaba a sentir una profunda satisfacción, una intangible gratificación, al amarla.

A pesar de sus temores, todavía quería eso, quería aferrarse a ello y asegurarlo con cada fibra de su ser, incluso si para ello tenía que aceptar el amor. El miedo al temor, a la desesperación y a la desolación no era suficiente para apartarlo de ese camino, para evitar buscar las alegrías del amor.

Sarah murmuró en sueños y se acurrucó aún más contra su cuerpo. Él la estrechó instintivamente entre sus brazos, luego recordó la herida y se obligó a aflojar el abrazo. Sarah estaba allí, con él. Era todo lo que importaba.

Había estado allí, con él, desde el instante en que la puerta se había cerrado a su espalda cuando la había seguido desde la salita. Sarah había tomado un baño antes; él se había asomado para asegurarse de que su doncella la estaba ayudando, sólo entonces Charlie se había retirado. Pero cuando regresó, y se quedaron solos, Sarah se había vuelto hacia él con vacilación, pero con un evidente propósito.

Charlie había estado preocupado por la herida de su esposa, por los movimientos apasionados que podrían provocarle dolor. Sarah le había dejado muy claro que era ella quien decidía ofrecerle su cuerpo y su amor y le había demostrado, implícita y explícitamente, que él era su objetivo, el centro de toda su atención.

Charlie se había rendido a ella, se había tendido en la cama y la había dejado tomarle a su manera, permitiendo que lo montara hasta alcanzar un dulce olvido. Lo había visto en la cara de Sarah, en sus ojos, y estaba seguro de que ella lo había visto en los de él. Había habido un momento memorable, en que se había entregado a ella de una manera inigualable, en que la gloria lo inundó y lo reclamó.

Con más intensidad esta vez.

Charlie sintió que ella estaba extrañamente satisfecha con él, con cómo se había comportado en el Manor, pero sabía que no habría podido comportarse de otra manera. Se había sentido algo incómodo al darse cuenta de lo manifiestamente posesivo y protector que había sido, pero a Sarah no parecía haberle importado.

Lo que por otro lado daba igual. No habría podido actuar de otra manera ni aunque hubiese querido.

Por el momento, todo parecía ir bien entre ellos y, aunque su relación progresaba muy lentamente, parecía seguir la dirección correcta. Charlie no siempre podía saber si ella aprobaba lo que él hacía, pero hasta entonces el instinto que lo guiaba no le había fallado.

Satisfecho, se permitió hundirse en el sueño, perderse en el velo de los recuerdos. Se vio a sí mismo en su desayuno de bodas haciendo una promesa, una que había olvidado de manera consciente. Luego, con un instinto infalible, le había prometido a Sarah hacerla feliz.

Estaba camino de cumplir esa promesa, y también de decirle que la amaba. De admitir en voz alta, ante todo aquel que quisiera escucharle, lo que sentía por ella.

Tenía una biblioteca llena de libros. En alguna parte encontraría las palabras adecuadas.

Si había una verdad que había reconocido finalmente, era que no se podía recibir amor sin ofrecerlo a cambio, y por último, confesarlo.

Casi todos los de su mismo sexo encontraban eso último bastante intimidante...

Comenzó a dormirse y a perder contacto con la realidad. Se hundió en el sueño, dejando sin resolver ese eterno misterio del universo.

La tarde del domingo siguiente, Malcolm Sinclair se encontraba paseando por los muelles de Watchet. Su fría mirada color avellana buscaba sin cesar, mirando a un hombre y luego a otro. Su presa no daba señales de vida. Había recorrido las calles del pueblo y las tiendas, asomándose a todas las tabernas y negocios.

Finalmente, con la rabia estremeciéndole el cuerpo, se detuvo al final de la calle Mayor. No tenía ni idea de dónde estaba Jennings. Lo había buscado durante toda la noche y lo que llevaba de día. Incluso se había arriesgado a buscarle por las colinas al norte de la granja Quilley, pero no lo había encontrado.

Deslizó la mirada por la calle Mayor y escudriñó, todo lo que podía abarcar desde allí. Había estado en Watchet con frecuencia durante las últimas semanas. Los lugareños sabían quién era y se habían acostumbrado a verle por el pueblo. Decidiendo que hablar con su hombre de confianza lo antes posible era más importante que correr el riesgo de que alguien les viera juntos, giró sobre sus talones y subió por la calle Mayor, luego tomó la última calle a la derecha.

Jennings había alquilado una diminuta casa de pescadores al final de esa calle. Malcolm la dejó atrás y recorrió el estrecho y rocoso camino que conducía a las colinas. Se detuvo un poco más adelante, se dio la vuelta y miró al mar, como si estuviera estudiando el acantilado y el trazado del pueblo.

La casita y el establo que tenía al lado estaban también en su línea de visión. No había ningún caballo en el establo.

Malcolm maldijo por lo bajo. Debatió consigo mismo, pero dada la última acción de Jennings, era imperativo pararle los pies al hombre.

Tras lanzar otra mirada a su alrededor, siguió avanzando por el camino, luego se dio la vuelta y finalmente entró en el porche trasero de la casa de pescadores. La puerta de atrás no estaba cerrada con llave.

No había nadie, así que no podía hacer nada más salvo dejar una nota. Arrancó una hoja de la libreta que siempre llevaba consigo y escribió con mayúsculas ya que era la mejor manera de disfrazar su letra, un mensaje simple:

«VEN A VERME ESTA NOCHE.»

Dejó la nota abierta sobre la mesa, debajo de un vaso.

Nadie podría deducir nada de esas palabras, pero Jennings sí sabría qué querían decir.

En silencio, salió de la casa y se alejó a toda prisa.

Malcolm llegó a Finley House cuando los últimos rayos del sol se desvanecían en el cielo. Metió la llave en la cerradura de la puerta y entró en la casa dirigiéndose en silencio hacia la biblioteca, la única habitación que utilizaba además del dormitorio de la planta superior.

Se hundió en el sillón ante el fuego de la chimenea, negando mentalmente con la cabeza mientras intentaba enfrentarse a la maraña de acontecimientos en la que tan inesperadamente se había visto atrapado. Levantó la mirada hacia el reloj de la repisa de la chimenea y vio la tarjeta que había dejado allí, una invitación de lady Conningham para que cenara con su familia y otros invitados esa misma noche.

Aquella imagen era un vívido recordatorio de lo que, de alguna manera, había llegado a ser muy importante para él sin proponérselo, y que ponía en riesgo su plan. Charlie, Sarah, y su vida juntos, allí en la paz y beatitud del campo.

Hasta ese momento, no había valorado lo preciosa que era esa realidad, no hasta que la había visto y experimentado a través de los ojos de Charlie y Sarah. Hasta entonces no había sabido lo mucho que había anhelado aquella clase de vida. Se daba cuenta ahora, al saber cuánto envidiaba a Charlie, una envidia sana hacia su buena fortuna. Quizá porque Charlie era muy parecido a él, no sólo en apariencia, sino en agudeza mental, en ingenio compartido, en su afición por las finanzas y el sencillo placer de ganar dinero.

Reconocía que Charlie caminaba por una línea recta y estrecha mientras que él encontraba excitante desviarse del camino, pero eso era el resultado de las influencias y la guía que cada uno de ellos había recibido en sus años de formación más que de cualquier diferencia intrínseca. Charlie había tenido a su familia y a los Cynster; él no había tenido a nadie, a menos que contase a su último y no llorado tutor, Lowther, quien se había visto obligado a pegarse un tiro en la cabeza para no tener que enfrentarse al escándalo por su participación en el comercio de trata de blancas.

Los negocios de Charlie eran cristalinos, mientras que los suyos permanecían ocultos entre las sombras, pero las bases eran muy parecidas.

Malcolm torció el gesto con pesar. Bajó la mirada y clavó los ojos en las llamas que lamían los leños que su ama de llaves había dejado ardiendo en la chimenea. Por mucho que quisiera imaginar lo contrario, sabía que jamás podría tener lo que Charlie tenía ahora mismo al alcance de la mano. Sin embargo, lo que realmente le irritaba, lo que realmente le fastidiaba y enfurecía, era cómo Charlie se negaba a apreciar lo que se le ofrecía, lo que la vida le había puesto en bandeja, que no lo tomara en sus manos y lo agradeciera.

Quizás eran los cinco años que los separaban —la madurez, la soledad que llenaba su vida cada día— lo que hacía que viera y apreciara lo que Charlie tenía, algo de lo que Malcolm carecía y que le hacía consciente de las oportunidades perdidas, de una vida más allá del dinero y desprovista de todo logro personal, algo que Charlie poseía y que debería valorar y aprovechar.

Ya que él no podía.

Aunque de una manera indirecta, no cabía duda de que tenía todo eso al alcance de su mano si quería. Y extrañamente aquello le importaba.

Con lo cual tenía que decirle a Jennings que se olvidara del orfanato. La incapacidad de contactar con su hombre de confianza le molestaba sobremanera —odiaba no tener el control absoluto—, pero Jennings acabaría por encontrar su nota y, como siempre, obedecería. Iría a su casa ya entrada la noche, refugiándose entre las sombras para que nadie lo viera.

Malcolm miró la invitación de lady Conningham. Incapaz de acudir a la iglesia por tener que buscar a Jennings, había enviado una nota a Morwellan Park esa mañana. El muchacho que la había llevado había regresado con unas líneas de Charlie asegurándole que la herida de Sarah era de poca importancia y que ya estaba en pie.

Si era así, lo más probable es que ella estuviera en la cena de su madre, y él quería —necesitaba— comprobar por sí mismo que Sarah no había sufrido ningún daño duradero por el evidente entusiasmo de Jennings.

Aquel impulso, atizado por una emoción que no comprendía, era extraño para él. Sabía que no sentía por la joven lo mismo que sentía Charlie, pero viéndola a través de los ojos de su amigo, había llegado a admirarla y respetarla como nunca antes había respetado a ninguna otra mujer. Pero no sólo deseaba que Sarah estuviera bien, quería que Charlie y ella fueran felices.

Ya que él no podía tener esa vida, se encargaría de que el conde sí la tuviera.

Malcolm se levantó. Jennings no llegaría hasta medianoche. No había ninguna razón para no pasar la tarde en el Manor en excelente compañía, para asegurarse de que Sarah estaba bien y para, si se le presentaba la oportunidad, dirigir —sutilmente— a Charlie para que aceptara y abrazara todo lo que su esposa le ofrecía, todo lo que podía tener.

Irónicamente asombrado de encontrarse siendo adalid de tal causa, fue arriba a cambiarse de ropa.

Charlie miró la mesa de comedor en Conningham Manor y agradeció todo lo que tenía. Sarah estaba sentada frente a él, evidentemente repuesta de su terrible experiencia, y sólo una ocasional punzada de dolor la hacía esbozar una mueca cuando se estiraba demasiado o se rozaba la espalda sin querer.

Él se había pasado todo el día en una montaña rusa emocional, al no poder envolverla en una capa protectora. Sabía lo irritante que ella encontraría eso, y cada vez que se había interesado por su estado, ella le había sonreído y le había asegurado que ya estaba recuperada del todo.

La luz en los ojos de su esposa, su suave sonrojo mientras se reía de alguna cosa que Malcolm, sentado a su lado, le había dicho, habían tranquilizado a Charlie como nunca lo hubieran hecho las palabras.

A pesar estar conversando con el señor Sinclair, Sarah era plenamente consciente de la mirada de Charlie, que no había variado de intensidad en lo más mínimo desde que el día anterior había ido a buscarla al Manor. La atención y los cuidados de su marido habían sido inquebrantables. Esa mañana la había dejado dormir, enviando a su doncella para que la despertara sólo cuando había llegado la hora de vestirse para ir a la iglesia. Había supuesto correctamente que ella no habría querido perderse el servicio, sobre todo para evitar las especulaciones que habría ante tal hecho. Pero en cuanto habían encabezado la salida de la congregación, Charlie la había guiado hasta el carruaje para volver a casa, evitando el habitual paseo y charla en el patio de la iglesia.

Sarah se había preparado para eso, pero se había sentido aliviada al no tener que forzarse mental o físicamente. Al llegar a casa, había insistido en que se encontraba bien para asistir a la cena de su madre, y Charlie le había dicho que enviaría a un mozo a casa de su madre confirmando su asistencia con la condición de que descansara hasta entonces. Luego él se había arrellanado en el sillón de la salita de Sarah para leer unos boletines informativos mientras su esposa echaba una siesta en la *chaise*.

Habían compartido el almuerzo ligero que había llevado Crisp, después del cual Sarah había descansado un poco más antes de darse un baño y cambiarse de vestido para la cena.

Charlie se había mostrado especialmente solícito durante el trayecto en el carruaje. Al llegar al Manor, Sarah hizo un esfuerzo por disipar la preocupación de su madre. Lo último que quería en ese momento —cuando Charlie estaba tan pendiente de ella— era que su madre y sus hermanas la atosigaran, aunque fuera con la mejor intención del mundo. Sarah quería aferrarse a esos momentos a solas, hacerlos durar tanto como fuera posible. Quería estar sola con Charlie tanto tiempo como pudiera. Pronto partirían a Londres, donde se reunirían con Serena y Augusta en Morwellan House para la temporada. Entonces no le quedaría más remedio que dejar que otros se entrometieran en su vida.

Hasta ese momento, Sarah quería concentrarse en acoplar sus vidas, y parecía que Charlie estaba de acuerdo con ella.

Saberlo hacía que resplandeciera de felicidad. Era plenamente consciente de lo feliz que le había hecho el cambio de actitud de su marido y si se sentía un poco vulnerable, como si aquello fuera demasiado bueno para ser verdad, lo veía como la cruz que debía cargar —un reto—, algo a lo que tenía que enfrentarse y obligarse a asumir hasta la muerte.

Mientras daba cuenta del postre, deslizó la mirada por la mesa. Sabía que todos los presentes la conocían; era una ocasión memorable.

Barnaby había estado ausente todo el día, registrando las aldeas y pueblos cercanos en busca del escurridizo agente. Había regresado decepcionado pero resuelto, a tiempo de cambiarse y acompañarlos en el carruaje. Ahora estaba sentado al lado de la madre de Sarah, entreteniéndola con el relato de algún escándalo londinense. Las absortas expresiones de las caras cercanas a él confirmaban su reputación como anecdotista.

El señor Sinclair estaba charlando con el señor Ravenswell, así que Sarah se giró hacia el señor Finsbury, sentado a su otro lado, cuando de repente se oyeron varios golpes distantes.

Alguien estaba aporreando la puerta principal.

Sarah intercambió una mirada alarmada con su padre mientras las conversaciones en torno a la mesa se interrumpían. Se oyeron voces urgentes de hombres.

Luego la puerta se abrió de golpe y Johnson, el mayordomo, irrumpió en la estancia. Sólo bastó mirarle a la cara para que todos los hombres se levantaran.

—Milord... —Jonson miró al padre de Sarah y luego a Charlie—, es el orfanato, milord... ¡está ardiendo!

Diez caóticos minutos después, Charlie, montado en uno de los caballos de caza de lord Conningham, y Sarah, que montaba una yegua moteada, se dirigían hacia al norte, hacia el resplandor rojizo que iluminaba el cielo nocturno, hacia el humo que envolvía la silueta de Crowcombe recortada contra las colinas Brendon.

Charlie miró a Sarah y escrutó su cara pálida. Barnaby cabalgaba al lado de ella, con Malcolm a la zaga. Los seguían un montón de mozos y empleados de los establos del Manor así como toda la ayuda que habían podido encontrar, como los jardineros, que habían cargado sus herramientas en una carreta y se dirigían por el camino al orfanato. Por otro lado los invitados de más edad que habían asistido a la cena habían tomado sus carruajes y se habían dirigido a sus propiedades para reclutar a más hombres.

Mirando hacia delante, Charlie maldijo para sus adentros. Por lo que podía observar a través del humo que envolvía el lugar, dos de las alas posteriores del orfanato estaban en llamas. La parte principal de la casa no parecía afectada por el momento; entrecerrando los ojos, vio la silueta de la estructura gris contra el resplandor de las llamas que se alzaban detrás.

Volvió a mirar a Sarah. Había insistido en cabalgar con ellos. Aunque él hubiera preferido que viajara en la carreta, sabía que llegarían más rápido campo a través y también sabía lo importante que era para ella poner orden en el inmenso revuelo que sin duda se habría formado en el orfanato. Por ello había contenido sus protestas y se había asegurado de que ella tomara una montura tranquila que no se encabritara ante el olor a quemado.

Volviendo la vista hacia delante, no se molestó en volver a maldecir. Era mejor ahorrar saliva, pues sabía que iba a necesitarla.

Saltaron por encima del riachuelo y comenzaron a subir la pendiente. Tuvieron que detenerse frente a la cerca; ningún caballo la saltaría voluntariamente con el infierno que se había desatado a pocos metros. Todos se apresuraron a desmontar, consternados ante lo que veían. Charlie ató las riendas de su caballo a la cerca y tomó las de la yegua de Sarah —que miraba aturdida el dantesco espectáculo— para atarlas también; luego se giró hacia ella. La tomó por los hombros y la obligó a volverse hacia él.

Capturó la mirada de su esposa.

—Te necesitan. —Sarah parpadeó, luego inspiró profundamente y asintió con la cabeza antes de volver a mirar las llamas. Cogiéndola por la cintura, la alzó y la dejó al otro lado de la cerca antes de cruzarla él mismo de un salto. El resto de los hombres los siguieron.

Era difícil saber por dónde empezar. Charlie se detuvo un segundo para hacer inventario, y luego agarró a Sarah de la manga.

—Reúne a los niños, a todos, y llévalos más allá del patio. Lo más lejos posible de la grava.

Sarah asintió con la cabeza, parpadeó y tosió cuando una nube de humo la rodeó. La joven cogió el chal y se cubrió la nariz y la boca con él.

Con una mirada, Charlie reunió a Barnaby y al resto de los hombres y se encaminó a la parte de atrás del edificio.

Había tenido razón. Dos de las alas estaban en llamas. La tercera, un poco más al norte, estaba algo chamuscada. El tejado de paja del porche estaba ennegrecido, pero no había ardido.

Había algunos hombres tratando de llevar agua al tejado de paja, pero estaba demasiado alto. Lo único que podían hacer era mojar las paredes y rezar. Otros luchaban por mantener a raya las llamas de las dos alas para que no alcanzaran el edificio principal, que, al tener los muros de piedra y el tejado de pizarra, no se había visto afectado por el momento.

El humo era cada vez más intenso. Charlie se abrió paso entre los hombres del pueblo de Crowcombe que habían llegado primero. Cargados con mantas y sacos, intentaban combatir las llamas mientras los demás corrían de un lado a otro con cubos y baldes, lanzando el agua tan alto como podían.

Reinaban el caos y la confusión mezclados con un pánico creciente. Los hombres del Manor buscaron sacos y cubos y corrieron a ayudar. Charlie se detuvo el tiempo suficiente para indicar a los hombres que concentraran sus esfuerzos en las zonas donde las alas se unían al edificio principal.

—El resto de esas dos alas se ha perdido, así que podemos ahorrarnos el esfuerzo. —Se interrumpió para toser, luego señaló el edificio principal—. Será mejor que nos centremos ahí. —Avanzó hacia el ala sur, dirigiéndose a los hombres a gritos y señalando su objetivo hasta que le entendieron.

Barnaby se acercó y gritó por encima del rugiente crepitar de las llamas.

—Les diré a los otros que se concentren en el ala norte. —Se alejó antes de que Charlie asintiera con la cabeza.

Logró llegar al pozo en medio del barullo, donde Kennett sacaba agua tan rápido como podía.

—Por fortuna el agua salada apaga las llamas igual que la potable. —Kennett sacó otro balde y vertió el contenido en el cubo que esperaba. Soltó el balde vacío atado a una cuerda en la boca del pozo, donde cayó con estrépito al agua; luego comenzó a izarlo otra vez.

Charlie echó un vistazo alrededor y divisó al jefe de cuadra del Manor.

—Jessup reúne a tus hombres más fuertes para que se ocupen del pozo.

—Sí, milord. —Jessup llamó a un mozo forzudo—. Miller, encárgate de esto. Enviaré a dos de los jardineros para que te ayuden cuando lleguen.

Charlie se acercó a Kennett.

—Tú conoces este lugar mejor que nadie. Tenemos que impedir que las llamas lleguen al edificio principal... y también al ala norte.

Kennett miró en la dirección a la que Charlie apuntaba con el dedo, luego tosió y asintió con la cabeza.

—Sí.

—Ya les he dicho a los que se encargan del ala sur que se centren en el edificio principal. Ocúpate tú del ala norte. Es la única que se puede llegar a salvar. —Charlie se interrumpió para toser, luego gritó—: Hay más hombres en camino. En cuanto lleguen diles que se concentren en apagar las llamas del edificio principal y el ala norte.

Kennett asintió con la cabeza y se alejó. Sólo había dado unos pocos pasos cuando fue tragado por el humo.

Charlie se detuvo sólo para meter su pañuelo en un cubo de agua; luego lo escurrió y se lo ató sobre la nariz, antes de zambullirse de vuelta en el barullo.

La escena era dantesca. Las dos enormes y viejas alas estaban completamente en llamas, salpicando el negro de la noche con remolineantes llamaradas naranjas y rojas envueltas en el humo gris. Las ráfagas de calor cortaban el aire circundante. El fuego era como un ser vivo que atronaba y silbaba, que rugía y tragaba, consumiendo y devorando todo lo que encontraba a su paso.

Charlie se dirigió al ala sur y avanzó lentamente entre la hilera de hombres, buscando a los niños. Los había visto antes; los más pequeños ofrecían su desesperada ayuda para salvar el único lugar al que habían llamado hogar.

Encontró a Maggs, pero cuando le ordenó que soltara el cubo y se fuera al patio, el chico apretó la mandíbula y sacudió la cabeza tozudamente.

—¡Vivimos aquí! —Cuando Charlie frunció el ceño y abrió la boca para discutir, Maggs gimió—: ¡Tenemos que ayudar!

Observó la cara de Maggs, manchada de hollín, sus cejas chamuscadas y su pelo polvoriento, y leyó la desesperada súplica juvenil en los ojos del chico. Vaciló y luego le dijo:

—Sólo los que tengan más de doce años. Todos los demás tienen que irse al patio con la condesa. —Agarró a Maggs por el hombro, le quitó el cubo de la mano y se lo dio a un hombre que pasaba. Inclinándose, le habló al oído—: Encárgate de reunir a todos los niños de más de doce años que puedan quedarse y ayudar si quieren, pero el resto que se vayan al patio.

En medio de la densa humareda, Charlie divisó una figura con coletas. Maldijo entre dientes.

—¿Quién es la niña de mayor edad?

—Ginny —dijo Maggs tosiendo.

—¿Está por aquí?

Maggs asintió con la cabeza.

—La he visto hace un rato.

—Encuéntrala. Dile que reúna a todas las niñas, a todas, y que las lleve al patio. Tendrán que ayudar a la condesa y al personal con los niños más pequeños.

Maggs asintió con la cabeza y señaló con la barbilla.

—Es esa de ahí. Se lo diré. —Maggs liberó el hombro de la mano de Charlie y partió en busca de Ginny.

—¡Maggs! —Charlie esperó a que el niño se detuviera y se volviera hacia él—. Vigila a los niños que se queden a ayudar. Si las cosas se ponen feas... —Charlie levantó la mirada a las llamas que engullían el ala sur y volvió a bajarla a los ojos de Maggs— quiero que me des tu palabra de que los reunirás a todos y los llevarás al patio. Sin discusión. Si Kennett o yo te decimos que te vayas, coges a los demás y te vas.

Maggs tragó saliva y retrocedió cuando las llamas surgieron como una oleada cerca de donde estaba parado. Levantó la mirada hacia Charlie y asintió con la cabeza.

—Sí, de acuerdo.

Se alejó tambaleándose. Charlie inspiró brevemente mientras contemplaba el ala sur, luego se volvió y vio llegar a más hombres de las propiedades de los hacendados que habían estado en el Manor.

Envió a algunos con Kennett y a otros a ayudar con el edificio principal. Llegaron más hombres con cubos, baldes y costales. Aún frescos, se enfrentaron a las llamas, permitiendo que aquellos que llevaban más tiempo luchando contra ellas se apartaran y recobraran el aliento.

Charlie corrió para combatir las llamas que comenzaban a surgir entre el edificio principal y el ala sur. Volvió a mojar el pañuelo en el agua y se lo ató de nuevo, mirando la hilera de hombres con los ojos entrecerrados. Todos estaban manchados de hollín y sucios. Eligió a Joseph Tiller, que jadeaba, y le quitó el cubo que llevaba en la mano.

Tomó también el saco de yute que había utilizado y se dirigió al ala sur para comprobar cómo le iba a Barnaby, lanzando gritos de ánimo allí por donde pasaba. Se encontró a Malcolm por el camino, también sucio y jadeante. El grupo de hombres que dirigía se esforzaban en apagar las llamas no para salvar lo que devoraban, sino para evitar que se propagaran.

Al llegar al ala sur, Charlie descubrió que el humo era más espeso allí que en los patios entre las otras alas. Tuvo que ir más despacio para no derribar a los demás hombres y que ellos a su vez pudieran verle y esquivarle.

Al igual que el ala sur, el ala central tenía algunos focos de fuego, pero como Charlie había dicho, Barnaby había preferido sacrificar parte de esa ala para tratar de evitar que las llamas se propagaran al edificio principal. A primera vista parecían haber tenido éxito, pero al entrecerrar los ojos y mirar más detenidamente, mientras se tropezaba con algunos hombres y los escombros de los patios entre las alas, Charlie creyó ver arder el tejado de paja cercano al edificio principal.

Sólo había unas llamas aquí y allá; brasas que lo habían alcanzado. Sin embargo, la mayor parte del tejado de paja anexo al edificio principal seguía intacto.

Después de intercambiar palabras con un Barnaby al que no hubiera reconocido ni su madre, Charlie procedió a buscar a Kennett. Se dirigió al ala norte notando que el sonido del fuego —el crepitar de las llamas, el constante silbido y el penetrante rugido— había decrecido gradualmente. Estaban ganando, obligando a las llamas a retirarse. El fuego estaba siendo vencido.

Kennett pensaba lo mismo.

—Aunque aún tenemos mucho trabajo por delante. Tenemos que mantener las llamas bajas y dejar que se apaguen por sí solas. No hay otra manera.

Charlie miró el tejado de paja con los ojos entrecerrados. En realidad no le gustaba el aspecto de aquel tejado.

—¿Hay alguna manera de que podamos aislar las alas del edificio principal? ¿Crear un cortafuegos o algo parecido?

Kennett hizo una mueca.

—Ojalá pudiésemos, pero las vigas del tejado de paja se conectan por debajo del tejado principal con las vigas maestras que se unen a los pilares. Si creyera que hubiera alguna manera de llegar hasta ellas, propondría tirarlas, pero son maderas muy gruesas, viejas y duras como el hierro. Se necesitarían explosivos para romperlas.

—O fuego —murmuró Charlie.

»Quizá podríamos humedecerlo todo desde abajo lo más deprisa posible —dijo tras un minuto—. Una vez que las llamas se apaguen, pondremos escaleras de mano contra el edificio principal y mojaremos el tejado de paja y las vigas.

Charlie se dio la vuelta cuando llegó una nueva oleada de hombres de los campos lejanos. Llevaban azadones, picos, palas... toda clase de herramientas, incluyendo algunos rastrillos de mango largo.

Charlie les hizo un gesto con la mano para que se acercaran.

—Moveos hacia las alas central y sur y derribad lo que ya esté quemado. Empezad por los extremos e id retrocediendo hasta la zona donde los hombres combaten el fuego.

La mayoría de los hombres asintieron con la cabeza y se fueron. Un hombre que llevaba un rastrillo de mango largo se quedó rezagado. Frunciendo el ceño, señaló con la cabeza el tejado de paja por debajo de los aleros del edificio principal.

—Creí que querrían que tirásemos esa sección primero para que el fuego no se extendiera al edificio principal.

Charlie intercambió una mirada con Kennett. Miró al hombre, pero fue Kennett quien respondió:

—No, muchacho. Estos días ha hecho frío y el tejado de paja está húmedo. Lo más probable es que eso ayude a proteger las vigas de las llamas. Lo dejaremos hasta el último minuto, e incluso así todavía tenemos que pensar cómo lo derribaremos.

—Oh —respondió el hombre.

Pero Charlie apenas lo oyó, mientras las palabras de Kennett y los extraños focos de fuego que había visto —¿había sido encima o debajo del tejado de paja?— se conectaban en su cabeza.

Centró su atención en el hombre.

—¿Había más hombres con rastrillos de mango largo como ése? ¿Además de los que acaban de llegar?

El hombre parpadeó ante el tono urgente de su voz; luego asintió con la cabeza.

—Sí. —Tosió—. Había algunos por el otro lado. —Indicó con un gesto el otro lado de la casa.

Charlie maldijo entre dientes, giró sobre sus talones y corrió.

19

Charlie corrió hacia el ala norte. Un montón de hombres estaban golpeando las paredes de ambos extremos. Desesperado, se abrió paso entre ellos y fue entonces cuando oyó el sonido que tanto había temido.

Una ráfaga repentina seguida de un fuerte silbido cuando una nueva llamarada surcó el aire con gran fuerza, haciendo que los hombres retrocedieran consternados mientras proferían gemidos y maldiciones.

Charlie corrió hacia el ala sur a toda velocidad. Se detuvo con un patinazo y levantó la mirada, entrecerrando los ojos para poder ver entre el denso humo, y entonces se confirmaron sus peores temores. Los hombres con los rastrillos de mango largo habían rodeado la parte sur de la casa y, pensando como el otro hombre, habían derribado el tejado de paja que había estado ardiendo lentamente.

Las llamas de debajo habían quedado al descubierto y habían comenzado a rugir, alimentándose vorazmente de todo lo que tenían por delante ahora que disponían de aire del que alimentarse.

Aunque se lo había esperado, Charlie se quedó mirándolas, cada vez más horrorizado. No habría manera de detener el fuego a partir de entonces.

Se había detenido en medio del ala sur y, a través de las paredes en llamas, podía ver lo que Kennett había dicho sobre las vigas de madera y el tejado ardiente que estaba unido a la estructura del edificio principal.

El fuego no se iba a detener al llegar a los muros de piedra... Iba a penetrar por aquellas vigas de madera hasta la casa principal.

Se oyeron unos repentinos rugidos y gritos provenientes de los patios interiores. Fue suficiente un vistazo para darse cuenta de que las llamas del ala sur habían alcanzado el ala central. El tejado de ésta también ardía ahora y el fuego se extendía por encima de los aleros del edificio principal.

Se oyó un enorme crujido, como el de una explosión, cuando una de las macizas vigas se agrietó. Un furioso rugido resonó sobre la cabeza de Charlie cuando el fuego se abrió paso por la brecha y, como una bestia voraz, cayó sobre el tejado de paja del ala norte.

En menos de un minuto había desaparecido cualquier esperanza de impedir que el fuego se extendiera.

Charlie miró a su alrededor y vio a Maggs. Estiró el brazo hacia el niño y lo agarró del codo, apartándole de las llamas.

—¡Vete! ¡Reúne a los demás y largaos!

Maggs miró a Charlie. Sus mejillas estaban manchadas de hollín y de las lágrimas provocadas por el humo y la desesperación. Vaciló; luego bajó la mirada, asintió con la cabeza y corrió.

Barnaby apareció tras Charlie.

—He sacado a todos los hombres de los patios. En cualquier momento esto se convertirá en una trampa mortal.

Miraron al ala sur, que ahora parecía resplandecer ominosamente por el fuego que había en el interior y que consumía el tejado de paja, elevándose cada vez más, totalmente descontrolado.

—Que todo el mundo se aleje de aquí. No podemos hacer nada más y las vidas de las personas son más importantes que este edificio —gritó Charlie.

Barnaby asintió con el rostro serio. Se volvió y agarró al primer hombre que vio para gritarle que se alejara del patio y que avisara a todos los hombres que pudiera. Charlie se abrió paso a lo largo del ala sur. Comprobó que alguien se hubiera encargado de sacar los caballos y los hubiera llevado a los campos antes de reunirse con Barnaby. Recorrieron la parte posterior de ese infierno avisando a todos cuantos se cruzaban en su camino, asegurándose de que nadie se quedara rezagado.

Las macizas vigas del ala sur se colapsaron y se derrumbó parte del tejado, lanzando una lluvia de chispas que alimentó el creciente rugido de las llamas.

El fuego era una bestia que no podían controlar.

Charlie y Barnaby tuvieron que sacar a rastras a Kennett del ala norte.

—¡No podemos salvarlo! —tuvo que gritarle Charlie a la cara antes de que finalmente se rindiera, dejara de luchar y permitiera que lo alejaran de allí.

Mientras se retiraban, Charlie se detuvo frente al ala norte y miró atrás, entrecerrando los ojos para ver entre la densa humareda, pero no vio a nadie, no había más movimiento que el del resplandor del fuego. Todos se habían alejado. Consolándose con eso, se dio la vuelta y corrió para alcanzar a Barnaby y a Kennett, que ya cruzaban el patio hacia donde la gente esperaba y observaba.

Había una multitud. Muchas de las mujeres del pueblo habían acudido para ayudar con los niños. Estaban sentadas en grupitos, intentando aplacar los temores de los pequeños.

Sintiéndose igual de atemorizado, Charlie buscó a Sarah con el corazón en un puño. No pudo verla de inmediato entre el desanimado gentío. Avanzó hasta el límite del patio sin dejar de escudriñar las caras y, de repente, la vio un poco más allá de donde él estaba. Estaba parada, clavando una mirada horrorizada en la casa, entonces se giró y lo vio.

—¡Faltan Quince y dos de los bebés! —gritó, recogiéndose las faldas y corriendo hacia él. Jadeando, lo agarró del brazo—. Antes la he visto traer al resto. Ha dicho que no necesitaba ayuda. Pero aquí sólo hay cuatro. Los ha dejado con varias mujeres y hemos pensado que los bebés que faltaban estaban con otras personas. Pero no es así y nadie ha visto a Quince desde hace rato. ¡No está aquí!

Charlie miró a la casa envuelta en llamas.

—¡Oh, no! —Sarah le apretó el brazo—. ¡Mira!

Su esposa señalaba la ventana más septentrional del ático. Detrás del grueso cristal se veía una figura oscura que luchaba por abrirla.

—Tiene el brazo roto —dijo Katy, que se había acercado a Sarah—. No conseguirá abrirla.

Joseph se acercó trastabillando.

—Las escaleras del ático están al fondo del ala sur. Ahora será imposible subir por ellas.

Charlie se giró hacia Kennett, que se había detenido a su lado con una mirada aturdida en el rostro. Posó las manos en sus hombros y lo sacudió.

—¿Dónde están las escaleras de mano?

Kennett lo miró con los ojos llenos de horror.

—Estaban en los patios. —Tragó saliva—. Habrán desaparecido.

Barnaby apareció a su lado.

—Ya los he revisado, no he encontrado ninguna escalera de mano. Van a ir a buscarlas a la posada de Crowcombe.

Todos miraron a la casa... A los áticos y a la figura frenética que luchaba con la ventana. El humo que se extendía por el tejado era cada vez más espeso y envolvía la parte delantera del edificio mientras las llamas resplandecientes se alzaban por detrás.

—No podemos esperar. —Soltándose de la mano de Sarah, Charlie atravesó el patio con paso enérgico, luego echó a correr.

Cuando llegó al porche que protegía la puerta principal, sabía qué hacer. Quince lo había visto venir. Charlie le había señalado la ventana central del ático, que quedaba justo encima de la puerta principal y el tejado del porche.

Había un enrejado a un lado del porche. Charlie rezó para que soportara su peso. Con mucho cuidado y distribuyendo su peso tan uniformemente como podía, comenzó a trepar por él. Las tablas de madera crujieron mientras él subía, pero consiguió llegar al alero del estrecho tejadillo del porche y encaramarse a él.

Barnaby lo observó. Cuando Charlie se alzó por encima del alero, le gritó:

—No pierdas el tiempo intentando romper el cristal de esa ventana. Es demasiado pequeña y el cristal muy grueso. ¿Puedes acercarte a la ventana de guillotina?

Charlie levantó la mirada, se puso en pie lentamente y mantuvo el equilibrio sobre el alero. El muro de piedra le dio algo sólido en lo que apoyarse. Pegando el pecho allí, llegó hasta la ventana de guillotina, que, gracias a la distribución simétrica de la fachada, estaba justo encima del tejado del porche. Puso los dedos bajo el borde de la ventana e intentó subirla. Estaba dura, pero insistió; entonces

Quince le echó una mano desde el otro lado y lograron abrir la ventana entre los dos.

La mujer respiró profundamente cuando el aire fresco entró en el ático.

—¡Gracias a Dios! Iré a por los bebés.

—No pienso esperar aquí —dijo Charlie. Se agarró al marco de la ventana y apoyando los pies en el muro de piedra se izó a sí mismo para entrar. Se dejó caer y sintió el calor que se filtraba por las tablas de madera del suelo.

Mientras intentaba ponerse en pie, oyó que alguien —Barnaby quizá— subía al tejadillo del porche.

Quince apareció entre el humo y le tendió un bebé. La mujer frunció el ceño.

—¿Qué...?

Él la silenció con un gesto de la mano.

—Ve a por el otro lo más rápido que puedas.

El fuego estaba ya en las vigas que sostenían el suelo. Charlie no sabía cuánto tiempo tardarían en ceder.

Se asomó a la ventana y pasó por el hueco el primer bebé, bien envuelto en una manta, aunque extrañamente silencioso, a las manos de Barnaby.

Observó cómo Barnaby se tambaleaba precariamente por el tejadillo. Su amigo se agachó al llegar al borde y le tendió el bebé a la multitud de manos que esperaba con impaciencia.

Charlie se dio la vuelta y cogió al otro bebé de las manos de Quince.

—¿Ya no quedan más?

—No. Bajaré...

—No te muevas. —Le imprimió a sus palabras cada pizca de autoridad que poseía—. Espérame aquí.

Charlie sentía el fuego bajo los pies. Podía escuchar el rugido ardiente. El piso inferior era pasto de las llamas. Era imposible salir por allí.

Quince se movió nerviosa, pero se quedó a su lado mientras él pasaba al último bebé. En cuanto dejó a la criatura en manos de Barnaby, Charlie se enderezó y dio un paso atrás.

—¿Qué...? —gritó Quince cuando él la cogió en brazos.

—Te toca —le dijo—. Es la única manera de salir de aquí.

Con el brazo roto ella no podía hacerlo sola. Quince tuvo que permitir que la ayudara a salir por la ventana antes de dejarla en manos de Barnaby, que la ayudó a bajar a donde Kennett esperaba para cogerla por las caderas y dejarla en el suelo.

En cuanto ella estuvo a salvo, Barnaby se volvió hacia Charlie con la cara tensa y pálida.

—¡Sal ya!

La última palabra quedó ahogada por un terrible ruido, el rugido de las llamas cuando atravesaron el techo por encima de la cabeza de Charlie.

Éste había sido consciente del fuego del piso inferior, pero no se le había ocurrido mirar hacia arriba.

El tejado de la casa estaba en llamas.

Barnaby saltó del tejadillo del porche.

Charlie se agarró a la repisa de la ventana y se lanzó de cabeza por el hueco. Aterrizó como un gato en el tejadillo. Antes de que éste cediera bajo su peso, se dejó caer al suelo. Aterrizó rodando y tosiendo, consciente de que todos se alejaban corriendo.

Jadeó; tenía los pulmones ardiendo. Levantó la cabeza y miró por encima del hombro. Los ojos le picaban por el humo y tuvo que parpadear varias veces para poder enfocar y ver el infierno en que se había convertido la casa.

Mientras seguía allí tirado observando, el tejado comenzó a caer, colapsándose finalmente con un rugido.

—¡Vamos! —Alguien le tiraba frenéticamente del hombro.

Charlie giró la cabeza y vio que era Sarah.

—¡Estamos demasiado cerca! —gritó la joven—. ¡Vamos, levántate! ¡Tenemos que alejarnos!

Charlie se sentía como si estuviera en una pesadilla. Le resultaba difícil mover las piernas. Se puso en pie con la ayuda de Sarah, pero sólo habían avanzado unos pasos cuando oyó una enorme explosión tras ellos. Sarah miró hacia atrás y gritó.

Charlie actuó por puro instinto, la agarró y la estrechó contra sí, protegiéndola con su cuerpo.

Algo le golpeó en la espalda, derribándolos a los dos.

Sintió un dolor punzante.

Sarah comenzó a retorcerse frenéticamente bajo él. Charlie no podía entender lo que le estaba diciendo. Entonces ella se levantó de un salto y, utilizando el chal para protegerse las manos, lo empujó hasta que el peso inerte de Charlie rodó a un lado.

Él intentó respirar y tosió tan fuerte que se sintió mareado y débil. Sarah le palmeó la espalda y los hombros con las manos envueltas en el chal, luego le agarró del brazo otra vez. Barnaby se detuvo patinando sobre la grava al lado de su amigo.

—Ponte en pie, Morwellan —dijo mientras lo agarraba del otro brazo.

Con la ayuda de Sarah, Barnaby y su propio esfuerzo, logró ponerse en pie y que las piernas le respondieran cuando permitió que lo guiaran sobre la grava hacia la gente que les esperaba con caras ansiosas, iluminadas por la luz de las llamas.

La multitud se hizo a un lado para dejarles paso. Barnaby le soltó. Charlie se sentó, dobló las rodillas y apoyó la frente en ellas, concentrándose en respirar.

Sarah se sentó a su lado. Supo que era ella sin ni siquiera mirar al sentir el frío roce de su mano en la mejilla. Luego le tomó la mano y se apoyó en él mientras el orfanato ardía por completo.

El aire frío le revivió. Mucho antes de que se derrumbaran los últimos muros y de que el fuego comenzara a apagarse, Charlie ya se había recuperado lo suficiente como para empezar a formular los planes necesarios para ocuparse del desastre.

Había sido un trozo de viga lo que les había golpeado a Sarah y a él cuando el suelo del ático cedió bajo sus pies y se desplomó sobre el piso inferior. La gran extensión del patio de grava había protegido al resto de los presentes de sufrir peligros similares, pero había mucha gente que había resultado herida al intentar combatir las llamas.

Los niños habían sido la máxima prioridad para Sarah y para él.

Levantándose lentamente, ayudó a su esposa a ponerse en pie. Le sostuvo la mano y bajó la mirada hacia su cara pálida y manchada de hollín.

—Lo reconstruiremos —dijo simplemente.

Ella sonrió débilmente, levantando una mirada empañada hacia él. Parpadeó con rapidez y luego asintió con la cabeza.

—Pero no con el tejado de paja.

Él sonrió.

—Hecho. Nada de tejados de paja.

—Intento decirme que no hemos perdido nada verdaderamente importante, que no había nada ahí dentro que no pudiera ser reemplazado, salvo los niños. Pero la mayoría han perdido lo poco que poseían.

—No podemos devolverles los recuerdos, pero quizá podamos darles otros nuevos —dijo él, finalmente—. Nuevos y mejores recuerdos. —Ella le brindó una amplia sonrisa. Él la miró a los ojos—. Veamos... ¿Cuántos niños hay? ¿En cuántos grupos podemos dividirlos? ¿Cuántos niños en cada uno?

Sarah abrió la boca para responder, pero vaciló un momento.

—Busquemos a Katy y a los demás. Deberíamos planearlo todos juntos.

Charlie asintió con la cabeza. Se abrieron paso entre la multitud dispuestos a ocuparse del problema de inmediato y seguir adelante, en vez de quejarse por lo que habían perdido. Aunque el fuego todavía ardía con una furia inclemente, lo ignoraron, mejor dicho, utilizaron su luz mientras, junto con el personal del orfanato y las personas que habían acudido a ayudar, comenzaban a reunir a los niños.

Maggs y Ginny se levantaron y esperaron pacientemente hasta que Sarah y Charlie se acercaron a ellos para preguntar:

—¿Podemos ir a buscar nuestras cosas, señorita? —inquirió Ginny.

Sarah intentó esbozar una sonrisa, pero fracasó.

—Lo siento mucho, Ginny. —Puso una mano en el hombro de la niña, señalando con la otra la destrozada casa—. Pero me temo que no queda nada.

Maggs le dio un codazo a Ginny.

—No se refería a eso. Nosotros... Todos nosotros, recogimos todo lo que pudimos y lo llevamos a la colina antes de que el fuego se extendiera. —Se movió inquieto y luego admitió mirando al suelo—: El personal del orfanato no quería que lo hiciéramos, pero bueno... algunos de nosotros ya habíamos estado antes en un incendio. Tomamos algunas precauciones. Así que mientras los mayores ayudábamos a apagar el fuego, los más pequeños recogieron tanto sus pertenencias como las nuestras. —Señaló con la barbilla detrás de la ardiente ruina—. Todas nuestras cosas están allí, sólo hay que ir a buscarlas. Sentimos no haber podido ayudar más, pero...

Todavía embargado por la culpa, siguió con la mirada clavada en el suelo.

Charlie le dio una palmadita en el hombro.

—Has tomado una decisión muy sabia. —Intercambió una mirada con Sarah—. Estoy seguro de que nadie, y muchos menos el personal, te reprochará haberte tomado tiempo para intentar salvar vuestras pertenencias. Todos hemos hecho lo que hemos podido, pero esta vez no ha sido suficiente.

Maggs levantó la mirada hacia Charlie para confirmar que hablaba en serio.

—Entonces, ¿podemos ir a buscar nuestras cosas?

—A ver si podemos encontrar ayuda. —Charlie escrutó a la multitud, luego hizo señas a Barnaby para que se acercara. Tras un rápido intercambio de palabras y un par de sugerencias por parte de Charlie, Barnaby reunió a un grupo de hombres que junto con los niños mayores y varios faroles se dirigieron a la colina detrás del orfanato, aún envuelto en llamas, para recoger sus pertenencias. Los más pequeños habían rescatado sus cosas antes y los mayores estaban encantados de devolverles el favor.

—Es un pequeño alivio —le dijo Sarah a Katy.

Entre Charlie, Sarah y el personal del orfanato habían convenido adónde iría cada niño y quién se encargaría de supervisarlo. En cuanto habían oído las sugerencias de Sarah y Charlie, el personal se había relajado visiblemente.

—Así que estamos todos de acuerdo —dijo Sarah—. Mantendremos juntos a los niños mayores. El mejor lugar para acomodarlos será Casleigh. Lord y lady Cynster sabrán cómo alojarlos y Joseph y Lily pueden acompañarlos. De esta manera podrán seguir con sus estudios y llevar una vida relativamente normal. —Continuó diciéndoles que los niños menores irían al Manor, donde su madre y sus hermanas, junto con Twitters, ayudarían a Jeannie y a Jim a mantener a las criaturas entretenidas y contentas—. Todos los bebés, Quince, Katy y Kennett vendrán al Park. Necesitaré que los tres estéis cerca para comenzar a hacer planes sobre el nuevo orfanato.

Los miembros del personal asintieron con la cabeza, agotados y aliviados al mismo tiempo.

Charlie le tocó el brazo a Sarah.

—Iré a comprobar cuántos carruajes ha pedido Gabriel. Puede que necesitemos más.

Sarah asintió con la cabeza y le apretó brevemente la mano, luego se la soltó y se volvió hacia el personal. Mientras se alejaba, Charlie la oyó organizar a los niños en grupos que ya estaban listos para partir.

Gabriel, Alathea y Martin Cynster habían acudido desde Casleigh. Aunque habían llegado demasiado tarde para ayudar a combatir las llamas, habían llevado consigo a numerosos mozos de cuadra. Además, mientras Alathea se había unido al doctor Caliburn para atender las heridas y curar las quemaduras, Gabriel y Martin se habían movido entre los presentes con el fin de determinar cuántos carruajes harían falta para transportar a los exhaustos hombres y mujeres a sus casas, y habían enviado a los mozos a las casas cercanas para que llevaran todas las carretas y carruajes que pudieran conseguir. No había nadie en el valle que se negara a ayudar a un Cynster.

Charlie buscó a Gabriel y le explicó con detalle las necesidades de los niños.

—Ya he pedido que traigan nuestros propios carruajes —dijo Gabriel—. Los niños y el personal pueden subirse primero. Ha sido una noche espantosa y necesitamos apartarlos del frío. Ya tienen de sobra con la conmoción que han sufrido.

Charlie miró a la casa, que seguía envuelta en llamas.

—Algunos nos quedaremos aquí hasta asegurarnos de que el fuego se ha extinguido.

Gabriel asintió con la cabeza.

—Necesitaremos carruajes y carretas para poder transportar a todos aquellos que estén demasiado exhaustos o heridos para ir a caballo.

Charlie siguió moviéndose entre la multitud. Barnaby regresó con la carreta del orfanato cargada hasta arriba. Esbozó una amplia sonrisa manchada por el hollín que le ennegrecía la cara.

—Los niños lo han hecho bien. Parece que han salvado sus posesiones favoritas.

Charlie levantó la mirada a la resplandeciente granja en ruinas y murmuró:

—Una pequeña merced.

Más tarde, acompañado de Barnaby y un puñado de hombres robustos, Charlie rodeó la edificación, observando las llamas, que languidecían y se apagaban, comprobando los alrededores para asegurarse de que no quedaban rescoldos arrojados por las numerosas explosiones. El establo, el granero y las dependencias anexas detrás del orfanato habían sobrevivido. Aunque la mayor parte de los muros del edificio principal seguían en pie, tendrían que derribarlos. Las paredes de madera del interior habían sido devoradas por las llamas.

—Tardará unos días en apagarse por completo —dijo Barnaby deteniéndose junto a él en el lado sur de la casa.

Charlie asintió con la cabeza. Paseó la mirada por los hombres que los habían ayudado.

—Gracias a todos. Esta noche ya hemos hecho todo lo que estaba en nuestras manos.

Los hombres le estrecharon la mano que les tendía, luego cruzaron el patio hacia donde esperaban los últimos carruajes para llevarlos a casa o los caballos que habían dejado atados un poco más allá. El personal del orfanato junto con los niños y sus pertenencias se habían marchado hacía rato. Alathea y Martin habían partido con los que habían sido destinados a Casleigh; Gabriel y Sarah se habían quedado con los últimos rezagados.

Con Barnaby a su lado, Charlie atravesó lentamente el patio. Algunas imágenes de aquella noche infernal cruzaron por su mente. Frunció el ceño y examinó a los pocos hombres que todavía quedaban.

—¿Has visto a Sinclair?

—Ha tenido que irse —dijo Barnaby—. Ha estado ayudando desde el principio. Más tarde, estaba a mi lado cuando te ayudé en el rescate. Cuando el edificio principal comenzó a arder, jamás había visto un horror tan desnudo en la cara de un hombre. De hecho, parecía tan mal que me pregunté si padecía del corazón. Cuando nos reunimos para organizarlo todo, me dijo que tenía que encargarse de algo. —Barnaby hizo una mueca—. Creo que trataba de lidiar con el horror que sentía. Parecía muy afectado.

Girando la cabeza, Barnaby estudió la cara de Charlie.

—¿Te has dado cuenta de que tienes la espalda de la chaqueta quemada?

Charlie arqueó las cejas.

—¿De veras? —Movió los hombros y sintió un tirón en la tela y un dolor sordo en la piel. Recordó cuando Sarah le había palmeado la espalda con las manos envueltas en el chal, y se encogió de hombros—. No es nada, sobreviviré.

Los dos se reunieron con Sarah y Gabriel cuando se marchaba el último carruaje.

—Ya hemos hecho todo lo que se podía hacer —dijo buscando la mirada de Sarah—. Deberíamos volver a casa.

La joven suspiró y asintió con la cabeza. Deslizando la mano en la de él, se dirigieron a donde estaban los caballos. Eran los últimos. Gabriel y Barnaby los siguieron.

—¿Alguna idea de qué provocó el incendio? —preguntó Gabriel.

Charlie y Sarah miraron por encima del hombro a tiempo de ver cómo Barnaby asentía con la cabeza.

Tenía una expresión sombría y resuelta en la cara.

—Algunos de los críos, los de mayor edad, Jim y Joseph Tiller, vieron cómo ocurrió. Alguien disparó flechas encendidas al tejado de paja de las alas, donde previamente había escondido telas empapadas de aceite entre los fajos. Quienquiera que fuera no quería correr el riesgo de que la paja no ardiera, como ocurrió en el ala norte, que estaba más expuesta al clima. De hecho podríamos haber controlado el incendio en esa ala de no haber sido por esos trapos ocultos entre la paja.

—Pero... —Charlie negó con la cabeza— ¿cuándo escondió esos trapos? El personal ha estado haciendo guardia incluso por la noche.

Barnaby se encogió de hombros.

Siguieron caminando con el ceño fruncido.

—Habrá sido hoy —dijo Sarah con un suspiro mientras volvía su mirada hacia ellos—. Es domingo. Tanto el personal como los niños van a la iglesia de Crowcombe. Debieron de estar ausentes durante hora u hora y media, quizá más. Sólo Quince se queda aquí, y la mayoría de las veces está con los bebés en el ático, donde las ventanas dan al patio. Aunque Quince haya echado algún vistazo de vez en cuando, si el hombre se acercó por detrás, no tuvo manera de verlo.

—Y las escaleras de mano estaban en los patios entre las alas. —Charlie sacudió la cabeza.

Llegaron a los caballos. Charlie ayudó a montar a Sarah y luego se subió a su montura de un salto.

Todos se detuvieron un instante para echar un último vistazo a los restos del orfanato, todavía envuelto en llamas resplandecientes que iluminaban la noche de invierno.

Gabriel habló por todos en tono duro.

—Quienquiera que sea ese canalla, tenemos que detenerle.

Malcolm tenía intención de hacer justo eso. Había cabalgado hasta Finley House en un estado deplorable, atormentado por lacerantes emociones que jamás había experimentado antes. Lo que había visto esa noche le había revuelto literalmente el estómago, más por el sentimiento de culpa que lo embargaba que por las náuseas.

Sentía como si le estuviera estrangulando el corazón o incluso el alma. Tenía que detenerse, tenía que detenerlo, ya. Esa misma noche.

Con esa sensación invadiendo su mente había conseguido calmarse, lavarse el hollín de la cara y las manos, cepillarse el pelo, ponerse ropa limpia y sentarse de nuevo tras el escritorio, donde había hecho un soberano esfuerzo por dejar la mente en blanco —despojándola de todo lo que había visto esa noche— e idear su plan de acción.

Como siempre, trazó su plan a sangre fría, calculando hasta el más mínimo detalle. Puede que sus planes no funcionaran a veces, pero no sería porque él no lo intentara.

Siguió esperando, sentado tras el escritorio débilmente iluminado por la luz titilante de la lumbre hasta que Jennings llamó a la puertaventana. Malcolm se levantó y dejó entrar a su hombre de confianza. En silencio le indicó la silla frente al escritorio. Cerró la puerta con llave y se la guardó en el bolsillo.

Luego volvió al escritorio.

Jennings se acomodó en la silla. Estiró las piernas y cruzó las manos sobre su creciente barriga. Sonrió con suficiencia mientras Malcolm rodeaba el escritorio para volver a sentarse.

—Recibí su nota. Pero espero que haya sido testigo de mi actuación en el orfanato esta noche. No cabe la menor duda de que la condesa venderá esta vez. Haría falta mucho dinero para volver a reconstruir el lugar.

Malcolm se dejó caer en su silla, luchando por controlar una oleada de furia helada. Jennings no se mostraba intranquilo por la falta de luz; Malcolm siempre había procurado que nadie los viera juntos ni siquiera por casualidad.

Esa noche la penumbra servía para otro propósito. Ocultaba la rabia en los ojos de Malcolm.

Se tomó un momento para estudiar a Jennings. No había cambiado mucho desde que Malcolm lo había conocido en Londres hacía casi dieciséis años. Por aquel entonces ya era un hombre grueso, con una cara redonda y anodina que inspiraba confianza. Su temple, su expresión sincera, la franqueza de sus discursos y una aguda inteligencia habían logrado que Malcolm lo tuviera en consideración. Ninguno de esos atributos había cambiado.

Lo que Malcolm no había sabido hasta hacía pocos días era que Jennings no tenía conciencia. Era cauto y poseía instinto de conservación, pero...

—El orfanato... —Malcolm se interrumpió hasta asegurarse de que tenía un perfecto control de su voz. Jennings estaba acostumbrado a esas largas pausas, pero un temblor furioso en su voz podría ponerle sobre aviso antes de lo que Malcolm deseaba—. ¿En algún momento se te ha ocurrido pensar que alguno de esos niños podría quedar atrapado por las llamas?

Jennings se encogió de hombros.

—Es posible, pero era un riesgo razonable. Tuvieron tiempo de salir. —Cuando Malcolm no respondió de inmediato, Jennings añadió—: Y no es como si no hubiéramos tenido alguna que otra muerte en el pasado.

Malcolm cerró el puño bajo el escritorio, pero mantuvo un tono suave y tranquilo cuando habló:

—Así es. No obstante, jamás te pregunté al respecto. ¿De cuántas muertes somos responsables en realidad?

Tamborileando con los pulgares, Jennings miró al techo e hizo una mueca.

—No es que haya llevado la cuenta exactamente, pero puede que sean diez o algo así.

—Ya veo. —A Malcolm le resultaba cada vez más difícil controlar su rabia fría, en especial cuando no sólo estaba dirigida a Jennings; más de la mitad iba dirigida a sí mismo. Se levantó lentamente y rodeó el escritorio mientras consideraba sus palabras—. No sé si te habrás dado cuenta, pero ésta es la primera vez que te veo en acción. En nuestros demás proyectos, visité brevemente la zona, reconocí los terrenos en cuestión y luego regresé a Londres para enviarte a adquirirlos. Jamás volví a pisar aquellas tierras. Sin embargo, en este caso, cuando vine aquí para explorar el lugar, me enamoré de este valle y decidí quedarme. Comencé a tratar con los lugareños y a valorar lo que tienen, las vidas que llevan en esta pequeña y tranquila comunidad. Por primera vez en mi vida pensé que había encontrado un lugar en el que me gustaría vivir, comprar una casa, establecerme, quizás incluso casarme y formar una familia.

Ni en su rostro ni en su voz asomaba un solo indicio de los turbulentos sentimientos que bullían bajo la superficie.

Sentándose en el borde del escritorio, inclinó la cabeza hacia Jennings.

—Reconozco que en algunos de nuestros primeros proyectos en común, cuando regresaste sin el título de la propiedad requerida y me sugeriste persuadir a los dueños de vender, pensé en varias maneras para conseguir que la gente, la gente normal con aspiraciones normales, se sintiera impulsada a separarse de sus tierras mediante supersticiones, accidentes y cosas similares. Desde mi punto de vista fue un consejo teórico. Imparcial y distante. Nunca supe si en realidad utilizabas o no esos métodos. —Hizo una pausa antes de añadir con una voz todavía desprovista de emoción—: Por ejemplo, jamás supe nada de esas muertes.

Jennings parpadeó sin tener muy claro adónde quería ir a parar.

—Es cierto.

—Por supuesto, si hubiera sabido algo al respecto, habría imaginado... las cosas que hacías. Habría sabido qué métodos utilizabas y, en general, habría comprendido lo que eso quería decir. Pero a menos que no vea las cosas que haces con mis propios ojos, tus métodos no dejan de ser algo abstracto para mí. No dejan de ser más que una teoría y por lo tanto no me afectan.

Finalmente buscó la mirada de Jennings y esbozó una débil sonrisa.

—Verás, hasta ahora no me había encontrado cara a cara con las consecuencias humanas y emocionales de nuestras acciones. Hasta ahora no había tenido que enfrentarme, ni siquiera imaginar, ninguna responsabilidad por el resultado de mis planes. —Sostuvo la mirada de Jennings—. Pero siento tener que decirte que haber presenciado nuestros métodos de persuasión en el orfanato me ha provocado cierta conmoción.

Ahora estaban lo suficientemente cerca para que Jennings notara las turbulentas emociones que Malcolm contenía. Jennings se removió en el asiento y frunció el ceño, perplejo.

—Pero... sólo he seguido sus órdenes. He hecho lo que pensaba que debía hacer.

—Oh, claro —admitió Malcolm levantando una mano—. Sin embargo, mi pregunta es: ¿cómo has podido hacerlo?

Jennings parpadeó.

Bruscamente, Malcolm dejó caer el escudo que ocultaba sus emociones.

—En esta ocasión se trataba de gente buena y generosa —estalló, dejando salir su furia y su condenación—. Gente que ayuda a los niños; niños huérfanos que no tienen a nada ni a nadie más en el mundo.

«Como él.»

Aspiró bruscamente al reconocer la verdad de ese hecho, luego continuó con voz dura e inclemente, y una dicción temiblemente precisa.

—Déjame explicarte cómo me siento tras haberme visto obligado a observar de primera mano las consecuencias de tus acciones en el orfanato. Supongo que tú estabas demasiado lejos para ver que yo estaba allí, ayudando a combatir el fuego.

La expresión de Jennings era una mezcla de incomprensión e incipiente sospecha, seguidas por un creciente temor.

Malcolm le sostuvo la mirada.

—Así que estaba allí para presenciar no sólo la devoción del personal del orfanato, sino cómo los demás habitantes de la zona acudían a ayudar. No sólo he visto lo importante que era para la condesa el orfanato y la angustia que nuestras acciones le han provocado, sino cómo el conde, a pesar de su evidente desaprobación hacia ese lugar, intentaba salvarlo. Estaba allí, Jennings, totalmente paralizado por un despreciable miedo mientras Meredith y su amigo arriesgaban sus vidas, pues ahora podrían estar muertos, para salvar a dos pobres bebés y a su niñera. Por primera vez en mi vida, Jennings, he comprendido qué quiere decir realmente «nobleza obliga», finalmente he entendido qué significan «caridad» y «valor».

Reprimiendo el impulso de levantarse y pasearse de arriba abajo, Malcolm permaneció sentado en el borde del escritorio sosteniendo la mirada de Jennings con firmeza.

—Hasta que vine aquí no creía en el amor, en la caridad ni en la nobleza ni en ninguna de esas cosas que se suponen son las mejores cualidades del hombre. Nunca creí que existieran. Jamás las había visto desfilar ante mí de una manera imposible de ignorar, jamás me había visto obligado a reconocer que son reales. Ahora, gracias a nuestro último proyecto y a tus acciones, tu personal interpretación de mi consejo sobre métodos de persuasión, he abierto los ojos.

Malcolm apoyó una mano de largos dedos en el muslo de manera relajada, mientras apoyaba la otra en el escritorio y observaba a Jennings.

—Por supuesto, ahora que comprendo todo el dolor, la angustia y la pena, el terror y la pérdida que han provocado tus acciones a partir de mis instrucciones, me he quedado muy afligido, Jennings, hasta lo más hondo de lo que creo que es mi alma. Jamás pensé que podría sentirme de esa manera, que podía sentir remordimientos. Pero ahora no puedo sentir otra cosa. Me siento vacío, deshonrado... culpable. —Hizo una pausa y luego añadió con suavidad—: Y tú, Jennings, tienes la culpa.

Jennings se agarró a los brazos de la silla, pero antes de que se levantara del asiento, Malcolm le atizó en la sien con un pequeño candelero de latón que había detrás de él en el escritorio. Jennings soltó un gemido y cayó al suelo inconsciente.

Malcolm se levantó, cogió la cuerda que había dejado tras el escritorio y ató con rapidez las manos de Jennings a su espalda, luego le inmovilizó los tobillos y sacó un pañuelo del bolsillo para amordazarlo.

Después de correr las cortinas de todas las ventanas, Malcolm regresó al escritorio y encendió la lámpara. En cuanto tuvo luz, se sentó de nuevo en la silla. Se preguntó si debía sentir lástima por Jennings, por involucrarlo en sus planes, pero parecía que ésa era una emoción que todavía no había desarrollado. Desde el principio había reconocido en Jennings la misma falta de conciencia, la misma ausencia de compasión, que él había tenido hasta hacía poco. Si no fuera por los planes de Malcolm, Jennings, al igual que su último y no llorado tutor, Lowther, habría encontrado otro camino a la perdición.

Puso una hoja en blanco sobre el papel secante, cogió la pluma y la mojó en el tintero; desvió la mirada a las otras tres cartas apiladas junto al papel secante y se detuvo.

Entonces, apretando los labios, se inclinó sobre el papel y escribió.

Las cartas habían llegado el día anterior mientras había estado buscando a Jennings. Pensando que no tenían importancia, las había dejado a un lado. Las había abierto hacía menos de una hora, cuando se había sentado a esperar a Jennings.

Eran de tres prestigiosos bufetes de abogados de Londres. Cada una de ellas le informaba de que una de sus empresas personales —de esas en las que Malcolm Sinclair aparecía como director— estaba siendo investigada por las autoridades. Cada uno de los abogados había tenido que entregar todos los documentos y registros de una compañía. Tres abogados. Tres empresas. Todas las cartas habían sido fechadas cuatro días antes.

Se había quedado sentado durante por lo menos diez minutos con los ojos clavados en las cartas, intentando imaginar por qué razón las autoridades habían decidido investigar esas empresas. No habían cometido ninguna acción ilegal, no estaban vinculadas de ninguna manera con ninguna de las otras compañías que él había utilizado para llevar a cabo sus especulaciones del ferrocarril, a no ser que...

De repente, entendió cuál había sido el fleco suelto en su magnífica creación, el hilo que conectaba sus empresas personales con las compañías creadas para invertir en el ferrocarril. Releyendo las cartas había encontrado la confirmación. Uno de los abogados había escrito que las autoridades estaban interesadas en un pago hecho por una de las compañías del ferrocarril a una de sus empresas personales.

El único cabo que jamás se le había ocurrido esconder y a alguien se le había ocurrido tirar de él.

Se había quedado sentado con la mirada perdida en la oscuridad dejando pasar el tiempo al comprender que aquello era su absoluta ruina. En cuanto surgiera su nombre y, teniendo en cuenta su reputación como inversor ferroviario, descubrirían la conexión. Y una vez que tuvieran su nombre no tardarían en encontrar pruebas suficientes para ahorcarle.

Había considerado el porvenir durante un buen rato. Luego se había encogido de hombros y se había centrado en su plan para encargarse de la situación actual. Ante eso, la ruina era lo de menos.

Escribió durante un buen rato.

Luego Jennings se removió. Dejando la pluma a un lado, Malcolm se levantó y rodeó el escritorio. Cogió a su agente del brazo y lo obligó a ponerse en pie.

—Camina.

Le había dejado la suficiente holgura en la cuerda con que le había atado los tobillos para que pudiera andar.

Atontado y aturdido, Jennings intentó resistirse, pero Malcolm le empujó fuera de la biblioteca y lo condujo por el pasillo hacia la cocina. La puerta de madera del sótano estaba abierta. Al verla, a Jennings le entró el pánico e intentó resistirse, pero con Malcolm —más alto, más pesado y, como Jennings iba a descubrir, más fuerte— detrás de él, no pudo evitar que lo empujara hacia aquella negrura abismal.

Malcolm se detuvo en el umbral y murmuró:

—Si no dejas de luchar y bajas las escaleras, tendré que empujarte por ellas.

Jennings vaciló, todavía tenso pero incapaz de salvarse de ninguna manera. Dejó de luchar. Asintió con la cabeza y dio un paso hacia delante con cuidado.

Malcolm cogió el farol que había dejado allí encendido y fue tras él. Agarraba con fuerza uno de los brazos de Jennings para sostenerle mientras bajaba tambaleante las escaleras.

Una vez llegaron al sótano, Malcolm le señaló un taburete situado delante de una columna. Jennings caminó hasta allí arrastrando los pies y se sentó en él. Antes de que supiera qué estaba ocurriendo, Malcolm le rodeó el pecho con otra cuerda y lo ató a la columna.

Colocándose de tal manera que Jennings pudiera verle, observó al hombre y se giró hacia las escaleras.

—¿Hummm?

Volviéndose con el farol en alto, Malcolm se cruzó con la mirada de Jennings.

—¿Por qué? —preguntó, inclinando la cabeza.

Malcolm vaciló.

—Porque, inesperada y tardíamente, parezco haber desarrollado una conciencia. —Luego hizo una pausa y añadió arqueando las cejas—: O puede que por fin me haya dado cuenta de que ya tengo una y quiera usarla.

Torció la boca secamente.

—¿Quieres saber qué voy a hacer? —Jennings asintió con la cabeza—. Supongo que, dado que llevamos juntos en esto casi diecisiete años, te lo debo.

Brevemente, Malcolm esbozó su plan.

—Aunque estoy perfectamente preparado para aceptar las responsabilidades de lo que he hecho, no aceptaré la responsabilidad por tus acciones. Aunque las ideas fueron mías, las decisiones que tomaste fueron tuyas. Durante los últimos quince años o más has trabajado bajo mis órdenes directas, pero lo has hecho tomando tus propias decisiones, según tu propia iniciativa.

Se interrumpió momentáneamente y luego dijo:

—¿Recuerdas a la señora Edith Balmain?

Sinclair esperó hasta que el reconocimiento iluminó los ojos embotados de Jennings.

—Exacto. Fue al principio de todo, cuando tratábamos con Lowther. Ante la muerte de Lowther, la señora Balmain fue lo suficientemente amable para darme un consejo. Me advirtió que me guardara mis pensamientos y mis planes para mí mismo. —Estudió a Jennings con atención y luego murmuró—: Hubiera sido mejor para los dos que lo hubiera hecho.

Bajó el farol y miró a Jennings en la penumbra una última vez.

—Vendrán a por ti mañana, imagino que antes del atardecer. Te aconsejo que implores clemencia al tribunal.

Malcolm se volvió y se dirigió a las escaleras. Una serie de gemidos ahogados le hizo darse la vuelta.

—¿Quieres saber qué voy a hacer yo?

Jennings asintió enérgicamente.

Malcolm sonrió con total sinceridad.

—Cuando vengan a por mí, ya me habré ido.

20

Con Sarah, Barnaby y Gabriel a la zaga, Charlie se dirigió hacia el sur a medio galope. Gabriel era quien más fresco estaba. Colocó su montura al lado de la de Barnaby y se mantuvo vigilante mientras atravesaban los montes de camino a casa.

Cuando llegaron a los establos del Park, Broker y uno de los mozos estaban esperándoles para encargarse de los caballos y dejar que se dirigieran a casa. La mirada alarmada en las caras de los hombres confirmaba lo sucios y andrajosos que estaban.

Gabriel permaneció en su montura. Mantuvo el caballo al paso mientras ellos salían lentamente al patio de los establos.

Sarah alzó la mirada hacia él.

—Es tarde. No creo que falte mucho para el amanecer. ¿Por qué no pasas aquí la noche? Te quedan unos cuantos kilómetros hasta Casleigh.

Gabriel sonrió y negó con la cabeza.

—Puede que sea tarde, pero Alathea no se dormirá hasta que regrese y le informe de que todo está bien... Tan bien como cabe esperar.

Al lado de Sarah, Charlie soltó un bufido.

—Por no decir que le prometiste que lo harías cuando la obligaste a subirse en el carruaje con los niños.

Gabriel se rio entre dientes.

—Tu comprensión del matrimonio está mejorando.

Charlie carraspeó.

Sarah, Barnaby y él se detuvieron y se despidieron de Gabriel con la mano. A lomos de la enorme montura, su figura oscura fue tragada con rapidez por las sombras cuando tomó el camino hacia el sur. Bajaron los brazos y caminaron lentamente hacia la puerta lateral.

Crisp y Figgs estaban esperando para recibirles con el fuego encendido y unas copas de vino especiado que Figgs insistió en que se bebieran. Incapaces de reunir la fuerza necesaria para discutir con sus sirvientes, hicieron todo lo que éstos pedían. Los dos contuvieron el deseo de preguntar por su aspecto andrajoso y, en lugar de ello, les relataron los preparativos hechos en su ausencia.

—Hemos instalado a los bebés en la vieja habitación infantil —dijo Figgs—. La señorita Quince y la señora Carter están en las habitaciones anexas, y hemos acomodado al señor Kennett en el ala de los sirvientes. Estaban en un estado lamentable y muy cansados. Una de las doncellas se encargará de cuidar a los bebés el resto de la noche.

Barnaby se terminó de golpe la copa de vino y la dejó en la bandeja que sostenía Crisp.

—Os veré en el desayuno —les dijo a Charlie y a Sarah mientras se despedía con un gesto de cabeza—. Entonces pensaremos cuál será la mejor manera de proceder.

Crisp le aseguró a Barnaby que le llevarían agua caliente a su habitación de inmediato, y dio la orden pertinente a un lacayo.

—Milord, milady —Crisp se volvió hacia Sarah y Charlie—, en este momento les están preparando un baño caliente en sus habitaciones. Si necesitan algo más, cualquier cosa...

—Gracias, Crisp, Figgs. —Sarah reunió fuerzas para tomar el mando. Sospechaba que, si no lo hacía, Charlie y ella serían tratados por los dos sirvientes como si fueran niños—. Vuestros preparativos han sido ejemplares, sabíamos que podíamos contar con vosotros. Su señoría y yo nos las arreglaremos perfectamente.

Tomó la copa vacía de los dedos de Charlie y la depositó junto con la suya en la bandeja de Crisp.

—¿Está esperándome Gwen?

—Así es, milady —respondió Crisp—. Está supervisando la preparación de su baño.

—En ese caso, creo que su señoría y yo no necesitamos nada más. —Enlazó su brazo con el de Charlie. Su marido había tenido la precaución de ocultarle la espalda a Crisp y a Figgs—. Hasta mañana. Bajaremos a desayunar a las diez.

—Tomo nota, milady. —Crisp hizo una reverencia, y Figgs también.

—Gracias a los dos —dijo Charlie, despidiéndose con un gesto de cabeza.

Se volvió hacia Sarah cuando ésta le tiró del brazo y juntos se encaminaron a la escalinata y a sus habitaciones del piso superior.

Detrás de ellos se oyeron gritos ahogados de horror.

—¡Milord! Su chaqueta... —dijo Crisp.

—¡Está quemada! —exclamó Figgs al mismo tiempo.

Con un suspiro de resignación, Sarah se detuvo y se volvió, alzando una mano para detenerlos cuando se precipitaron hacia ellos.

—No es tan malo como parece. El doctor Caliburn ya lo ha examinado y me ha dado un bálsamo. —Sacó una botellita del bolsillo—. Me ha dicho lo que debo hacer. Ahora, si nos disculpáis, vamos a retirarnos para que pueda atender las heridas de su señoría.

Observando la escena por encima del hombro, Charlie asintió brevemente y siguió adelante con Sarah colgada de su brazo.

Cuando subieron las escaleras y ya estaban fuera del alcance del oído de sus sirvientes, Charlie se inclinó hacia ella y murmuró:

—Me preguntaba cómo diablos lograríamos librarnos de ellos. Desde luego, Crisp y Figgs podrían darles lecciones de entrometimiento a Serena y a Alathea. —Bajó la mirada a la cara de la joven—. Gracias por salvarme.

—Teniendo en cuenta que resultaste herido mientras intentabas salvarme, me pareció lo más justo —se rio Sarah.

Charlie soltó una risita.

—Pero tuve que salvarte porque tú ya me habías salvado a mí, ¿recuerdas?

—Pero te caíste porque te habías subido al tejadillo del porche para salvar a los bebés y a Quince. —Habían llegado a la puerta de sus habitaciones. Sarah se detuvo y le miró a la cara. Sonriendo suavemente, acarició la mejilla de su esposo—. Los dos hemos puesto algo de nuestra parte esta noche, pero sobre todo tú. —Poniéndose de puntillas, le rozó los labios con los suyos—. Gracias.

Charlie bajó la mirada hacia sus ojos y le devolvió otra suave sonrisa.

—Ha sido... —vaciló, luego dijo—: un honor y un placer para mí.

Abrió la puerta y entraron en el vestíbulo; luego se dirigieron al dormitorio.

Sarah se fue directamente a la cámara contigua para comprobar que les habían preparado el baño y que tenían todo lo necesario; luego le dio permiso a Gwen para que se fuera a la cama.

Regresó al dormitorio, donde Charlie se retorcía delante del espejo de cuerpo entero, intentando verse la espalda.

—Ven aquí... no, no intentes quitarte aún la chaqueta.

Sarah lo empujó hacia el cuarto de baño y le hizo sentarse en un taburete cerca de un aparador con una palangana encima. Había una esponja flotando en el agua caliente. Ella la escurrió y luego la apretó contra las partes quemadas de la espalda de Charlie.

Con suavidad, humedeció cada una de las quemaduras antes de desplazarse a la siguiente. Charlie se quedó quieto, presa de un repentino cansancio.

—¿Me examinó Caliburn las quemaduras?

—Lo hizo cuando se lo pedí... ¿no te diste cuenta? No necesitó examinarlas detenidamente, vio lo que había sucedido. Tienes la chaqueta quemada, y también el chaleco, pero la camisa apenas está chamuscada y la piel sólo está enrojecida.

—Porque me quitaste la viga de la espalda con rapidez.

—Hummm...

Charlie tuvo la impresión de que ella estaba concentrada en curarle y que se suponía que él no debía distraerla con su charla. Quizá, como Gabriel había dicho, su comprensión del matrimonio estaba mejorando.

Curvó los labios y sonrió ampliamente. Vagamente fue consciente de que, a pesar de todo lo que había ocurrido durante esa larga noche, aún era capaz de sonreír, de que lo hacía con facilidad, con una dulce felicidad que le calentaba el corazón, y aquello era una extraña bendición.

Otro regalo que le debía a su esposa.

Sarah terminó de humedecer la tela quemada y lo urgió a ponerse en pie para ayudarle a quitarse la chaqueta y el chaleco juntos. Charlie sostuvo la chaqueta en alto para examinar los daños, pero Sarah se la quitó de los dedos y la dejó caer al suelo.

—La camisa... —Lo ayudó con los botones, pero lo detuvo antes de que intentara deshacerse de la prenda, haciendo que esperara mientras volvía a humedecer las zonas quemadas.

La joven se puso a su espalda y le ayudó a quitarse la camisa por los brazos. Antes de que él pudiera darse la vuelta, la arrojó al suelo junto con la chaqueta y procedió a humedecerle los hombros y la espalda.

—Ahora al baño... Es lo que ordenó el doctor Caliburn. Luego tengo que aplicarte el bálsamo.

Charlie no dudaba de las órdenes del médico, sólo de la manera en que ella creía que debía aplicarlas, pero dócilmente se sentó en el taburete y se quitó las botas con la ayuda de Sarah, luego se puso en pie y se deshizo de los pantalones.

Sarah se había acercado a la bañera para comprobar la temperatura del agua.

Esperó a que ella regresara para cogerla de la mano y arrastrarla hasta la bañera. Allí la tomó entre sus brazos. Sordo a sus protestas, la despojó del sucio y desastrado vestido, de las enaguas y de la camisola, lanzándolos junto al montón de ropa descartada. Luego la alzó en sus brazos y, durante un momento, se recreó en el tacto de su piel sedosa contra la suya y de su cuerpo curvilíneo contra el suyo. Entró en la bañera, sentándose lentamente y acomodándola delante de él.

Ella gimió y se retorció para quedar frente a él. Agarró la esponja de la bandeja donde la había dejado, la sumergió en el agua y, con una expresión resuelta y una mirada de advertencia, la apretó contra la piel de Charlie y procedió a lavar el hollín y la suciedad de sus brazos y su pecho.

Él curvó los labios y apoyó el cuello en el borde de la bañera procurando que los hombros no lo hicieran, y dejó que Sarah continuara con su labor. La miró a la cara mientras tanto. Una extraña y tranquilizadora calma los envolvió y los inundó cuando él alargó la mano y tomó la esponja de la de ella para deslizarla por sus brazos marfileños. Se retorcieron en la bañera aseándose mutuamente, aliviándose y calmándose, lavándose el pelo el uno al otro hasta que los dos estuvieron limpios.

Charlie se puso en pie y cogió los cubos de agua caliente que estaban al lado de la bañera, enjuagándola primero a ella y luego a sí mismo. Se secaron con las toallas que previamente habían calentado ante el fuego; luego, agarrados de la cintura, se apoyaron el uno en el otro mientras se dirigían a la cama.

Los dos estaban exhaustos, pero Sarah lo hizo sentarse en el borde de la cama y Charlie dejó que le aliviara la piel quemada. Subió las piernas a la cama y se tumbó de lado para que a ella le resultara más fácil aplicarle el bálsamo.

Le rozó suavemente con los dedos mientras extendía la crema fría por la piel ardiente de sus hombros y su espalda.

Charlie cerró los ojos y disfrutó de su tacto. Si hubiera sido un gato, habría ronroneado.

En algún momento, durante sus cuidados, él se quedó dormido.

Se despertó tumbado boca abajo con las mantas apoyadas sobre una almohada a un lado y en la propia Sarah al otro, para evitar que le rozaran las heridas.

Sarah debía de haberle colocado de esa manera después de que él se quedara dormido. Aquel pensamiento conjuró una imagen que le hizo sonreír.

Cerró los ojos, y se dejó llevar de nuevo hacia aquel profundo sueño. Lleno de una paz que jamás había experimentado antes de que ella entrara en su vida, apartó de sus pensamientos los acontecimientos de esa noche y lo que le esperaba al día siguiente.

A pesar de los horrores del incendio, se sentía embargado por una sensación de victoria. Puede que hubieran perdido la casa de la granja, pero no el orfanato en sí, a los niños y al personal. Y había sido gracias a la ayuda de todos —ya fueran de la clase acomodada o no— los que habían aunado sus fuerzas cuando habían visto que el lugar corría peligro.

Había algo muy poderoso en aliarse para derrotar a un enemigo común que amenazaba a una institución tan apreciada por toda la comunidad.

A raíz del incendio, al día siguiente tendrían que dedicarse a organizar, coordinar, arreglar y decidir.

Podía imaginar lo ocupados que estarían Sarah y él cada uno por su lado y, aunque una parte de su mente protestaba por tener que pasar algún tiempo separados, otra le recordaba lo maravillosa que era esa sensación de unión que ahora compartían. Todo lo que necesitaban era una mirada, una caricia, y aquella sensación aparecía, ya estuvieran en una habitación abarrotada de gente o a solas.

Sarah era suya y siempre lo sería a partir de entonces. Aferrarse a su esposa, tener el valor de hacerlo, la había hecho suya. Y ella lo había hecho suyo.

Pero aparte de eso había mucho más que celebrar.

Incluyendo el hecho de que Sarah estaba realmente embarazada... Estaba seguro de ello. Cuando la había sostenido contra sí, con la cabeza apoyada en su hombro, y le había lavado el vientre con suavidad, se había dado cuenta de que estaba un poco más redondeado de lo que lo había estado antes. Se había sentido tentado —muy tentado— de decirle a Sarah en ese mismo momento cuánto la amaba. Era imposible sentir otra cosa cuando su amor, el de los dos, los envolvía con una fuerza casi tangible.

Pero no había encontrado ninguna palabra, ninguna que considerara apropiada, ninguna que pudiera expresar con sinceridad todo lo que sentía, y cuando lo hiciera quería dejar muy claro que cada palabra provenía directamente de su corazón.

Pero quizá buscar las palabras adecuadas no fuera necesario.

Había estado a punto de hablar, de confiar en sus instintos y en la comprensión de Sarah, pero ella había levantado una mano para ahogar un bostezo y Charlie se había dado cuenta de lo exhausta que estaba, tan exhausta como él. El impulso de hablar había desaparecido. Cuando finalmente pronunciara aquellas palabras quería que su esposa las recordara y no que imaginara más tarde que lo había soñado.

No obstante, se las diría pronto.

Sarah, así como Alathea, Gabriel y todos los demás, tenía razón. Valía la pena luchar por un matrimonio basado en el amor.

Y también merecía la pena hacer cualquier sacrificio por él.

Mientras el resto del mundo dormía y la noche se desvanecía suavemente con la llegada del amanecer, Malcolm Sinclair permanecía sentado en el escritorio de la biblioteca de su casa sin dejar de deslizar la pluma por el papel. Fue apilando una página tras otra al lado de su codo. No tenía ninguna duda sobre lo que quería escribir.

El amanecer teñía con su luz trémula el horizonte cuando finalmente suspiró y se enderezó. Firmó con una floritura al pie de la última página, y le pasó cuidadosamente el papel secante. Juntó las páginas y las dobló, encendió una vela, derritió un poco de cera y las lacró con su sello.

Entonces y sólo entonces se detuvo. Sostuvo la pluma en alto sobre el fajo de páginas y curvando los labios escribió con fluidez: «A quien corresponda.»

Listo. Se recostó en la silla y observó las páginas que había escrito. Poco a poco su mirada se fue volviendo distante. Frunció el ceño en un gesto que endureció su bien parecido rostro, pero luego sacudió la cabeza y colocó dos nuevas páginas en blanco ante él.

Tardó unos minutos en escribir las nuevas notas. Las firmó y las selló antes de levantarse y colocar el fajo de páginas sobre el escritorio. Apagó la lámpara y, recogiendo las dos notas, caminó hasta la puertaventana y descorrió las cortinas. Bajo la débil luz que iluminaba la estancia se dirigió a la mesa auxiliar que había al lado de la chimenea.

Abrió el cajón de la mesita y sacó el diario de Edith Balmain. Apoyando una rodilla en el suelo, contempló en silencio el hermoso volumen con cubiertas plateadas durante un minuto, luego se giró y, con el libro entre las manos, salió de la habitación.

Abrigada y relajada, Sarah se despertó sola en la cama, sintiéndose curiosamente contenta. Mientras se desperezaba, recordó los acontecimientos de la noche anterior y supo por qué se sentía feliz.

Su tía Edith —que había sido una mujer muy sabia— le había dicho con frecuencia que de algo malo siempre surgía algo bueno.

La joven se levantó y llamó a Gwen, luego se aseó y se vistió. Dejó a su doncella exclamando horrorizada por el estado en que se encontraba la ropa que se habían quitado la noche anterior y se dirigió al comedor del desayuno.

El orfanato se había quemado hasta los cimientos, pero Sarah jamás se había sentido más segura y en paz consigo misma.

Charlie estaba sentado a la cabecera de la mesa, y Barnaby, a su derecha. Su esposo levantó la vista cuando ella entró y la miró directamente a los ojos. Sarah le brindó una sonrisa radiante y feliz, sabiendo por la mirada de Charlie que él se sentía exactamente igual que ella.

Aquella mañana era el principio del resto de sus vidas. De su vida juntos. Si algo habían demostrado los acontecimientos de la noche anterior, había sido eso.

El futuro que se extendía ante ellos sería como ellos quisieran que fuera y la unión de sus vidas era ya un hecho.

Como Charlie había dicho, reconstruirían el orfanato y todo sería mucho mejor.

Sarah se llenó el plato, sorprendida de lo hambrienta que estaba. Prescindió de cualquier formalidad y se sentó a la izquierda de Charlie, que había estado esperando para acercarle la silla.

En cuanto se sentó, fue Barnaby quien tomó la palabra.

—Saldré dentro de unos minutos. Ya he pedido que me ensillen el caballo. —Miró a Charlie y luego le explicó—: Hemos decidido que tenemos que informar a las autoridades sobre todo lo que ha ocurrido. Cabalgaré hasta Londres y se lo contaré a Stokes, luego regresaré y seguiré buscando a ese dichoso agente. Todavía andará por aquí, esperando que vendas, aunque es muy probable que aguarde unos días antes de hacer su siguiente oferta. Sin embargo, después del incendio en el orfanato, tenemos que resolver esta investigación de inmediato y es necesario que tanto Stokes como el resto sepan lo que está ocurriendo. Que sepan cuál es el juego que se traen entre manos y que están jugando en serio.

Se tomó el último bocado de jamón.

—También me dará la oportunidad de comprobar si Diablo y Montague han encontrado alguna pista.

Sarah asintió con la cabeza.

—Aquí tenemos mucho que hacer. Tenemos que organizar a los niños y al personal y ver qué hacemos con la granja.

Charlie asintió con la cabeza. Cogiendo la mano de su esposa, la envolvió con la suya.

—Iré a la granja con Kennett. Examinaremos el lugar para ver qué se ha salvado de la ruina. Tardarán unos días en apagarse los últimos rescoldos, pero empezaremos a valorarlo todo hoy.

—Y también están los animales —dijo Sarah—. Jim los envió al campo norte. ¿Podría el terrateniente Mack encargarse de ellos por el momento?

Charlie asintió con la cabeza.

—Se lo preguntaré.

—Entretanto —Sarah arrugó la nariz—, voy a tener que escribirle al obispo. «Lamento decirle, señoría, que el orfanato ha sido destruido por el fuego.» Sólo Dios sabe cómo voy a decírselo.

—No te preocupes por el obispo. Estoy seguro de que comprenderá la situación —dijo Charlie—. Haz una lista con todo lo que van a necesitar los niños y el personal. Seguro que recibirás visitas de tu madre, de la señora Duncliffe, de Alathea y de Celia y de muchas más damas de la comunidad; todas querrán saber qué pueden hacer para ayudar. Probablemente te darán un día de gracia, pero por tu propia paz mental, te recomiendo que tengas la lista hecha para mañana.

Sarah se rio. Charlie tenía razón.

—Ya me las arreglaré.

Se oyó el chirrido de una silla cuando Barnaby, sonriendo, dejó la servilleta sobre la mesa y se levantó.

—Os dejaré con vuestras obligaciones y yo seguiré con las mías. —Les hizo un gesto con la mano cuando empezaron a levantarse—. Conozco la salida y los dos tenéis que desayunar. No tardaré en volver. Estaré aquí antes de que os deis cuenta. —Su expresión suave se tornó dura, y un destello depredador brilló en sus ojos—. Éste es un malhechor cuya caída no quiero perderme.

Se despidió con un gesto de cabeza y abandonó el comedor, dirigiéndose a paso vivo al vestíbulo.

Cuando se desvaneció el sonido de sus pasos, Sarah prestó atención a su plato, lo mismo que Charlie. Comieron en un agradable silencio; luego Sarah suspiró, saciada, y se recostó en la silla.

Charlie se tomó el café con la mirada fija en la cara de su esposa.

Ella sonrió, sólo para él, dejándole ver su felicidad.

—Será mejor esta vez, ¿verdad?

Él le sostuvo la mirada mientras dejaba la taza a un lado, luego le cogió la mano y se la llevó a los labios. Se la besó sin apartar la mirada de sus ojos.

—Mejor que nunca —confirmó. Después de un rato, añadió—: Muchísimo mejor.

Una hora más tarde, Malcolm Sinclair esperaba a su ama de llaves —una mujer del pueblo que limpiaba y cocinaba para él— en la puerta de su casa.

Le brindó una encantadora sonrisa.

—Señora Perkins, discúlpeme por no habérselo mencionado ayer, pero no la necesitaré la semana que viene. Tengo que ausentarme por un tiempo y debo partir esta misma tarde. Acepte esto... —le entregó una bolsa llena—. El sueldo de esta semana más una gratificación por sus servicios. La avisaré cuando esté de regreso.

La señora Perkins contó las monedas con rapidez y descubrió que la «gratificación» cubriría una semana completa de sus servicios. Le sonrió feliz.

—Por supuesto, señor. Ha sido un placer trabajar para usted. Estaré encantada de regresar cuando esté de vuelta.

Le hizo una reverencia y emprendió el camino de vuelta, sin duda planeando qué hacer con aquel inesperado tiempo libre.

Malcolm se quedó en la puerta hasta que ella atravesó el portón y desapareció calle abajo. Dio un paso atrás y cerró la puerta. Luego se quitó la chaqueta de vestir.

Se puso una de trabajo y un sombrero de ala ancha en la cabeza para que le cubriera su reconocible pelo rubio; luego se ajustó unos gruesos guantes de jardinero antes de ir a recoger el saco de herramientas que había dejado tras la puerta. Se lo echó sobre un hombro y recorrió el pasillo con sus viejas botas resonando pesadamente en el suelo de madera pulida. Atravesó la biblioteca y salió por la puertaventana; le aguardaba su caballo ya ensillado.

Charlie examinó las ennegrecidas ruinas de la granja Quilley. Las alas se habían visto reducidas a montones de brasas ardientes de madera quemada y escombros manchados de hollín, pero aún había llamas pequeñas en el edificio principal, devorando el esqueleto de vigas de madera enterrado bajo los muros de piedra.

En algunos lugares, las paredes habían cedido y algunos pesados bloques de piedra se habían desmoronado sobre el suelo. Y aquellos muros que aún permanecían en pie parecía que iban a caerse de un momento a otro.

—Tendremos que derribarlos nosotros —señaló Charlie—. No podemos arriesgarnos a que le caigan a alguien encima.

—Sí. —A su lado, Kennett asintió con la cabeza con aire sombrío—. Haremos lo que podamos hoy, pero tendremos que hacerlo poco a poco, según se vaya extinguiendo el fuego en cada sección.

Charlie consideró los inestables muros y los montones de escombros detrás de la casa principal.

—Dejaremos los muros para última hora de hoy. Tenemos que esparcir los escombros de la parte de atrás y asegurarnos de que no quedan rescoldos.

Se volvió para mirar al grupo de hombres que subían la cuesta. Muchos cargaban herramientas. Los primeros habían aparecido después de que Kennett y él atravesaran Crowcombe a caballo.

Saludó a los recién llegados y se volvió hacia la casa principal. Después de indicarles lo que había que hacer, cogió un rastrillo y se puso manos a la obra.

Durante toda la mañana, trabajó codo con codo con los hombres. Mientras se dedicaban a esa tarea relativamente mecánica, hablaron entre ellos. Al principio los hombres vigilaron sus palabras cuando lo tenían cerca, pero poco a poco se fueron relajando y finalmente acabaron charlando con él, preguntándole qué opinaba sobre la caza, sobre los nuevos tramos de ferrocarril que atravesarían el valle y muchos otros temas relacionados con la zona, sobre los cuales él tenía su propio punto de vista y mucha influencia.

Cuando se tomaron un descanso a media mañana para tomar las cervezas que les había enviado el posadero de Crowcombe, Charlie había averiguado más sobre los problemas que afectaban a la gente de la comunidad hablando con esos hombres que tras horas escuchando a sus administradores.

Se apoyó en el rastrillo en mangas de camisa —hacía rato que había dejado la chaqueta sobre una valla cercana— y bebió un largo trago de cerveza, luego se secó el sudor de la frente con la manga. El día era frío pero soleado, y la brisa traía el aroma de la primavera.

Echó un vistazo a los hombres que le rodeaban; todos habían aceptado su autoridad sin cuestionarla. De hecho, la habían buscado. Para ellos era correcto que él, un Morwellan, el conde de Meredith, estuviera allí dándoles órdenes, asumiendo su responsabilidad. Eso era lo que hacía que las comunidades prosperaran.

Pero él llevaba años alejado de la zona y, si no hubiera sido por su esposa, no estaría allí en ese momento. Sin su vínculo con ella, habría sido el padre de Sarah quien se habría encargado de aquello, pero a su edad habría enviado a uno de sus hombres de confianza, y definitivamente no era lo mismo.

Los Cynster estaban más al sur, esa zona era el dominio de los Meredith, y él no era sólo el conde, sino mucho más joven y físicamente capaz que la mayor parte de sus vecinos.

Su sitio estaba allí, entre esas personas. Con los pies bien plantados en el suelo para saber cuáles eran sus problemas y ayudarlos.

Su responsabilidad estaba allí, no en Londres.

Y lo que más le asombraba de todo era lo bien que le sentaba aquello, lo cómodo que se sentía en aquel papel.

El deber siempre había formado parte de su vida, aunque no había pensado demasiado en esa faceta. Pero ahora había aceptado ese nuevo aspecto de su vida y había hecho los cambios oportunos para encajarlo en ella. Quizás ése fuera otro aspecto que como en todos los demás encajaría bien. Mejor que la vida que había imaginado que tendría con su esposa ideal en Londres, lejos de lo que ahora comprendía era una parte esencial de él, de quien era en realidad, del hombre que quería ser ahora.

—¿Milord?

Se volvió para ver a uno de los hombres mayores, que lo llamaba por señas.

—Hemos dado con una sección de la cerca que está quemada. Parece que una parte del tejado de paja cayó sobre ella. ¿Puede venir y decirnos qué quiere que hagamos?

Charlie se enderezó, dejó a un lado el rastrillo y siguió al hombre rodeando el edificio.

Después del mediodía, Malcolm Sinclair se puso una elegante chaqueta, unos ceñidos pantalones de ante y una inmaculada camisa blanca. Cuando cruzó la corta distancia que separaba el portón de su casa de Crowcombe, era la viva imagen de un caballero londinense.

Se detuvo ante el pórtico de piedra del despacho del notario. Rara vez contrataba a alguien de la localidad, pero en ese caso, usar los servicios de Skeggs le parecía lo más apropiado e inteligente.

Se giró lentamente y contempló la ancha franja de tierra por encima del pueblo, todavía negra y humeante, que eran los escombros de la granja Quilley. Reflexionó sobre la imagen, preguntándose si alguien la consideraría un símbolo perfecto del fin de sus ambiciones.

Tras un momento, se dio la vuelta y, abriendo la puerta del despacho de Skeggs, adoptó un aire sereno y entró.

Sarah no tuvo la oportunidad de escribirle al obispo hasta primera hora de la tarde, cuando hubieron alimentado a los seis bebés y los acostaron para que durmieran la siesta. La joven encontraba a aquellas personas diminutas y perfectas totalmente fascinantes... muchísimo más de lo que las había encontrado unas semanas antes.

Puede que ésa fuera una señal más de su estado. Todavía no estaba segura del todo... pero esperaba y rogaba con todas sus fuerzas no estar equivocada. Sentía que ésa sería la culminación de sus aspiraciones, el broche perfecto para el inicio de su nueva vida. Pero quería estar segura antes de decírselo a nadie. Ni siquiera a Charlie.

En especial a Charlie.

El día de su boda había observado la expresión de su mirada cuando Dillon y Gerrard habían hablado de sus hijos. No necesitaba preguntarse cuál sería su reacción si le decía que estaba embarazada. Pero precisamente porque sabía cuánto significaba esto para él, tenía que estar segura de ello. Totalmente segura.

Su salita se había visto invadida por una ingente cantidad de ropa blanca, así que se refugió en la biblioteca de Charlie. Se acomodó en la silla tras el escritorio y cogió una pluma del juego que su marido mantenía en buen estado.

Buscó papel y tinta y procedió a realizar su tarea. Como había previsto, encontrar las palabras adecuadas para comunicar tan ingrata noticia no era un asunto fácil, pero cuando el reloj repicó una hora después, había logrado lo que consideraba un resultado satisfactorio. Cerró la carta, le puso el sello de Charlie, y la dejó sobre el papel secante para que su esposo la franqueara.

En ese momento oyó que alguien llamaba a la puerta y la abría. Levantó la mirada y vio que era Crisp.

—Ah... aquí está, milady. Uno de los chicos de Crowcombe ha traído una nota del señor Sinclair.

—Gracias, Crisp. —Sarah cogió la nota sellada de la bandejita que le tendía el mayordomo.

—El chico ha dicho que no era necesaria una respuesta inmediata, milady. —Crisp hizo una reverencia y se retiró.

Sarah cogió el abrecartas de Charlie para romper el sello y abrió la nota.

—¡Oh, es maravilloso! —Sinclair le había escrito para decirle que había encontrado el diario de su tía en «el lugar más sorprendente». Sarah se preguntó dónde habría sido, luego siguió leyendo con rapidez.

Por desgracia, escribía Sinclair, tenía que marcharse para encargarse de unos asuntos urgentes y, dada la cantidad de recados que tenía que hacer antes de irse, no podía permitirse el lujo de acercarse hasta allí para entregárselo. Sin embargo, le preguntaba si tendría un momento libre para reunirse con él en el puente de la cascada, ya que se había prometido a sí mismo que no dejaría la zona sin disfrutar de la vista de la famosa cascada de Will's Neck. Pensaba pasar por allí a eso de las tres y, si ella podía acercarse a esa hora, podría entregarle el diario y explicarle dónde lo había encontrado.

Si por cualquier motivo no podía reunirse con él, había escrito, Malcolm le devolvería el diario cuando regresara a Crowcombe, aunque no podía precisar cuándo sería eso. Dado el valor nostálgico y personal que para ella tenía el diario, no quería confiarle su devolución a otras personas.

Sarah miró el reloj. Eran las dos y cuarto; tenía tiempo de sobra para cambiarse de ropa y llegar hasta la cascada.

Ella quería el diario y quería saber dónde lo había encontrado. Tras la cantidad de humo que había inhalado la noche anterior, el aire fresco y el ejercicio le vendrían bien.

Fue una de las decisiones más fáciles que había tomado ese día. Se levantó y se dirigió a la puerta para ordenar que ensillaran a *Blacktail* mientras ella se ponía el traje de montar.

Veinte minutos más tarde, Charlie se encontraba organizando a un grupo de hombres con mazos y carretillas, comprobando la estabilidad de los muros que todavía estaban en pie, cuando un muchacho de Crowcombe se acercó a él.

—Un mensaje, milord. —El niño se quitó la gorra y le tendió

una nota doblada y sellada—. Es del señor Sinclair. Del hombre que se aloja en Finley House.

Charlie cogió la nota. Rebuscó en el bolsillo y le dio una moneda al muchacho antes de darle permiso para que se fuera.

Les lanzó una mirada a los hombres, pero éstos sabían lo que se hacían. Dio un paso atrás y se apoyó contra la cerca, luego rompió el sello de la nota de Malcolm, la desdobló y leyó.

La sangre huyó de su rostro.

Sin ni siquiera un saludo, el mensaje de Malcolm iba directo al grano.

En poco tiempo tendré a tu mujer en mi poder. Para cuando leas estas palabras, Sarah estará de camino al puente de la cascada de Will's Neck. Si deseas volver a verla, tendrás que hacer exactamente lo que te digo. No vaciles, no pienses y, lo más importante, no intentes comprender lo que he planeado. Ni se te ocurra organizar nada o dar la alarma. Recuerda que la distancia entre la granja Quilley y el puente es una línea recta y que te estoy observando con un catalejo.

Abandona la granja y cabalga hasta el puente. Haz lo que te digo y Sarah todavía será tuya, totalmente ilesa, al final del día.

Muévete, hazlo ya o la perderás.

Te estaré esperando en el puente de la cascada.

Charlie clavó una mirada ciega en las letras negras que bailaban ante sus ojos.

Un frío temor fluyó por sus venas hasta que se cerró como un puño gélido sobre su corazón. Jamás se había sentido tan solo en toda su vida. Ni tan frío.

Pero sabía lo que tenía que hacer. Justo lo que Malcolm le pedía.

Respiró hondo luchando contra la fuerte opresión que sentía en el pecho, pero se mantuvo calmado exteriormente y se obligó a pensar...

No tenía alternativa. No podía contactar con nadie, ni tampoco pedir ayuda.

En especial cuando sabía que Malcolm Sinclair no bromeaba.

Se metió la nota en el bolsillo y se dirigió a donde había dejado atado a *Tormenta*. Presionado por el tiempo, desató al caballo.

—¡Tengo que irme, he recibido un mensaje! —le gritó desde lejos a Kennett—. Intentaré regresar más tarde. Hasta que vuelva, encárgate de todo.

El gesto despreocupado y lacónico de Kennett daría a entender a cualquier observador que él no le había dicho nada preocupante o alarmante.

Cogió las riendas de *Tormenta*, se subió a la grupa de un salto, y se alejó tan rápido como pudo por la carretera de Crowcombe que conducía al puente de la cascada de Will's Neck.

21

Sarah guió a *Blacktail* por la última y pronunciada cuesta que conducía al puente de la cascada de Will's Neck. No se apresuró. Estaba segura de que llegaría a tiempo. Balanceándose con el paso de *Blacktail*, disfrutó de la vista de las solitarias colinas salpicada por vislumbres ocasionales de los exuberantes valles y el centelleo del mar distante que se entreveía entre los árboles que bordeaban el camino.

Las nubes matutinas se habían dispersado, permitiendo que un sol radiante bañara la tierra. Con cada aliento de aire puro y frío venía la promesa de la primavera, de un nuevo comienzo.

Sarah curvó los labios. Se sentía llena de confianza y determinación. El edificio del orfanato había desaparecido, pero todos habían sobrevivido y esa terrible experiencia los haría más fuertes y mejores.

Charlie y ella habían encontrado su camino a pesar de las dificultades iniciales en su matrimonio, y también ellos eran más fuertes y se sentían más seguros conforme pasaban los días.

La sensación de paz y la promesa del futuro la embargaban cuando llegó al claro donde la gente solía dejar atados los caballos mientras se acercaban a ver la cascada desde el puente.

Había un enorme caballo negro con una silla de montar de hombre esperando pacientemente. Sarah ató a *Blacktail* a una rama baja junto al claro y luego, recogiéndose las faldas, se dirigió por el estrecho camino que llevaba al puente.

El puente, que se extendía sobre el profundo desfiladero por el que descendía la cascada, estaba al doblar la siguiente curva. Era posible cruzarlo a caballo, pero conducía a un camino sin salida. La mayor parte de la gente acudía para ver las vistas, y luego se iba por donde había venido.

Al doblar la curva vio el puente, cuatro metros de tablas de madera unidas entre sí y sujetas por gruesas cuerdas atadas a los macizos postes de madera que se hundían en la roca a ambos lados. Malcolm esperaba en el centro, con las manos apoyadas en el pasamanos de cuerda y la vista clavada en el profundo desfiladero que desembocaba en el valle mucho más abajo.

Sinclair oyó los pasos de Sarah y se giró hacia ella. Sonriendo, le extendió una mano, mostrándole la cubierta plateada del diario de Edith. Encantada, Sarah le devolvió la sonrisa; luego dirigió la mirada a la pequeña cuesta que llevaba hasta el puente, suspendido un poco más abajo del camino. Los caballos podían salvar el desnivel con facilidad, pero cuando —como ahora— el suelo estaba húmedo y resbaladizo, el descenso era complicado para las personas. Por fortuna, alguien había colocado unas piedras pulidas para formar una serie de escalones irregulares a un lado de la cuesta. Sarah se recogió la cola del vestido sobre un brazo y comenzó a bajar con mucho cuidado.

El puente tenía cuatro metros de largo pero apenas uno de ancho. Malcolm estaba justo en el centro, donde las vistas eran mejores. Cuando pisó las tablas del puente, Sarah sintió que éste se movía más de lo que había esperado, pero se estabilizó de inmediato. Quizá fuera cosa de su equilibrio, ¿acaso no se mareaban las embarazadas?

O quizá se debiera al efecto casi desorientador del increíble rugido que surgía del agua embravecida que pasaba bajo el puente. A causa del reciente deshielo, el torrente de la cascada había crecido. El agua caía a borbotones, rugiendo como una bestia viviente, chocando, brincando, lanzándose en picado hacia el profundo abismo de roca.

De vez en cuando, una nube de espuma fina envolvía el puente.

Malcolm estaba esperándola, observándola con una de sus agradables sonrisas, una que ella reconocía como sincera. Era un hombre muy parecido a Charlie, con el mismo encanto natural, pero que ella había llegado a conocer muy bien. Devolviéndole la misma sonrisa sincera, se acercó él.

—Gracias por venir. —Malcolm tuvo que inclinar la cabeza y acercarse más a ella para escucharla por encima del rugido de la cascada. Le tendió el diario de Edith.

Sarah lo cogió y le dio la vuelta entre sus manos, hojeando las páginas con rapidez. Parecía intacto.

—¿Dónde lo encontró?

Levantó la mirada hacia la cara de Malcolm.

Él la miró directamente a los ojos. La sonrisa se había desvanecido de su rostro y en su lugar había aparecido una expresión sincera aunque sombría.

—Estaba en el cajón de la mesita auxiliar en la biblioteca de Finley House.

—¿Cómo...? —Sarah se interrumpió y frunció el ceño—. ¿En Finley House? ¿No es allí donde usted reside?

—Sí. Yo lo guardé allí.

Sinclair hizo la declaración con tal franqueza que Sarah no estuvo segura de haberle entendido bien.

—Usted lo cogió en el Park... —De repente, recordó que él los había visitado el día que ella había descubierto la desaparición del diario. Había hablado con ella en la rosaleda y antes había estado con Charlie en la biblioteca. Cuando lo vio, se dirigía hacia los establos tras haber pasado por la puertaventana de su salita.

Su mirada se clavó en la de ella.

—Veo que ya recuerda... Tardé sólo un minuto en cogerlo de su escritorio.

Atónita, Sarah frunció el ceño.

—Pero ¿por qué?

Sinclair miró al diario.

—Porque su tía y yo nos conocíamos. Cuando hubiera llegado a las anotaciones del mes de mayo, habría leído lo que su tía pensaba de mí, que, a pesar de no ser directamente responsable, era yo quien había ideado un plan que involucraba un comercio de trata de blancas que las autoridades acababan de sacar a la luz. —Torció los labios—. Tenía razón.

La mirada de Malcolm se volvió distante.

—Su tía fue una mujer notable, quizás algo mayor y débil, pero con una mente muy perspicaz. Al parecer, había conocido a mis padres bastante bien. Vino a verme y me dijo sin ningún rodeo que sabía que era yo quien había ideado aquel plan, que aunque no fuera el canalla que lo había puesto en marcha, eso no me absolvía de la culpa. Me advirtió que no debía permitir que mis planes, como ella los llamaba, fueran usados por otros en el futuro. —Hizo una mueca y miró el diario—. Luego lo escribió todo ahí, y lo dejó para que me atormentara en el futuro.

Sarah continuó frunciendo el ceño.

—Pero si mi tía dijo que usted no era culpable, y las autoridades no vieron razón para acusarle, lo que ella escribió, aunque fuera cierto, hablaría de usted como el joven que había sido en 1816. Como el joven que cometió una locura de juventud. Puede que yo leyera lo que ella escribió, pero no habría dicho nada.

Malcolm la miró a los ojos y sonrió.

—No, no lo habría hecho público. Pero yo había decidido quedarme a vivir aquí, comprar una propiedad y construir mi propia casa, y había llegado a apreciar la buena opinión que tanto usted como Charlie tenían de mí. De hecho, dado el interés de su marido por invertir en el ferrocarril, no podía arriesgarme a que le mencionara lo que Edith había escrito, ni a que le mostrara las anotaciones de ese diario.

—¿Por qué? —La sospecha se alzaba, instintiva y compulsiva, pero Sarah aún no veía la relación—. ¿Qué hubiera visto Charlie en el diario de mi tía que no debía ver?

Malcolm sostuvo su mirada un largo rato y luego dijo:

—Con lo que Charlie sabe de mí y de mi reputación, combinado con el profundo conocimiento que Edith tenía de mi manera de pensar, Charlie podría haber llegado a preguntarse, dado que en una ocasión me había desviado del camino recto, si podría volver a hacerlo.

»Y a mí —endureció la voz— no me pareció inteligente permitirlo. Para una mente tan brillante como la de Charlie no habría sido difícil pasar de la mera conjetura a percibir todas las posibilidades. A imaginar qué clase de planes podría haber ideado después. Y una vez que lo hubiera hecho, se habría sentido impulsado a investigar, y dar con algún tipo de información que sugiriera que al menos uno de mis planes estaba en marcha. Y aunque no pudiera vincularlo conmigo, el hecho de que tuviera la más mínima sospecha habría sido muy incómodo para mí.

Sarah se humedeció los labios repentinamente secos.

—¿Acaba de admitir que tiene un plan? ¿Qué clase de plan?

Los ojos color avellana de Malcolm capturaron los de ella. Cuando curvó los labios de nuevo, Sarah sintió como si él pudiera leerle el pensamiento.

—Realmente, Charlie no la merece. Es usted mucho más lista de lo que él piensa. Pero sí, ha supuesto bien... Como lo habría hecho Charlie si alguna vez hubiera leído las palabras de su tía Edith. El inversor que está detrás de las ofertas de compra por la granja Quilley soy yo.

Sarah se lo quedó mirando. A pesar de lo que había dicho, no podía creérselo.

—¿Es usted el malnacido que está detrás de... de los accidentes en la granja?

El temperamento de Sarah comenzó a inflamarse. Alzó el brazo y señaló al otro lado del valle, hacia la estrecha franja de tierra donde los negros escombros aún humeaban.

—¿Es usted quien ha incendiado el orfanato? —Bruscamente, ella se dio cuenta de lo evidente, parpadeó y dejó caer la mano—. No, no puede haber sido usted. —Se sintió confusa y volvió a mirarle a los ojos—. Usted estaba con nosotros, estaba sentado a mi lado en el comedor de mis padres mientras alguien disparaba flechas de fuego al tejado de paja del orfanato.

Él la miró como si le irritara que ella hubiera interrumpido sus acusaciones, como si le molestara que no siguiera acusándolo. Como si quisiera que se ensañara con él.

Cuando Sarah no lo hizo y se limitó a mirarle con el ceño fruncido, esperando una explicación, él también frunció el ceño.

—No, no lo hice. —Su voz se había vuelto irritable. Apretó los labios—. Pero ésa no es la cuestión. Si lo leyeras —golpeó ligeramente el diario de tía Edith con el dedo—, lo entenderías. Yo jamás he hecho nada ilegal. Jamás le he hecho daño a nadie ni he provocado accidentes ni, muchísimo menos, he planeado la muerte de nadie. No he cometido ningún crimen. No personalmente. Sin embargo, tal como dice Edith, eso no me absuelve de la culpa.

No había alzado la voz, pero sí la intensidad de su tono, tan intenso como el resplandor de su mirada, con la que la inmovilizaba, como si la mente aguda de Sarah se hubiera vuelto obtusa de repente.

—No fui yo quien provocó el incendio del orfanato, y no, no sabía qué iba a pasar. Nunca, jamás he dado ninguna orden que implicara al orfanato. Me quedé horrorizado cuando supe que le habían disparado y herido. Me pasé los dos días siguientes buscando a mi hombre para ordenarle que detuviera los ataques. Lo único que le dije fue que quería el título de propiedad de la granja Quilley, y que no había ninguna prisa con tal de que finalmente acabara en mis manos.

Atrapada por su mirada, Sarah vio la angustia, real y sincera, que llameaba en los ojos de Sinclair.

—La noche pasada estaba con usted, con Charlie y con todos los demás cuando llegaron con la noticia de que el orfanato estaba ardiendo. Cabalgué con ustedes hasta la granja y trabajé con Charlie y los demás para intentar, de una manera totalmente inútil, apagar las llamas. —La taladró con la mirada—. Nadie tenía una razón mejor que yo para combatir ese fuego. Pero no pude hacer nada para detenerlo... tuve que quedarme allí, observando cómo el lugar se quemaba, viendo y oyendo el terror y la angustia de los niños, sabiendo que todo eso lo habían provocado mis planes. —Él le sostuvo la mirada con firmeza sin ocultar las turbulentas emociones que lo embargaban—. Y por si eso no fuera suficiente, tuve que observar cómo Charlie y Barnaby arriesgaban sus vidas para salvar a unos bebés que yo mismo había puesto en peligro. Y sé, sin ningún tipo de duda, que no poseo ni el coraje ni la compasión de esos hombres.

Hizo una pausa y luego continuó con voz baja pero firme:

—Tuve que quedarme allí sabiendo con una angustiosa certeza que todo aquello era culpa mía. Que como Edith me había advertido años atrás, debería haberme guardado mis planes para mí.

Una vez más su mirada se volvió distante. Sarah lo observó tan perpleja por sus revelaciones que no podía ni moverse ni pensar. Pero a pesar de todas aquellas confesiones, no se sentía amenazada por él.

—Siempre he pensado que era muy listo, que saldría airoso de todo. —Su voz se había convertido en un murmullo y ella tuvo que aguzar el oído para escucharle por encima del ensordecedor ruido de la cascada—. Pero lo cierto es que no soy más que un absoluto fracaso.

Volvió a centrar su atención en ella, luego respiró hondo y pareció salir de su ensimismamiento, regresando al presente. Esbozó una sonrisa irónica y pesarosa a la vez. Levantó la voz y ella pudo escucharle con más facilidad.

—Y ahora todo se desmorona. Las autoridades están por fin tras mi pista, y sea o no responsable directo de los crímenes, no me dejarán escapar esta vez.

—¿Por qué me lo cuenta todo a mí? —preguntó ella, mirándolo fijamente.

—Porque quiero que me entienda. Quiero que alguien lo entienda todo antes de que me vaya. —Escrutó sus ojos, preguntándose claramente si ella lo hacía—. No sabe cuánto lamento no haber seguido el consejo de su tía. Si lo hubiera hecho... Pero no puedo cambiar el pasado. En mi arrogancia, hice precisamente aquello que ella me advirtió que no hiciera jamás, y ahora recojo lo que he sembrado.

Sarah le miró directamente a los ojos y supo que era sincero. De lo que no estaba tan segura es de si estaba en su sano juicio. Parecía resuelto a aceptar su culpa, a reconocerla... a confesarlo todo. Pero incluso así tenía intención de escapar.

Sin embargo, a pesar de que la confesión de Sinclair la había puesto en guardia, seguía sin sentirse amenazada por él. Sin importar lo que dijera, le costaba trabajo temerle. Sinceramente esperaba que sus sentidos no se sintieran confundidos por lo mucho que ese hombre se parecía a Charlie.

—Y... —se humedeció los labios—, ¿ahora qué?

—Ahora... —Sinclair había apartado los ojos de ella para mirar el camino que conducía al puente, como si hubiera oído algo.

Sarah miró hacia atrás al tiempo que le oía hablar con una voz que volvía a ser casi inaudible:

—Ahora tengo intención de poner las cosas en orden antes de irme, algo que Edith Balmain sí aprobaría, ya que resultará beneficioso para su sobrina.

Sarah se volvió para mirarlo directamente a la cara. Había algo en ella, un firme propósito en su expresión que le puso los pelos de punta.

Con suma rapidez él le agarró la muñeca. Ella la retorció intentando liberarse, pero aunque su agarre no era lo suficientemente fuerte para causarle dolor, era inquebrantable.

—No luche contra mí. —La miró brevemente antes de volver a mirar por encima de su cabeza el camino—. No tengo intención de hacerle daño de ninguna manera ni a usted ni a Charlie. —Aunque pareciera increíble dada la situación, Sinclair esbozó una sonrisa—. Sería contraproducente, por no decir otra cosa.

Sarah clavó los ojos en él, furiosa.

—Me está hablando en clave. —«Se ha vuelto loco.»

Él la miró; ahora tenía su habitual expresión impasible.

—He dicho todo lo que tenía que decirte. —Levantó la cabeza y miró al camino—. Pero aún no he hablado con Charlie.

Finalmente, la joven oyó con claridad el sonido de cascos de caballo que él había estado oyendo, y que cada vez era más audible por encima del rugido ensordecedor de la cascada.

Sintiéndose de repente insegura de su integridad física —y de la cordura de Sinclair—, Sarah lo miró.

—¿De qué va todo esto?

Por un momento ella pensó que no contestaría, pero luego habló fría y tranquilamente:

—Como ya le he dicho, toda mi vida se desmorona ante mí, no tengo control sobre nada, pero sí sobre esto.

El sonido de cascos estaba cada vez más cerca. Ella levantó la cabeza y vio cómo Charlie refrenaba su montura justo en lo alto de la empinada cuesta. Con expresión pétrea bajó la mirada hacia ella y Malcolm. Desde donde estaba, su marido podía ver cómo Sinclair la agarraba por la muñeca con firmeza y cómo ella sostenía el diario de Edith en la otra mano.

Charlie se apeó sin decir nada. Anudó las riendas de *Tormenta* en la silla de montar antes de palmearle el anca para que se dirigiera al claro donde estaban los otros caballos.

Luego comenzó a bajar la cuesta sin vacilación. El rugido de la cascada hacía inútil hablar hasta que estuviera más cerca.

—¡Detente!

Charlie alzó la vista ante la orden de Malcolm. Dio un paso más hacia el penúltimo escalón delante del puente. Estudió a Sarah. Parecía estar tan conmocionada como él, puede que incluso más confundida e insegura, aunque todavía conservaba la calma.

Charlie se paró y miró a Malcolm. A pesar de lo que sabía ahora, de todo lo que había adivinado, aún podía ver en los ojos color avellana de Malcolm al mismo hombre que había admirado hasta media hora antes.

—Eres tú, ¿verdad? El inversor que quiere adquirir la granja Quilley. Eres quien está detrás de todas las operaciones especulativas que involucran al ferrocarril.

A pesar de la falta de pruebas, las piezas habían encajado en la mente de Charlie. Incluso podía explicarse por qué estaban allí. Malcolm había sabido que podía conseguir llevar a Sarah hasta aquel lugar con la excusa del diario de su tía, y atraerlo a él por medio de Sarah. Pero lo que esperaba sacar Sinclair de todo aquello quedaba lejos de su comprensión.

Vio que alzaba las cejas pero que mantenía la expresión impasible.

—Me preguntaba cuánto tiempo tardarías en llegar a esa conclusión. No pensé que sería tan pronto. —El tono de su voz sugería que se había quedado gratamente impresionado, pero al instante parpadeó y cualquier atisbo de admiración desapareció de su rostro. Después de un momento, dijo—: Ah, por supuesto... debí haberme dado cuenta antes. Eras tú quien estaba detrás de todas esas investigaciones sobre la procedencia de los fondos en lugar de averiguar quién recibía los beneficios, ¿verdad?

Charlie le sostuvo la mirada pero no respondió.

Malcolm esbozó una sonrisa.

—Por supuesto, ¿quién más podría ser?

Había un gran problema en el escenario que se había formado en la mente de Charlie. Había visto el horror de Malcolm cuando oyó que habían disparado a Sarah, lo había visto combatir el fuego que había engullido el orfanato con la misma desesperación que ellos. Entrecerró los ojos y ladeó la cabeza.

—¿Qué pasó? ¿Tu secuaz se volvió loco? —Cuando Malcolm siguió guardando silencio, le preguntó—: ¿Quién es?

Malcolm descartó la pregunta con un movimiento rápido de su mano libre. Con la otra seguía sujetando con firmeza la muñeca de Sarah, justo encima del pasamanos de cuerda.

—No te preocupes por él, muy pronto conocerás su nombre. Ahora no es él quien me preocupa. —La voz de Malcolm se endureció—. Sino tú.

Charlie vaciló, luego extendió los brazos con las palmas hacia arriba.

—Me pediste que viniera y aquí estoy.

Dio un paso hasta el último escalón.

—¡No! —El tono de Malcolm lo dejó paralizado. Mirándolo a los ojos, Malcolm indicó con la cabeza las cuerdas que sujetaban el puente—. Mira las cuerdas.

Charlie lo hizo y se quedó sin aliento. Las gruesas cuerdas que habían sostenido el puente durante años estaban cortadas y unidas con otras más finas. Las cuerdas que ahora anclaban el puente en el que se encontraban Malcolm y Sarah eran significativamente menos resistentes y por lo tanto menos capaces de soportar más peso.

—En ambos lados —dijo Malcolm. Cuando la mirada de Charlie se desplazó al otro extremo para comprobarlo, continuó hablando—: He calculado la fuerza, la tensión... tú sabes bien cómo se hace. Las cuerdas que hay ahora soportarán el peso de dos personas, pero no de tres. —Malcolm hizo una pausa, luego continuó—: Así que, si tratas de acercarte a nosotros, el puente cederá y caerá, y tú serás el responsable de la muerte de todos nosotros, incluida tu esposa.

Con un gesto de cabeza señaló la rugiente cascada que rompía sobre las dentadas rocas de abajo.

—Sin duda, nos esperaría una muerte segura.

—Dice la verdad. —Sarah habló por primera vez desde que Charlie había llegado. Buscó los ojos de su marido con una expresión pálida y horrorizada—. El puente se ha tambaleado cuando lo he pisado. —Desplazó la mirada al final de las cuerdas—. Pero no he comprendido por qué.

Malcolm dejó pasar un momento mientras ellos asimilaban la situación, luego le habló a Charlie:

—Como sin duda te habrás dado cuenta ya, no hay otra manera de resolver este asunto salvo que yo suelte a Sarah y deje que abandone el puente.

Ignorando el pánico devastador que amenazaba con asfixiarle y la sombría furia que lo embargaba, Charlie sostuvo la mirada de Malcolm. Dejó pasar también otro momento mientras se estrujaba el cerebro, intentando buscar una salida.

—¿Qué tengo que hacer para que liberes a Sarah? —preguntó finalmente.

Malcolm sonrió.

—Diría que nada excesivo, pero... sólo tienes que hacer dos cosas. La primera es escuchar.

Charlie buscó los ojos de Sarah. Sí, ella tenía miedo, pero aún no era presa del pánico. A pesar de su confusión, su esposa parecía mucho más serena que Malcolm o él mismo. Conseguir que Sinclair siguiera hablando mientras decidía qué hacer parecía lo más inteligente.

Clavando la mirada en la cara de Malcolm, arqueó las cejas.

—¿Escuchar qué?

—Una historia de amor... y pérdida. —Malcolm también arqueó las cejas en un gesto vagamente desafiante—. Una historia familiar en ciertos aspectos, pero muy desagradable en otros.

Charlie vio la mirada desconcertada que Sarah le lanzó a Malcolm y se preguntó si su esposa estaría comenzando a dudar de la cordura de Malcolm, igual que lo estaba haciendo él. La escena parecía cada vez más rocambolesca, pero si Sinclair quería seguir hablando y que él le escuchase, estaba más que dispuesto a complacerle. Mientras hablaba, Malcolm no prestaba atención a Sarah, y resultaba evidente que no tenía planes inmediatos de hacerle ningún daño. Muy bien. Charlie era perfectamente capaz de escuchar con atención mientras planeaba qué hacer.

Asintiendo con la cabeza para indicarle que estaba escuchando, que podía seguir contando esa historia que tantas ganas tenía de narrarles, Charlie se afianzó sobre la roca con los pies separados. Durante las negociaciones, las manos a menudo revelaban más de lo que uno quería, así que se las metió en los bolsillos de los pantalones.

Malcolm sonrió, pero la sonrisa no le llegó a los ojos.

—Durante estas últimas semanas, he llegado a respetar tu inteligencia, tu perspicacia; ciertamente eres tan listo como yo. Pero hay un tema en el que eres un tonto redomado. Considero que los ejemplos siempre son mejores que las advertencias y, ya que somos tan parecidos, déjame describirte cómo podría haber sido tu vida. Tú, al igual que yo, podrías haber nacido de unos padres que jamás hubieran tenido tiempo para ti. En una familia sin hermanos, sin vínculos familiares, podrías, al igual que yo, haber crecido completamente solo.

»Y al igual que yo, podrías haber educado tu mente sumergiéndote en problemas puramente teóricos, de los que se aprenden en la escuela. Sin nadie a tu alrededor a quien le importaras, ni padres ni tutores. Podrías, al igual que yo, haber llegado a la edad adulta conociendo sólo los retos y los triunfos de una mente brillante y sin ninguna de las alegrías que tantos dan por supuestas, como los simples placeres de las relaciones humanas.

»Sin embargo... —Malcolm hizo una pausa.

Charlie parpadeó, desconcertado por completo ante la inesperada dirección que habían tomado las palabras de Sinclair.

Malcolm esbozó una sonrisa y continuó:

—... tu vida jamás ha sido así. Naciste en el seno de una familia que te quería, pasaste todos los años de formación rodeado de personas a las que les importabas. Y a las que tú amabas y por las que te preocupabas a su vez. Incluso más, como el heredero de un condado, has estado condicionado desde tu más tierna infancia a recibir los elogios que eso conlleva. Tu posición tiene responsabilidades, sí, pero también tiene intangibles recompensas. No sólo es la posición que ocupas, sino el reconocimiento que te supone, algo que marca una auténtica diferencia con la vida de otras personas... y que todo el mundo aprecia. Tú posees el poder, y la habilidad para ejercerlo como quieras, de influenciar en la vida de mucha gente y hacerla mejor. Puedes llevar consuelo y felicidad a otros, mientras que yo sólo les he traído oscuridad y desesperación.

Malcolm sostuvo la mirada de Charlie con ojos penetrantes.

—Pero no ha sido hasta hace poco que has aceptado dedicar tu tiempo y energía a tales actos. Por tu bien, espero que lo ocurrido en el orfanato te haya cambiado para siempre.

La cara de Charlie parecía de piedra.

—¿Hablas de mi legado?

Malcolm curvó los labios. Asintió con la cabeza.

—Si quieres llamarlo así. Pero la posición que ocupas como conde no es más que uno de los muchos puntos sobre los que quería hablarte.

»Antes de irme, quería decirte, ya que nadie más lo hará, y nadie más podría hacerlo con la misma comprensión que yo, que serás un tonto redomado durante el resto de tu vida si no intentas aceptar el amor y todo lo que éste te ofrece. Si no aceptas a Sarah de la manera en que ella se ha ofrecido a ti.

Charlie se lo quedó mirando, totalmente perplejo.

—En efecto. —Una vez más, Malcolm curvó los labios en una desdeñosa sonrisa—. No, no es un tema sobre el que los caballeros hablen habitualmente. No obstante, lo haré y tú escucharás. —Capturó los ojos de Charlie con una mirada fija e inquebrantable—. El amor es lo que da sentido a la vida... lo que da sentido a la vida de un hombre. Si no hay amor, la vida carece de sentido, por mucho que yo y los que son como yo queramos desear lo contrario. He comprendido eso ahora. Mi vida ha sido una concha vacía, una cáscara que una vez que os deje se llevará el viento con la misma ligereza que pasa el tiempo.

Mantenía la misma voz neutra, pero en su tono se percibían la pasión y la sinceridad.

—Jamás busqué el amor, jamás lo deseé ardientemente, porque nunca supe lo que era, ni mucho menos lo que podría significar para mí. Al observaros a Sarah y a ti juntos, se me abrieron los ojos y entendí la verdad. Sólo podría haberme ocurrido contigo, Charlie, porque por una ironía del destino, yo podría haber sido tú y viceversa.

Esta vez, cuando hizo una pausa, Charlie sintió que Malcolm miraba su propio interior, cavilando con aire crítico su propia confesión; luego pareció salir de su ensimismamiento, respiró hondo y volvió a mirar los ojos de Charlie.

—Mi tiempo ha pasado, ya es muy tarde para que aprenda otra manera de vivir la vida. Pero tú... Tú tienes ante ti la oportunidad que yo querría, una por la que mataría, ahora que sé lo suficiente para apreciarla. —Una expresión de impaciencia cruzó brevemente los rasgos de Malcolm—. ¿Tienes idea de lo frustrante que es haber observado cómo te equivocas al no aceptar el amor? Tu indiferencia, tu rechazo a un regalo por el que yo mataría, ha sido y es un insulto rotundo. Todo lo que tenías que hacer era extender la mano y tomarlo, pero no. Has vacilado, una y otra vez, en aceptar algo por lo que yo daría cualquier cosa.

Entrecerró los ojos y pareció leer los pensamientos de Charlie, su reacción. Negó con la cabeza lentamente.

—Sí, te envidio todo eso, pero sé que no es para mí. Sarah y todo lo que ella te ofrece no son para mí. Dejaré que rectifiques y que tu vida sea todo lo que pueda ser, y espero que después de todo lo que te he dicho aprecies cada regalo como se merece.

De una manera indefinible Malcolm pareció erguirse, como si hubiera retrocedido mentalmente. Vaciló y luego continuó:

—Y quizá, cuando todo esto haya acabado, cuando te acuerdes de mí, espero que también recuerdes que Malcolm Sinclair habría sido un hombre muy diferente si la vida, el destino, hubiera puesto en su camino la mitad de las cosas que tú tienes.

Sostuvo la mirada de Charlie.

—Dale gracias a Dios por tu vida, acéptala con todo lo que ésta te ofrece.

Charlie tenía intención de hacer exactamente eso. Aunque no había necesitado que Malcolm se lo señalara, no podía negar los dones que la vida le había ofrecido. Pero había sido por el acuerdo que tenía con Sarah y toda la charada que habían interpretado en presencia de Malcolm por lo que éste había creído su equívoca actitud ante el amor, ante la familia y su posición.

Malcolm se había quedado callado. Reflexionando sobre sus propios sentimientos turbulentos, sobre todo lo que había expuesto Malcolm, Charlie asintió con la cabeza para demostrarle que le había entendido.

—¿Cuál es la segunda cosa que tengo que hacer para que sueltes a Sarah? —le preguntó entonces.

La sonrisa que curvó lentamente los labios de Malcolm fue extraña e hipnótica.

—Es muy sencillo. —Su voz apenas era lo suficientemente fuerte como para oírse por encima del rugido del agua—. Dile a ella por qué debería soltarla.

Charlie miró a los ojos color avellana de Malcolm y entendió perfectamente lo que había querido decir. Pero la paz que veía en los ojos de Malcolm hizo que se cuestionara de nuevo la cordura de ese hombre. Se humedeció los labios, repentinamente secos.

—¿Por qué estás haciendo esto?

Sarah estaba todavía en el puente, al lado de Malcolm, que la retenía por la muñeca. La joven había oído su discurso sin decir nada. En algún momento había sentido el impulso de hablar, incluso había abierto la boca —para defenderle, sin duda—, pero al final había optado por guardar silencio, algo que Charlie le agradecía profundamente.

Pero en sus ojos había ahora una expresión cautelosa. Al igual que él, no sabía adónde quería llegar Malcolm.

Al igual que Charlie, no sabía si podía confiar en él.

Malcolm suspiró.

—Porque aún no le has dicho las palabras, ¿verdad? Sarah necesita oírlas, y yo también. Es mi última petición, o mi precio, como quieras llamarlo. Si pronuncias esas palabras, sabré que has aceptado lo que he dicho, no me importa que lo hagas a regañadientes.

Charlie ya había aceptado más allá de lo que Malcolm pretendía, ya había aceptado el amor y lo que éste significaba en su vida. Pero aunque tenía intención de decir las palabras no quería tener que hacerlo bajo coacción. Le molestaba pensar que la primera vez que Sarah las oyera sería de esa manera.

No quería eso. Y no creía que ella lo quisiera tampoco.

Pero las diría, eso y cualquier otra cosa que Malcolm quisiera, aunque todavía seguía dudando de la cordura de éste. Ahora que había oído lo que Sinclair pensaba de sus vidas, la envidia que había confesado sentir, ¿no podía ser que bajo todo eso sintiera un enconado resentimiento? Y si era así, ¿hasta dónde supuraba el veneno?

¿Hasta qué punto se habría visto afectada su inteligencia? ¿Y su voluntad? Evidentemente la integridad, en vista de los hechos, nunca había sido su fuerte.

Todos esos pensamientos y especulaciones zumbaban en la mente de Charlie; había sopesado las distintas opciones, evaluando impactos y reacciones, calculando los riesgos mientras escuchaba el discurso de Malcolm.

Finalmente, todo —la vida de Sarah y la suya— dependía de un solo acto, de una reacción. Si admitía su amor por Sarah, si ponía voz a sus palabras para que tanto Malcolm como Sarah las oyeran, ¿qué haría Sinclair después?

¿Cumpliría su extraño trato y dejaría que Sarah saliera del puente hacia un lugar seguro? Y luego, ¿qué?

¿No podría ser todo una trampa? ¿No podría Malcolm dejarse llevar por la envidia y atacar a Charlie, arrebatándole el amor de la manera más cruel posible, una vez que éste hubiera confesado lo que sentía por su esposa?

Sabía que Malcolm podía coger a Sarah por la cintura, alzarla y tirarla por encima de las cuerdas antes de que él pudiera impedirlo.

Como Malcolm había dejado muy claro, sólo les esperaba una muerte segura allí abajo.

A pesar de todo, de todas las posibilidades y consideraciones,

¿podía confiar Charlie lo suficiente en la cordura de Malcolm como para arriesgar la vida de Sarah?

Respiró hondo y miró a su esposa a los ojos y supo que ella no confiaba en Malcolm hasta ese punto. Dado que...

La vacilación de Charlie había irritado a Sinclair.

—Di las palabras. —La impaciencia le teñía la voz—. Ésta es mi última acción antes de irme, mi único gesto totalmente altruista. Pero... —aguzó la mirada— no lo hagas, no la rechaces, disfruta de esa emoción todo lo que puedas. —Hizo una pausa y luego añadió—: Ha llegado el momento de que empieces a hablar.

Charlie tomó aire, miró a Sarah y vio su propia pregunta reflejada en sus ojos: «¿Qué era lo más conveniente?» Sólo podía darle una respuesta.

—Confía en mí.

Sacó las manos de los bolsillos y bajó al puente de un salto.

La sorpresa en la cara de Malcolm fue totalmente genuina.

Charlie agarró a Sarah, la liberó de un tirón de la mano de Malcolm, se dio la vuelta sin dejar de agarrarla y la lanzó hacia la cuesta, al lado de los escalones de piedra.

El puente comenzó a tambalearse. Charlie se agarró al pasamanos de cuerda, que estaba tirante y a punto de soltarse. Sintió que las tablas oscilaban bajo sus pies y se precipitó hacia delante, buscando el poste de anclaje más próximo.

Lo alcanzó con una mano, pero no pudo agarrarse a él con la suficiente fuerza para ponerse a salvo.

Detrás de él oyó cómo Malcolm maldecía:

—¡Maldito tonto!

Las tablas se balancearon sobre el vacío; dos de los anclajes se habían soltado, uno en cada extremo, y los otros dos apenas podían soportar aquella sobrecarga. No había tiempo que perder.

Charlie se impulsó hacia arriba, intentando agarrarse mejor a la superficie resbaladiza y redondeada del poste, que estaba cubierto totalmente de humedad, y sintió que Malcolm se acercaba por detrás.

Unas manos firmes le agarraron una de las botas y de repente se vio empujado hacia arriba.

Charlie rodeó el poste de anclaje con un brazo. Sarah se apoyó en el mismo poste y le agarró por el hombro y la manga. Entonces desplazó la mirada tras él y soltó un grito.

Charlie miró atrás.

Al principio no comprendió lo que veía.

Con su peso fuera del puente, éste estaba ligeramente ladeado, pero aunque las dos últimas cuerdas estaban bajo una fuerte presión, seguían aguantando.

Sin embargo, Malcolm tenía un cuchillo en la mano e intentaba cortar la cuerda atada al poste de anclaje.

Mientras Charlie miraba, la cuerda cedió.

Malcolm levantó la cabeza y sus miradas se encontraron durante un instante.

Luego el puente cayó y chocó contra la roca del lado opuesto; Malcolm había desaparecido.

Durante un buen rato, Charlie y Sarah se quedaron mirando al vacío. Charlie aguzó el oído, pero no oyó nada más que un chapoteo entre el ruido ensordecedor del agua; luego el rugido continuó y la corriente siguió su curso.

Por encima de él, Sarah tragó saliva, luego lo agarró con más firmeza por la chaqueta y tiró con fuerza.

—¡Sube!

Antes de que cayese él también.

Sarah había gritado cuando había visto a Malcolm detrás de Charlie, sacando el cuchillo de su bota, pero Sinclair ni siquiera había mirado a Charlie.

Ahora lo entendía. No había sido ése su propósito. Jamás había sido su objetivo hacerles daño. Le había dicho que jamás atentaría contra la vida de Charlie o la de ella... que sería contraproducente. Recordó la extraña sonrisa en sus labios cuando le había dicho eso, y tragó saliva.

Tiró con fuerza y soltó aire cuando Charlie comenzó a subir lentamente. El barranco estaba desgastado por el tiempo y la roca era lisa. Había muy pocas grietas o surcos en los que poder apoyarse. Sarah aspiró profundamente, volvió a tirar de la chaqueta de su marido y retrocedió cuando, con su ayuda, él comenzó a subir, trepando por el poste hasta que finalmente pudo poner el pie en los escalones.

Se dejó caer hacia atrás, sin importarle que pudiera estropeársele la falda de terciopelo y sin soltar la chaqueta de Charlie, hasta que éste se dejó caer de espaldas a su lado en lo alto de la cuesta. Una cuesta que ahora conducía directamente al abismo. Sarah comprobó que ninguno de los dos corría peligro de caerse ni de deslizarse, entonces se dejó caer de espaldas al lado de Charlie.

Se quedaron allí tumbados uno al lado del otro, simplemente respirando. Miraron el cielo azul con sólo unas pocas nubes flotando en el aire.

Durante largos momentos permanecieron quietos y en silencio. Sarah no sabía por dónde empezar, pero luego la mano de Charlie encontró la suya y se cerró en torno a ella.

—Malcolm tenía razón en un montón de cosas, pero se equivocaba en una. Una declaración de amor forzada no tiene ningún valor. —Hizo una pausa y luego continuó mientras le apretaba la mano—: Te amo. Ya lo sabes. Hace tiempo que busco las palabras adecuadas para decírtelo, pero éstas son las únicas que conozco. Lo eres todo para mí. Mi sol, mi luna, mis estrellas... mi vida. Sin ti no sé qué sería de mí... te necesito, te deseo. Daría mi vida por ti en cualquier momento o lugar sin dudarlo siquiera. Pero preferiría vivir una vida a tu lado, cuidándote y amándote tanto tiempo como me lo permita el destino. Ésa es la única realidad que conozco. Y, aunque no he tenido el valor de decirte estas palabras antes, intentaré decírtelas todos los días durante el resto de nuestras vidas. Te amo. —Se llevó la mano de Sarah a los labios y le besó los dedos entrelazados con los suyos—. Jamás lo dudes.

Sarah había girado la cabeza para observar el perfil de Charlie mientras hablaba.

—Yo también te amo —le dijo con los ojos empañados—, y siempre lo he hecho... como ya sabes. —Apoyándose en un codo, Sarah se inclinó hacia delante y le besó en la mejilla. Estudió el rostro de su marido durante un rato y añadió—. Siempre lo has sabido, ¿verdad?

Él vaciló, luego la miró a los ojos.

—No de manera consciente, pero tal vez lo supiera a un nivel más profundo. —Levantó la mano y le colocó el pelo detrás de la oreja—. Puede que ésa sea la razón por la que me fijé en ti.

Sarah se recostó sobre él y apoyó la frente en su hombro. Volvieron a mirar al cielo.

—Todavía no puedo creer lo que... hizo.

—Yo no estoy seguro de que pueda llegar a comprenderlo —dijo Charlie tras un rato.

—Antes de que llegaras, me dijo que antes de irse quería hacer una buena acción, algo que mi tía hubiera aprobado —dijo la joven tras un momento de vacilación—. Creo que se refería a enderezar nuestro matrimonio.

—No puedo culparle por eso, nuestro matrimonio es importante. Y el vínculo entre él y yo, nuestra amistad, también. Sin tener en cuenta sus intenciones, a pesar de que nos haya puesto en peligro en el puente. —Levantando una mano, Charlie le acarició la cabeza, alisándole el pelo—. Y no pienses que no te habría dicho cuánto te amo si él no me hubiera presionado.

Sarah encontró la otra mano de Charlie y entrelazó sus dedos con los suyos.

—Pensé, cuando te exigió que lo escucharas y luego empezó a hablar, que debía de estar loco. Comencé a asustarme. No podía imaginar lo que haría una vez que hicieras lo que te exigía.

—Lo sé. Yo tampoco podía imaginarlo. Por eso salté a por ti.

Sus corazones ya se habían tranquilizado. Sarah suspiró.

—No tenía otra intención, ¿verdad? Desde el principio pensaba en morir.

Los dos habían nacido en la zona. Conocían la cascada. Sabían que sería un milagro que Malcolm hubiera sobrevivido.

—Sí. —Charlie respiró hondo y soltó el aire—. Éste era otro de sus inteligentes planes diseñados para lograr muchas cosas. Para devolverte el diario de tu tía, para forzarme a escuchar su perorata sobre el amor, para obligarme a decirte que te amo antes de tener que abandonar esta vida. Si hubiera querido salvarse, podría haberlo hecho con facilidad. Cuando salté al puente y te liberé, lo único que tenía que haber hecho era correr al otro lado. No hay duda de que tenía tiempo de sobra para ponerse a salvo. Es imposible que no lo supiera. Pero en lugar de eso, se acercó a mí y se aseguró de que yo estuviera a salvo.

—Y luego cortó la cuerda.

Charlie pensó en eso.

—Ha venido preparado con el cuchillo porque asumió que yo hablaría, y que luego tú saldrías del puente. Una vez hubieras hecho eso, él habría cortado las cuerdas mientras yo te ayudaba a subir. Ninguno de los dos habría podido detenerle.

Pasó otro largo rato, luego Sarah suspiró y se incorporó. Charlie hizo lo mismo. Él le pasó el brazo por los hombros y juntos miraron el profundo abismo que se abría a sus pies.

—Era un hombre extraño —dijo ella.

Charlie asintió con la cabeza.

—Un hombre que jamás había conocido el amor —añadió, como si fuera un epitafio.

Se pusieron en pie y se sacudieron el uno al otro la suciedad y las hojas húmedas de la ropa como mejor pudieron. Sarah recuperó el diario de Edith de donde lo había dejado tirado, y caminaron lentamente hacia el claro donde los aguardaban los caballos.

22

Entraron en el patio de los establos del Park en medio de un fuerte estrépito. Charlie todavía se sentía algo desorientado, aún se estremecía por todo lo que había ocurrido en el puente, intentaba asimilar aquellos hechos y emociones tan complejos.

Croker se acercó a coger las riendas de los caballos. Soltó una exclamación ahogada ante el estado de Charlie y Sarah, pero aceptó la suave afirmación de Sarah de que a pesar de las apariencias los dos se encontraban perfectamente.

—Volvemos a estar hechos un desastre —le murmuró Charlie mientras atravesaban el césped hacia la casa—. Sin duda Crisp y Figgs no lo aprobarán.

Sarah bajó la mirada al diario plateado que sostenía entre las manos. Su leve sonrisa se desvaneció.

—¿Qué le diremos a la gente?

Su marido comprendió lo que le estaba preguntando. Durante el lento viaje de regreso desde la cascada, Sarah le había contado todo lo que Malcolm había dicho antes de que él llegara al puente. Pero ahora que Malcolm estaba muerto, ¿era necesario hacer público todo lo que sabían?

—Creo...

Se interrumpió al oír el retumbar de cascos de caballos. Se giraron para observar cómo tres hombres a caballo se acercaban galopando a través de los campos y entraban en el patio de los establos.

Gabriel, que iba a la cabeza, los vio. Tiró de las riendas del semental y lo puso al trote.

Barnaby lo siguió, acompañado por un individuo con un gabán, a quien Charlie reconoció.

—Es el inspector Stokes —le murmuró a Sarah. Había coincidido con Stokes en muchas ocasiones.

—¿Qué ha ocurrido? —preguntó Gabriel entrecerrando los ojos ante el aspecto deplorable que presentaban.

—Ahora os cuento. —Charlie pasó la mirada de Stokes a Barnaby—. No has tenido tiempo de llegar a Londres, ¿qué te ha hecho regresar tan pronto?

Con una expresión pétrea, Barnaby lo miró a los ojos.

—No te lo vas a creer, pero nuestro especulador es Sinclair.

Charlie asintió con la cabeza.

—Nos hemos enterado hace un rato. —Miró a Sarah antes de volver su mirada a los tres hombres—. ¿Por qué no dejáis los caballos con Croker y nos esperáis en la biblioteca? Dadnos unos minutos para que nos cambiemos de ropa y luego nos contáis lo que habéis averiguado y os diremos lo que sabemos.

Barnaby frunció el ceño, pero Gabriel asintió con la cabeza.

—Buena idea.

Se dio la vuelta y Stokes le siguió. Barnaby se vio obligado a aceptar ese plan a pesar de la impaciente mirada de curiosidad que apareció en sus ojos.

Veinte minutos más tarde Charlie abrió la puerta de la biblioteca y la sostuvo para que Sarah entrara; luego la siguió. Los otros tres hombres se habían acomodado en los sillones delante de la chimenea. Cuando Sarah se acercó a ellos, todos se levantaron.

Charlie la presentó a Stokes.

El inspector, un hombre alto y moreno, que vestía de una manera sobria y pulcra, le hizo una reverencia.

—Es un placer conocerla, condesa.

Sarah sonrió.

—He ordenado que nos traigan té y buñuelos. —Paseó la mirada por los tres hombres—. Estoy segura de que todos necesitamos un tentempié.

Se sentó en la *chaise*; Charlie se sentó a su lado mientras todos los demás volvían a tomar sus respectivos asientos. Miró a Barnaby.

431

—Tú primero.

Barnaby vaciló pero asintió.

—No llegué a Londres. Me topé con Stokes cerca de Salisbury. Venía a contarnos lo que Montague había descubierto.

Barnaby miró a Stokes, quien continuó relatando los hechos.

—Montague tuvo en cuenta la sugerencia que hiciste —dijo Stokes, señalando a Charlie con la cabeza— y comenzó a investigar la procedencia de los fondos utilizados para comprar las tierras con las que luego se especulaba. Se concentró en una única propiedad, en una única suma de dinero, y de esa manera sus pesquisas lo condujeron hasta una cuenta a nombre de Malcolm Sinclair, descubriendo así la implicación de éste. Montague le contó sus sospechas a su excelencia, el duque de St. Ives.

—Diablo investigó un poco más —dijo Barnaby—. Habló con Wolverstone, quien a su vez informó a Dearne y a Paignton. —Miró a Sarah—. Al parecer la esposa de Paignton, Phoebe, es familiar tuyo.

—¿La prima Phoebe? —Sarah frunció el ceño, luego abrió mucho los ojos—. Estuvo un tiempo viviendo con tía Edith. ¿Conocía Phoebe a Malcolm Sinclair?

Barnaby negó con la cabeza, desconcertado.

—No, no lo conocía. Pero su marido, Paignton, sí. Cuando era joven, Malcolm Sinclair estuvo involucrado junto con su tutor en un plan relacionado con el comercio de trata de blancas. En 1816, Paignton, Dearne y otros más lo sacaron todo a la luz.

—Pero no acusaron a Malcolm Sinclair—dijo Sarah—, aunque se sospechaba que había sido el cerebro del plan.

Barnaby clavó la mirada en ella.

—¿Cómo lo has sabido?

Sarah sostuvo en alto el diario plateado que había llevado consigo.

—Mi tía Edith lo sospechó, y le dijo a Sinclair lo que pasaría si no se reformaba. Lo escribió todo aquí. Hace tiempo heredé uno de los volúmenes de sus diarios.

—Como puedes ver, es un diario fácilmente reconocible. Sinclair lo vio y se lo robó a Sarah para que no descubriéramos la verdad sobre su pasado —dijo Charlie—, y para que yo no pudiera sospechar que su interés por el ferrocarril se debiera a algo más que a la pura inversión.

—En efecto... —comenzó a decir Stokes, pero se interrumpió

cuando se abrió la puerta. Esperó mientras Crisp y un lacayo entraban portando unas bandejas con té, tostadas y buñuelos. La tentación de la miel, la mermelada y la mantequilla fresca provocó una pausa temporal. Luego, tras zamparse un buñuelo, Stokes tomó un sorbo de té y dejó la taza en la mesita.

Miró a Charlie.

—Tenemos pruebas más que suficientes para arrestar al señor Sinclair y muchas preguntas que hacerle. Venía hacia aquí para llevarle detenido a Londres cuando me he topado con el señor Adair. Sus noticias sobre el incendio en el orfanato sólo nos dan más razones para detener a Sinclair de inmediato.

—Han pasado por Casleigh para contarme lo que habían averiguado. —La sonrisa de Gabriel era la de un depredador—. Como es natural, me he unido al grupo.

—Y, por supuesto, nos hemos detenido aquí por si querías acompañarnos. —Barnaby frunció el ceño mientras estudiaba la expresión fría e impasible de Charlie—. Después de todo, ¿quién lo conoce mejor que tú?

Charlie suspiró.

—Sinclair está muerto.

El anuncio fue recibido con exclamaciones de incredulidad. Cuando se desvanecieron, Charlie les explicó lo que había ocurrido: Sinclair había utilizado el diario de Edith para conseguir que Sarah fuera al puente de la cascada y de esa manera atraerlo a él hasta allí.

—Me lo ha confesado todo —dijo Sarah—. Estaba muy arrepentido, no se ha molestado en negar su implicación en los hechos. Eran sus planes y aceptaba la culpa que recaía sobre sus hombros.

—Pero, si no he entendido mal, tenía un cómplice que resultó ser demasiado entusiasta a la hora de interpretar sus órdenes. —Charlie entrecerró los ojos, recordando—. Sinclair nos ha dicho que muy pronto conoceremos la identidad de ese hombre, pero no ha añadido nada más al respecto.

—¿Cómo ha muerto? —preguntó Barnaby. Stokes y él se inclinaron hacia delante para conocer el final de la historia.

Charlie miró a Gabriel.

—Aflojó las cuerdas que sostenían el puente de manera que sólo pudiera soportar el peso de dos personas. Cuando yo he llegado, Sarah y él estaban allí. Después de hacer su confesión y decir todo lo que quería decir, ha soltado a Sarah y la ha dejado salir del puente. En cuanto ella ha estado a salvo, ha cortado la cuerda... y ha caído.

Era la historia que Sarah y él habían acordado contar. El resto de las revelaciones de Malcolm Sinclair sólo era asunto de ellos tres.

Gabriel palideció.

—Santo Dios.

Stokes paseó la mirada de Gabriel a Charlie.

—¿Está seguro de que ha muerto?

Gabriel miró a Stokes fijamente.

—Inspector, le llevaremos al puente o, mejor dicho, al lugar donde éste estaba, y podrá verlo por sí mismo. Es imposible que nadie sobreviva a una caída como ésa. —Gabriel miró a Charlie—. No hay duda de que Sinclair se ha quitado la vida.

No obstante, Barnaby y Stokes decidieron ir a registrar la casa de Malcolm en Crowcombe. Mientras ellos cabalgaban hacia el norte, Charlie y Gabriel organizaron la búsqueda del cuerpo de Sinclair.

Una hora más tarde, después de enviar a varios grupos de búsqueda para que registraran la corriente más allá de la cascada, Charlie, Gabriel y Sarah habían extendido un mapa detallado de la zona en el escritorio de la biblioteca cuando oyeron el sonido de unos pasos enérgicos en el pasillo que anunciaba el regreso de Stokes y Barnaby.

Ambos hombres entraron en la habitación con una expresión aún más aturdida si cabe que cuando se habían marchado.

—¿Qué ha pasado? —preguntó Charlie.

Barnaby se dejó caer en una silla.

—Es increíble. —Negó con la cabeza—. Ha dejado una confesión sobre su escritorio que abarca más de una década de planes con los suficientes detalles para contentar a cualquier juez, todo pulcramente rubricado y sellado, con una nota diciéndonos que encontraríamos a su secuaz atado en el sótano, y que deberíamos hablar con el notario de la localidad para obtener más información.

Stokes, que se había acercado a mirar el mapa, levantó la mirada a los demás.

—Cuando decidió enmendar sus errores, Sinclair no dejó ningún cabo suelto. Su confesión ahorrará mucho trabajo a las autoridades, así como tiempo y dinero público. Al bajar al sótano, hemos encontrado a su cómplice, el agente al que el señor Adair buscaba, maniatado.

—No confesará, pero con todo lo que nos ha dejado Sinclair, eso no será problema. —La mirada de Barnaby se endureció—. No hemos llegado a leer toda la confesión de Sinclair, pues eran muchísimas páginas, pero sí hemos leído lo suficiente como para estar seguros de que Jennings, su agente, será ahorcado.

—Pero ahí no acaba todo —continuó Stokes—. Hemos ido a ver al notario a su despacho de la calle Mayor. Al parecer, Sinclair redactó ayer un nuevo testamento. —Stokes miró a Sarah y a Charlie—. En él pide que se indemnicen a todas aquellas personas que se hayan visto perjudicadas por sus planes en el pasado, aunque también señala que las compañías ferroviarias no deberán recibir ninguna compensación, pues fue la ineficacia y avaricia de éstas lo que le permitió obtener tanto dinero. Después de que se hayan pagado todas las indemnizaciones pertinentes, dispuso que se cedieran sus bienes residuales al orfanato de la granja Quilley para su reconstrucción, pero no en el mismo lugar. El resto de los fondos debería utilizarse para el mantenimiento del orfanato y para fundar otros donde sean necesarios. —Stokes hizo una pausa—. Os ha nombrado —señaló a Charlie y Sarah con la cabeza— albaceas de su testamento y de los fideicomisos que el orfanato financie.

Esta vez fueron Charlie y Sarah quienes se quedaron perplejos.

Gabriel habló con voz ronca:

—Dijisteis que habíais detectado veintitrés casos de usura. Aun después de pagar una generosa indemnización a los perjudicados, si he oído bien sobre la inmensa fortuna de Sinclair, quedará una importante cantidad de dinero para el fondo del orfanato.

—Asumiendo que el Parlamento permita que se ejecute el testamento —intervino Barnaby—. Pero incluso sin encontrar el cuerpo de Sinclair, sus activos serán confiscados por haber derivado de lo que en principio fueron ganancias ilícitas.

Stokes asintió con la cabeza.

—Incluso él pensó en eso, y por ese motivo también dejó una carta rogándole al Parlamento que permitiera la ejecución del testamento. Y dadas las circunstancias en que se ha desarrollado todo, al confesar y entregar a su cómplice, al quitarse la vida, ahorrándonos, por así decirlo, un juicio y una ejecución, imagino que sus señorías verán con buenos ojos que el dinero sea utilizado para beneficio de los niños huérfanos. —Stokes se encogió de hombros—. ¿Quién sabe? Puede que incluso les haya ahorrado la molestia de tener que decidir qué hacer con tal cantidad de dinero.

Gabriel sonrió ampliamente.

—Podemos dejar eso en manos de Diablo y Chillingworth. No creo que muchos pares vieran con buenos ojos que tal fortuna fuera a parar a las arcas de la Corona.

Sintiéndose un poco mareada, Sarah se hundió lentamente en la silla detrás del escritorio.

—Él dijo que quería hacer algo bien, algo bueno. —Observó a Charlie.

Él le sostuvo la mirada.

—Pues yo creo que es algo muy bueno el uso que quiso darles a esos fondos que consiguió invirtiendo legalmente sus ganancias ilícitas.

Barnaby meneó la cabeza lentamente.

—Todavía me cuesta creerlo: la confesión completa, la entrega de su cómplice, el testamento, su muerte. Es como si hubiera despertado de repente y se hubiera escandalizado de sus propios actos.

—Sucede a veces —dijo Stokes—. Suele haber un desencadenante, algo que les hace darse cuenta de lo que han hecho, en lo que se han convertido, y de repente no pueden soportarlo más.

—Le asqueaba en lo que se había convertido. —Charlie miró a Sarah, y luego a Barnaby—. Eso fue evidente cuando hablamos con él.

—Pero —Barnaby se inclinó hacia delante— ¿qué provocó su arrepentimiento?

Charlie miró de nuevo a Sarah, pero no respondió. Eso y otras muchas cosas que Malcolm les había contado a él y a su esposa, y que, ahora comprendía un poco más, eran algo que Charlie consideraba demasiado personal para contar. Algo que sólo ellos sabían, que los dos habían compartido y que ahora, por fin, entendían.

Malcolm Sinclair había desaparecido y les había dejado vivir. Aún más, había intentado que vivieran una vida más plena.

Sarah le dirigió a Charlie una suave sonrisa y tampoco dijo nada.

—Entonces —dijo Stokes mirando el mapa—, ¿aquí estaba el puente?

Gabriel asintió con la cabeza. Luego trazó con el dedo el camino que seguía la corriente más allá de la cascada.

—La cascada mira hacia el oeste, pero aquí, un poco después, la corriente se encuentra con un saliente y gira al norte, y más adelante al este, hasta que finalmente desemboca en este lago. —Golpeó levemente el mapa—. Es pequeño pero profundo. Desde allí el agua sale al río, que sigue dirección norte hasta desembocar en Bridgwater Bay.

—Así que lo más probable es que encontremos el cuerpo entre la cascada y el lago. —Barnaby se había parado al lado de Stokes.

Charlie intercambió una mirada con Gabriel.

—Hemos enviado gente a rastrear la zona. El cauce del río es muy rocoso en esa parte y, con el reciente deshielo, ha crecido la corriente. Si no encontramos el cuerpo en el lago, o en las orillas, es probable que no lo encontremos nunca.

Stokes se enderezó.

—Iré y echaré un vistazo a la cascada, luego hablaré con los rastreadores.

Barnaby asintió con la cabeza.

—Iré con usted. —Le dirigió a Charlie una mirada—. Será mejor que acabemos con esto de una vez.

Ni Charlie ni Gabriel vieron ningún sentido a unirse a la búsqueda. Puede que encontraran el cuerpo de Sinclair o que no lo hicieran nunca.

Acompañado de Sarah, Charlie se dirigió a los establos para despedirse de los demás. Gabriel se fue a Casleigh, para contarles las noticias a Alathea, a Martin y a Celia, que también habían conocido a Malcolm Sinclair.

Barnaby se fue con Stokes.

Charlie y Sarah regresaron lentamente a la casa cogidos de la mano.

Un rato después, Stokes se encontraba al pie de la cascada meneando la cabeza mientras miraba los escalones de piedra que habían conducido al puente.

—Debe de haber sido impresionante salir de ese puente y luego ver caer al señor Sinclair.

—Mira esto. —Barnaby cogió una tablilla astillada entre dos rocas. Había más de cincuenta metros de rocas dentadas bajo la rugiente cascada, hasta las rocas quebradas sobre las que el agua se arremolinaba.

Apartándose de la corriente que discurría velozmente, Barnaby le mostró la tabla a Stokes.

—Es un trozo del puente. A pesar de que la madera es dura, los bordes han quedado totalmente destrozados. —Se volvió a mirar la cascada—. Imagina lo que puede haber ocurrido con el cuerpo de Sinclair.

Stokes hizo una mueca y también observó la cascada.

—Cierto, sólo la intervención divina podría haber hecho que un hombre pudiera sobrevivir a una caída como ésa, y dudo que Sinclair haya sido tocado por la mano de Dios.

No obstante, Stokes y Barnaby emprendieron una minuciosa búsqueda siguiendo la corriente, preguntando en vano a los rastreadores con los que se encontraban y enviándolos de vuelta al Park.

Ya estaba anocheciendo cuando llegaron al lago. Había tres hombres allí. Harris, el jardinero jefe del Park, fue quien se acercó a hablar con ellos.

—Es la segunda vez que buscamos en esta zona, señor. No hemos visto ningún cuerpo entre la maleza de la orilla, ni lo hemos divisado en el lago. Sin embargo, como puede ver... —señaló con la cabeza hacia donde la corriente agitaba la superficie del lago— la corriente es tan fuerte y el agua discurre tan deprisa que a estas alturas bien podría haber arrastrado el cuerpo hasta el centro del canal de Bristol.

Miraron en la dirección que Harris les indicaba, hacia la superficie plomiza del canal, no muy lejos de allí.

Stokes hizo una mueca.

—Hemos hecho todo lo posible. —Se despidió de Harris con un gesto de cabeza—. Será mejor que nos retiremos antes de que caiga la noche.

—Sí, señor. —Harris se tocó la gorra y reunió a sus muchachos con una mirada y luego se dirigieron al lugar donde habían dejado los caballos.

Barnaby y Stokes habían dejado sus monturas en el punto donde la corriente de la cascada se unía al lago y echaron a andar hacia allí.

—Tengo que admitir —dijo Stokes— que nunca pensé que todo esto terminaría tan pronto, ni con tanta pulcritud. —Miró a Barnaby—. Sin duda tu padre estará encantado, y también las demás autoridades. —Stokes sonrió ampliamente y miró hacia delante—. Y tú volverás a Londres a tiempo de asistir a todos esos bailes y fiestas de la temporada.

Barnaby gimió.

—Es el único fallo que veo a la excepcional planificación de Sinclair. Preferiría estar inmerso en la investigación de cualquier crimen con tal de que mi padre impidiera que mi madre cayera sobre mí... literalmente. Ahora tendré que inventarme alguna investigación que excuse mi falta de interés hasta que me vea envuelto en una de verdad.

Stokes le lanzó una mirada afectuosa al ver su expresión apesadumbrada.

—Pero yo pensaba que es eso lo que hacen los aristócratas como tú. Echarles un vistazo a las señoritas que se presentan en sociedad y elegir a una de ellas como esposa. ¿Acaso no es así?

—En teoría sí, siempre y cuando uno tenga intención de casarse. Pero yo soy el tercer hijo. No tengo ningún motivo para dejarme cazar, sin importar lo que mi madre y sus amigas piensen al respecto. No es que tenga nada contra el matrimonio, está bien para otros. Bueno, sólo hay que ver a Gerrard y Jacqueline, Dillon y Pris, y ahora Charlie y Sarah; aprecio lo que tienen, pero...

—No es para ti, ¿verdad?

Barnaby se preguntó cómo habían acabado hablando de eso, pero Stokes y él se conocían desde hacía años y habían trabajado juntos. Si había alguien que podía comprender su posición, ése era Stokes.

—No, no es para mí. Sinceramente, ¿puedes imaginar a una dama...? Y te recuerdo, Stokes, que mi madre no aprobaría a ninguna mujer que no fuera una dama y con un rango adecuado además... así que, ¿puedes imaginar a una dama de esa clase feliz al verme dedicar tanto tiempo a algo tan inmencionable en algunos círculos sociales como las investigaciones criminales? ¿Que de vez en cuando lo tenga que dejar todo y salir precipitadamente del país? ¿O que me disfrace y desaparezca en los bajos fondos de Londres a la caza y captura de algún malhechor?

—Hummm. —Stokes había asistido de manera oficial a suficientes fiestas sociales para comprender lo que Barnaby quería decir.

—Por no mencionar que se arriesgaría a sufrir un estigma social, y que coquetearía constantemente con la posibilidad de que la sociedad la excomulgara por cualquier error que yo cometiera. —Barnaby bufó—. Jamás funcionaría. Se pondría histérica en menos de una semana.

Hizo una pausa y luego continuó:

—Para mí... investigar, y todo lo que eso conlleva, es lo que más me gusta hacer. Se me da bien, y tú, mi padre y otras autoridades me necesitáis. No hay nadie más que pueda hacer este tipo de trabajo dentro de la sociedad. —Vaciló y luego continuó, más para sí mismo que para Stokes—: Es mi profesión. Me he abierto camino, y no tengo intención de detenerme ahora; no existe mujer en la tierra capaz de conseguir que le dé la espalda a mi trabajo.

Stokes no respondió. Barnaby no esperaba respuesta alguna. Llegaron a los caballos, montaron y se miraron.

—¿Y ahora? —preguntó Barnaby.

Stokes reflexionó antes de responder:

—Soy de los que piensan que, a caballo regalado, no le mires el diente. Con su ataque de remordimientos, Sinclair nos ha facilitado las cosas y ha sido de gran ayuda. Mañana regresaré a Londres e informaré de la presunta muerte de Malcolm Sinclair. —Stokes volvió la mirada atrás, a lo largo de la corriente rocosa—. No creo que lleguemos a encontrar ningún rastro de él.

Barnaby asintió con la cabeza. Agitaron las riendas de sus caballos y se encaminaron hacia el Park.

Esa misma noche, en el dormitorio del conde, en su cama, Sarah yacía en brazos de su marido, abrigada, saciada y satisfecha, más feliz de lo que jamás había sido en su vida. Bajo su mejilla, el corazón de Charlie latía fuerte y regular. Aunque sentía el cansancio en cada músculo de su cuerpo, Sarah lo rodeó con los brazos.

—Hubo un momento en la cascada... un horrible instante en el que pensé que podría perderte. —Levantó la cabeza y le miró a la cara y a los ojos en sombras—. Acababas de lograr agarrarte al poste de anclaje y yo trataba de subirte cuando... Malcolm sacó un cuchillo de su bota.

Charlie le sostuvo la mirada. Alzando una mano, apartó el pelo de la cara de su esposa y le acunó la mejilla.

—¿Pensaste que iba a apuñalarme?

Ella asintió con la cabeza.

—Sólo por un instante. —Sarah se estremeció y volvió a apoyar la cabeza en el pecho de Charlie, nutriéndose de su calor, de él, de la palpable realidad de su cuerpo bajo el de ella—. Pero fue suficiente. —Lo estrechó entre sus brazos con más fuerza—. No quiero perderte nunca. Ni siquiera quiero pensar en la posibilidad de perderte de nuevo.

El pecho de Charlie se estremeció al soltar una risita irónica. Luego la besó en la frente.

—Ahora sabes cómo me siento. La mera idea de perderte es suficiente para que me resulte imposible pensar.

Jugueteó con el pelo de Sarah, se lo alisó y acarició.

—No sabía que él se hubiera dado cuenta de todas esas cosas que me dijo. Pero no todo es cierto, yo ya me había dado cuenta; tú me abriste los ojos, me hiciste afrontar la realidad y ver la necesidad de cambiar. En ese momento, en todo lo que podía pensar era en lo que él podría hacerte una vez que comprendiera que no iba a discutir, una vez que comprendiera que ya había aceptado todo eso que él quería que aceptara. En lugar de escuchar su monólogo, estaba pensando en cómo ponerte a salvo.

Sarah esbozó una sonrisa y le plantó un beso en el pecho.

—Yo no sabía lo que pensaba hacerme, pero jamás me sentí amenazada. Pero con respecto a ti, no estaba tan segura.

—Y ahora todo ha acabado. Como si hubiéramos salido victoriosos de una dura prueba, el futuro se extiende ante nosotros para hacer con él lo que queramos. —Hizo una pausa y luego continuó—: Sé lo que quiero. —Tomó la mano de Sarah sobre su pecho y entrelazó sus dedos—. Si estás de acuerdo, viviremos aquí todo el año, salvo las pocas semanas que pasemos en Londres, en primavera, durante la temporada, como tú deseas, y en otoño, durante las sesiones del Parlamento. Pero el resto del tiempo nos quedaremos aquí, donde quedan tantas cosas por hacer. Aquí, donde estaremos rodeados de la familia, de la hacienda y de la comunidad. De la gente que nos necesita.

Con la cabeza sobre su pecho, Sarah suspiró y luego dijo:

—Y es aquí donde debemos criar a nuestra familia, ¿no crees? En este lugar, donde nosotros crecimos, del que conocemos cada centímetro de tierra y donde todo el mundo nos conoce y conocerá a nuestros hijos; será lo mejor para ellos, ¿verdad?

—¿Ellos? —preguntó después de permanecer callado durante un buen rato.

La joven clavó la mirada en sus manos entrelazadas sobre el pecho de Charlie.

—Es probable que esté embarazada, pero no estoy del todo segura.

Levantó la cabeza y lo miró directamente a los ojos. Lo que vio en ellos la hizo entrecerrar los suyos.

—Lo sabías, ¿verdad?

La mirada que le devolvió Charlie decía que no estaba seguro de qué decir.

—Yo... eh... me lo imaginaba.

Sarah observó en sus ojos algo parecido al pánico por cómo podría reaccionar ella. La joven sonrió como un gato ante un plato con crema, se estiró y lo besó.

—En ese caso podemos imaginárnoslo un poquito más. No quiero decírselo a nadie hasta que estemos seguros.

Él asintió con la cabeza.

—Sí. Estoy de acuerdo.

Sarah frunció el ceño mientras se echaba hacia atrás.

—Ni siquiera a Dillon y a Gerrard.

—Ni se me había pasado por la cabeza. —Parpadeó antes de continuar—: En cualquier caso, si no te sientes cómoda con todo eso y no quieres ir a Londres esta temporada, mamá lo entendería.

Sarah se rio, sintiéndose alegre y despreocupada.

—No hay ninguna posibilidad de que eso ocurra. —Se acurrucó en los cálidos brazos de Charlie—. Hay mucha gente esperando conocernos en la capital y un simple embarazo no es excusa suficiente. —Le clavó el dedo en el pecho—. Y si piensas utilizar mi embarazo para encerrarme, te sugiero que lo pienses de nuevo.

—Si no puedo encerrarte, ¿puedo mimarte al menos? —preguntó Charlie después de un rato, sosteniéndola firmemente entre sus brazos.

Sarah ladeó la cabeza considerando sus palabras. Sonrió feliz.

—No me importaría dejar que me mimaras. —Luego la joven se rio entre dientes—. Charlie... no es propio de ti pedir permiso.

Charlie sonrió, acercándola más a él, estrechándola con más fuerza contra su cuerpo.

—He cambiado. —Lo había hecho. Y le sorprendía cuánto. Le dio un beso en el pelo—. Te amo, y es aquí donde quiero estar. En el Park, contigo y con nuestros hijos, cuando lleguen.

Charlie había comprendido por fin por qué Gerrard y Gabriel y todos los demás habían abandonado con tanta facilidad la vida en Londres después de que se hubieran casado. Las delicias de Londres poseían poco encanto comparado con lo que le esperaba allí, con lo que había aceptado. Bajó la mirada hacia Sarah.

—Éste es mi sitio.

Lo sería ahora y por siempre jamás.

Todo estaba bien, todo era perfecto entre ellos, aunque había algo que Charlie le debía a su esposa. La miró a la cara, la parte de ésta que podía verle mientras estaba acurrucada y segura entre sus brazos.

—Esto, nuestro amor, todavía me asusta un poco —le dijo—. Sé que es algo que puede llegar a controlarme y sin duda lo hará más en los años venideros. Y eso me preocupa.

Sarah levantó la cabeza y le miró, luego colocó las manos en su pecho y apoyó la barbilla en ellas para poder mirarle a la cara, a los ojos.

—¿Por qué?

A pesar de que su primer impulso fue echarse atrás, se obligó a responderle.

—Me asusta que eso me haga hacer cosas que no debería, que me haga correr riesgos que finalmente podrían ponerte a ti, a nuestros hijos, al condado y todo lo que eso conlleva, en peligro. —Hizo una pausa y luego, mirándola a los ojos, añadió—: Como le pasó a mi padre.

La expresión de perplejidad de Sarah era en sí misma una pregunta.

Charlie tomó aire.

—Mi padre nos quería. Nos quería muchísimo, quizá demasiado. Se obsesionó con conseguir una vida mejor para nosotros y fue esa obsesión lo que le hizo correr riesgos, riesgos financieros. —Hizo una pausa y luego continuó—: Casi llevó al condado a la ruina. Si Alathea no hubiera intervenido, lo habría hecho.

Los ojos de Sarah se iluminaron con una comprensión y compasión que él no había esperado.

—¿Es por eso por lo que no querías amarme? ¿Por lo que intentaste que nuestro amor no saliera de esta habitación?

Charlie asintió con la cabeza.

—Pensé que si podía mantenerlo aquí dentro... Jamás tomo decisiones financieras aquí.

Sonaba ridículo ahora que sabía en qué consistía el amor, pero Sarah no se rio. Se limitó a observarle, luego estiró los brazos y le tomó la cara entre las manos, mirándole profundamente a los ojos.

—Tú no eres tu padre.

Cuando Charlie abrió la boca para replicar, ella le hizo guardar silencio volviendo a tomar la palabra.

—Yo le conocía, ¿recuerdas? No te pareces nada a él, no por dentro. Eres como Serena: competente, práctico y perspicaz. Jamás cometerías los mismos errores que cometió tu padre. Sólo tienes que ver tu reputación como inversor, la alta estima en que te tiene Gabriel, cómo te describió Malcolm. Pero dejando a un lado todo eso, eres mucho más fuerte de lo que tu padre lo fue nunca. Puede que el amor llegue a controlarte, pero jamás hará que pierdas de vista el único deber que tienes por encima de todo. Jamás me pondrás a mí, ni a nadie por quien te sientas responsable, ni mucho menos al amor, en peligro. No dejarás que nada corra peligro.

Sarah le brindó una cálida sonrisa.

—Quizá no lo veas con la misma claridad que yo, o que cualquier otra persona que te conoce, pero tú eres tú, Charlie, siempre lo has sido y siempre lo serás. Eres un hombre protector, nunca harías daño a nadie, nunca lo pondrías en peligro. Ni siquiera el amor, con todo su poder, puede cambiar lo que está en tu corazón... y en realidad el amor no haría eso. El amor está de tu lado, no en tu contra. Te hará fuerte, no débil.

Sarah hizo una pausa y le sostuvo la mirada antes de añadir quedamente:

—El amor no es peligroso, ni tampoco lo es amarme. No es peligroso para mí que tú me ames.

La joven siguió con la mirada clavada en los ojos de su marido, y lo que vio en ellos hizo que el corazón le diera un brinco. Luego sonrió, se inclinó hacia él y le rozó los labios con los suyos.

—Y por eso, nuestro matrimonio funcionará... por nuestro amor.

Charlie esperó a que ella se echara hacia atrás para poder mirarla a los ojos.

—Eso y la fuerza. Tu fuerza. La mía no cuenta.

Ella sonrió ampliamente.

—Y la prudencia... tuya y mía.

Él torció los labios.

—Y la comprensión. Tuya, más que mía. —Sostuvo la mirada de su esposa y sintió que se ahogaba en sus ojos azules, en el amor que brillaba en ellos con tal fuerza que casi lo dejó sin aliento—. Y otra cosa. Confianza. Confío en que tú sepas qué hacer con el amor.

Sarah sonrió.

—Y yo confío en ti por ser como eres, que es justo lo que yo deseo. Y por eso, siempre sabré qué hacer con nuestro amor.

Sarah atrajo sus labios a los de ella y le besó, y dejó que él la besara, permitió que el amor floreciera, que la pasión creciera y el deseo ardiera hasta arrebatarlos una vez más.

Hasta el paraíso que ahora compartían, hasta el éxtasis de la unión que habían creado. Que habían aceptado.

Más tarde, Charlie los acomodó de nuevo sobre las almohadas. La luna brillaba con intensidad, su trémula luz entraba por la ventana iluminando la cama. Sintiéndose bendecido más allá de lo posible, agradecido y honrado hasta lo más profundo de su alma, Charlie extendió la mano intentando atrapar el rayo de luz en la palma, medio esperando, dada la magia que les envolvía, ser capaz de sentir su peso.

Y mientras dejaba que la luz plateada iluminara su mano, Charlie recordó una fascinación anterior. Una que lo había tentado, que lo había llevado hasta ese momento, al amor y la vida que ahora abrazaba incondicionalmente. Al futuro y todo lo que éste traería consigo.

Era la fascinación que había sentido por Sarah y por el esquivo y adictivo sabor de la inocencia.

La misma luna que arrojaba sus rayos como una bendición sobre la cama de Charlie y Sarah brillaba, pálida y fría, sobre el canal de Bristol y el estuario del Severn. Caía sobre la oscura y ondulante superficie del agua, tiñendo de plata una silueta negra que la marea había depositado en una playa desierta de la costa de la bahía de Bridgwater.

Empapado y con la ropa hecha trizas, un náufrago yacía sobre la áspera arena, donde lo habían abandonado las olas.

Pero no había nadie cerca para verlo. Nadie que se preguntara quién era, de dónde era o por qué estaba allí.

Nadie a quien le preocupara.

Y allí se quedó mientras la luna cedía su lugar en el cielo.

Hasta que al final, inevitablemente, apareció el sol y el mundo volvió de nuevo a la vida.